# SCANDINAVIAN FOLK & FAIRY TALES

"Twigmuntus, Cowbelliantus, Perchnosius? Can you give me an answer
to that?" the lad asked. (An illustration to the "Twigmuntus" story by
Carl Larsson, "the Prince of Swedish illustrators.")

# SCANDINAVIAN FOLK & FAIRY TALES

Edited by Claire Booss

## TALES FROM NORWAY · SWEDEN · DENMARK · FINLAND · ICELAND

*Illustrated*

**AVENEL BOOKS**
*New York*

This 1984 edition is published by Avenel Books, distributed
by Crown Publishers, Inc., One Park Avenue, New York,
New York 10016.

The tales and illustrations that appear in the
section entitled "Traditional Finnish Tales" were published
originally in *Tales of a Finnish Tupa*, copyright © 1936, 1964 by
Albert Whitman & Company, Chicago, and are reprinted here
by permission of the publisher.

Manufactured in the United States of America

Designed by Mary McBride

**Library of Congress Cataloging in Publication Data**
Main entry under title:

Scandinavian folk & fairy tales.

  Summary: A collection of folk literature from five countries,
with illustrations.
  1. Tales—Scandinavia.   [1. Folklore—Scandinavia] I. Booss,
Claire.   II. Title: Scandinavian folk and fairy tales.
PZ8.1.S277   1984       398.2'0948       84-442

ISBN: 0-517-43620-5

h  g  f  e  d  c  b  a

# CONTENTS

INTRODUCTION                                                xiii

## TALES FROM NORWAY

The Man Who Was Going to Mind the House            3
The Giant Who Had No Heart                         4
The Pancake                                       10
The Lad and the Devil                             12
The Greedy Youngster                              14
The Seven Fathers in the House                    22
The Smith and the Devil                           24
The Three Billy-Goats Who Went Up into the Hills to
    Get Fat                                       29
Peter Gynt                                        30
Legends of the Mill                               34
The Lad and the North Wind                        41
Peik                                              44
Foolish Men and Scolding Wives                    49
The Parson and the Clerk                          52
The Giant and Johannes Blessom                    53
The Box with the Funny Thing in It                56
The Widow's Son                                   56
East of the Sun and West of the Moon              63
Ashiepattle Who Made the Princess Tell the Truth at
    Last                                          71
An Evening in the Squire's Kitchen               72
Hans, Who Made the Princess Laugh                84
A Summer Night in a Norwegian Forest             89
The Witch                                         99
The Charcoal-Burner                              106
The Fisherman and the Draug                      111
The Honest Penny                                 118

The Death of Chanticleer                        121
Reynard and Chanticleer                         124
The Companion                                   125
Death and the Doctor                            134
The Way of the World                            136
Pork and Honey                                  138
Slip Root, Catch Reynard's Foot                 139
Bruin and Reynard Partners                      140
Master Tobacco                                  141
The Three Lemons                                144
The Trolls in Hedale Wood                       149
The Skipper and Old Nick                        150
How to Win a Prince                             151
Boots and the Beasts                            152
How They Got Hairlock Home                      157
Little Freddy with His Fiddle                   160

# TALES FROM SWEDEN

## PART ONE—FROM SWEDEN AT LARGE

"Lars, My Lad!"                                 169
The Sausage                                     179
The Old Woman and the Tramp                     182
What Shall Baby's Name Be?                      186
St. Peter and the Two Women                     190
The Valiant Chanticleer                         194
Twigmuntus, Cowbelliantus, Perchnosius          199
The Lad and the Fox                             203
Old Nick and the Girl                           203
The Stone Statue                                206
The Artful Lad                                  208
"All I Possess!"                                221
The Cock and the Crested Hen                    223
Old Nick and the Pedlar                         224
Why the Executioner Is Called Assessor          229
The Parson and the Clerk                        232

## PART TWO—FROM THE REGIONS
### SKÅNE

The Sure Shot                                   238
Stompe Pilt                                     239

The Lord of Rosendal 240
The Master of Ugerup 242
The Ghost at Fjelkinge 244
Ljungby Horn and Pipe 246

## BLEKINGE

The Swan Maiden 248
The Knight of Ellenholm 250

## SMÅLAND

The Trolls of Skurugata 251
Dame Soåsan 252
The Giant Puke 256
Katrineholm Manor 257
Ebbe Skamelson 260
Johan and the Trolls 262
The Lost Treasure 265

## GÖTLAND

The Ten Fairy Servants 265
The Sea Nymph 268
The Byse 269

## ÖLAND

The Bridge over Kalmarsound 270

## HALLAND

The Young Lady of Hellerup 271
Elstorps Woods 272

## BOHUSLÄN

The Giant Maiden in Boråseröd Mountain 274
The Bridal Present 276
Hålde Hat 276
The Golden Cradle 277

## VESTERGÖTLAND

The Knights of Ållaberg 279
The Countess of Höjentorp 279
The Giant of Skalunda 280
The Trolls in Resslared 282

Bishop Svedberg and the Devil    283
The Treasure in Säby Creek    284

### ÖSTERGÖTLAND

The Tomts    285
The Urko of North Wij    286
The Troll Shoes    289

### DAL

The Wood and Sea Nymphs    290
The Mountain Kitchen    290

### VERMLAND

Saxe of Saxeholm    292
The Polite Coal Burner    293
The Harvesters    293

### NÄRIKE

The Ulfgryt Stones    294
Kate of Ysätter    296
The Elves' Dance    298
The Fiddler and the Sea Nymph    299

### VESTERMANLAND

The Snipe    300
Tibble Castle and Klinta Spring    300
The Coal Burner and the Troll    302
Bolstre Castle    305

### SÖDERMANLAND

The Changelings    306
Lake Goldring    307
The Troll's Garden at Stallsbacke    309

### UPLAND

The Werwolf    309
The Herd-boy    316

### DALARNE

The Water Nymph    324
The Treasure Seekers    324
The Lapp in Magpie Form    326

### GESTRIKLAND

The Vätters 327

### MEDELPAD

Starkad and Bale 328

### HERJEDALEN

The Vätt's Storehouse 330

### VESTERBOTTEN

The Voyage in a Lapp Sled 332

### LAPPLAND

The Lapp Genesis, or the First of Mankind 332
The Giant's Bride 333
The Cunning Lapp 334

# TALES FROM DENMARK

## PART ONE—TALES BY HANS CHRISTIAN ANDERSEN

The Ugly Duckling 339
The Wild Swans 345
The Old House 356
The Elf of the Rose 362
Soup from a Sausage Skewer 367
The Little Mermaid 377
The Girl Who Trod on the Loaf 393
The Swineherd 398
Little Claus and Big Claus 402
The Flying Trunk 410
The Nightingale 415
The Goblin and the Huckster 422
The Marsh King's Daughter 426
The Tinder-Box 454
The Bottle Neck 460
Little Tuk 468
She Was Good for Nothing 472

## PART TWO—TRADITIONAL TALES

Toller's Neighbors 479
The Troll's Hammer 482

The Magician's Pupil                                    485
Temptations                                             488
The Girl Clad in Mouseskin                              493
The Outlaw                                              496
The Little Chicken Kluk and His Companions              500

# TALES FROM FINLAND

### PART ONE—WEIRD TALES FROM NORTHERN SEAS (TOLD BY NORWEGIANS ABOUT FINNS)

Jack of Sjöholm and the Gan-Finn                        503
Finn Blood                                              518

### PART TWO—TRADITIONAL FINNISH TALES
#### TALES OF MAGIC

Vaino and the Swan Princess                             528
Lippo and Tapio                                         532
The Wooing of Seppo Ilmarinen                           536
The Mouse Bride                                         541
Antti and the Wizard's Prophecy                         547
Jurma and the Sea God                                   554
Severi and Vappu                                        559
Leppä Polkky and the Blue Cross                         564
Liisa and the Prince                                    573

#### DROLL STORIES

The Pig-Headed Wife                                     579
Stupid Peikko                                           581

#### FABLES

The End of the World                                    589
Farmers Three                                           590
The Vain Bear                                           591
The Wisdom of the Rabbit                                592

# TALES FROM ICELAND

#### STORIES OF ELVES

Túngustapi                                              595
The Genesis of the Hid-Folk                             598

The Fisherman of Götur 599
The Grateful Elfwoman 600
Thórdur of Thrastastadir 600
Grímsborg 601
The Father of Eighteen Elves 602
The Bishop and the Elves 604
Who Built Reynir Church? 605
Katla's Dream 606
The Man-Whale 609
Valbjörg the Unelfed 612
Una the Elfwoman 617
Hildur, the Queen of the Elves 619
The Man-Servant and the Water-Elves 624
The Crossways 625

### STORIES OF WATER-MONSTERS

The Merman 626
Nennir, or the One Who Feels Inclined 628
The Lake-Monster 628
Naddi 629

### STORIES OF TROLLS

Troll's Stone 629
Gellivör 630
The Shepherdess 633
Jóra the Troll 633
Katla 634
Olafur and the Trolls 635
The Troll in the Skrúdur 636
The Shepherd of Silfrúnarstadir 638
The Night-Trolls 642
The Story of Bergthór of Bláfell 642
Gryla 643

### STORIES OF GHOSTS AND GOBLINS

Murder Will Out 643
Ketill, the Priest of Húsavík 644
White Cap 644
A Ghost's Vengeance 645
The Boy Who Did Not Know What Fear Was 646
The Two Sigurdurs 651

The Deacon of Myrká 653
The Son of the Goblin 655

## MISCELLANEOUS TALES

The Story of Jón Asmundsson 657
The Skeleton in Hólar Church 665

# INTRODUCTION

SCANDINAVIAN TALES, like Scandinavian art and the people themselves, are earthy, vital, and filled with contrasts of light and dark. They are ghostly and terrible, joyous and lighthearted, realistic and sexy, poetic, comic, and bizarre. These contrasts create a richer woven fabric than in any other folk or fairy lore.

Why this is, I cannot say, but perhaps it is because the people who produced them have had to endure, through centuries, extremes of climate and geography that other cultures have not. Their fierce winters, their incredibly long nights, the terrain itself which is difficult to farm and must be coaxed to sustain life, and often even difficult to travel through, may explain it.

However it came to be, it is the sense of extremes that gives these stories their power to terrify, haunt, and delight.

It is strange therefore that, until this time, there has not been a popular, complete, and definitive collection of the folklore of all five northern countries. There are collections by separate country, by the great tale masters, such as Denmark's Hans Christian Andersen, and the great collector-editors such as Asbjörnsen and Moe of Norway; there are even anthologies that combine two or three countries, but, somehow, collections of all five countries and all genres is something totally unknown.

This is a curious lapse because the national character of each country individually is unique and strong, and together they are complementary and compelling. Their qualities are fully reflected in their stories. The Norwegians, for example, descendants from the fierce, untamed Vikings, are a hardy, courageous and independent people, but with a love of home and domestic life. This makes their stories as varied as the lyrical "East of the Sun and West of the Moon"—a classic recounting of the arduous travels of a beautiful, brave, and devoted young woman to the ends of the earth and beyond to reclaim her lost husband—and the robust, down-to-earth rendering of "The Man Who Was Going to Mind the House," with its early hint of feminism, or the marvelous "Seven Fathers in the House," which is not only mythical but also intensely domestic.

All Scandinavian tale-spinners seem to share the inimitable story-making qualities of a strong sense of wonder, a fierce loyalty to ideals, and a great sense of humor. Their stories have a wealth of supernatural creatures—fairies, elves, ghosts, goblins, dwarfs, giants, trolls, and spirits of the house and barnyard, such as nisses and tomts. Take the trolls, for example, perhaps the single most celebrated creation of the Scandinavian imagination. Their form varies from country to country, but although they are usually grotesque, evil-looking creatures, they somehow still manage to be a little pathetic and touching and comic to the reader's eye. They reward human kindness with powerful tools, but *usually* with strings attached! And they can be vengeful. They often put a curse on any natural object or person that has had anything to do with stopping them from getting their way. There is recourse for the victimized mortal, though: religion—and specifically, in these Scandinavian stories, Christianity, the early and prime faith of the North—is fatal to trolls and many other supernatural beings. Should they be within hearing of church bells, or otherwise fall under religious influence, their power is destroyed. Modern readers may at first find the periodic references to Christianity strange or distracting, but they should understand that Christianity and its practice were considered salvation against the powers of evil and the supernatural in general.

The tales in this collection come from sources ranging in time from the fifteenth to the twentieth centuries, and from all the different genres of anthology. Although all of the stories have their *initial* roots in true folklore—tales passed down through the ages by word of mouth—some of them have come further from their origins than others, having been transformed, polished, or updated more by the craftsmen, or series of craftsmen, who put them into print. In this volume I have kept the stories in their original groupings as much as possible so that the tone and flavor of the source is maintained and there is a continuous flow.

Although the overall structure of the book is organized by country, subdivided at times by region or subject matter, in this introduction I will discuss the stories in terms of their progressive evolution from the earliest sources in the age-old tales.

Closest to their sources are the "traditional tales," represented by the stories in Part Two of the Danish section. They were collected and edited in the mid-nineteenth century, but some are genuine productions of the fifteenth and sixteenth centuries. These early tales usually include the names of towns and regions.

It is interesting to note that, even in these earliest works, sexuality, both implicit and explicit, hovers in the background, if not the foreground, as in "The Girl Clad in Mouseskin" and the charming "Temptations." In the latter, all efforts to tempt an extremely honest young man fail, but in the end, as the concluding poem makes clear, sexual delights do succeed in weakening this fellow's resolve:

> Dainty the fare, sweet was the mead,
> The lady's arm was soft and round,

The sparkling cup my senses drown'd,
And thus I lost my master's steed.

These earliest works as well as some later ones contain occasional ar-
chaic language—expressions that may sound curious or mysterious to
the modern ear. I have retained most of these in the interests of authen-
ticity and flavor. Some examples are "scrip," a knapsack in which a lunch
was often packed; "goodman," the head of a household; "goodwife," the
mistress of the household; and finally, "goody," a less dignified version of
"goodwife," indicating a woman, usually married, of lowly or peasant
status. However, wherever it has been absolutely necessary for understanding, some words have been translated or substituted.

The traditional Danish tales were reprinted from *Yule-Tide Stories*
(1888), edited by Benjamin Thorpe. (He in turn reprinted most of them
from a compilation done by Carit Etlar in 1847.) Also from Thorpe's
volume, but one step further removed from its sources, are the Swedish
stories from Upland, "The Werwolf" and "The Herdboy." Thorpe tells
us that the original editors of those and other (Swedish) tales in his
collection traveled long and hard through the provinces, "committing the
stories to writing from the lips of the people," keeping the basic narra-
tives intact but believing that, because of the roughness of the peasant
narrators, the external form "naturally called for some remodelling."
And, in fact, the reader of Thorpe's book will note that the Swedish tales
flow more smoothly and felicitously.

The two Upland stories appear here within the regional section of
Swedish tales, all of which have specific locales and are grouped according to the province from which they came. This will increase their appeal
to anyone with a knowledge of the country. But the rough, idiosyncratic
character of these sometimes violent and often unpredictable early tales
will appeal to all who appreciate earthy humor, realism, and grotesques.
All the other early Swedish regional tales in this volume come from
*Swedish Fairy Tales* by Herman Hofberg, translated by W. H. Myers (1895).
Hofberg's book was the first formulation of traditional Swedish folklore,
and, thus, is historically significant.

The tales from the Hofberg collection are short, but poetic, and frequently have a moral. Seven stories, four from the province of Småland
alone, demonstrate the great variety of these tales: "Dame Soåsan" and
"The Giant Puke" illustrate the dangers of disobeying the strictures that
come with gifts from trolls or giants. "The Trolls in Skugurata" is terrible
and grim, while "Ebbe Skamelson" is a lovely love story, with a sad ending—once again, someone doesn't keep his promise! "The Troll Shoes,"
from Ostergötland, and "The Vätt's Storehouse," from Heriedalen,
are funny, while "The Coal Burner and the Trolls," from Vesterman-
land, includes an illegitimate pregnancy and—very rare—trolls who are
outwitted!

The next category of source includes those masters of the nineteenth
century who found, collected, and edited the early tales with so much
talent and faithfulness that their styles are as remarked upon as their
subject matter. They include Asbjörnsen and Moe of Norway, and Jón

Arnason, who has rightly been called the "Grimm of Iceland."

All of the Icelandic tales herein are taken from Arnason's *Icelandic Legends* (1864), translated by George E. J. Powell and Eiríkur Magnússon. Jón Arnason (1819–1888), a librarian and teacher, spent thirty years exhaustively searching for these treasures, which he gathered from every nook and cranny of Iceland. It was his major work and has been translated all over the world. Arnason also adhered closely to locale, conveying a perfect picture of the life and spirit of the times. Although his tales were grouped by the supernatural creatures that dominate them—elves, water-monsters, trolls, ghosts, and goblins—rather than by locality, the places of origin are prominent in the stories. Arnason's enormous task was eased by the fact that, since ancient times, Icelanders have been great story-tellers, and their legends contain primary wit and wisdom. These stories will be of particular interest to adults, although children certainly can enjoy them. The emotional tone of these tales is very defined. "Túngustapi," for example, the first elf story, is cruel but haunting, while "The Crossways," the last elf story, is hilarious.

Like the earliest tales mentioned above, many of the Icelandic legends include references to sexuality, but there is also a variation on the theme wherein elves or other supernatural creatures mate with humans and produce young, with eerie but intriguing results—as in "The Man-Whale" and "Valbjörg the Unelfed."

Cruelty also plays a prominent role in many of the Icelandic tales, as it does in Scandinavian folklore in general, and, indeed, in folk literature the world over. Grimm's famous tales, for instance, have given many a sensitive parent cause for concern. In this anthology the stories of cruelty and violence have not been deleted altogether and hardly ever expurgated, but they do not dominate in quite the proportion they did in their original settings.

And now we come to Peter Christen Asbjörnsen (1812–1885), a giant in the field, who, together with Jörgen Moe (1813–1882), did more to find, preserve, and immortalize Norwegian folklore than any other writer. The major portion of the tales from Norway in this collection (from the first story through "The Charcoal Burner") are taken from Asbjörnsen's *Round the Yule Log*, translated by H. L. Braekstad in 1881. I can do no better in describing his achievements than to quote from Edmund W. Gosse's fine introduction to that edition. He calls Asbjörnsen, a zoologist, "a man of science whose irresistible bias towards literary style may be said to have made a poet of him against his will." And he notes that "when a great writer first dares, in a ripe literature, to write exactly as people commonly speak, we can scarcely realize how startling a thing it is. This is what the author of these tales has done. . . . He has cast to the winds the rules of composition, the balance of clauses, the affected town-phrases, and all the artificial forms hitherto deemed requisite . . . and he has had the courage to note down the fine idiomatic speech of the mountaineer in its native freshness."

Asbjörnsen's profession took him from one end of the country to the other, and his fondest pastime was to take walking tours and fishing trips with his old friend the lyrical poet and pastor Jorgen Moe, to coax stories out of every peasant whom they met. Later they set the tales down into books; the first was *Norwegian Folk and Fairy Tales* in 1842. Though Asbjörnsen created the greater number of books and his name is better known, Moe's gentle assistance was undoubtedly invaluable throughout. Gosse notes that they were barely in time to save the stories from extinction: In many districts they had already ceased to exist; in others they remained solely in the memories of a few aged persons. They obtained most of their best tales from "minstrels at bridal-feasts, boatmen on the fjords, from old blind vagabonds and the household paupers who form so strange a feature of the Norse peasant community."

Gosse concluded his tribute:

> It is difficult to doubt that though Asbjörnsen is himself a learned saw in this species of science, it is mainly the tale that has delighted him, the quaint wit, the savage pathos, the intimate and tender sympathy with all that is wild and solitary in the nature of his fatherland. And as a literary artist this is his highest praise, that he has contrived to lay the peculiarities of Norwegian landscape before his readers with a subtlety of touch such as no other poet or proseman has achieved—not by description so much as by a series of those sympathetic and brilliant touches which make us forget the author, and fancy that we are walking in the body through the country of his affection. In Asbjörnsen's tales the English reader will find, in its quintessence, the genius and temper of the Norwegian peasant.

As mentioned, the first and major portion of the tales from Norway come from Braekstad's translation of Asbjörnsen and Moe. The remainder, with one exception noted below, are from Sir George Dasent's *Tales from the Fjeld* (1908), which consists of translations of Asbjörnsen's *Popular Tales from the Norse*. Dasent tells his tales in a very warm, intimate, conversational tone. The writers themselves had earlier described Dasent's translations of their works as "the best and happiest rendering of our tales that has appeared." Certainly neither Braekstad nor Dasent was wanting in this area. (The American reader today may be somewhat more conscious of Anglicisms in Dasent's work, particularly the omnipresence of the nickname Boots for the youngest member in the family, on whom all the dirty work falls.)

Scandinavian tales are often symbolic and allegorical but in a way that is realistic and easy to accept. Two such tales from the Dasent translations are "Death and the Doctor" and "The Way of the World."

A few of the Norwegian tales, including "Legends of the Mill" and "An Evening in the Squire's Kitchen," contain stories within stories. They are set in a framework formed by the imaginary adventures of English sportsmen on the fjeld, or fells—a barren plateau of the upland—in Norway.

An intriguing and significant sort of Norwegian folk tale is the changeling story, in which a troll's offspring is switched in the cradle with a human child. "The Greedy Youngster" and "The Witch" are important examples in this collection. One wonders if these plots originated with parents desiring to explain odd, unpredictable, or wicked behavior in their young, effectively laying the blame elsewhere.

Before finally turning from the discussion of Norwegian tales, I must draw attention to what is possibly the most arresting tale of all: "The Fisherman and the Draug." It comes from a collection well named *Weird Tales from Northern Seas* (1893), by Jonas Lie, translated by R. Nisbet Bain. Lie (1833–1908), a Danish novelist and folklorist, excelled in describing the wild and dangerous seas of northern Norway and the hardy sailors who fought a bitter struggle for survival there. His tales capture the savage, lonely aura—where even the supernatural beings appear to be only malevolent and to hate man. "The Fisherman and the Draug" is a thrilling and frightening story, beautifully told, with vivid, realistic descriptions that include interesting bits of sailing technique. Two of Lie's other fine stories from that collection appear in the Finnish section.

Not nearly as well known outside its country of origin, Sweden, but certainly characteristic and delightful, is the work of Baron G. Djurklou, *Fairy Tales from the Swedish* (1901), also translated by H. L. Braekstad. All of the tales in the section "From Sweden at Large" have been taken from that collection. The translator notes that the originals were "written in the dialect of the Swedish peasantry . . . and . . . the translator has tried to retain as far as possible the humorous and colloquial style of the original."

It is true of fairy tales in general, and truer of them than of folk tales, that goodness is rewarded and evil punished. The dictionary distinction between folk and fairy tales is that fairy tales usually involve supernatural beings and are never true, whereas folk tales, handed down through the ages, may possibly have been based on a true occurrence. And these Swedish fairy tales are no exception to the rule: goodness triumphs, often with the help of supernatural creatures or people who have supernatural powers. An outstanding example of this is the splendid, comic opening story, "Lars, My Lad!"

In the Djurklou collection, despite its frequent humor, life is seen as a harsh struggle for existence against hunger and poverty—the twin plagues of the peasant farmer—and people are either good and generous, helping one another or stingy and selfish; in keeping with the requirement of fairy tales, the latter are usually punished. The endings, in fact, may be a bit grim, but they are just. The clever and pungent "All I Possess!" is the perfect example: a rich but stingy farmer starves his wife, but her successor outwits him.

In these struggles between good and evil, the power of darkness often figures. The Norwegians call this power "the Devil"; the Swedes here identify "Old Nick" and "Katie Gray," his female counterpart. The Icelanders are also fascinated by the black arts and even tell of a "black school."

Part One of the Finnish tales is about as internationally Scandinavian as one can get. It consists of two more selections from Lie's *Weird Tales from Northern Seas*, told by Norwegians, about Finns, and taken from the Danish. "Jack of Sjöhölm and the Gan-Finn" is haunting, while "Finn Blood" is a charming love story set against a background of the superstitious beliefs and wild imaginings of the Nordland fishermen.

A word should be said here about the *Kalevala* (1838–1849), Finland's great national epic and the reasons why no selections from that world-famous work are included here. Actually, the reasons are rather interesting. Recent scholarship has revealed that the *Kalevala* is not a true folk epic, as was previously thought, but rather is largely the composition of Dr. Elias Lönrott (1802–1884), a philologist, poet, and folklorist, who also practiced medicine in country districts of Finland where he transcribed traditional ballads. As Jaakko Ahokas has pointed out in *A History of Finnish Literature* (Indiana University Press, 1973), Lönrott believed these to be fragments of a great epic such as *The Iliad*, and in an attempt to restore the work, he actually composed one that in and of itself was not a genuine folk epic, although most of his materials were authentic.

This is not to demean the quality of that wondrous work, which has inspired, among other things, Sibelius's major musical compositions and Longfellow's *Hiawatha*, and which probably was primarily responsible for awakening a sense of national cultural pride in nineteenth-century Finland as well as helping to bring Finland to the cultural awareness of the Western world.

In any event, there would have been an additional obstacle to reproducing selections from that piece here: There is such a strong narrative line that, even though there are individual incidents and events within it that could be excerpted, much of the cumulative power of the work would be lost if it were excerpted.

The traditional tales in Part Two of the Finnish section are truly authentic folklore, although, because they were translated in the twentieth century, they do have a decidedly modern cast.

The Finns are a hardy, stubborn people whose small nation, geographically isolated and linguistically different from its neighbors, lies in the shadow of the powerful Soviet Union. These factors have probably contributed to the Finns' strongly developed individualism, endurance, and love of liberty, characteristics evident in the stories presented here, which come from *Tales from a Finnish Tupa** (1936), by James Cloyd Bowman and Margery Bianco, from a translation by Aili Kolehmainen. As Mr. Bowman states:

> The heart of Finnish folklore is magic . . . the magic of words . . . .
> These folk tales make much and varied use of the power

* A *tupa* is a peasant's cottage.

of words, but they also depict the life of a strange people. Their customs, their beliefs, their sorrows, and their laughter, in short their entire culture, is herein recorded for all time.

The Finns were a pastoral people. They loved their fields and their flocks, their rivers and lakes, and their deep, wild forests. They loved peace, and hated violence. They approved of strength and courage and right doing, and liked nothing better than to trip up the heels of the oppressor and the deceiver. . . .

On the surface they were cold and inexpressive, and seemed as frozen over as their lakes in winter. But beneath their fur coats their hearts were warm, and deep within their hearts, when least expected, there was a droll laughter, and a keen sense of human values.

The tales in this book that have traveled farthest from their sources are those of Denmark's master storyteller, Hans Christian Andersen (1805–1875), and indeed many of his stories were totally his inventions. But no one would say that their charm has suffered as a result. In fact, his inspired tale-spinning has done much to bring converts to the world of folk and fairy lore, as well as enchanting children and adults for the century-and-a-quarter since they were written.

Although the greater number of Andersen's stories were creations of his imagination, in some cases they were suggested by early tales and legends told to him in his childhood, as well as by Danish history and themes from foreign literature. Examples of the first are "The Tinder-Box," "The Wild Swans," "Little Claus and Big Claus," and "The Swineherd," while "The Elf of the Rose" was borrowed from a novel of Boccaccio's.

The stories in this collection have been reprinted from *The Complete Hans Christian Andersen Fairy Tales* (Avenel Books, 1981), edited by Lily Owens, a compilation of tales translated in the nineteenth century by Mrs. H. B. Paull and others, but they appear here with an entirely new selection of illustrations. Some of the tales are familiar and beloved classics, among them "The Ugly Duckling," "The Nightingale," and "The Little Mermaid," but there are also a number of lesser known, equally charming tales.

Unlike typical fairy tales, many of Andersen's do not end happily. Since many of his ideas came from his personal experiences, the difficulties and sufferings of his life were probably responsible. He was the son of a poor shoemaker, and although he had the brilliance of a scholar, his parents had no money to educate him. His father died when he was a child. Acutely sensitive and high-strung, he was bullied by other children. Later, Andersen failed in his attempts to become a performing artist: he tried acting, singing, and dancing, and failed to make a career in any of these endeavors. Then he attempted playwriting, but he earned only modest sums. Only with his fairy tales did he achieve success and fame. Ugly and unworldly, he was persistently unlucky in romance. His poignant remark as an old bachelor was: "I have imagined so much and had so little."

Andersen wrote his tales for the pleasure of adults as well as children; he often read to the King of Denmark two of the king's favorites, "The Nightingale" and "The Swineherd." Andersen's fairy tales have since joined the ranks of the most published works of literature for all ages, and they have been translated into every known language in the world.

Certainly not the least of this gathering of Scandinavian riches is the art, unique yet so various in mood, and expressive of the many different regions. The illustrations represent a full range in terms of time, fame, and emotional tone: from the unknown nineteenth-century artists that illustrate the early Icelandic tales with their stark, haunting images, to the happy, mischievous drawings of the noted twentieth-century American artist Laura Bannon that decorate the traditional Finnish tales.

The Norwegian tales were illustrated by several artists, some well known, some anonymous. The best known are probably Otto Sinding (1842–1909) and Peter Arbo (1831–1892), Norwegians whose work accompanies the Braekstad translations in the first part of the section; the Dasent translations were illustrated by Moyr Smith, a nineteenth-century British artist. The striking art for *Weird Tales from Northern Seas* was done by the illustrious Laurence Housman (1865–1959).

The tales in the section "From Sweden at Large" were illustrated by the noted Norwegian artist Theodor Kittelsen (1857–1914); and although Herman Hofberg has stated that the drawings for the regional Swedish tales are by some of the best Swedish artists, he does not give their names.

The stories of Hans Christian Andersen have been illustrated so many times and in so many different ways that the editor was hard pressed to decide whose art to include. The work of several nineteenth-century English artists is represented here: Alfred Walter Bayes, Arthur J. Gaskin, V. Pedersen, and M. L. Stone.

As a footnote, it should be mentioned that the alert reader will notice that occasionally the plot of a story from one country will turn up in another tale from a different one although usually with some variation. This is an interesting and well-known phenomenon in folk literature, and scholars have set forth several explanations. It suffices here merely to note the occurrence and to challenge the reader to see if he can find some examples. The example that stands out here is the age-old "Henny Penny" or "Chicken Little" story. It appears in this volume as "Little Chicken Cluck and his Companions" from Denmark and "The End of the World" from Finland.

Although I have tried to do so here, it is almost impossible to fully convey the feeling of excitement inherent in these tales. It is the power of the real, combined with the darkness of the unknown, and delight of the impossible. Then, too, there is a lyrical, happy, romantic side to these tales, and the earthy, lusty quality that makes Scandinavians unafraid to refer to sex, illegitimacy, and to imagine the mating of mortals and supernatural creatures.

Although I have suggested all this, the reader must really turn to the tales themselves in order to really enjoy all these qualities. Take a journey through Scandinavia, through the centuries, and through the range of experiences that life offers, as well as some that can be found only in the realms of imagination.

New York City                                    CLAIRE BOOSS
1984

## ACKNOWLEDGMENTS

A book such as this cannot be compiled without the valued assistance and suggestions of many others. I would particularly like to thank the folk-lore book specialists Elliot Klein of New York City and Paris, and Kristen Cummings of Stillwater, Minnesota, as well as Alvalene P. and T. Edward Karlsson of the Swedish Book Nook in New York City and Marion F. Adler, children's book specialist of Stockbridge, Massachusetts. Administrators of the library at the Consulate General of Finland were also very helpful.

                                                        C.B.

# TALES FROM NORWAY

THE MAN WHO WAS GOING TO MIND THE HOUSE

# THE MAN WHO WAS GOING TO MIND
## THE HOUSE

THERE WAS once upon a time a man who was always cross and surly, and he was always telling his wife that she didn't do enough work in the house. So one evening in the hay-making time he came home and began to scold and swear all over the house. "Dear me, don't get into such a temper," said the wife; "tomorrow we will try and change our work. I'll go with the mowers and mow the hay, and you can stop at home and mind the house." Yes, the husband rather liked that, and he was quite willing for his part. Early next morning the wife took a scythe on her shoulder, and went out in the fields with the hay-mowers to mow. But the man was to do the work in the house.

He thought he would churn the butter first of all, but when he had churned a while, he became thirsty and went down into the cellar to draw some beer. While he was busy filling the bowl, he heard that the pig had got into the room above. Away he ran up the cellar stairs with the tap in his hand, just to see the pig didn't upset the churn, but when he saw that the pig had already knocked the churn over, and stood there licking up the fine cream, which was running over the floor, he got so furiously wild that he forgot the beer-barrel and turned round on the pig. He got hold of it in the doorway and gave it such a tremendous kick, that it killed the poor pig on the spot. All at once he remembered the tap he had in his hand, but when he went down into the cellar, all the beer had run out of the barrel.

He then went into the larder, and found cream enough to fill the churn again, and so he commenced churning once more, for butter he would have by dinner-time. When he had churned some time he recollected that the cow, which they kept at home, hadn't been let out of the cow-house, and hadn't had a straw of hay or anything to drink, although it was late in the day. He thought it was too far to take the cow to the field where she generally grazed, so it struck him he would put her on the roof; the cottage had a turf-roof, and there was a splendid crop of grass growing there. The cottage lay close to a steep little hill, and if he placed a plank between this and the roof, he thought he could easily get the cow

3

up there. But he could not leave the churn very well, because the baby was crawling about on the floor and he thought the child might easily upset it. He took therefore the churn on his back and went out, but he thought he had better water the cow first, before he put her on the roof. So he took a bucket to get some water from the well; but as he stooped down to pull the bucket up, all the cream ran out of the churn over his neck and down into the well. It would soon be dinner-time, and still he hadn't got any butter, so he thought he had better boil the porridge for dinner, and hung a pot with water over the fire. When he had done this, he began to feel afraid that the cow might fall off the roof and break her legs or her neck, so he went up on the roof to tie her up. The one end of the rope he tied round the neck of the cow, and the other he let down the chimney and tied round his leg when he came down, for the water was boiling already, and he must put the oatmeal in and begin to make the porridge. While he was stirring it, the cow fell off the roof and dragged the man up the chimney by the rope which was tied to his leg; there he stuck, and the cow hung outside against the wall between heaven and earth, for she could neither get up nor down. The wife had waited in seven lengths and seven breadths for her husband to come and call the people home to dinner; but she saw no sign of him, so she thought at last she would wait no longer, but go home. When she saw the cow hanging so awkwardly, she went at once and cut the rope with her scythe, but at the same moment her husband came down the chimney, and when the wife went inside he was standing on his head in the porridge pot.

# THE GIANT WHO HAD NO HEART

THERE WAS once upon a time a king who had seven sons. He loved them all so much that he could never do without them all at once; one had always to be with him. When they were grown up, six of them set out to woo. But the father kept the youngest son at home, and for him the others were to bring back a princess to the palace. The king gave the six the finest clothes you ever set your eyes upon, and you could see the glitter of them a long way off, and each had his own horse, which cost many, many hundred dollars, and so they set out on the journey.

After having been to many royal palaces and seen all the princesses there, they came at last to a king who had six daughters; such lovely princesses they had never seen, and so each of them began wooing one of the six sisters, and when they had got them for sweethearts, they set out for home again; but they quite forgot to bring a princess with them for Ashiepattle,* who was left at home, so busy were they making love to their sweethearts.

*The favourite hero of many Norwegian fairy tales is called "Askeladen," a sort of a male "Cinderella," and is always the youngest son of the family.

THE MAN WHO WAS GOING TO MIND THE HOUSE

When they had journeyed a good bit of the way, they passed close to the side of a steep mountain, where there was a giant's castle. As soon as the giant saw them, he came out and turned them all, princes and princesses, into stone. But the king waited and waited for his six sons, but no sons came. He was very sad, and said that he should never be glad again. "Had you not been left to me," he said to Ashiepattle, "I should not care to live any longer. I am so sad because I have lost your brothers."—"But I have been thinking to ask for leave to set out and find them, I have," said Ashiepattle.—"No, I cannot let you go," said his father; "I shall lose you as well." But Ashiepattle would go, and he begged and prayed till the king gave him leave to go. The king had no other horse to give him but an old jade, for his six brothers and their men had taken all the other horses, but Ashiepattle did not mind that; he mounted the shabby old nag.

"Good-bye, father," said he to the king, "I shall come back, sure enough, and who knows but I shall have my six brothers with me as well," and off he started.

Well, when he had got a bit on his way, he came to a raven, which was lying in the road flapping his wings, and was unable to get out of his way, it was so famished. "Oh, dear friend, give me something to eat, and I will help you in your utmost need," said the raven.—"Very little food have I," said the prince, "and you don't look as if you could help me much either, but a little I must give you, for you want it badly, I see," and then he gave the raven some of the food he had with him. When he had travelled some distance further, he came to a stream. There he saw a big salmon, which had got ashore and was dashing and knocking himself about and could not get into the water again. "Oh, dear friend! help me into the water again," said the salmon to the prince, "and I will help you in your utmost need."—"I don't suppose it can be much of a help you can give me," said the prince, "but it is a pity you should lie there and very likely perish," so he shoved the fish into the stream again. So he travelled a long, long way, till he met a wolf, which was so famished that he was only able to drag himself along the road. "Dear friend, give me your horse," said the wolf. "I am so hungry, I hear the wind whistling in my empty stomach. I have had nothing to eat for two years."—"No," said Ashiepattle, "I can't do it; first I came to a raven which I had to give all my food to; then I came to a salmon which I had to help back into the water; and now you want my horse. But that is impossible, for then I should have nothing to ride upon."—"Yes, yes, my friend, but you must help me," said the wolf, "you can ride on me instead; I shall help you again in your utmost need."— "Well, the help you can give me will not be great; but I suppose you must have the horse then, since you are so needy," said the prince. And when the wolf had finished the horse Ashiepattle took the bridle and put the bit in the wolf's mouth and the saddle on his back, and the wolf felt now so strong and well after what he had had to eat, that he set off with the prince as if he were nothing at all; Ashiepattle had never ridden so fast before. "When we get a little bit further I will show you a giant's castle," said the wolf, and in a little while they came there. "See, here is the giant's castle," said the wolf again, "and there you see all your six brothers, whom the giant has turned into stone, and there are their six brides. Over yonder is the door of the castle, and you must go in there."—"I dare not," said the prince, "the giant will kill me."—"Not at all," answered the wolf; "when you go in there you will meet a princess. She will tell you what to do to make an end of the giant. Only do as she tells you." Well, Ashiepattle went into the castle, but to tell the truth he felt rather afraid. When he got inside, he found the giant was out; but in a chamber sat the princess, just as the wolf had said. Such a lovely maiden Ashiepattle had never seen before.

"Good heavens! what has brought you here?" said the princess, as soon as she saw him. "It's sure to be your death; no one can kill the giant who lives here, for he hasn't got any heart."—"But now when I am here, I suppose I had better try my strength with him," said Ashiepattle, "and I must see if I can't release my brothers who are standing outside here, turned into stone, and I will try to save you as well."—"Well, since you will stop, we must try and do the best we can," said the princess. "You must creep under the bed over there and listen well to what he says when I speak with him, and be sure to lie as quiet as you can."

So Ashiepattle crept under the bed, and no sooner had he done so than the giant came home. "Ugh, what a smell of Christian blood there is here," shouted the giant.—"Yes, a magpie flew over the house with a man's bone and let it fall down the chimney," said the princess; "I made haste to throw it out, but the smell doesn't go away so soon." So the giant said no more about it, and when evening came, they went to bed. When they had lain a while, the princess said: "There is one thing I wanted so very much to ask you about, if I only dared."—"Well, what can that be?" asked the giant.—"I should so like to know where your heart is, since you don't carry it about you," said the princess.—"Oh, that's a thing you needn't know anything about," said the giant, "but if you must know, it's under the stone slab in front of the door."—"Ah, ha! we shall soon see if we can't find that," said Ashiepattle to himself under the bed.

Next morning the giant got up very early and set out for the wood, but no sooner was he out of sight than Ashiepattle and the princess commenced looking for the heart under the door-slab, but although they dug and searched all they could, they could not find anything. "He has made a fool of me this time," said the princess; "but I must try him again." So she picked all the prettiest flowers she could find and strewed them over the door-slab, which they put in its right place again. When the time came for the giant to return home, Ashiepattle crept under the bed, and he had scarcely got well under before the giant came in. "Ugh, what a smell of Christian blood there is here," screamed the giant.—"Yes, a magpie flew over the house and dropped a man's bone down the chimney," said the princess; "I made haste to clear it away, but I suppose the smell hasn't gone away yet."—So the giant said no more about it, but in a little while he asked who it was that had been strewing flowers around the door-slab. "Why, I, of course," said the princess.—"And what's the meaning of it?" asked the giant.—"Well, you know I am so fond of you," said the princess, "that I couldn't help doing it when I knew that your heart was lying under there."—"Ah, indeed," said the giant, "but it isn't there after all."

When they had gone to bed in the evening, the princess asked again where his heart was, because she was so very fond of him, she said, that she would so like to know it. "Oh, it's over in the cupboard on the wall there," said the giant. Ah, ha, thought both Ashiepattle and the princess, we will soon try to find it. Next morning the giant was early out of bed, and made for the wood again, but the moment he was gone Ashiepattle and the princess were looking in the cupboard for the heart, but they looked and searched and found no heart. "Well, we must try once more," said the princess. She hung flowers and garlands around the cupboard, and when the evening came Ashiepattle crept under the bed again. Shortly the giant came in. "Ugh, Ugh!" he roared, "what a smell of Christian blood there is here."—"Yes, a magpie flew past here just now, and dropped a man's bone down the chimney," said the princess; "I made haste to throw it out, but I suppose that's what you still smell." When the giant heard this, he said no more about it; but as soon as he saw the cupboard decked out with flowers and garlands, he asked who it was that had done that. It was the princess, of course. "But what's the meaning of all this foolery?" asked the giant.—"Well, you know how fond I am of you," said the princess; "I couldn't help doing it, when I knew your heart was there."—"How can you be so foolish to believe it?" said the giant.—"Well, how can I help believing it when you say so?" answered the princess.— "Oh, you are a foolish creature," said the giant, "you can never go where my heart is!"—"Ah, well," said the princess, "but I should like to know for all that where it is."—So the giant could not refuse to tell her any longer, and he said: "Far, far away in a lake lies an island,—on that island stands a church,—in that church there is a well,—in that well swims a duck,—in that duck there is an egg,—and in the egg—well, there is my heart."

Early next morning, almost before the dawn of day, the giant set out for the wood again. "Well, I suppose I had better start as well," said Ashiepattle; "I wish I only knew the way!" He said farewell to the princess for a time, and when he came outside the castle there was the wolf still waiting for him. He told the wolf what had happened inside, and that he was now going to set out for the well in the church, if he only knew the way. The wolf asked him to jump on his back,—he would try and find the way, sure enough, he said, and away they went over hills and mountains, over fields and valleys, while the wind whistled about them. When they had travelled many, many days, they came at last to the lake. The prince did not know how he should get across it; but the wolf asked him only not to be afraid, and then he plunged into the water with the prince on his back and swam across to the island. When they came to the church, they found the key for the church-door hanging high, high up on the steeple, and at first the young prince did not know how to get hold of it. "You will have to call the raven," said the wolf, which the prince did. The raven came at once, and flew up for the key, and so the prince got inside the church. When he came to the well, the duck was

The Giant Who Had No Heart

there sure enough. It was swimming about just as the giant had said. He commenced calling and calling, and at last he lured her up to him and caught her. But just as he was lifting her out of the water, the duck let the egg fall in the well; and Ashiepattle didn't know how to get it up again. "You had better call the salmon," said the wolf, which the prince did. The salmon came and fetched the egg from the bottom of the well. The wolf then told him to squeeze the egg, and as soon as Ashiepattle squeezed it, they heard the giant screaming. "Squeeze it once more," said the wolf, and when the prince did so, the giant screamed still more piteously, and prayed so nicely and gently for himself; he would do all the prince wished, if he only wouldn't squeeze his heart to pieces.—"Tell him, that if he will give you back again alive your six brothers and their brides, which he turned into stone, you will spare his life," said the wolf, and Ashiepattle did so.—Yes, the giant would do that at once, and he restored the six princes and the six princesses to life.—"Now, squeeze the egg to pieces," said the wolf. Ashiepattle squeezed it flat between his hands, and the giant burst.

So when Ashiepattle had got rid of the giant, he rode back again on his friend, the wolf, to the giant's castle, and there stood all his six brothers and their brides, all alive, and then Ashiepattle went into the mountain for his own bride, and they all set out for their home, the royal palace. The old king was pleased, I can tell you, when all his seven sons came back, each with his bride. "But the loveliest of the princesses is Ashiepattle's bride after all," said the king, "and he shall sit at the top of the table with her."

And then the wedding came off, and the king gave a grand feast which lasted for many a day, and if they have not done feasting by this, why, they are still at it.

# THE PANCAKE

ONCE UPON a time there was a good housewife, who had seven hungry children. One day she was busy frying pancakes for them, and this time she had used new milk in the making of them. One was lying in the pan, frizzling away—ah! so beautiful and thick,—it was a pleasure to look at it. The children were standing round the fire, and the goodman sat in the corner and looked on.

"Oh, give me a bit of pancake, mother, I am so hungry!" said one child.
"Ah, do! dear mother," said the second.
"Ah, do! dear, good mother," said the third.
"Ah, do! dear, good, kind mother," said the fourth.
"Ah, do! dear, good, kind, nice mother," said the fifth.
"Ah, do! dear, good, kind, nice, sweet mother," said the sixth.
"Ah, do! dear, good, kind, nice, sweet, darling mother," said the

seventh. And thus they were all begging for pancakes, the one more prettily than the other, because they were so hungry, and such good little children.

"Yes, children dear, wait a bit till it turns itself," she answered—she ought to have said "till I turn it"—"and then you shall all have pancakes, beautiful pancakes, made of new milk,—only look how thick and happy it lies there."

When the pancake heard this, it got frightened, and all of a sudden, it turned itself and wanted to get out of the pan, but it fell down in it again on the other side, and when it had been fried a little on that side too, it felt a little stronger in the back, jumped out on the floor, and rolled away, like a wheel, right through the door and down the road.

"Halloo!" cried the goodwife, and away she ran after it, with the frying-pan in one hand and the ladle in the other, as fast as she could, and the children behind her, while the goodman came limping after, last of all.

"Halloo, won't you stop?—Catch it, stop it. Halloo there!" they all screamed, the one louder than the other, trying to catch it on the run, but the pancake rolled and rolled, and before long, it was so far ahead, that they could not see it, for the pancake was much smarter on its legs than any of them.

When it had rolled a time, it met a man.

"Good day, pancake!" said the man.

"Well met, Manny Panny," said the pancake.

"Dear pancake," said the man, "don't roll so fast, but wait a bit and let me eat you."

"When I have run away from Goody Poody and the goodman and seven squalling children, I must run away from you too, Manny Panny," said the pancake, and rolled on and on, till it met a hen.

"Good day, pancake," said the hen.

"Good day, Henny Penny," said the pancake.

"My dear pancake, don't roll so fast, but wait a bit and let me eat you," said the hen.

"When I have run away from Goody Poody and the goodman and seven squalling children, and from Manny Panny, I must run away from you too, Henny Penny," said the pancake, and rolled on like a wheel down the road. Then it met a cock.

"Good day, pancake," said the cock.

"Good day, Cocky Locky," said the pancake.

"My dear pancake, don't roll so fast, but wait a bit and let me eat you," said the cock.

"When I have run away from Goody Poody and the goodman and seven squalling children, from Manny Panny, and Henny Penny, I must run away from you too, Cocky Locky," said the pancake, and rolled and rolled on as fast as it could. When it had rolled a long time, it met a duck.

"Good day, pancake," said the duck.

"Good day, Ducky Lucky," said the pancake.

"My dear pancake, don't roll so fast, but wait a bit and let me eat you," said the duck.

"When I have run away from Goody Poody and the goodman and

seven squalling children, from Manny Panny, and Henny Penny, and Cocky Locky, I must run away from you too, Ducky Lucky," said the pancake, and with that it fell to rolling and rolling as fast as ever it could. When it had rolled a long, long time, it met a goose.

"Good day, pancake," said the goose.

"Good day, Goosey Poosey," said the pancake.

"My dear pancake, don't roll so fast, but wait a bit and let me eat you," said the goose.

"When I have run away from Goody Poody and the goodman and seven squalling children, and Manny Panny, and Henny Penny, and Cocky Locky, and Ducky Lucky, I must run away from you too, Goosey Poosey," said the pancake, and away it rolled. So when it had rolled a long, very long time, it met a gander.

"Good day, pancake," said the gander.

"Good day, Gander Pander," said the pancake.

"My dear pancake, don't roll so fast, but wait a bit and let me eat you," said the gander.

"When I have run away from Goody Poody and the goodman and seven squalling children, and from Manny Panny, and Henny Penny, and Cocky Locky, and Ducky Lucky, and Goosey Poosey, I must run away from you too, Gander Pander," said the pancake, and rolled and rolled as fast as it could. When it had rolled on a long, long time, it met a pig.

"Good day, pancake," said the pig.

"Good day, Piggy Wiggy," said the pancake, and began to roll on faster than ever.

"Nay, wait a bit," said the pig, "you needn't be in such a hurry-scurry; we two can walk quietly together and keep each other company through the wood, because they say it isn't very safe there."

The pancake thought there might be something in that, and so they walked together through the wood; but when they had gone some distance, they came to a brook.

The pig was so fat it wasn't much trouble for him to swim across, but the pancake couldn't get over.

"Sit on my snout," said the pig, "and I will ferry you over."

The pancake did so.

"Ouf, ouf," grunted the pig, and swallowed the pancake in one gulp, and as the pancake couldn't get any farther,—well, you see we can't go on with this story any farther, either.

# THE LAD AND THE DEVIL

ONCE UPON a time there was a lad, who went along a road cracking nuts. He happened to find one which was worm-eaten, and shortly afterwards he met the devil. "Is it true," said the lad, "what they say, that the devil

THE LAD AND THE DEVIL

can make himself as small as he likes, and go through a pin-hole?" "Yes, of course," answered the devil. "Well, let me see you do it; creep into this nut if you can," said the lad. And the devil did it. But he had no sooner got through the worm-hole, than the lad put a small peg in the hole. "I have got you safe, now," he said, and put the nut in his pocket. When he had walked some distance he came to a smithy. He went in there and asked the smith if he would crack that nut for him. "Yes, that's easily done," said the smith, and took the smallest hammer he had, laid the nut on the anvil, and gave it a blow, but it didn't break. So he took a somewhat bigger hammer, but that wasn't heavy enough either; then he took a still bigger one, but no,—the nut would not break. This made the smith angry, and he seized the big sledge-hammer. "I shall soon make bits of you," he said, and he gave the nut such a blow that it went into a thousand pieces, and sent half the roof of the smithy flying in the air. Such a crash! just as if the hut were tumbling together.

"I think the devil was in the nut," said the smith.

"So he was," said the lad.

# THE GREEDY YOUNGSTER

Once upon a time there were five women who were in a field reaping corn. None of them had any children, but they were all wishing for a child. All at once they found a big goose egg, almost as big as a man's head.

"I saw it first," said one. "I saw it just as soon as you did," shouted another. "But I'll have it," screamed the third, "I saw it first of all."

Thus they kept on quarrelling and fighting about the egg, and they were very near tearing each other's hair. But at last they agreed that it should belong to them all, and that they should sit on it as the geese do and hatch a gosling. The first woman sat on it for eight days, taking it very comfortably and doing nothing at all, while the others had to work hard both for their own and her living. One of the women began to make some insinuations to her about this.

"Well, I suppose you didn't come out of the egg either before you could chirp," said the woman who was on the egg. "But I think there is something in this egg, for I fancy I can hear some one inside grumbling every other moment: 'Herring and soup! Porridge and milk!' You can come and sit for eight days now, and then we will sit and work in turn, all of us."

So when the fifth in turn had sat for eight days, she heard plainly some one inside the egg screeching for "Herring and soup! Porridge and milk!" And so she made a hole in it; but instead of a gosling out came a baby, but it was awfully ugly, and had a big head and a tiny little body. The first thing it screamed out for, as soon as it put its head outside the egg, was "Herring and soup! Porridge and milk!" And so they called it "the greedy youngster."

Ugly as he was, they were fond of him at first; but before long he became so greedy that he ate up all the meat they had. When they boiled a dish of soup or a pot of porridge which they thought would be sufficient for all six, he finished it all by himself. So they would not have him any longer.

"I have not had a decent meal since this changeling crept out of the eggshell," said one of them, and when the youngster heard that they were all of the same opinion, he said he was quite willing to go his way; "if they did not want him, he was sure he did not want them," and with that he left the place.

After a long time he came to a farm where the fields were full of stones, and he went in and asked for a situation. They wanted a labourer on the farm, and the farmer put him to pick up stones from the field. Yes, the youngster went to work and picked up the stones, some of which were so big that they would make many cart-loads; but whether they were big or small, he put them all into his pocket. It did not take him long to finish that job, so he wanted to know what he should do next.

"You will have to get all the stones out of the field," said the farmer. "I suppose you can't be ready before you have commenced?"

But the youngster emptied his pockets and threw all the stones in a heap. Then the farmer saw that he had finished the work, and he thought he ought to look well after one who was so strong. He must come in and get something to eat, he said. The youngster thought so too, and he alone ate what was prepared both for master and servants, and still he was only half satisfied.

"He is the right sort of man for a labourer, but he is a terrible eater, to be sure," thought the farmer. "A man like him would eat a poor farmer out of house and home before anybody knew a word about it," he said. He had no more work for him; it was best for him to go to the king's palace.

The youngster set out for the palace, where he got a place at once. There was plenty of food and plenty of work. He was to be errand boy, and to help the girls to carry wood and water and do other odd jobs. So he asked what he was to do first.

"You had better chop some wood in the meantime," they said. Yes, he commenced to chop and cut wood till the splinters flew about him. It was not long before he had chopped up everything in the place, both firewood and timber, both rafters and beams, and when he was ready with it, he came in and asked what he was to do now.

"You can finish chopping the wood," they said.

"There is no more to chop," he answered.

That could not be possible, thought the overlooker, and had a look into the wood-shed. But yes, the youngster had chopped up everything; he had even cut up the timber and planks in the place. This was vexatious, the overlooker said; and then he told the youngster that he should not taste food until he had gone into the forest and cut just as much timber as he had chopped up for firewood.

The youngster went to the smithy and got the smith to help him to make an axe of five hundredweight of iron, and then he set out for the forest and began to make a regular clearance, not only of the pine and the lofty fir trees, but of everything else which was to be found in the king's forests, and in the neighbours' as well. He did not stop to cut the branches or the tops off, but he left them lying there as if a hurricane had blown them down. He put a proper load on the sledge and put all the horses to it, but they could not even move it; so he took the horses by the heads to give the sledge a start, but he pulled so hard that the horses' heads came off. He then turned the horses out of the shafts and drew the load himself.

When he came to the palace, the king and his overlooker were standing in the hall to give him a scolding for having destroyed the forest—the overlooker had been there and seen what he had been doing. But when the king saw the youngster dragging half the forest after him, he got both angry and afraid; but he thought he had better be a little careful with him, since he was strong.

"Well, you are a wonderful workman, to be sure," said the king; "but how much do you eat at a time, because I suppose you are hungry now?"

Oh, when he was to have a proper meal of porridge, it would take twelve barrels of meal to make it, thought the youngster; but when he had put that away, he could wait a while, of course, for his next meal.

It took some time to boil such a dish of porridge, and meantime he was to bring in a little firewood for the cook. He put a lot of wood on a sledge, but when he was coming through the door with it, he was a little rough and careless again. The house got almost out of shape, and all the joists creaked; he was very near dragging down the whole palace. When the porridge was nearly ready, they sent him out to call the people home from the fields. He shouted so that the mountains and hills around rang with echoes, but the people did not come quick enough for him. He came to blows with them, and killed twelve of them.

"You have killed twelve men," said the king; "and you eat for many times twelve; but how many do you work for?"

"For many times twelve as well," answered the youngster.

When he had finished his porridge, he was to go into the barn to thrash. He took one of the rafters from the roof and made a flail out of it, and when the roof was about to fall in, he took a big pine tree with branches and all and put it up instead of the rafter. So he went on thrashing the grain and the straw and the hay all together. This was doing more damage than good, for the corn and the chaff flew about together, and a cloud of dust arose over the whole palace.

When he had nearly finished thrashing, enemies came into the country, as a war was coming on. So the king told the youngster that he should take men with him to go and meet the enemy and fight them, for the king thought they would surely kill him.

No, he would not have any men with him to be cut to pieces; he would fight by himself, answered the youngster.

"So much the better," thought the king; "the sooner I shall get rid of him; but he must have a proper club."

They sent for the smith; he forged a club which weighed a hundred-weight. "A very nice thing to crack nuts with," said the youngster. So the smith made one of three hundredweight. "It would do very well for hammering nails into boots," was the answer. Well, the smith could not make a bigger one with the men he had. So the youngster set out for the smithy himself, and made a club that weighed five tons, and it took a hundred men to turn it on the anvil. "That one might do for lack of a better," thought the youngster. He wanted next a bag with some provisions they had to make one out of fifteen oxhides, and they filled it with food, and away he went down the hill with the bag on his back and the club on his shoulder.

When he came so far that the enemy saw him, they sent a soldier to ask him if he was going to fight them.

"Yes; but wait a little till I have had something to eat," said the youngster. He threw himself down on the grass and began to eat with the big bag of food in front of him.

But the enemy would not wait, and commenced to fire at him at once, till it rained and hailed around him with bullets.

"I don't mind these crowberries a bit," said the youngster, and went on eating harder than ever. Neither lead nor iron took any effect upon him, and his bag with food in front of him guarded him against the bullets as if it were a rampart.

So they commenced throwing bomb-shells and firing cannons at him. He only grinned a little every time he felt them.

"They don't hurt me a bit," he said. But just then he got a bomb-shell right down his windpipe.

"Fy!" he shouted, and spat it out again; but then a chain-shot made its way into his butter-can, and another carried away the piece of food he held between his fingers.

That made him angry; he got up and took his big club and struck the ground with it, asking them if they wanted to take the food out of his mouth, and what they meant by blowing crowberries at him with those pea-shooters of theirs. He then struck the ground again till the hills and rocks rattled and shook, and sent the enemy flying in the air like chaff. This finished the war.

When he came home again, and asked for more work, the king was taken quite aback, for he thought he should have got rid of him in the war. He knew of nothing else but to send him on a message to the devil.

"You had better go to the devil and ask him for my ground-rent," he said. The youngster took his bag on his back, and started at once. He was not long in getting there, but the devil was gone to court, and there was no one at home but his mother, and she said that she had never heard talk of any ground-rent. He had better call again another time.

"Yes, call again to-morrow is always the cry," he said; but he was not going to be made a fool of, he told her. He was there, and there he would remain till he got the ground-rent. He had plenty of time to wait. But when he had finished all the food in his bag, the time hung heavy on his hands, and then he asked the old lady for the ground-rent again. She had better pay it now, he said.

"No, she was going to do nothing of the sort," she said. Her words were as firm as the old fir tree just outside the gates, which was so big that fifteen men could scarcely span it.

But the youngster climbed right up in the top of it and twisted and turned it as if it was a willow, and then he asked her if she was going to pay the ground-rent now.

Yes, she dared not do anything else, and scraped together as much money as he thought he could carry in his bag. He then set out for home with the ground-rent, but as soon as he was gone, the devil came home. When he heard that the youngster had gone off with his bag full of money, he first of all gave his mother a hiding, and then he started after him, thinking he would soon overtake him.

He soon came up to him, for he had nothing to carry, and now and then he used his wings; but the youngster had of course to keep to the ground with his heavy bag. Just as the devil was at his heels, he began to jump and run as fast as he could. He kept his club behind him to keep the devil off, and thus they went along, the youngster holding the handle and the devil trying to catch hold of the other end of it, till they came to a deep valley. There the youngster made a jump across from the top of one hill to the other, and the devil was in such a hurry to follow him that he ran his head against the club and fell down into the valley and broke his leg, and there he lay.

"There is the ground-rent," said the youngster when he came to the palace, and threw the bag with the money to the king with such a crash that you could hear it all over the hall.

The king thanked him, and appeared to be well pleased, and promised him good pay and leave of absence if he wished it, but the youngster wanted only more work.

"What shall I do now?" he said.

As soon as the king had had time to consider, he told him that he must go the hill-troll, who had taken his grandfather's sword. The troll had a castle by the sea, where no one dared to go.

The youngster put some cartloads of food into his bag and set out again. He travelled both long and far, over woods and hills and wild moors, till he came to the big mountains where the troll, who had taken the sword of the king's grandfather, was living.

But the troll seldom came out in the open air, and the mountain was well closed, so the youngster was not man enough to get inside.

So he joined a gang of quarrymen who were living at a farm on top of the hill, and who were quarrying stones in the hills about there. They had never had such help before, for he broke and hammered away at the rocks till the mountain cracked, and big stones of the size of a house rolled down the hill. But when he rested to get his dinner, for which he was going to have one of the cartloads in his bag, he found it was all eaten up.

"I have generally a good appetite myself," said the youngster; "but the one who has been here can do a trifle more than I, for he has eaten all the bones as well."

Thus the first day passed; and he fared no better the second. On the third day he set out to break stones again, taking with him the third load of food; but he lay down behind the bag and pretended to be asleep. All of a sudden, a troll with seven heads came out of the mountain and began to eat his food.

"It's all ready for me here, and I will eat," said the troll.

"We will see about that," said the youngster, and hit the troll with his club, so the heads rolled down the hill.

So he went into the mountain which the troll had come out of and in there stood a horse eating out of a barrel of glowing cinders, and behind it stood a barrel of oats.

"Why don't you eat out of the barrel of oats?" asked the youngster.

"Because I cannot turn around," said the horse.

"But I will soon turn you round," said the youngster.

"Rather cut my head off," said the horse.

So he cut its head off, and the horse turned into a fine handsome fellow. He said he had been bewitched, and taken into the mountain and turned into a horse by the troll. He then helped the youngster to find the sword, which the troll had hidden at the bottom of the bed, and in the bed lay the old mother of the troll, asleep and snoring hard.

So they set out for home by water, but when they had got some distance out to sea the old mother came after them. As she could not overtake them, she lay down and began to drink the sea, and she drank till the water fell; but she could not drink the sea dry, and so she burst.

When they came to land, the youngster sent word that the king must come and fetch the sword. He sent four horses, but no, they could not move it; he sent eight, and he sent twelve; but the sword remained where it was. They were not able to stir it from the spot. But the youngster took it and carried it up to the palace alone.

The king could not believe his eyes when he saw the youngster back again. He appeared however to be pleased to see him, and promised him land and riches. When the youngster wanted more work, the king said he might set out for an enchanted castle he had, where no one dared to live, and he would have to stop there till he had built a bridge over the sound, so that people could get across to the castle.

If he was able to do this he would reward him handsomely, yes, he would even give him his daughter in marriage, said he.

"Well, I think I can do it," said the youngster.

No one had ever got away alive; those who had got as far as the castle, lay there killed and torn to pieces as small as barley, and the king thought he should never see him any more if he would go thither.

But the youngster started on his expedition; he took with him the bag of food, a crooked, twisted block of a fir tree, an axe, a wedge, and some chips of the fir root, and the small pauper boy at the palace.

When he came to the sound, he found the river full of ice, and the current ran as strong as in a waterfall; but he stuck his legs to the bottom of the river and waded till he got safe across.

When he had warmed himself and had something to eat, he wanted to go to sleep, but before long he heard such a terrible noise, as if they were turning the castle upside down. The door burst wide open, and he saw nothing but a gaping jaw extending from the threshold up to the lintel.

"There is a mouthful for you," said the youngster, and threw the pauper boy into the swallow; "taste that! But let me see now who you are! Perhaps you are an old acquaintance?"

And so it was; it was the devil who was about again.

They began to play cards, for the devil wanted to try and win back some of the ground-rent which the youngster had got out of his mother by threats, when he was sent by the king to collect it; but the youngster was always the fortunate one, for he put a cross on the back of all the good cards, and when he had won all the money which the devil had upon him, the devil had to pay him out of the gold and silver which was in the castle.

Suddenly the fire went out, so they could not tell the one card from the other.

"We must chop some wood now," said the youngster, who drove the axe into the fir block, and forced the wedge in; but the twisted, knotty block would not split, although the youngster worked as hard as he could with the axe.

"They say you are strong," he said to the devil; "just spit on your hands, stick your claws in, and tear away, and let me see what you are made of."

The devil did so, and put both his fists into the split and pulled as hard as he could, when the youngster suddenly struck the wedge out, and the devil stuck fast in the block and the youngster let him also have a taste of the butt end of his axe on his back. The devil begged and prayed so nicely to be let loose, but the youngster would not listen to anything of the kind unless he promised that he would never come there any more and create any disturbance. He also had to promise that he would build a bridge over the sound, so that people could pass over it at all times of the year, and it should be ready when the ice was gone.

"They are very hard conditions," said the devil; but there was no other way out of it—if the devil wanted to be set free, he would have to promise it. He bargained, however, that he should have the first soul that went across the bridge. That was to be the toll.

Yes, he should have that, said the youngster. So the devil was let loose, and he started home. But the youngster lay down to sleep, and slept till far into the day.

When the king came to see if he was cut and chopped into small pieces, he had to wade through all the money before he came to his bedside. There was money in heaps and in bags which reached far up the wall, and the youngster lay in bed asleep and snoring hard.

"Lord help me and my daughter," said the king when he saw that the youngster was alive. Well, all was good and well done that no one could deny; but there was no hurry talking of the wedding before the bridge was ready.

One day the bridge stood ready, and the devil was there waiting for the toll which he had bargained for.

The youngster wanted the king to go with him and try the bridge, but the king had no mind to do it. So he mounted a horse himself, and put

THE GREEDY YOUNGSTER

the fat dairy-maid in the palace on the pommel in front of him; she looked almost like a big fir-block, and so he rode over the bridge, which thundered under the horse's feet.

"Where is the toll? Where have you got the soul?" cried the devil.

"Why, inside this fir-block," said the youngster; "if you want it you will have to spit in your hands and take it."

"No, many thanks! if she does not come to me, I am sure I sha'n't take her," said the devil. "You got me once into a pinch, and I'll take care you don't get me into another," and with that he flew straight home to his old mother, and since that time he has never been heard or seen thereabouts.

The youngster went home to the palace and asked for the reward the king had promised him, and when the king wanted to get out of it, and would not stick to what he had promised, the youngster said it was best he got a good bag of food ready for him, and he would take his reward himself.

Yes, the king would see to that, and when the bag was ready the youngster asked the king to come outside the door. The youngster then gave the king such a kick, which sent him flying up in the air. The bag he threw after him that he might not be without food, and if he has not come down again by this, he is floating about with his bag between heaven and earth to this very day.

# THE SEVEN FATHERS IN THE HOUSE

THERE WAS once upon a time a man who was travelling about, and he came at length to a big and fine farm; it was such a fine mansion that it might well have been a little palace. "It would be a nice thing to get a night's rest here," said the man to himself, when he came inside the gate. Close by stood an old man with grey hair and beard, and chopped wood. "Good evening, father," said the traveller; "can I get lodgings here to-night?" "I am not the father in the house," said the old man, "go into the kitchen and speak to my father!" The traveller went into the kitchen; there he met a man who was still older, and he was lying on his knees in front of the hearth, blowing into the fire. "Good evening, father; can I get lodgings here to-night?" asked the traveller. "I am not the father in the house," said the old man; "but go in and speak to my father; he is sitting by the table in the parlour." So the traveller went into the parlour and spoke to him who was sitting by the table; he was much older than the other two, and he sat there with chattering teeth, shaking, and reading in a big book, almost like a little child. "Good evening, father; can you give me lodgings here to-night?" said the man. "I am not the father in the house; but speak to my father over there, he who sits on the bench," said the man who was sitting at the table with chattering teeth, and shaking and shivering. So the traveller went to him who was sitting

THE SEVEN FATHERS IN THE HOUSE

on the bench; he was getting a pipe of tobacco ready; but he was so bent with age, and his hands shook so much, that he was scarcely able to hold the pipe. "Good evening, father," said the traveller again; "can I get lodgings here to-night?"—"I am not the father in the house," said the old, bent-up man; "but speak to my father, who is in the bed over yonder." The traveller went to the bed, and there lay an old, old man, and the only thing about him that seemed to be alive was a pair of big eyes. "Good evening, father; can I get lodgings here to-night?" said the traveller. "I am not the father in the house; but speak to my father, who lies in the cradle yonder," said the man with the big eyes. Yes, the traveller went to the cradle; there was a very old man lying, so shrivelled up, that he was not larger than a baby, and one could not have told that there was life in him if it had not been for a sound in his throat now and then. "Good evening, father; can I get lodgings here to-night?" said the man. It took some time before he got an answer, and still longer before he had finished it; he said, like the others, that he was not the father in the house; "But speak to my father; he is hanging up in the horn against the wall there." The traveller stared round the walls, and at last he caught sight of the horn; but when he looked for him who hung in it, there was scarcely anything to be seen but a lump of white ashes, which had the appearance of a man's face. Then he was so frightened, that he cried aloud: "Good evening, father; will you give me lodgings here to-night?" There was a sound like a little tomtit's chirping, but it was no more than he was just able to understand that it meant, "Yes, my child." And now a table came in which was covered with the costliest dishes, with ale and brandy; and when he had eaten and drunk, in came a good bed with reindeer skins, and the traveller was very glad indeed that he at last had found the right father in the house.

# THE SMITH AND THE DEVIL

ONCE UPON a time, in those days when the saints used to wander about on earth, two of them came to a smith. He had made a bargain with the devil that he should belong to him after seven years, if he during that time was to be the master over all masters in his profession. Both he and the devil had put their names to this contract. So the smith wrote with great letters over the smithy door: "Here lives the master over all masters." When the two saints saw this, they went in to the smith, and the elder asked him: "Who are you?"—"Read what there's written over the door," answered the smith; "but perhaps you cannot read writing, so you had better wait till some one comes by who can help you." Before the saint could answer him a man came with his horse, which he asked the smith to shoe for him. "Will you let me shoe it?" asked the saint. "You may try," said the smith; "you cannot do it so badly but I shall be able to put it right again." The saint went out and took one leg off the horse and put it in the fire on the forge and made the shoe red hot; he then sharpened the points, clenched the nails, and put the leg back in its place again. When he had done with that leg, he took the other fore-leg, and did the same with it; and when he had put that in its place, he took the hind-legs, first the right and then the left, put them in the fire, made the shoes red hot, sharpened the points and clenched the nails, and then he put them on the horse again. The smith stood and looked on all the while. "You are not such a bad smith after all," he said. "Ah, you think so," said the saint.

Just then the smith's mother came across to the smithy and asked him to come home and eat his dinner; she was very old, and had a crooked back and big wrinkles in her face, and she was scarcely able to walk.

"Take notice of what you now will see," said the saint. He took the woman, put her in the fire, and forged a young, lovely maiden out of her. "I say what I said before," said the smith, "you are not at all a bad smith. You will find over my door: 'Here lives the master over all masters,' but for all that, I now see that one learns as long as he lives"—and with that he went home and ate his dinner.

As soon as he came back to the smithy, a man came riding, who wanted to have his horse shod. "I shall soon do that for you," said the smith; "I have just learned a new way to shoe horses, and a very good one it is when the days are short;" and so he commenced cutting and breaking away at the horse's legs, till he got them all off—"for I don't see the use of going forwards and backwards with one at a time," he said—and put the legs in the fire as he had seen the saint do. He put plenty of coals on, and let his boy work the bellows smartly; but it went as one might expect—the legs were burnt up, and the smith had to pay for the horse. This was not exactly to his liking, but at that moment a poor old woman, who went about begging, came past, and he thought if one thing does not succeed another may. So he took the old woman and put her in the fire, and although she cried and begged for her life, it was of no use. "You don't know what is good for you, although you are so old," said the smith; "I will make a young woman of you in half a minute, and I shan't charge as much as a penny for the job."

It fared no better with the poor old woman than with the horse's legs. Just then the saints came round again to him. "That was ill done," said the saint. "Oh, I don't think there are many who will be asking after her," answered the smith; "but it is a great shame that the devil doesn't hold to what is written over the door."—"If you might have three wishes from me," said the saint, "what would you wish for yourself?" "Try me," answered the smith, "and you will get to know."

The saint then gave him three wishes. "First of all, I wish that when I ask anybody to climb up in the pear-tree just outside the smithy, he must sit there till I myself ask him to come down again," said the smith. "Secondly, I wish that any one whom I ask to sit down in the arm-chair in the smithy there must remain in it till I myself ask him to get up; and, last of all, I wish that if I ask anybody to creep into the steel-ring purse which I have in my pocket, he must remain there till I give him leave to creep out again."

"You have wished like a foolish man," said the other saint. "First of all you should have wished for leave to get into paradise."—"I dared not ask for that," said the smith, and bade the saints farewell.

Well, days came and days passed, and when the time was up, the devil came to fetch the smith according to the agreement.

"Are you ready now?" he said, as he put his nose in at the door of the smithy. "Well, yes; but I want to finish the head of this nail first," said the smith; "just climb up into the pear-tree and take a pear. You must be both hungry and thirsty after your journey." The devil thanked him for the kind offer, and climbed up into the tree.

"Now that I think of it," said the smith, "I don't think I shall get this head finished for the next four years, for this iron is so terribly hard. You can't come down in that time, but you may sit there and rest yourself." The devil begged and prayed that he might get leave to come down again, but all in vain. At last he had to promise that he would not come back till the fours years were out, and so the smith said: "Well, on that condition you may come down."

When the time was up, the devil came again to fetch the smith. "You are ready now, I suppose?" he said. "I think you have had time to finish the head of that nail by this." "Yes, I have finished the head, of course," answered the smith; "but still you have come a trifle too early, because I have not sharpened the point yet; such hard iron I have never in my life worked at before. While I hammer down the point of the nail, you might as well sit down in my arm-chair and rest yourself, for I suppose you are pretty tired."

The devil thanked him for his kindness, and sat down in the arm-chair; but he had no sooner sat down for a good rest than the smith said, that taking everything into consideration, he could not get the point properly sharpened in less than four years. The devil at first begged very prettily to be let out of the chair, and after a time he grew angry and began to threaten; but the smith excused himself the best way he could, and said it was all the fault of the iron, for it was really so terribly hard, and gave the devil the consolation that he sat very comfortably in the arm-chair, and that he in four years' time would let him out exactly to the minute. There was no other help for it; the devil had to promise that he would not come to fetch the smith till the four years were out, and so the smith said: "Well, on that condition you may go," and away the devil went as fast as he could.

In four years' time the devil came again to fetch the smith. "You are ready now, of course?" said the devil, as he put his nose in at the door of the smithy. "Ready, quite ready," answered the smith; "we can start when you like. But there is one thing," he continued, "which I have been standing here and thinking about for a long time, to ask you about. Is it true, what they say, that the devil can make himself as small as he likes?"—"Yes, of course," answered the devil.—"Ah, perhaps you could do me the favour to creep into this steel-ring purse and see if there are any

THE SMITH AND THE DEVIL

holes at the bottom," said the smith; "I am so afraid I shall lose my money for the journey."—"Oh, yes, with pleasure," said the devil, and made himself small and crept into the purse. But he had scarcely got inside when the smith closed the purse.

"It is safe and sound everywhere," said the devil inside the purse.

"I am glad to hear you say that," answered the smith; "but it is better to be prudent beforehand than wise afterwards. I think I will weld the joints a little better together, just for safety's sake you know," and with that he put the purse in the fire and made it red hot.

"Oh dear! oh dear!" cried the devil; "are you mad? Don't you know I am inside the purse?"

"Yes, but I can't help you," said the smith. "There's an old saying, that 'one must strike while the iron is hot,' " and so he took his big sledge-hammer, put the purse on the anvil, and hammered away as hard as he could.

"Oh dear! oh dear! oh dear!" screamed the devil inside the purse. "Dear friend, do let me out and I shall never come back again."

"Well, I think the joints are pretty well welded together now," said the smith, "so now you may come out again." With this he opened the purse, and the devil rushed away in such a hurry that he did not even look behind him.

Some time after this, the smith began thinking that he had perhaps done a foolish thing by making the devil his enemy. "For suppose the saints above won't have me," he said, "I may run the risk of being home-less altogether, since I have fallen out with the old man down below." He thought it would be as well to try and get into one of the two places at once, better early than late; and so he took his sledge-hammer on his shoulder and started. When he had gone some distance, he came to a place where the road divides into two—one leading to paradise, and the other to the devil. Just at this point he overtook a tailor, who was hurry-ing along with his smoothing-iron in his hand. "Good day," said the smith, "where are you off to?"—"To paradise, if I can get in there," answered the tailor; "and you?"—"Well, I shan't have the pleasure of your company for long then," answered the smith; "I have made up my mind to try the other place first, because I happen to know the old man a little already." So they bade one another "Farewell," and each went his way.

But the smith was a strong, powerful man, and he walked much faster than the tailor, so it did not take him long to get to his destination. He told the gatekeeper to go and tell his master that there was some one outside who wished to speak with him.

"Go and ask who he is," said the devil to the gatekeeper, who went out and asked the smith.

"Give your master my compliments, and tell him that it is the smith who has that purse which he knows of," said the smith; "and just ask him kindly to let me in at once, for I have been working in the smithy till dinner-time, and since I have walked all the way."

When the devil heard this, he ordered the gatekeeper to lock all the nine locks on the gate—"and put on an extra padlock as well," said the devil, "for if he comes inside, he will upset the place altogether."—"Well, there is no shelter to be got here, I see," said the smith, when he heard them locking the gate more securely; "I had better try my luck in paradise." And with that he turned round and went back till he reached the cross road. There he followed the road which the tailor had taken. As he was rather angry at having had to walk all the way to the devil's and back for no good, he hurried on as fast as he could and reached the gate of paradise just as St. Peter opened it a little, that the thin, skinny tailor might slip in. The smith was still six or seven paces from the gate. "I think it's best to make haste now," said the smith. He took the sledge-hammer and hurled it into the opening of the door just as the tailor got inside.

If the smith didn't get it through the opening that time, I don't know what has become of him since.

# THE THREE BILLY-GOATS WHO WENT UP INTO THE HILLS TO GET FAT

THERE WERE once upon a time three Billy-goats, who were going up into the hills to get fat. On the way there was a bridge over a torrent which they had to cross. Under the bridge lived a big, ugly troll, with eyes as big as saucers, and a nose as long as a rake-handle.

First of all came the youngest Billy-goat, and was going over the bridge. Trip trap, trip trap, went the bridge.—"Who is that tripping over my bridge?" shouted the troll.—"Oh! it's only the smallest Billy-goat; I'm going up into the hills to get fat," said the goat; he had such a small voice.—"I'm coming to take you!" said the troll.—"Oh no! please don't take me, for I am so little. Wait a while till the next Billy-goat comes; he is much bigger."—"Very well!" said the troll.

In a little while came the next Billy-goat, and was going over the bridge. Trip trap, trip trap, trip trap went the bridge.—"Who is that tripping over my bridge?" shouted the troll.—"Oh, it's only the second Billy-goat; I'm going up into the hills to get fat," said the goat; he hadn't such a small voice as the first one.—"I'm coming to take you," said the troll.— "Oh no! please don't take me, but wait till the big Billy-goat comes; he is much bigger."—"Very well then!" said the troll.

Just then came the big Billy-goat. Trip trap, trip trap, trip trap went the bridge. He was so heavy that the bridge creaked and groaned under him.—"Who is that tramping over my bridge?" shouted the troll.—"It's the big Billy-goat!" said the goat; he had an awful hoarse voice.—"I'm coming to take you," screamed the troll.

"Come on, and blinded you shall reel
From my two spears, whose points are steel.
Like grain between two granite stones
I'll crush your marrow and your bones!"

said the big Billy-goat, and flew straight at the troll and poked his eyes out, crushed him, bones and all, to pieces, and pushed him out into the torrent, and then he went up into the hills. There the Billy-goats got so fat, that they were scarcely able to walk home again, and if the fat hasn't gone off them, they are still as fat as ever. And snip, snap, snout, here my tale is out.

# PETER GYNT

IN THE olden days there lived in Kvam a hunter, whose name was Peter Gynt, and who was always roaming about in the mountains after bears and elks, for in those days there were more forests on the mountains than there are now, and consequently plenty of wild beasts. One evening late in the autumn, long after the cattle had left the mountains, Peter set out on one of his usual expeditions. All the dairy-maids had also gone away, except the three girls at the Vala dairy. When Peter came up towards Hövring, where he intended to stay for the night in a deserted dairy, it was so dark that he could scarcely see an arm's length before him. The dogs began barking violently, and it was altogether very dismal and unpleasant. All of a sudden he ran against something, and when he put his hand out, he felt it was cold and slippery and very big. As he didn't think he had gone off the road, he had no idea of what this something could be, but unpleasant it was at any rate.

"Who is it?" asked Peter, for he could now feel it was moving.

"Oh, it's Humpy," was the answer.

Peter was no wiser for this, but walked on one side for some distance, thinking that so he would be able to pass the mysterious presence. But he ran against something again, and when he put his hand out he felt it was very big, cold, and slippery.

"Who is it?" asked Peter Gynt.

"Oh, it's Humpy," was the answer again.

"Well, you'll have to let me pass, whether you are Humpy or not," said Peter, for he guessed now that he was walking round in a ring, and that the monster had circled itself round the dairy. Just then the monster shifted itself a little, and Peter got past and soon found the house. When he came inside he found it was no lighter in there than outside. He was feeling his way about along the wall to put his gun away and hang his bag up, but while he was groping about in this way, he felt again something cold, big, and slippery.

PETER GYNT

"Who is it?" shouted Peter.

"Oh, it's the big Humpy," was the answer. Wherever he put his hands out or tried to get past he ran against the monster.

"It's not very pleasant to be here, I am sure," thought Peter, "since this Humpy is both outside and inside, but I'll try if I can't shunt this intruder out of my way."

So he took his gun and went outside, feeling his way carefully, till he found what he thought was the head of the monster, which he felt sure was a monster troll.

"What are you, and who are you?" asked Peter.

"Oh, I am the big Humpy from Etnedale," said the troll. Peter did not lose a moment, but fired three shots right into the troll's head.

"Fire another," said the troll. But Peter knew better; if he had fired another shot, the bullet would have rebounded against himself.

Both Peter and the dogs then commenced dragging the troll out of the house, so that they might come inside and make themselves comfortable. Whilst he was so employed he heard jeers and laughter in the hills round about.

"Peter dragged a bit, but the doggies dragged more," said a voice.

Next morning he went out stalking. When he came in between the hills, he saw a lassie, who was calling some sheep up a hill-side. But when he came up to the place, she was gone and the sheep too, and he saw nothing but a pack of bears.

"Well, I never saw bears in a pack before," said Peter to himself. When he went nearer, they had all disappeared, except one.

> "Look after your pig,
> For Peter Gynt is out
> With his gun so big,"

shouted a voice over in the hill.

"Ah, he can't hurt my pig; he hasn't washed himself to-day," said another voice in the hill. Peter washed his hands with some water he had with him. He fired, and shot the bear. Then he heard more jeers and laughter in the hill.

"You should have looked after your pig!" cried a voice.

"I forgot he carried water with him," answered another.

Peter skinned the bear and buried the carcass. On his way home he met a fox.

"Look at my lamb! How fat it is," said a voice in a hill.

"Look at Peter, he is lifting that gun of his," said another voice, just as Peter put his gun up and shot the fox. He skinned the fox also, and took the skin with him. When he came to the dairy, he put both the head of the fox and the bear on the wall outside the house, with their jaws wide open. So he lighted a fire and put a pot on to boil some soup, but the chimney smoked so terribly that he could scarcely keep his eyes open, and had therefore to open a small window. Some time after a troll came and poked his nose in; the nose was so long that it reached across the room to the fireplace.

"Here is a proper nose, if you like," said the troll.

"And here is proper soup! You never tasted the like;" and with that he poured the boiling soup over the troll's nose. The troll ran away wailing and crying, but in all the hills around they were jeering and laughing, and the voices shouted:

"Nosey stew! Nosey stew!"

It was now quiet for some time. Shortly Peter heard a great noise and bustle outside the house. He looked out, and saw a big carriage drawn by bears. They were carting away the big monster into the mountain. Suddenly a bucket of water was thrown down the chimney; the fire was put out, and Peter sat all in the dark. Then a laughing and chuckling commenced in all corners of the room, and a voice said:—

"Now Peter is no better off than the girls at Vala."

So Peter made the fire again, shut up the dairy, and set off for the Vala dairy, taking the dogs with him. When he had gone some distance he saw such a glare of light in the direction of the dairy that it seemed to him the house must be on fire. Just then he came across some wolves. Some of these he shot, and some his dogs killed. But when he came to the dairy it was all dark there; there was no sign of any fire. There were three strangers in the room amusing themselves with the dairy-maids, and one outside the door. They were four hill-trolls, and their names were Gust, Tron, Tjöstöl, and Rolf. Gust was standing outside keeping watch, while the others were inside courting the girls. Peter fired at Gust, but missed him. But the troll ran away frightened, and when Peter came inside he found the trolls flirting with the girls more desperately than ever. Two of them were terribly frightened and were saying their prayers, but the third, who was called Mad Kari, wasn't a bit afraid. They might come there for all she cared; she would like to see what sort of fellows they were. But when the trolls found that Peter was in the room they began whining, and told Rolf to get a light. And then the dogs rushed at Tjöstöl and knocked him over on his back into the burning embers of the fire, so the sparks flew about him.

"Did you see any of my snakes about, Peter?" asked Tron—that was what he called the wolves.

"I'll send you the same way as the snakes," said Peter, and fired a shot at him, and then he killed Tjöstöl with the butt-end of his rifle. Rolf had fled through the chimney.

So when he had cleared all the trolls out, the girls packed up their things, and Peter accompanied them home. They dared not stay any longer up on the hills.

Shortly before Christmas, Peter set out again on another expedition. He had heard of a farm on Dovrefell which was invaded by such a number of trolls every Christmas-eve that the people on the farm had to move out, and get shelter at some of their neighbours. He was anxious to go there, for he had a great fancy to come across the trolls again. He dressed himself in some old ragged clothes, and took a tame white bear, which he had, with him, as well as an awl, some pitch, and twine. When he came to the farm he went in and asked for lodgings.

"God help us!" said the farmer; "we can't give you any lodgings. We have to clear out of the house ourselves soon and look for lodgings, for every Christmas-eve we have the trolls here."

But Peter thought he should be able to clear the trolls out—he had done such a thing before; and then he got leave to stay, and a pig's skin into the bargain. The bear lay down behind the fireplace, and Peter took out his awl, and pitch, and twine, and began making a big, big shoe, which it took the whole pig's skin to make. He put a strong rope in for laces, that he might pull the shoe tightly together, and, finally, he armed himself with a couple of handspikes.

Shortly he heard the trolls coming. They had a fiddler with them, and some began dancing, while others fell to eating the Christmas fare on the table—some fried bacon, and some fried frogs and toads, and other nasty things which they had brought with them. During this some of the trolls found the shoe Peter had made. They thought it must belong to a very big foot. They all wanted to try it on at once, so they put a foot each into it; but Peter made haste and tightened the rope, took one of the handspikes and fastened the rope around it, and got them at last securely tied up in the shoe.

Just then the bear put his nose out from behind the fireplace, where he was lying, and smelt they were frying something.

"Will you have a sausage, pussy?" said one of the trolls, and threw a hot frog right into the bear's jaw.

"Scratch them, pussy!" said Peter.

The bear got so angry that he rushed at the trolls and scratched them all over, while Peter took the other handspike and hammered away at them as if he wanted to beat their brains out. The trolls had to clear out at last, but Peter stayed and enjoyed himself with all the Christmas fare the whole week. After that the trolls were not heard of there for many years.

Some years afterwards, about Christmas-time, the farmer was out in the forest cutting wood for the holidays, when a troll came up to him and shouted—

"Have you got that big pussy of yours, yet?"

"Oh, yes, she is at home behind the fireplace," said the farmer; "and she has got seven kittens all bigger and larger than herself."

"We'll never come to you any more, then," said the troll.


# LEGENDS OF THE MILL


WHEN THE world goes against me, and it is very seldom it forgets to do so whenever there is an opportunity, I have always felt a relief in taking walks in the open air as an alleviation of my portion of troubles and anxieties. What there was the matter with me on this occasion I cannot now remember, but what I clearly recollect is, that one summer afternoon

LEGENDS OF THE MILL

some years ago I took my fishing-rod and strolled through the fields on the eastern side of the Akers river, on my way to the outlet of the Maridale lake.

The bright air, the scent of the new-mown hay, the fragrance of the flowers, the singing of the birds, the walk and the fresh breezes from the river, greatly revived my spirits. When I came to the bridge by the outlet, the sun was sinking behind the ridge of the hills, at one moment lighting up the evening clouds with all his lustre, that they for a brief time might rejoice in their borrowed splendour and reflect themselves in the clear waters of the lake, and then for another brief moment breaking through the clouds and sending forth a ray of light, which formed golden paths in the dark pine-forests of the farther shore. After the hot day the evening breeze carried a refreshing fragrance from the pine-trees, and the distant expiring notes of the cuckoo's evening song disposed the mind to sadness. My eyes followed mechanically the drifting flies as they floated down the river with the stream.

But look! there rose a silvery fish; the line ran whizzing off the reel, and when I stopped it the rod stood bent into a hoop; it must be a trout of about two pounds! There was now no time for going into raptures about the fragrance of the pine-trees or the cuckoo's notes; I wanted all my presence of mind to land the fish. The current was strong and the fish fought bravely, and as I had no landing-net I had to pay out more line, and wind in again twice or thrice, before I could bring him with the current into a small bay, where he was successfully landed and found to be a fine purple-spotted fish of the size I had supposed.

I went on trying for fish along the western bank down the river, but only small trout rose at my flies, and a score was the total catch.

When I came to the saw-mill at Brække, the sky was overcast, it was already growing dark, only above the level of the northwestern horizon there appeared a streak of light, which threw a subdued glimmer on the tranquil surface of the mill-pond. I went out on the timber boom and made a few casts, but with little success. Not a breath of air was stirring, the winds seemed to have gone to rest. My flies alone disturbed the placid waters.

A half-grown-up lad, who was standing behind me on the bank, advised me to "troll with bait"—a cluster of worms fastened to the hook, which is dragged in jerks over the surface of the water—and offered to find the bait for me. I took his advice, and the trial succeeded beyond expectation; a trout of a pound weight rose to the bait, and was not without some difficulty landed on the inconvenient spot where I was standing. But with this the day's sport seemed to be over; no fish ruffled the tranquil pond, the bats alone, which shot backwards and forwards in the air, produced sometimes, when they pounced down after the insects, trembling ripples which quivered over the bright surface of the water.

Before me was the saw-mill; its interior was lighted up by a blazing fire on the open hearth. The mill was in full work, but its wheels, its saws and levers, no longer appeared to be guided or directed by any human will or hand; it seemed to be a mere toy under the invisible power, and subject to the whim, of the mill goblin. Soon, however, human forms became visible. One of these went out on the timber raft lying in the mill-pond, and with an immense pitchfork guided the logs into the channel towards the mill, setting the whole raft rocking with a wave-like motion; another rushed hurriedly about with an axe in his hand, shaping and squaring the huge logs, while the loose chips and bits of bark rushed into the roaring eddies below. From inside the mill there came a whizzing, whirring, and clashing sound, and now and then a bright saw-blade flashed in the air, as if in combat with the spirits of the night, to cut the stumps and uneven ends off the logs.

Some cold gusts of a northerly wind coming down the course of the river made me feel that I was wet and tired, and I decided therefore on going into the saw-mill to get a little rest by the fire. I called to the boy, who was still standing on the bank, to take the fish-basket, which I had left behind, and follow me over the barrier; the slippery logs of which this was composed were rocking up and down, and were engulfed in the water at every step I took.

By the hearth in the mill sat an old grey-bearded peasant, with a red cap down over his ears, whose presence I did not at first discern, as the shadow of the hearth hid him from me. When he heard that I wished to rest and warm myself, he at once prepared a seat for me on a block by the fire.

"That's a splendid fish," said the old man as he took the last trout I had caught in his hand; "and it's one of the golden ones too! It weighs almost two pounds. You have caught it in the mill-pond here, I suppose?"

On my assenting to this, the old man, who appeared to be an ardent fisherman, told me of the large trout he caught in the neighbourhood thirty years ago, when he came here from Gudbrandsdale, and made the most heartrending complaints of the decrease of fish and increase of saw-dust, just as Sir Humphrey Davy makes in his *Salmonia*.

"The fish are becoming more and more scarce," he said in a voice that penetrated clearly to me through the noise in the mill; "such a trout as that, small as it is, is a rare thing to catch now, but the saw-dust increases year by year. You cannot wonder that the fish doesn't go into the river, for if he opens his mouth to get a mouthful of clear water, he gets his gills choked with saw-dust and shavings. Drat that saw-dust, although I shouldn't forget it is the mill that feeds me and mine, but I get so wild when I think of the big fellows I have landed here in days gone by."

The boy had in the meantime arrived with the basket, but he seemed to be ill at ease amid the noise and commotion which prevailed in the mill. He stepped cautiously over the boards, and in his face was depicted fear and anxiety at the rush of the water between the wheels underneath the floor where he was standing.

"This is an awful place to be in," he said. "I wish I was safe at home again."

"Don't you belong to these parts?" I asked.

"Where do you come from?" asked the old man.

"Oh, I come from the Old Town," answered the lad, who all the time kept himself as close to me as possible. "I have been over to the clerk at Brække with a letter for the bailiff; and I am so afraid to go alone in the dark."

"You ought to be ashamed of yourself, such a big lad as you are," said the old man, but added in a comforting tone, "the moon will be up shortly, and perhaps you may go in company with this stranger here."

I promised the lad my company as far as the Beier bridge, which seemed to reassure him somewhat. In the meantime the saw was stopped and two of the men began filing and sharpening the blades, which produced such a piercing sound that it went through bone and marrow. It is very often heard at night through the rush of the waters as far as the town below. It seemed to have a very unpleasant effect upon the nerves of the frightened lad.

"Ugh! I dared not stay here a night for all the world!" he said, and stared around him, as if he expected to see a mill-goblin rise through the floor, or a brownie in every corner.

"Well, I have been here many a night," said the old man, "and little reward have I had for it."

"My mother has told me that there is witchcraft and all sorts of evil spirits in these mills," remarked the lad, somewhat alarmed.

"I can't say I have seen anything," said the old man. "The water has, to be sure, been shut off and turned on at times, when I have had a little nap in the mill during the night, and I have heard noises in the back-shed, but I have never seen anything. Folks don't believe in such beings nowadays," he continued, with an inquiring look towards me, "and there-fore they daren't show themselves. Folks are too sensible and too well read in our days."

"You are perhaps right there," I said, for I could perceive there was a meaning in his look, and I preferred that he should tell me some old stories rather than I should dispute his doubts or question his belief that civilization was a terror to brownies and other supernatural beings. "You are right to some extent in what you say. In the olden days people had a stronger belief in all kinds of witchery; now they pretend not to believe in it, that they may be looked upon as sensible and educated people, as you say. But far up in the country, in the mountain districts, we still often hear of fairies having been seen, of their spiriting people away into the mountains, and such like. Now, I'll tell you a story," I continued, that I might give him some encouragement to start one; "I'll tell you a story, which took place somewhere, but where and when I cannot exactly re-member.

"There was a man who had a flour-mill, close to a waterfall, and there was a mill-goblin in that mill. Whether the man used to give him Christ-mas cakes and beer, as they do in some places, I don't know, but I should think he didn't, for every time he went to grind his corn the goblin got hold of the tub-wheel and stopped the mill, and he couldn't get any corn ground. The man knew very well it was the goblin who had his hand in this, and one evening when he went to the mill, he took a big pot full of pitch-tar with him and put it on the fire. He turned the water on to the wheel and the mill went for a while, but suddenly it stopped, as he expected it would. He seized a long pole and struck at the mill-goblin round about the wheel, but all in vain. At last he opened the door which led out to the wheel, and there stood the mill-goblin in the door, gaping. His jaw was so big that it reached from the threshold up to the lintel.

" 'Have you ever seen such a jaw?' said the goblin.

"The man ran for the pot and pitched the boiling tar into the gaping jaw, and said, 'Have you ever felt anything so hot?'

"The goblin uttered a terrible shriek, and let go the wheel. He has never been seen or heard there after that time, nor has the mill been stopped since."

"Yes," said the boy, who had listened to my story with a mixture of fear and curiosity; "I have heard my grandmother tell that story, and she used also to tell another about a mill-goblin somewhere up in the country, where no one could get anything ground at the mill, it was so bewitched. But one evening came a beggar-woman, who badly wanted to get a little corn ground, and she asked if she could not get leave to stay there for the night and do it.

" 'Oh, dear no!' said the owner of the mill; 'you can't stay there at night; neither you nor the mill would have any peace for the goblin.' But the beggar-woman wanted so badly to get her corn ground, for she had not a spoonful of meal to make either soup or porridge for the children at home. Well, at last she got leave to go into the mill and grind her corn at night. When she came there, she made a fire on the hearth, where a big pot of tar was hanging. She started the mill, and sat down by the hearth with her knitting. In a while a girl came into the mill and said 'Good evening' to her.

" 'Good evening,' answered the beggar-woman, and went on with her knitting.

"But very soon the strange girl began raking the fire out over the hearth, but the beggar-woman raked it together again.

" 'What's your name?' said the fairy, as you already will have guessed that the strange girl was.

" 'My name is Self!' answered the beggar-woman.

"The girl thought that was a strange name, and began raking the fire about again. This made the beggar-woman angry, and she began scolding and raking the fire together. They were thus employed for some time, when the beggar-woman, watching her opportunity, upset the boiling tar over the girl, who began screaming and screeching, and as she ran out of the mill, she cried:

" 'Father, father, Self has burnt me!'

" 'Well, if you have burnt yourself, you have only yourself to blame,' said a voice in the hill."

"It was a good thing for the woman it didn't fare worse with her," said the old man with the grey beard; "she might have been burnt, both she and the mill, for where I come from I heard tell of something similar, which happened there long ago. There was a farmer who had a mill that was burnt down two Whitsun-nights in succession. The third year he had a tailor staying with him before Whitsuntide, making new clothes for the holidays.

" 'I wonder if anything will happen to the mill this year?' said the farmer. 'Perhaps it will burn to-night too!'

" 'No fear of that,' said the tailor; 'give me the key and I'll look after the mill.'

"The farmer was well pleased with that, and when the evening came the tailor got the key and went down into the mill. It was almost empty, as it had only just been finished. He sat down in the middle of the floor, took his chalk out and marked a large ring around him, and round about this he wrote the Lord's Prayer, and then he did not feel afraid even if Old Nick himself should come.

"Towards midnight the door flew suddenly open, and in rushed such a number of black cats that the whole room swarmed with them. They were not long in getting a pot on the fire, and then they put more and more wood on, till the pot, which was full of pitch-tar began to boil and sputter.

" 'Ho, ho!' said the tailor to himself, 'that's the way you do it, eh?' and no sooner had he spoken, than one of the cats put her paw behind the pot and was about to upset it.

" 'Psht! cat! You'll burn yourself,' said the tailor.

" 'Psht! cat! You'll burn yourself! says the tailor to me,' said the cat to the other cats, and away they ran from the fire, and began jumping and dancing round the ring; but very soon the cat stole over to the fire again with the intention of upsetting the pot.

" 'Psht! cat! You'll burn yourself!' cried the tailor, and frightened it away from the fire.

" 'Psht! cat! You'll burn yourself! says the tailor to me,' said the cat to the other cats; and they all began to dance and jump about, but the next moment they tried again to upset the pot.

" 'Psht! cat! You'll burn yourself!' shouted the tailor so loudly, that he frightened them away. They scampered away over the floor, the one over the other, and began jumping and dancing as before.

"They then formed a circle outside the ring, and took to dancing round it, quicker and quicker, till the tailor thought the mill was going round too. The cats glared at him with such big, terrible eyes, as if they were going to eat him.

"But while they were in the middle of the dance, the cat which had been trying to upset the pot put her paw inside the ring as if she wanted to get hold of the tailor. But when he saw this he loosened his sheath-knife and held it ready. All at once the cat thrust her paw inside the ring again, but the tailor was quick as lightning and chopped the paw off. The cats set up a terrible howl, and away they rushed through the door as fast as they could.

"But the tailor laid himself down in the ring and slept till the sun shone far into the mill. Then he rose, locked up the mill, and went up to the farm.

"When he came in both the farmer and his wife were still in bed, for it was Whitsunday morning.

" 'Good morning,' said the tailor, and shook hands with the farmer.

" 'Good morning,' said the farmer, who, as you may guess, was both glad and surprised to see the tailor safe back again.

" 'Good morning, mother,' said the tailor, and offered the goodwife his hand.

" 'Good morning,' said the wife; but she was so pale, and looked so queer and confused, and kept her right hand under the bedclothes. At last she offered the tailor her left hand. The tailor then guessed how matters stood, but what he said to the husband, and how it fared with the wife after that, I never heard."

"The farmer's wife must have been a witch then?" asked the lad, who had been listening intently.

"Yes, of course she was," said the old man.

We could scarcely hear each other's voices any longer; the saw was again hard at work and making a terrible noise. The moon had now risen. I felt refreshed after the short rest, and bade the old man farewell and started for town in company with the scared lad, following the foot-path below the Grefsen hill. A white mist floated over the course of the river and the marshes in the valley below. Above the smoky veil over the town rose Akerhus fort, with its towers standing out in sharp relief against the mirror of the fjord, beyond where the Nœs point loomed as a black shadow.

The sky was almost cloudless. Scarcely any draught could be noticed in the air. The light of the moon was blended with the gloaming of the summer night and softened the outlines of the landscape in the fore-ground, which lay before us. But the distant fjord lay bathed in the bright and beaming moonlight, while the Asker and Bœrum hills loomed high up in the sky and formed the distant frame of the picture.

Refreshed by their cooling bath of evening dew, the violets and other nocturnal flowers emitted a pleasant fragrance over the fields, but from the bogs and the rivulets came up now and then damp, penetrating gusts, that sent an icy chill through me.

"Ugh! how it makes one shudder," cried my companion on such occa-sions. He believed that these gusts were the breath of passing spirits of the night, and thought he saw a witch or cat with glowing eyes in every bush which the wind put in motion.

# THE LAD AND THE NORTH WIND

ONCE UPON a time there was an old woman who had a son, and as she was very weak and feeble, she sent her son across the yard to the store-house to fetch the meal for the porridge for dinner. But when he got outside on the steps, the north wind came rushing past, took the meal out of his bowl, and away it flew through the air.

The lad went back to the storehouse to fetch more, but when he came out on the steps the north wind came whistling past again, and away went the meal; and when the lad went back the third time for the meal, the north wind played him the same trick over again. The lad got angry at this, and thought it wasn't right of the north wind to behave in this manner, so he made up his mind to give the north wind a call, and ask him for his meal.

Well, the lad started off, but it was a long way, and he walked and walked—and came at last to the north wind.

"Good day," said the lad, "and thanks for calling to see me yesterday." "Good day," answered the north wind—his voice was hoarse and gruff— "no thanks required. What do you want?" "Oh," said the lad, "I was only going to ask you to be good enough to let me have back that meal you took from me on the steps, because we haven't much, and if you are going on in this way, and take what little we have, we shall starve." "I haven't got any meal," said the north wind, "but since you are so hard up, you shall have a table-cloth, which will provide you with everything you wish, if you only say, 'Cloth, spread yourself and serve up all kinds of fine dishes!' "

The lad was well satisfied with this. But as the way was so long that he couldn't get home that night, he went into a roadside inn, and when they were going to have supper, he put the cloth on a table which stood in the corner, and said, "Cloth, spread yourself, and serve up all kinds of fine dishes."

He had scarcely said these words before the cloth did as it was told, and all in the room thought it was a very nice thing to have, but no one liked it better than the innkeeper's wife. She thought that would be the very thing for her. It would save her such a lot of trouble in frying and boiling, laying the cloth, and putting the things on the table, and so on.

So in the middle of the night, when all were asleep, she took the cloth from the lad, and put another one in its stead, just like the one he had got from the north wind, but her cloth couldn't, of course, serve up as much as an oatmeal cake.

When the lad awoke, he took the cloth and set out on his journey, and that day he got back to his mother. "Well," he said, "I have been to the north wind, I have! He is a decent fellow, I think, because he gave me this cloth, and I have only to say, 'Cloth, spread yourself, and serve up all kinds of fine dishes,' and then I get the best of everything I want to eat and drink."

"Ah, indeed! I daresay," said the mother, "but I don't believe it, till I see it." So the lad lost no time, but took a table, laid the cloth on it, and said, "Cloth, spread yourself, and serve up all kinds of fine dishes," but the cloth didn't serve up so much as a dry crust.

"Ah, well!" said the lad, "there's no help for it, I must go to the north wind again," and away he went. Towards evening, he came to where the north wind lived.

"Good evening," said the lad. "Good evening," said the north wind. "I want my rights for the meal you took from us," said the lad, "for that cloth you gave me is not good for anything." "I haven't any meal," said the north wind, "but here is a goat for you, which makes only golden ducats, if you only say, 'Goat of mine, make money!' "

THE LAD AND THE NORTH WIND

That pleased the lad, but as it was too late to get home that day, he went into the same inn where he had been before. But before he called for anything, he wanted to try the goat and see if it was true what the north wind had said about it, and sure enough the goat made only golden ducats.

But when the innkeeper saw what kind of goat the lad had, he thought this was a goat worth having, so when the lad had fallen asleep, he took another goat which couldn't make any golden ducats, and put that in its place.

Next morning the lad started off home, and when he came in to his mother, he said, "The north wind is a good fellow after all; this time he has given me a goat that makes only golden ducats, if I only say, 'Goat of mine, make money!' "

"Ah, to be sure!" said his mother, "that's all rubbish,—and I don't believe it till I see it." "Goat of mine, make money!" cried the lad, but not a shilling could the goat make.

So the lad went back again to the north wind, and said that the goat wasn't worth anything, and he wasn't going to be done out of his meal, not he!

"Well," said the north wind, "I have nothing else to give you but that old stick over there in the corner; but it is a good stick, and if you only say, 'Stick of mine, lay on,' it lays on, till you say, 'Stick of mine, leave off.' "

But it was a long way home, and the lad went into the old inn where he had slept before; and as he pretty well guessed how he had lost the cloth and the goat, he lay down at once on the bench and began snoring as if he were asleep.

The innkeeper, who thought that the stick must be good for something also, looked for a stick like the one the lad had, and was going to change the sticks while the lad was snoring away, but just as the innkeeper was going to take the stick, the lad cried out, "Stick of mine, lay on," and the stick commenced beating the poor innkeeper, till he jumped over chairs and tables, while he shouted and yelled: "Oh dear! oh dear! Tell the stick to leave off, or else it will kill me; you shall have both your cloth and your goat back again!"

When the lad thought that the innkeeper had had enough, he said, "Stick of mine, leave off;" took his cloth and put it in his pocket, and with the stick in his hand, and leading the goat by a string, he started off home. And now, thought the lad, he had been very well paid for the meal he had lost.

# PEIK

THERE WAS once on a time a man and a woman; they had a son and a daughter who were twins, and they were so like each other that you could not tell the one from the other, except by their clothes.

The boy they called Peik. He was of little use on the farm while the parents lived, for he did not care for anything else but playing tricks upon people, and he was so full of tricks and pranks, that no one was left in peace for him. But when the parents died he grew worse and worse,— he would not do anything; he only did his best to make an end of what there was left after them, and to quarrel with everybody. The sister worked and toiled all she could, but it was of little help, and so she told him how wrong it was that he would not do anything useful, and asked him:

"What do you think we shall live upon, when you have finished everything?"

"Oh, I'll go and play a trick upon somebody," said Peik.

"Yes, you are always ready and willing when you are bent upon that," said his sister.

"Well, I'll try my best," said Peik.

So when he had made an end of everything, and there was nothing more in the house, he set out on his journey, and walked and walked till he came to the king's palace.

The king was standing at the door, and when he saw the lad he said:

"Where are you off to to-day, Peik?"

"Oh, I am off to see if I cannot play a trick upon somebody," said Peik.

"Can't you play a trick upon me, then?" said the king.

"No, I don't think I can, because I have left my trickery-sticks at home," said Peik.

"Can't you go and fetch them?" said the king; "I should like to see, if you are such a clever trickster as folks make you out to be."

"I am not able to walk so far now," said Peik.

"I'll lend you a horse and saddle," said the king.

"I don't think I am able to ride either," said Peik.

"We'll lift you up," said the king, "and I suppose you'll be able to stick on to the horse."

Well, Peik rubbed and scratched his head, as if he was going to pull all his hair off, but he let himself be lifted on top of the horse at last; there he sat, and swung backwards and forwards and sideways as long as the king could see him, and the king laughed till the tears came into his eyes, for he had never seen such a sorry horseman before. But as soon as Peik came into the wood behind the hill, where the king could see him no longer, he sat straight and steady as if he was nailed to the horse and started off as if he had stolen both horse and bridle, and when he came to the town he sold them both.

In the meantime the king walked up and down and waited for Peik. He longed to see him coming back with his trickery-sticks; he could not help laughing when he called to mind how pitiable he looked, as he sat rolling to and fro on the horse like a haybag which didn't know which side to fall off on; but hours went and hours came,—and no Peik came. So the king guessed at last that he had been played a trick, and done out of his horse and saddle as well, although Peik did not have his trickery-sticks with him. But then things took another turn, for the king got in a rage and made up his mind to take Peik's life.

But Peik got to know the day when he was coming, and told his sister to put the porridge-pot on the fire with some water in it. But just before the king came in he took the pot off the fire and put it on the chopping-block and began making the porridge on the block.

The king wondered at this, and was so taken up with the wonderful pot that he forgot what he had come there for.

"What do you want for that pot?" said he.

"I can't spare it very well," said Peik.

"Why can't you spare it?" said the king; "I'll make it worth your while to sell it."

"Well, it saves me both money and trouble, chopping and carrying," said Peik.

"Never mind, I'll give you a hundred dollars for it," said the king; "you did me out of horse and saddle the other day, and the bridle too, but I'll let bygones be bygones, if I get the pot."

"Well, I suppose you must have it then," said Peik.

When the king came back to the palace he sent out invitations to a great feast, but the meat was to be boiled in the new pot, which was put in the middle of the floor.

The guests thought the king was out of his mind, and went about nudging each other and laughing at him. But he walked round the pot and cackled and chuckled to himself, saying all the time, "All right, all right! wait a bit! it will boil directly;" but there was no sign of any boiling.

So the king guessed that Peik had been playing a trick upon him again, and he set out to kill him.

When the king came to his place Peik was standing by the barn.

"Wouldn't it boil?" he said.

"No, it would not," said the king; "but now you shall suffer for it," he said, and was going to get his knife ready.

"I believe you there," said Peik, "for you did not have the block."

"I shouldn't wonder if you are telling a lie again," said the king.

"It's all for the want of the block," said Peik; "the pot won't boil without it."

Well, what was he going to have for it?

"It was worth three hundred dollars at least, but for his sake it should go for two," said Peik.

So the king got the block, and set off for home. He invited guests again to a feast and put the pot on the block in the middle of the room. The guests thought the king was gone sheer mad, and went about making game of him. He cackled and chuckled round the pot, saying all the time, "Wait a bit, it will boil soon,—it will boil directly;" but there was no more chance of its boiling on the block than on the floor.

So the king guessed that he had been tricked by Peik that time as well. He tore his hair, and would not rest till he set out to kill him; he should not spare him this time, whether he had got anything to say for himself or not.

But Peik was prepared to receive him again. He killed a wether and took the bladder and filled it with the blood of the slaughtered animal. He then put the bladder in his sister's bosom and told her what she should say when the king came.

"Where is Peik?" shouted the king. He was in such a rage that his voice trembled.

"He is so poorly, that he is not able to move," answered the sister, "and so he thought he would try and get some sleep."

"You must wake him up!" said the king.

No, she dared not do it; he was so hasty.

"Well, I am still more hasty," said the king; "and if you don't wake him I'll——" and with that he put his hand to his side for his knife.

No, no! she would rather wake him; but Peik turned round in his bed in great rage, pulled out his knife and stabbed her in the bosom, but the knife hit only the bladder; a stream of blood gushed out, and she fell down on the floor as if she were dead.

"What a villain you are, Peik," said the king, "you have stabbed your own sister and that while the king stands by and looks at it."

"Oh, there isn't much danger, as long as I have got breath in my nostrils," said Peik, and took a ram's horn, which he began blowing; and when he had blown a wedding march on it he put the horn to his sister's nostrils and blew life into her again and she rose up as if nothing had been the matter with her.

"Why, bless me, Peik! Can you kill people and blow life into them again?" said the king.

"Well, yes, what would become of me if I couldn't?" said Peik. "You see, I am so hasty, and I can't help killing every one who comes near me and annoys me."

"I am also very hasty," said the king, "and I must have that horn; I'll give you a hundred dollars for it, and I'll forgive you besides for doing me out of the horse and cheating me on the pot and block business, and all the rest."

Peik could not very well spare the horn, but for his sake he should have it, and so the king got it, and set out home as fast as he could.

He had no sooner come home before he must try the horn. He began quarreling and scolding the queen and his eldest daughter, and they scolded him again, but before they knew a word about it he pulled out his knife and stabbed them both, so they fell down stone dead, and all who were in the room ran out; they were so afraid.

The king walked up and down the floor for some time and kept on saying there was no danger so long as there was breath in his nostrils, and a great deal more nonsense which had flowed out of Peik's mouth. He then took the horn and began blowing, but although he blew all he could that day and the day after as well, he could not blow life into the bodies; they were dead, and dead they remained, both the queen and his daughter, and so he had to bury them, and to give a grand funeral in the bargain.

When this was done the king set out to settle with Peik and to take his life, but Peik had everything prepared, for he knew the king was coming, and he said to his sister:

"You must change clothes with me and be off! You may take all we have with you."

Yes, she changed clothes with him, packed up her things, and started off as fast as she could, while Peik sat all by himself in his sister's clothes.

"Where is that Peik?" said the king, as he came in a great rage through the door.

"He's gone away," said he who sat in the sister's clothes.

"Well, had he been at home now he wouldn't have had long to live," said the king; "it's no use sparing the life of such a scamp."

"He knew your majesty was coming to punish him for having played so many tricks upon you, and so he ran away and left me behind here both without food or money," said Peik, trying to appear like a shy bashful maiden.

"Come along with me to the palace, and you shall get enough to live on; there is little use in sitting in the cottage here and starving," said the king.

Yes, he would willingly do that, and so the king took him and let him learn everything, and kept him as one of his own daughters; in fact the king felt now as if he had all his three daughters again, for Peik stitched and sewed and sung and played with them, and was in their company early and late.

Some time afterwards a prince came to the palace to woo one of the princesses.

"Yes, I have three daughters," said the king; "you have only to say which one you will have."

So the prince got leave to go up in their bower and get acquainted with them. In the end he liked Peik best, and threw a silk handkerchief into his lap, and so they began getting everything ready for the wedding, and shortly the prince's relations arrived at the palace, and the wedding festivities commenced in earnest with feasting and drinking; but on the wedding day, as night was coming on, Peik dared not remain any longer, and he stole out of the palace and ran across the fields; and there was no bride to be found.

And worse remains to be told, for the two princesses were suddenly taken ill, and all the guests had to break up and take their departure just as they were in the middle of all the fun and feasting.

The king was both enraged and sorrowful at these misfortunes, and began to wonder what could really be the cause of them.

So he mounted his horse and rode out, for he thought it was so lonely to say alone by himself at home; but when he came out in the fields he saw Peik sitting there on a stone, playing a Jew's harp.

"Halloh! are you sitting there, Peik?" asked the king.

"Of course I am," said Peik, "I can't sit in two places at once."

"Well, you have played such vile tricks on me time after time," said the king, "that you will have to come with me and get your deserts."

"Well, I suppose there's no help for it," said Peik, "so I may as well jump into it as creep into it."

When they came to the palace the king gave orders to get ready a barrel, which Peik was to be put in, and when it was ready they carted it up on a high mountain, where he was to lie in the barrel for three days to think on all that he had done, before they rolled the barrel down the mountain into the sea.

On the third day a rich man came past as Peik lay in the barrel singing—

> "To paradise, to paradise I am bound,
> Safe in my barrel as it turns round and round."

When the man heard this, he asked Peik what he would take to let him
take his place.

"I ought to be well paid for that," said Peik, "for there isn't such a
chance every day to go straight to paradise."

The man was willing to give him all he possessed, and so he knocked
out the bottom of the barrel and crept into it instead of Peik.

In the evening the king came to roll the barrel down the mountain.

"A safe journey to you!" said the king; he thought it was Peik who was
in it. "You'll roll faster into the sea than if you were drawn by the swiftest
reindeer, and now there will be an end both to your and your tricks."

Before the barrel was half way down the mountain there wasn't a whole
stave or bit of it left, nor of the man who was inside. But when the king
came home to the palace, Peik was there before him. He sat on the steps
and played upon the Jew's harp.

"What! are you sitting here, Peik?" said the king.

"Of course I am," said Peik. "I suppose I may have lodgings and shelter
for all my horses, my cattle and my money."

"Where did I roll you to, that you got all these riches?" asked the king.

"Oh, you rolled me into the sea," said Peik, "and when I came to the
bottom there was more than enough to take both of horses and cattle, of
gold and goods. They went about in flocks, and the gold lay in heaps as
big as houses.

"What will you take to roll me the same way?" said the king.

"Oh, that shan't cost you much," said Peik. "Since you didn't take
anything of me, I won't take anything of you either."

So he put the king into a barrel and rolled him down the mountain;
and when he thus had got the king out of the way, he went home to the
palace and married the youngest princess and had a grand wedding.
Afterwards he ruled his land and kingdom well and wisely, but he left
off playing tricks upon people and he was never spoken of as Peik any
more, but as His Royal Majesty the King!


# FOOLISH MEN AND SCOLDING WIVES


THERE WERE once upon a time two women, who were always quarrelling,
and one day when they had nothing else to quarrel about, they began
arguing about their husbands, as to who was the most foolish.

The longer they argued the more angry they got, and at last they were very near pulling each other's hair, for, as every one knows, it is easier to begin a quarrel than to end it, and it's a bad look-out if sense is wanting in such a predicament.

One of them said there was nothing which she could not get her husband to believe, if she only said it, for he was so stupid as the trolls, and believed anything. The other said that there was nothing so silly that she could not get her husband to do, if she only said it ought to be done, for he was so foolish and stupid that you could not easily find his like.

"Well, let us try who can make the biggest fool of our husbands, and then we'll see which one is the most stupid," they said one day, and to this they both agreed.

When the husband of the first of these women came home from the wood, his wife said: "Goodness gracious! what ails you? You must be ill, you look as if you were dying."

"Want of something to eat and drink is all that ails me," said the husband.

"But gracious goodness!" screeched the woman, "you are looking worse and worse every minute! You look like a corpse! You must go to bed! Dear, or dear, this can never last long." And in this way she went on, till she got her husband to believe that he was on the point of dying, and she got him to go to bed, folded his hands, and closed his eyes; next she laid him out and put him into a coffin, and that he might not be smothered while he was there, she had some holes made in the boards, so he could both breathe and look out.

The other woman took a pair of carding-combs and began to card, but she had no wool upon them. The man happened to come in and see this foolish operation.—"There is little help in a spinning-wheel without yarn, but carding-combs without wool is the height of nonsense," said her husband.

"Without wool?" said the woman, "why I have wool! But you don't see it, for it is of a very fine sort, I can tell you." When she had done the carding, she brought out her spinning-wheel and began spinning.—"But this is foolish work," said the man; "you are sitting there spinning and spoiling your wheel all the time, since you have got nothing on it!"— "Nothing on it?" said the woman, "but the thread is so fine, that it wants better eyes than yours to see it," she said.

When she was ready with the spinning she took the yarn off the wheel and set up her loom and began weaving the cloth. She then took it off her loom, pressed it and cut it out, and sewed new clothes of it for her husband; and when they were ready she hung them up in the loft of the storehouse. The husband could see neither the cloth nor the clothes, but he had got the belief into his head the cloth was so fine that he could not see, and so he only said: "Well yes, if it is so fine, it's very fine indeed."

But one day his wife said to him: "You must go to the funeral to-day; our neighbour, who died the other day, is going to be buried to-day, and so you had better use your new clothes."—Yes, he would go to the funeral, and she helped him to put the clothes on, for they were so fine, that he might easily tear them to pieces if he put them on himself. When he came to his neighbour's farm the funeral feast had already begun,

FOOLISH MEN AND SCOLDING WIVES

and the guests had been drinking hard; their grief did not increase much you may depend, when they saw the last arrival in his new clothes.

But when they set out for the churchyard, and the dead man peeped out through the holes in his coffin, he burst out laughing till the coffin shook.

"Well, well," he cried; "I can't help laughing when I see Joe Southend walking stark naked at my funeral!"

When the people heard this, they were not slow in taking the lid off the coffin, and the man in the new clothes asked how it was that the man whose funeral they had been feasting at was lying in the coffin, talking and laughing; "it would be more seemly if he was crying and weeping."

"Well, tears never dug any one out of his grave yet," said the others, and so the two husbands found out at last how their wives had been plotting the whole thing against them. Then they went home and did something which they never had done in their lives, and if there is anybody who likes to know what that was he must go and ask the birch rod over the door.

# THE PARSON AND THE CLERK

ONCE UPON a time there was a parson, who was such a bully, that he screamed out a long way off, when anybody came driving against him in the main road: "Out of the way, out of the way! Here comes the parson himself!"

One day, when he was driving along and carrying on in this way, he met the king. "Out of my way, out of my way!" he shouted, ever so far off. But the king drove straight on and took no notice of him, so that time the parson had to pull his horse on one side. When the king came alongside him, he said: "To-morrow, you will have to appear at the palace, and if you cannot answer the three questions which I will ask you, you shall lose both your gown and your collar, for your pride's sake."

That was something different to what the parson was used to. He could bawl and shout and carry on terribly, but to bother his brains with problems and answers was out of the question. So he went to the clerk, who they said had a much smarter tongue than the parson. He told the clerk he had no mind to go, "for a fool can ask more than ten wise men can answer," said the parson, and so he got the clerk to go instead.

Well, the clerk set out and came to the palace dressed in the parson's gown and collar. The king received him at the door with crown and sceptre, and was so fine that he glittered a long way off.

"Oh, you are there, are you?" asked the king.

Yes, he was there, sure enough.

"Now, tell me first," said the king, "how far is it from east to west?"

"Why, a day's journey," said the clerk.

"How do you make that out?" asked the king.

"Well, don't you see, the sun rises in the east and sets in the west, and he does it easily enough in a day," said the clerk.

"Very well," said the king; "but tell me now, what you think I am worth, as I stand here before you."

"Well, our Lord was valued at thirty silver pieces, and I suppose I cannot put you higher than twenty-nine," said the clerk.

"So, so!" said the king, "since you are so very clever at everything, tell me what it is I am thinking about just now?"

"Why, you are surely thinking it is the parson who stands here before you; but so help me, if you don't think wrong,—for I am the clerk."

"Be off with you,—go home, and you be the parson and let him be clerk," said the king, and so it was.


# THE GIANT AND JOHANNES BLESSOM


ABOVE VAAGE parsonage rises a hill or small mountain, crowned with tall and majestic pine-trees. It is called the "Jutulsberg," or the giant's mountain, by the Vaage people. It is very steep and is full of deep dark crevices. By a freak of nature a formation of the rocks, somewhat resembling a large gateway, can be seen in one of its more bare and weatherbeaten sides. If you stand on the bridge over the wild Finne river, or on the further side of the fields, and look up at the gate above the overhanging garlands and luxuriant foliage of the weeping birch which grows out of the fissures in the rock, and if, in addition, you call your imagination to your assistance, the formation takes the appearance of a double gateway, which at the top is joined in a gothic arch.

Old, white-stemmed birch trees stand as pillars at its sides, but their lofty crowns do not reach up to where the arch begins. If the gateway extended into the mountain the length of a church, you could put Vaage church with roof and spire into it. It is not an ordinary door or gate,—it is the entrance to the giant's castle—the giant's gate as it is called, under which the biggest troll with fifteen heads can comfortably pass without bending his neck.

If any one in the olden days, when there was more intercourse between human beings and trolls, wanted to borrow anything from the giant, or to speak with him on other business, it was customary to throw a stone at the gate and say: "Open, Jutul!"

One afternoon, a couple of years ago, I came on a visit to the parsonage. The family had gone up to their mountain dairy and there was no one at home but an old peasant, who, on being requested to show me the way, went with me up to the giant's gate. We knocked, but no one came to open it. It was not to be wondered at that the giant would not receive us, or that he at his advanced age so seldom receives visitors, for if we were to judge by the numerous marks of stones having been thrown at the gate, he must have been exceedingly troubled with visits.

"One of the last who saw him," said my companion, "was Johannes Blessom, the parson's neighbour. But I should think he wished he never had seen him," he added.

"This Johannes Blessom was once down in Copenhagen about a law-suit—for there was no justice to be had here in the country in those days, and if any one wished for 'fair play' there was no help for it but to go down there. His father, who also had a lawsuit, did the same thing before him. Well, it was a Christmas eve, when Johannes had finished his busi-ness with the grand folks, and was ready to start home; he walked along the streets in a gloomy mood, for he was longing to be at home up in the far north, and knew there was no way of getting home till long after Christmas. Suddenly a person, who by his dress appeared to be a peasant from his own parish of Vaage, passed him in a great hurry. He was a big, tall man, with large silver buttons as big as dollar pieces in his white jacket. Johannes thought he knew him, but he walked past him so quickly that he did not get a good sight of his face.

" 'You are in a great hurry,' said Johannes.

" 'Yes, I have to make haste,' answered the stranger; 'I have to be at Vaage to-night!'

" 'I wish I could get there as well,' said Johannes.

" 'Well, you can stand behind on my sledge,' said the stranger, 'for I have a horse who does the mile in twelve strides.'

"Johannes thanked him for the offer, went with him to the stable, and off they started. Johannes was only just able to stick on to the sledge, for away they went like the wind through the air. He could neither see earth nor sky.

"At one place they stopped to rest. Johannes could not tell where it was, but just as they were starting again he saw a skull on a pole. When they had travelled some distance Johannes began to feel cold.

" 'Ugh! I forgot one of my mittens where we rested,' said he; 'my fingers are freezing!'

" 'You'll have to stand it, Johannes Blessom,' said the stranger, 'it isn't far to Vaage now. Where we rested was half-way!'

"The stranger stopped just before they came to the bridge over the Finne river to put Johannes down.

" 'You are not far from home, now,' said he, 'and you must promise me not to look behind you if you hear any rumble or see any light around you.'

"Johannes promised this and thanked him for the lift. The stranger proceeded on his way over the Finne bridge, and Johannes walked up the hill-side to his farm. But all of a sudden he heard a rumble in the giant's mountain, and the road in front of him was suddenly lighted up—he thought he could have seen to pick up a needle. He forgot what he had promised, and turned his head to see what it was. The gate in the mountain was wide open and there came a light from it as from many thousand candles. Right in the middle of the gate he saw the giant him-self,—it was the stranger he had been driving with. But from that day,

The Giant and Johannes Blessom

Johannes Blessom's head was all on one side, and so it remained as long as he lived."

# THE BOX WITH THE FUNNY THING IN IT

ONCE UPON a time there was a little boy, who was walking along a road. When he had gone some distance he found a box. "There must be something funny in that box," he said to himself; but although he twisted and turned it he was not able to get it open. When he had walked some distance farther he found a little key. He was tired, and sat down by the roadside. He thought it would be great fun to see if the key fitted the box, for there was a little keyhole in it. He took the little key out of his pocket; he blew first into the pipe of the key, and then he blew into the keyhole; he put the key into the keyhole and turned it round. "Click," said the lock, and when he tried the lid the box was open. But can you guess what there was in the box? Why, it was a calf's tail, and if the calf's tail had been longer this tale would have been longer too.

# THE WIDOW'S SON

THERE WAS once a poor, very poor widow, who had an only son. She pulled through with the boy till he was confirmed; but then she told him that she could not feed him any longer; he would have to go out and earn his own bread.

The lad wandered out into the world, and when he had walked a day or so he met a stranger.—"Where are you going to?" asked the man.—"I'm going out into the world to try and get some work," said the lad.—"Will you come into my service?" asked the man.—"Well, why not! just as well with you as with anybody else," answered the lad.—"You will find it a very good place," said the man; "you are only going to keep me company and do nothing else besides."

So the lad went with him home, and he got plenty of food and drink, and had little or nothing to do; but on the other hand he never saw a living soul come near the man.

So one day the man said to him: "I'm going away for eight days, and during that time you will be here all alone, but you must not go into any of these four rooms here. If you do I will take your life when I come back."—No, said the lad, he should not go into any of the rooms.

But when the man had been away three or four days the lad could not help going into one of the rooms. He looked round, but saw nothing but a shelf over the door, on which lay a brier twig. Well, this is surely something to forbid my seeing, thought the boy.

When the eight days were gone the man returned.—"You haven't been into any of the rooms, I suppose?" said he.—"No, not at all," said the lad.—"Well, we shall soon see," said the man, and with that he went into the room where the lad had been. "But I find you have been there after all," said the man, "and now you shall lose your life."

The lad cried and begged for himself till he got off with his life; but he got a good thrashing. When that was over they were as good friends as ever.

Some time afterwards the man went away again; he was going to stay away for a fortnight this time, but first he told the lad that he must not put a foot in any of the rooms where he had not already been; he might, however, go into that room where he had been.

Well, it happened just as the last time, only that the lad waited eight days before he went into the second room. In this room he saw nothing but a shelf over the door, and a piece of rock and a water-jug on it. Well, that's something to be so afraid of, thought the lad again.

When the man came back he asked the lad if he had been into any of the rooms.—No, not likely, the lad hadn't been there!—"We shall soon see," said the man, but when he saw that the lad had been into one of the rooms after all, he said: "I shall spare you no longer now; you will lose your life this time!"

But the lad cried and begged for himself again, and he got off with a good thrashing again, but this time he got as much as he could possibly stand. When he had got over the effects of the thrashing he led the same comfortable life as before, and he and the man were the best of friends again.

Some time after the man had to go on a journey again, and this time he should be away for three weeks, and so he said to the lad that if he went into the third room during his absence, he would not have the slightest chance of escaping with his life.

When fourteen days had gone the lad could not help himself; but stole into the third room; he saw nothing in there except a trap-door in the floor. When he lifted it up and looked down into the room below he saw a big copper kettle which stood there and boiled and bubbled; but he saw no fire under it.

It would be great fun to feel if it is hot, thought the boy, and put his finger into the kettle, but when he pulled it out again it was gilded all over. The boy scraped and washed it, but the gilding would not come off, so he tied a rag round it, and when the man came home and asked what was the matter with his finger the lad said that he had cut himself very badly. But the man tore off the rag, and then he saw easily enough what really ailed the finger.

He was at first going to kill the lad; but as he began crying and praying for himself again, he gave him such a sound thrashing instead that he had to keep his bed for three days, and then the man took a jar down from the wall, and rubbed the lad with some of its contents and he was as well as ever again.

Before long the man went away again, and was not coming back for a month. But he told the lad that if he went into the fourth room he must not have any hope of escaping with his life that time.

For two or three weeks the lad managed to resist the temptation, but then he couldn't help himself any longer,—he must and would go into that room, and so he did. There stood a big black horse in a box by himself, and with a manger of glowing cinders at his head, and a truss of hay at his tail. The lad thought this was altogether wrong; he changed them about and put the truss of hay at the horse's head.

So the horse said: "Since you have such a good heart that you let me have something to eat, I will save you from the troll, for that's what the man is that you are with. But now you must go up into the room just above here and take a suit of armour out of those hanging there, and mind you do not take any of the bright ones, but the most rusty you see. Take that one! And sword and saddle you must look out for yourself in the same way."

The lad did as he was told, but it was very heavy work to carry it all at once. When he came back the horse told him to take all his clothes off and jump into the kettle which stood and boiled in the room below, and to have a good dip there.

"I shall be an awful sight then," thought the lad, but he did as the horse had told him. When he had finished his bath he became handsome and smart, and as red and white as blood and milk, and much stronger than before.

"Do you feel any different?" asked the horse.—"Yes," said the lad.— "Try if you can lift me," said the horse.—Oh, yes, he could do that; and the sword, why, he swung it about his head as if it were nothing at all. "Now, put the saddle on me," said the horse, "and put the suit of armour on you, and then don't forget the brier-twig, the piece of rock, the water-jug, and the jar of ointment, and then we'll be off."

The lad had no sooner got on the horse than off they went at such a rate that he couldn't tell how fast they got on. When he had been riding for some time the horse said to him: "I think I hear a rumbling of something! Just look round; can you see anything?"—"Yes, there are a great, great many coming after us; at least a score," said the lad.—"Well, that's the troll," said the horse; "he is coming after us with his imps."

The rode on for a while, until they who were coming after them were close upon them. "Now throw your brier-twig over your shoulder," said the horse, "but throw it a good distance behind me!" The lad did so, and suddenly a big, close brier-wood grew up behind them. So the lad rode a long, long way, while the troll had to go home and fetch something to hew his way through the wood.

But in a while the horse said again: "Look behind! Can you see anything now?"—"Yes, a great many," said the lad; "as many as would fill a church."—"Ah ha! that's the troll,—he has taken more with him this time. Throw the piece of rock you have, but throw it far behind me!"

As soon as the lad had done what the horse had said, a great steep mountain rose behind him, and so the troll had to go home and fetch something to mine his way through the mountain, and while the troll was doing this the lad rode again some distance on his way. But before long the horse asked him to look behind him again, and then the lad saw a crowd like a big army in bright armour, which glistened in the sun. "Ah ha!" said the horse, "that's the troll,—now he has got all his imps with him. Take the water-jug and throw all the water out behind you, but mind you do not spill any of it on me!"

The lad did as he was told, but for all the care he took, he happened to spill a drop on the horse's flank. Well, the water he threw behind him became a great lake, but on account of the drop he spilled on the horse he found himself far out in the water, but the horse swam safely to land with him. When the trolls came to the lake they laid down to drink it dry, but they drank till they burst. "Now we have got rid of them," said the horse.

So when they had travelled a long, long time, they came to a green plain in a wood. "Now you must take off your whole suit of armour and only put your own ragged clothes on," said the horse, "and then take the saddle off me and let me go; but hang all the things inside this big hollow lime-tree here. You must then make yourself a wig of pine-moss and go up to the king's palace, which is close by; there you must ask for service. Whenever you want me, only come and shake the bridle, and I'll come to you."

Yes, the lad did as the horse had told him, and when he put the wig of moss on his head he became so ugly, and pale, and miserable-looking that no one would know him again. He then went to the palace and asked first, if he could get some work in the kitchen and carry water and wood for the cook; but the cook asked: "Why do you wear that ugly wig? Take it off you! I won't have such a fright in here."—"I can't do that," answered the lad, "I am not all right in my head."—"Do you think I will have you here near the food, if that's the case?" said the cook; "go down to the coachman; you are better suited for cleaning out the stable."

But when the coachman asked him to take off his wig and got the same answer he would not have him either. "You had better go to the gardener," he said; "you are more fit for digging in the garden." Yes, the gardener would take him, and gave him leave to stay with him, but none of the other servants would sleep with him, so he had to sleep by himself under the steps of the summer-house. It stood on posts, and a high staircase led up to it; under this he put some moss for a bed, and there he lay as well as he could.

When he had been some time at the palace, it happened one morning, just as the sun was rising, that the lad had taken off his wig of moss and was washing himself; he then looked so handsome that it was a pleasure to look at him.

The princess saw the lad from her window, and she thought that she never had seen any one so handsome. She asked the gardener why the lad slept out there under the steps. "Oh, none of his fellow-servants will sleep with him," said the gardener. "Let him come up and lie outside the door of my chamber," said the princess, "and then I suppose they will not think themselves too good to sleep in the same room as he."

The gardener told the lad of it. "Do you think I'll do that?" said the lad; "they would say that I was running after the princess."—"Yes, you are very likely to be suspected of that," said the gardener, "you are so good-looking!"—"Well, if she orders it so, I suppose I must go," said the lad.

When he was going up stairs in the evening he tramped and stamped so terribly that they had to tell him to walk more softly, that the king should not get to know it. So he lay down by the door and began to snore.

The princess then said to her maid: "Just go quietly to him and pull off his wig." The maid was just going to snatch it off his head, when he took hold of it with both his hands and said that she should not have it; and with that he lay down again and began snoring. The princess gave the maid a sign again, and that time she snatched the wig off him, and there lay the lad so lovely and red and white, just as the princess had seen him in the morning sun. After that the lad slept every night outside the princess's chamber.

But before long the king got to hear that the gardener's boy lay outside the princess's chamber every night, and he was so enraged at this that he almost took the lad's life. He did not do this, however, but threw him into the prison tower. He shut up his daughter in her chamber, and told her she should not have leave to go out day or night. She cried and prayed for herself and the lad, but all to no purpose. The king only got more vexed at it.

In a while a war broke out in the land, and the king had to take up arms against another king, who wanted to take the kingdom from him. When the lad heard this he asked the keeper to go to the king and ask for a suit of armour and a sword and permission to go to the war. All laughed when the keeper delivered his message, and asked the king to give him some old rusty suit, that they might have the fun of seeing this poor wretch going to fight in the war. So the lad got permission and an old, wretched horse in the bargain, who jogged along on three legs and dragged the fourth after him.

So they all set out to meet the enemy; but they had not got far from the palace before the lad got stuck in a bog with his nag. There he sat and kicked away and cried: "Gee up, gee up!" to his nag. All amused themselves at this sight, and laughed and made game of the lad as they rode past.

But no sooner were they out of sight than the lad ran to the lime-tree, put on his suit of armour, and shook the bridle. The horse appeared at once, and said: "You do your best, and I will do mine!" When the lad came up the battle had already begun, and the king was in a bad plight; but the lad rushed into the thick of the fight and put the enemy to flight. The king and his people wondered much who it could be who had come to help them; but no one came so near him as to be able to talk to him, and when the battle was over he was gone. When they rode home, they found the lad still stuck in the bog, kicking away at his three-legged

THE WIDOW'S SON

nag, and they began laughing again. "Just look! there sits that fool still!" they said.

The next day when they set out again, the lad was still sitting there; they laughed again and made game of him, but no sooner had they ridden past him, before the lad ran to the lime-tree, and all happened just as on the first day. Every one wondered who this strange warrior could be that had helped the king. No one, of course, guessed it could be the lad!

When they were on their way home at night and saw the lad still sitting there on his horse, they jeered at him again, and one of them shot an arrow at him and hit him in the leg. He began to cry and wail so pitiably, that the king threw his pocket-handkerchief to him to tie round the wound.

The third morning when they set out, they found the lad still on his nag in the bog. "Gee up, gee up!" he was shouting to his horse. "I am afraid he will be sitting there till he starves to death," said one of the king's soldiers, as they rode past him, and laughed at him till they were nearly falling off their horses. But when they were gone, he ran again to the lime-tree, and came up to the battle in the very nick of time. That day he killed the king of the enemy, and so the war was all over.

When the battle was over, the king happened to discover his handkerchief, which the strange warrior had tied round his leg, and he had no difficulty then in guessing who he was. They received him with great joy, and brought him with them to the palace, and the princess, who saw him from her window, became so glad, that no one could believe it, and she exclaimed joyfully: "There comes my love."

He then took the pot of ointment and rubbed himself on the leg, and afterwards he rubbed all the wounded, so that all were well there and then.

So he married the princess, but on the very day when the wedding took place, he went down into the stable to his horse, who was standing there quite sullen and dejected; his ears hung down, and he would not eat anything. When the young king—for he was now made king, and had got half the kingdom—spoke to him and asked what was the matter with him, the horse said: "I have now helped you through, and I do not care to live any longer. You must take the sword and cut my head off."

"No, I will do nothing of that sort," said the young king; "but you shall have everything you want and do no more work."—"Well, if you don't do as I tell you," said the horse, "you had better look out for your life, which is in my hands entirely." So the king had to do what was asked of him; but when he lifted the sword and was about to strike, he felt so grieved that he had to turn his face away, because he would not see the blow; but no sooner had he cut the head off, than the loveliest prince stood on the spot where the horse had stood.

"Where in all the world did you come from?" asked the king.

"It was I who was the horse," answered the prince. "At one time I was king in the land where the king came from that you killed in the battle yesterday. It was he who turned me into a horse and sold me to the troll. But now that he is killed, I shall get my kingdom back again, and you and I will be neighbouring kings; but we will never make war on one another."

And no more they did; they were friends as long as they lived, and they used to go and visit each other very often.

# EAST OF THE SUN AND WEST OF THE MOON

THERE WAS once a poor tenant who had many children, but very little food or clothes to give them; they were all pretty children, but the prettiest was the youngest daughter, who was so lovely that there was almost too much of her loveliness.

So one Thursday evening, late in the autumn, when there was terrible weather and it was dreadfully dark out of doors, and it rained and blew as well till the wall creaked, they were all sitting by the hearth busy with something or other. All at once some one knocked three times on the window-pane. The goodman went out to see what was the matter; when he came outside he saw a great big white bear.

"Good evening!" said the white bear.—"Good evening!" said the man.— "Will you give me your youngest daughter, and I will make you as rich as you now are poor," said the bear.—Yes; the man thought it would be very nice to be so rich, but he must speak with his daughter first; so he went in and told her that a great white bear was outside, who promised that he would make them rich if he could only get her. She said "No," and would not agree to any such arrangement; so the man went out and arranged with the white bear that he should come again next Thursday evening for an answer. In the meantime they talked her round, and told her of all the riches they would come in possession of, and how fine she herself would have it in her new home; so at last she gave in to their entreaties and began washing and mending her few rags and made herself look as well as she could, and was at last ready for the journey. Her baggage, of course, was not much to speak of.

Next Thursday evening the white bear came to fetch her; she got up on his back with her bundle, and away they went. When they had gone some distance the white bear said: "Are you afraid?"—No, she wasn't afraid.—"Well, only hold tight by my coat and there's no danger," said the bear.

And so she rode far, far away, and came at last to a big mountain. The white bear knocked at it and a gate was opened, and they came into a castle where there were a great many rooms all lit up and gleaming with silver and gold, and amongst these was a great hall, where a table stood ready laid; in fact, all was so grand and splendid that you would not believe it unless you saw it. So the white bear gave her a silver bell, which she was to ring whenever there was anything she wanted, and her wishes would be attended to at once.

Well, when she had eaten, it was getting late in the evening, and she became sleepy after the journey, so she thought she would like to go to bed. She rang the bell, and had scarcely touched it, before she was in a room, where she found such a beautiful bed as any one could wish for, with silken pillows and curtains, and gold fringes; everything else in the room was made of gold and silver. But when she had gone to bed and put out the light, she heard some one coming into the room and sitting down in the big armchair near the bed. It was the white bear, who at night could throw off his shape, and she could hear by his snoring as he sat in the chair that he was now in the shape of a man; but she never saw him, because he always came after she had put out the light, and in the morning before the day dawned he was gone.

Well, for a while everything went on happily, but then she began to be silent and sorrowful, for she went about all day alone, and no wonder she longed to be home with her parents and her sisters and brothers again. When the white bear asked what ailed her, she said she was so lonely there, she walked about all alone, and longed for her home and her parents and brothers and sisters, and that was the reason she was so sad.

"But you may visit them, if you like," said the white bear, "if you will only promise me one thing. You must never talk alone with your mother, but only when there are others in the room. She will take you by the hand and try to lead you into a room to speak with you all by yourself; but you must not do this by any means, or you will make us both unhappy, and bring misfortune over us."

One Sunday the white bear came and told her that they were now going to see her parents. Away they went, she sitting on his back, and they travelled far and long; at last they came to a grand white farmhouse, where her sisters and brothers were running about. Everything was so pretty that it was a pleasure to see it.

"Your parents are living there," said the bear; "but mind you don't forget what I have said, or you will make us both unhappy." No, she would not forget it. When they came to the farm, the bear turned round and went away.

There was such a joy when she came in to her parents that there was no end to it. They said they did not know how to thank her fully for what she had done for them. They had everything they wanted, and everybody asked after her and wanted to know how she was getting on, and where she was living. She said that she was very comfortable and had everything she wished for; but what she otherwise answered I don't know, but I believe they did not get much out of her.

But one day after dinner it happened exactly as the white bear had said; her mother wanted to speak with her alone in her chamber. But she recollected what the bear had told her, and would not go with her. "What we have got to talk about, we can do at some other time," she said. But somehow or other her mother talked her round at last, and so she had to tell her everything. She told her how a man came into her room every night as soon as she had put out the light, and how she never saw him, for he was always gone before the day dawned. She was sorrowful at this, for she thought she would so like to see him; and in the day time she walked about there all alone and felt very lonely and sad.

"Oh, dear me!" said her mother, "it may be a troll for all we know! But I will tell you how you can get a sight of him. You shall have a piece of candle from me, and this you must take with you home in your bosom. When he is asleep, light that candle, but take care not to drop any of the tallow on him."—Yes, she took the candle and hid it in her bosom, and in the evening the white bear came and fetched her.

When they had gone some distance of the way the bear asked her if everything hadn't happened as he had said. Yes, she couldn't deny that.— "Well, if you have listened to your mother's advice you will make us both unhappy, and all will be over between us," said the bear.—No, that she hadn't!

When she came home and had gone to bed, the same thing occurred as before. Some one came into the room and sat in the arm-chair by her bedside, but in the middle of the night when she heard that he was asleep, she got up and struck a light, lit the candle, and let the light fall on him. She then saw that he was the loveliest prince any one could wish to see, and she fell at once in love with him; she thought that if she could not kiss him there and then she would not be able to live. And so she did, but she dropped three hot drops of tallow on him, and he woke up.

"What have you done?" he said, "you have now made us both unhappy for ever, for if you had only held out one year I should have been saved. I have a stepmother who has bewitched me, and I am now a white bear by day and a man by night. But now all is over between us, and I must leave you and go back to her; she lives in a castle which lies east of the sun and west of the moon, and in the same castle there is a princess with a nose two yards long, and now I must marry her."

She wept and cried, but there was no help for it; he must go and leave her. So she asked him if she might not go with him. No, that was impossible!—"But if you will tell me the way, I will try and find you," she said. "I suppose I may have leave to do that!"—Yes, she could do that, he said, but there was no road to that place; it lay east of the sun and west of the moon, and she could never find her way there.

Next morning when she awoke, both the prince and the castle were gone; she lay on a little green field far in the middle of the dark thick forest, and by her side lay the same bundle with her old rags which she had brought with her from home. When she had rubbed the sleep out of her eyes and wept till she was tired, she set out on her way and walked for many, many a day, till she at last came to a big mountain.

Close to it an old woman sat and played with a golden apple. She asked her if she knew the way to the prince who lived with his stepmother in a castle that lay east of the sun and west of the moon, and who was going to marry a princess with a nose two yards long.—"How do you know him?" asked the old woman, "perhaps it was you who should have had him?"—Yes, it was she. "Ah, indeed! is that you?" said the woman; "well, all I know is that he lives in that castle which lies east of the sun and west of the moon, and thither you will come late or never, but I will lend you my horse, and on him you can ride to my neighbour, an old friend of mine; perhaps she can tell you. When you have got there, just give my horse a blow with your whip under the left ear and ask him to go home again;—and you had better take this golden apple with you."

So she got up on the horse and rode a long, long time till she at last came to a mountain, where an old woman was sitting with a golden carding-comb. She asked her if she knew the way to the castle which lay east of the sun and west of the moon. She answered like the first old woman, that she didn't know anything about it, but it was sure to be east of the sun and west of the moon, "and thither you will come, early or late, but I will lend you my horse as far as my neighbour; perhaps she can tell you. When you have got there, just give my horse a blow under the left ear and ask him to go home again." And the old woman gave her the golden carding-comb, which might come in useful for her.

The young girl got up on the horse and rode for a long, long weary time, and came at last to a large mountain, where an old woman was sitting and spinning on a golden spinning-wheel. She asked her if she knew the way to the prince, and where the castle was that lay east of the sun and west of the moon. And so came the same question: "Perhaps it is you who should have had the prince?"—Yes, it was! But the old woman knew the way no better than the other two. It was east of the sun and west of the moon,—she knew that,—"and thither you will come, early or late," she said, "but I will lend you my horse, and then I think you had better ride to the east wind and ask him. Perhaps he is known about those parts and can blow you there. When you have got there, just touch the horse under the ear and he'll go home again." And so she gave her the golden spinning-wheel. "You might find use for it," said the old woman.

She rode on many days for a long weary time before she got to the east wind, but after a long time she did reach it, and so she asked him if he could tell her the way to the prince, who lived east of the sun and west of the moon. Yes, he had heard tell of that prince, said the east wind, and of the castle too, but he didn't know the way thither, for he had never blown so far. "But if you like, I'll go with you to my brother, the west wind. Perhaps he may know it, for he is much stronger. Just get up on my back and I'll carry you thither."

Yes, she did so, and away they went at a great speed. When they got to the west wind, they went in to him, and the east wind told him that his companion was the one who should have had the prince who lived in the castle, which lay east of the sun and west of the moon; she was now on her way to find him again, and so he had gone with her to hear if the west wind knew where that castle was.—"No, I have never blown so far," said the west wind, "but if you like I'll go with you to the south wind, for he is much stronger than any of us, and he has been far and wide; perhaps he may tell you. You had better sit up on my back and I'll carry you thither."

Well, she got on his back, and off they started for the south wind; they weren't long on the way, I can tell you! When they got there, the west wind asked his brother if he could tell him the way to that castle which lay east of the sun and west of the moon. His companion was the one who should have had the prince who lived there.—"Oh, indeed!" said

EAST OF THE SUN AND WEST OF THE MOON

the south wind, "is that she? Well, I have been to many a nook and corner in my time, but so far I have never blown. But if you like, I'll go with you to my brother, the north wind; he is the oldest and strongest of all of us, and if he doesn't know where it is you will never be able to find any one who can tell you. Just get up on my back and I'll carry you thither."

Yes, she sat up on his back, and away they went at such a rate, that the way didn't seem to be very long.

When they got to where the north wind lived he was so wild and unruly that cold gusts were felt a long way off. "What do you want?" he shouted from far away, but still it made them shiver all over.—"Oh, you needn't be so very harsh," said the south wind, "it's I, your own brother; and then I have got her with me who should have had the prince who lives in that castle which lies east of the sun and west of the moon, and she wants to ask you if you have ever been there and if you can tell her the way. She is so very anxious to find him again."—"Well, yes, I do know where it is," said the north wind; "I once blew an aspen leaf thither, but I was so tired that I wasn't able to blow for many days after. But if you really intend going there and you are not afraid to come with me, I will take you on my back and try if I can blow you so far."—Yes, she was willing; she must go thither, if it were possible, one way or another, and she wasn't a bit afraid, go how it would.

"Very well!" said the north wind, "you must stop here to-night then, for we must have a whole day before us and perhaps more, if we are to reach it."

Early next morning the north wind called her, and then he blew himself out and made himself so big and strong that he was terrible to look at. Away they went, high up through the air at such a fearful speed, as if they were going to the end of the world. There was such a hurricane on land that trees and houses were blown down, and when they came out on the big sea ships were wrecked by hundreds. And onwards they swept, so far, far, that no one would believe how far they went, and still farther and farther out to sea, till the north wind got more and more tired and so knocked up that he was scarcely able to give another blow, and was sinking and going down more and more; and at last they were so low that the tops of the billows touched their heels.

"Are you afraid?" said the north wind.—"No," she said, she wasn't a bit afraid. But they were not so very far from land either, and the north wind had just sufficient strength left to reach the shore and put her off just under the windows of the castle which lay east of the sun and west of the moon; but he was then so tired and worn out that he had to rest for many days before he could start on his way home again.

Next morning she sat down under the castle windows, and began playing with the golden apple, and the first one she saw was the princess with the long nose, whom the prince was going to marry.

"What do you want for that golden apple of yours?" she asked, and opened the casement.—"It is not for sale, neither for gold nor money," said the girl.—"If it isn't for sale for gold or money, what do you want for it then?" said the princess; "I'll give you what you ask!"—"Well, if I to-night may sit in the arm-chair by the bedside of the prince who lives

EAST OF THE SUN AND WEST OF THE MOON

here, you shall have it," said the girl who came with the north wind.—
Yes, she might do that, there would be no difficulty about that.

So the princess got the golden apple; but when the girl came up into
the prince's bedroom in the evening, he was fast asleep; she called him
and shook him, and now and then she cried and wept; but no, she could
not wake him up so that she might speak to him. Next morning, as soon
as the day dawned, the princess with the long nose came and turned her
out of the room.

Later in the day she sat down under the castle windows and began
carding with her golden carding-comb, and then the same thing happened again. The princess asked her what she wanted for the carding-
comb, and she told her that it wasn't for sale neither for gold nor money,
but if she might get leave to sit in the arm-chair by the prince's bedside
that night, she should have it. But when she came up into the bedroom
she found him fast asleep again, and for all she cried and shook him, for
all she wept, he slept so soundly that she could not get life into him; and
when the day dawned in the early morning, in came the princess with
the long nose and turned her out of the room again.

So as the day wore on, she sat down under the castle windows and
began spinning on the spinning-wheel, and that the princess with the
long nose wanted also to have. She opened the casement and asked the
girl what she wanted for it. The girl told her, as she had done twice
before, that it was not for sale either for gold or money, but if she might
sit in the arm-chair by the prince's bedside that night she should have it.
Yes, she might do that. But there were some Christian people who had
been carried off and were imprisoned in the room next to the prince's,
and they had heard that some woman had been in his room and wept
and cried and called his name two nights running, and this they told
the prince.

In the evening, when the princess came and brought him his drink, he
made appear as if he drank, but he threw it over his shoulder, for he felt
sure she had put a sleeping draught in his drink.

So when the girl came into his room that night she found the prince
wide awake, and then she told him how she had come there. "You have
just come in time," said the prince, "for to-morrow I was to be married
to the princess; but I won't have that Longnose, and you are the only one
that can save me. I will say that I shall want to see what my bride can do,
and if she is fit to be my wife; then I will ask her to wash the shirt with
the three tallow stains on it. She will try, for she does not know that it is
you who dropped the tallow on the shirt; but that can only be done by
Christian folks, and not by a pack of trolls like we have in this place; and
so I will say that I will not have anybody else for a bride except the one
who can wash the shirt clean, and I know you can do that." And they felt
very glad and happy, and they went on talking all night about the joyful
time in store for them.

The next day, when the wedding was to take place, the prince said: "I
think I must see first what my bride can do!"—"Yes, quite so!" said the
stepmother.—"I have got a very fine shirt, which I am going to use for
my wedding shirt; but there are three tallow stains on it which I wanted

washed out; and I have made a vow that I will not take any other woman for a wife than the one who is able to do that; if she cannot do that, she is not worth having," said the prince. "Well, that was easy enough," said the stepmother and agreed to this trial. Well, the princess with the long nose set to washing the best she could, but the more she washed the bigger grew the stains. "Why, you cannot wash," said the old witch, her step-mother; "let me try!"—but no sooner did she take the shirt than it got still worse, and the more she washed and rubbed the bigger and blacker the stains grew.

So did the other trolls try their hands at washing, but the longer they worked at it the dirtier the shirt grew, till at last it looked as if it had been up the chimney. "Ah, you are not worth anything, the whole lot of you!" said the prince; "there's a poor girl under the window just outside here, and I am sure she can wash much better than any of you. Come in, my girl!" he shouted out to her.—Yes, she would come in.—"Can you wash this shirt clean?" asked the prince.—"Well, I don't know," she said, "but I will try."

And no sooner had she taken the shirt and dipped it in the water, than it was as white as the driven snow, if not whiter. "Yes, you shall be my wife," said the prince. But the old witch flew into such a rage that she burst; and the princess with the long nose and all the trolls must have burst also, for I never heard of them since. The prince and his bride then set free all the people who had been carried off and imprisoned there, and so they took as much gold and silver with them as they could carry, and moved far away from the castle which lay east of the sun and west of the moon.

# ASHIEPATTLE WHO MADE THE PRINCESS TELL THE TRUTH AT LAST

THERE WAS once upon a time a king, who had a daughter, and she was such an awful story-teller, that you couldn't find a greater anywhere. So the king made known, that if any one could outdo her in telling stories and make her tell the truth, he should have her for a wife and half the kingdom in the bargain.

There were many who tried, for everybody would be glad to get the princess and half the kingdom, but they all fared badly.

Well, there were three brothers, who were also going to try their luck, and the two elder set out first, but they fared no better than all the others. So Ashiepattle thought he would try, and set out for the palace.

He met the princess outside the cow-house. "Good day," said he.— "Good day," said she; "I suppose you haven't got such a big cow-house as we. When two boys stand, one at each end, and blow their horns, they can't hear each other!"—"Oh, indeed," said Ashiepattle, "ours is a great deal bigger! If a young calf starts to go from one end of it to the other, he is a big bull by the time he comes out."

"May be," said the princess; "but then you haven't got so big a bull as we have! Look, there he is!—When two men sit, one on each horn, they can't touch each other with a yard measure."—"Why, that's nothing," said Ashiepattle; "we have a bull so big, that when two men sit, one on each horn, and blow their horns, they can't hear each other."

"Oh, indeed," said the princess, "but you haven't got so much milk as we anyhow, for we milk our cows into great tubs and empty them into great big coppers, and make such awful big cheeses."

"Well, we milk into great big casks, which we cart into the dairy, and put the milk into great brewing vats and make cheeses as big as houses. Once we had a cream-coloured mare, which we put into the vat to tread the cheese together, and she had her foal with her, but one day she lost the foal in the cheese and we couldn't find it. But after we had been eating the cheese for seven years, we came across a great big cream-coloured horse who was walking about in the cheese. I was going to drive that horse to the mill one day and all of a sudden his back broke right off; but I knew how to put that right. I took a pine-twig and stuck it in his back, and he had no other back-bone as long as we had him. But that twig grew and grew so tall, that I climbed right up to the clouds by it, and when I got there I saw the north wind sitting there spinning a rope of mutton broth. Suddenly the top of the pine-tree broke off, and there I was. But the north wind let me down by one of the ropes, and I came right into a fox's hole; and who do you think were sitting there?—Why, my mother and your father of course, both mending boots; and all of a sudden my mother gave your father such a blow with an old boot, that the scurf* flew out of his hair!"

"There you tell a lie," shouted the princess; "my father never was scurfy!"

And so Ashiepattle won!

# AN EVENING IN THE SQUIRE'S KITCHEN

IT WAS a miserable evening; outside it was snowing and blowing, and in the squire's parlour the candle burned so dimly that you could scarcely distinguish anything in the room but a clock-case with some Chinese ornaments, a large mirror in an old-fashioned frame, and a silver family tankard. The squire and I were the only occupants of the room. I sat in a corner of the sofa with a book in my hand, while the squire himself had taken a seat in the other corner buried in the perusal of the manuscript of a political treatise, which he had called: "Attempts at a few well-

*Scurf—dry flakes, like dandruff.

An Evening in the Squire's Kitchen

meant patriotic utterances for the welfare of my country, by Anonymous," as he called himself out of modesty.

To the profound study of this intellectual gold mine, many shrewd
opinions, as might easily be imagined, owed their birth. That he himself,
at least, was convinced of their excellence, the cunning look in the grey
blinking eyes which he directed towards me left me no doubt; there was,
however, no want of "well-meant patriotic utterances" in his conversation,
the quality of which can best be judged by those who have had the
opportunity of glancing over the above-named treatise, or his large un-
printed essay about the tithes. But all this display of wisdom was lost
upon me; I had it at my fingers' ends, having now heard it for the twenty-
third time. I am not endowed with the patience of an angel; but what
could I do? The retreat to my room was cut off,—they had been washing
the floor for Sunday, and the room was no doubt steaming with vapour
from the damp boards. Having made a few vain attempts at engrossing
my attention in my book, I was obliged to let myself be carried away by
the impetuous torrent of the squire's eloquence. The squire was now on
his hobby-horse, as we say; he had placed the old worn fur cap by his
side on the sofa, leaving his bald head and grey hairs exposed. He became more and more excited; he rose from the sofa, walked up and
down the floor with hurried steps and fought with his hands in the air,
till the light flickered hither and thither, while the sweeping tail of his
long grey home-spun coat described long circles every time he swung
himself round and raised himself on his longer leg, for, like Tyrtæus and
Peter Solvold of our parish, he was afflicted with a limp. His impassioned
words buzzed about my ears like cockchafers round the top of the lime-
trees. He thundered away about lawsuits and judgments in the High
Court of Justice, about disputes with the Court of Chancery, about clearing out the forests, about luxury, the rule of the majority in the national
assembly, and the blowing up of the rocks in the Mörkefos, about the
corn duty and the cultivation of the Jœdern district, about industries and
centralisations, about the insufficiency of the currency, about official ar-
istocracy and all other "ocracies" in the world, from King Nebuchadnez-
zar down to Peter Solvold's democracy.

It was impossible to endure the jargon and the affected pathos of the
squire any longer. Out in the kitchen one peal of laughter succeeded
another; Kristen, the smith on the farm, was the spokesman out there—
he had evidently just finished a story, and another hearty laugh echoed
through the room.

"No, I must go out and hear what the smith is telling," I said, inter-
rupting the eloquent squire, and made a dart for the kitchen, leaving
him behind in the room in company with the dimly burning candle and
his own disturbed reflections.

"Stuff and nonsense, and lying rigmaroles!" he growled, as I vanished
through the door; "it's a disgrace to see learned people—But well-meant
patriotic words, no——" I heard no more.

Light, life, and merriment prevailed in the lofty airy kitchen. A great
fire blazed on the large open hearth and lighted up the room even in its
farthest corners. By the side of the hearth presided the squire's wife with

her spinning-wheel. Although she, for many years had waged continual war against rheumatism, her pleasant face shone like the full moon from under the white head-gear, while she had protected herself against any possible attack of the enemy by a multiplicity of petticoats and jackets; and as an outer fortification she had put on a monster of a frieze cloak. Along the edge of the hearth sat the children, and cracked nuts. Round about them was a circle of girls and wives of the neighbouring tenants; "they trod the spinning-wheels with diligent feet, or were using the scraping carding-combs," as an author has it. In the passage outside the door, the threshers, who had done their day's work, were stamping the snow off their feet before they came in,—their hair full of chaff. They sat down by the big old-fashioned table, where the cook soon brought them their supper, consisting of a large dish of thick porridge and a bowl of milk.

The smith was leaning against the wall by the hearth; he was smoking a long cutty-pipe, and on his countenance, which bore traces of smithy-soot, lay a dry, serious expression, which told he had been telling some story, and that to his own satisfaction.

"Good evening, Kristen," said I; "what are you telling that creates such fun?"

"Hee, hee, hee!" screamed the youngsters, with great glee depicted in their faces; "Kristen has told us about the smith and the devil, and then about the lad who got him into the nut, and now he says he's going to tell us about Peter Sannum, whose horse the fairies stopped on the Asmyr hill."

"Yes," began the smith, "that Peter belonged to one of the Sannum farms north of the church. He was a wise man, and he was often fetched with sledge and horse to cure both man and beast, just like old Mother Bertha Tuppenhaug here. But somehow or other he could not have been clever enough, for the fairies tied him up once in a field near his farm, where he had to stand the whole night with his mouth all on one side; and that time I was going to tell you about he fared no better either. You see, this Peter could never agree with people, he was just like—ahem!—hem!—well yes, he was a regular disagreeable fellow, who had lawsuits with everybody. Well, he had once a case before the Court of Appeal in Christiania, and he had to be in court at ten o'clock in the morning. He thought he had better start from home the evening before to be in time, which he did; but when he came to the Asmyr hill his horse was stopped. There is something not quite right thereabouts; many years ago some one hung himself there, and there are many who have heard music there, both on fiddles and clarionettes and flutes and other wind instruments. Yes, old Mother Bertha could tell something about that; she has heard it and she says she never heard anything so beautiful, it was just like the grand band which was over at the bailiff's in 1814. Isn't that true, Bertha?" asked the smith.

"Yes, every word of it, my lad," said Mother Bertha, who was sitting near the hearth carding.

"Well, as I told you, the horse was stopped," continued the smith, "and it would not move from the spot. For all he whipped and shouted the horse only danced round in a ring, but he couldn't get him to move either forward or backward. Hour passed after hour, but there the horse stood—and thus the whole night through. He knew some one must be holding the horse, for although he cursed and went on at an awful rate, he did not get a step farther. Towards the morning, just in the grey dawn, he got off the horse and went up to Ingebret Asmyr, and got him to bring a firebrand with him, and when he had got in the saddle again, he asked him to throw the firebrand over the horse. I should say he got a start then; away he went at full gallop; Peter could scarcely stick to the horse, and did not stop till he reached town; but then the horse was burst."

"I have heard of this before," said old Bertha, and left off carding; "but I would never believe that Peter Sannum didn't know better than that: but since you, Kristen, say so, I suppose I must believe it."

"Yes, you may," answered the smith; "for I heard it from Ingebret Asmyr himself, who carried the firebrand and threw it over the horse for him."

"He should have looked down over the horse's head between the ears, shouldn't he, Bertha?" asked one of the boys.

"Yes, that he should," answered Bertha; "for then he would have seen who held the horse, and then they would have had to let his horse go. I have heard that from one who knew more about such things than anybody; they called him 'Hans Cheerful' at home in Halland. In other parishes they called him, 'Hans Decency,' for he always used the expression, 'everything with decency.' He was taken into the mountain by the fairies, and had been with them for many years, and at last they wanted him to marry their daughter, who was always hanging about after him. But this he wouldn't, and when he had been rung for from several churches,* the fairies took him at last and threw him from a high knoll far out into the parish. He thought himself he would have gone right out into the fjord. From that time he became half-witted. He was then put out on the parish, and went from farm to farm and told all sorts of wonderful stories, but all of a sudden he would laugh and say:

" 'Hee, hee, hee! Kari, Karina, I see you!' for the huldre girl was always after him.—While he was with the fairies, he told us, he had always to go with them when they were out to provide themselves with food and milk, for everything which the sign of the cross had been made over they had no power to touch, and then they said to Hans: 'You'll have to take this, for this has been crossed,' and so he filled their bags with tremendous loads of all sorts of food; but if it ever began to thunder, they used to run away as fast as they could, so Hans could scarcely follow them. He was generally in company with one called Vaatt, and he was so strong, that he took both Hans and his load and carried them under his arms when such weather came upon them suddenly. Once they met the sheriff of Ringerike in a deep valley up in Halland, and Vaatt took hold of the horse and stopped him, and the sheriff shouted and whipped and pulled

---

*It was an old custom to ring the bells of the parish church if any one was supposed to have been carried off into the mountains by the fairies.

the poor horse about till he was pitiful to look at. But the sheriff's boy got off the sledge and looked over the horse's head between the ears, and then Vaatt had to let go his hold, 'and I should say they went off then,' said Hans, 'the boy had scarcely time to get on the sledge again, and we burst out with such laughter, that the sheriff turned round and looked behind——' "

"Yes," said a tenant from a distant part of the parish, "I have heard something like that about a parson in Lier. He was once on his way to an old woman, who was on her death-bed and who had led a wicked life. When he got into the forest his horse was stopped for him; but he knew what to do,—he was a smart fellow that Lier parson,—in one jump he was up on the back of the horse, and looked over his head between his ears, and then he saw an ugly old man, who was holding the reins. They say, it was old Nick himself.

" 'Leave go,—you sha'n't have her,' said the parson. He had to leave go, but he gave the horse such a smart blow at the same time, that the horse started off at such a pace that the sparks flew about under his hoofs, and the boy could scarcely stick on to the sledge. That time the parson came riding on horseback to a dying parishioner."

"But I don't know how it will fare with the cows, ma'am," said Mary, the dairymaid, who came toiling in with a pail of milk; "I do believe they'll starve. Just look here, ma'am, what little milk we get."

"Yet must take hay from the stable, Mary," said the squire's wife.

"Yes, I ought to try that!" answered Mary; "if I go there, the men get as savage as wild geese."

"I'll give you a good piece of advice, Mary," said one of the boys with a sly look. "You must boil cream-porridge and put it in the stable-loft every Thursday night, and you will find that the brownie helps you to carry hay to the cows, while the men are asleep."

"Well, yes, if there only were any brownie here, I would do it," answered the old dairymaid quite innocently; "but believe me, there is no brownie on this farm; why, our master and mistress don't believe in such—no, on Nœs with the captain's, that time I served there, there was the brownie sure enough!"

"How do you know that, Mary?" asked the squire's wife. "Did you see him?"

"See him? yes, of course; I've seen him, sure enough," answered Mary.

"Oh, tell us, tell us all about it," shouted the boys.

"Well, yes! I can do that," said the dairymaid and began:

"When I was in service at the captain's I told you of, the stableboy said to me one Saturday night:

" 'If you'll fodder the horses for me to-night, Mary, I'll do you a good turn some day.'

" 'All right,' said I, 'I'll do that for you,' for he was going to see his sweetheart, you know.

"So towards evening when the horses should have their fodder, and I had given it to a couple of them, I took an armful of hay to give to the captain's own horse,—he was always so fat and glossy, you could almost see yourself in his shiny coat,—but just as I was going into the box to him, he fell right into my arms——"

"Who, who? the horse?" asked the boys.

"No, of course not! It was the brownie; I got so frightened, that I dropped the hay on the spot and ran away as fast as I could. When Peter, the lad, came home, I said to him: 'I have foddered the horses for you once, my dear Peter, but believe me, I sha'n't do it again. The captain's horse didn't get as much as a straw, he didn't!' and so I told him all about it.

" 'Ah, that didn't matter a bit,' said Peter, 'the captain's horse has got some one that looks after him anyhow, he has!' "

"What did the brownie look like, Mary?" asked one of the boys.

"Well, you see, I didn't see him exactly!" she said, "it was so dark I couldn't see a hand before me, but I felt him as plainly as now, when I touch you; he was hairy, and didn't his eyes glisten?"

"Oh, it was only a cat!" objected another of the boys.

"Cat?" said Mary with the greatest contempt, "why, I felt every one of his fingers; he had only four, and they were hairy all over! If that wasn't the brownie, may I never leave this spot alive!"

"Of course, that must have been the brownie sure enough," said the smith, "for he hasn't got any thumbs, and he's hairy on his fists—I've never shaken hands with him, but I've heard say so; and we all know he minds the horses, and is about the best stableboy you could have. There are a great many he is very useful to; but it's not only he that may be useful to the farmers, for up in Ullensaker," he said, as he began a new story, "there was a man who once found the fairies just as useful to him as the brownie is to others. He lived on Rögli farm, and knew well enough that the huldre was there, for once when he was going to town— it was in the spring just as the snow was melting away on the roads—and had got as far as Skjœllebœk and had watered his horses, he met a herd of red cows, so big and fat that it was a pleasure to look at them, and after them came several cartloads of tubs and buckets and all sorts of things, with fine fat horses for the carts; but in front went a fine lassie with a snow-white milking pail in her hand.

" 'But where are you going to, this time of the year?' asked the Rögli man, surprised.

" 'Oh, we are going to the Rögli pastures in Ullensaker,' answered she who went in front; 'there is plenty of grass there.'

"He thought it was rather strange that they were going to graze on his pastures, but no one else but he either saw or heard anything of them. He asked several whom he met on the road, but no one had seen any cattle.

"At home on his farm several strange things happened too, sometimes. If he did any work after sunset it was always destroyed during the night, and at last he had to give up working after the sun had set.

"But now I must tell you about that time I told you they did him a good turn. One autumn he was walking about in his fields, feeling if his crop of barley was dry; it was very late in the autumn and he thought it wasn't quite dry enough to cart it in yet, but then he heard a voice over in a hill saying quite plainly: 'You had better cart in your crops! To-morrow it'll be snowing!' And he began carting as fast as he could, and carted till long past midnight, till he got his crop in; but the next morning the snow lay shoe-deep in the fields."

"But it is not always that the fairies are so good," said one of the boys. "What about the huldre who stole the wedding fare at Eldstad, and left her cup behind her?"

"Yes, I'll tell you all about that," said the smith, who eagerly took this hint to begin a new story.

"There was once a wedding at Eldstad in Ullensaker, but as they hadn't any oven on the farm, they had to send the joints to the neighbouring farm, where they had an oven, to get them roasted. In the evening, the boy on the farm, where the wedding took place, was to fetch them. As he was driving over one of the moors, he plainly heard a voice shouting—

> " 'If you are going to Eldstad,
>    Just tell our Deld, from her sire,
>    That Dild fell in the fire.'

"The boy was frightened, and drove so fast that the wind whistled in his nostrils, for the weather was cold, and the roads were in a splendid condition. He heard the voice calling after him several times, so he remembered the words well. He came safely home with his load, and went into a room, where the servants were helping themselves to something to eat at the end of a big table, as they found time to get a few mouthfuls.

" 'Holloa, lad! has Old Nick brought you here already, or haven't you gone for the joints yet!' asked one of the people belonging to the house.

" 'Yes, of course I have,' said the lad; 'there you see the joints coming in through the door. But I drove as fast as the horse could gallop, for when I came over the moor I heard a voice shouting after me:

> " ' "If you are going to Eldstad,
>    Just tell our Deld, from her sire,
>    That Dild fell in the fire." '

" 'Oh, that's my child,' shouted a voice from amongst the guests in the next room, and in an instant a woman rushed out as if she had lost her senses. She ran against one after the other, and nearly knocked them over, but suddenly her hat fell off, and it was then evident that it was a huldre; she had been stealing both meat and bacon, butter and cake, beer and brandy, and all that was good. But she became so upset on hearing about the youngster, that she left behind her a silver cup in the beer bowl, and didn't notice that her hat had fallen off. They took both the cup and the hat and kept them at Eldstad; and the hat had this property, that whoever put it on was invisible to every other mortal, except to such as were gifted with second sight; but whether the hat is there still, I cannot say for certain, for I have not seen it, nor have I had it on either."

"Yes, these huldres are very smart at thieving, I have always heard that," said old Bertha Tuppenhaug, "but particularly in the summer time when the cattle are up in the mountains. It's regular holiday time for both huldres and other fairies then, for while the dairymaids go about thinking of their sweethearts, they forget to make crosses over the milk and cream and their food, and then the fairies can take what they like. It isn't often they are seen, but it does happen now and then, as it happened once at the Neberg dairy up here.

"There were some wood-cutters up there at work, and as they were going towards the dairy for supper, they heard a voice over in the forest shouting to them:

" 'Tell Kilde, both her sonnies fell in the soup-kettle and burnt themselves.'

"When the wood-cutters came to the dairy they told the girls of this, and said: 'As we were going home to supper, just as we had shouldered our axes, we heard some one shouting over in the forest:

" ' "Tell Kilde, both her sonnies fell in the soup-kettle and burnt themselves." '

" 'Oh, they're my children,' some one shouted in the pantry, and suddenly a huldre rushed out with a milk-pail in her hand, which she dropped as she ran, splashing the milk all about the room."

"Ah, well! you hear so many tales," said the smith with a sneer, as if he had his doubts about the truth of this story; it was, however, perfectly evident that the remark was made out of vexation at being interrupted, when he had once fairly started with his own stories. No one in the whole parish was richer than he in a stock of the most wonderful stories and tales about the huldres and fairies; and his belief in these supernatural beings was on a par with the credulity of the most superstitious. "You hear so many things," he continued, "you cannot believe them all. But what has happened to your own kith and kin you are bound to believe! Now, I'll tell you something that happened to my father-in-law; he was a most serious and credible man, so what he said you may depend upon was true. His name was Joe, and he lived at Skroperud in Ullensaker. He built himself a new house there, and he had two or three fat cows and a horse, the like of which was not to be found in the whole parish; the horse was often used as post-horse between Mo and Trögstad, and Joe didn't seem to care much how the beast was used,—for fat he was and fat he remained. Joe was a hunter, and a fiddler as well. He was often about in the parish playing, but at home it was impossible to get him to touch the fiddle; even if the room was full of lads and lasses he refused to play. But one evening some lads from the neighbouring farm came to see him, and they brought some brandy with them in their pocket-flasks. They treated Joe, and when they had made him tipsy, more lads came in, and although he refused to play at first, eventually he took down the fiddle. But after he had played for some time he put it away, for he knew that the fairies were not far off, and that they didn't like the noise and disturbance. But the lads persuaded him to play again; and thus it happened two or three times that he put the fiddle away, and that the lads coaxed him to play again. At last he hung his fiddle up on the wall, and swore he wouldn't play another stroke that night, and with that he turned them all out, lads and lasses! He was just going to bed, and was standing in his shirtsleeves by the hearth lighting his pipe for the night with a brand, when a large party of old and young people came in and filled the whole room.

" 'Now, are you there again?' said Joe. He thought at first they were the same as had been there dancing, but when he saw they were strangers he felt a little frightened, took his daughters, who were already in bed, and threw them out on the floor—he was a big strong man—and asked: 'What people are these? Do you know them?'

"The lasses were sleepy, and didn't know what to answer. So he took his gun down from the wall and turned round towards the people who had come in, and threatened them with the butt end of his rifle. 'If you don't get out of this quickly, I'll turn you out in such a way that you won't know whether you are standing on your heads or your heels!' Away they rushed, yelling out of the door, the one on top of the other, and he fancied they all looked like a lot of grey balls of worsted rolling out through the door. But when Joe had put his gun away and come over to the hearth to light his pipe again, he found an old man sitting on the stool by the fire,—he had such a long beard, that it reached down to his knees,—it must have been a yard long, and he also had a pipe, which he was trying to light with a firebrand like Joe,—one moment it was alight and the next it went out.

" 'And you,' said Joe, 'do you belong to the same gang of tramps, you too? Where do you come from?'

" ' Oh, I don't live far away, I can tell you,' said the man, 'and I would advise you to take more care and not make such a noise and disturbance after this, or I'll make you a poor man.'

" 'So,' said Joe, 'where do you live then?'

" 'I live close by, under the corn-drying room,' said the man; 'and if we hadn't been living there it would have been gone long ago, for you have been firing over much now and then, and it has been hot enough there I can tell you; but the whole building is not so strong, but that it'll fall in a heap if I touch it with my finger. Now you know it, so you had better mind after this!'

"There was no more dancing and playing to be heard at Skroperud after that; Joe parted with his fiddle, and they could never get him to touch another since."

During the latter part of this story, the squire had been making a commotion in the parlour; cupboard doors were opened and shut; we heard the keys rattle, and we knew he was busy locking up the silver plate and other portable property, from the silver tankard down to the leaden tobacco-box. Just as the smith had finished his story, the squire opened the door and popped in his head with his cap on one side.

"So you are at your cock and bull stories and lies again?" he asked.

"Lies?" said the smith very much offended, "I have never told lies, sir! And this story is true enough, for I am married to one of the daughters. My wife, Dorthe, she was lying in bed and saw the old man with the beard. These girls were a little queer, to be sure, almost half-witted, but that came from their having seen fairies," he added, with an indignant look at the squire.

"Half-witted?" said the squire, "yes, I should think so; and that's what you are too, when you are not tipsy, and then you are raving mad. Come, boys!—Go to bed, and don't sit here and listen to such rubbish and nonsense."

"I don't think that's kindly spoken on your part, sir," answered the smith, with an air of superiority; "the last time I heard rubbish and nonsense spoken, was when you made the speech on the Neberg hill the last Anniversary of our Independence."

"Confounded rubbish!" muttered the squire, as he came trudging through the kitchen with the candle in one hand and a bundle of Acts and some newspapers under his arm.

"Oh, wait a bit, sir," said the smith, evidently with the intention of teasing the squire, "and let the boys stay a little longer too. You might like to hear a trifle also. It doesn't do you good to be always reading in the law books either. I'll tell you about a dragoon who was married to a huldre. I know it's true, for I've heard it of old Bertha, and she's from the very parish where it happened."

The squire banged the door after him angrily, and we heard him tramping up the stairs.

"Well, well, since the squire won't listen, I'll tell it to you, my lads," said the smith, addressing the boys, on whom all grandfatherly authority was lost when the smith promised to tell tales.

"Many years ago," he began, "there lived a wealthy old couple on a farm in Halland. They had a son, who was a dragoon,* and a fine big fellow he was. They had a dairy up in the mountains, but it wasn't like the dairies you generally see, it was a nice and well-built dairy, with a regular chimney and roof and windows too. They stayed there all the summer, but when they left in the autumn, some woodcutters, or hunters, or fishermen, or such people who knock about in the mountains at that time, had noticed that the huldre people moved in there with the cattle. And amongst them was a lass, who was so lovely that they had never seen her like.

"The son had often heard people speak of this, and one autumn when they had left the dairy he dressed himself in full uniform, put the dragoon-saddle on his horse, and the pistols in the holsters, and off he started. When he came in sight of the dairy, it was all ablaze with light, and he guessed then that the huldre people had come already. So he tied his horse to the stump of a pine-tree, took one of the pistols with him, and stole quietly up to the window and looked in. In the room sat an old man and an old woman, who were so crooked and so wrinkled with age, and so dreadfully ugly, that he had never seen anything so hideous in his life; but then there was a lass who was so lovely that he thought he could not live if he did not make her his own. They had all cow's tails, the lovely lass as well. He could see that they had only lately arrived, for the room appeared to have been very lately put in order. The lass was busy washing the ugly old man, while the woman was lighting a fire under the big cheese-kettle on the hearth.

*Dragoon—A military horseman.

"All of a sudden the dragoon pushed the door open, and fired his pistol right over the head of the lassie, which sent her rolling over on to the floor. But at the same moment she turned just as ugly as she had been beautiful before, and her nose grew as long as the pistol.

" 'You can take her now; she is yours now!' said the old man. But the dragoon was almost spell-bound; he remained standing on the same spot and could not move a step either forwards or backwards. The old man began to wash the lass, and she looked a little better after that, the nose decreased to about half the size, and the ugly cow's tail was tied up, but it would be a sin to say she was anything like pretty.

" 'She is yours now, my brave dragoon! Put her in front of you on the pommel of the saddle, and ride through the parish with her and celebrate your wedding. For us two, you can prepare something in the small chamber in the wash-house, for we don't care to mix with the other wedding-guests,' said the old ugly one, who was the father of the lass; 'but when the loving cup is passing round you may as well look in on us.'

"He dared not do otherwise; he took the lassie with him on the pommel of the saddle and made preparations for the wedding. But before they went to church, the bride asked one of the bridesmaids to stand close behind, that no one should see the cow's tail fall off when the parson put his hand on her head.

"So the wedding was celebrated, and when the loving cup was passing round, the bridegroom went across to the chamber, where a table had been laid for the old huldrefolks. He did not notice anything there that time, but when the guests had departed and he went in to see to the old folks again they were gone, but he found such a lot of gold and silver which they must have left behind, that he had never seen so much treasure before.

"So everything went comfortably for a long time; and whenever they had any friends with them, the wife got something ready for the old couple in the little chamber, who always left so much money behind them that the young people did not know what to do with it. But the huldre wife was ugly and remained ugly, and the young husband began to get tired of her, and I believe he was unkind to her now and then, and even attempted to strike her.

"One day late in the autumn he was going to town, but the early frost had set in and the roads were slippery, so he had to get his horse shod first. He went to the smithy,—for he was a clever smith himself,—but whichever way he twisted and turned the iron, the shoes were either too large or too small, and he could not get them to fit. He had only that horse at home on the farm, so he had no choice but to work away at the shoeing. But dinner time came, and the afternoon wore on, and still the horse was unshod.

" 'Will you never get those shoes ready?' asked his wife. 'You are not much of a husband of late, and I think you are still less a smith. I see no help for it but to go myself to the smithy and shoe your horse. If I make the shoe too big you can make it smaller, and if I make it too small you can make it bigger.' She went into the smithy, and the first thing she did was to take the shoe in her hands and pull the iron out straight.

" 'Look here,' she said, 'this is the way you are to do it!' So she bent the shoe together as if it were of lead. 'Now hold his foot up,' she said, and the shoe fitted exactly; the best smith could not have done it better.

" 'You seem to be very strong in your fingers,' said her husband, as he looked at her.

" 'Do you think so?' she said. 'How do you think it would have fared with me, if you had been as strong in your fingers? But I care for you too much to use my strength against yours.'

"From that day he was most kind and good to her."

"Well, I think we have had enough for to-night," said the squire's wife, when the smith had finished this story, and got up from her comfortable seat.

"Yes, I suppose we must be going, since the old man has gone to roost," said the smith, and bade the children "Good night;" but he had to promise them to tell more the next evening, having made the condition that he was to have a "quarter of tobacco."

Next afternoon, when I went into the smithy, I found the smith chewing very hard, which was always the case when he had been drinking.

In the evening he went to some of the neighbouring farms to get more drink. When I saw him again some days afterwards, he was gloomy and chary of words. He would not tell any stories, although the boys promised him both tobacco and brandy. The girls whispered, that the fairies had got hold of him and knocked him over in the Asmyr hill. A carter had found him lying there early in the morning, and then he spoke incoherently.


# HANS, WHO MADE THE PRINCESS LAUGH


ONCE UPON a time there was a king, who had a daughter, and she was so lovely that the reports of her beauty went far and wide; but she was so melancholy, that she never laughed, and besides she was so grand and proud that she said "No" to all who came to woo her—she would not have any of them, were they ever so fine, whether they were princes or noblemen.

The king was tired of this whim of hers long ago, and thought she ought to get married like other people; there was nothing she need wait for,—she was old enough and she would not be any richer either, for she was to have half the kindgom, which she inherited after her mother.

So he made known every Sunday after the service, from the steps outside the church, that he that could make his daughter laugh should have both her and half the kingdom. But if there were any one who tried and could not make her laugh, he would have three red stripes cut out of his back and salt rubbed into them—and, sad to relate, there were many sore backs in that kingdom. Lovers from south and from north, from east and from west came to try their luck—they thought it was an easy thing to make a princess laugh. They were a queer lot altogether, but for all their cleverness and for all the tricks and pranks they played, the princess was just as serious and immovable as ever.

But close to the palace lived a man who had three sons, and they had also heard that the king had made known that he who could make the princess laugh should have her and half the kingdom.

The eldest of the brothers wanted to try first, and away he went; and when he came to the palace, he told the king he wouldn't mind trying to make the princess laugh.

"Yes, yes! that's all very well," said the king; "but I am afraid it's of very little use, my man. There have been many here to try their luck, but my daughter is just as sad, and I am afraid it is no good trying. I do not like to see any more suffer on that account."

But the lad thought he would try anyhow. It couldn't be such a difficult thing to make a princess laugh at him, for had not everybody, both grand and simple, laughed so many a time at him when he served as soldier and went through his drill under Sergeant Nils.

So he went out on the terrace outside the princess's windows and began drilling just as if Sergeant Nils himself were there. But all in vain! The princess sat just as serious and immovable as before, and so they took him and cut three broad, red stripes out of his back and sent him home.

He had no sooner arrived home, than his second brother wanted to set out and try his luck. He was a schoolmaster, and a funny figure he was altogether. He had one leg shorter than the other, and limped terribly when he walked. One moment he was no bigger than a boy, but the next moment when he raised himself up on his long leg he was as big and tall as a giant—and besides he was great at preaching.

When he came to the palace, and said that he wanted to make the princess laugh, the king thought that it was not so unlikely that he might; "but I pity you, if you don't succeed," said the king, "for we cut the stripes broader and broader for every one that tries."

So the schoolmaster went out on the terrace, and took his place outside the princess's window, where he began preaching and chanting, imitating seven of the parsons, and reading and singing just like seven of the clerks whom they had had in the parish.

The king laughed at the schoolmaster till he was obliged to hold on to the door-post, and the princess was just on the point of smiling, but suddenly she was as sad and immovable as ever, and so it fared no better with Paul the schoolmaster than with Peter the soldier—for Peter and Paul were their names, you must know!

So they took Paul and cut three red stripes out of his back, put salt into them, and sent him home again.

Well, the youngest brother thought he would have a try next. His name was Hans. But the brothers laughed and made fun of him, and showed him their sore backs. Besides, the father would not give him leave to go, for he said it was no use his trying, who had so little sense; all he could do was to sit in a corner on the hearth, like a cat, rooting about in the ashes and cutting chips. But Hans would not give in—he begged and prayed so long, till they got tired of his whimpering, and so he got leave to go to the king's palace and try his luck.

When he arrived at the palace, he did not say he had come to try to make the princess laugh, but asked if he could get a situation there. No, they had no situation for him; but Hans was not so easily put off; they might want one to carry wood and water for the kitchenmaid in such a big place as that, he said. Yes, the king thought so too, and to get rid of the lad he gave him leave to remain there and carry wood and water for the kitchenmaid.

One day, when he was going to fetch water from the brook, he saw a big fish in the water just under an old root of a fir-tree, which the current had carried all the soil away from. He put his bucket quietly under the fish and caught it. As he was going home to the palace, he met an old woman leading a golden goose.

"Good day, grandmother!" said Hans. "That's a fine bird you have got there; and such splendid feathers too! he shines a long way off. If one had such feathers, one needn't be chopping firewood."

The woman thought just as much of the fish which Hans had in the bucket, and said if Hans would give her the fish he should have the golden goose; and this goose was such, that if any one touched it he would be sticking fast to it if he only said: "If you'll come along, then hang on."

Yes, Hans would willingly exchange on those terms. "A bird is as good as a fish any day," he said to himself. "If it is as you say, I might use it instead of a fish-hook," he said to the woman, and felt greatly pleased with the possession of the goose.

He had not gone far before he met another old woman. When she saw the splendid golden goose, she must go and stroke it. She made herself so friendly and spoke so nicely to Hans, and asked him to let her stroke that lovely golden goose of his.

"Oh, yes!" said Hans, "but you mus'n't pluck off any of its feathers!"

Just as she stroked the bird, Hans said: "If you'll come along, then hang on!"

The woman pulled and tore, but she had to hang on, whether she would or no, and Hans walked on, as if he only had the goose with him.

When he had gone some distance, he met a man who had a spite against the woman for a trick she had played upon him. When he saw that she fought so hard to get free and seemed to hang on so fast, he thought he might safely venture to pay her off for the grudge he owed her, and so he gave her a kick.

"If you'll come along, then hang on!" said Hans, and the man had to hang on and limp along on one leg, whether he would or no; and when he tried to tear himself loose, he made it still worse for himself, for he was very nearly falling on his back whenever he struggled to get free.

So on they went till they came in the neighbourhood of the palace. There they met the king's smith; he was on his way to the smithy, and had a large pair of tongs in his hand. This smith was a merry fellow, and was always full of mad pranks and tricks, and when he saw this procession coming jumping and limping along, he began laughing till he was

Hans, Who Made the Princess Laugh

bent in two, but suddenly he said:

"This must be a new flock of geese for the princess; but who can tell which is goose and which is gander? I suppose it must be the gander toddling on in front. Goosey, goosey!" he called, and pretended to be strewing corn out of his hands as when feeding geese.

But they did not stop. The woman and the man only looked in great rage at the smith for making game of them. So said the smith: "It would be great fun to see if I could stop the whole flock, many as they are!"— He was a strong man, and seized the old man with his tongs from behind in his trousers, and the man shouted and struggled hard, but Hans said:

"If you'll come along, then hang on!"

And so the smith had to hang on too. He bent his back and stuck his heels in the ground when they went up a hill and tried to get away, but it was of no use; he stuck on to the other as if he had been screwed fast in the great vice in the smithy, and whether he liked it or not, he had to dance along with the others.

When they came near the palace, the farm-dog ran against them and barked at them, as if they were a gang of tramps, and when the princess came to look out of her window to see what was the matter, and saw this procession, she burst out laughing. But Hans was not satisfied with that. "Just wait a bit, and she will laugh still louder very soon," he said, and made a tour round the palace with his followers.

When they came past the kitchen, the door was open and the cook was just boiling porridge, but when she saw Hans and his train after him, she rushed out of the door with the porridge-stick in one hand and a big ladle full of boiling porridge in the other, and she laughed till her sides shook; but when she saw the smith there as well she thought she would have burst with laughter. When she had had a regular good laugh, she looked at the golden goose again and thought it was so lovely that she must stroke it.

"Hans, Hans!" she cried, and ran after him with the ladle in her hand; "just let me stroke that lovely bird of yours."

"Rather let her stroke me!" said the smith.

"Very well," said Hans.

But when the cook heard this, she got very angry. "What is it you say!" she cried, and gave the smith a smack with the ladle.

"If you'll come along, then hang on!" said Hans, and so she stuck fast to the others too, and for all her scolding and all her tearing and pulling, she had to limp along with them.

And when they came past the princess's window again, she was still there waiting for them, but when she saw that they had got hold of the cook too, with the ladle and porridge-stick, she laughed till the king had to hold her up. So Hans got the princess and half the kingdom, and they had a wedding which was heard of far and wide.

# A SUMMER NIGHT IN A NORWEGIAN FOREST

*The evening shadows now unfold*
*Their curtain o'er the lonely wold;*
*The night wind sighs with dreary moan,*
*And whispers over stock and stone.*
*Tramp, Tramp! the trolls come trooping, hark!*
*Across the moor to the deep woods dark.*

*—GEIJER*

WHEN I was a boy about fourteen years old I came one Saturday afternoon in the middle of the summer to Upper Lyse, the last farm in Sörkedale. I had frequently walked or driven over the main road between Christiania and Ringerike, and I had now, after having been at home on a short visit, taken the road past Bokstad to Lyse for a change, with the intention of making a short cut through the north part of the Krog-wood.

I found all the doors of the farmhouse wide open, but I looked in vain in the parlour, in the kitchen, and in the barn, for a human being whom I could ask for a drink and who could give me some direction about the road.

There was no one at home but a black cat, who was sitting quite content and purring on the hearth, and a dazzling white cock, who was walking up and down the passage breasting himself and crowing incessantly, as much as to say: "Now I am the cock of the walk!" The swallows, which had been tempted here in great numbers on account of the quantity of insects to be found in proximity to the wood, and had established themselves in the barn and under the caves, were gambolling, circling, and twittering fearlessly about in the sunshine.

Tired with the heat and my walk, I threw myself down on the grass in the shadow of the house, where I lay half-asleep enjoying a quiet rest, when I was startled by an unpleasant clamour,—the jarring voice of a woman, who was trying by alternately scolding and using pet names to pacify a litter of grunting pigs on the farm. By following the sound I came upon a bare-footed old woman with a yellow dried-up countenance, who was bending down over the pigs' trough, busy filling it with food, for which the noisy little creatures were fighting, tearing, pushing, and yelling, with expectation and delight.

On my questioning her about the road, she answered me by asking me another question, while she, without raising herself up, turned her head half away from her pets to stare at me.

"Where might you come from?"

When she had got a satisfactory answer to this, she continued, while she repeatedly addressed herself to the young pigs:

"Ah, so!—you are at school at the parson's, eh!—hush, hush! little piggies then!——The road to Stubdale, do you say?——Just look at that one now! Will you let the others get something as well, you rascal! Hush, hush! Be quiet, will you! Oh, poor fellow, did I kick you then?——Yes, yes, I'll tell you the road directly,—it's—it's straight on through the wood till you come to the big water-wheel!"

As this direction seemed to me to be rather vague for a road of about fourteen miles length through a forest, I asked her if I could not hire a lad who knew the road, to go with me.

"No, bless you! Is it likely?" she said, as she left the piggery and came out on the slope before the farm. "They are so busy now with the hay-making, that they've scarcely time to eat. But it's straight through the wood, and I'll explain it to you right enough, as if you saw the road before you. First you go up the crag and all the hills over yonder, and when you have got up on the heights, you have the straight road right before you to Heggelie. You have the river on your left hand all the way, and if you don't see it, you'll hear it. But just about Heggelie there is a lot of twistings and turnings, and now and then the road is lost altogether for some distance—if one is a stranger there, it's not an easy thing to find one's way, but you are sure to find it as far as Heggelie, for that's close to the lake. Afterwards you go along the lake, till you come to the dam across a small tarn, just like a bridge, as they call it; bear away to the left there, and then turn off to the right, and you have the road straight before you to Stubdale in Aasa."

Although this direction was not quite satisfactory, particularly as it was the first time I had started on an excursion off the mainroad, I set out confidently and soon all hesitation vanished. From the heights a view was now and then obtained between the lofty pine and fir-trees of the valley below with its smiling fields and variegated woods of birch and alder trees, between which the river wound like a narrow silvery streak. The red-painted farm-houses, peculiar to Norway, lay picturesquely scattered on the higher points of the undulating valley, where men and women were busy haymaking. From some chimneys rose columns of blue smoke, which appeared quite light against the dark background of thickly studded pine forests on the mountain slopes.

Over the whole landscape lay a repose and a peace so perfect that no one could have suspected the close proximity of the capital. When I had advanced some distance into the forest, I heard the notes of the bugle and the distant baying of hounds in full cry, which gradually ceased, till nothing but a faint echo of the bugle reached my ear. I now heard the roar of the river, which rushed wildly past at some distance on my left, but as I advanced the road seemed gradually to approach it, and soon the valley in some parts grew narrower and narrower, till I at last found myself at the bottom of a deep, gloomy gorge, the greatest part of which was taken up by the river. But the road left the river again; there were certainly twistings and turnings, as the old woman had said, for at one moment it wound hither and the next thither, and at some places it was almost imperceptible. Now it went up a steep incline, and when I had passed the brow of the hill, I saw between the fir-trees a couple of twinkling tarns before me, and on the margin of one of these a dairy on a verdant slope, bathed in the golden light of the evening sun. In the shady retreat under the hill grew clusters of luxuriant ferns; the wild French willow stood proudly with its lofty crest of red and gorgeous flowers between the pebbles, but the sedate monk's hood lifted its head still higher and looked gloomily and wickedly down on it, while it nodded and kept time to the cuckoo's song, as if it were counting how many days it had to live. On the verdant slope and down by the edge of the water, the bird-cherry and the mountain ash displayed their flowery garb of summer. They sent a pleasant and refreshing fragrance far around, and shook sorrowfully the leaves of their white flowers over the reflected picture of the landscape in the mirror of the lake, which on all sides was surrounded by pine trees and mossy cliffs.

There was no one at home in the dairy. All doors were locked,—I knocked everywhere, but no answer,—no information as to the road. I sat down on a rock and waited a while, but no one appeared. The evening was setting in; I thought I could not stay there any longer, and started again. It was still darker in the forest, but shortly I came to a timber-dam across a bit of river between two tarns. I supposed this was the place where I "should bear off first to the left, and then to the right." I went across, but on the other side of the dam there were only—as it appeared to me—flat, smooth, damp rocks and no trace of a road; on the opposite side, the right side of the dam, there was a well-trodden path. I examined both sides several times, and although it appeared to be contrary to the direction I had received, I decided on choosing the broader road or path, which was continued on the right hand side of the water. As long as it followed the course of the dark tarn, the road was good and passable, but suddenly it turned off in a direction which, according to my ideas, was the very opposite of the one I should take, and lost itself in a con- fused net of paths and cattle-tracks amid the darkness of the forest. Inexpressibly tired of this anxious intricate search I threw myself down on the soft moss to rest for a while, but the fatigue conquered the fears of the lonely forest, and I cannot now tell how long I dozed. On hearing a wild cry, the echo of which still resounded in my ears when I awoke, I jumped to my feet. I felt comforted by the song of the redbreast, and I thought I felt less lonely and deserted as long as I heard the merry notes of the thrush.

The sky was overcast and the darkness of the forest had increased considerably. A fine rain was falling, which imparted renewed life to the plants and trees and filled the air with a fresh, aromatic fragrance; it also seemed to call to life all the nocturnal sounds and notes of the forest. Among the tops of the fir-trees above me, I heard a hollow, metallic sound, like the croaking of the frog and a penetrating whistling and piping. Round about me was a buzzing sound, as if from a hundred spinning-wheels, but the most terrible of all these sounds was, that they at one time seemed close to your ear, and in another moment far away; now they were interrupted by frolicsome, wild cries and a flapping of wings,—now by distant cries of distress, on which a sudden silence fol- lowed again. I was seized by an indescribable fear; these sounds sent a chill through me, and my terror was increased by the darkness between the trees, where all objects appeared distorted, moving and alive, stretching forth thousands of hands and arms after the stray wanderer. All the fairy tales of my childhood were conjured up before my startled imagination, and appeared to be realised in the forms which surrounded me; I saw the whole forest filled with trolls, elves, and sporting dwarfs. In thoughtless and breathless fear I rushed forward to avoid this host of demons, but while flying thus still more frightful and distorted shapes appeared,—and I fancied I felt their hands clutching me. Suddenly I heard the heavy tread of some one, who moved over the crackling branches of the underwood. I saw, or fancied I saw, a dark shape, which approached me with a pair of eyes shining like glowing stars. My hair stood on an end; I believed my fate was inevitably sealed, and shouted almost unconsciously as if to give myself new courage:

"If there's anybody there, tell me the way to Stubdale!" A deep growl was the answer I received, and the bear, for such it was, walked quickly away in the same direction whence he had come. I stood for some time and listened to his heavy steps and the crackling of the branches under his feet. I mumbled to myself: "I wish it was daylight and that I had a gun with me, and you should have had a bullet, Master Bruin, for frightening me thus!"

With this wish and childish threat all fear and thoughts of danger vanished, and I walked on again quite composed, on the soft mossy ground. There was now no sign of either road or path; but it grew lighter between the trees in front of me, the forest became more open, and I found myself on the slope leading down to the shores of a large lake, surrounded on all sides by pine forests, which on the distant shores vanished under the misty veil of the night.

By the red glimmering of the northern sky, which was reflected in the dark surface of the lake, over which the bats fluttered and circled, while large birds higher up in the air shot swiftly across with that croaking and penetrating whistle which not long ago had appeared so terrible to me, I found I had gone in a north-easterly direction instead of to the west.

While I was meditating whether I should remain here till the sun rose, or try to find my way back to the dam, I discovered to my inexpressible joy on this side of the lake a glimpse of a fire between the trees. I ran towards it, but I soon discovered that it was farther off than it at first appeared to be, because, after having walked about a mile, I found myself still separated from it by a deep valley.

When after considerable trouble I had forced my way through the chaos of fallen trees, which the wind had torn up in this exposed wild region, and had ascended the other steep hill-side, I had still a good distance to walk across an open wooded heath, where the firs stood in rows like lofty pillars and where the ground resounded under my steps.

On the outskirt of this wood trickled a small brook, where the alder and the pine trees again sought to maintain their place, and on a small plot on the slope on the other side of a brook burned a great log-fire, which threw its red light far in between the trees. In front of the fire sat a dark figure, which, on account of its position between me and the blazing fire, appeared to me to be of supernatural proportions. The old stories about robbers and thieves in this forest came suddenly back to

A Summer Night in a Norwegian Forest

me, and I was on the point of running away when my eyes caught sight
of a hut, made out of fir-branches, close to the fire, and two other men,
who sat outside it, and the many axes, which were fixed into the stump
of a felled tree, and it became evident to me that they were wood-cutters.

The dark figure, an old man, was speaking,—I saw him move his lips;
he held a short pipe in his hand, which he only put to his mouth now
and then to keep it alight by these occasional pulls. When I approached
the group, the story had either come to an end or he had been interrupted, he stooped forward, put some glowing embers in his pipe, smoked
incessantly and appeared to be attentively listening to what a fourth
person, who had just arrived, had to say. This person, who apparently
also belonged to the party, was carrying a bucket of water from the
brook. His hair was red, and he was dressed in a long jersey jacket, and
had more the appearance of a tramp than a wood-cutter. He looked as if
he had been frightened by something or other.

The old man had now turned round towards him, and as I had crossed
the brook and was approaching the party from the side, I could now see
the old man plainly in the full glare of the fire. He was a short man with
a long hooked nose. A blue skull-cap with a red border scarcely covered
his head of bristly grey hair, and a short-bodied but long Ringerike coat
of dark grey frieze with worn velvet borders served to make the round-
ness and crookedness of his back still more conspicuous.

The new-comer appeared to be speaking about a bear.

"Well, who would believe it?" said the old man, "what did he want
there? It must have been some other noise you heard, for there doesn't
grow anything on the dry heath hereabout which he would be after. No,
not Bruin, not he," he added; "I almost think you are telling lies, Peter!
There's an old saying, that red hair and firs don't thrive in good soil," he
continued half aloud. "If it had been down in the bear's den or in Styg-
dale, where Knut and I both heard him and saw him the other day—but
here?—No, no! he doesn't come so near the fire, he doesn't! You have
been frightening yourself!"

"Frightening myself? Oh, dear no! Didn't I hear him moving and
crushing through the underwood, my canny Thor Lerberg?" answered
the other, somewhat offended and chagrined at the old man's doubts and
taunts.

"Well, well, my boy," continued Thor in his former tone, "I suppose it
was something bigger than a squirrel anyhow!"

I now stepped forward, and said it must have been me that he had
heard, and told them how I had lost my way, and the fright I had undergone, and how hungry and tired I was. I asked whereabouts I was now,
and if one of them would show me the way to Stubdale.

My appearance created considerable surprise to the party, which however was not so much apparent in their words, as in the attention with
which they regarded me and heard my story. The old man, whose name
I had heard was Thor Lerberg, seemed particularly interested in it; and
as it appeared that he was accustomed to thinking aloud, I could, on
hearing some of the remarks which he now and then mumbled to himself, participate in his reflections, thus:

"No, no, that was the wrong way!—He should have gone over the dam there—Stubdale way—he went wrong altogether—he is too young—he isn't used to the woods—ah, that was the woodcock—and the goat-sucker—yes, yes! it sounds strange to him, that hasn't heard him—oh, yes! the loon does shriek dreadfully—particularly when there's fine rain—ah, ah! yes, that must have been the bear he met—he is a brave boy after all!"

"Yes!" I said boldly, and gave vent to my awakening youthful courage in about the same words as the man who once came across a bear asleep on a sunny hill side: "If it had been daylight, and if I had been a hunter and had a loaded gun with me, and if I could have made it go off, why, by my faith, the bear should have lain dead on the spot, he should."

"Yes, of course, hah, hah, hah!" laughed old Thor, and chuckled till the others joined in the laughter; "of course he would have lain dead on the spot,—that's plain! hah, hah, hah!"

"But you are now by Storflaaten, the biggest lake in the forest here," he said, addressing himself to me, when I had finished my story; "towards morning we'll help you on your way, for we have got a boat, and when you have got across the water you haven't far to go to Stubdale then. But I suppose you would like to rest yourself a little now, and get something to eat! I have nothing but some peas-pudding and rancid bacon, and may be you are not used to that kind of food; but if you are hungry, perhaps you would like some fish? I have been out fishing, and fine fish I got too,—yes, in the lake I mean!"

I thanked him for his offer, and he told one of his companions to take a "regular good 'un" off the string and roast it in the glowing embers of the fire.

In the meantime the old man asked a number of questions about myself, and by the time I had answered all these the fish was ready, and I began my meal with great appetite. He now asked one of his companions to tell us something about what he once said had happened to his father, when he was out cutting timber.

"Well, that's very soon told," answered the lad, a strapping young fellow of a smart, undaunted appearance, and not much over the twenties. "Father was then working for the squire in Ask, and was cutting timber up in the squire's forest; he used to sleep at a cottage further down the valley, at Helge Myra's place,—you knew Helge, didn't you Thor?—Well, one day he had been taking too long a nap after dinner,—such a heavy sleep came over him,—and when he awoke the sun was already setting behind the hills. But he would finish his day's work before he left off, and he began cutting away till the splinters flew about him in all directions, but it grew darker and darker; there was still a small pine left, which he was determined to have down, but no sooner had he given it the first cut, than the axe head flew off the handle. He set about looking for it and found it at last in a hollow. But suddenly he thought he heard some one calling him by name; he could not make out who it could be, for Helge Myra could not have any business thereabouts, and no one else lived there for miles around. He listened again, but did not hear anything, so he thought he might have been mistaken. He began cutting

again, but all at once the axe-head flew off the handle again. He found it
this time also after a long search, but when he was going to cut the tree
on the north side of its stem, he heard plainly a voice shouting in the
mountain:

" 'Halvor, Halvor! Early you come and late you go,'——'but as soon as
I heard that,' said my father, 'I felt as if I had lost the use of my legs and
I could scarcely get the axe out of the stem of the pine tree, but when I
did take to my legs I didn't stop until I came to Helge's cottage.' "

"Yes, I have heard that story before," said old Thor, "but that wasn't
the one I meant; it was about the time he was at the wedding at the dairy
on Kile hill."

"Oh, that time!" answered the indefatigable lad; "that was in the spring,
just before Easter 1815, when father lived at Oppen-Eie—the snow wasn't
gone yet, but he had to set out for the forest to cut and drag home some
wood. He went up in the Helling hill, where he found a withered fir,
which he commenced cutting down at once. While cutting away at it, he
thought he saw withered firs all around him, but while he was staring
and wondering at this, up came a procession of eleven horses,—all of a
mouse-grey colour; it appeared to him to be a wedding-party.

"What people are these, who are coming this way over the hill?" he
asked.

"Oh, we are from Östhalla," says one of them, "we are going to the
Veien dairy to keep the wedding; the one who drives in front is the
parson, next are the bride and bridegroom, and I am his father-in-law.
You had better stand behind on my sledge and come along."

"When they had travelled some distance, the father-in-law said: 'Will
you take these two bags with you and go to the Veien farm and get two
barrels of potatoes in them by the time we go home?'

"My father promised to do this. They came soon to a place which he
thought he knew, and so it was. It was just north of the Kill hill, where
the old dairy stood; but there was no dairy there then, but a great fine
building, and here they all entered. Some one met them on the steps to
give the guests a glass of welcome, and they gave father a glass also, but
he said, 'No, thanks!' he would not have anything he said, for he had only
his old clothes on, and would not intrude on such fine folks. 'Never mind
this man,' said one of them, 'take a horse and see him on his way home,'
which they did; they put him in a sledge with a mouse-grey horse before
it, and one of them sat up and drove the horse. When they got as far as
the little valley north of Oppenhagen—where the land-slip took place—
he thought he sat between the ears of a bucket; but shortly this vanished
also, and it was only then he really came to himself again. He began
looking for his axe, and found it sticking in the same withered fir-tree he
had begun to cut down. When he came home, he was so confused and
queer, that he could not tell now many days he had been away; but he
was only away from the morning to the evening,—and for some time
afterwards he was not himself——"

"Yes, many a queer thing happens hereabout," said old Thor; "and I
for my part have also seen a little—well, witchcraft I mean,—and if you

A Summer Night in a Norwegian Forest

like to sit up a little longer, I'll tell you what has happened to me,—in this here forest, I mean."

Yes, they would all like to hear it;—to-morrow was Sunday, and it didn't much matter if they went to bed late.

"Well, it might be about ten or twelve years ago," he answered, "I was burning charcoal over in the Kampenhaug forest. In the winter I had two horses there to cart the coals to the Bærum works. One day I happened to stop too long at the works, for I met some old friends from Ringerike there, and we had a good talk about one thing or another, and a little drop to drink too,—yes, brandy I mean—and so I did not come back to the kiln before ten o'clock in the evening. I made a fire, so I could see loading the sledges, for it was terribly dark, and I had to get the carts loaded in the evening, for I had to be off at three o'clock next morning, if I was to get to the works and back again the same day while it was light,—back to the kiln I mean. When I had got the fire to burn up, I began loading the sledges. But just as I was turning round to the fire again a drift of snow came sweeping down upon it and put it out entirely,—the fire I mean. So I thought to myself: 'Why, bless me, the old witch in the hill here is vexed to-night, because I come home so late and disturb her.' I struck a light and made a new fire. But, strange to say, the shovel would not drop all the coals into the basket,—more than half went over the sides. At last I got the sledges loaded, and I was going to put the ropes round them, but will you believe me, every one of them broke, the one after the other,—the ropes I mean. So I had to get new ropes, and at last got the sledges ready, gave the horses their fodder, and went to bed. But do you think I awoke at three? No, not till long after the sun had risen, and still I felt heavy and queer, both in my head and my body. Well, I had something to eat and went then to look to the horses, but the shed was empty and the horses were gone. I got rather out of temper at this, and I am afraid I swore a little into the bargain, but I thought I had better try and find some tracks of them. During the night there had fallen a little fresh snow, and I could see they had not gone off in the direction of the valley or the works. I found, however, the track of two horses and of a couple of broad large feet in a northerly direction; I followed these for two or three miles, when the tracks parted, and the foot-marks vanished altogether, one horse had gone to the east, and the other to the west, and after following up one first for five or six miles, I came upon him at last. I had to take him home to the hut and tie him up, before I could start looking for the other horse. By the time I got hold of him it was near upon noon, and so there was no use going to the works that day. But I promised I should never disturb the old witch any more,—in the evening I mean.

"But these promises are strange things sometimes,—if you keep a promise to Christmas you are pretty sure to break it before next Michaelmas. The year after I made a trip to Christiania late in the autumn,— the roads were in a fearful bad condition and it was already very late in the afternoon before I left town, but I wanted to get home that night. I was on horseback and took the road by Bokstad, which is the shortest, as you know,—to Ausfjerdingen I mean. The weather was wet and ugly, and it was beginning to grow dark when I started. But when I came over the bridge by Heggelie I saw a man coming towards me,—he wasn't very tall, but terribly big; he was as broad as a barn-door across his shoulders, and his hands were nearly a foot across the knuckles. He carried a leather bag in one hand, and seemed to be talking to himself. When I came nearer to him, his eyes glistened like burning cinders, and they were as big as saucers. His hair stood out like bristles, and his beard was no better; I thought he was a terrible, ugly brute, and I prayed for myself the little I could, and just as I came to the end, down he sank,—in the ground I mean.

"I rode on, humming an old psalm, but suddenly I met him again coming down a hill; his eyes and his hair and beard too sparkled with fire this time. I began praying again, and had no sooner finished than he was gone. But I had scarcely ridden a mile, before I met him once more as I was crossing a small bridge. His eyes flashed like lightning and sparks flew out of his hair and beard, and so he shook his bag, till you could see blue and yellow and red tongues of fire shooting out of it. But then I lost my temper right out, and instead of praying I swore at him, and he vanished on the spot. But as I rode on, I began to be afraid that I should meet this brute again, so when I came to Lövlie I knocked at the door, and asked for lodgings till daylight, but do you think they would let me in? No. I could travel by day, like other folks, they said, and then I needn't ask for lodgings!—So I guessed the old brute had been there before me and frightened them, and I had to set out again. But then I started another old psalm, till the mountains rang with it, and I came at last safe to Stubdale, where I got lodgings—but it was almost morning then."

The manner in which he told these stories was, like his speech, slow and expressive, and he had the custom of repeating single words, or part of his sentences at the end of these, or adding one or another superfluous explanation. He generally applied these remarks after one of his many exertions to keep his pipe alight, and they had such a comical effect on me, that I had great difficulty to refrain from laughing outright. I was in a merry mood after having safely got through my nocturnal expedition, and to this I must ascribe the fact that his stories did not make the impression upon me which, after what I had gone through, might have been expected.

The dawn of the day was now appearing, and old Thor told one of his companions to row me across the lake, and put me on my right road.


# THE WITCH


ON A hill, some distance from the main road in the middle of Gudbrands-dale, some years ago stood a cottage. Perhaps it is there still. It was mild April weather,—the snow was melting, the brooks rushed wildly down the mountain sides, the fields were nearly bare, the thrushes were scolding each other in the woods, all the groves resounded with the twittering of birds,—in short there was every sign of an early spring.

In the mighty birch tree and lofty mountain ash, which stretched out their naked branches over the roof of the cottage in the glittering sunlight, some busy tomtits whisked about, while a chaffinch, who had perched himself in the top of the birch tree, sung out at the top of his voice.

Inside in the smoky room with the raftered ceiling, it was dark and dismal. A middle-aged peasant woman of a very common and unintellectual appearance was busy blowing into a blaze some branches and sticks of wood under the coffee-kettle on the open hearth. Having at last succeeded in this, she raised herself up, rubbed the smoke and the ashes out of her smarting eyes, and said:

"People say there's no use in this lead-melting,—for the child hasn't got the wasting sickness; they say it's a changeling. There was a fell-maker here the other day and he said the same, for when he was a youngster, he had seen a changeling in Ringerike somewhere, and that one was as soft in its body and as loose about its joints as this one."

While she spoke, her simple face had assumed an expression of anxiety, which showed what impression the fell-maker's words had made upon her superstitious mind.

She addressed her words to a big bony woman, whose age might be about sixty. She was unusually tall, but when she was sitting, she appeared to be of low stature, and this peculiarity she had to thank for the nickname of "Longlegs," which the people had added to her name of Gubjör. In the gang of tramps with whom she used to roam about, she had other names. Grey hairs straggled out from under her head-gear, which surrounded a dark face with bushy eyebrows and a long knotted nose. The original unintellectual expression of her face, which was clearly indicated by a low forehead and great breadth between the cheekbones, contrasted greatly with the unmistakable cunning in her small sparkling eyes. Her dress betokened her as a straggler from some northern district; her whole appearance denoted that if she were not a witch, she was at least a tramp, who would be now impudent and audacious, now humble and cringing, according to circumstances.

While the peasant woman was speaking and attending to the coffee-kettle, Gubjör was keeping in motion a hanging cradle in which lay a child of a sickly appearance, by giving it now and then a push with her hand. She replied to the peasant woman in a calm tone of superiority, although her sparkling eyes and the quivering muscles round her mouth showed that she was not satisfied with the statement of the fell-maker.

"Folks will talk so much about things they don't understand, my dear Marit," she said; "they talk fast and loose, and, as for the fell-maker, he may understand sheep's skin well enough, but sickness and changelings he knows nothing about, I say and maintain!—I should think I ought to know something about changelings, for I have seen enough of them. That changeling he spoke about must have been Brit's from Froen, for I recollect she had a changeling; she got it soon after she was married,— she had a very good and nice child, but it was changed for a troll's brat as ill-tempered and unruly as if it belonged to the fiend himself. He would never speak a word,—only eat and cry, and she hadn't the heart to strike it or illtreat the youngster either; but somebody taught her a charm to make him speak, and then she found out what kind of a brat he really was. She got hold of him one day and began to thrash him soundly and called him all sorts of names, when suddenly the door flew open and somebody,—whom of course she couldn't see,—rushed into the room, tore the changeling away from her, and threw her own child on to the floor with such violence that it began to cry.—Or perhaps it was the changeling that Siri Strömhugget had? That was an old-fashioned, dried-up youngster, and I don't think he had any joints at all,—but he was no more like your child here than this old cap of mine! I recollect her youngster well enough too. I served at the parish clerk's at that time, when I saw it more than once, and I also recollect how she got rid of it. There was a great deal of talk about it at the time, for Siri, as you know, came from this parish. When she was quite young, she served at Kvam; after that she moved to Strömhugget, where she was married to Ola,— the son there. Soon after her first child was born, a strange woman came into the room and took the child from the bed and put another in its place. Siri, who was ill in bed, tried to get up and get her child back,— she struggled with all her might, but she could not move from the spot,— she was spell-bound and quite powerless. She was going to call her aunt, who was in the next room, but she could not open her mouth, and she was just as frightened as if they had been going to take her life. It was easy enough to see that the child was a changeling, for it wasn't like other children at all—it screamed and cried, as if a knife stuck in it, and it wheezed and hit about with its arms like a huldre-cat, and was as ugly as sin. It was always eating, and poor Siri didn't for the life of her know how to get rid of it. But at last she heard of a woman who knew something about these things, and she told her to take the youngster and flog him with a proper rod three Thursday evenings in succession.—Yes, she did so, and the third Thursday evening a woman came flying over the barn-roof, and threw a child away from her and took up the changeling. But as she rushed off she struck Siri across the fingers; and she carries the marks to this day, and I have seen them with my own eyes," added Gubjör, as a further proof of the truth of her story. "No, this child is no more a changeling than I am; and how could it happen, that they could change yours after all the trouble you have taken to prevent it?" she asked.

"Well, no! that's what I cannot make out either," said the mother quite innocently, "for I've had castor in the cradle,—I have crossed him, and I put a silver brooch in his shirt, and I stuck a knife in the beam over the door, so I don't know how they could have managed to change him."

"Well then, they can't have had any power over him either. I know all about that, I should think," began Gubjör again, "for in a parish close to Christiania I once knew a woman who had a child, which she was so very careful about,—she made crosses over it and used castor and everything else she had heard of, for there was plenty of witchcraft thereabout, I can tell you; but one night, as she lay in bed, with the child by her side near the edge of the bed, her husband, who was lying near the wall, awoke suddenly and saw such a red glare all over the room, just like when one stirs the fire,—and sure enough, there was some one stirring the fire too, for when he looked towards the fireplace, he saw an old man sitting there raking the fire together. He was an ugly brute,—uglier than I can describe,—and he had a long grey beard. When he had got the fire to give a good light, he began stretching his arms out for the child, but he could not move from the stool he sat on. His arms grew longer and longer, till they reached half way across the room, but he didn't stir from the fire, and couldn't reach the child. He sat thus for some time, while the husband was so frightened that he didn't know what to do. He then heard some one moving outside the window.

" 'I say, Peter, why don't you come?' asked a voice outside.

" 'Hold your tongue, woman!' said the old man, who was sitting by the fire, 'they have been crossing and fiddling over this youngster, so I can't get it.'

" 'Well, you might come back, so we can be off,' said the voice again. It was the old man's wife, who was waiting outside to receive the youngster.

"But just look at this fine little boy!" said the sorceress with affected kindness, as she took the child, who had just woke up, and vigorously resisted the strange woman's caresses and began crying at the apparently coaxing, but really repulsive, expression of the woman; "he is as white as snow and pure as an angel; he is rather weak about the joints, that he is,—but to say he is a changeling, that's a mistake, I say.—No, it's wasting sickness," she added, as she turned round to the mother with a lofty air of conviction; "it's wasting sickness!"

"Hush, I fancy I heard some one knocking outside. Mercy on me, if it's my husband who has come back!" said Marit, terrified at being surprised by her husband in company with the sorceress over a cup of coffee. She ran to the door and looked out, but there was nobody there but a brindled cat, which sat on the steps licking her paws after a hunt in the neighbouring bush, and a woodpecker, which was pecking away at the sunburnt logs of the cottage wall, trying to wake up the drowsy insects from their winter sleep in the holes and crevices in the timber, and turning his head every moment, as if he was looking for some one, but it was only an April shower he was expecting.

"Is there anybody there?" asked Gubjör. On receiving an answer in the negative, she continued: "Well, we had better leave the door open, so we can have the benefit of the sun and see when your husband comes home,—for I suppose he's coming that way."

"He went with his sledge to get a load of leaves for the goats," answered Marit; "but I'm so afraid he'll be finding us out. Last time when he heard that you had been here, he was that wild that I didn't know what to say. He said he would give me money to go to the doctor with, for he won't hear of any such goings on, or any magic curing; for he is well read, and doesn't believe in the fairies any longer, since he went about with that schoolmaster of ours."

"To the doctor's? Bah!" said the sorceress, and spat upon the floor. "Yes, I would advise anybody to go to that stuck-up grandee with this

THE WITCH

wee bit of a body. If one doesn't come with gold and fine presents," she continued, with an affected air of superior knowledge, "he bites and worries you as if you were dogs, and not people. Why, what happened that time Gjertrud Kostibakken lay with the last gasp of breath in her body? He wouldn't go to a tramp, for he was at a Christmas party at the magistrates', nor did he go either till he was threatened both with bishop and judge; and he might have saved himself the trouble, for when he came to the door the poor woman was dead. No! to go to the doctor's with a child like this,—suffering with wasting sickness, is madman's work! But, dear me!" she said with a sneer, "you may go to him for what I care, but if he can help you as much as this—, may I never be able to cure another in my life. They don't know anything about this wasting sickness, bless you! There's nothing about it in their books, and they don't know of any remedy for it!—and they know that well enough too,—that's the reason they don't give any powders or drugs and such nasty stuff for it. No, there's no other remedy but lead-melting, but they don't know anything about that."

"Let's put the ladle on, mother," she began in a different tone, "it's getting on towards noon. If we have melted twice, we'll have to melt the third time as well, or we don't know what might happen. The child has the wasting sickness, but there are nine sorts of that disease in the world, as I've told you already,—and you saw yourself he had both the goblin-spell and the water-spell, for the first Thursday the lead showed a man with two big horns and a tail. That was the goblin-spell. Last time it was a mermaid, you saw it as plainly as if it had been drawn. That was the water-spell. But now Thursday has come round again, and the question is what will it show now? The third time is the most important, you must know. There, take the child," she said, as she gave it to its mother. "Let me finish this drop of coffee, and I'll set to at once."

When the coffee was drunk, and the cup was put away with many thanks and blessings, she went demurely to the hearth, and pulled out a snuff-horn.

"Since last Thursday," she said, "I've been in seven parishes and scraped lead off the frames of church-windows at midnight, for I used the last of my lead last Thursday. It's trying both to mind and body," she mumbled to herself, while she shook out from the snuff-horn some of the lead, which, according to her statement, she had collected under so many difficulties.

"I suppose you have brought some water from a brook running north at midnight?" she inquired further.

"Yes. I was down by the mill-stream last night; it's the only stream running north for a long way round," answered the peasant woman, as she brought out a carefully closed pail, from which she poured the water into a large beer-bowl. Across this was placed a thin oatmeal cake, through which a hole was made with a darning needle. When the lead was melted, Gubjör went to the door, looked up at the sun, took the ladle and poured the melted lead slowly through the hole into the water, while she mumbled some words over it which seemed to be to this effect:—

"I conjure for sickness, I conjure for pain—
I conjure it off, and I call it again—
I conjure the weather, the wind, and the rain!
I have spells for the north, I have charms for the west,
And the south and the east must obey my behest—
I conjure in water, I conjure on land,
I conjure in rocks, and I conjure in sand—
I conjure pain into the alder-tree root—
I conjure disease into tiny foal's foot—
Where the flame of Gehenna comes bellowing forth,
Or where the charmed waters flow on to the north,
There, there shall pain wither, consumed by my spell,
And with the poor babe all shall henceforth be well!"

As was only natural, the boiling lead hissed and spluttered as it was poured into the water.

"Just listen to the wickedness of it,—it must come out now," said the sorceress to the peasant woman, who with a mixed feeling of fear and awe, stood listening with the child in her arms. When the oatmeal cake was taken off the bowl, a couple of figures formed by the melted lead were seen in the water. The sorceress regarded them for some time, with her head on one side; she then began nodding it and said:—

"Corpse-spell, corpse-spell!—first goblin-spell, then water-spell, and now corpse-spell. One of them would have been enough!" she added, shaking her head. "Yes, I now see how it all has happened," she continued aloud, and turned round to the mistress of the house. "First, you travelled through a wood and past a hill while the trolls were out, there you blessed the child. You then crossed a river, and there you also blessed the child; but when you came past the churchyard,—it was before the cock crowed,—you forgot to bless the child, and there it caught the corpse-spell."

"Bless me,—how do you know that?" exclaimed Marit with great surprise. "Every word you say is true. When we left the dairy last summer on our way home, it was rather late before we started, as some of the sheep got astray from us, and it was growing dark by the time we got down into the valley,—once I thought I saw the glimmer of a light over in the forest and I heard something like a gate being opened in the Vesæt hill,—they say there are fairies there—and then I blessed the child. When we crossed the river, I heard a terrible cry, and I blessed the child again,—the others said it was only the loon, which screamed for bad weather."

"Yes, that would have been sufficient, if there was nothing else but the loon," said Gubjör; "when it screams at a new-born babe, that child is bewitched."

"Yes, I have also heard that," said the mother; "but when we came past the churchyard,—it was just past midnight—then the bull got unruly and we had such trouble to keep the cattle together, that I forgot to bless the child there."

"That's where the child caught it then, you may be sure, for the corpse-spell comes from the churchyard. Just look yourself in the bowl here: there stands a coffin and there is a church steeple, and in the coffin lies a corpse, spreading out its fingers," said the sorceress with great importance, as she explained these mystic figures of the melted lead.

"Humph,—but there is a remedy!" she mumbled to herself again, but sufficiently loud to be heard by the other.

"What remedy is that?" asked the mother, both glad and curious.

"There's a remedy,—it does try one, but never mind," said Gubjör; "I shall make a dummy baby, which I shall bury in the churchyard, and then the dead will believe they have got the child,—take my word, they won't know but what it is the real baby! But we must have some family silver to go with it! Have you got any?"

"Yes, I have a couple of old silver coins, which were given me when I was baptized, and I didn't want to touch them;—but if life depends upon it—" said the anxious mother, and she began at once searching in an old chest.

"Yes,—one I shall put in the hill,—the other in water, the third I shall bury in consecrated ground, where the disease was caught. I must have three in all," said the sorceress, "and some old rags to make a dummy of."

She got what she asked for. A big doll was soon made up in the shape of a wrapped-up baby. The sorceress rose from her seat, took the dummy baby and her stick, and said:

"I'm going now to the churchyard to bury it. The third Thursday from to-day I shall be back again,—then we'll see! If there is going to be life, you can see yourself in the pupils of the child's eye, but if he is going to die you'll see something black and nothing else. And now I must be off to Joramo. I haven't been there for a long time; but they sent word to me to come and see a youngster who has got the troll-spell. But that's an easy matter! I'll push him under a piece of turf the contrary way to which the sun goes, and then he'll be a man again."

During this time the mistress of the house began to show unmistakable signs of uneasiness, and the story-teller also noticed them.

"What's the matter?" said the witch. "Oh, I see!—it's your husband that's coming," she continued, as she looked out through the open door, and added in a grave tone: "There's no room here for Gubjör any longer; but don't you be afraid, mother;—I'll go round by the churchyard, and then he won't see me."

# THE CHARCOAL-BURNER

THERE WAS once upon a time a charcoal-burner who had a son, and he was also a charcoal-burner. When the father died, the son got married, but he would not do any work, and he neglected also to look after his kilns, and very soon no one would have him to burn charcoal any more for them.

But one day he had got a kiln of charcoal ready burnt, and he set out for town with some loads of it and sold them. When he had done his business, he loitered down some of the streets and looked about him. On his way home he fell in with some neighbours and other people from the same parish, and he talked and bragged to them about all that he had seen in town.

The most remarkable thing he saw, he said, was the great number of parsons he met, and all the people in the streets took off their hats to them. "I wish I was a parson," he said, "perhaps the people would take off their hats to me too; now, they don't appear to see me at all."

"Well, your clothes are black enough, anyhow," said his neighbours; "but now that we are on the way, we may as well call in at the sale at the old parson's, and get a glass with the others,—and you can buy yourself a gown and ruff* at the same time."

Yes, he did so, and when he came home he hadn't a penny left.

"I suppose you have brought both money and good manners home with you from town this time?" said his wife.

"Good manners! yes, I should think so," said the charcoal-burner. "Just look here! I am a parson now. Here is both the gown and the ruff!"

"Yes, very likely!" said his wife; "strong beer makes big words, it appears! You don't care how things go!"

"You shouldn't boast or bother about the coals you are burning, till they are ready," answered the husband.

But one day a great many people, dressed like parsons, passed the charcoal-burner's house on their way to the palace, and it was plain to see that something was going to take place there, so the charcoal-burner thought he would go as well, and put on the old parson's clothes. His wife thought it would be wiser of him to stay at home, for even if he got the chance to hold a horse for some grand person, she was afraid the sixpence he got for it would vanish down his throat, which usually was the case. "Yes, everybody talks about the drink, but no one about the thirst, do they mother?" said the husband; "the more one drinks, the more one thirsts," and with that he started for the palace. All the strangers were invited to come into the presence of the king, and the charcoal-burner entered with the others. The king then told them that he had lost his most costly ring, and he felt sure it had been stolen. He had therefore called together all the learned clergy in the country, to hear if any of them could tell him who the thief was. And the king promised that he would handsomely reward the one who could tell him about it,—if he was a curate, he should get a living; if he was a rector, he should be made a dean; if he was a dean, he should be made a bishop; and if he was a bishop, he should be the first man after the king. So the king went from one to the other, and asked them all if they could tell him who the thief was, and when he came to the charcoal-burner, he said: "Who are you?"

---

*The Norwegian clergy wear a long black gown and an Elizabethan ruff.

"I am the wise parson and the true prophet," said the charcoal-burner.

"Then you can tell me who has taken my ring?" said the king.

"Well, it isn't beyond sense and reason, that what has happened in the dark might be brought to light," said the charcoal-burner; "but it isn't every year that the salmon plays in the fir-tops. I have now been studying and working for seven years to get bread for myself and my family, but I haven't got a living yet, so if the thief is to be found, I must have plenty of time and paper, for I must write and reckon early and late."

Yes, he should have as much time and paper as he wished, if he only could find the thief.

So he got a room to himself in the palace, and before long they found out that he must know something more than writing a sermon, for he used so much paper that it lay about in heaps; but there wasn't one who could make out a word of all he had written, for it was only pothooks and marks like a crow's toes. But the time wore on, and he could not find any trace of the thief.

So the king got tired of waiting, and told him that if he couldn't find the thief in three days, he should lose his life.

"Ah, but he that rules must not be hasty, but wait till his temper cools," said the charcoal-burner. "One can't begin and rake out the coals, till they are thoroughly burnt and the fire has gone out."

But the king stuck to what he said, and the charcoal-burner felt his life wasn't worth much. Now it so happened, that it was three of the king's servants who waited upon him day by day in turn that had stolen the ring between them.

So one day, when one of the servants came into his room and cleared away the table after supper, and was just about leaving the room, the charcoal-burner heaved a deep sigh and looked after him and said:

"There goes the first of them"; but he only meant the first of the three days he still had to live. "This parson knows all about it," said the servant, when he got his comrades by themselves, and told them that the parson had said, "that he was the first of them."

The second servant, who was to wait upon him the next day, was to notice what he would say then, and sure enough, as he was going out after having cleared the table, the charcoal-burner gazed steadily at him, sighed and said: "There goes the second of them." So the third servant was to observe what happened the third day; it got worse and worse he thought, for when the servant came to the door and was going out with all the plates and dishes, the charcoal-burner folded his hands and said: "There goes the third of them," and then he sighed as if his heart would break.

The servant came breathlessly out to his comrades and told them it was clear enough that the parson knew all about it, and so they went into his room and fell on their knees before him, and prayed and begged of him, that he would not tell it was they who had taken the ring; they would give him a hundred dollars each, if he only would not bring them into trouble.

He promised faithfully, that no one should get into trouble if he got the money, the ring, and a lump of porridge. He put the ring into the porridge, and told one of them to give it to the biggest pig belonging to the king.

Next morning the king came; it was easy to see he would not be played with; he would know all about the thief.

"Well, I have written and reckoned far and wide," said the charcoal-burner, "but I find it's not a man who has stolen the ring."

"Pooh! who is it then?" said the king. "Oh, it's that big pig which belongs to your majesty," said the charcoal-burner.

Well, they brought out the pig and killed it, and, sure enough, the ring was found inside it. So the charcoal-burner got a living, and the king was so pleased that he gave him a farm and horse and a hundred dollars in the bargain. It did not take the charcoal-burner long to move, and the first Sunday after he had settled in his parish he was going to church to read his first sermon. But before he started he had to get some breakfast, and so he put the sermon on the bread plate; but he made a mistake and took the sermon instead of the bread, and dipped it into the soup, and when he felt it was so tough to chew, he gave it all to his dog, and the dog made short work of it and swallowed it all.

When he found out his mistake, he was at a loss what to do. But he had to go to church, for his congregation was waiting for him; and when he came there, he went straight up into the pulpit. He put on such a grand air while he was getting ready for the sermon, that all thought he must be a very fine preacher. But when he did begin, it wasn't so very fine after all.

"The words, my dear brethren, which you were going to hear this day, have gone to the dogs; but come again, some other Sunday, my dear parishioners, and you shall hear something else! And thus endeth this sermon!"

Well, all the people thought he was a queer parson, for they had never heard such a sermon; but then they thought he might improve, and if not—why, they would know how to deal with him. Next Sunday the church was so crowded by people who wanted to hear the new parson, that there was scarcely room for them all in the church. As soon as the parson arrived, he went straight up into the pulpit, and then he stood for some time without saying a word, but all at once he made a start and cried out: "I say, old mother Berit, why do you sit so far back in the church?"—"Oh, my boots are in such a bad state, your reverence!" said she.—"But you could have got an old pig's skin and made yourself a new pair of boots, and then you could have come to the front like other decent people.—Besides, I wish you would all consider which way you are going, for I see that some of you, when you are coming to church, come from the north, and others come from the south, and the same when you leave church; but I suppose you stop and gossip on the way, and then they wonder at home what has become of you. Yea! who knows what will become of us all? And then I have to give notice, that the old parson's widow has lost her black mare. She had fetlocks round her hoofs, and a long mane, and more of this kind which I sha'n't mention in this place. And then I have a big hole in my old breeches pocket, which I know, but you don't! But whether any of you have a piece of some stuff, which would suit the hole, neither you nor I know."

Some of the people were well satisfied with the sermon, and believed that he in time would make a good parson, but most of them thought it was really too bad; and when the dean came round on one of his visits, they complained to him of the parson and said that such sermons were never heard before, and one of them happened to recollect the last one about the old widow's mare and repeated it all to the dean.

"That was a very good sermon," said the dean; "he spoke very likely in parables and impressed upon you to seek the light and to shun the darkness and its deeds, when he spoke about those who were walking on the broad or the narrow road; and particularly do I consider his notice about the old widow's mare a splendid parable as to how it will fare with us all in the end. The breeches pocket with the hole in it referred to his wants, and the piece of stuff was the offerings and gifts he expected from his congregation," said the dean.

"Yes, we thought as much," they said; "it was all about his offerings, sure enough!"

And so the dean said that he thought the parish had got such a good, sensible parson, that they should not complain of him, and the end was, that they got no other parson; but as time wore on he got worse instead of better, and so they complained to the bishop.

Well, after a long time the bishop came round on a visitation, but the charcoal-burner had been in the church the day before without anybody knowing of it, and had sawed the pulpit in several places, so it only hung together when one walked up the steps carefully.

So when the congregation had assembled, and the parson was to preach before the bishop, he stole quietly up the steps and began his sermon in his usual style, but after having gone on for some time he spoke up, threw up his arms, and cried out:

"If there is any one here, who has any evil deed or thought in his mind, it were better he left this place, for to-day, this very day, there will be a fall, the like of which has not taken place since the creation of the world;" and with that he struck the pulpit with his hands, and down tumbled both pulpit and parson with such a crash, that the congregation took to their heels and ran out of the church, as if the day of judgment had come.

So the bishop told the people that he wondered that the congregation could complain of a parson, who was so gifted and had such wisdom, that he could prophesy things that were to come. He thought he ought at least to be dean, and it was not long before he was made one. There was no help for it; they had to put up with him.

Now it so happened, that the king and queen in that country had no children, but when the king heard that he was to have one he was curious to know whether he was to get a son and heir to his broad lands and acres, or if he only would get a princess. So all the learned men in the land were called to the palace to say which it would be. But as none of them were able to do this, both the king and the bishop happened to think of the new dean, and it did not take long till they had him brought before them and began questioning him. No, he could not tell, he said, for it wasn't easy to guess what no one could know anything about.

"Well, well!" said the king, "I don't care whether you know it or not; but you are the wise parson and the true prophet, who can foretell things to come, and if you won't tell me, you'll lose both your gown and your ruff! But never mind, I'll give you a trial first," and so he took the biggest silver tankard he had and went down to the sea shore with the parson. "Can you tell me now, what I have got in this tankard?" said the king; "and if so, you can tell me the other thing I asked you as well," and he held the lid of the tankard tight. The charcoal-burner wrung his hands in despair and cried: "Oh, you unfortunate crawling crab of this earth, what have you now in return for all your toil and trouble!" "Ah, there you see! You did know it after all!" said the king, for he had put a crab in the tankard.

So the charcoal-burner had to go back to the palace, where he was shown into the queen's drawing-room. He took a chair and sat down in the middle of the room; while the queen walked up and down the floor.

"One should never make a stall for the unborn calf, and never quarrel about the baby's name before it is born," said the charcoal-burner, "but I never saw anything like this before; when the queen comes towards me, I fancy it will be a prince, and when she walks away from me, it seems to me as if it will be a princess." It turned out in time to be twins, and so the charcoal-burner had made a lucky hit that time also. And thus for telling what no one could know anything about he got loads of money, and he became next man to the king. Snip, snap, snout, that man knew what he was about.

# THE FISHERMAN AND THE DRAUG*

ON KVALHOLM, down in Helgeland, dwelt a poor fisherman, Elias by name, with his wife Karen, who had been in service at the parson's over at Alstad. They had built them a hut here, and he used to go out fishing by the day about the Lofotens.

There could be very little doubt that the lonely Kvalholm was haunted. Whenever her husband was away, Karen heard all manner of uncanny shrieks and noises, which could mean no good. One day, when she was up on the hillside, mowing grass to serve as winter fodder for their couple of sheep, she heard, quite plainly, a chattering on the strand beneath the hill, but look over she durst not.

They had a child every year, but that was no burden, for they were both thrifty, hard-working folks. When seven years had gone by, there were six children in the house; but that same autumn Elias had scraped together so much that he thought he might now venture to buy a *Sexær-*

*A demon peculiar to the north Norwegian coast. It rides the seas in a half-boat.

*ing,*[1] and henceforward go fishing in his own boat.

One day, as he was walking along with a *Kvejtepig*[2] in his hand, and thinking the matter over, he unexpectedly came upon a monstrous seal, which lay sunning itself right behind a rock on the strand, and was as much surprised to see the man as the man was to see the seal. But Elias was not slack; from the top of the rock on which he stood, he hurled the long heavy Kvejtepig right into the monster's back, just below the neck.

The seal immediately rose up on its tail right into the air as high as a boat's mast, and looked so evilly and viciously at him with its bloodshot eyes, at the same time showing its grinning teeth, that Elias thought he should have died on the spot for sheer fright. Then it plunged into the sea, and lashed the water into bloody foam behind it. Elias didn't stop to see more, but that same evening there drifted into the boat place on Kvalcreek, on which his house stood, a Kvejtepole, with the hooked iron head snapped off.

Elias thought no more about it, but in the course of the autumn he bought his *Sexæring,* for which he had been building a little boat-shed the whole summer.

One night as he lay awake, thinking of his new *Sexæring,* it occurred to him that his boat would balance better, perhaps, if he stuck an extra log of wood on each side of it. He was so absurdly fond of the boat that it was a mere pastime for him to light a lantern and go down to have a look at it.

Now as he stood looking at it there by the light of the lantern, he suddenly caught a glimpse in the corner opposite, on a coil of nets, of a face which exactly resembled the seal's. For an instant it grinned savagely at him and the light, its mouth all the time growing larger and larger; and then a big man whisked out of the door, not so quickly, however, but that Elias could catch a glimpse, by the light of the lantern, of a long iron hooked spike sticking out of his back. And now he began to put one and two together. Still he was less anxious about his life than about his boat; so he there and then sat him down in it with the lantern, and kept watch. When his wife came in the morning, she found him sleeping there, with the burnt-out lantern by his side.

One morning in January, while he was out fishing in his boat with two other men, he heard, in the dark, a voice from a skerry at the very entrance of the creek. It laughed scornfully, and said, "When it *comes to a Femböring,*[3] Elias, look to thyself!"

But there was many a long year yet before it *did* come to that; but one autumn, when his son Bernt was sixteen, Elias knew he could manage it, so he took his whole family with him in his boat to Ranen,[4] to exchange his *Sexæring* for a *Femböring.* The only person left at home was a little

---

[1] A boat with three oars on each side.

[2] A long pole, with a hooked iron spike at the end of it, for spearing Kvejte or hallibut with.

[3] A large boat with five oars on each side, used for winter fishing in northern Norway.

[4] The chief port in those parts.

Finn girl, whom they had taken into service some few years before, and who had only lately been confirmed.

Now there was a boat, a little *Femböring*, for four men and a boy, that Elias just then had his eye upon—a boat which the best boat-builder in the place had finished and tarred over that very autumn. Elias had a very good notion of what a boat should be, and it seemed to him that he had never seen a *Femböring* so well built *below* the water-line. *Above* the water-line, indeed, it looked only middling, so that, to one of less experience than himself, the boat would have seemed rather a heavy goer than otherwise, and anything but a smart craft.

Now the boat-master knew all this just as well as Elias. He said he thought it would be the swiftest sailer in Ranen, but that Elias should have it cheap, all the same, if only he would promise one thing, and that was, to make no alteration whatever in the boat, nay, not so much as adding a fresh coat of tar. Only when Elias had expressly given his word upon it did he get the boat.

But the devil who had taught the boat-master how to build his boats so cunningly *below* the water-line—*above* the water-line he had had to use his native wits, and they were scant enough—must surely have been there beforehand, and bidden him both sell it cheaply, so that Elias might get it, and stipulate besides that the boat should not be looked at too closely. In this way it escaped the usual tarring fore and aft.

Elias now thought about sailing home, but went first into the town, provided himself and family with provisions against Christmas, and indulged in a little nip of brandy besides. Glad as he was over the day's bargain, he, and his wife too, took an extra drop in their e'en, and their son Bernt had a taste of it too.

After that they sailed off homewards in their new boat. There was no other ballast in the boat but himself, his old woman, the children, and the Christmas provisions. His son Bernt sat by the main-sheet; his wife, helped by her next eldest son, held the sail-ropes; Elias himself sat at the rudder, while the two younger brothers of twelve and fourteen were to take it in turns to bail out.

They had eight miles of sea to sail over, and when they got into the open, it was plain that the boat would be tested pretty stiffly on its first voyage. A gale was gradually blowing up, and crests of foam began to break upon the heavy sea.

And now Elias saw what sort of a boat he really had. She skipped over the waves like a sea-mew; not so much as a splash came into the boat, and he therefore calculated that he would have no need to take in all his clews (rings in the corner of the sail) against the wind, which an ordinary *Femböring* would have been forced to do in such weather.

Out on the sea, not very far away from him, he saw another *Femböring*, with a full crew, and four clews in the sail, just like his own. It lay on the same course, and he thought it rather odd that he had not noticed it before. It made as if it would race him, and when Elias perceived that, he could not for the life of him help letting out a clew again.

And now he went racing along like a dart, past capes and islands and rocks, till it seemed to Elias as if he had never had such a splendid sail before. Now, too, the boat showed itself what it really was, the best boat in Ranen.

The weather, meantime, had become worse, and they had already got a couple of dangerous seas right upon them. They broke in over the mainsheet in the forepart of the boat where Bernt sat, and sailed out again to leeward near the stern.

Since the gloom had deepened, the other boat had kept almost alongside, and they were now so close together that they could easily have pitched the baling-can from one to the other.

So they raced on, side by side, in constantly stiffer seas, till night-fall, and beyond it. The fourth clew ought now to have been taken in again, but Elias didn't want to give in, and thought he might bide a bit till they took it in in the other boat also, which they needs *must* do soon. Ever and anon the brandy-flask was brought out and passed round, for they had now both cold and wet to hold out against.

The sea-fire, which played on the dark billows near Elias's own boat, shone with an odd vividness in the foam round the other boat, just as if a fire-shovel was ploughing up and turning over the water. In the bright phosphorescence he could plainly make out the rope-ends on board her. He could also see distinctly the folks on board, with their sou'westers on their heads; but as their larboard side lay nearest, of course they all had their backs towards him, and were well-nigh hidden by the high heeling hull.

Suddenly a tremendous roller burst upon them. Elias had long caught a glimpse of its white crest through the darkness, right over the prow where Bernt sat. It filled the whole boat for a moment, the planks shook and trembled beneath the weight of it, and then, as the boat, which had lain half on her beam-ends, righted herself and sped on again, it streamed off behind to leeward.

While it was still upon him, he fancied he heard a hideous yell from the other boat; but when it was over, his wife, who sat by the shrouds, said, with a voice which pierced his very soul: "Good God, Elias! the sea has carried off Martha and Nils!"—their two youngest children, the first nine, the second seven years old, who had been sitting in the hold near Bernt. Elias merely answered: "Don't let go the lines, Karen, or you'll lose yet more!"

They had now to take in the fourth clew, and, when this was done, Elias found that it would be well to take in the fifth and last clew too, for the gale was ever on the increase; but, on the other hand, in order to keep the boat free of the constantly heavier seas, he dare not lessen the sail a bit more than he was absolutely obliged to do; but they found that the scrap of sail they could carry gradually grew less and less. The sea seethed so that it drove right into their faces, and Bernt and his next eldest brother Anthony, who had hitherto helped his mother with the sail-lines, had, at last, to hold in the yards, an expedient one only resorts to when the boat cannot beat even the last clew—here the fifth.

The companion boat, which had disappeared in the meantime, now suddenly ducked up alongside again, with precisely the same amount of sail as Elias's boat; but he now began to feel that he didn't quite like the look of the crew on board there. The two who stood and held in the yards (he caught a glimpse of their pale faces beneath their sou'westers) seemed to him, by the odd light of the shining foam, more like corpses than men, nor did they speak a single word.

A little way off to larboard he again caught sight of the high white back of a fresh roller coming through the dark, and he got ready betimes to receive it. The boat was laid to with its prow turned aslant towards the on-rushing wave, while the sail was made as large as possible, so as to get up speed enough to cleave the heavy sea and sail out of it again. In rushed the roller with a roar; again, for an instant, they lay on their beam ends; but, when it was over, the wife no longer sat by the sail ropes, nor did Anthony stand there any longer holding the yards—they had both gone overboard.

This time also Elias fancied he heard the same hideous yell in the air; but in the midst of it he plainly heard his wife anxiously calling him by name. All that he said when he grasped the fact that she was washed overboard, was, "In Jesus' Name!" His first and dearest wish was to follow after her, but he felt at the same time that it became him to save the rest of the freight he had on board, that is to say, Bernt and his other two sons, one twelve, the other fourteen years old, who had been baling out for a time, but had afterwards taken their places in the stern behind him.

Bernt had now to look to the yards all alone, and the other two helped as best they could. The rudder Elias durst not let slip, and he held it fast with a hand of iron, which continuous exertion had long since made insensible to feeling.

A moment afterwards the comrade boat ducked up again: it had vanished for an instant as before. Now, too, he saw more of the heavy man who sat in the stern there in the same place as himself. Out of his back, just below his sou'wester (as he turned round it showed quite plainly), projected an iron spike six inches long, which Elias had no difficulty in recognising again. And now, as he calmly thought it all over, he was quite clear about two things: one was that it was the *Draug* itself which was steering its half-boat close beside him, and leading him to destruction; the other was that it was written in heaven that he was to sail his last course that night. For he who sees the Draug on the sea is a doomed man. He said nothing to the others, lest they should lose heart, but in secret he commended his soul to God.

During the last hour or so he had been forced out of his proper course by the storm; the air also had become dense with snow; and Elias knew that he must wait till dawn before land could be sighted. Meanwhile he sailed along much the same as before. Now and then the boys in the stern complained that they were freezing; but, in the plight they were now in, that couldn't be helped, and, besides, Elias had something else to think about. A terrible longing for vengeance had come over him, and, but for the necessity of saving the lives of his three lads, he would have tried by a sudden turn to sink the accursed boat which kept alongside of him the whole time as if to mock him; he now understood its evil errand only too well. If the *Kvejtepig* could reach the Draug before, a knife or a gaff might surely do the same thing now, and he felt that he would gladly have given his life for one good grip of the being who had so mercilessly torn from him his dearest in this world and would fain have still more.

At three or four o'clock in the morning they saw coming upon them through the darkness a breaker of such a height that at first Elias thought they must be quite close ashore near the surf swell. Nevertheless, he soon recognised it for what it really was—a huge billow. Then it seemed to him as if there was a laugh over in the other boat, and something said, "There goes thy boat, Elias!" He, foreseeing the calamity, now cried aloud: "In Jesus' Name!" and then bade his sons hold on with all their might to the withy-bands by the rowlocks when the boat went under, and not let go till it was above the water again. He made the elder of them go forward to Bernt; and himself held the youngest close by his side, stroked him once or twice furtively down the cheeks, and made sure that he had a good grip. The boat, literally buried beneath the foaming roller, was lifted gradually up by the bows and then went under. When it rose again out of the water, with the keel in the air, Elias, Bernt, and the twelve-year-old Martin lay alongside, holding on by the withy-bands; but the third of the brothers was gone.

They had now first of all to get the shrouds on one side cut through, so that the mast might come to the surface alongside instead of disturbing the balance of the boat below; and then they must climb up on the swaying bottom of the boat and stave in the key-holes, to let out the air which kept the boat too high in the water, and so ease her. After great exertions they succeeded, and Elias, who had got up on the top first, now helped the other two up after him.

There they sat through the long dark winter night, clinging convulsively on by their hands and knees to the boat's bottom, which was drenched by the billows again and again.

After the lapse of a couple of hours died Martin, whom his father had held up the whole time as far as he was able, of sheer exhaustion, and glided down into the sea. They had tried to cry for help several times, but gave it up at last as a bad job.

Whilst they two thus sat all alone on the bottom of the boat, Elias said to Bernt he must now needs believe that he too was about to be "along o' mother!" but that he had a strong hope that Bernt, at any rate, would be saved, if he only held out like a man. Then he told him all about the *Draug,* whom he had struck below the neck with the *Kvejtepig,* and how it had now revenged itself upon him, and certainly would not forbear till it was "quits with him."

It was towards nine o'clock in the morning when the grey dawn began to appear. Then Elias gave to Bernt, who sat alongside him, his silver watch with the brass chain, which he had snapped in two in order to drag it from beneath his closely buttoned jacket. He held on for a little time longer, but, as it got lighter, Bernt saw that his father's face was deadly pale, his hair too had parted here and there, as often happens when death is at hand, and his skin was chafed off his hands from holding on to the keel. The son understood now that his father was nearly at the last gasp, and tried, so far as the pitching and tossing would

THE FISHERMAN AND THE DRAUG

allow it, to hold him up; but when Elias marked it, he said, "Nay, look to thyself, Bernt, and hold on fast. I go to mother—in Jesus' Name!" and with that he cast himself down headlong from the top of the boat.

Every one who has sat on the keel of a boat long enough knows that when the sea has got its own it grows much calmer, though not immediately. Bernt now found it easier to hold on, and still more of hope came to him with the brightening day. The storm abated, and, when it got quite light, it seemed to him that he knew where he was, and that it was outside his own homestead, Kvalholm, that he lay driving.

He now began again to cry for help, but his chief hope was in a current which he knew bore landwards at a place where a headland broke in upon the surge, and there the water was calmer. And he did, in fact, drive closer and closer in, and came at last so near to one of the rocks that the mast, which was floating by the side of the boat all the time, surged up and down in the swell against the sloping cliff. Stiff as he now was in all his limbs from sitting and holding on, he nevertheless succeeded, after a great effort, in clambering up the cliff, where he hauled the mast ashore, and made the Femböring fast.

The Finn girl, who was alone in the house, had been thinking, for the last two hours, that she had heard cries for help from time to time, and as they kept on she mounted the hill to see what it was. There she saw Bernt up on the cliff, and the over-turned Femböring bobbing up and down against it. She immediately dashed down to the boat-place, got out the old rowing-boat, and rowed along the shore and round the island right out to him.

Bernt lay sick under her care the whole winter through, and didn't go a fishing all that year. Ever after this, too, it seemed to folks as if the lad were a little bit daft.

On the open sea he never would go again, for he had got the sea-scare. He wedded the Finn girl, and moved over to Malang, where he got him a clearing in the forest, and he lives there now, and is doing well, they say.

# THE HONEST PENNY

ONCE UPON a time there was a poor woman who lived in a tumble-down hut far away in the wood. Little had she to eat, and nothing at all to burn, and so she sent a little boy she had out into the wood to gather fuel. He ran and jumped, and jumped and ran, to keep himself warm, for it was a cold grey autumn day, and every time he found a bough or a root for his billet, he had to beat his arms across his breast, for his fists were as red as the cranberries over which he walked, for very cold. So when he had got his billet of wood and was off home, he came upon a clearing of stumps on the hillside, and there he saw a white crooked stone.

"Ah! you poor old stone," said the boy; "how white and wan you are! I'll be bound you are frozen to death;" and with that he took off his jacket and laid it on the stone. So when he got home with his billet of wood his mother asked what it all meant that he walked about in wintry weather in his shirtsleeves. Then he told her how he had seen an old crooked stone which was all white and wan for frost, and how he had given it his jacket.

"What a fool you are!" said his mother; "do you think a stone can freeze? But even if it froze till it shook again, know this—every one is nearest to his own self. It costs quite enough to get clothes to your back, without your going and hanging them on stones in the clearings;" and as she said that, she hunted the boy out of the house to fetch his jacket.

So when he came where the stone stood, lo! it had turned itself and lifted itself up on one side from the ground. "Yes! yes! this is since you got the jacket, poor old thing," said the boy.

But when he looked a little closer at the stone, he saw a money-box, full of bright silver, under it.

"This is stolen money, no doubt," thought the boy; "no one puts money, come by honestly, under a stone away in the wood."

So he took the money-box and bore it down to a tarn hard by and threw the whole hoard into the tarn; but one silver penny-piece floated on the top of the water.

"Ah! ah! that is honest," said the lad; "for what is honest never sinks."

So he took the silver penny and went home with it and his jacket. Then he told his mother how it had all happened, how the stone had turned itself, and how he had found a money-box full of silver money, which he had thrown out into the tarn because it was stolen money, and how one silver penny floated on the top.

"That I took," said the boy, "because it was honest."

"You are a born fool," said his mother, for she was very angry; "were naught else honest than what floats on water, there wouldn't be much honesty in the world. And even though the money were stolen ten times over, still you had found it; and I tell you again what I told you before, every one is nearest to his own self. Had you only taken that money we might have lived well and happy all our days. But a ne'er-do-weel thou art, and a ne'er-do-weel thou wilt be, and now I won't drag on any longer toiling and moiling for thee. Be off with thee into the world and earn thine own bread."

So the lad had to go out into the wide world, and he went both far and long seeking a place. But wherever he came, folk thought him too little and weak, and said they could put him to no use. At last he came to a merchant, and there he got leave to be in the kitchen and carry in wood and water for the cook. Well, after he had been there a long time, the merchant had to make a journey into foreign lands, and so he asked all his servants what he should buy and bring home for each of them. So, when all had said what they would have, the turn came to the scullion too, who brought in wood and water for the cook. Then he held out his penny.

"Well, what shall I buy with this?" asked the merchant; "there won't be much time lost over this bargain."

"Buy what I can get for it. It is honest, that I know," said the lad.

That his master gave his word to do, and so he sailed away.

So when the merchant had unladed his ship and laded her again in foreign lands, and bought what he had promised his servants to buy, he came down to his ship, and was just going to shove off from the wharf. Then all at once it came into his head that the scullion had sent out a silver penny with him, that he might buy something for him.

"Must I go all the way back to the town for the sake of a silver penny? One would then have small gain in taking such a beggar into one's house," thought the merchant.

Just then an old wife came walking by with a bag at her back.

"What have you got in your bag, mother?" asked the merchant.

"Oh! nothing else than a cat. I can't afford to feed it any longer, so I thought I would throw it into the sea, and make away with it," answered the woman.

Then the merchant said to himself, "Didn't the lad say I was to buy what I could get for his penny?" So he asked the old wife if she would take four farthings for her cat. Yes! the goody was not slow to say "done," and so the bargain was soon struck.

Now when the merchant had sailed a bit, fearful weather fell on him, and such a storm, there was nothing for it but to drive and drive till he did not know whither he was going. At last he came to a land on which he had never set foot before, and so up he went into the town.

At the inn where he turned in, the board was laid with a rod for each man who sat at it. The merchant thought it very strange, for he couldn't at all make out what they were to do with all these rods; but he sat him down, and thought he would watch well what the others did, and do like them. Well! as soon as the meat was set on the board, he saw well enough what the rods meant; for out swarmed mice in thousands, and each one who sat at the board had to take to his rod and flog and flap about him, and naught else could be heard than one cut of the rod harder than the one which went before it. Sometimes they whipped one another in the face, and just gave themselves time to say, "Beg pardon," and then at it again.

"Hard work to dine in this land!" said the merchant. "But don't folk keep cats here?"

"Cats?" they all asked, for they did not know what cats were.

So the merchant sent and fetched the cat he had bought for the scullion, and as soon as the cat got on the table, off ran the mice to their holes, and folks had never in the memory of man had such rest at their meat.

Then they begged and prayed the merchant to sell them the cat, and at last, after a long, long time, he promised to let them have it; but he would have a hundred dollars for it; and that sum they gave and thanks besides.

So the merchant sailed off again; but he had scarce got good sea-room before he saw the cat sitting up at the mainmast head, and all at once again came foul weather and a storm worse than the first, and he drove and drove till he got to a country where he had never been before. The merchant went up to an inn, and here, too, the board was spread with rods; but they were much bigger and longer than the first. And, to tell the truth, they had need to be; for here the mice were many more, and every mouse was twice as big as those he had before seen.

So he sold the cat again, and this time he got two hundred dollars for it, and that without any haggling.

So when he had sailed away from that land and got a bit out at sea, there sat Grimalkin again at the masthead; and the bad weather began at once again, and the end of it was, he was again driven to a land where he had never been before.

He went ashore, up to the town, and turned into an inn. There, too, the board was laid with rods, but every rod was an ell and a half long, and as thick as a small broom; and the folk said that to sit at meat was the hardest trial they had, for there were thousands of big ugly rats, so that it was only with sore toil and trouble one could get a morsel into one's mouth, 'twas such hard work to keep off the rats. So the cat had to be fetched up from the ship once more, and then folks got their food in peace. Then they all begged and prayed the merchant, for heaven's sake, to sell them his cat. For a long time he said "No;" but at last he gave his word to take three hundred dollars for it. That sum they paid down at once, and thanked him and blessed him for it into the bargain.

Now, when the merchant got out to sea, he fell a-thinking how much the lad had made out of the penny he had sent out with him.

"Yes, yes, some of the money he shall have," said the merchant to himself, "but not all. Me it is that he has to thank for the cat I bought; and besides, every man is nearest to his own self."

But as soon as ever the merchant thought this, such a storm and gale arose that every one thought the ship must founder. So the merchant saw there was no help for it, and he had to vow that the lad should have every penny; and no sooner had he vowed this vow, than the weather turned good, and he got a snoring breeze fair for home.

So, when he got to land, he gave the lad the six hundred dollars, and his daughter besides; for now the little scullion was just as rich as his master, the merchant, and even richer; and, after that, the lad lived all his days in mirth and jollity; and he sent for his mother, and treated her as well as or better than he treated himself; "for," said the lad, "I don't think that every one is nearest to his own self."

# THE DEATH OF CHANTICLEER

ONCE UPON a time there was a Cock and a Hen, who walked out into the field, and scratched, and scraped, and scrabbled. All at once Chanticleer found a burr of hop, and Partlet found a barleycorn; and they said they would make malt and brew Yule ale.

"Oh! I pluck barley, and I malt malt, and I brew ale, and the ale is good," cackled dame Partlet.

"Is the wort strong enough?" crew Chanticleer, and as he crowed he flew up on the edge of the cask, and tried to have a taste; but, just as he bent over to drink a drop, he took to flapping his wings, and so he fell head over heels into the cask, and was drowned.

When dame Partlet saw that, she clean lost her wits, and flew up into the chimney-corner, and fell a-screaming and screeching out. "Harm in the house! harm in the house!" she screeched out all in a breath, and there was no stopping her.

"What ails you, dame Partlet, that you sit there sobbing and sighing?" said the Handquern.

"Why not," said dame Partlet, "when goodman Chanticleer has fallen into the cask and drowned himself, and lies dead? That's why I sigh and sob."

"Well, if I can do naught else, I will grind and groan," said the Handquern; and so it fell to grinding as fast as it could.

When the Chair heard that, it said—

"What ails you, Handquern, that you grind and groan so fast and oft?"

"Why not, when goodman Chanticleer has fallen into the cask and drowned himself; and dame Partlet sits in the chimney and sighs and sobs? That's why I grind and groan," said the Handquern.

"If I can do naught else I will crack," said the Chair; and with that he fell to creaking and cracking.

When the Door heard that, it said—

"What's the matter? Why do you creak and crack so, Mr. Chair?"

"Why not?" said the Chair; "goodman Chanticleer has fallen into the cask and drowned himself; dame Partlet sits in the chimney sighing and sobbing; and the Handquern grinds and groans. That's why I creak and crackle, and croak and crack."

"Well," said the Door, "if I can do naught else, I can rattle and bang, and whistle and slam;" and with that it began to open and shut, and bang and slam, it grieved one to hear, and all one's teeth chattered.

All this the Stove heard, and it opened its mouth and called out—

"Door! Door! why all this slamming and banging?"

"Why not," said the Door, "when goodman Chanticleer has fallen into the cask and drowned himself; dame Partlet sits in the chimney sighing and sobbing; the Handquern grinds and groans; and the Chair creaks and cracks. That's why I bang and slam."

"Well," said the Stove, "if I can do naught else, I can smoulder and smoke;" and so it fell a-smoking and steaming till the room was all in a cloud.

The Axe saw this as it stood outside, and peeped with its shaft through the window.

"What's all this smoke about, Mrs. Stove?" said the Axe in a sharp voice.

"Why not," said the Stove, "when goodman Chanticleer has fallen into the cask and drowned himself; dame Partlet sits in the chimney sighing and sobbing; the Handquern grinds and groans; the Chair creaks and cracks; and the Door bangs and slams. That's why I smoke and steam."

"Well, if I can do naught else, I can rive and rend," said the Axe; and with that it fell to riving and rending all around about.

This the Aspen stood by the saw.

"Why do you rive and rend everywhere so, Mr. Axe?" said the Aspen.

"Goodman Chanticleer has fallen into the ale-cask and drowned himself," said the Axe; "dame Partlet sits in the chimney sighing and sobbing; the Handquern grinds and groans; the Chair creaks and cracks; the Door slams and bangs; and the Stove smokes and steams. That's why I rive and rend all about."

"Well, if I can do naught else," said the Aspen, "I can quiver and quake in all my leaves;" so it grew all of a quake.

The Birds saw this, and twittered out—

"Why do you quiver and quake, Miss Aspen?"

"Goodman Chanticleer has fallen into the ale-cask and drowned himself," said the Aspen, with a trembling voice; "dame Partlet sits in the chimney sighing and sobbing; the Handquern grinds and groans; the Chair creaks and cracks; the Door slams and bangs, the Stove steams and smokes; and the Axe rives and rends. That's why I quiver and quake."

"Well, if we can do naught else, we will pluck off all our feathers," said the Birds; and with that they fell a-pilling and plucking themselves till the room was full of feathers.

This the Master stood by and saw, and, when the feathers flew about like fun, he asked the Birds—

"Why do you pluck off all your feathers, you Birds?"

"Oh! goodman Chanticleer has fallen into the ale-cask and drowned himself," twittered out the Birds; "dame Partlet sits sighing and sobbing in the chimney; the Handquern grinds and groans; the Chair creaks and cracks; the Door slams and bangs; the Stove smokes and steams; the Axe rives and rends; and the Aspen quivers and quakes. That's why we are pilling and plucking all our feathers off."

"Well, if I can do nothing else, I can tear the brooms asunder," said the man; and with that he fell tearing and tossing the brooms till the birch-twigs flew about east and west.

The goody stood cooking porridge for supper, and saw all this.

"Why, man!" she called out, "what are you tearing the brooms to bits for?"

"Oh!" said the man, "goodman Chanticleer has fallen into the ale-vat and drowned himself; dame Partlet sits sighing and sobbing in the chimney; the Handquern grinds and groans; the Chair cracks and creaks; the Door slams and bangs; the Stove smokes and steams; the Axe rives and rends; the Aspen quivers and quakes; the Birds are pilling and plucking all their feathers off; and that's why I am tearing the brooms to bits."

"So, so!" said the goody; "then I'll dash the porridge over all the walls," and she did it; for she took one spoonful after the other, and dashed it against the walls, so that no one could see what they were made of for very porridge.

That was how they drank the burial ale after goodman Chanticleer, who fell into the brewing-vat and was drowned; and, if you don't believe it, you may set off thither and have a taste both of the ale and the porridge.


# REYNARD AND CHANTICLEER


ONCE UPON a time there was a cock who stood on a dung-heap and crew and flapped his wings. Then the fox came by.

"Good day," said Reynard. "I heard you crowing so nicely; but can you stand on one leg and crow, and wink your eyes?"

"Oh, yes," said Chanticleer, "I can do that very well." So he stood on one leg and crew; but he winked only with one eye, and when he had done that he made himself big and flapped his wings, as though he had done a great thing.

"Very pretty, to be sure," said Reynard. "Almost as pretty as when the parson preaches in church; but can you stand on one leg and wink both your eyes at once? I hardly think you can."

"Can't I, though!" said Chanticleer, and stood on one leg, and winked both his eyes, and crew. But Reynard caught hold of him, took him by the throat, and threw him over his back, so that he was off to the wood before he had crowed his crow out, as fast as Reynard could lay legs to the ground.

When they had come under an old spruce fir, Reynard threw Chanticleer on the ground, and set his paw on his breast, and was going to take a bite!

"You are a heathen, Reynard!" said Chanticleer. "Good Christians say grace, and ask a blessing before they eat."

But Reynard would be no heathen. God forbid it! So he let go his hold, and was about to fold his paws over his breast and say grace—but pop! up flew Chanticleer into a tree.

"You shan't get off for all that," said Reynard to himself. So he went away, and came again with a few chips which the woodcutters had left. Chanticleer peeped and peered to see what they could be.

"Whatever have you got there?" he asked.

"These are letters I have just got," said Reynard; "won't you help me to read them, for I don't know how to read writing?"

"I'd be so happy, but I dare not read them now," said Chanticleer, "for here comes a hunter; I see him, I see him, as I sit by the tree trunk."

When Reynard heard Chanticleer chattering about a hunter, he took to his heels as quick as he could.

This time it was Reynard who was made game of.

# THE COMPANION

ONCE UPON a time there was a farmer's son who dreamt that he was to marry a princess far, far out in the world. She was as red and white as milk and blood, and so rich there was no end to her riches. When he awoke he seemed to see her still standing bright and living before him, and he thought her so sweet and lovely that his life was not worth having unless he had her too. So he sold all he had, and set off into the world to find her out. Well, he went far, and farther than far, and about winter he came to a land where all the high-roads lay right straight on end; there wasn't a bend in any of them. When he wandered on and on for a quarter of a year he came to a town, and outside the church door lay a big block of ice, in which there stood a dead body, and the whole parish spat on it as they passed by to church. The lad wondered at this, and when the priest came out of church he asked him what it all meant.

"It is a great wrong-doer," said the priest. "He has been executed for his ungodliness, and set up there to be mocked and spat upon."

"But what was his wrong-doing?" asked the lad.

"When he was alive here he was a vintner," said the priest, "and he mixed water with his wine."

The lad thought that no such dreadful sin.

"Well," he said, "after he had atoned for it with his life, you might as well have let him have Christian burial and peace after death."

But the priest said that could not be in any wise, for there must be folk to break him out of the ice, and money to buy a grave from the church; then the gravedigger must be paid for digging the grave, and the sexton for tolling the bell, and the clerk for singing the hymns, and the priest for sprinkling dust over him.

"Do you think now there would be any one who would be willing to pay all this for an executed sinner?"

"Yes," said the lad. If he could only get him buried in Christian earth, he would be sure to pay for his funeral ale out of his scanty means.

Even after that the priest hemmed and hawed; but when the lad came with two witnesses, and asked him right out in their hearing if he could refuse to sprinkle dust over the corpse, he was forced to answer that he could not.

So they broke the vintner out of the block of ice, and laid him in Christian earth, and they tolled the bell and sang hymns over him, and the priest sprinkled dust over him, and they drank his funeral ale till they wept and laughed by turns; but when the lad had paid for the ale he hadn't many pence left in his pocket.

He set off on his way again, but he hadn't got far ere a man overtook him, who asked if he didn't think it dull work walking on all alone.

No; the lad did not think it dull. "I have always something to think about," he said.

Then the man asked if he wouldn't like to have a servant.

"No," said the lad; "I am wont to be my own servant, therefore I have need of none; and even if I wanted one ever so much, I have no means to get one, for I have no money to pay for his food and wages."

"You do need a servant, that I know better than you," said the man, "and you have need of one whom you can trust in life and death. If you won't have me as a servant, you may take me as your companion; I give you my word I will stand you in good stead, and it shan't cost you a penny. I will pay my own fare, and as for food and clothing, you shall have no trouble about them."

Well, on those terms he was willing enough to have him as his companion; so after that they travelled together, and the man for the most part went on ahead and showed the lad the way.

So after they had travelled on and on from land to land, over hill and wood, they came to a crossfell that stopped the way. There the companion went up and knocked, and bade them open the door; and the rock opened sure enough, and when they got inside the hill up came an old witch with a chair, and asked them, "Be so good as to sit down. No doubt ye are weary."

"Sit on it yourself," said the man. So she was forced to take her seat, and as soon as she sat down she stuck fast, for the chair was such that it let no one loose that came near it. Meanwhile they went about inside the hill, and the companion looked round till he saw a sword hanging over the door. That he would have, and if he got it he gave his word to the old witch that he would let her loose out of the chair.

"Nay, nay," she screeched out; "ask me anything else. Anything else you may have, but not that, for it is my Three-Sister Sword; we are three sisters who own it together."

"Very well; then you may sit there till the end of the world," said the man. But when she heard that, she said he might have it if he would set her free.

So he took the sword and went off with it, and left her still sitting there.

When they had gone far, far away over naked fells and wide wastes, they came to another crossfell. There, too, the companion knocked and bade them open the door, and the same thing happened as happened before; the rock opened, and when they had got a good way into the hill another old witch came up to them with a chair and begged them to sit down. "Ye may well be weary," she said.

"Sit down yourself," said the companion. And so she fared as her sister had fared; she did not dare to say nay, and as soon as she sat down on the chair she stuck fast. Meanwhile the lad and his companion went about in the hill, and the man broke open all the chests and drawers till he found what he sought, and that was a golden ball of yarn. That he set his heart on, and he promised the old witch to set her free if she would give him the golden ball. She said he might take all she had, but that she could not part with; it was her Three-Sister Ball. But when she heard that she should sit there till doomsday unless he got it, she said he might take it all the same if he would only set her free. So the companion took the golden ball, but he left her sitting where she sat.

So on they went for many days, over waste and wood, till they came to a third crossfell. There all went as it had gone twice before. The companion knocked, the rock opened, and inside the hill an old witch came up, and asked them to sit on her chair, they must be tired. But the companion said again, "Sit on it yourself," and there she sat. They had not gone through many rooms before they saw an old hat which hung on a peg behind the door. That the companion must and would have; but the old witch couldn't part with it. It was her Three-Sister Hat, and if she gave it away, all her luck would be lost. But when she heard that she would have to sit there till the end of the world unless he got it, she said he might take it if he would only let her loose. When the companion had got well hold of the hat, he went off, and bade her sit there still, like the rest of her sisters.

After a long, long time, they came to a Sound; then the companion took the ball of yarn, and threw it so hard against the rock on the other side of the stream, that it bounded back, and after he had thrown it backwards and forwards a few times it became a bridge. On that bridge they went over the Sound, and when they reached the other side, the man bade the lad to be quick and wind up the yarn again as soon as he could, for, said he—

"If we don't wind it up quick, all those witches will come after us, and tear us to bits."

So the lad wound and wound with all his might and main, and when there was no more to wind than the very last thread, up came the old witches on the wings of the wind. They flew to the water, so that the spray rose before them, and snatched at the end of the thread; but they could not quite get hold of it, and so they were drowned in the Sound.

When they had gone on a few days farther, the companion said, "Now we are soon coming to the castle where she is, the princess of whom you dreamt, and when we get there, you must go in and tell the king what you dreamt, and what it is you are seeking."

So when they reached it he did what the man told him, and was very heartily welcomed. He had a room for himself, and another for his companion, which they were to live in, and when dinner-time drew near, he was bidden to dine at the king's own board. As soon as ever he set eyes on the princess he knew her at once, and saw it was she of whom he had dreamt as his bride. Then he told her his business, and she answered that she liked him well enough, and would gladly have him; but first he must undergo three trials. So when they had dined she gave him a pair of golden scissors, and said—

"The first proof is that you must take these scissors and keep them, and give them to me at mid-day tomorrow. It is not so very great a trial, I fancy," she said, and made a face, "but if you can't stand it you lose your life; it is the law, and so you will be drawn and quartered, and your body will be stuck on stakes, and your head over the gate, just like those lovers of mine, whose skulls and skeletons you see outside the king's castle."

"That is no such great art," thought the lad.

But the princess was so merry and mad, and flirted so much with him, that he forgot all about the scissors and himself, and so while they played and sported, she stole the scissors away from him without his knowing it. When he went up to his room at night, and told how he had fared, and what she had said to him, and about the scissors she gave him to keep, the companion said—

"Of course you have the scissors safe and sure?"

Then he searched in all his pockets, but there were no scissors, and the lad was in a sad way when he found them wanting.

"Well! well!" said the companion; "I'll see if I can't get you them again."

With that he went down into the stable, and there stood a big, fat Billygoat, which belonged to the princess, and it was of that breed that it could fly many times faster through the air than it could run on land. So he took the Three-Sister Sword, and gave it a stroke between the horns, and said—

"When rides the princess to see her lover tonight?"

The Billygoat baaed, and said it dared not say, but when it had another stroke, it said the princess was coming at eleven o'clock. Then the companion put on the Three-Sister Hat, and all at once he became invisible, and so he waited for her. When she came, she took and rubbed the Billygoat with an ointment which she had in a great horn, and said—

"Away, away, o'er roof-tree and steeple, o'er land, o'er sea, o'er hill, o'er dale, to my true love who awaits me in the fell this night."

At the very moment that the goat set off, the companion threw himself on behind, and away they went like a blast through the air. They were not long on the way, and in a trice they came to a crossfell. There she knocked, and so the goat passed through the fell to the Troll, who was her lover.

"Now, my dear," she said, "a new lover is come, whose heart is set on having me. He is young and handsome, but I will have no other than you," and so she coaxed and petted the Troll.

"So I set him a trial, and here are the scissors he was to watch and keep; now do you keep them," she said.

So the two laughed heartily, just as though they had the lad already on wheel and stake.

"Yes! yes!" said the Troll; "I'll keep them safe enough."

> "And I shall sleep on the bride's white arm,
> While ravens round his skeleton swarm."

And so he laid the scissors in an iron chest with three locks; but just as he dropped them into the chest, the companion snapped them up. Neither of them could see him, for he had on the Three-Sister Hat; and so the Troll locked up the chest for naught, and he hid the keys he had in the hollow eye-tooth in which he had the toothache. There is would be hard work for any one to find them, the Troll thought.

So when midnight was passed she set off home again. The companion got up behind the goat, and they lost no time on the way back.

Next day, about noon, the lad was asked down to the king's board; but then the princess gave herself such airs, and was so high and mighty, she would scarce look towards the side where the lad sat. After they had dined, she dressed her face in holiday garb, and said, as if butter wouldn't melt in her mouth—

"May be you have those scissors which I begged you to keep yesterday?"

"Oh, yes, I have," said the lad, "and here they are," and with that he pulled them out, and drove them into the board till it jumped again. The princess could not have been more vexed had he driven the scissors into her face; but for all that she made herself soft and gentle, and said—

"Since you have kept the scissors so well, it won't be any trouble to you to keep my golden ball of yarn, and take care you give it me to-morrow at noon; but if you have lost it, you shall lose your life on the scaffold. It is the law."

The lad thought that an easy thing, so he took and put the golden ball into his pocket. But she fell a-playing and flirting with him again, so that he forgot both himself and the golden ball, and while they were at the height of their games and pranks, she stole it from him, and sent him off to bed.

Then when he came up to his bedroom, and told what they had said and done, his companion asked—

"Of course you have the golden ball she gave you?"

"Yes! yes!" said the lad, and felt in his pocket where he had put it; but no, there was no ball to be found, and he fell again into such an ill mood, and knew not which way to turn.

"Well! well! bear up a bit," said the companion. "I'll see if I can't lay hands on it;" and with that he took the sword and hat and strode off to a smith, and got twelve pounds of iron welded on to the back of the sword-blade. Then he went down to the stable, and gave the Billygoat a stroke between his horns, so that the brute went head over heels, and he asked—

"When rides the princess to see her lover tonight?"

"At twelve o'clock," baaed the Billygoat.

So the companion put on the Three-Sister Hat again, and waited till she came, tearing along with her horn of ointment, and greased the Billygoat. Then she said, as she had said the first time—

"Away, away, o'er roof-tree and steeple, o'er land, o'er sea, o'er hill, o'er dale, to my true love who awaits me in the fell this night."

In a trice they were off, and the companion threw himself on behind the Billygoat, and away they went like a blast through the air. In the twinkling of an eye they came to the Troll's hill, and, when she had knocked three times, they passed through the rock to the Troll, who was her lover.

"Where was it you hid the golden scissors I gave you yesterday, my darling?" cried out the princess. "My wooer had it and gave it back to me."

"That was quite impossible," said the Troll; "for he had locked it up in a chest with three locks and hidden the keys in the hollow of his eye-tooth." But when they unlocked the chest and looked for it, the Troll had no scissors in his chest.

So the princess told him how she had given her suitor her golden ball. "And here it is," she said; "for I took it from him again without his knowing it. But what shall we hit upon now, since he is master of such craft?"

Well, the Troll hardly knew; but, after they had thought a bit, they made up their minds to light a large fire and burn the golden ball; and so they would be cocksure that he could not get at it. But, just as she tossed it into the fire, the companion stood ready and caught it; and neither of them saw him, for he had on the Three-Sister Hat.

When the princess had been with the Troll a little while, and it began to grow towards dawn, she set off home again, and the companion got up behind her on the goat, and they got back fast and safe.

Next day, when the lad was bidden down to dinner, the companion gave him the ball. The princess was even more high and haughty than the day before, and, after they had dined, she perked up her mouth, and said in a dainty voice—

"Perhaps it is too much to look for that you should give me back my golden ball, which I gave you to keep yesterday?"

"Is it?" said the lad. "You shall soon have it. Here it is, safe enough;" and as he said that he threw it down on the board so hard, that it shook again; and as for the king, he gave a jump high up into the air.

The princess got as pale as a corpse, but she soon came to herself again, and said, in a sweet, small voice—

"Well done! well done!" Now he had only one more trial left, and it was this:

"If you are so clever as to bring me what I am now thinking of by dinner-time to-morrow, you shall win me, and have me to wife."

That was what she said.

The lad felt like one doomed to death, for he thought it quite impossible to know what she was thinking about, and still harder to bring it to her; and so, when he went up to his bedroom, it was hard work to comfort him at all. His companion told him to be easy, he would see if he could not get the right end of the stick this time too, as he had done twice before. So the lad at last took heart, and lay down to sleep.

Meanwhile, the companion went to the smith and got twenty-four pounds of iron welded on to his sword; and, when that was done, he went down to the stable and let fly at the Billygoat between the horns with such a blow, that he went right head over heels against the wall.

"When rides the princess to her lover to-night?" he asked.

"At one o'clock," baaed the Billygoat.

So when the hour drew near, the companion stood in the stable with his Three-Sister Hat on; and, when she had greased the goat, and uttered the same words that they were to fly through the air to her true love, who was waiting for her in the fell, off they went again on the wings of the wind; and, all the while, the companion sat behind.

But he was not light-handed this time; for, every now and then he gave the princess a slap, so that he almost beat the breath out of her body.

And when they came to the wall of rock, she knocked at the door, and it opened, and they passed on into the fell to her lover.

As soon as she got there, she fell to bewailing, and was very cross, and said she never knew the air could deal such buffets; she almost thought, indeed, that some one sat behind, who beat both the Billygoat and herself; she was sure she was black and blue all over her body, such a hard flight had she had through the air.

Then she went on to tell how her lover had brought her the golden ball too; how it happened, neither she nor the Troll could tell.

"But now do you know what I have hit upon?"

No, the Troll did not.

"Well," she went on, "I have told him to bring me what I was then thinking of by dinner-time to-morrow, and what I thought of was your head. Do you think he can get that, my darling?" said the princess, and began to fondle the Troll.

"No, I don't think he can," said the Troll. "He would take his oath he couldn't;" and then the Troll burst out laughing, and both the princess and the Troll thought the lad would be drawn and quartered, and that the crows would peck out his eyes, before he could get the Troll's head.

So when it turned towards dawn, she had to set off home again; but she was afraid, she said, for she thought there was some one behind her, and so she was afraid to ride home alone. The Troll must go with her on the way. Yes, the Troll would go with her, and he led out his Billygoat (for he had one that matched the princess's), and he smeared it and greased it between the horns. And when the Troll got up, the companion crept on behind, and so off they set through the air to the king's grange. But all the way the companion thrashed the Troll and his Billygoat, and gave them cut and thrust and thrust and cut with his sword, till they got weaker and weaker, and at last were well on the way to sink down into the sea over which they passed. Now the Troll thought the weather was so wild, he went right home with the princess up to the king's grange, and stood outside to see that she got home safe and well. But just as she shut the door behind her, the companion struck off the Troll's head and ran up with it to the lad's bedroom.

"Here is what the princess thought of," said he.

Well, they were merry and joyful, one may think, and when the lad was bidden down to dinner, and they had dined, the princess was as lively as a lark.

"No doubt you have got what I thought of?" said she.

"Aye, aye; I have it," said the lad, and he tore it out from under his coat, and threw it down on the board with such a thump that the board, trestles and all, was upset. As for the princess, she was as though she had been dead and buried; but she could not say that this was not what she was thinking of, and so now he was to have her to wife, as she had given her word. So they made a bridal feast, and there was drinking and gladness all over the kingdom.

But the companion took the lad on one side, and told him that he must just shut his eyes and sham sleep on the bridal night; but if he held his life dear, and would listen to him, he wouldn't let a wink come over them till he had stripped her of her troll-skin, which had been thrown over her, but he must flog it off her with a rod made of nine new birch twigs, and he must tear it off her in three tubs of milk: first he was to scrub her in a tub of year-old whey, and then he was to scour her in the tub of buttermilk, and lastly, he was to rub her in a tub of new milk. The birch twigs lay under the bed, and the tubs he had set in the corner of the room. Everything was ready to his hand. Yes; the lad gave his word to do as he was bid, and to listen to him. So when they got into the bridal bed at even, the lad shammed as though he had given himself up to sleep. Then the princess raised herself up on her elbow and looked at him to see if he slept, and tickled him under the nose; but the lad slept on still. Then she tugged his hair and his beard; but he lay like a log, as she thought. After that she drew out a big butcher's knife from under the bolster, and was just going to hack off his head; but the lad jumped up, dashed the knife out of her hand, and caught her by the hair. Then he flogged her with the birch rods, and wore them out upon her till there was not a twig left. When that was over he tumbled her into the tub of whey, and then he got to see what sort of beast she was: she was black as a raven all over her body; but when he scrubbed her well in the whey, and scoured her with buttermilk, and rubbed her well in new milk, her troll-skin dropped off her, and she was fair and lovely and gentle; so lovely she had never looked before.

Next day the companion said they must set off home. Yes; the lad was ready enough, and the princess too, for her dower had been long wait-ing. In the night the companion fetched to the king's grange all the gold and silver and precious things which the Troll had left behind him in the fell, and when they were ready to start in the morning the whole grange was so full of silver, and gold, and jewels, there was no walking without treading on them. That dower was worth more than all the king's land and realm, and they were at their wits' end to know how to carry it with them. But the companion knew a way out of every strait. The Troll left behind him six billygoats, who could all fly through the air. Those he so laded with silver and gold that they were forced to walk along the ground, and had no strength to mount aloft and fly, and what the billygoats could not carry had to stay behind in the king's grange. So they travelled far and farther than far, but at last the billygoats got so footsore and tired they could not go another step. The lad and the princess knew not what to do; but when the companion saw they could not get on, he took the whole dower on his back, and the billygoats a-top of it, and bore it all so far on that there was only half a mile left to the lad's home.

Then the companion said, "Now we must part. I can't stay with you any longer."

But the lad would not part from him, he would not lose him for much or little. Well, he went with them a quarter of a mile more, but farther he could not go, and when the lad begged and prayed him to go home and stay with him altogether, or at least as long as they had drunk his home-coming ale in his father's house, the companion said, "No. That could not be. Now he must part, for he heard heaven's bells ringing for him." He was the vintner who had stood in the block of ice outside the church door, whom all spat upon; and he had been his companion and

THE COMPANION

helped him because he had given all he had to get him peace and rest in Christian earth.

"I had leave," he said, "to follow you a year, and now the year is out."

When he was gone, the lad laid together all his wealth in a safe place, and went home without any baggage. Then they drank his home-coming ale, till the news spread far and wide over seven kingdoms, and when they had got to the end of the feast, they had carting and carrying all the winter both with the billygoats and the twelve horses which his father had before they got all that gold and silver safely carted home.

# DEATH AND THE DOCTOR

ONCE UPON a time there was a lad who had lived as a servant a long time with a man of the North Country. This man was a master at ale-brewing; it was so out-of-the-way good the like of it was not to be found. So, when the lad was to leave his place and the man was to pay him the wages he had earned, he would take no other pay than a keg of Yule-ale. Well, he got it and set off with it, and he carried it both far and long, but the longer he carried the keg the heavier it got, and so he began to look about to see if any one were coming with whom he might have a drink, that the ale might lessen and the keg lighten. And after a long, long time, he met an old man with a big beard.

"Good day," said the man.

"Good day to you," said the lad.

"Whither away?" asked the man.

"I'm looking after some one to drink with, and get my keg lightened," said the lad.

"Can't you drink as well with me as with any one else?" said the man. "I have fared both far and wide, and I am both tired and thirsty."

"Well! why shouldn't I?" said the lad; "but tell me, whence do you come, and what sort of man are you?"

"I am 'Our Lord,' and come from Heaven," said the man.

"Thee will I not drink with," said the lad; "for thou makest such distinction between persons here in the world, and sharest rights so unevenly that some get so rich and some so poor. No! with thee I will not drink," and as he said this he trotted off with his keg again.

So when he had gone a bit farther the keg grew too heavy again; he thought he never could carry it any longer unless some one came with whom he might drink, and so lessen the ale in the keg. Yes! he met an ugly, scrawny man who came along fast and furious.

"Good day," said the man.

"Good day to you," said the lad.

"Whither away?" asked the man.

"Oh, I'm looking for some one to drink with, and get my keg lightened," said the lad.

"Can't you drink with me as well as with any one else?" said the man; "I have fared both far and wide, and I am tired and thirsty."

"Well, why not?" said the lad; "but who are you, and whence do you come?"

"Who am I? I am the De'il, and I come from Hell; that's where I come from," said the man.

"No!" said the lad; "thou only pinest and plaguest poor folk, and if there is any unhappiness astir, they always say it is thy fault. Thee I will not drink with."

So he went far and farther than far again with his ale-keg on his back, till he thought it grew so heavy there was no carrying it any farther. He began to look round again if any one were coming with whom he could drink and lighten his keg. So after a long, long time, another man came, and he was so dry and lean 'twas a wonder his bones hung together.

"Good day," said the man.

"Good day to you," said the lad.

"Whither away?" asked the man.

"Oh, I was only looking about to see if I could find some one to drink with, that my keg might be lightened a little, it is so heavy to carry."

"Can't you drink as well with me as with any one else?" said the man.

"Yes; why not?" said the lad. "But what sort of man are you?"

"They call me Death," said the man.

"The very man for my money," said the lad. "Thee I am glad to drink with," and as he said this he put down his keg, and began to tap the ale into a bowl. "Thou art an honest, trustworthy man, for thou treatest all alike, both rich and poor."

So he drank his health, and Death drank his health, and Death said he had never tasted such drink, and as the lad was fond of him, they drank bowl and bowl about, till the ale was lessened, and the keg grew light.

At last Death said, "I have never known drink which smacked better, or did me so much good as this ale that you have given me, and I scarce know what to give you in return." But, after he had thought awhile, he said the keg should never get empty, however much they drank out of it, and the ale that was in it should become a healing drink, by which the lad could make the sick whole again better than any doctor. And he also said that when the lad came into the sick man's room, Death would always be there, and show himself to him, and it should be to him for a sure token if he saw Death at the foot of the bed that he could cure the sick with a draught from the keg; but if he sat by the pillow, there was no healing nor medicine, for then the sick belonged to Death.

Well, the lad soon grew famous, and was called in far and near, and he helped many to health again who had been given over. When he came in and saw how Death sat by the sick man's bed, he foretold either life or death, and his foretelling was never wrong. He got both a rich and powerful man, and at last he was called in to a king's daughter far, far away in the world. She was so dangerously ill no doctor thought he could do her any good, and so they promised him all that he cared either to ask or have if he would only save her life.

Now, when he came into the princess's room, there sat Death at her pillow; but as he sat he dozed and nodded, and while he did this she felt herself better.

"Now, life or death is at stake," said the doctor; "and I fear, from what I see, there is no hope."

But they said he *must* save her, if it cost land and realm. So he looked at Death, and while he sat there and dozed again, he made a sign to the servants to turn the bed round so quickly that Death was left sitting at the foot, and at the very moment they turned the bed, the doctor gave her the draught, and her life was saved.

"Now you have cheated me," said Death, "and we are quits."

"I was forced to do it," said the doctor, "unless I wished to lose land and realm."

"That shan't help you much," said Death; "your time is up, for now you belong to me."

"Well," said the lad, "what must be must be; but you'll let me have time to read the Lord's Prayer first?"

Yes, he might have leave to do that; but he took very good care not to read the Lord's Prayer; everything else he read, but the Lord's Prayer never crossed his lips, and at last he thought he had cheated Death for good and all. But when Death thought he had really waited too long, he went to the lad's house one night, and hung up a great tablet with the Lord's Prayer painted on it over against his bed. So when the lad woke in the morning he began to read the tablet, and did not quite see what he was about till he came to Amen; but then it was just too late, and Death had him.

# THE WAY OF THE WORLD

ONCE UPON a time there was a man who went into the wood to cut hop-poles, but he could find no trees so long and straight and slender as he wanted, till he came high up under a great heap of stones. There he heard groans and moans as though some one were at Death's door. So he went up to see who it was that needed help, and then he heard that the noise came from under a great flat stone which lay upon the heap. It was so heavy it would have taken many a man to lift it. But the man went down again into the wood and cut down a tree, which he turned into a lever, and with that he tilted up the stone, and lo! out from under it crawled a Dragon, and made at the man to swallow him up. But the man said he had saved the Dragon's life, and it was shameful thanklessness in him to want to eat him up.

"May be," said the Dragon, "but you might very well know I must be starved when I have been here hundreds of years and never tasted meat. Besides, it's the way of the world—that's how it pays its debts."

The man pleaded his cause stoutly, and begged prettily for his life; and at last they agreed to take the first living thing that came for a daysman,* and if his doom went the other way the man should not lose his life, but if he said the same as the Dragon, the Dragon should eat the man.

The first thing that came was an old hound, who ran along the road down below under the hillside. Him they spoke to, and begged him to be judge.

"God knows," said the hound, "I have served my master truly ever since I was a little whelp. I have watched and watched many and many a night through while he lay warm asleep on his ear, and I have saved house and home from fire and thieves more than once; but now I can neither see nor hear any more, and he wants to shoot me. And so I must run away, and slink from house to house, and beg for my living till I die of hunger. No! it's the way of the world," said the hound; "that's how it pays its debts."

"Now I am coming to eat you up," said the Dragon, and tried to swallow the man again. But the man begged and prayed hard for his life, till they agreed to take the next comer for a judge; and if he said the same as the Dragon and the hound, the Dragon was to eat him, and get a meal of man's meat; but if he did not say so, the man was to get off with his life.

So there came an old horse limping down along the road which ran under the hill. Him they called out to come and settle the dispute. Yes; he was quite ready to do that.

"Now, I have served my master," said the horse, "as long as I could draw or carry. I have slaved and striven for him till the sweat trickled from every hair, and I have worked till I have grown lame, and halt, and worn out with toil and age; now I am fit for nothing. I am not worth my food, and so I am to have a bullet through me, he says. Nay! nay! It's the way of the world. That's how the world pays its debts."

"Well, now I'm coming to eat you," said the Dragon, who gaped wide, and wanted to swallow the man. But he begged again hard for his life.

But the Dragon said he must have a mouthful of man's meat; he was so hungry, he couldn't bear it any longer.

"See, yonder comes one who looks as if he was sent to be a judge between us," said the man, as he pointed to Reynard the fox, who came stealing between the stones of the heap.

"All good things are three," said the man; "let me ask him, too, and if he gives doom like the others, eat me up on the spot."

"Very well," said the Dragon. He, too, had heard that all good things were three, and so it should be a bargain. So the man talked to the fox as he had talked to the others.

"Yes, yes," said Reynard, "I see how it all is;" but as he said this he took

*judge

the man a little on one side.

"What will you give me if I free you from the Dragon?" he whispered into the man's ear.

"You shall be free to come to my house, and to be lord and master over my hens and geese every Thursday night," said the man.

"Well, my dear Dragon," said Reynard, "this is a very hard nut to crack. I can't get it into my head how you, who are so big and mighty a beast, could find room to lie under yon stone."

"Can't you?" said the Dragon; "well, I lay under the hill-side, and sunned myself, and down came a landslip, and hurled the stone over me."

"All very likely, I dare say," said Reynard; "but still I can't understand it, and what's more I won't believe it till I see it."

So the man said they had better prove it, and the Dragon crawled down into his hole again; but in the twinkling of an eye they whipped out the lever, and down the stone crashed again on the Dragon.

"Lie now there till doomsday," said the fox. "You would eat the man, would you, who saved your life?"

The Dragon groaned, and moaned, and begged hard to come out; but the two went their way and left him alone.

The very first Thursday night Reynard came to be lord and master over the hen-roost, and hid himself behind a great pile of wood hard by. When the maid went to feed the fowls, in stole Reynard. She neither saw nor heard anything of him; but her back was scarce turned before he had sucked blood enough for a week, and stuffed himself so that he couldn't stir. So when she came again in the morning, there Reynard lay and snored, and slept in the morning sun, with all four legs stretched straight; and he was as sleek and round as a German sausage.

Away ran the lassie for the goody, and she came, and all the lasses with her, with sticks and brooms to beat Reynard; and, to tell the truth, they nearly banged the life out of him; but, just as it was almost all over with him, and he thought his last hour was come, he found a hole in the floor, and so he crept out, and limped and hobbled off to the wood.

"Oh, oh," said Reynard; "how true it is. 'Tis the way of the world; and this is how it pays its debts."

# PORK AND HONEY

AT DAWN the other day, when Bruin came tramping over the bog with a fat pig, Reynard sat up on a stone by the moorside.

"Good day, grandsire," said the fox; "what's that so nice that you have there?"

"Pork," said Bruin.

"Well, I have got a dainty bit too," said Reynard.

"What is that?" asked the bear.

"The biggest wild bee's comb I ever saw in my life," said Reynard.

"Indeed, you don't say so," said Bruin, who grinned and licked his lips. He thought it would be so nice to taste a little honey. At last he said, "Shall we swop our fare?"

"Nay, nay!" said Reynard, "I can't do that."

The end was that they made a bet, and agreed to name three trees. If the fox could say them off faster than the bear, he was to have leave to take one bite of the bacon; but if the bear could say them faster, he was to have leave to take one sup out of the comb. Greedy Bruin thought he was sure to sup out all the honey at one breath.

"Well," said Reynard, "it's all fair and right, no doubt, but all I say is, if I win, you shall be bound to tear off the bristles where I am to bite."

"Of course," said Bruin, "I'll help you, as you can't help yourself."

So they were to begin and name the trees.

"FIR, SCOTCH FIR, SPRUCE," growled out Bruin, for he was gruff in his tongue, that he was. But for all that he only named two trees, for Fir and Scotch Fir are both the same.

"Ash, Aspen, Oak," screamed Reynard, so that the wood rang again.

So he had won the wager, and down he ran and took the best part out of the pig at one bite, and was just running off with it. But Bruin was angry because he had taken the best bit out of the whole pig, and so he laid hold of his tail and held him fast.

"Stop a bit, stop a bit," he said, and was wild with rage.

"Never mind," said the fox, "it's all right; let me go, grandsire, and I'll give you a taste of my honey."

When Bruin heard that, he let go his hold, and away went Reynard after the honey.

"Here, on this honeycomb," said Reynard, "lies a leaf, and under this leaf is a hole, and that hole you are to suck."

As he said this he held up the comb under the bear's nose, took off the leaf, jumped up on a stone, and began to gibber and laugh, for there was neither honey nor honeycomb, but a wasp's nest, as big as a man's head, full of wasps, and out swarmed the wasps and settled on Bruin's head, and stung him in his eyes and ears, and mouth and snout. And he had such hard work to rid himself of them that he had no time to think of Reynard.

And that's why, ever since that day, Bruin is so afraid of wasps.

# SLIP ROOT, CATCH REYNARD'S FOOT

ONCE UPON a time there was a bear, who sat on a hillside in the sun and slept. Just then Reynard came slouching by and caught sight of him.

"There you sit taking your ease, grandsire," said the fox. "Now, see if

I don't play you a trick." So he went and caught three field-mice and laid them on a stump close under Bruin's nose, and then he bawled out into his ear, "Bo! Bruin, here's Peter the Hunter, just behind this stump;" and as he bawled this out he ran off through the wood as fast as ever he could.

Bruin woke up with a start, and when he saw the three little mice, he was as mad as a March hare, and was going to lift up his paw and crush them, for he thought it was they who had bellowed in his ear.

But just as he lifted it he caught sight of Reynard's tail among the bushes by the woodside, and away he set after him, so that the underwood crackled as he went, and, to tell the truth, Bruin was so close upon Reynard, that he caught hold of his off hind-foot just as he was crawling into an earth under a pine-root. So there was Reynard in a pinch; but for all that he had his wits about him, for he screeched out, "SLIP THE PINE-ROOT AND CATCH REYNARD'S FOOT," and so the silly bear let his foot slip and laid hold of the root instead. But by that time Reynard was safe inside the earth, and called out—

"I cheated you that time, too, didn't I, grandsire!"

"Out of sight isn't out of mind," growled Bruin down the earth, and was wild with rage.

# BRUIN AND REYNARD PARTNERS

ONCE UPON a time Bruin and Reynard were to own a field in common. They had a little clearing up in the wood, and the first year they sowed rye.

"Now we must share the crop as is fair and right," said Reynard. "If you like to have the root, I'll take the top."

Yes, Bruin was ready to do that; but when they had threshed out the crop, Reynard got all the corn, but Bruin got nothing but roots and rubbish. He did not like that at all; but Reynard said it was how they had agreed to share it.

"This year I have the gain," said Reynard; "next year it will be your turn. Then you shall have the top, and I shall have to put up with the root."

But when spring came, and it was time to sow, Reynard asked Bruin what he thought of turnips.

"Aye, aye!" said Bruin, "that's better food than corn;" and so Reynard thought also. But when harvest came Reynard got the roots, while Bruin got the turnip-tops. And then Bruin was so angry with Reynard that he put an end at once to his partnership with him.

# MASTER TOBACCO

ONCE UPON a time there was a poor woman who went about begging with her son; for at home she had neither a morsel to eat nor a stick to burn. First she tried the country, and went from parish to parish; but it was poor work, and so she came into the town. There she went about from house to house for awhile, and at last she came to the Lord Mayor. He was both open-hearted and open-handed, and he was married to the daughter of the richest merchant in the town, and they had one little daughter. As they had no more children, you may fancy she was sugar and spice and all that's nice, and in a word there was nothing too good for her. This little girl soon came to know the beggar-boy as he went about with his mother; and as the Lord Mayor was a wise man, as soon as he saw what friends the two were, he took the boy into his house, that he might be his daughter's playmate. Yes, they played and read and went to school together, and never had so much as one quarrel.

One day the Lady Mayoress stood at the window, and watched the children as they were trudging off to school. There had been a shower of rain, and the street was flooded, and she saw how the boy first carried the basket with their dinner over the stream, and then he went back and lifted the little girl over, and when he set her down he gave her a kiss.

When the Lady Mayoress saw this, she got very angry. "To think of such a ragamuffin kissing our daughter—we who are the best people in the place!" That was what she said. Her husband did his best to stop her tongue. "No one knew," he said, "how children would turn out in life, or what might befall his own: the boy was a clever, handy lad, and often and often a great tree sprang from a slender plant."

But no! it was all the same, whatever he said and whichever way he put it. The Lady Mayoress held her own, and said beggars on horseback always rode their cattle to death, and that no one had ever heard of a silk purse being made out of a sow's ear; adding, that a penny would never turn into a shilling, even though it glittered like a guinea. The end of it all was that the poor lad was turned out of the house, and had to pack up his rags and be off.

When the Lord Mayor saw there was no help for it, he sent him away with a trader who had come thither with a ship, and he was to be cabin-boy on board her. He told his wife he had sold the boy for a roll of tobacco.

But before he went the Lord Mayor's daughter broke her ring into two bits, and gave the boy one bit, that it might be a token to know him by if they ever met again; and so the ship sailed away, and the lad came to a town, far, far off in the world, and to that town a priest had just come who was so good a preacher that every one went to church to hear him, and the crew of the ship went with the rest the Sunday after to hear the sermon. As for the lad, he was left behind to mind the ship and to cook the dinner. So while he was hard at work he heard some one calling out across the water on an island. So he took the boat and rowed across, and there he saw an old hag, who called and roared.

"Aye," she said, "you have come at last! Here have I stood a hundred years calling and bawling, and thinking how I should ever get over this water; but no one has ever heard or heeded but you, and you shall be well paid if you will put me over to the other side."

So the lad had to row her to her sister's house, who lived on a hill on the other side close by; and when they got there, she told him to beg for the old table-cloth which lay on the dresser. Yes! he would beg for it; and when the old witch who lived there knew that he had helped her sister over the water, she said he might have whatever he chose to ask.

"Oh," said the boy, "then I won't have anything else than that old table-cloth on the dresser yonder."

"Oh," said the old witch, "that you never asked out of your own wits."

"Now I must be off," said the lad, "to cook the Sunday dinner for the church-goers."

"Never mind that," said the first old hag; "it will cook itself while you are away. Stop with me, and I will pay you better still. Here have I stood and called and bawled for a hundred years, but no one has ever heeded me but you."

The end was he had to go with her to another sister, and when he got there the old hag said he was to be sure and ask for the old sword, which was such that he could put it into his pocket and it became a knife, and when he drew it out it was a long sword again. One edge was black and the other white; and if he smote with the black edge everything fell dead, and if with the white everything came to life again. So when they came over, and the second old witch heard how he had helped her sister across, she said he might have anything he chose to ask for her fare.

"Oh," said the lad, "then I will have nothing else but that old sword which hangs up over the cupboard."

"That you never asked out of your own wits," said the old witch; but for all that he got the sword.

Then the old hag said again, "Come on with me to my third sister. Here have I stood and called and bawled for a hundred years, and no one has heeded me but you. Come on to my third sister, and you shall have better pay still."

So he went with her, and on the way she told him he was to ask for the old hymn-book; and that was such a book that when any one was sick and the nurse sang one of the hymns, the sickness passed away, and they were well again. Well! when they got across, and the third old witch heard he had helped her sister across, she said he was to have whatever he chose to ask for his fare.

"Oh," said the lad, "then I won't have anything else but granny's old hymn-book."

"That," said the old hag, "you never asked out of your own wits."

When he got back to the ship the crew were still at church, so he tried his table-cloth, and spread just a little bit of it out, for he wanted to see what good it was before he laid it on the table. Yes! in a trice it was covered with good food and strong drink, enough and to spare. So he just took a little snack, and then he gave the ship's dog as much as it could eat.

When the church-goers came on board, the captain said, "Wherever did you get all that food for the dog? Why, he's as round as a sausage, and as lazy as a snail."

"Oh, if you must know," said the lad, "I gave him the bones."

"Good boy," said the captain, "to think of the dog."

So he spread out the cloth, and at once the whole table was covered all over with such brave meat and drink as they had never before seen in all their born days.

Now when the boy was again alone with the dog, he wanted to try the sword, so he smote at the dog with the black edge, and it fell dead on the deck; but when he turned the blade and smote with the white edge, the dog came to life again and wagged his tail and fawned on his playmate. But the book—that he could not get tried just then.

Then they sailed well and far till a storm overtook them, which lasted many days; so they lay to and drove till they were quite out of their course, and could not tell where they were. At last the wind fell, and then they came to a country far, far off, that none of them knew; but they could easily see there was great grief there, as well there might be, for the king's daughter was a leper. The king came down to the shore, and asked was there any one on board who could cure her and make her well again.

"No, there was not." That was what they all said who were on deck.

"Is there no one else on board the ship than those I see?" asked the king.

"Yes; there's a little beggar-boy."

"Well," said the king, "let him come on deck."

So when he came, and heard what the king wanted, he said he thought he might cure her; and then the captain got so wroth and mad with rage that he ran round and round like a squirrel in a cage, for he thought the boy was only putting himself forward to do something in which he was sure to fail, and he told the king not to listen to such childish chatter.

But the king only said that wit came as children grew, and that there was the making of a man in every child. The boy had said he could do it, and he might as well try. After all, there were many who had tried and failed before him. So he took him home to his daughter, and the lad sang a hymn once. Then the princess could lift her arm. Once again he sang it, and she could sit up in bed. And when he had sung it thrice the king's daughter was as well as you and I are.

The king was so glad, he wanted to give him half his kingdom and the princess to wife.

"Yes," said the lad, "land and power are fine things to have half of," and was very grateful; "but as for the princess, he was betrothed to another," he said, "and he could not take her to wife."

So he stayed there awhile, and got half the kingdom; and when he had not been very long there, war broke out, and the lad went out to battle with the rest, and you may fancy he did not spare the black edge of his sword. The enemy's soldiers fell before him like flies, and the king won the day. But when they had conquered, he turned the white edge, and they all rose up alive and became the king's soldiers, who had granted them their lives. But then there were so many of them that they were badly off for food, though the king wished to send them away full, both of meat and drink. So the lad had to bring out his table-cloth, and then there was not a man that lacked anything.

Now when he had lived a little longer with the king, he began to long to see the Lord Mayor's daughter. So he fitted out four ships of war and set sail; and when he came off the town where the Lord Mayor lived, he fired off his cannon like thunder, till half the panes of glass in the town were shivered. On board those ships everything was as grand as in a king's palace; and as for himself, he had gold on every seam of his coat, so fine he was. It was not long before the Lord Mayor came down to the shore and asked if the foreign lord would not be so good as to come up and dine with him. "Yes, he would go," he said; and so he went up to the mansion-house where the Lord Mayor lived, and there he took his seat between the Lady Mayoress and her daughter.

So as they sat there in the greatest state, and ate and drank and were merry, he threw the half of the ring into the daughter's glass, and no one saw it; but she was not slow to find out what he meant, and excused herself from the feast and went out and fitted his half to her half. Her mother saw there was something in the wind and hurried after her as fast as she could.

"Do you know who that is in there, mother?" said the daughter.

"No!" said the Lady Mayoress.

"He whom papa sold for a roll of tobacco," said the daughter.

At these words the Lady Mayoress fainted and fell down flat on the floor.

In a little while the Lord Mayor came out to see what was the matter, and when he heard how things stood he was almost as uneasy as his wife.

"There is nothing to make a fuss about," said Master Tobacco. "I have only to claim the little girl I kissed as we were going to school."

But to the Lady Mayoress he said—

"You should never despise the children of the poor and needy, for none can tell how they may turn out; for there is the making of a man in every child of man, and wit and wisdom come with growth and strength."

# THE THREE LEMONS

ONCE UPON a time there were three brothers, who had lost their parents; and as they had left nothing behind them on which the lads could live, they had to go out into the world to try their luck. The two elder fitted themselves out as well as they could; but the youngest, whom they called Taper Tom, because he always sat in the chimney-corner and held tapers of pine-wood, him they would not have with them.

The two set out early in the grey dawn; but, however fast they went, or did not go, Taper Tom came just as soon as the others to the king's palace. So when they got there, they asked for work. The king said he had nothing for them to do; but as they were so pressing, he'd see if he could not find them something—there must be always something to do in such a big house. Yes! they might drive nails into the wall; and when they had done driving them in, they might pull them out again. When they had done that, they might carry wood and water into the kitchen.

Taper Tom was the handiest in driving nails into the wall and in pulling them out again, and he was the handiest also in carrying wood and water. So his brothers were jealous of him, and said he had given out that he was good enough to get the king the prettiest princess who was to be found in the twelve kingdoms; for you must know the king had lost his old dame and was a widower. When the king heard that, he told Taper Tom he must do what he had said, or else he would make them lay him on the block and chop his head off.

Taper Tom answered he had never said nor thought anything of the kind, but, as the king was so stern, he would try what he could do. So he got him a scrip of food over his shoulders, and set off from the palace; but he had not gone far on the road before he grew hungry, and wanted to taste the food they had given him when he set out. So when he had seated himself to rest at his ease under a spruce by the roadside, up came an old hag hobbling, who asked what he had in his scrip.

"Salt meat and fresh meat," said the lad. "If you are hungry, granny, come and take a snack with me."

Yes! she thanked him, and then she said may be she would do him a good turn herself; and away she hobbled through the wood. So when Taper Tom had eaten his fill and had rested, he threw his scrip over his shoulder and set off again; but he had not gone far before he found a pipe. That, he thought, would be nice to have with him and play on by the way; and it was not long before he brought the sound out of it, you may fancy. But then there came about him such a swarm of little Trolls, and each asked the other in full cry—

"What has my lord to order? What has my lord to order?"

Taper Tom said he never knew he was lord over them; but if he was to order anything, he wished they would fetch him the prettiest princess to be found in twelve kingdoms. Yes! that was no great thing, the little Trolls thought; they knew well enough where she was, and they could show him the way, and then he might go and get her for himself, for they had no power to touch her.

Then they showed him the way, and he got to the end of his journey well and happily. There was not any one who laid so much as two sticks across in his way. It was a Troll's castle, and in it sat three lovely princesses; but as soon as ever Taper Tom came in, they all lost their wits for fear, and ran about like scared lambs, and all at once they were turned into three lemons that lay in the window. Taper Tom was so sorry and unhappy at that, he scarce knew which way to turn. But when he had thought a little, he took and put the lemons into his pocket, for he thought they would be good to have if he got thirsty by the way, for he had heard say lemons were sour.

So when he had gone a bit of the way, he got so hot and thirsty; water was not to be had, and he did not know what he should do to quench his thirst. So he fell to thinking of the lemons, and took one of them out and bit a hole in it. But lo! inside sat the princess as far as her armpits, and screamed out—

"Water!—water!" Unless she got water, she must die, she said.

Yes! the lad ran about looking for water as though he were a mad thing; but there was no water to be got, and all at once the princess was dead.

So when he had gone a bit farther, he got still hotter and thirstier; and as he could find nothing to quench his thirst, he pulled out the second lemon and bit a hole in it. Inside it was also a princess, sitting as far as her armpits, and she was still lovelier than the first. She, too, screamed for water, and said if she could not get it she must die outright. So Taper Tom hunted under stone and moss, but he could find no water; and so the end was the second princess died too.

Tamper Tom thought things got worse and worse, and so it was, for the farther he went the hotter it got. The earth was so dry and burnt up, there was not a drop of water to be found, and he was not far off being half dead of thirst. He kept himself as long as he could from biting a hole in the lemon he still had, but at last there was no help for it. So when he had bitten the hole, there sat a princess inside it also; she was the loveliest in twelve kingdoms, and she screamed out if she could not get water she must die at once. So Taper Tom ran about hunting for water; and this time he fell upon the king's miller, and he showed him the way to the mill-dam. So when he came to the dam with her and gave her some water, she came quite out of the lemon, and was stark naked. So Taper Tom had to let her have the wrap he had to throw over her, and then she hid herself up a tree while he went up to the king's palace to fetch her clothes, and to tell the king how he had got her, and, in a word, told him the whole story.

But while this was going on, the cook came down to the mill-dam to fetch water; and when she saw the lovely face which played on the water, she thought it was her own, and grew so glad she fell a-dancing and jumping because she had grown so pretty.

"The devil carry water," she cried, "since I am so pretty;" and away she threw the water-buckets. But in a little while she got to see that the face in the mill-dam belonged to the princess who sat up in the tree; and then she got so cross, that she tore her down from the tree, and threw her out into the dam. But she herself put on Taper Tom's cloak, and crept up into the tree.

So when the king came and set eyes on the ugly swarthy kitchen-maid, he turned white and red; but when he heard how they said she was the loveliest in twelve kingdoms, he thought he could not help believing there must be something in it; and besides, he felt for poor Taper Tom, who had taken so much pains to get her for him.

"She'll get better, perhaps, as time goes on," he thought, "when she is dressed smartly and wears fine clothes;" and so he took her home with him.

THE THREE LEMONS

Then they sent for all the wig-makers and needlewomen, and she was dressed and clad like a princess; but for all they washed and dressed her, she was still as ugly as ever.

After a while the kitchen-maid was to go to the dam to fetch water, and then she caught a great silver fish in her bucket. She bore it up to the palace, and showed it to the king, and he thought it grand and fine; but the ugly princess said it was some witchcraft, and they must burn it, for she soon saw what it was. Well! the fish was burnt, and next morning they found a lump of silver in the ashes. So the cook came and told it to the king, and he thought it passing strange; but the princess said it was all witchcraft, and bade them bury it in the dung-heap. The king was much against it; but she left him neither rest nor peace, and so he said at last they might do it.

But lo! next day stood a tall lovely linden tree on the spot where they had buried the lump of silver, and that linden had leaves which gleamed like silver. So when they told the king that, he thought it passing strange; but the princess said it was nothing but witchcraft, and they must cut down the linden at once. The king was against that; but the princess plagued him so long that at last he had to give way to her in this also.

But lo! when the lasses went out to gather the chips of the linden to light the fires, they were pure silver.

"It isn't worth while," one of them said, "to say anything about this to the king or the princess, or else they too will be burnt and melted. It is better to hide them in our drawers. They will be good to have when a lover comes, and we are going to marry."

Yes! they were all of one mind as to that; but when they had borne the chips awhile, they grew so fearfully heavy that they could not help looking to see what it was; and then they found the chips had been changed into a child, and it was not long before it grew into the loveliest princess you ever set eyes on.

The lasses could see very well that something wrong lay under all this. So they got her clothes, and flew off to find the lad who was to fetch the loveliest princess in twelve kingdoms, and told him their story.

So when Taper Tom came, the princess told him her story, and how the cook had come and torn her from the tree and thrown her into the dam; and how she had been the silver fish, and the silver lump, and the linden, and the chips, and how she was the true princess.

It was not so easy to get the king's ear, for the ugly cook hung over him early and late; but at last they made out a story, and said that a challenge had come from a neighbour king, and so they got him out; and when he came to see the lovely princess, he was so taken with her, he was for holding the bridal feast on the spot; and when he heard how badly the ugly cook had behaved to her, he said they should take her and roll her down-hill in a cask full of nails. Then they kept the bridal feast at such a rate that it was heard and talked of over twelve kingdoms.

# THE TROLLS IN HEDALE WOOD

Up at a place in Vaage, in Gudbrandsdale, there lived once on a time in the days of old a poor couple. They had many children, and two of the sons who were about half grown up had to be always roaming about the country begging. So that they were well acquainted with all the highways and byways, and they also knew the short cut into Hedale.

It happened once that they wanted to go thither, but at the same time they heard that some falconers had built themselves a hut at Maela, and so they wished to kill two birds with one stone, and see the birds, and how they are taken, and so they took the cut across Longmoss. But you must know it was far on towards autumn, and so the milkmaids had all gone home from the huts, and they could neither get shelter nor food. Then they had to keep straight on for Hedale, but the path was a mere track, and when night fell they lost it; and, worse still, they could not find the falconers' hut either, and before they knew where they were, they found themselves in the very depths of the forest. As soon as they saw they could not get on, they began to break boughs, lit a fire, and built themselves a bower of branches, for they had a hand-axe with them; and, after that, they plucked heather and moss and made themselves a bed. So a little while after they had lain down, they heard something which sniffed and snuffed so with its nose; then the boys picked up their ears and listened sharp to hear whether it were wild beasts or wood Trolls, and just then something snuffed up the air louder than ever, and said—

"There's a smell of Christian blood here!"

At the same time they heard such a heavy footfall that the earth shook under it, and then they knew well enough the Trolls must be about.

"Heaven help us! what shall we do?" said the younger boy to his brother.

"Oh! you must stand as you are under the fir, and be ready to take our bags and run away when you see them coming; as for me, I will take the hand-axe," said the other.

All at once they saw the Trolls coming at them like mad, and they were so tall and stout, their heads were just as high as the fir-tops; but it was a good thing they had only one eye between them all three, and that they used turn and turn about. They had a hole in their foreheads into which they put it, and turned and twisted it with their hands. The one that went first he must have it to see his way, and the others went behind and took hold of the first.

"Take up the traps," said the elder of the boys, "but don't run away too far, but see how things go; as they carry their eye so high aloft they'll find it hard to see me when I get behind them."

Yes! the brother ran before and the Trolls after him, meanwhile the elder got behind them and chopped the hindmost Troll with his axe on the ankle, so that the Troll gave an awful shriek, and the foremost Troll got so afraid he was all of a shake and dropped the eye. But the boy was not slow to snap it up. It was bigger than two quart pots put together, and so clear and bright, that though it was pitch dark, everything was as clear as day as soon as he looked through it.

When the Trolls saw he had taken their eye and done one of them harm, they began to threaten him with all the evil in the world if he didn't give back the eye at once.

"I don't care a farthing for Trolls and threats," said the boy, "now I've got three eyes to myself and you three have got none, and besides two of you have to carry the third."

"If we don't get our eye back this minute, you shall be both turned to stocks and stones," screeched the Trolls.

But the boy thought things needn't go so fast; he was not afraid for witchcraft or hard words. If they didn't leave him in peace he'd chop them all three, so that they would have to creep and crawl along the earth like cripples and crabs.

When the Trolls heard that they got still more afraid, and began to use soft words. They begged so prettily that he would give them their eye back, and then he should have both gold and silver and all that he wished to ask. Yes! that seemed all very fine to the lad, but he must have the gold and silver first, and so he said if one of them would go home and fetch as much gold and silver as would fill his and his brother's bags, and give them two good cross-bows beside, they might have their eye, but he should keep it until they did what he said.

The Trolls were very put out, and said none of them could go when he hadn't his eye to see with; but all at once one of them began to bawl out for their goody; for you must know they had a goody between them all three as well as an eye. After a while an answer came from a knoll a long way off to the north. So the Trolls said she must come with two steel cross-bows and two buckets full of gold and silver; and then it was not long, you may fancy, before she was there. And when she heard what had happened, she too began to threaten them with witchcraft. But the Trolls got so afraid, and begged her beware of the little wasp, for they couldn't be sure he would not take away her eye too. So she threw them the cross-bows and the buckets and the gold and the silver, and strode off to the knoll with the Trolls; and since that time no one has ever heard that the Trolls have walked in Hedale Wood snuffing after Christian blood.

# THE SKIPPER AND OLD NICK

ONCE UPON a time there was a skipper who was so wonderfully lucky in everything he undertook; there was no one who got such freights, and no one who earned so much money, for it rolled in upon him on all sides, and, in a word, there was no one who was good to make such voyages as he, for whithersoever he sailed, he took the wind with him—nay, men did say he had only to turn his hat and the wind turned the way he wished it to blow.

So he sailed for many years, both in the timber trade and to China, and he had gathered money together like grass. But it so happened that once he was coming home across the North Sea with every sail set, as though he had stolen both ship and lading; but he who wanted to lay hold on him went faster still. It was Old Nick, for with him he had made a bargain, as one may well fancy, and that very day the time was up, and he might look any moment that Old Nick would come and fetch him.

Well, the skipper came up on deck out of the cabin and looked at the weather; then he called for the carpenter and some others of the crew, and said they must go down into the hold and hew two holes in the ship's bottom, and when they had done that they were to lift the pumps out of their beds and drive them down tight into the holes they had made, so that the sea might rise high up into the pumps.

The crew wondered at all this, and thought it a funny bit of work, but they did as the skipper ordered; they hewed holes in the ship's bottom and drove the pumps in so tight that never a drop of water could come to the cargo, but up in the pump itself the North Sea stood seven feet high.

They had only just thrown the chips overboard after their piece of work when Old Nick came on board in a gust of wind and caught the skipper by the throat.

"Stop, father!" said the skipper; "there's no need to be in such a hurry," and as he said that he began to defend himself and to loose the claws which Old Nick had stuck into him by the help of a marling-spike.

"Haven't you made a bargain that you would always keep the ship dry and tight?" asked the skipper. "Yes! you're a pretty fellow; look down the pumps; there's the water standing seven feet high in the pipe. Pump, devil, pump! and pump the ship dry, and then you may take me and have me as soon and as long as you choose."

Old Nick was not so clever that he was not taken in; he pumped and strove, and the sweat ran down his back like a brook, so that you might have turned a mill at the end of his backbone, but he only pumped out of the North Sea and into the North Sea again. At last he got tired of that work, and when he could not pump a stroke more, he set off in a sad temper home to his grandmother to take a rest. As for the skipper, he let him stay a skipper as long as he chose, and if he isn't dead, he is still perhaps sailing on his voyages whithersoever he will, and twisting the wind as he choses only by turning his hat.

# HOW TO WIN A PRINCE

ONCE UPON a time there was a king's son who made love to a lass, but after they had become great friends and were as good as betrothed, the prince began to think little of her, and he got it into his head that she wasn't clever enough for him, and so he wouldn't have her.

So he thought how he might be rid of her; and at last he said he would take her to wife all the same if she could come to him—

> "Not driving,
>  And not riding;
> Not walking,
>  And not carried;
> Not fasting,
>  And not full-fed;
> Not naked,
>  And not clad;
> Not in the daylight,
>  And not by night."

For all that he fancied she could never do.

So she took three barleycorns and swallowed them, and then she was not fasting, and yet not full-fed; and next she threw a net over her, and so she was

> Not naked,
> And yet not clad

Next she got a ram and sat on him, so that her feet touched the ground; and so she waddled along, and was

> Not driving,
> And not riding;
> Not walking,
> And not carried.

And all this happened in the twilight, betwixt night and day.

So when she came to the guard at the palace, she begged that she might have leave to speak with the prince; but they wouldn't open the gate, she looked such a figure of fun.

But for all that the noise woke up the prince, and he went to the window to see what it was.

So she waddled up to the window, and twisted off one of the ram's horns, and took it and rapped with it against the window.

And so they had to let her in and have her for their princess.


# BOOTS AND THE BEASTS

ONCE UPON a time there was a man who had an only son, but he lived in need and wretchedness, and when he lay on his deathbed, he told his son he had nothing in the world but a sword, a bit of coarse linen, and a few crusts of bread—that was all he had to leave him. Well, when the man was dead, the lad made up his mind to go out into the world to try his luck; so he girded the sword about him, and took the crusts and laid them in the bit of linen for his travelling fare; for you must know they lived far away up on a hillside in the wood, far from folk. Now the way he went took him over a fell, and when he had got up so high that he could look over the country, he set his eyes on a lion, a falcon, and an ant, who stood there quarrelling over a dead horse. The lad was sore afraid when he saw the lion, but he called out to him and said he must come and settle the strife between them and share the horse, so that each should get what he ought to have.

So the lad took his sword, and shared the horse as well as he could. To the lion he gave the carcass and the greater portion; the falcon got some of the entrails and other tit-bits; and the ant got the head. When he had done, he said—

"Now I think it is fairly shared. The lion shall have most, because he is biggest and strongest; the falcon shall have the best, because he is nice and dainty; and the ant shall have the skull, because he loves to creep about in holes and crannies."

Yes! they were all well pleased with his sharing; and so they asked him what he would like to have for sharing the horse so well.

"Oh," he said, "if I have done you a service, and you are pleased with it, I am also pleased; but I won't be paid."

Yes; but he must have something, they said.

"If you won't have anything else," said the lion, "you shall have three wishes."

But the lad knew not what to wish for; and so the lion asked him if he wouldn't wish that he might be able to turn himself into a lion; and the two others asked him if he wouldn't wish to be able to turn himself into a falcon and an ant. Yes! all that seemed to him good and right; and so he wished these three wishes.

Then he threw aside his sword and wallet, turned himself into a falcon, and began to fly. So he flew on and on, till he came over a great lake; but when he had almost flown across it he got so tired and sore on the wing he couldn't fly any longer; and as he saw a steep rock that rose out of the water, he perched on it and rested himself. He thought it a wondrous strong rock, and walked about it for a while; but when he had taken a good rest, he turned himself again into a little falcon, and flew away till he came to the king's grange. There he perched on a tree, just before the princess's windows. When she saw the falcon, she set her heart on catching it. So she lured it to her; and as soon as the falcon came under the casement she was ready, and, pop! she shut-to the window, and caught the bird, and put him into a cage.

In the night the lad turned himself into an ant and crept out of the cage; and then he turned himself into his own shape, and went up and sat down by the princess's bed. Then she got so afraid, that she fell to screeching out and awoke the king, who made into her room and asked whatever was the matter.

"Oh!" said the princess, "there is some one here."

But in a trice the lad became an ant, crept into the cage, and turned himself into a falcon. The king could see nothing for her to be afraid of; so he said to the princess it must have been the nightmare riding her. But he was hardly out of the door before it was the same story over again. The lad crept out of the cage as an ant, and then became his own self, and sat down by the bedside of the princess.

Then she screamed loud, and the king came again to see what was the matter.

"There is some one here," screamed the princess. But the lad crept into the cage again, and sat perched up there like a falcon. The king looked and hunted high and low; and when he could see nothing, he got cross that his rest was broken, and said it was all a trick of the princess.

"If you scream like that again," he said, "you shall soon know that your father is the king."

But for all that, the king's back was scarcely turned before the lad was by the princess's side again. This time she did not scream, although she was so afraid she did not know which way to turn.

So the lad asked why she was so afraid.

Didn't he know? She was promised to a hill-ogre, and the very first time she came under bare sky he was to come and take her; and so when the lad came she thought it was the hill-ogre. And besides, every Thursday morning came a messenger from the hill-ogre, and that was a dragon, to whom the king had to give nine fat pigs every time he came; and that was why he had given it out that the man who could free him from the dragon should have the princess and half the kingdom.

The lad said he would soon do that; and as soon as it was daybreak the princess went to the king and said there was a man in there who would free him from the dragon and the tax of pigs. As soon as the king heard that, he was very glad, for the dragon had eaten up so many pigs, there would soon have been no more left in the whole kingdom. It happened that day was just a Thursday morning, and so the lad strode off to the spot where the dragon used to come to eat the pigs, and the shoeblack in the king's grange showed him the way.

Yes, the dragon came, and he had nine heads, and he was so wild and wroth, that fire and flame flared out of his nostrils when he did not see his feast of pigs; and he flew upon the lad as though he would gobble him up alive. But, pop! he turned himself into a lion, and fought with the dragon, and tore one head off him after another. The dragon was strong, that he was, and he spat fire and venom. But as the fight went on he hadn't more than one head left, though that was the toughest. At last the lad got that torn off too; and then it was all over with the dragon.

So he went to the king, and there was great joy all over the palace; and the lad was to have the princess. But once on a time, as they were walking in the garden, the hill-ogre came flying at them himself, and caught up the princess and bore her off through the air.

As for the lad, he was for going after her at once; but the king said he mustn't do that, for he had no one else to lean on now he had lost his daughter. But for all that, neither prayers nor preaching were any good;

BOOTS AND THE BEASTS

the lad turned himself into a falcon and flew off. But when he could not see them anywhere, he called to mind that wonderful rock in the lake, where he had rested the first time he ever flew. So he settled there; and after he had done that, he turned himself into an ant, and crept down through a crack in the rock. So when he had crept about awhile, he came to a door which was locked. But he knew a way how to get in, for he crept through the keyhole, and what do you think he saw there? Why, a strange princess combing a hill-ogre's hair that had three heads.

"I have come all right," said the lad to himself; for he had heard how the king had lost two daughters before, whom the Trolls had taken.

"Maybe I shall find the second also," he said to himself, as he crept through the keyhole of a second door. There sat a strange princess combing a hill-ogre's hair who had six heads. So he crept through a third keyhole still, and there sat the youngest princess combing a hill-ogre's hair with nine heads. Then he crept up her leg and stung her, and so she knew it was the lad who wished to talk to her; and then she begged leave of the hill-ogre to go out.

When she came out the lad was himself again, and so he told her she must ask the hill-ogre whether she would never get away and go home to her father. Then he turned himself into an ant and sat on her foot, and so the princess went into the house again, and fell to combing the hill-ogre's hair.

So when she had done this awhile she fell a-thinking.

"You're forgetting to comb me," said the hill-ogre. "What is it you're thinking of?"

"Oh, I am doubting whether I shall ever get away from this place, and home to my father's grange," said the princess.

"Nay, nay, that you'll never do," said the hill-ogre; "not unless you can find the grain of sand which lies under the ninth tongue of the ninth head of the dragon to which your father paid tax; but that no one will ever find; for if that grain of sand came over the rock, all the hill-ogres would burst, and the rock itself would become a gilded palace, and the lake green meadows."

As soon as the lad heard that, he crept out through the keyholes, and through the crack in the rock, till he got outside. Then he turned himself into a falcon, and flew whither the dragon lay. Then he hunted till he found the grain of sand under the ninth tongue of the ninth head, and flew off with it; but when he came to the lake he got tired, so tired that he had to sink down and perch on a stone by the strand. And just as he sat there he dozed and nodded for the twinkling of an eye; and meantime the grain of sand fell out of his bill down among the sand on the shore. So he searched for it three days before he found it again. But as soon as he had found it he flew straight off to the steep rock with it, and dropped it down the crack. Then all the hill-ogres burst, and the rock was rent, and there stood a gilded castle, which was the grandest castle in all the world; and the lake became the loveliest fields and the greenest meadows any one ever saw.

So they travelled back to the king's grange, and there arose, as you may fancy, joy and gladness. The lad and the youngest princess were to have one another; and they kept up the bridal feast over the whole kingdom for seven full weeks.

# HOW THEY GOT HAIRLOCK HOME

ONCE UPON a time there was a goody who had three sons. The first was called Peter, the second Paul, and the third Osborn Boots. One single nanny-goat she had who was called Hairlock, and she never would come home in time for tea. Peter and Paul both went out to get her home, but they found no nanny-goat; so Boots had to set off, and when he had walked a while he saw Hairlock high, high upon a crag.

"Dear Hairlock, pretty Hairlock," he cried, "you can't stand any longer on yon crag, for you must come home in good time for tea to-day."

"No, no, that I shan't," said Hairlock; "I won't wet my socks for any one; and if you want me, you must carry me."

But Osborn Boots would not do that, so he went and told his mother.

"Well," said his mother, "go to the fox and beg him to bite Hairlock." So the lad went to the fox.

"My dear fox! bite Hairlock, for Hairlock won't come home in good time for tea to-day."

"No," said the fox, "I won't blunt my snout on pig's bristles and goat's beards."

So the lad went and told his mother.

"Well, then," she said, "go to Greylegs, the wolf." So the lad said to Greylegs—

"Dear Greylegs! do, Greylegs, tear the fox, for the fox won't bite Hairlock, and Hairlock won't come home in good time for tea to-day."

"No," said Greylegs, "I won't wear out my paws and teeth on a dry fox's carcass."

So the lad went and told his mother.

"Well, then, go to the bear," said his mother, "and beg him to slay Greylegs."

So the lad said to the bear—

"My dear bear! do, bear, slay Greylegs, for Greylegs won't tear the fox, and the fox won't bite Hairlock, and Hairlock won't come home in good time for tea to-day."

"No, I won't," said the bear; "I won't blunt my claws in that work, that I won't."

So the lad told his mother.

"Well, then," she said, "go to the Finn and beg him to shoot the bear." So the lad said to the Finn—

"Dear Finn! do, Finn, shoot the bear, for the bear won't slay Greylegs, Greylegs won't tear the fox, the fox won't bite Hairlock, and Hairlock won't come home in good time for tea to-day."

"No, that I won't," said the Finn; "I'm not going to shoot away my bullets for that."

So the lad told his mother.

"Well, then," she said, "go to the fir, and beg him to fall on the Finn."

So the lad said to the fir—

"My dear fir! do, fir, fall on the Finn, for the Finn won't shoot the bear, the bear won't slay the wolf, the wolf won't tear the fox, the fox won't bite Hairlock, and Hairlock won't come home in good time for tea to-day."

"No, that I won't," said the fir; "I'm not going to break off my boughs for that."

So the lad told his mother.

"Well, then," said she, "go to the fire and beg it to burn the fir."

So the lad said to the fire—

"My dear fire! do, fire, burn the fir, for the fir won't fall on the Finn, the Finn won't shoot the bear, the bear won't slay the wolf, the wolf won't tear the fox, the fox won't bite Hairlock, and Hairlock won't come home in good time for tea to-day."

"No, that I won't," said the fire; "I'm not going to burn myself out for that, that I won't."

So the lad told his mother.

"Well, then," she said, "go to the water and beg it to quench the fire."

So the lad said to the water—

"My dear water! do, water, quench the fire, for the fire won't burn the fir, the fir won't fall on the Finn, the Finn won't shoot the bear, the bear won't slay the wolf, the wolf won't tear the fox, the fox won't bite Hairlock, and Hairlock won't come home in good time for tea to-day."

"No, I won't," said the water; "I'm not going to run to waste for that, be sure."

So the lad told his mother.

"Well, then," she said, "go to the ox, and beg him to drink up the water."

So the lad said to the ox—

"My dear ox! do, ox, drink up the water, for the water won't quench the fire, the fire won't burn the fir, the fir won't fall on the Finn, the Finn won't shoot the bear, the bear won't slay the wolf, the wolf won't tear the fox, the fox won't bite Hairlock, and Hairlock won't come home in good time for tea to-day."

"No, I won't," said the ox; "I'm not going to burst asunder in doing that, I trow."

So the lad told his mother.

"Well, then," said she, "you must go to the yoke, and beg him to pinch the ox."

So the lad said to the yoke—

"My dear yoke! do, yoke, pinch the ox, for the ox won't drink up the water, the water won't quench the fire, the fire won't burn the fir, the fir won't fall on the Finn, the Finn won't shoot the bear, the bear won't slay the wolf, the wolf won't tear the fox, the fox won't bite Hairlock, and Hairlock won't come home in good time for tea to-day."

"No, that I won't," said the yoke; "I'm not going to break myself in two in doing that."

So the lad told his mother.

"Well, then," she said, "you must go to the axe, and beg him to chop the yoke."

So the lad said to the axe—

"My dear axe! do, axe, chop the yoke, for the yoke won't pinch the ox, the ox won't drink up the water, the water won't quench the fire, the fire won't burn the fir, the fir won't fall on the Finn, the Finn won't shoot the bear, the bear won't slay the wolf, the wolf won't tear the fox, the fox won't bite Hairlock, and Hairlock won't come home in good time for tea to-day."

"No, that I won't," said the axe; "I'm not going to spoil my edge for that, that I won't."

So the lad told his mother.

"Well, then," she said, "go to the smith, and beg him to hammer the axe."

So the lad said to the smith—

"My dear smith! do, smith, hammer the axe, for the axe won't chop the yoke, the yoke won't pinch the ox, the ox won't drink up the water, the water won't quench the fire, the fire won't burn the fir, the fir won't fall on the Finn, the Finn won't shoot the bear, the bear won't slay the wolf, the wolf won't tear the fox, the fox won't bite Hairlock, and Hairlock won't come home in good time for tea to-day."

"No, I won't," said the smith; "I'm not going to burn up my coal and wear out my sledge-hammer for that," he said.

So the lad told his mother.

"Well, then," she said, "you must go to the rope, and beg it to hang the smith."

So the lad said to the rope—

"My dear rope! do, rope, hang the smith, for the smith won't hammer the axe, the axe won't chop the yoke, the yoke won't pinch the ox, the ox won't drink up the water, the water won't quench the fire, the fire won't burn the fir, the fir won't fall on the Finn, the Finn won't shoot the bear, the bear won't slay the wolf, the wolf won't tear the fox, the fox won't bite Hairlock, and Hairlock won't come home in good time for tea to-day."

"No," said the rope, "that I won't; I'm not going to fray myself out for that."

So the lad told his mother.

"Well, then," she said, "you must go to the mouse, and beg him to gnaw the rope."

So the lad said to the mouse—

"My dear mouse! do, mouse, gnaw the rope, for the rope won't hang the smith, the smith won't hammer the axe, the axe won't chop the yoke, the yoke won't pinch the ox, the ox won't drink up the water, the water won't quench the fire, the fire won't burn the fir, the fir won't fall on the Finn, the Finn won't shoot the bear, the bear won't slay the wolf, the wolf won't tear the fox, the fox won't bite Hairlock, and Hairlock won't come home in good time for tea to-day."

"No, I won't," said the mouse; "I'm not going to wear down my teeth for that."

So the lad told his mother.

"Well, then," she said, "you must go to the cat, and beg her to catch the mouse."

So the lad said to the cat—

"My dear cat! do, cat, catch the mouse, for the mouse won't gnaw the rope, the rope won't hang the smith, the smith won't hammer the axe, the axe won't chop the yoke, the yoke won't pinch the ox, the ox won't drink up the water, the water won't quench the fire, the fire won't burn the fir, the fir won't fall on the Finn, the Finn won't shoot the bear, the bear won't slay the wolf, the wolf won't tear the fox, the fox won't bite Hairlock, and Hairlock won't come home in good time for tea to-day."

"Well," said the cat, "just give me a drop of milk for my kittens, and then—" that's what the cat said; and the lad said, yes, she should have it.

So the cat bit mouse, and mouse gnawed rope, and rope hanged smith, and smith hammered axe, and axe chopped yoke, and yoke pinched ox, and ox drank water, and water quenched fire, and fire burnt fir, and fir felled Finn, and Finn shot bear, and bear slew Greylegs, and Greylegs tore fox, and fox bit Hairlock, so that she sprang home and knocked one of her hindlegs against the barn wall.

So there lay the nanny-goat, and now she limps about on three legs.

But as for Osborn Boots, he said it served her just right, because she would not come home in good time for tea that very day.


# LITTLE FREDDY WITH HIS FIDDLE

ONCE UPON a time there was a cottager who had an only son, and this lad was weakly, and hadn't much health to speak of; so he couldn't go out to work in the field.

His name was Freddy, and undersized he was too; and so they called him Little Freddy. At home there was little either to bite or sup, and so his father went about the country trying to bind him over as a cow-herd or an errand-boy; but there was no one who would take his son till he came to the sheriff, and he was ready to take him, for he had just packed off his errand-boy, and there was no one who would fill his place, for the story went that he was a skinflint.

But the cottager thought it was better there than nowhere; he would get his food, for all the pay he was to get was his board—there was nothing said about wages or clothes. So when the lad had served three years he wanted to leave, and then the sheriff gave him all his wages at one time. He was to have a penny a year. "It couldn't well be less," said the sheriff. And so he got threepence in all.

As for little Freddy, he thought it was a great sum, for he had never owned so much; but for all that, he asked if he wasn't to have something more.

"You have already had more than you ought to have," said the sheriff.

"Shan't I have anything, then, for clothes?" asked little Freddy; "for those I had on when I came here are worn to rags, and I have had no new ones."

And, to tell the truth, he was so ragged that the tatters hung and flapped about him.

"When you have got what we agreed on," said the sheriff, "and three whole pennies beside, I have nothing more to do with you. Be off!"

But for all that, he got leave just to go into the kitchen and get a little food to put in his scrip; and after that he set off on the road to buy himself more clothes. He was both merry and glad, for he had never seen a penny before; and every now and then he felt in his pockets as he went along to see if he had all three. So when he had gone far and farther than far, he got into a narrow dale, with high fells on all sides, so that he couldn't tell if there were any way to pass out; and he began to wonder what there could be on the other side of those fells, and how he ever should get over them.

But up and up he had to go, and on he strode; he was not strong on his legs, and had to rest every now and then—and then he counted and counted how many pennies he had got. So when he had got quite up to the very top, there was nothing but a great plain overgrown with moss. There he sat him down, and began to see if his money was all right; and before he was aware of him a beggar-man came up to him, and he was so tall and big that the lad began to scream and screech when he got a good look of him, and saw his height and length.

"Don't you be afraid," said the beggar-man; "I'll do you no harm. I only beg for a penny, in God's name."

"Heaven help me!" said the lad. "I have only three pennies, and with them I was going to the town to buy clothes."

"It is worse for me than for you," said the beggar-man. "I have got no penny, and I am still more ragged than you."

"Well, then, you shall have it," said the lad.

So when he had walked on awhile he got weary, and sat down to rest again. But when he looked up there he saw another beggar-man, and he was still taller and uglier than the first; and so when the lad saw how very tall and ugly and long he was, he fell a-screeching.

"Now, don't you be afraid of me," said the beggar; "I'll not do you any harm. I only beg for a penny, in God's name."

"Now, may Heaven help me!" said the lad. "I've only got two pence, and with them I was going to the town to buy clothes. If I had only met you sooner, then——"

"It's worse for me than for you," said the beggar-man. "I have no penny, and a bigger body and less clothing."

"Well, you may have it," said the lad.

So he went awhile farther, till he got weary, and then he sat down to rest; but he had scarce sat down than a third beggar-man came to him.

He was so tall and ugly and long, that the lad had to look up and up, right up to the sky. And when he took him all in with his eyes, and saw how very, very tall and ugly and ragged he was, he fell a-screeching and screaming again.

"Now, don't you be afraid of me, my lad," said the beggar-man; "I'll do you no harm; for I am only a beggar-man, who begs for a penny in God's name."

"May Heaven help me!" said the lad. "I have only one penny left, and with it I was going to the town to buy clothes. If I had only met you sooner, then——"

"As for that," said the beggar-man, "I have no penny at all, that I haven't, and a bigger body and less clothes, so it is worse for me than for you."

"Yes," said little Freddy, he must have the penny then—there was no help for it; for so each would have what belonged to him, and he would have nothing.

"Well," said the beggar-man, "since you have such a good heart that you gave away all that you had in the world, I will give you a wish for each penny." For you must know it was the same beggar-man who had got them all three; he had only changed his shape each time, that the lad might not know him again.

"I have always had such a longing to hear a fiddle go, and see folk so glad and merry that they couldn't help dancing," said the lad; "and so, if I may wish what I choose, I will wish myself such a fiddle, that everything that has life must dance to its tune."

"That he might have," said the beggar-man; but it was a sorry wish. "You must wish something better for the other two pennies."

"I have always had such a love for hunting and shooting," said little Freddy; "so if I may wish what I choose, I will wish myself such a gun that I shall hit everything I aim at, were it ever so far off."

"That he might have," said the beggar-man; but it was a sorry wish. "You must wish better for the last penny."

"I have always had a longing to be in company with folk who were kind and good," said little Freddy; "and so, if I could get what I wish, I would wish it to be so that no one can 'Nay' to the first thing I ask."

"That wish was not so sorry," said the beggar-man; and off he strode between the hills, and he saw him no more. And so the lad lay down to sleep, and the next day he came down from the fell with his fiddle and his gun.

First he went to the storekeeper and asked for clothes, and at one farm he asked for a horse, and at another for a sledge; and at this place he asked for a fur coat, and no one said him "Nay"—even the stingiest folk, they were all forced to give him what he asked for. At last he went through the country as a fine gentleman, and had his horse and his sledge; and so when he had gone a bit he met the sheriff with whom he had served.

"Good day, master," said little Freddy, as he pulled up and took off his hat.

"Good day," said the sheriff. And then he went on, "When was I ever your master?"

"Oh, yes," said little Freddy. "Don't you remember how I served you three years for three pence?"

"Heaven help us!" said the sheriff. "How you have got on all of a hurry! And pray, how was it that you got to be such a fine gentleman?"

"Oh, that's tellings," said little Freddy.

"And are you full of fun, that you carry a fiddle about with you?" asked the sheriff.

"Yes, yes," said Freddy. "I have always had such a longing to get folk to dance; but the funniest thing of all is this gun, for it brings down almost anything that I aim at, however far it may be off. Do you see that magpie yonder, sitting in the spruce fir? What'll you bet I don't bag it as we stand here?"

On that the sheriff was ready to stake horse and groom, and a hundred dollars beside, that he couldn't do it; but as it was, he would bet all the money he had about him; and he would go to fetch it when it fell—for he never thought it possible for any gun to carry so far.

But as the gun went off down fell the magpie, and into a great bramble thicket; and away went the sheriff up into the brambles after it, and he picked it up and showed it to the lad. But in a trice little Freddy began to scrape his fiddle, and the sheriff began to dance, and the thorns to tear him; but still the lad played on, and the sheriff danced, and cried, and begged till his clothes flew to tatters, and he scarce had a thread to his back.

"Yes," said little Freddy, "now I think you're about as ragged as I was when I left your service; so now you may get off with what you have got."

But first of all, the sheriff had to pay him what he had wagered that he could not hit the magpie.

So when the lad came to the town he turned aside into an inn, and he began to play, and all who came danced, and he lived merrily and well. He had no care, for no one would say him "Nay" to anything he asked.

But just as they were all in the midst of their fun, up came the watchmen to drag the lad off to the townhall; for the sheriff had laid a charge against him, and said he had waylaid him and robbed him, and nearly taken his life. And now he was to be hanged—they would not hear of anything else. But little Freddy had a cure for all trouble, and that was his fiddle. He began to play on it, and the watchmen fell a-dancing, till they lay down and gasped for breath.

So they sent soldiers and the guard on their way; but it was no better with them than with the watchmen. As soon as ever little Freddy scraped his fiddle, they were all bound to dance, so long as he could lift a finger to play a tune; but they were half dead long before he was tired. At last they stole a march on him, and took him while he lay asleep by night; and when they had caught him, he was doomed to be hanged on the spot, and away they hurried him to the gallows-tree.

There a great crowd of people flocked together to see this wonder, and the sheriff, he too was there; and he was so glad at last at getting amends for the money and the skin he had lost, and that he might see him hanged with his own eyes. But they did not get him to the gallows very fast, for little Freddy was always weak on his legs, and now he made himself weaker still. His fiddle and his gun he had with him also—it was hard to part him from them; and so, when he came to the gallows, and had to mount the steps, he halted on each step; and when he got to the top he sat down, and asked if they could deny him a wish, and if he might have leave to do one thing? He had such a longing, he said, to scrape a tune and play a bar on his fiddle before they hanged him.

"No, no," they said; "it were sin and shame to deny him that." For, you know, no one could gainsay what he asked.

But the sheriff he begged them, for God's sake, not to let him have leave to touch a string, else it was all over with them altogether; and if the lad got leave, he begged them to bind him to the birch that stood there.

So little Freddy was not slow in getting his fiddle to speak, and all that were there fell a-dancing at once, those who went on two legs, and those who went on four; both the dean and the parson, and the lawyer, and the bailiff, and the sheriff, masters and men, dogs and swine—they all danced and laughed and screeched at one another. Some danced till they lay for dead; some danced till they fell into a swoon. It went badly with all of them, but worst of all with the sheriff; for there he stood bound to the birch, and he danced and scraped great bits off his back against the trunk. There was not one of them who thought of doing anything to little Freddy, and away he went with his fiddle and his gun, just as he chose; and he lived merrily and happily all his days, for there was no one who could say him "Nay" to the first thing he asked for.

LITTLE FREDDY WITH HIS FIDDLE

# TALES FROM SWEDEN

"Lars, My Lad!"

# PART ONE
*From Sweden at Large*

## "LARS, MY LAD!"

THERE WAS once a prince or a duke, or something of that sort, but at any rate he belonged to a very grand family, and he would not stay at home. So he travelled all over the world, and wherever he went he was well liked, and was received in the best and gayest families, for he had no end of money. He made friends and acquaintances, as you may imagine, wherever he went, for he who has a well-filled trough is sure to fall in with pigs who want to have their fill. But he went on spending his money until he came to want, and at last his purse became so empty that he had not even a farthing left. And now there was an end to all his friends as well, for they behaved like the pigs; when the trough was empty and he had no more to give them, they began to grunt and grin, and then they ran away in all directions. There he stood alone with a long face. Everybody had been so willing to help him to get rid of his money, but nobody would help him in return; and so there was nothing for it but to trudge home and beg for crusts on the way.

So late one evening he came to a great forest. He did not know where he should find a shelter for the night, but he went on looking and searching till he caught sight of an old tumble-down hut, which stood in the middle of some bushes. It was not exactly good enough for such a fine cavalier, but when you cannot get what you want you must take what you can get. And, since there was no help for it, he went into the hut. Not a living soul was to be seen; there was not even a stool to sit upon, but alongside the wall stood a big chest. What could there be inside that chest? If only there were some bits of mouldy bread in it! How nice they would taste! For, you must know, he had not had a single bit of food the whole day, and he was so hungry and his stomach so empty that it groaned with pain. He lifted the lid. But inside the chest there was another chest, and inside that chest there was another; and so it went on, each one smaller than the other, until they became quite tiny boxes. The more there were the harder he worked away, for there must be something very fine inside, he thought, since it was so well hidden.

At last he came to a tiny, little box, and in this box lay a bit of paper— and that was all he got for his trouble! It was very annoying, of course,

169

but then he discovered there was something written on the paper, and when he looked at it he was just able to spell it out, although at first it looked somewhat difficult.

"Lars, my lad!"

As he pronounced these words something answered right in his ear:

"What are master's orders?"

He looked round, but he saw nobody. This was very funny, he thought, and so he read out the words once more:

"Lars, my lad!"

And the answer came as before:

"What are master's orders?"

But he did not see anybody this time either.

"If there is anybody about who hears what I say, then be kind enough to bring me something to eat," he said. And the next moment there stood a table laid out with all the best things one could think of. He set to work to eat and drink, and had a proper fill. He had never enjoyed himself so much in all his life, he thought.

When he had eaten all he could get down, he began to feel sleepy, and so he took out the paper again:

"Lars, my lad!"

"What are master's orders?"

"Well, you have given me food and drink, and now you must get me a bed to sleep in as well. But I want a really fine bed," he said, for you must know he was a little more bold now that his hunger was stayed. Well, there it stood, a bed so fine and dainty that even the king himself might covet it. Now this was all very well in its way; but when once you are well off you wish for still more, and he had no sooner got into bed than he began to think that the room was altogether too wretched for such a grand bed. So he took out the paper again:

"Lars, my lad!"

"What are master's orders?"

"Since you are able to get me such food and such a bed here in the midst of the wild forest, I suppose you can manage to get me a better room, for you see I am accustomed to sleep in a palace, with golden mirrors and draped walls and ornaments and comforts of all kinds," he said. Well, he had no sooner spoken the words than he found himself lying in the grandest chamber anybody had ever seen.

Now he was comfortable, he thought, and felt quite satisfied as he turned his face to the wall and closed his eyes.

But that was not all the grandeur; for when he woke up in the morning and looked round, he saw it was a big palace he had been sleeping in. One room led into the other, and wherever he went the place was full of all sorts of finery and luxuries, both on the walls and on the ceilings, and they glittered so much when the sun shone on them, that he had to shade his eyes with his hand, so strong was the glare of gold and silver wherever he turned. He then happened to look out of the window. Good gracious! How grand it was! There was something else than pine forests and juniper bushes to look at, for there was the finest garden any one could wish for, with splendid trees and roses of all kinds. But he could not see a single human being, or even a cat; and that, you know, was rather lonely, for otherwise he had everything so grand and had been set up as his own master again.

So he took out the bit of paper:

"Lars, my lad!"

"What are master's orders?"

"Well now you have given me food and bed and a palace to live in, and I intend to remain here, for I like the place," he said, "yet I don't like to live quite by myself. I must have both lads and lasses whom I may order about to wait upon me," he said.

And there they were. There came servants and stewards and scullery maids and chambermaids of all sorts, and some came bowing and some curtseying. So now the duke thought he was really satisfied.

But now it happened that there was a large palace on the other side of the forest, and there the king lived who owned the forest, and the great, big fields around it. As he was walking up and down in his room he happened to look out through the window and saw the new palace, where the golden weathercocks were swinging to and fro on the roof in the sunlight, which dazzled his eyes.

"This is very strange," he thought; and so he called his courtiers. They came rushing in, and began bowing and scraping.

"Do you see the palace over there?" said the king.

They opened their eyes and began to stare.

Yes, of course they saw it.

"Who is it that has dared to build such a palace in my grounds?" said the king.

They bowed, and they scraped with their feet, but they did not know anything about it.

The king then called his generals and captains.

They came, stood to attention and presented arms.

"Be gone, soldiers and troopers," said the king, "and pull down the palace over there, and hang him who has built it; and don't lose any time about it!"

Well, they set off in great haste to arm themselves, and away they went. The drummers beat the skins of their drums, and the trumpeters blew their trumpets, and the other musicians played and blew as best they could, so that the duke heard them long before he could see them. But he had heard that kind of noise before, and knew what it meant, so he took out his scrap of paper:

"Lars, my lad!"

"What are master's orders?"

"There are soldiers coming here," he said, "and now you must provide me with soldiers and horses, that I may have double as many as those over in the wood, and with sabres and pistols, and guns and cannons with all that belongs to them; but be quick about it."

And no time was lost; for when the duke looked out, he saw an immense number of soldiers, who were drawn up around the palace.

When the king's men arrived, they came to a sudden halt and dared not advance. But the duke was not afraid; he went straight up to the colonel of the king's soldiers and asked him what he wanted.

The colonel told him his errand.

"It's of no use," said the duke. "You see how many men I have; and if the king will listen to me, we shall become good friends, and I will help him against his enemies, and in such a way that it will be heard of far and wide," he said.

The colonel was of the same opinion, and the duke then invited him and all his soldiers inside the palace, and the men had more than one glass to drink and plenty of everything to eat as well.

But while they were eating and drinking they began talking; and the duke then got to hear that the king had a daughter who was his only child, and was so wonderfully fair and beautiful that no one had ever seen her like before. And the more the king's soldiers ate and drank the more they thought she would suit the duke for a wife.

And they went on talking so long that the duke at last began to be of the same opinion. "The worst of it," said the soldiers, "is that she is just as proud as she is beautiful, and will never look at a man."

But the duke laughed at this. "If that's all," said the duke, "there's sure to be a remedy for that complaint."

When the soldiers had eaten and drunk as much as they could find room for, they shouted "Hurrah!" so that it echoed among the hills, and then they set out homewards. But, as you may imagine, they did not walk exactly in parade order, for they were rather unsteady about the knees, and many of them did not carry their guns in regulation manner. The duke asked them to greet the king from him. He would call on him the following day, he said.

When the duke was alone again, he began to think of the princess, and to wonder if she were as beautiful and fair as they had made her out to be. He would like to make sure of it; and as so many strange things had happened that day that it might not be impossible to find that out as well, he thought.

"Lars, my lad!"

"What are master's orders?"

"Well, now you must bring me the king's daughter as soon as she has gone to sleep," he said; "but she must not be awakened either on the way here or back. Do you hear that?" he said. And before long the princess was lying on the bed. She slept so soundly and looked so wonderfully beautiful, as she lay there. Yes, she was as sweet as sugar, I can tell you.

The duke walked round about her, but she was just as beautiful from whatever point of view he looked at her.

The more he looked the more he liked her.

"Lars, my lad!"

"What are master's orders?"

"You must now carry the princess home," he said, "for now I know how she looks, and to-morrow I will ask for her hand," he said.

Next morning the king looked out of the window. "I suppose I shall not be troubled with the sight of that palace any more," he thought. But, zounds! There it stood just as on the day before, and the sun shone so brightly on the roof, and the weathercocks dazzled his eyes.

He now became furious, and called all his men.

They came quicker than usual.

The courtiers bowed and scraped, and the soldiers stood to attention and presented arms.

"Do you see the palace there?" screamed the king.

They stretched their necks, and stared and gaped.

Yes, of course, that they did.

"Have I not ordered you to pull down the palace and hang the builder?" he said.

Yes, they could not deny that; but then the colonel himself stepped forward and reported what had happened and how many soldiers the duke had, and how wonderfully grand the palace was.

And next he told him what the duke had said, and how he had asked him to give his greetings to the king, and all that sort of thing.

The king felt quite confused, and had to put his crown on the table and scratch his head. He could not understand all this, although he was a king; for he could take his oath it had all been built in a single night; and if the duke were not the evil one himself, he must in any case have done it by magic.

While he sat there pondering, the princess came into the room.

"Good morning to you, father!" she said. "Just fancy, I had such a strange and beautiful dream last night!" she said.

"What did you dream then, my girl?" said the king.

"I dreamt I was in the new palace over yonder, and that I saw a duke there, so fine and handsome that I could never have imagined the like; and now I want to get married, father," she said.

"Do you want to get married? you, who never cared to look at a man! That's very strange!" said the king.

"That may be," said the princess; "but it's different now, and I want to get married, and it's the duke I want," she said.

The king was quite beside himself, so frightened did he become of the duke.

But all of a sudden he heard a terrible noise of drums and trumpets and instruments of all kinds; and then came a message that the duke had just arrived with a large company, all of whom were so grandly dressed that gold and silver glistened in every fold. The king put on his crown and his coronation robes, and then went out on the steps to receive them. And the princess was not slow to follow him.

The duke bowed most graciously, and the king of course did likewise, and when they had talked a while about their affairs and their grandeur they became the best of friends. A great banquet was then prepared, and the duke was placed next to the princess at the table. What they talked about is not easy to tell, but the duke spoke so well for himself that the princess could not very well say "no" to anything he said, and then he went up to the king and asked for her hand. The king could not exactly say "no" either, for he could very well see that the duke was a person with whom it were best to be on friendly terms; but give his sanction there and then, he could not very well do that either. He wanted to see the duke's palace first, and find out about the state of affairs over there, as you may understand.

So it was arranged that he should visit the duke and take the princess with him to see his palace; and with this they parted company.

When the duke returned home, Lars became busier than ever, for there was so much to attend to. But he set to work and strove hard; and when the king and his daughter arrived everything was so magnificent and splendid that no words can describe it. They went through all the rooms and looked about, and they found everything as it should be, and even still more splendid, thought the king, and so he was quite pleased.

The wedding then took place, and that in grand style; and on the duke's arrival home with his bride he too gave a great feast, and then there was an end to the festivities.

Some time passed by, and one evening the duke heard these words:

"Are you satisfied now?"

It was Lars, as you may guess, but the duke could not see him.

"Well, I ought to be," said the duke. "You have provided me with everything I have," he said.

"Yes, but what have I got in return?" asked Lars.

"Nothing," said the duke; "but, bless me, what could I have given you, who are not of flesh and blood, and whom I cannot see either?" he said. "But if there is anything I can do for you, tell me what it is, and I shall do it."

"Well, I should like to ask you for that little scrap of paper which you found in the chest," said Lars.

"Nothing else?" said the duke. "If such a trifle can help you, I can easily do without it, for now I begin to know the words by heart," he said.

Lars thanked the duke, and asked him to put the paper on the chair in front of the bed, when he retired to rest, and he would be sure to fetch it during the night.

The duke did as he was told; and so he and the princess lay down and went to sleep.

But early in the morning the duke awoke and felt so cold that his teeth chattered, and when he had got his eyes quite open he found he was quite naked and had not even as much as a thread on his back; and instead of the grand bed and the beautiful bedroom, and the magnificent palace, he lay on the big chest in the old tumble-down hut.

He began to shout:

"Lars, my lad!" But he got no answer. He shouted once more:

"Lars, my lad!" But he got no answer this time either. So he shouted all he could:

"Lars, my lad!" But it was all in vain.

Now he began to understand how matters stood. When Lars had got the scrap of paper he was freed from service at the same time, and now he had taken everything with him. But there was no help for it. There stood the duke in the old hut quite naked; and as for the princess she was not much better off, although she had her clothes on, for she had got them from her father, so Lars had no power over them.

The duke had now to tell the princess everything, and ask her to leave him. He would have to manage as best he could, he said. But she would not hear of it. She well remembered what the parson had said when he married them, and she would never, never leave him, she said.

In the meantime the king in his palace had also awakened, and when he looked out of the window he did not see any sign whatever of the other palace, where his daughter and son-in-law lived. He became uneasy, as you may imagine, and called his courtiers.

They came in, and began to bow and scrape.

"Do you see the palace over yonder behind the forest?" he asked.

They stretched their necks and stared with all their might.

No, they did not see it.

"Where has it gone to, then?" asked the king.

Well, really they did not know.

It was not long before the king had set out with all his court through the forest; and when he arrived at the place where the palace with the beautiful gardens should have been, he could not see anything but heather and juniper bushes and firs. But then he discovered the old tumble-down hut, which stood there among the bushes. He entered the hut and—mercy on us!—what a sight met his eyes! There stood his son-in-law, quite naked, and his daughter, who had not very many clothes on either, and who was crying and moaning.

"Dear, dear! what does all this mean?" said the king; but he did not get any answer, for the duke would rather have died then tell him.

The king did his utmost to get him to speak; but in spite of all the king's promises and threats the duke remained obstinate and would not utter a word.

The king then became angry—and no wonder, for now he could see that his grand duke was not what he pretended to be, and so he ordered the duke to be hanged, and that without any loss of time. The princess begged and prayed for mercy; but neither prayers not tears were of any help now; for an impostor he was, and as an impostor he should die, said the king.

And so it had to be. They erected a gallows, and placed the rope round the duke's neck. But while they were getting the gallows ready, the princess got hold of the hangman, and gave both him and his assistant some money, that they should so manage the hanging of the duke that he should not lose his life, and in the night they were to cut him down, so that he and the princess might then flee the country. And that's how the matter was arranged.

In the meantime they had strung up the duke, and the king and his court and all the people went their way.

The duke was not in great straits. He had, however, plenty of time to reflect how foolish he had been in not saving some of the crumbs when he was living in plenty, and how unpardonably stupid he had been in letting Lars have the scrap of paper. This vexed him more than all. If only he had it again, he thought, they should see he had been gaining some sense in return for all he had lost. But it is of little use snarling if you haven't got any teeth. "Ah, well, well!" he sighed, and so he dangled his legs, which was really all he could do.

The day passed slowly and tediously for him, and he was not at all displeased when he saw the sun setting behind the forest. But just before it disappeared he heard a fearful shouting, and when he looked down the hill, he saw seven cart-loads of worn-out shoes, and on the top of the hindmost cart he saw a little old man in grey clothes and with a red pointed cap on his head. His face was like that of the worst scarecrow, and the rest of him was not very handsome either.

He drove straight up to the gallows, and when he arrived right under it he stopped and looked up at the duke, and then burst out laughing, the ugly old fellow!

"How stupid you were!" he said; "but what should the fool do with his stupidity if he did not make use of it?" And then he laughed again. "Yes, there you are hanging now, and here am I carting away all the shoes I have worn out for your whims. I wonder if you can read what is written on this bit of paper, and if you recognize it?" he said with an ugly laugh, holding up the paper before the duke's eyes.

But all who hang are not dead, and this time it was Lars who was befooled.

The duke made a clutch, and snatched the paper from him.

"Lars, my lad!"

"What are master's orders?"

"Well, you must cut me down from the gallows and put the palace and all the rest in its place again, exactly as it was before, and when the night has set in you must bring back the princess."

All went merrily as in a dance, and before long everything was in its place, just as it was when Lars took himself off.

When the king awoke the next morning he looked out of the window, as was his custom, and there stood the palace again, with the weather-cocks glittering so beautifully in the sunshine. He called his courtiers, and they came and began to bow and scrape.

They stretched their necks as far as they could, and stared and gaped.

"Do you see the palace over there?" said the king.

Yes, of course they did.

The king then sent for the princess, but she was not to be found. He then went out to see if his son-in-law was still hanging on the gallows, but neither son-in-law nor gallows was to be seen.

He had to lift off his crown and scratch his head. But that did not improve matters; he could not make head or tail of either one thing or the other. He set off at once with all his court through the forest, and when he came to the place where the palace should stand, there it stood sure enough. The gardens and the roses were exactly as they used to be, and the duke's people were to be seen everywhere among the trees. His son-in-law and his daughter received him on the steps, dressed in their finest clothes.

"Well, I never saw the like of this," said the king to himself; he could scarcely believe his own eyes, so wonderful did it all seem to him.

"God's peace be with you, father, and welcome here!" said the duke.

The king stood staring at him.

"Lars, My Lad!"

"Are you my son-in-law?" he asked.

"Well, I suppose I am," said the duke. "Who else should I be?"

"Did I not order you to be hanged yesterday like any common thief?" said the king.

"I think you must have been bewitched on the way," said the duke, with a laugh. "Do you think I am the man to let myself be hanged? Or is there any one here who dares to believe it?" he said, and looked so fiercely at the courtiers that they felt as if they were being pierced through and through.

They bowed and scraped and cringed before him.

"Who could believe such a thing? Was it at all likely?"

"Well, if there is any one who dares to say the king could have wished me such evil, let him speak out," said the duke, and fixed his eyes upon them still more fiercely than before.

They went on bowing and scraping and cringing.

How could any one dare to say such a thing? No, they had more sense than that, they should hope.

The king did not know what to believe, for when he looked at the duke he thought he never could have wished him such evil; but still he was not quite convinced.

"Did I not come here yesterday, and was not the whole palace gone, and was there not an old hut in its place? And did not I go into that hut, and did not you stand stark naked right before my eyes?" he asked.

"I wonder the king can talk so," said the duke. "I think the trolls must have bewitched your eyes in the forest and made you quite crazy; or what do you think?" he said, and turned round to the courtiers.

They bowed and bowed till their backs were bent double, and agreed with everything he said, there could be no mistake about that. The king rubbed his eyes, and looked round about him.

"I suppose it is as you say, then," he said to the duke, "and it is well I have got back my proper sight and have come to my senses again. For it would have been a sin and a shame if I had let you be hanged," he said; and so he was happy again, and nobody thought any more about the matter.

"Once bitten, twice shy," as the proverb says; and the duke now took upon himself to manage and look after most of his affairs, so that it was seldom Lars had to wear out his shoes. The king soon gave the duke half the kingdom into the bargain; so he had now plenty to do, and people said they would have to search a long time to find his equal in wise and just ruling.

Then one day Lars came to the duke, looking very little better than the first time he had seen him; but he was, of course, more humble, and did not dare to giggle and make grimaces.

"You do not want my help any longer, now," he said; "for although I did wear out my shoes at first, I am now unable to wear out a single pair, and my feet will soon be covered all over with moss. So I thought I might now get my leave of absence," he said.

The duke quite agreed with him. "I have tried to spare you, and I almost think I could do without you," he said. "But the palace and all the rest I do not want to lose, for such a clever builder as you I shall never get again; nor do I ever want to adorn the gallows again, as you can well understand; so I cannot give you back the paper on any account," he said.

"Well, as long as you have got it, I need not fear," said Lars; "but if anybody else should get hold of it there will be nothing but running and trudging about again, and that's what I want to avoid; for when one has been tramping about for a thousand years, as I have done, one begins to get tired of it," he said.

But they went on talking, and at last they agreed that the duke should put the paper in the box, and then bury it seven ells under the ground, under a stone fixed in the earth. They then thanked one another for the time they had spent in each other's company, and so they parted.

The duke carried out his part of the agreement, for he was not likely to want to change it. He lived happy and contented with the princess, and they had both sons and daughters. When the king died, he got the whole of the kingdom, and you may guess he was none the worse off for that; and there no doubt he still lives and reigns, if he is not dead.

But as for that box with the scrap of paper in it, there are many who are still running about looking for it.

# THE SAUSAGE

THERE WAS once an old woman, who was all alone one evening in her cottage, occupied with her household affairs. While she was waiting for her husband, who was away at work over in the forest, and while she was bustling about, a fine, grand lady came in, and so the woman began to curtsey and curtsey, for she had never seen such a grand person before.

"I should be so much obliged if you would lend me your brewing pan," said the lady, "for my daughter is going to be married, and I expect guests from all parts."

Oh, dear, yes! That she might have, said the woman, although she could not remember whether she had ever seen her before, and so she went to fetch the pan.

The lady took it, and thanked the woman, saying that she would pay her well for the loan of it, and so she went her way.

Two days afterwards the lady came back with it, and this time she also found the woman alone.

"Many thanks for the loan," said the lady, "and now in return you shall have three wishes."

And with this the lady left, and vanished so quickly that the old woman had not even time to ask her name or where she lived. But that did not matter, she thought, for now she had three wishes, and she began to think what she should wish for. She expected her husband back soon, and she thought it would be best to wait till he came home and could have a say in the matter. But the least they could wish for must be a fine big farm—the best in the parish, and a box full of money, and just fancy how happy and comfortable they would be then, for they had worked so hard all their days! Ah, yes, then the neighbours would have something to wonder at, for you may guess how they would stare at all the fine things she would have.

But since they were now so rich it was really a shame that there should be nothing but some blue, sour milk and some hard crusts of bread in the cupboard for her husband when he came home tired and weary, he who was fond of hot food. She had just been to her neighbour's, and there she had seen a fine big sausage, which they were going to have for supper.

"Ah, deary me, I wish I had that sausage here!" sighed the old woman; and the next moment a big sausage lay on the table right before her.

She was just going to put it in the pan when her husband came in.

"Father, father!" cried the woman, "it's all over with our troubles and hard work now. I lent my brewing pan to a fine lady, and when she brought it back she promised we should have three wishes. And now you must help me to wish for something really good, for you're so clever at hitting upon the right thing—and it's all true, for just look at the sausage, which I got the moment I wished for it!"

"What do you mean, you silly old woman?" shouted the husband, who became angry. "Have you been wishing for such a paltry thing as a sausage, when you might have had anything you liked in the world? I wish the sausage were sticking to your nose, since you haven't any better sense."

All at once the woman gave a cry, for sure enough there was the sausage sticking to her nose; and she began tearing and pulling away at it, but the more she pulled the firmer it seemed to stick. She was not able to get it off.

"Oh, dear! oh, dear!" sobbed the woman. "You don't seem to have any more sense than I, since you can wish me such ill luck. I only wanted something nice for you, and then——, oh, dear! oh, dear!" and the old woman went on crying and sobbing.

The husband tried, of course, to help his wife to get rid of the sausage; but for all he pulled and tugged away at it he did not succeed, and he was nearly pulling his wife's head off her body.

But they had one wish left, and what were they now to wish?

Yes, what were they to wish? They might, of course, wish for something very fine and grand; but what could they do with all the finery in the world, as long as the mistress of the house had a long sausage sticking to the end of her nose? She would never be able to show herself anywhere!

"You wish for something," said the woman in the midst of her crying.

"No, you wish," said the husband, who also began crying when he saw the state his wife was in, and saw the terrible sausage hanging down her face.

So he thought he would make the best use he could of the last wish, and said:

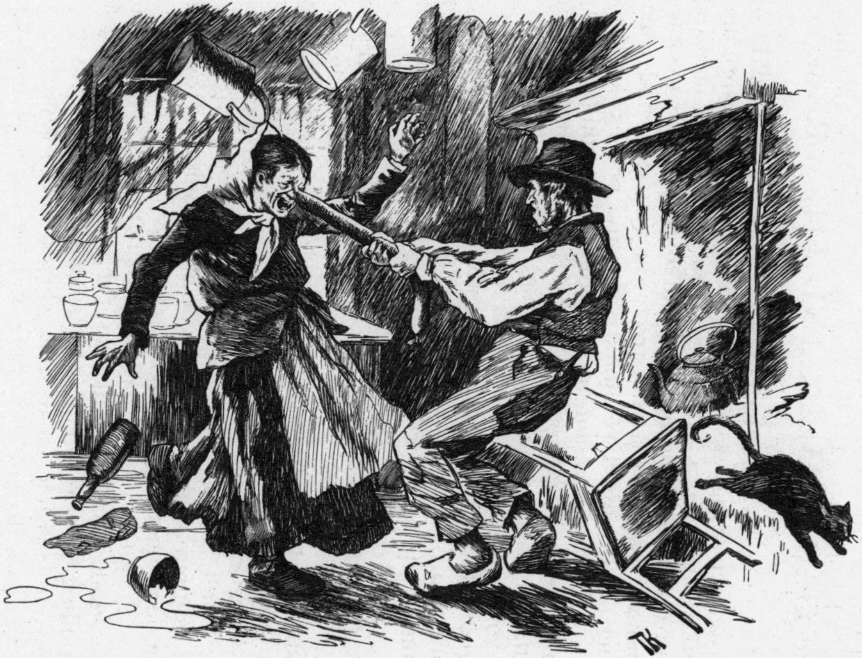

THE SAUSAGE

"I wish my wife was rid of that sausage."

And the next moment it was gone!

They both became so glad that they jumped up and danced round the room in great glee—for you must know that although a sausage may be ever so nice when you have it in your mouth, it is quite a different thing to having one sticking to your nose all your life.

# THE OLD WOMAN AND THE TRAMP

THERE WAS once a tramp, who went plodding his way through a forest. The distance between the houses was so great that he had little hope of finding a shelter before the night set in. But all of a sudden he saw some lights between the trees. He then discovered a cottage, where there was a fire burning on the hearth. How nice it would be to roast one's self before that fire, and to get a bite of something, he thought; and so he dragged himself towards the cottage.

Just then an old woman came towards him.

"Good evening, and well met!" said the tramp.

"Good evening," said the woman. "Where do you come from?"

"South of the sun, and east of the moon," said the tramp; "and now I am on the way home again, for I have been all over the world with the exception of this parish," he said.

"You must be a great traveller, then," said the woman. "What may be your business here?"

"Oh, I want a shelter for the night," he said.

"I thought as much," said the woman; "but you may as well get away from here at once, for my husband is not at home, and my place is not an inn," she said.

"My good woman," said the tramp, "you must not be so cross and hard-hearted, for we are both human beings, and should help one another, it is written."

"Help one another?" said the woman, "help? Did you ever hear such a thing? Who'll help me, do you think? I haven't got a morsel in the house! No, you'll have to look for quarters elsewhere," she said.

But the tramp was like the rest of his kind; he did not consider himself beaten at the first rebuff. Although the old woman grumbled and complained as much as she could, he was just as persistent as ever, and went on begging and praying like a starved dog, until at last she gave in, and he got permission to lie on the floor for the night.

That was very kind, he thought, and he thanked her for it.

"Better on the floor without sleep, than suffer cold in the forest deep," he said; for he was a merry fellow, this tramp, and was always ready with a rhyme.

When he came into the room he could see that the woman was not so badly off as she had pretended; but she was a greedy and stingy woman of the worst sort, and was always complaining and grumbling.

He now made himself very agreeable, of course, and asked her in his most insinuating manner for something to eat.

"Where am I to get it from?" said the woman. "I haven't tasted a morsel myself the whole day."

But the tramp was a cunning fellow, he was.

"Poor old granny, you must be starving," he said. "Well, well, I suppose I shall have to ask you to have something with me, then."

"Have something with you!" said the woman. "You don't look as if you could ask any one to have anything! What have you got to offer one, I should like to know?'

"He who far and wide does roam sees many things not known at home; and he who many things has seen has wits about him and senses keen," said the tramp. "Better dead than lose one's head! Lend me a pot, granny!"

The old woman now became very inquisitive, as you may guess, and so she let him have a pot.

He filled it with water and put it on the fire, and then he blew with all his might till the fire was burning fiercely all round it. Then he took a four-inch nail from his pocket, turned it three times in his hand and put it into the pot.

The woman stared with all her might.

"What's this going to be?" she asked.

"Nail broth," said the tramp, and began to stir the water with the porridge stick.

"Nail broth?" asked the woman.

"Yes, nail broth," said the tramp.

The old woman had seen and heard a good deal in her time, but that anybody could have made broth with a nail, well, she had never heard the like before.

"That's something for poor people to know," she said, "and I should like to learn how to make it."

"That which is not worth having, will always go a-begging," said the tramp.

But if she wanted to learn how to make it she had only to watch him, he said, and went on stirring the broth.

The old woman squatted on the ground, her hands clasping her knees, and her eyes following his hand as he stirred the broth.

"This generally makes good broth," he said; "but this time it will very likely be rather thin, for I have been making broth the whole week with the same nail. If one only had a handful of sifted oatmeal to put in, that would make it all right," he said. "But what one has to go without, it's no use thinking more about," and so he stirred the broth again.

"Well, I think I have a scrap of flour somewhere," said the old woman, and went out to fetch some, and it was both good and fine.

The tramp began putting the flour into the broth, and went on stirring, while the woman sat staring now at him and then at the pot until her eyes nearly burst their sockets.

"This broth would be good enough for company," he said, putting in one handful of flour after another. "If I had only a bit of salted beef and a few potatoes to put in, it would be fit for gentlefolks, however particular they might be," he said. "But what one has to go without, it's no use thinking more about."

When the old woman really began to think it over, she thought she had some potatoes, and perhaps a bit of beef as well; and these she gave the tramp, who went on stirring, while she sat and stared as hard as ever.

"This will be grand enough for the best in the land," he said.

"Well, I never!" said the woman; "and just fancy—all with a nail!"

He was really a wonderful man, that tramp! He could do more than drink a sup and turn the tankard up, he could.

"If one had only a little barley and a drop of milk, we could ask the king himself to have some of it," he said; "for this is what he has every blessed evening—that I know, for I have been in service under the king's cook" he said.

"Dear me! Ask the king to have some! Well, I never!" exclaimed the woman, slapping her knees. She was quite awestruck at the tramp and his grand connections.

"But what one has to go without, it's no use thinking more about," said the tramp.

And then she remembered she had a little barley; and as for milk, well, she wasn't quite out of that, she said, for her best cow had just calved. And then she went to fetch both the one and the other.

The tramp went on stirring, and the woman sat staring, one moment at him and the next at the pot.

Then all at once the tramp took out the nail.

"Now it's ready, and now we'll have a real good feast," he said. "But to this kind of soup the king and the queen always take a dram or two, and one sandwich at least. And then they always have a cloth on the table when they eat," he said. "But what one has to go without, it's no use thinking more about."

But by this time the old woman herself had begun to feel quite grand and fine, I can tell you; and if that was all that was wanted to make it just as the king had it, she thought it would be nice to have it just the same way for once, and play at being king and queen with the tramp. She went straight to a cupboard and brought out the brandy bottle, dram glasses, butter and cheese, smoked beef and veal, until at last the table looked as if it were decked out for company.

Never in her life had the old woman had such a grand feast, and never had she tasted such broth, and just fancy, made only with a nail!

She was in such a good and merry humour at having learnt such an economical way of making broth that she did not know how to make enough of the tramp who had taught her such a useful thing.

So they ate and drank, and drank and ate, until they became both tired and sleepy.

The tramp was now going to lie down on the floor. But that would never do, thought the old woman; no, that was impossible. "Such a grand person much have a bed to lie in," she said.

THE OLD WOMAN AND THE TRAMP

He did not need much pressing. "It's just like the sweet Christmas time," he said, "and a nicer woman I never came across. Ah, well! Happy are they who meet with such good people," said he; and he lay down on the bed and went asleep.

And next morning when he woke the first thing he got was coffee and a dram.

When he was going the old woman gave him a bright dollar piece.

"And thanks, many thanks, for what you have taught me," she said. "Now I shall live in comfort, since I have learnt how to make broth with a nail."

"Well it isn't very difficult, if one only has something good to add to it," said the tramp as he went his way.

The woman stood at the door staring after him.

"Such people don't grow on every bush," she said.

# WHAT SHALL BABY'S NAME BE?

THERE WAS once upon a time a worthy and well-to-do couple, who lived on the fat of the land, and had their house full of everything that was good and nice. But of children they had not many, for there was only one daughter in the house, and her they called Peggy, although she was christened Margaret, as you may guess.

Whatever the cause might be, whether the girl was ugly or whether there was anything else the matter with her, she grew up to be a big wench of full five and twenty years, and yet there was no suitor who would look at her.

"It's very strange," thought the father to himself; for all the lads in the parish knew, of course, that he had one of the finest farms, and many, many hundreds of dollars in money as well, and that he could give his daughter as a dowry both oxen and cows, goats and sheep, and that he would let his son-in-law take over the whole of the farm and keep the old folks till they died. He was never sparing with words on this subject. "Yes, they must be a silly, crack-brained lot when they don't avail themselves of such an opportunity, and get hold of one's only daughter," thought both the man and his wife. Peggy thought the same, although she did not say as much; but the lads seemed to keep away just as much as ever, for day after day passed, and year after year, but still no suitor came.

So one summer evening, as the man sat looking down the road and longing that a suitor might come, it happened that one of the best and smartest lads from one of the farms in the parish came strolling up the hill.

"Mother, mother!" cried the man. "I think he's coming at last! Come and have a look!"

His wife came running into the room and began staring out through the window.

"Well, what did I say?" she exclaimed. "If it isn't Peter South-farm! Sure enough it's he!"

She rushed out of the room again and began to bustle about and tidy her chamber, and called Peggy.

"Look out, wench! Now he's coming!"

"Whom do you mean, mother?"

"Why, your sweetheart, of course."

"Eh, you don't say so, mother!" cried Peggy, and became so pleased that she was quite beside herself.

And now they set to work to tidy and smarten themselves, and prepare something for the stranger who was coming up the road, for such a rare guest one could not expect every day.

In the meantime the suitor—for they had guessed quite rightly, a suitor it was—had entered the room, and greeted the man with a "good evening."

"Good evening," replied the man, and asked him to sit down. "One needs some rest, when one has walked up a steep hill like this," he said.

But the lad needed some pressing, it seemed.

He did not know if he would be welcome, he said; and so it was best that he should remain at the door till he had told his errand.

The man felt his heart leaping in his breast.

For many years he had longed for some one to come on such an errand, for he knew well what the lad was after.

"What errand might that be?" he asked.

"Well it's rather an important matter," said the suitor.

The man called his wife, and she came in and greeted the lad.

"Excuse me—but may I ask," said the lad, "if there is a nice young girl here called Margaret?"

Yes, indeed there was—their only child, a big grown-up wench! And so clever with her hands—she could sew and stitch, spin and weave, both plain and striped and patterned—and she wasn't above taking off her gold ring and giving a hand at heavy work, if it was wanted. And then she was their only daughter, and was going to have the whole of the farm, the oxen and cows, the goats and sheep, and silver and gold, the clothes, the money and woven stuffs of all kinds as her dowry.

Both the man and his wife went on jabbering and chattering at the same time, and got so excited that it was with the greatest difficulty that the suitor was allowed to explain his errand.

She was just the girl he was looking out for, he said, and as he had no spokesman with him he would have to speak for himself, and tell them how he was off at home, and hear if they, who were her parents, would be satisfied with a son-in-law like him, he said.

"Well, that is quite possible," said the man. He himself was now so old and worn out and broken down with rheumatics that he wanted some one to take over the farm, so he could not very well refuse a good offer, he said. But one could not talk over such matters at the door; the lad must come inside, and partake of what his wife could offer.

"But this much I may say, at any rate," said the man, trying to put on a grand air, "that many have already spoken to me on the subject; but it is you, do you see, just you, that I have been waiting for," he said; "and you may reckon yourself lucky that you have not come too late. And, mother, you see, she agrees with everything I say—or, what do you think, mother?"

She had so much to attend to and look after, she said, but she was of the same mind as her husband. "And Peggy," said the man, "she is a good and obedient child. She does everything we tell her."

Peggy stood outside the door and kept it ajar, while she peeped through the opening, and would have said "yes" there and then, if it had only been proper. But she could not show herself too willing, either.

The man and the suitor now began to help themselves to the refreshments, and to talk about their farms and about the harvest, and about the number of cattle each of them could feed during the winter on their farms, and such things, while the wife was busy smartening up Peggy, whose head was so full of courtship and marriage that she was quite unfit to do anything for herself. But when she was dressed she looked very smart and shone like the sun, and then, as you may guess, she was to go in and see her suitor.

But she could not go in empty handed, and so here mother hit upon the idea—for women are always so artful—that Peggy should go down to the cellar for beer, and then come in to her suitor with the large silver cup in her hand.

While she was on her way down to the cellar she began thinking that when she was married it might easily happen that she, like others, would have a child; and then she went on thinking and pondering what she should call her first baby, for a name it must have, of course; but what should it be? Yes, what ought she to call it!

But she could not make up her mind about it, although she thought and pondered all she could, till at last she quite forgot both the cellar and the beer, the suitor and the rest of the world. It was really not an easy matter either, for she could not know whether it would be a boy or a girl; but whatever it might be, the baby must have a name, and a really fine name, too, you must know.

But what should it be?

Yes, what should baby's name be?

While she stood there meditating her father and the suitor sat in the room partaking of the refreshments before them—smoked ham and cheese and other good things which the wife had in her cupboard.

One oatmeal cake after the other disappeared while they were waiting for the beer and the girl, and they began to think that the wolves must have got hold of her, since she did not come back.

"She is so shy and childish, that girl of mine," said the wife, "and I shouldn't wonder if she is afraid to come in. I shall have to fetch her, I suppose!"

And she hurried out to look for Peggy, whom she found standing outside the cellar-door, pondering and thinking.

"You are like Noah's raven, you are! How can a big wench like you

stand there like that? I do believe you have lost your senses! Why
don't you go in to your suitor?" said her mother. "What is it you are
thinking about?"

"Oh, my dear mother," said Peggy, "I am just thinking what my first
baby should be called. Can you tell me, mother?"

"Bless me, girl, if I can," said the woman; "but a name it must
have, the little angel—and a fine name it must be. But what shall it be?
Let me see."

And she too began thinking and remained standing there.

As neither his daughter nor his wife came back the man became
uneasy.

"This is really too bad," he said, "that Peggy should make herself so
precious. She is not generally so contrary, and I am sure that she'll say
'yes' just as willingly as we do," he said. "I suppose I must go myself and
fetch her."

And so he limped out of the room as quickly as he could.

When he saw his wife and daughter standing outside the cellar-door
he burst into a furious rage and shouted:

"I think you must have gone out of your minds, standing there like a
pair of sundials, while you have got a suitor in the house! Just come in,
will you?"

"Yes, yes," said the wife; "but I must tell you, we have been trying to
settle a very ticklish business."

"Well, then, what might that be?" said the man.

"Why,—what shall Peggy's first baby be called?"

"Oh, is that it?" said the man, looking as tender and pleased as if he
had the youngster on his arm. "So, that's it, is it?—Well, the baby must
have a really fine name,—the little angel! But what shall we call it?—Yes,
what shall we call it?

He began to scratch his head and to think and ponder. He did not
know either whether it would be a boy or a girl,—but no matter which it
was, the baby must have a name, and what should it be called?—yes, what
should they call it?"

He couldn't make up his mind either, and so he remained standing
there as well.

In the meantime the suitor had been sitting all by himself in the parlour, and was getting tired of waiting. So, as neither the maiden nor the
old folks came back, he thought they must be doing it purposely, and had
made up their minds to make a fool of him; whereupon he became
furious, and took his hat and went.

When he came out into the farmyard he saw them all three standing
outside the cellar-door.

The man caught sight of him first. "I must tell you, my lad," he said,
"we have been standing here thinking over a very important matter,—
and that is, what shall Peggy's first baby be called?"

"Good gracious!" said the suitor, "that'll surely bear thinking over, and
you may have to think it over for a long time," he said, "for the baby will
not be called after me! That's as certain as the sun rose this morning."
And with that he lifted his hat and went down the hill.

The old man began to shout after him, but it was of no use. He went down the road and never came back again.

What happened afterwards I have not heard a word about; but if a suitor ever did call again, they would, no doubt, take care not to lose their heads over such useless speculations,—for we all know that there is a time for everything, and that we should strike while the iron is hot.

# ST. PETER AND THE TWO WOMEN

IN THE days when St. Peter walked about on earth he came late one evening to a large farm, and asked for shelter for the night. The master was not at home, but his wife was sitting all alone; and although she was very rich and had an abundance of everything one could wish, she was stingy beyond all belief. She could not give him shelter—was it likely she could?—and what should she give him to eat, and where should she put him? No, he would have to try somewhere else, she said; and, as there was no help for it, so he did.

When he had gone a little way he came to a small cottage, where there lived a poor widow, who struggled and toiled at spinning and weaving in order to scrape together a little food for herself and her children. St. Peter went into the parlour and told her his errand. The woman said, what was only too true, that she had little either of money or of food, but the little she had she would willingly share with him, since he had to go from house to house and beg for scraps of food—for she did not know it was St. Peter, nor did he say anything about it himself either.

So he got permission to stop there for the night, and he was quite welcome to what she could give him to eat. Early next morning he thanked her for her kindness and got ready to go.

"I have no money to pay you with," he said; "but what I can give I will give you. The first thing you do to-day you shall be doing all the day," he said.

The woman could not understand what he meant by this; but as soon as he was gone she took her yard-measure, for she had finished a piece of weaving and was going to take it off the loom in the evening, as she wanted to know how long it was.

She began to measure and to count, and she got to seventy, eighty, ninety and one hundred; but it was the most remarkable piece of cloth she had ever seen, for the more she measured the longer it became. The whole room became full of it, so that she had to go into the passage, but still there was no end to the piece.

The passage, too, became filled, so she had to go out on the grass. She measured and measured, but still the cloth grew longer, much longer than she could measure. She would not give in, but kept unceasingly at it the whole day. Towards evening the rich farmer's wife came past the

St. Peter and the Two Women

cottage, and when she saw what the widow was doing she stopped all at once and wondered greatly at what she saw, for such a piece of weaving no human being had surely ever seen.

"What in all the world are you doing?" she asked.

"Twenty-three, twenty-four, twenty-five! Measuring a piece of weaving," said the widow. She was far on in the thirteenth hundred.

"Where in all the world have you got such a long piece from?" asked the woman.

"Twelve and twenty, thirteen and twenty, nineteen and twenty," said the widow—she had lost count, but still she kept on measuring. "Yes, you may well ask that," she said, and went on measuring. "A man came here last night and got a night's lodging, and when he left here this morning he said that the first thing I began with I should be doing the whole day; and now I have been measuring this cloth, which seems never to come to an end."

"Oh dear! oh dear! How stupid I was! How terribly stupid I was to let him go!" said the farmer's wife; "for he came to our place also, you must know. But, my dear, if he should ever come this way again and look in upon you you might send him to me, since you have been so lucky," she said.

Yes, that she would be glad to do, said the widow. She wished other people might be just as fortunate as she herself had been, although she had nothing to thank the farmer's wife for.

Of course, the widow could not use all the cloth herself, so she went to some of her neighbours to hire some oxen to cart it to town; and, just fancy, the cloth filled three cart-loads! Such a quantity of cloth had never been seen in one day in the market place; but she got rid of every yard for all that, and returned home with so much money that she had no longer any need to trouble about clothes and food.

But the rich farmer's wife went home and began to bustle about and get things ready, so that she should be able to treat the stranger in good style if he should come back to her; but she knew no more than the widow that the stranger was St. Peter.

She went about in great expectation, and dared scarcely go out of the room, so afraid was she that he should come in her absence and that she should miss him. She had bought a very fine piece of cloth and placed it on the loom, and the measure was lying on the top of it, so she was fully prepared for him; but day after day passed and week after week, and she grew angry and impatient because he was such a silly fellow not to have the sense to find his way there.

Late one evening there was a knock at the door.

The woman went out into the passage and pulled back the bolt. It was St. Peter, who asked for shelter for the night. Yes, that he should have, sure enough; and the woman curtseyed and behaved in a way that was quite ridiculous.

She then put the best she had on the table, so that he should be quite satisfied. In the morning he thanked her for her kindness and the good food, and prepared to go.

"Just one word, my good man," said the woman; "when you got shelter

ST. PETER AND THE TWO WOMEN

at my neighbour's some time ago you gave her a promise, and you might as well give me one," she said, and curtseyed and made herself most agreeable and pleasant.

"What promise might that be?" asked St. Peter.

"Well, you said that whatever she began with she should be doing all the day," said the woman.

"Would you also like that?" said St. Peter.

"Should I like it? Why, my good man, of course, I should," said the woman. "I have the measure in my hand and the cloth handy."

"Well, I suppose I must do the same for you as for her then," said St. Peter; "so the first thing you do when I am gone you shall be doing the whole day. But, whatever you do, think it well over first," he said.

The woman curtseyed and thanked him, and was very happy and contented.

"Now I shall measure so much cloth that I shall have more than the poor body over yonder," she thought; and turned round and went back into the room.

Suddenly she remembered she ought to have drawn some water from the pump for her kettle, so that she could go on measuring the cloth without being disturbed. So she went to the pump and began to draw the water; but as this was the first thing she did after St. Peter was gone, there was no help for it—she must go on pumping water the whole day. The water came rushing out of the pump and ran all over the yard. It rose higher and higher as the hours crept by, and the woman began to shout and cry for help; but no one came to her assistance, and probably no one could have helped her either. When the sun was about to set the water had reached up to her chin. She was now quite exhausted, and all of a sudden she sank back into the water and was drowned. The yard measure and the cloth floated about on the water, and they may be floating there still for all I know.

# THE VALIANT CHANTICLEER

THERE WAS once upon a time a married couple who had no children, and they did not know what to do to get a child. The husband did not seem to mind so much, but the wife could not rest till she had a child. She must have one, whatever happened; and she went to doctors and wise men, and consulted all who knew a little more than other people, but to no avail. There was no one who could give her any advice.

So one evening an old woman came and asked for shelter for the night, which she got. But when women get together they always find something to talk about, and before long the wife had told the old woman all about herself and her affairs, and what a pity it was that she had no children.

"Is it no worse than that?" said the woman. "There's a way out of that!

Look," she said, "here is an egg for you, and when you put it in your bosom and keep it nice and warm, you will soon have a little one, and a wonderful child it will be; such a child you have never seen," she said.

The wife thought this was strange, but there are so many strange things in this world that it was hardly worth while to wonder much about it. She took the egg and thanked the woman for her good advice, and said she would do as she was bid, and with this they parted.

She put the egg in her bosom and tended it well and carefully, and kept it as warm as she possibly could, and after a time a little cockerel flew out of it. The wife was not very pleased at this, you can understand, for she had not expected it would end in this way.

But as she had hatched him herself, she supposed he must be her child after all, such as he was. She looked after him and gathered food together for him, and cackled to him, and made herself as much like a hen as she could. And so he grew up and got both feathers and comb, and became so big, so big, that his equal had never been seen before.

When he was full-feathered he had to go out and find what he could, and he began to kick and scratch about in the dust heap, so that the rubbish was thrown up in the air so high that no one could see what became of it. But he wanted to try if he could do more than that, and so he strutted out into the corn-field, where the master of the house was toiling away and ploughing with the one ox he possessed. But he got on very slowly, so the cock thought he ought to help him. So he was yoked to the plough; and then things took a different turn, for now they went at such a speed that the master had to run as fast as he could, and in a little while the cock had ploughed the whole field. He now thought he was a full-grown fellow, and that he could get married; but not to a little farm-yard hen, that would never do for him. No, he must look higher, and so he flapped his wings and crowed.

"The king's daughter shall be mine!" and he wanted to set out for the king's palace.

But he must have a suitable conveyance for the bride, he thought, even if he had to drag it himself; and as there was nothing else to be found, he took the big soup-ladle. The wife cried and cackled after him, but out into the world he must go, and away he went.

All at once he met a fox.

"Where are you going?" asked the fox.

"To the king's palace," crowed the cock.

"May I come with you?" said the fox.

"Sit up behind," cried the cock; and the fox took a seat in the ladle, and away they went.

Then he met a wolf.

"Where are you going?" asked the wolf.

"To the king's palace," crowed the cock.

"May I come with you?" said the wolf.

"Sit up behind," cried the cock; and then the wolf seated himself in the ladle, and away they went.

Then the cock met a bear.

"Where are you going?" asked the bear.

"To the king's palace," crowed the cock.

"May I come with you?" said the bear.

"Sit up behind," cried the cock; and then the bear took a seat in the ladle, and away they went.

All at once they came to a lake.

"Where are you going?" asked the lake.

"To the king's palace," crowed the cock.

"May I come with you?" said the lake.

"Sit up behind," cried the cock; and then the lake began to heave, so that the one billow after the other washed up into the ladle, and soon the whole lake was in it. The cock's companions got a little wet about the feet, but there was no help for that. The cock set off with them, and so they came to the king's palace. The cock now flew up on the roof of the palace and crowed:

"The king's daughter shall be mine!"

The king heard this.

"That's a strange cock!" he thought. And then he gave orders that his men should catch him, and all of them began to run after the cock and call him. But when they got so near to him that they could almost catch him, he flew up on the roof again, and then he crowed:

"The king's daughter shall be mine!"

It was all in vain, they could not catch him.

"I suppose you must have her, then," said the king, with a laugh; and then the cock allowed himself to be caught at once.

But as soon as the king had got him he was sorry for what he had promised, for a king's word is a king's word; but a better son-in-law he might surely have got—he who had such a fair and beautiful daughter, and his only daughter into the bargain. But how should he get rid of him?

"If I let him into the goose-pen, the geese are sure to finish him off," he thought; and so he let the cock in among the geese. They began to pinch and peck at him with their beaks and to pluck his feathers out, but just then he crowed for the fox:

"Cock-a-doodle-do! Foxie, come and help!"

And the fox came sneaking along, and he was not slow in getting in among the geese, and there he ravaged about in such a way that they were all dead in less than no time.

The cock then flew up on the roof, and crowed:

"The king's daughter shall be mine!"

"Such a dreadful cock I have never set eyes on!" thought the king. "Now he has killed all my geese! How shall I get rid of him? What if I let him in among my cattle? They'll be sure to finish him," he thought, and so he let him into the cow-shed. The king had a large herd of cattle, and they seized the cock with their horns and tossed him about between them like a ball.

But the cock flew up on top of the bull and crowed for the wolf:

"Cock-a-doodle-do! Wolfie, come and help!"

The wolf was not long in coming, and he had such a feast that there

THE VALIANT CHANTICLEER

wasn't a single beast left alive.

The cock flew up on the roof again, and then he crowed:

"The king's daughter shall be mine!"

"Has any one seen the like of that cock?" said the king. "Now he has finished all my geese and all my cattle. How shall I get rid of him? What if I let him in among the horses? They'll be sure to finish him," he thought; and so he let the cock into the stable.

The king had a lot of horses, and they began to rear and kick with all their might, so that the cock was knocked about from one to the other like a wheel rolling down the street, and he soon got tired of that kind of knocking about. So he crowed for the bear.

"Cock-a-doodle-do! Bruin, come and help!"

And the bear was not long in coming, and he began to strike and tear, till there was not one of the king's horses left.

The cock then flew up on the roof again, and crowed:

"The king's daughter shall be mine!"

"That's the worst cock I ever came across," said the king. "First he kills all my geese and all my cattle, and now he has finished my horses as well. I shall be quite ruined. But now I'll put him on the spit and roast him and eat him myself, and it'll be a wonder if I don't get rid of him then." That was what must be done; and so they took the cock and put him on the spit, and the kitchenmaids made such a big fire, that it fizzled all round him. But the cock crowed for the lake.

"Cock-a-doodle-do! Lakey, come and help!"

And the lake came rolling in and put out the fire. But it was only just in the nick of time,—for the cock was half roasted. But as they could not get him done any better, he would have to do as he was; and so they carried him up on a silver dish and placed him on the table. The king was so angry that he swallowed him in one gulp.

"Now I suppose I'm rid of him," he thought.

But had anybody heard the like?

As soon as the cock got into the king's stomach he began to revive again and to crow:

"The king's daughter shall be mine!" And he tumbled about so terribly down there that the king could not keep him down, and so had to vomit him. But no sooner had the cock recovered than he began to flap his wings, and he flew up and perched on the top of the king's crown, and there he crowed:

"The king's daughter shall be mine!"

The king was in despair; he did not know what to do, and flung his crown away.

"Well, you had better take her then, you bird of ill-omen, and half the kingdom as well; only leave me in peace!" he cried.

The cock was now to have the princess. She cried and wept bitterly, for you can easily understand she did not want such a bridegroom. She was not a hen, and did not want to become one.

But all her crying and her wailings were of no avail, she would have to marry the cock and be satisfied with him. He tried to comfort her as best he could, and swept the table with his wings, and breasted and plumed himself in a cock's very best manner; but she went on crying and weeping, and as he was not able to console her, he at last asked her to wring his neck. No, that she would not do, for life may be dear, even to a cock, she thought. But he begged and prayed so hard that at last she did it, and the next moment a prince stood before her, and he was so fine and handsome as to beggar all description; and yet he was the cock! There was soon an end to the crying and wailing, and things took another turn, for both the princess and the king were so happy that no one can believe how happy they were.

To the wedding came people from all parts of the country, and the man and his wife were there as well. The fox and the wolf and the bear waited at the table, and the lake washed up the dishes, and altogether it was the grandest wedding I have ever been to in all my days.

# TWIGMUNTUS, COWBELLIANTUS, PERCHNOSIUS

ONCE UPON a time there was a king who was so very learned that no parson in the whole world could surpass him; in fact, he was so learned that ordinary folks could hardly understand what he said, nor could he understand them either. But in order to have some one to talk with he procured seven wise professors, who were not quite so learned as himself, but who were just able to interpret his learned sayings, so that people could apprehend them, and who could twist and turn about the talk of ordinary folk so that it became sufficiently learned and complicated for the king to understand it.

The king had no son, but he had a daughter, and in order that she should be happily married, and the country governed according to the fundamental principles of his learning, he issued an edict that he who was so learned as to put the king and his professors to silence should have his daughter and half the kingdom there and then. But any one who attempted the task and did not succeed, should lose his head for having dared to exchange words with the king.

That was no joke; but the princess was so fair and beautiful that it was no joke to gaze at her either. And the king did not keep her caged up, for anyone who wished could see her.

There came princes and counts and barons and parsons and doctors, and learned persons from all quarters of the world; and no sooner did they see the princess than they one and all wanted to try their luck. But, however learned they were, their learning never proved sufficient, and every one of them lost his head.

Over in a corner of the kingdom there lived a farmer, who had a son. This lad was not stupid; he was quick of apprehension and sharp witted, and he was not afraid of any thing.

When the king's edict came to this out-of-the-way place, and the parson had read it from the pulpit, the lad wanted to try his luck. "He who nothing risks, nothing wins," thought the lad; and so he went to the parson and told him that if he would give him lessons in the evenings, he would work for the parson in the daytime, but he wanted to become so learned that he could try a bout with the king and his professors.

"Whoever means to compete with them must be able to do something more than munch bread," said the parson.

"That may be," said the lad; "but I'll try my luck."

The parson thought, of course, that he was mad; but when he could get such a clever hand to work for him only for his keep, he thought he could not very well say no; and so the lad got what he wanted.

He worked for the parson in the daytime, and the parson read with him in the evening; and in this way they went on for some time, but at last the lad grew tired of his books.

"I am not going to sit here and read and grind away, and lose what few wits I have," he said; "and it won't be of much help either, for if you are lucky things will come right of themselves, and if you are not lucky you'll never make a silk purse out of a sow's ear."

And with this he pitched the books on the shelf and went his way.

All at once he came to a large forest, where the trees and the bushes were so thick that it was with difficulty he could get along. While he was thus pushing his way through, he began wondering what he should say when he came to the king's palace, and how best he could make use of the learning he had picked up from the parson. All of a sudden the twig of a tree struck him across his mouth, so that his teeth rattled.

"That is Twigmuntus," he said.

A little while after he came to a meadow, where a cow was standing bellowing so furiously that it almost deafened him.

"That is Cowbelliantus," he said.

He then came to a river; but as there was neither bridge nor planks across it, he had to put his clothes on his head and swim across.

While he was swimming a perch came and bit him on the nose.

"That is Perchnosius," he said.

At last he came to the king's palace, where things did not look at all pleasant, for there were men's heads stuck on long stakes round about, and they grinned so horribly that they were enough to frighten any one out of his wits. But the lad was not easily frightened.

"God's peace!" he said, and raised his cap. "There you stick and grin at me; but who knows if I may not be keeping you company before the day is over, and be grinning with you at others? But if I happen to be alive, you shall not stick there any longer gaping at people," he said.

So he went up to the palace and knocked at the gate.

The guard came out and asked what he wanted.

"I have come to try my luck with the princess," said the lad.

"You?" said the guard, "well, you're a likely one, you are! Have you lost your senses? There have been princes and counts and barons and parsons and doctors and learned persons here, and all of them have had to pay with their heads for that pleasure; and yet you think you'll succeed!" he said.

"I should say it is no concern of yours," said the lad; "just open the

Twigmuntus, Cowbelliantus, Perchnosius

gate, and you'll see one who's not afraid of anything."

But the guard would not let him in.

"Do as I tell you," said the lad, "or there'll be a fine to-do!"

But the guard would not.

The lad then seized him by the collar and flung him against the wall, so that it creaked; and then he walked straight in to the king, who sat in his parlour with all his seven professors about him. Their faces were long and thin, and they looked like puny sickly persons about to die. They were sitting with their heads on one side meditating and staring at the floor.

Then one of them, who looked up, asked the lad in ordinary language: "Who are you?"

"A suitor," said the lad.

"Do you want to try for the princess's hand?"

"Well, that's about it!" said the lad.

"Have you lost your wits? There have been princes and counts and barons and parsons and doctors and learned persons here, and all of them have gone headless away; so you had better turn about and get away while your head is on your shoulders," he said.

"Don't trouble yourself on that account, but rather think of the head on your own shoulders," said the lad. "You look after yours, and I'll take care of mine! So just begin, and let me hear how much wit you have got, for I don't think you look so very clever," he said.

The first professor then began a long harangue of gibberish; and when he had finished the second went on; and then the third; and in this way they continued till at length it was the turn of the seventh. The lad did not understand a single word of it all, but he didn't lose courage for all that. He only nodded his approval to all of it.

When the last had finished his harangue he asked:

"Can you reply to that?"

"That's easy enough," said the lad. "Why, when I was in my cradle and in my go-cart I could twist my mouth about and prate and jabber like you," he said. "But since you are so terribly learned, I'll put a question to you, and that shall not be a long one:

"Twigmuntus, Cowbelliantus, Perchnosius? Can you give me an answer to that?"

And now you should have seen how they stretched their necks and strained their ears. They put on their spectacles and began to look into their books and turn over the leaves.

But while they were searching and meditating, the lad put his hands in his trouser pockets, and looked so frank and fearless that they could not help admiring him, and wondering that one who was so young could be so learned and yet look just like other people.

"Well, how are you getting on?" said the lad. "Cannot all your learning help you to open your mouths, so that I can have an answer to my question?" he said.

Then they began to ponder and meditate, and then they glanced at the ceiling, and then they stared at the walls, and then they fixed their eyes upon the floor. But they could not give him any answer, nor could the king himself, although he was much more learned than all the others together. They had to give it up, and the lad got the princess and half the kingdom. This he ruled in his own way, and if it did not fare better, it did not fare worse for him than for the king with all his fundamental principles.

# THE LAD AND THE FOX

THERE WAS once upon a time a little lad, who was on his way to church, and when he came to a clearing in the forest he caught sight of a fox, who was lying on the top of a big stone fast asleep, so that the fox did not know the lad had seen him.

"If I kill that fox," said the lad, taking a heavy stone in his fist, "and sell the skin, I shall get money for it, and with that money I shall buy some rye, and that rye I shall sow in father's cornfield at home. When the people who are on their way to church pass by my field of rye they'll say: 'Oh, what splendid rye that lad has got!' Then I shall say to them: 'I say, keep away from my rye!' But they won't heed me. Then I shall shout to them: 'I say, keep away from my rye!' But still they won't take any notice of me. Then I shall scream with all my might: 'Keep away from my rye!' and then they'll listen to me."

But the lad screamed so loudly that the fox woke up and made off at once for the forest, so that the lad did not even get as much as a handful of his hair.

No; it's best always to take what you can reach, for of undone deeds you should never screech, as the saying goes.

# OLD NICK AND THE GIRL

THERE WAS once a girl who was so mad about dancing that she nearly went out of her mind whenever she heard a fiddle strike up.

She was a very clever dancer, and a smarter girl to whirl round in a dance or kick her heels was not easily to be found, although she only had shoes made of birch-bark, and knitted leggings on her feet. She swept past at such a rate that the air whistled round her like a humming top. She might have whirled round still more quickly and lightly, of course, if she had had leather shoes. But how was she to get them, when she had no money to pay for them? For she was very poor, this girl, and could ill afford them.

So one day, when the fair was being held at Amberg Heath, whom should she meet but Old Nick!* He was going to see the fun of the fair, as you may guess, for all sorts of tramps and vagabonds and watch-dealers and rogues go there; and where such gentry are to be found, others of the same feather are sure to flock together.

"What are you thinking about?" asked Old Nick, who knew well enough how matters stood.

"I am wondering how I shall be able to get a pair of leather shoes to dance in," said the girl; "for I haven't any money to pay for them," she said.

"Is that all? We'll soon get over that," said Old Nick, and produced a pair of leather shoes, which he showed her. "Do you like these?" he asked.

The girl stood staring at the shoes. She could never have believed that there were such fine, splendid shoes, for they were not common ones sewn with pitched thread, but real German shoes with welted soles, and looked as French as one could wish.

"Is there a spring in them as well?" she asked.

"Yes, that you may be sure of," said Old Nick. "Do you want them?"

Yes, that she did; there could be no doubt about that, and so they began bargaining and higgling about the payment, till at last they came to terms. She was to have the shoes for a whole year for nothing, if only she would dance in his interest, and afterwards she should belong to him.

She did not exactly make a good bargain, but Old Nick is not a person one can bargain with. But there was to be such a spring in them that no human being would be able to swing round quicker in a dance or kick higher than she did; and if they did not satisfy her, he would take them back for nothing, and she should be free.

With this they parted.

And now the girl seemed to wake up thoroughly. She thought of nothing else but going to dances, wherever they might be, night after night. Well, she danced and danced, and before she knew it the year came to an end, and Old Nick came and asked for his due.

"They were a rubbishy pair of shoes you gave me," said the girl; "there was no spring at all in them," she said.

"Wasn't there any spring in the shoes? That's very strange," said Old Nick.

"No, there wasn't!" said the girl. "Why, my bark shoes are far better, and I can get on much faster in them than in these wretched things."

"You twist about as if you were dancing," said Old Nick; "but now I think you will have to dance away with me after all."

"Well, if you don't believe my words, I suppose you'll believe your eyes," she said. "Put on these grand shoes of yours, and try them yourself," she said, "and I'll put on my bark shoes, and then we'll have a race, so that you can see what they are good for," she said.

*The Devil

Well, that was reasonable enough, he thought, and, no doubt, he felt there was very little danger in trying it. So they agreed to race to the end of Lake Fryken and back, one on each side of the lake, which, as you know, is a very long one indeed. If she came in first she was to be free, but if she came in last she was to belong to him.

But the girl had to run home first of all, for she had a roll of cloth for the parson, which she must deliver before she tried her speed with Old Nick. Very well, that she might, for he went in fear of the parson; but the race should take place on the third day afterwards.

Now, as bad luck would have it for Old Nick, it so happened that the girl had a sister, who was so like her that it was impossible to know one from the other, for they were twins, the two girls.

But the sister was not mad about dancing, so Old Nick had not got scent of her. The girl now asked her sister to place herself at Frykstad, the south end of the lake, and she herself took up her position at Fryksend, the north end of it.

She had the bark shoes on, and Old Nick the leather ones; and so they set off, each on their side of the lake. The girl did not run very far, for she knew well enough how little running she need do; but Old Nick set off at full speed, much faster than one can ride on the railway.

But when he came to Frykstad he found the girl already there; and when he came back to Fryksend there she was too.

"Well, you see now?" said the girl.

"Of course I see," said Old Nick, but he was not the man to give in at once. "One time is no time, that you know," he said.

"Well, let's have another try," said the girl.

Yes, that he would, for the soles of his shoes were almost worn out, and then he knew what state the bark shoes would be in.

They set off for the second time, and Old Nick ran so fast that the air whistled round the corners of the houses in Sonne and Emtervik parishes; but when he came to Frykstad, the girl was already there, and when he got back to Fryksend, she was there before him this time also.

"Can you see now who comes in first?" she said.

"Yes, of course I can," said Old Nick, and began to dry the perspiration off his face, thinking all the time what a wonderful runner that girl must be. "But you know," he said, "twice is hardly half a time! It's the third time that counts."

"Let's have another try, then," said the girl.

Yes, that he would, for Old Nick is very sly, you know, for when the leather shoes were so torn to pieces that his feet were bleeding, he knew well enough what state the bark shoes would be in.

And so they set off again. Old Nick went at a terrible speed; it was just like a regular north-wester rushing past, for now he was furious. He rushed onwards, so that the roofs were swept away and the fences creaked and groaned all the way through Sonne and Emtervik parishes. But when he got to Frykstad the girl was there, and when he got back to Fryksend then she was there too.

His feet were now in such a plight that the flesh hung in pieces from them, and he was so out of breath, and groaned so hard, that the sound echoed in the mountains. The girl almost pitied the old creature, disgusting as he was.

"Do you see, now," she said, "that there's a better spring in my bark shoes than in your leather ones? There's nothing left of yours, while mine will hold out for another run, if you would like to try," she said.

No, Old Nick had now to acknowledge himself beaten, and so she was free.

"I've never seen the like of such a woman," he said; "but if you go on dancing and jumping about like that all your days we are sure to meet once more," he said.

"Oh, no!" said the girl. And since then she has never danced again, for it is not every time that you can succeed in getting away from Old Nick.

# THE STONE STATUE

THERE WERE once two men who were walking across a churchyard—and there was nothing remarkable about that; but when one of them lifted his cap, as one should do in such a place, and said: "God's peace to all who rest here!" then the other said: "They lie as they have made their bed, and they get what they deserve!" It was very wicked to talk in that way; and no sooner had he spoken these words than he was changed into a stone statue, and thus he stood for many, many years. The one parson after the other came and prayed and chanted over him, but no one was able to exorcise the soul out of the petrified body.

It so happened that a new parson came to the parish, and he was much more learned than all the others. He was a model parson in every respect; but he was somewhat hasty, and his wife was not one to be trifled with either. When he saw the stone statue and heard why it stood there, he wanted also to try to get its soul to rest in peace. He had the statue carried into his study, so that he could pray over it every day, both in the morning and in the evening and at all hours of the day, which he did. But the first time he read the evening prayers and came to the words: "God banish everything that is evil from this house!" he heard something like a titter over in the corner where the statue stood, but he could not make out from whom it proceeded. Next evening when he came to these words the same thing happened, but he became none the wiser this time either.

The third evening he again heard the same tittering; but this time he kept a better watch, and then he discovered it was the statue over in the corner that had tittered.

"Can you laugh?" said the parson. "If so, I suppose you can tell me what you are laughing at?"

Yes, that the statue could.

THE STONE STATUE

"You see, reverend father," said the statue, "you are wonderfully learned in all sorts of divine teachings, and you live, no doubt, according to what you teach; but you quarrel a little too much with your wife, and therefore all the house swarms with little imps during the day. When you read the evening prayers and come to the words: 'God banish every thing that is evil from this house!' they have to take themselves off; and there is one among them, a little fellow who limps and who tosses his body about in such a funny way when he trudges along, that one cannot help laughing at him. But although they take to flight when you read the prayers, it is not long before they are back again; and as soon as you and your wife begin to quarrel this limping little rascal comes hobbling in, and then all the other little devils come prowling after him, one after the other."

Those words made the parson's heart ache, for when stones begin to talk it is well to listen.

And this he did. He became more forbearing to his wife, and as she herself was not particularly fond of these crawling little things, whom she could not see, but who swarmed around her, she also tried, as well as she could, to control her temper. And as both of them were now more friendly to one another and more inclined to give way to each other, they began little by little to agree and to get on well together. And after a while the statue was not heard to say anything either; and some little time afterwards the parson asked it if it now saw any signs of the little hobbling imp and his companions.

"Well, I have seen him holding the door ajar and peeping in, but he has not ventured across the threshold," said the statue; "but now I think he has become tired of it, for he has not been here for many days, and now I only see God's angels around you."

The parson rejoiced at hearing these words, and thanked God for having put an end to all their dissensions.

"But how is it with yourself now?" he asked the statue.

"Well, I shall also find peace now," said the statue; "for now I have done a good deed, and I am only waiting for the last prayer."

And it was not long before it came. The parson read the best prayer he knew, and when he had finished the statue became flesh and blood again, but he drew his last breath at the same moment. The parson put him in a coffin and gave him a respectable burial, and in this way they both benefited.

# THE ARTFUL LAD

THERE WERE once two farmers whose farms lay side by side in the same parish. Their land was of the same size and equally taxed, so that by rights both the farmers ought to have been equally well off. But they were not; for the one was rich, and the other was only just able to keep body and soul together. You may think this was strange, since the one was just as industrious as the other; but it was not so very strange after all, for the rich farmer had a servant lad to help him—and a very clever lad he was, while the other had to do all the work himself, and did not even get any help from his wife, for she suffered so much from internal complaints, she said, that she was unable to do any work in the fields. Nor did she do much indoor work, at which she had to sit quiet; but spin and wind yarn, and run about from one room to the other, that she could do. And as for her complaint, it could not be as bad as she pretended, for she did not look either ill or ailing. No, on the contrary she was stout and trim, and red in the face like a peony; and although she was short and stout, she was broad both across her shoulders and hips, so that no one could find anything amiss with her. But she was one of those who will steal away from work and idle her time away; and that was about all that ailed her. And she had the habit of hiding away all that her husband brought home with him in his ox-cart, and so you may guess things could not last very long. The farmer was greatly to be pitied, although no one thought of pitying him; for if only he had given his wife a talking-to now and then it would have been all the better for him. But this he neglected to do, and so he had to suffer for it; there was no help for it.

So one Sunday morning, when his wife was out gallivanting about, as was her custom early and late, the farmer was sitting alone in his parlour, and a strange lad happened to come in.

"Good evening, master!" said the lad.

"Good evening!" said the farmer.

"Do you want a servant lad, master?"

"A servant lad? God help me," said the farmer, "how can I afford that? I can scarcely manage to keep and feed myself, worse luck!"

"Is that so?" said the lad. "But that's just the reason why you want some one to help you."

"You talk as if you hadn't any sense," said the farmer. "If two mouths can empty a dish, does one get any the more when a hungry body stands by staring at one? And if the stuff for one's breeches is not enough for two legs, is it likely to be sufficient for four?"

"Of course," said the lad, "if only you use your wits; for if you use them, you need not be without either bread or breeches, that's certain, and that you may depend upon. And I'll take care to manage things, and to stretch the stuff for the breeches, so that it will be sufficient both for you and for me—that's to say, if the missus does not wear the breeches," he said.

"You have a bold tongue, my lad," said the farmer; "but it's one thing to boast and brag, and another to work and drag; and braggarts are generally the greatest sluggards,—have you heard that?"

"Yes, I have. I have heard that and a good deal more," said the lad. "But that's neither here nor there. I like this place, and here I'll remain, and as for wages we are sure to agree about them. I don't want to take anything from you till I've earned it."

"How you do talk!" said the farmer. "You talk and you talk till my ears tingle, but that's an easy matter, and big words often lead to a big fall;

but if you can manage to get along on scanty fare, there will not be much risk about it," he said.

"Well, you take the risk, master, and you'll not regret it," said the lad. "For I am the lad who's not afraid of anything."

The farmer began to scratch his head. He liked the lad, for you must know he was a big, strong fellow, and if he were only half as strong as he looked, he would still be one of the strongest in the parish. But it would require more than water-gruel to feed such a fellow properly. What should he feed him on? And his wife was not at home either. What would she say when she found she had such a big eater in the house? What should they give him to eat?

"Well," said the boy, who began to be impatient, "what's your answer?"

"Well, that's just what I am thinking about," said the farmer.

"But that's of little good to me," said the lad. "Listen to me! Don't sit pondering and pondering, or it'll fare with you as with the parson who walked up and down the vestry pondering upon his first sermon till all the people had left the church. No, that won't do! Quick thoughts belong to a quick head, so don't make yourself more stupid than you are! Here's my hand!" he said.

Well, the farmer had to hold out his hand too, which the lad squeezed so hard that the farmer yelled; and that was the whole contract. But what was done was done; and the wife might think what she liked, for the lad went to his work at once, he did.

All at once the wife came rushing in.

"Good evening! Glad to see you back!" said the farmer.

"Good evening, husband!" said the wife. "How have you been amusing yourself while I have been out?" she said, in an insinuating voice and with a mild look in her eyes.

"Well, I've taken a servant lad!" said the farmer.

"Servant lad?" said the wife. "Have you gone clean out of your senses? Taken a servant lad, you say?"

"Yes, just so!" said the farmer.

"Bless me!" said the woman, clasping her hands in surprise. "Has any one ever heard the like? What are we going to pay him and feed him with, I should like to know?"

"His wages will be my affair, and the feeding yours," said the farmer.

"I pity him, poor fellow," said the wife.

"You needn't pity me at all," said the lad, "for I'm the sort of lad that isn't afraid. How do you do, mother? We shall be the best of friends and get on well together," he said.

The wife had to shake hands with him; and when she looked a little closer at him, she saw he was a fine fellow, who had his wits about him. 'That fellow is not to be trifled with,' she thought, but she did not say a word. And the lad did not speak a word either. He only stared at her, as she sat by the hearth, looking as fat and round in the face as a pancake; and then he looked at the farmer and saw how thin and gaunt and sallow he was. "What a fiend of a woman! She must eat something better than water-gruel," thought the lad.

On the following Monday the farmer and the lad set out early in the morning to the forest to cut trees for hurdles. When they got there, the lad remembered that he had forgotten his axe. So he had to run home again. He went into the parlour and found that his mistress was out, but there was a cloth on the table, and he could see she had not put it there to be bleached by the sun, for there was bread and butter and cheese and even brandy on the table. Had any one ever seen such a woman? That was quite another sort of breakfast to the water-gruel and bread-crumbs she gave her husband.

"There's something wrong in this house," he thought, "but take your time and you'll see." And so he crept into the settle-bed, and shut down the lid over him, and then he cut a little peep-hole in the side of the bed.

All at once the woman came hurrying in, bringing her neighbour with her. She asked him to sit down and make himself at home, which he lost no time in doing.

"I heard you were going to the forest to-day, and so I thought you would like a tit-bit and a dram," she said, and made herself as caressing and pleasant as a westerly breeze on a midsummer night. Her guest needed no persuasion, and it wasn't necessary to ask him twice. He ate and drank and helped himself to one dram after another. The woman was not backward either. She drank a glass with him, and chattered away and made herself as pleasant as she could. In the meantime the lad lay inside the settle-bed, chewing a bit of straw and peeping through the hole and listening all the while.

When the neighbour had finished his breakfast, he had eaten so much that he had to loosen the strap of his leathern apron, and then he got ready to go.

"Just wait a bit," said the woman. "Where will you be working to-day?"

"I shall be in the forest close to where your people are cutting," he said.

"Will you be alone?" she asked.

Yes, that he would, he said, for his lad had gone to the mill.

"If you will mark the trees and drop branches in the path, I'll come and bring you some dinner," she said.

"Thank you," said the neighbour as he went out; and so the woman went into the kitchen.

Then the lad jumped out of the settle-bed and made his way back to the forest.

Well, the neighbour did as the woman had told him, but as he went through the forest and lopped off branches, the lad, who was following behind, picked them up and marked the path leading to the place where his master was working.

He thought he had managed things very well.

In the meantime his master had been hewing away till the splinters flew, and swore because the lad did not come back.

"How stupid I was! What did I want with a lazy-bones like that," he thought. "He can boast and brag, but he is not so smart on his legs as with his tongue, that I can see; and if he goes on like this the first day, what will the end be?"

Just then the lad came back. He had lost his way in the forest, he said, and he had had to turn his jacket three times* before he got on the right path.

"With the lazy ox the Huldre drives best," the farmer said; "and I should like to know whether you belong to her people or mine," he said, and was very angry.

"Bide your time, and you'll see," said the lad, and set to work with a will.

He cut away till the forest thundered and rang with his blows, so that in short time he had felled more trees than the farmer.

"Will that do?" he said.

"It will," said the farmer.

The lad then put down the axe and began to look round.

"What are you staring after?" said the farmer.

"I can see by the sun that it's dinner-time," said the lad; "and I am looking for my mistress, for I think it's about time that she ought to be here with our dinner."

"Is that what you are staring after?" said the farmer. "If so, you'll be staring till your eyes start out of your head, for mother said she hadn't got anything for us; so we shall have to cut and hew as long as we are able, and even when we get home I don't think we shall be able to scrape much together."

"Bless me!" said the lad, "we mustn't think it'll be as bad as that? Oh no, the mistress will be coming, you'll see, and you may depend she'll give us a good meal."

"Well, believe it if you like," said the farmer. "But if you can manage with that sort of food till this evening you'll not be difficult to keep," he said.

And with this he tightened the leather apron round his waist and began to fell trees again.

"Look there, master!" said the lad.

The farmer did stare, you may guess, for he saw his wife stealing along between the bushes with a big bag of food on her arm.

She did not take her eyes off the ground, as she was looking for the branches, and she didn't know where she was till she was close up to her husband.

"Well, mother!" said the farmer.

His wife gave a start.

"Good gracious, is that you?" she said.

"Of course it's me," said the farmer, and laughed. "Surely you ought to know that when you come here with the dinner. But sit down, and let me see what you have been able to scrape together for us."

He then took the bag and began to see what she had brought.

There was butter and cheese and there was pease pudding. "Ey, hey!" said the farmer, smacking his lips. And there was sweet cheese and cheese cakes, too.

"I can hardly believe my eyes! Why, this'll be quite a grand feast,

---

*Any one led astray by the Huldre (the fairy of the wood of the North) must, according to popular belief, turn his jacket inside out three times before he can find his way.

mother!" said he. He then found a little bottle. What could there be in that bottle? He took out the cork. It was brandy. He became so pleased that he gave his wife a dig in the ribs, so that she went sprawling along the ground.

"I say, mother," he cried, "where have you got all these good things from? You haven't stolen them, I hope?"

"Oh, they are some trifles I have been saving up," she said, "and I thought they would just do to-day, since it is the first dinner we give our new lad," she said; but most likely she wished both the lad and her husband as far away as possible, and a little bit farther, as you may guess, for it was their neighbour she was looking for, and he, poor fellow, would not even be able to get a sniff of the good things.

But she was a cunning woman, and that kind of woman always finds a way out of difficulties.

"I say, husband," she said, "our neighbour is in the forest too to-day, and we have never offered him any hospitality. Won't you ask him to come here and have something?"

The farmer was not particularly anxious to get any help, for there was not overmuch of food in the bag, and he and the lad could easily manage what there was, he thought; but he was not mean, nor did he want to go against his wife either.

"Run and ask our neighbour, then," he said to the lad; and off went the lad, but first he took a large piece of cheese with him. He would eat that on the way, he said, for the water-gruel and bread-crumbs which he had had for breakfast had disappeared long ago, so he was very hungry, he said. But he broke the cheese in pieces instead, and dropped them on the path as he went along.

And so he came to where the neighbour was.

"I say, mister!" said the lad. "You'll have to be on the look out, for my master has discovered that my mistress asks you to our house when he is away, so now there'll be a fine kettle of fish."

And then he ran back to his master.

"Master!" he cried. "For God's sake, master, make haste and take the axe with you. Our neighbour has felled a big tree, which has fallen right across him."

"Dear, dear! What a misfortune!" cried the farmer; and set off running with the axe in his hand.

When the neighbour caught sight of him running towards him in this way he remembered what the lad had said, and took to his heels as fast as he could. The farmer stared after him in surprise; at the same time he was glad to see he was unhurt. "Wait a bit!" he cried. "Wait a bit, do you hear? I have got something nice for you over here."

Something nice? No, thank you; he was much obliged, but he thought it was best to keep away, for that kind of treat he could do without. He took to running still faster; he never said a word—he only ran.

"I should say he has gone mad," said the farmer; "for as a rule he does not want much pressing. But to run the flesh off your bones to get people to eat up your food when you're hungry, why, only a fool would do that," he said, and so he went back.

But then he saw the pieces of cheese which the lad had dropped along the path.

"What a careless boy!" he thought; and began to pick up the pieces as he went along.

In the meanwhile the lad was sitting beside his mistress, eating and drinking and gorging himself from the bag.

"What's father picking up over there?" said the woman.

"Pebbles," said the lad.

"Pebbles?" said the woman. "What is he going to do with them?"

"How should I know?" said the lad. "But you had better take care, mistress, for my master knows how you carry on with our neighbour when he is away. He knows it was for our neighbour, and not for him, that you brought this dinner; and now there'll be a nice kettle of fish."

The woman, as you may guess, turned red and became quite frightened.

"Heaven help me! heaven help me!" she muttered; and then she set off homewards.

The farmer shouted after her; but she would not hear him—she only ran as fast as she could.

"I think she is gone mad as well; he said; "or what is it she is running after?"

"Indeed, I don't know," said the lad; "unless the house is on fire."

"You don't say so!" shouted the farmer; and he took to his heels as well.

But his wife was more nimble on her legs, and she got home first. She ran into the kitchen and hid herself in the baker's oven. The farmer rushed to the well and filled a bucket with the water, and ran into the kitchen. But he could see no fire anywhere.

"I wonder if it's in the baker's oven!" he said; and opened the door and threw the whole bucket of water into it. The wife began to shout and cry: "My dear, kind husband! Don't be angry with me! I will never ask our neighbour here any more when you are out, and I'll never take him any food either."

"Ah ha!" said the farmer. "Is that how matters stand? It's no wonder then that you have nothing but water-gruel for me! Did ever one hear the like? But I'll not stand it any longer; no, I'll not stand it!"

And he dragged his wife out of the oven and began to beat her as hard as he could.

The wife cried and screamed, but all of no avail; the more she screamed the more he belaboured her, for now he was fairly started.

Just then the lad came in.

"I think you had better take a rest now, master," he said; "for I suppose you have been thanking mistress for the grand feast."

"You think so?" said the farmer. "No—o! She must have more!" And so he wanted to begin again.

"No, stop!" said the lad; "it's enough now."

"Is it?" said the farmer. "I suppose it'll have to do then. But I haven't let him have anything yet."

"You mustn't either," said the lad.

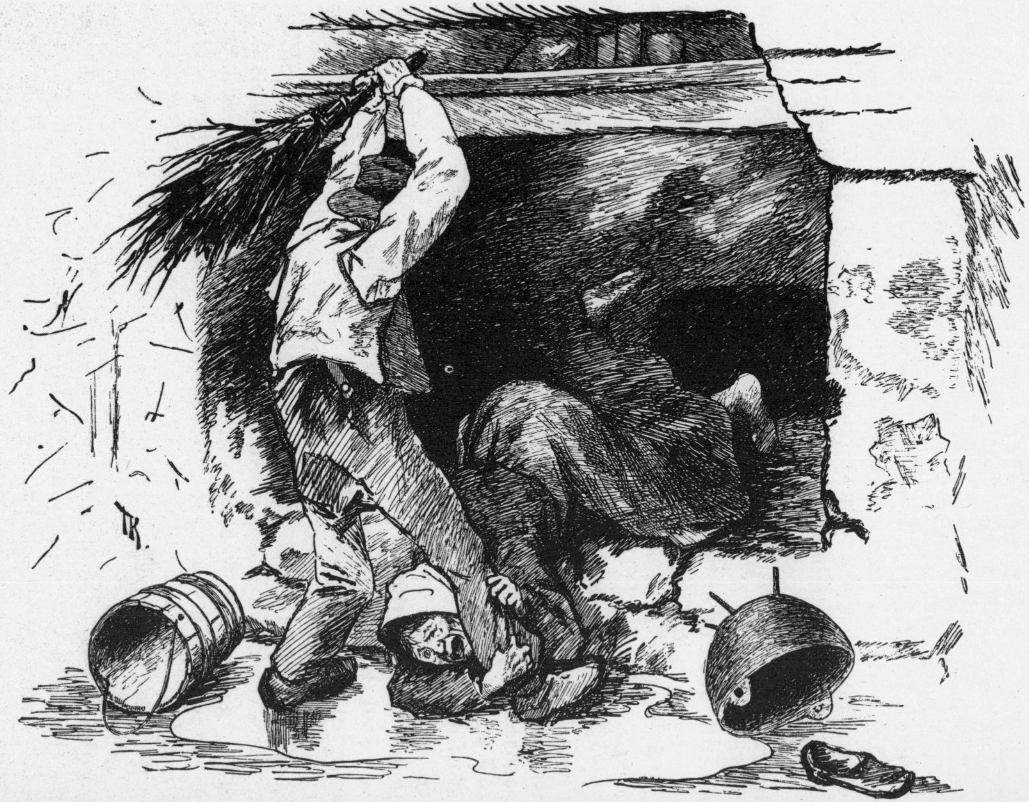

The Artful Lad

"Mustn't I? yes, indeed I will; and in such a way that I'll break every bone of that rascal's back."

"No, indeed you mustn't," said the lad. "I'll manage him."

"Will you?" said the farmer; and he did not at all object to this, for he had seen sufficient to know that the lad was able to manage it better than he, and that it was no joke when any one got into his clutches.

"Well, you had better do it, then!" he said.

So the lad went to the neighbour.

"Good evening!" he said.

"Good evening! How are things going?" said the neighbour.

"Very badly," said the lad; "for I must tell you that master is sharpening his axe, and is so furious with you that if you don't take care of yourself you'll never know what will happen. He has sworn he'll cut those shanks of yours to bits because you carry on with his wife when he is away."

"Oh dear, oh dear! What a scrape I have got into! What can a wretched man like me do?"

"Well, you must listen to what I say," said the lad; "you see, they have scarcely any corn left at our place and if you will give me two barrels of rye, half a barrel of peas, and a quartern of wheat, I shall be able to keep him quiet."

"Are you mad? so much for so little?"

"How do I know if it's too much or too little?" said the lad; "but I'll ask your wife about it, and then we shall soon know."

"No, stop!" said the farmer. "My wife, you see, has such a hasty temper. "But one barrel of rye I might be able to manage, if only she doesn't get to hear of it."

"Two barrels," said the lad.

"One barrel," said the farmer.

"Two," said the lad, "or else——"

"No, no! stop! You shall have them then."

But the lad was not yet satisfied. He wrangled and bargained so long that he got the quartern of wheat, but of the peas he could only get half of what he wanted, for else they would run out of pease-meal altogether. The other quartern he would owe him. The lad was satisfied with this; and he was to come at midnight to fetch the corn, so that the neighbour's wife should not know anything about it; and with this they parted.

When the lad came back the farmer asked him: "Well, have you given him what he deserved?"

"Yes, you may be sure of that," said the lad. "He has now got enough to make his back smart for some time to come, and more he may get whenever I have a chance. But this you must keep to yourself, and you mustn't let either him or any of his notice anything. You understand that? And not a word to mistress either."

Yes, that the farmer promised.

"I say, master," said the lad, "I think you have now taught mistress to be obedient and to look after the crumbs better; but she has scarcely a morsel in the house, so I will be off to the mill, so that she can get her barrels and bins filled."

"To the mill?" said the farmer. "What are you going to grind? We have scarcely anything else but siftings in the bins."

"Oh, I'll see to that," said the lad. "Go to bed, and don't trouble about it."

"That's a wonderful lad!" thought the farmer. And then he did as the lad had told him; but the lad went into the cart-house and greased the wheels of the cart and got ready to start. In the middle of the night he called at the neighbour's for the corn, and then he drove to the mill.

But we know what womenfolk are. Even if they never go farther than from the hearth to the kitchen shelf they know what's going on in other people's houses for all that. And if they don't know they begin to wonder, and don't rest till they have found out. The neighbour's wife knew well enough how things were at the other farm, and when she heard they had taken on a servant lad, she wondered what they were going to give him to eat, and when she was told they had a cartload of corn at the mill, she began to wonder still more. Yes, she wondered and wondered, and could not rest till she had found out where they had got the corn from. She had her mother living with her—an old crone between eighty and ninety, or thereabout. But, old as she was, she was just as inquisitive as her daughter. And they kept on wondering so long till at last they hit upon a plan; and then the woman went to her neighbour.

"Good morning!" she said.

"Good morning!" said the farmer.

"We are all going to a party," she said, "and will you kindly let me leave a chest with you, while we are away? For I am rather anxious about the chest, I must tell you, as all the best we have is in it."

But the best was really her mother, who was hidden in the chest, and was to listen to what the people talked about. But nothing was said about this, of course.

"Oh, there won't be any difficulty about that," said the farmer; and so the woman and her servant girl carried in the chest, and then they set out for the party.

Soon afterwards the lad came back from the mill. And now his mistress had all kinds of flour, and she began to make both bread and pancakes.

All at once the lad saw the chest.

"What chest is that?" said he.

"Oh, it belongs to our neighbour," said the farmer. "They have gone to a party and have left it with us; for there is something very precious in it," he said.

"Ah, indeed!" said the lad. "I wonder what that can be? But I suppose we can have a look at it," he said; and so he took his axe and forced open the lid.

He then saw the old woman inside the chest.

"Hullo! Here's something precious indeed!" he said. "Just come and look!"

The farmer and his wife looked into the chest, and to their horror saw the old woman lying there as if she were dead.

"I think she is dead," said the farmer.

"And so do I," said the lad; "but we may as well try and see if there is

life in her, or what can be the matter." And so he struck the side of the
chest with his axe, to see if she would wake up and come to her senses.

But the old woman did not move a limb; she lay as stiff as a log.

Then he struck the chest again, but still she did not stir.

"Dead she is," said the lad; "but she must have come here alive, at any
rate, for she has pancake and ham with her."

He took a piece of the pancake and put it in her mouth, whereupon
he closed the lid again, so that no one could see it had been opened.

Later on the neighbour's wife came to fetch the chest, which she took
away with her. Now she would get to know a lot of news, she thought,
and she was quite looking forward to it.

But there was little occasion for joy, as you may imagine, when she
opened the chest and found that her mother was dead, and had a piece
of the pancake in her mouth.

"Oh dear! oh dear! She had been suffocated!" she cried. "Oh dear!
how stupid I was not to give her as much as a drop of beer with her! Oh!
what a misfortune!" and she cried and wailed till it was terrible to hear.

But what was done could not be undone, and since she could not cry
life into the old mother, they would have to think of the funeral. And a
grand funeral it should be; that was only fair and reasonable, in return
for all her mother had suffered.

And this was done; the clerk chanted over the corpse till the walls
creaked, and the parson preached about her life and good deeds till
every nook in the church resounded with his words. The festivities were
on the same scale; all the parish was there, with the exception of the lad,
for they thought they had nothing to thank him for.

But the lad thought otherwise; and as he could not join in the eating
and drinking, he thought he would find something else to do. He went
to the churchyard about midnight and dug up the old woman, carried
her in his arms and put her in the cellar among the beer barrels. The
beer he carried across in pails to his master's cellar and poured it into
his barrels, but the taps he placed in the old woman's hand, and then he
went his way.

In the morning the neighbour's wife had to go to the cellar for beer,
for the guests were thirsty, and wanted something to moisten their parched
throats with. But you may imagine how terrified she was when she saw
her mother sitting there.

"Oh dear! oh dear! That's because I left mother in the chest without
giving her anything to drink," she said.

She ran to her husband, and he hurried to the parson to come and
make his mother-in-law listen to reason. The parson told him to make
his mind easy, and if he would promise to pay for a new funeral, he
would read such prayers over the corpse that she would be sure to rest
in her grave, said the parson; and the clerk would chant so that it could
be heard all over the parish; and that would help a good bit too, added
the clerk.

The new funeral took place on the following Sunday, and this time
they did not forget the old custom of sewing the stockings together on
the corpse and to put a thunderbolt in the coffin. Yes, they even put a

whole bottle of beer beside her; and now they thought she could surely have nothing to look for in her son-in-law's house. And if the feasting wasn't greater, it wasn't at any rate less than at the first funeral; for everything was so grand that the old woman ought surely to rest satisfied, they thought. And so she might perhaps, if only the lad had been asked to the feast. But they had not asked him this time either, and so he went to the churchyard and dug her up again and carried her back to the farm. He placed her in the pea-bin in the barn, with a corn shovel in each hand. The peas he took away with him, for there was scarcely more than the quartern which the farmer owed him, and so he went away, leaving the door wide open.

In the morning they saw the barn door was open, and the farmer went to see what was the reason. But he nearly went out of his mind when he saw his mother-in-law sitting in the pea-bin, and found what havoc she had made there. "Did you ever see anything like it? This time she wanted to pay us out for the pancake which choked her," he said. "It's quite impossible to please that woman."

But there she sat in any case; and since she would not take herself off, there was no help for it but to go to the parson again. He wondered greatly at the old woman, who would not take any notice of all they had read and chanted over her. But if the man would pay him double fees, he would read so many prayers over her that she must remain in her grave; "there could be no question about that," said the parson. And the clerk would have to get some assistance, and they would sing so that it would be heard over seven parishes; "and that would be sure to help," said the clerk. The third funeral then took place, and they had now taken every care that the old woman should remain where she was. Yes, the parson read, the clerk chanted, and all the relatives, both in and outside the parish, were asked to the funeral feast.

But when the devil is abroad, it's little use to bar and bolt, and the lad was not asked this time either.

Close upon midnight the farmer said to the parson: "I am afraid that my mother-in-law is not satisfied this time either! Won't you let me drive you to the church, so that you could read over her once more, and then she would surely be at rest?" The parson would rather be excused, for he was enjoying himself at the funeral feast; but the farmer begged and prayed so hard that the parson promised to go, and so they drove off. When they came to the churchyard, the lad had already been there and dug up the old woman, but he had not got further than behind the church, and there he sat in a corner with the body in his lap.

The moon was shining, and the farmer had a foal, which was frolicking about after the mare. While the parson was reading over the grave the lad got hold of the foal, and then he took a stake and fixed it to the old woman's back, so that she could keep upright, and then he placed her across the foal.

When the parson had finished he and the farmer set out on their way back.

"Now I think your mother-in-law will rest where she is," said the parson; but the same moment the old woman rushed past as swiftly as an arrow on the foal's back. The parson stood aghast and did not know what to say, and the farmer was quite at his wit's end; neither the parson nor the clerk could manage her. All the guests were lost in wonder, and pitied the farmer all they could, but they could not give him any advice.

At last his neighbour said to him: "I think we'll have to send for my servant lad. He may be able to manage the matter, for he is never at a loss."

"Ah, but what can he do? Is he better than the parson and the clerk?" they all said. But the farmer was quite certain that his lad was not to be despised, and since there was nothing else to be done they might as well try what he could do. And so they sent for him, and he came.

"Can you tell me how I shall make peace with my mother-in-law?" asked the farmer.

"I should think I can," said the lad. "That's not a difficult matter. Let me have the old woman and I'll read so many prayers over her that she'll keep quiet for good," he said. "But I must have a hundred dollars for my trouble."

That was a lot of money, but if she would only leave him in peace it might not be so unreasonable after all, thought the farmer.

The lad then took the old woman and carried her to the churchyard and buried her; and as he did not dig her up again she remained where she ought to be.

And the people of the parish now began to say the lad was a far better hand at reading over the dead than the parson himself.

He got the hundred dollars; and he well deserved them, thought the farmer; for if it had not been for the lad his mother-in-law would have worried him into his grave, he declared. But he was anything but pleased about all the money he had had to pay the parson, for his chest was now cleaned out altogether.

From that time there was a change in the parish. The farmer who had been rich only just managed to keep things going, but the poor farmer got on well and prospered in everything, so that he was worth several hundred dollars more at the end of the year. This he had to thank the lad for: it was only the truth, and he should honestly reward him, he said.

But the lad was a wonderful fellow. He had a head of his own, and he would not have any payment for all the help he had given the farmer.

"A hundred dollars is sufficient payment for a servant lad," he said; "and I have got that from our neighbour, so you do not owe me anything."

"It's seldom you come across such a lad," said the farmer, who did not want to let him go.

"I think you must stop here another year," he said.

But the lad thanked him for his good offer; he could not stop any longer, he said.

"Why?" asked the farmer.

"Well, the parson has engaged me to help him," he said.

How he fared afterwards I have not heard; but if that lad has not become a parson, or a dean, or a bishop, then no one else has.

# "ALL I POSSESS!"

THERE WAS once a farmer who was so stingy and close fisted that he could scarcely find it in his heart to eat anything; and as for giving anything away to anybody, that was quite out of the question. He also wanted to accustom his wife to do without eating, but it fared with her as with the pedlar's mare; she died from an overdose of that doctrine, and so he had to find another wife in her stead.

And although he was what he was, there were plenty of girls who made themselves agreeable to him and were willing to begin where his wife had left off. For you must know he was rich, the ugly fellow, and it was his money they were after, although they knew they would have to suffer a little in return.

But he was not satisfied with any of them, for if they ate ever so little, they were sure to want something to eat. Those who were stout and comely would be too expensive to keep, and those who were thin and slender were sure to have a big appetite; so he was not able to find any one to his liking, although he had been all over the parish looking for one.

But the lad on the farm came to his assistance. He had heard of a girl in one of the neighbouring parishes, who was not even able to eat as much as a whole pea at one meal, but made it do for two.

The farmer was glad to hear of this; she was the girl he would like to have, and although she was somewhat deaf, so that she never heard more than half of what people said to her, he lost no time in proposing to the girl. Her father and mother said yes at once, seeing that the suitor was so rich, and it did not take him long to persuade the girl herself. A husband she must have some time or other, and so they clinched the matter, and the farmer entered into wedlock for the second time.

But after a time he began to wonder how his wife really managed to keep alive, for he noticed that she never took a morsel of food, or even drank so much as a drop of water, and this he thought was altogether too little. But she seemed to thrive very well for all that, and he even thought she was getting a little stouter.

"I wonder if she's deceiving me?" he thought.

So one day, when he was driving home from his work in the fields, he happened to meet his wife, who was coming from the cowshed with the milk.

"I wonder if she doesn't take a sip of the milk when she is straining it," he thought, and so he asked the lad to help him up on the roof and pull the damper aside, for he wanted to look down the chimney and see what his wife was doing. And this he did. He climbed up on the roof and put his head down the chimney, peering and prying all he could.

The lad then went in to his mistress.

"Master is now looking down the chimney," he said.

"Down the chimney?" said the wife. "Well, then you must put some faggots on the hearth and make a fire.

"I daren't," said the lad.

"If you daren't, I dare," said the woman, and so she made a fire and blew into it.

The farmer began shouting, for the smoke was nearly suffocating him.

"Bless me, is that you, husband?" said his wife.

"Yes, of course it is," said the farmer.

"What are you hanging there for?" she said.

"Oh, I was longing so much for you, wifey, that I went the shortest way," he said, and then he fell down on the hearth, and burned himself a good deal.

Some days passed and his wife neither ate nor drank, but if she did not grow stouter she did not become thinner.

"I wonder if she doesn't eat some of the bacon when she goes to the storehouse," he thought; and so he stole into the storehouse and ripped up one end of a large feather bed which was lying there. He crept into it and asked the lad to sew the ticking together again.

The lad did as he was bid, and then he went in to his mistress.

"Master is now lying inside the feather bed in the storehouse," he said.

"Inside the feather bed in the storehouse?" said the wife. "You must go and beat it well, so that neither dust nor moths get into it," she said, and so she took down a couple of stout hazel sticks and gave them to the lad.

"I daren't," said the lad.

"If you daren't, I dare," said the wife, and she went to the storehouse and began to beat the feather bed with all her might, so that the feathers flew about, and the farmer began shouting, for the blows hit him right across the face.

"Bless me, is that you, husband?" said the woman.

"Yes, of course it is," said the farmer.

"What are you lying there for?" said his wife.

"I thought I would lie on something better than straw for once," said the husband. They then ripped open the feather bed, and when he came out the blood was still streaming down his face.

Some days then passed and the wife neither ate nor drank, but her husband thought she was growing still stouter and more cheerful than ever.

"The devil knows what's at the bottom of all this," he thought. "I wonder if she drinks the beer when she goes into the cellar?"

And so he went down into the cellar and knocked the bottom out of an empty beer-barrel, and then he crept into the barrel, and asked the lad to put the bottom in again. The lad did as he was bid, and then he went in to his mistress.

"Master is now lying in the beer-barrel in the cellar," said the lad.

"In the beer-barrel in the cellar?" said the wife. "You must fill it with boiling juniper lye, for it's getting sour and leaky," she said.

"I daren't," said the lad.

"If you daren't, I dare," said the wife, and so she began boiling juniper lye, and then she poured it into the barrel. The farmer began to shout, but she poured a whole kettleful into the barrel, and yet another after that.

The man went on shouting louder and louder.

"Bless me, is that you, husband?" said the wife.

"Yes, of course it is," yelled the farmer.

"What are you lying there for?" said his wife.

But the farmer was not able to give any answer. He only moaned and groaned, for he was terribly scalded, and when they got him out of the barrel he was more dead than alive, and they had to carry him to his bed.

He now wished to see the parson, and while the lad went to fetch him the wife began to prepare some tasty dishes and to make cheese cakes and other nice things for the parson, so that he should not go away with an empty stomach.

But when the farmer saw how lavish she was in preparing all the dishes he shouted still louder than when he was scalded:

"All I possess! All I possess!" he cried, for he now believed they were going to eat up everything he had, and he knew that both the parson and the clerk were people who could make themselves at home and make a clean sweep of the table.

When the parson arrived the farmer was still shouting:

"All I possess! All I possess!"

"What is it your husband is saying?" said the parson.

"Oh, my husband is so terribly good and kind," said the wife. "He means that I shall have all he possesses," she said.

"His words must then be considered and looked upon as an intimation of his last will and testament," said the parson.

"Just so!" said the wife.

"All I possess! All I possess!" cried the farmer, and then he died.

His wife then had him buried, and afterwards she went to the proper authorities about her husband's affairs. And as both the parson and the clerk could give evidence that the farmer's last words were that she should have all he possessed she got it all. And when a year was gone she married the lad on the farm, but whether after that time she was just as hard of hearing I have never heard.


# THE COCK AND THE CRESTED HEN


THERE WAS once a cock who had a whole farmyard of hens to look after and manage; and among them was a tiny little crested hen. She thought she was altogether too grand to be in company with the other hens, for they looked so old and shabby; she wanted to go out and strut about all by herself, so that people could see how fine she was, and admire her pretty crest and beautiful plumage.

So one day when all the hens were strutting about on the dust-heap and showing themselves off and picking and clucking, as they were wont to do, this desire seized her, and she began to cry:

"Cluck, cluck, cluck, cluck, over the fence! cluck, cluck, cluck, over the fence!" and wanted to get away.

The cock stretched his neck and shook his comb and feathers, and cried:

"Go not there!" And all the old hens cackled:

"Go-go-go-go not there!"

But she set off for all that; and was not a little proud when she got away, and could go about pluming and showing herself off quite by herself.

Just then a hawk began to fly round in a circle above her, and all of a sudden he swooped down upon her. The cock, as he stood on top of the dust-heap stretching his neck and peering first with one eye and then with the other, had long noticed him, and cried with all his might:

"Come, come, come and help! Come, come, come and help!" till the people came running to see what was the matter. They frightened the hawk so that he let go the hen, and had to be satisfied with her tuft and her finest feathers, which he had plucked from her. And then, you may be sure, she lost no time in running home; she stretched her neck, and tripped along, crying:

"See, see, see, see how I look! See, see, see, see how I look!"

The cock came up to her in his dignified way, drooped one of his wings, and said:

"Didn't I tell you?"

From that time the hen did not consider herself too good to be in the company of the old hens on the dust-heap.

# OLD NICK AND THE PEDLAR

THERE WAS once a pedlar who travelled all over the world with his bag on his back, and a yard measure in his hand. But he did not get on as well as other pedlars, for while they got rid of two or three bagfuls, he was not able to get one bag emptied.

So one evening, as he dragged himself wearily along the roadside, he happened to meet Old Nick, who was lying in wait; for since people had become so Christian, Old Nick had to content himself with pedlars, and such like.

"How is business?" asked Old Nick.

"Oh, times are very bad," said the pedlar. "Wherever I put my head in through the door, I find some of my mates have been before me, and the

OLD NICK AND THE PEDLAR.

womenfolk will buy no more, and the men look angry," he said.

"Well, there's a remedy for that," said Old Nick. "If you will come to an arrangement with me you'll find that things will be different," he said.

Yes, the pedlar had no objection to that, for Old Nick would be sure to have him in the end at any rate; and so they made a bargain that the pedlar should sell all he bought, but if the bags ever became quite empty he should belong to Old Nick there and then.

That was a good bargain, thought the pedlar, for he would take care to manage it so that his bags never became quite empty; and then he set off home and got a horse and cart and goods of all kinds on credit. Then he drove from farm to farm and from one fair to another, and before long he had to go into town again for more goods. But however briskly business went, he always managed to have something left in his bags.

But Old Nick is not one to let anything slip through his fingers if he has once got hold of it, and so he followed close upon his heels, although the pedlar could not see him.

So one day he came to Hinnersmess fair, where there were crowds of people, and business was so brisk that it was as much as he could do to get out his stuff and measure what they wanted. For no doubt Old Nick had managed it so that his goods attracted the people's attention most.

There were other pedlars at the fair, of course; but neither words nor tricks were of any avail, for, in spite of all their gesticulations and persuasive ways, they sold little or nothing, as most of the people went to Old Nick's pedlar.

In order to get some share of the business they had to sell their goods to him, and no sooner were they on his stall than they were sold there and then.

But a pedlar is also a human being, if not exactly one of the best sort; and although he was doing a brisk business he was obliged to leave his stall for a short time, and so he asked one of his mates to attend to his customers in his absence.

While he was away, a man came and asked how much the whole lot would cost, for he wanted to buy it all, and the horse and cart and the bags as well.

"Six hundred crowns," said the pedlar, for you see he thought he might be beaten down. But the man did not even try to bargain by as much as a penny; he put the money at once on the stall.

"And now it's all mine, you understand," he said; and then he laughed. "Tell your mate I shall come to-night to fetch the goods, and then we shall have a drink together on the strength of the bargain," he said; and then he laughed once more, and to such an extent that it sounded like thunder, and the next moment he was gone. It was easy to guess who the person was, for the whole market-place smelt of sulphur.

When the pedlar came back, he asked: "Have you sold anything?"

"Yes, of course I have," said his mate. "I have done a grand business, too! I have sold the whole lot, and the horse and cart, and the bags as well, for four hundred crowns; and here they are," he said, and gave them to him. But the other two hundred crowns he put in his own

OLD NICK AND THE PEDLAR

pocket, for he wasn't a pedlar for nothing, you see.

"The Lord have pity on me then, poor wretch that I am!" moaned the pedlar. "Now I am completely undone."

"Have you gone out of your senses?" said his mate. "He was one of the right sort, I can tell you. He did not even beat me down a stiver, and to-night he is coming to have a drink with you on the strength of the bargain."

"Oh dear, oh dear!" cried the pedlar; and he wailed and moaned so terribly that everybody pitied him, for they thought he had gone out of his mind.

Just then a woman came by.

"What is it you are crying and groaning about?" she asked. But the pedlar went on moaning, for now he felt there was no help for him.

"Be quiet!" said the woman; "don't go on like that, my man! It can never be so bad but it can be bettered, I say; for I am Katie Grey,* and I can always help people out of their trouble, even if it be Old Nick himself you have fallen out with," she said. "Come, let me only hear what's the matter, and we'll find a way out of it."

The pedlar then told her all about his trouble.

If that was all, she said, she would be able to help him, if he only did what she told him; which he, of course, was willing to do, as long as he could save his skin.

When the night had set in Old Nick lost no time in coming to fetch him.

"You thought perhaps you could cheat me, but now you'll have to come with me after all," he said.

"There's no help for it, I suppose," said the pedlar; "but tell me, master, what did we arrange? Was it the whole lot you bought?" he asked.

"Yes, of course," said Old Nick; "I bought the whole lot, and horse and cart, and the bags too, and you remember the contract, I suppose?"

"Well, then, you bought what I have got here in this bag as well," said the pedlar, pointing to a great big bag which stood in a corner.

"Yes, it's all mine," said Old Nick. "But what sort of goods have you got in that bag? It looks so strange!"

"It's the best of all I have," said the pedlar, and opened the bag, and who should peep out but Katie Grey!

But then Old Nick opened his eyes and gave a start like a scared hare.

"Whew!" he shouted. "I haven't bought that bag, for any one who knows that fiendish creature would not have her as a gift."

"Yes, but then you haven't bought all of it," said the pedlar, "for she is mine as well, and she must go with the lot," he said.

"No, thank you!" said Old Nick. "I can easily do without a pedlar, for there are more of them; but if I take Katie Grey into the bargain I shall never have any peace. I know that terrible creature," he said.

With that he released the pedlar from his bond, and flew up through the chimney, carrying off the roof with him.

What happened afterwards I have never been able to find out; but if

---

*An evil old woman who had formerly outwitted Old Nick.

Old Nick could not get on with Katie Grey, the pedlar is not likely to have been any the better by the exchange either.

# WHY THE EXECUTIONER IS CALLED ASSESSOR

MANY, MANY years ago—well, it's so very, very long ago that no one can really tell how long ago it was—a number of grandees entered into a conspiracy against the king. But in spite of their power and arrogance he succeeded in laying them by the heels, and those who were not willing to swear submission to him there and then were all to lose their heads, which was only fair and just; for if one has not got more sense in one's head than to engage in such foolish undertakings, one may as well do without a head.

But since they were all such grand folks, the king himself wanted to see that everything was carried out properly; and so he set out for the spot where the execution was to take place, which was some distance away in the country. The executioner was, of course, going there as well; but he was not then such a great personage as he is now, and did not travel in such state, either at the public expense or at his own. Oh no, he had to trudge and plod along on his own legs, were the distance ever so great.

So it happened that he got into the middle of a big forest just as night was setting in, and as there was no sign of any house where he could get lodgings, he looked about for a place where he could lie down and rest. But while he was walking about looking for one, he saw some smoke rising out of the earth, and then he discovered in the ground a trap door covered with turf. If the smoke had not been coming out through the chinks he would never have noticed it.

While he stood wondering where the smoke came from, the trap door was lifted up, and the sooty and dishevelled head of a woman appeared in the opening.

"Bless the man!" said the woman, "have you lost your senses, standing there staring like that? The robbers will be home directly, and if they see you they'll pay you out for prying about here, and you'll never hear the cuckoo again," she said, and then she disappeared into the ground again.

The executioner was not easily frightened, but, 'he who does take care, will always safest fare;' and so he quietly slunk away.

But as he trudged along he marked the trees with his axe; for 'when one knows where the wolf lives, one need not go to the furrier for his skin,' he thought.

So by dint of walking and running he came at last to his destination; and what he had come there to do he did so satisfactorily that he was well rewarded, and the king himself thanked him for his able assistance.

But since the king was so condescending as to speak to one whom other people would not be seen with, the executioner thought he might as well have his say also, and so he told the king what he had seen in the forest. The king was greatly pleased to hear of this, for these robbers had done so much mischief to him and other folks that he would like to get hold of them.

"If I could only get some people to come with me," said the executioner, "I should be sure to catch them, for now I know where they are."

"Yes, that was all very well," thought the king; but he wanted to do this business in his own way, for he was strong and bold beyond all bounds. He was so powerful, indeed, that no one ventured to wrestle with him, for he could throw one and all to the ground in less than no time.

"What do we want with people?" he said. "If you will only come with me and show me the way, I think we two might venture a bout with them," he said; "for you look no weakling either."

Well, the executioner had no objection to that, for it wasn't every day he was in such company, and so they settled how they should set about it.

The king took off his crown and all his finery, and then they dressed themselves up like the worst of tramps, and blackened their faces and tore their clothes into pieces, so that the rags hung and dangled about them. The king put a sword inside his trousers, and the executioner hid his axe under his jacket; and so they set out.

No sooner had they got into the forest than they met the robbers, of whom there were altogether twelve.

"Who are you?" asked he who seemed to be their chief.

"We are a couple of miserable wretches, who are obliged to beg our bread," said the executioner. "We haven't tasted a morsel the whole day, and don't know what we are going to do for the night either," he said.

"There isn't much to be got out of you, poor beggars!" said the robber; "but that makes no difference. Since you have got into the forest you'll have to die, and no mistake," he said.

"God bless you for your pretty speech!" said the executioner, looking as miserable as he possibly could. "How lucky we were to fall in with you, for you know very well it's no pleasure to live when your stomach groans for food, and when you cannot get a morsel to satisfy it with. But since you are such a mighty lord, you might give us a good feed first, for, after all, it's hard to die on an empty stomach."

This greatly amused the robber, who laughed; and then the others began to laugh, so that their laughter could be heard all over the forest.

"Have you never had a good feed, poor wretches?" he asked. "Well, I'll be extravagant for once in my life. So come along, and you shall have as much as you can put into your carcasses. But to tell the truth, nobody who falls in with me need trouble much about food for the rest of their life," he said; and so he laughed, and then the other robbers laughed till the forest trembled.

They then set out for the robbers' cave, and there they lifted up the trap door, and slid down under the ground one after the other, and the two tramps as well.

There was a large room down there, and a long table in the middle,

WHY THE EXECUTIONER IS CALLED ASSESSOR

which stood ready laid. The woman with the sooty face carried in the food on silver dishes to the robbers, who sat side by side on the bench along the wall. They feasted and drank burnt brandy out of large chalices, and talked and bragged about all their valiant deeds, while they were having their fill.

When the robbers had had enough both of food and drink, the tramps were allowed to sit down to the table, but on the opposite side to the robbers.

The woman put both beef and pork before them, and each of them got his cup filled with brandy. But no sooner had she placed the food on the table than matters took quite a different turn. They planted their feet firmly on the ground, and pushed the table with such force against the robbers, that they were fixed against the wall as if they were nailed to it. Then they threw the brandy into the robbers' eyes, and the king drew forth his sword and the executioner his axe, and before the robbers could rub the brandy out of their eyes they were all killed.

This was a big capture, and no mistake; and the king was greatly pleased with it. All that was found in the robbers' cave he wanted to give to the executioner; but "no thank you," he answered, "there was something else he would like to have."

"Well, what might that be?" asked the king.

"Well, your majesty," he said, "if an executioner becomes ever so rich he's always looked upon as a butcher; and the people spit after him just as if he were Old Nick himself, and he is hardly ever allowed to mix with respectable people, however honest he may be. I would therefore most humbly ask your majesty to ordain it so that an executioner shall be respected like other people," he said.

"Yes, that is fair and reasonable," said the king; "and so it shall be."

The king accordingly issued an edict that no one must dare to spit after the executioner, for his calling was just as respectable as any other; and in order that no one should be ashamed to be in his company he was to have the title of Assessor, and wear a three-cornered hat when he was in full dress. Such was the edict, and so it is to this day.

But as the executioner would not accept what the robbers had hoarded, the king gave it to the woman who had served with them; and when she had combed the hair away from her eyes and washed the soot off her face she turned out to be quite a handsome woman. The executioner then thought that as the king had been so generous to him he would not be behindhand either, and so he made her the Lady Assessor; and thus after all he became possessor of all that the robbers had hoarded up.

# THE PARSON AND THE CLERK

THERE WAS once upon a time a parson who was such a miser that he even begrudged the beggars a meal; and as for giving a poor fellow a shelter

THE PARSON AND THE CLERK

for the night, he would not hear of it.

But he was a great preacher; and when he had once begun he would shout and thunder and strike the pulpit with his fists so that every corner in the church rang with his words. And his parishioners had nothing to complain about in this respect; but they did not like his meanness, and they thought it was a shame they had to put up with such a parson.

The parson's wife suffered not a little in consequence; for she was a kind and good woman, but she could do nothing with her husband.

Just before Christmas, when the poor were most importunate, the parson used to dress himself up like a tramp and sit in the kitchen in the evenings; and when some poor fellow came and asked for shelter for the night, the parson's wife had to say that they already had one to find room for, and would then tell him to go to the clerk, who was their nearest neighbour. The clerk, as you may guess, would have been just as pleased if he had not been troubled with these guests; for he thought—as was only too true—that it was more the parson's duty than his to feed and shelter the poor. But the clerk was a sly dog and full of fun and mischief, as parish clerks generally are.

It would be a strange thing, he thought, if there were not a remedy for meanness as well as for other ailments; so one evening, shortly before Christmas, he dressed himself like a tramp, and went to the parsonage and asked for shelter for the night.

Yes, that he should have had with pleasure, but they already had a stranger in the house, said the parson's wife, pointing to the other tramp, who was stitting by the hearth—for, of course, she never said a word about him being the parson. As matters stood she thought he had better go to the clerk, for they were not likely to have any strangers over there.

"Haven't they?" said the clerk. "Why, they have their place so full they have scarcely any room for themselves; for I have just come from there," he said, "and I don't think you would like me to sleep in the fields and freeze to death, would you?"

Oh, dear no, it wasn't likely; she could not be so unchristian; but as she had no place to put him she could not very well do anything for him, she said.

"I think you can," said the clerk; "if you can shelter one you can shelter two, and I don't suppose that this mate of mine is going to sleep in the parson's bed, is he?" he asked, and slapped the parson so hard on his back that he nearly tumbled on the hearth.

"We must be content, and be thankful as well, whichever way the world treats us," said the parson.

"What you say is quite true," said the clerk; "and I'll be quite content, and share the bed with you, if the lady of the house allows it, and she will then shelter two men to-night instead of one. For there is no help for it, as far as I can see," he said.

The parson's wife resisted his importunities as long as she could, for she thought the tramp would not be a pleasant bedfellow for her husband; but the clerk would by no means listen to her, so she had to give in at last.

They were to sleep in the servant lad's room in the brew-house, as he was away at the mill—the parson in the settle-bed, and the clerk on the bench.

That was her order; but the clerk was not satisfied with the arrangement, and when he came into the room he threw himself into the settle-bed, and the parson had to content himself with the bench.

Before long the clerk stole out of the room, and when he came back he woke the parson and said:

"I have served out that miserly parson, I can tell you! I have made a hole in the loft of his wood-shed, so that all the corn he had stored in the room above is running down among his stacks of wood."

"Oh dear! oh dear!" wailed the parson.

"What's the matter with you?" said the clerk.

"I feel so bad, so bad!" said the parson, and off he ran to the wood-shed.

"I think I have given him something to do now, and why should I lie on this wretched straw? I shall find better quarters in the house," thought the clerk; and so he went into the house and sat down in the parlour by the fire. The door was open to the parson's bedroom, and in order that the wife should think it was her husband who had come in he imitated the parson's voice.

"I have been lying so uncomfortably," he said in a pitiful voice, "for that scamp of a tramp made me lie on the bench, so I thought I would come here and rest for a little while."

"Of course, of course, my dear," said the wife. "But why should you be so hard-hearted with people? It is a sin and shame, that it is,—and it brings you no happiness either."

"Ah well, that may be," said the clerk, all the time imitating the parson. "I have been suffering so much to-night that I shall be better after this."

"God bless you for those words!" said the parson's wife.

In a little while the clerk said: "I must go now to that tramp, so that he does not find out where I am."

And off he went, and only just managed to lie down in time before the parson returned.

The parson had in the meantime been hard at work in the wood-shed trying to stop the hole in the loft, and had fallen head over heels many times among the logs and firewood, before he succeeded in doing so; but by that time nearly all the corn had found its way down into the wood-shed.

He came back to the servant-lad's room puffing and groaning like a smith's bellows, and lay down on the bench. As soon as the clerk saw that he had settled down and got the blanket over his head, he stole out of the room again.

When he came back he woke the parson and said:

"I have now served the parson a still better trick. When I came outside and heard the wolves howling over the hills, I went into the cow-house and let out all the cattle."

"Oh dear! oh dear!" shouted the parson, and started as if he had been shot.

"What's the matter with you?" said the clerk.

"I feel so bad, so bad! said the parson; and the next moment he was gone.

"I think you'll have enough to do for a long while now," said the clerk; and so he went back to the parlour.

"Are you there again?" asked the parson's wife from the bedroom.

"Yes, my dear," said the clerk, imitating the parson's voice. "I sent that tramp on a fool's errand; and I have been suffering so much on the bench that I thought I would come here and rest again for a while."

"Yes, my dear, that you must," said the wife; and the clerk settled down in the chair by the fire.

In a while the clerk said: "I must go back to that tramp again, so that he does not find out where I am;" and then he went back to his bed.

In the meanwhile the parson had been running about the fields and hills, and had fallen several times on his face, while he rushed about calling and driving in the cattle. He had a terrible struggle to get all the beasts back to the cow-house, for he had a large herd of cattle.

The clerk had not been long in bed when the parson came rushing into the room, puffing and groaning, so that one could not help pitying him; for he seemed to have lost his breath altogether.

"You were long away this time," said the clerk. "But in the meantime I have served out that miserly parson once more."

"What's that you say?" said the parson, who began to feel so ill at ease that he could scarcely keep on his legs.

"Yes," said the clerk; but this time he did not speak the truth. "I have been down in the cellar; and I have poured two buckets of ditch water in the beer barrel in the far off corner, for I thought the parson ought to have something to give his clerk at Christmas."

"Oh dear! oh dear!" shouted the parson.

"What's the matter with you?" asked the clerk.

"I feel so bad, so bad!" said the parson.

"Yes, I can imagine that," said the clerk; "and I pity you so much that now you may lie in my bed. It'll soon be morning, and I must be getting away. I don't expect I shall get any breakfast from this miserable parson, do you? Well, good-bye, then," he said; and off he went.

"Phew!" sighed the parson. He felt as if the whole parish had been lifted off his back; and no sooner was the clerk gone than he dragged himself in to his wife.

"Are you there again, husband?" she said.

"A-gain?" said the parson; it was with the greatest difficulty he was able to speak, so exhausted was he.

"Yes; you have been here twice before during the night," said his wife.

"Tw-ice?" groaned the parson.

"Yes, of course," said his wife.

"You have been dreaming!" said the parson.

"Oh dear, no; I don't dream when I don't sleep," said his wife. "But, my dear good husband, don't play such pranks another time!"

"No-o!" said the parson. "Better to give to the poor than to go through such misery as I have done to-night," he said, forcing the words out; and then he fell asleep.

All at once he started up and shouted to his wife: "My dear!"

"Well, my dear?" said his wife.

"The beer barrel in the furthest corner you must send to the clerk," he said.

"Bless my soul, but that's too much," said his wife.

"It's just—about right," moaned the parson; and then he fell asleep again.

Next morning the wife had the barrel of beer sent across to the clerk's house. He was much pleased to receive it, and sent back his thanks for it; for *he* knew the beer had not been tampered with. But the parson had the greatest trouble to sort out the corn from the splinters and rubbish in the wood-shed. But they kept on cleaning and shaking and sorting so long that at last they saved all the corn, with the execption of a few barrels.

But the parson never forgot that terrible night. He was cured of his meanness, and became quite a different person. He never refused any poor people either food or lodgings; and when the farmers came to pay their tithes in the autumn he gave them such a grand feast that his parishioners said they could never have wished for a better parson.

It was indeed worth a barrel of beer to have such a parish clerk!

# PART TWO
## From the Regions

## SKÅNE

## THE SURE SHOT

IT IS not alone in Bohemia's mountainous regions that the romantic characters are found which form the basis of Weber's immortal fictions. Similar traditions are current in many lands, especially in Sweden, one of which we will now relate.

In the artless fancy of the peasantry the means of acquiring the power of unerring aim are many, the most usual by compact with the Fairies or Wood Nymphs. While the compact lasts the possessor, sitting at his hut door, needs only to wish, and the game of his choice springs into view, and within range of his never-failing gun. Such a compact, however, invariably ends in the destruction of the hunter.

Many years ago there was a watchman up in the Göinge regions, a wild fellow, who, one evening, while drinking with his neighbors, more tipsy and more talkative as the hour grew late, boasted loudly of his marksmanship, and offered to wager that, with his trusty gun, he could give them such an exhibition of skill as they had never before seen.

"There goes, as I speak," said he, "a roe on Halland's Mountains."

His companions laughed at him, not believing that he could know what was transpiring at a distance of several miles, which was the least that lay between them and the spot indicated.

"I will wager you that I need go no farther than the door to shoot him for you," persevered the watchman in defiant tones.

"Nonsense!" said the others.

"Come, will you wager something worth the while? Say two cans of ale."

"Done! Two cans of ale, it shall be." And the company betook themselves to the yard in front of the hut.

It was a frosty autumn evening. The wind chased the clouds over the sky, and the half moon cast fitful reflections through the breaks over the neighborhood. In a few minutes a something was seen moving rapidly along the edge of a thicket on the farther side of a little glade. The watchman threw his gun carelessly to his shoulder and fired. A derisive laugh was echo to the report. No mortal, thought they, in such uncertain light and at such a distance, could shoot a deer in flight.

238

The watchman, certain of his game, hastened across the glade, followed by his companions, to whom the event meant, at least, two cans of ale.

It would not be easy to picture the surprise of the doubters, when, upon arriving at the thicket, they discovered, lying upon the ground, bathed in foam and his tongue hanging from his mouth, a magnificent stag, pierced through the heart by the deadly bullet, his life blood fast coloring his bed of autumn leaves a brighter hue.

What unseen power has brought this poor animal from Halland's Mountains in a bare half hour? Such were the thoughts of the watchman's companions as they retired in silence to the hut.

The watchman received his two cans of ale, but no one seemed inclined to join him in disposing of them. They now understood with what sort of a man they were having to do. It was evident to them that the watchman was in league with the Evil One himself, and they henceforth guarded themselves carefully against companionship with him after dark.

# STOMPE PILT

AT A little distance from Baal Mountain, in the parish of Filkestad, in Willand's Härad, lies a hill where, formerly, lived a giant named Stompe Pilt.

It happened one day, that a Goatherd came that way, driving his goats before him, up the hill.

"Who comes there?" demanded the Giant, rushing out of the hill, with a large flint stone in his fist, when he discovered the Goatherd.

"It is I, if you will know," responded the Herder, continuing his way up the hill with his flock.

"If you come up here I will squeeze you into fragments as I do this stone," shrieked the Giant, and crushed the stone between his fingers into fine sand.

"Then I will squeeze water out of you as I do out of this stone," replied the Herder, taking a new-made cheese from his bag and squeezing it so that the whey ran between his fingers to the ground.

"Are you not afraid?" asked the Giant.

"Not of you," replied the Herder.

"Then let us fight," continued Stompe Pilt.

"All right," responded the Goatherd, "but let us first taunt each other so that we will become right angry, for taunting will beget anger and anger will give us cause to fight."

"Very well, and I will begin," said the Giant.

"Go ahead, and I will follow you," said the Herder.

"You shall become a crooked nose hobgoblin," cried the Giant.

"You shall become a flying devil," retorted the Herder, and from his bow shot a sharp arrow into the body of the Giant.

"What is that?" inquired the Giant, endeavoring to pull the arrow from his flesh.

"That is a taunt," replied the Herder.

"Why has it feathers?" asked the Giant.

"In order that it may fly straight and rapidly," answered the Herder.

"Why does it stick so fast?" asked the Giant.

"Because it has taken root in your body," was the answer.

"Have you more of such?" inquired the Giant.

"There, you have another," said the Herder, and shot another arrow into the Giant's body.

"Aj! aj!" shrieked Stompe Pilt; "are you not angry enough to fight?"

"No, I have not yet taunted you enough," replied the Herder, setting an arrow to his bowstring.

"Drive your goats where you will. I can't endure your taunting, much less your blows," shrieked Stompe Pilt, and sprang into the hill again.

Thus the Herder was saved by means of his bravery and ingenuity.

# THE LORD OF ROSENDAL

In the beginning of the Sixteenth Century there lived in Skåne a nobleman, Andres Bille, Lord of Rosendal, who was very severe toward his dependents, and it was not unusual that a disobedient servant was put in chains, and even into the castle dungeons.

One day Bille's intended wife made a visit to Rosendal. Upon entering the court-yard almost the first object that attracted her attention was a peasant tethered like a horse. She inquiring as to the cause of such treatment, Bille informed her that the servant had come late to work, and was now suffering only well-merited punishment. The young woman begged Bille to set the man at liberty, but this he refused to do, and told her, emphatically, that she must not interpose in his affairs.

"When the intended wife," said the young lady, as she returned to her carriage, "is refused a boon so small, what will be the fate of the wife?" and thereupon she commanded her coachman to drive her home at once, and resolved to come no more to Rosendal.

People predicted that such a heartless man could not possibly be at rest in his grave, and true to the prediction, Bille, after his death and burial, came every night, in spirit, to Rosendal. Halting his white team in the court-yard, with stealthy steps he would make his way to his former bed-chamber where he would spend the night until cock-crow. If the bed had been prepared all was quiet in the chamber, otherwise such a dreadful noise followed that there was no such thing as sleep in the castle. Always, upon going to the room in the morning, the bed clothes were found tossed about and soiled as if a dog had occupied the bed.

THE LORD OF ROSENDAL

When the specter had gone on in this manner for a number of years, the new owner of the estate applied to a pious priest in Hässlunda, Master Steffan, and begged him to put a stop to these troublesome visits. To this end the priest, one day, accompanied by a fellow priest, set out for Kropp's Church, where Bille was buried. On the stroke of 12 o'clock, midnight, the grave opened and the ghost of the dead lord stepped forth. Father Steffan's companion at once took to his heels, but Father Steffan remained and began to read from a book he had with him. During the reading the ghost became larger and larger, but the priest would not be frightened. Finally the apparition interrupted the reading and addressed the priest.

"Is that you, Steffan, the goose thief?"

"It is, indeed, I," replied the priest, "and it is true that in my boyhood I stole a goose, but with the money received for the goose I bought a Bible, and with that Bible I will send you to hell, you evil spirit." Whereupon he struck the specter such a blow on the forehead with the Bible that it sank again into purgatory.

Unfortunately, because of the truth of Bille's accusation and that it came from Bille, the priest's prayers and reading lost much of potency, and he was unable to enforce upon the ghost entire quietude. Nevertheless, so much was accomplished that Bille now comes to Rosendal only once a year.

# THE MASTER OF UGERUP

IN THE parish of Köpinge, on the northern bank of a stream which, a short distance below Lake Helga, flows into the river Helga, lies an old mansion, Ugerup or Ugarp, known in early days as the seat of the Ugerup family, famous in the history of Denmark.

In the middle of the Sixteenth Century the estate was owned by Senator Axel Ugerup. On the Näs estate, a few miles distant, dwelt the wealthy Tage Thott, at that time one of the richest men in Skåne.

Herr Arild, Alex Ugerup's son, and Thale, Tage Thott's fair daughter, had, it may be said, grown up together, and even in childhood, had conceived a strong love for each other.

When Arild was yet a young man he was made ambassador to Sweden by the Danish Government, in which capacity he took part in the coronation of Erik XIV. Upon his return to Ugerup he renewed his attentions to his boyhood's love, and without difficulty obtained her consent and that of her parents to a union.

Not long thereafter war broke out between Sweden and Denmark. With anxiety and distress the lovers heard the call to arms. The flower of Danish knighthood hastened to place themselves under the ensign of their country, where even for Arild Ugerup a place was prepared. At leave-taking the lovers promised each other eternal fidelity, and Arild was soon in Copenhagen, where he was given a position in the navy.

In the beginning the Danes met with some success, but soon the tables were turned. At Öland Klas Kristenson Horn defeated the united Danish and Leibich flotillas, capturing three ships, with their crews and belongings. Among the captured was Arild Ugerup, who was carried, a prisoner, to Stockholm, where three short years before he was an honored visitor and won his knightly spurs.

The friends of Arild entertained little hope that they would ever see him again, and his rivals for the hand of Thale persistently renewed their suits. Tage Thott, who saw his daughter decline the attentions of one lover after another, decided, finally, that this conduct must not continue, and made known to his daughter that she must choose a husband from among the many available and desirable young men seeking her hand. Thale took this announcement very much to heart, but her prayers and tears were without avail. Spring succeeded winter and no Arild came. Meanwhile, the unrelenting father had made a choice and fixed upon a day when the union should take place.

During this time Arild, languishing in his prison, busied his brain in the effort to find some means of escape, but plan after plan was rejected as impracticable, until it occurred to him to make use of his rank and acquaintance with the King. So, not long thereafter, he sent to King Erik a petition, asking permission to go home on parole, for the purpose of solemnizing his wedding, also to be permitted to remain long enough in Ugerup to sow and gather his crops. The King readily granted his petition, since Arild promised, on his knightly honor, to return to his confinement as soon as his harvest was ripe.

He at once hastened to Skåne where he was not long in learning what had transpired during his absence, and that Thale, at her father's bidding, was about to be wedded to another. Continuing his journey to Näs, where his arrival caused both rejoicing and consternation, he presented himself to Tage and demanded Thale to wife, as had been promised him. Knight Tage, however, would not listen to such a thing as a change from his plans, and declared firmly that his daughter should belong to him whom he had selected for her, but Arild made a speedy end to the trouble. By strategy, he carried his bride away in secret to Denmark, where they were shortly afterward married. Tage, outwitted, made the best of the matter and accepted the situation, whereupon Arild and his wife returned to Ugerup.

Arild now had time to think about his promise to the King, and how he might, at the same time, keep it and not be separated from his wife. It would now profit to sow seeds that would not mature soon, so the fields that had heretofore been devoted to corn were planted with the seeds of the pine tree.

When the autumn had passed, and the King thought the harvest must, by this time, have been gathered, he sent Arild a request to come to Stockholm. But Arild convinced the messenger that his seeds had not yet sprouted, much less ripened.

When King Erik was made acquainted with the state of affairs, he could do no less than approve the ingenious method adopted by Arild to obtain his freedom without breaking his word, and allowed the matter to rest.

The product of Arild's pine seeds is now shown in a magnificent forest at Ugerup.

Many other stories are told in Skåne about Arild Ugerup and his wife. Among others, it is related of the former that he was endowed with marvelous strength, and that in the arch of the gateway opening into the estate was a pair of iron hooks, which, when coming home from Helsingborg, Arild was wont to catch hold of, and lift himself and horse together some distance off the ground, after which little exercise he would ride on.

His wife, Thale, was, like her husband, very strong, very good and benevolent, likewise very generous toward her dependents. A story is told of her, that one mid-summer evening, when the servants of the estate were gathered on the green for a dance, she requested her husband to give the people as much food and drink as she could carry at one load, and her request being, of course, granted, she piled up two great heaps of beef, pork and bread, which, with two barrels of ale, one under each arm, she carried out onto the green, with ease.

# THE GHOST AT FJELKINGE

DURING THE early half of the Seventeenth Century many of the best estates in Skåne belonged to the family of Barkenow, or more correctly, to the principal representative of the family, Madame Margaretta Barkenow, daughter of the renowned general and governor-general, Count Rutger Von Ascheberg, and wife of Colonel Kjell Kristofer Barkenow.

A widow at twenty-nine, she took upon herself the management of her many estates, in the conduct of which she ever manifested an indomitable, indefatigable energy, and a never-ceasing care for her numerous dependents.

On a journey over her estates, Madame Margaretta came, one evening, to Fjelkinge's inn, and persisted in sleeping in a room which was called the "ghost's room." A traveler had, a few years before, slept in this room, and as it was supposed had been murdered, at least the man and his effects had disappeared, leaving no trace of what had become of them. After this his ghost appeared in the room nightly, and those who were acquainted with the circumstance, traveled to the next post, in the dark, rather than choose such quarters for the night. Margaretta was, however, not among this number. She possessed greater courage, and without fear chose the chamber for her sleeping room.

After her evening prayers she retired to bed and sleep, leaving the lamp burning. At twelve o'clock she was awakened by the lifting up of

THE GHOST AT FJELKINGE

two boards in the floor, and from the opening a bloody form appeared, with a cloven head hanging upon its shoulders.

"Noble lady," whispered the apparition, "I beg you prepare, for a murdered man, a resting place in consecrated ground, and speed the murderer to his just punishment."

Pure in heart, therefore not alarmed, Lady Margaretta beckoned the apparition to come nearer, which it did, informing her that it had entreated others, who after the murder had slept in the room, but that none had the courage to comply. Then Lady Margaretta took from her finger a gold ring, laid it in the gaping wound, and bound the apparition's head up with her pocket handerchief. With a glance of unspeakable thankfulness the ghost revealed the name of the murderer and disappeared noiselessly beneath the floor.

The following morning Lady Margaretta instructed the bailiff of the estate to assemble the people at the post house, where she informed them what had happened during the night, and commanded that the planks of the floor be taken up. Here, under the ground, was discovered a half decomposed corpse, with the countess' ring in the hole in its skull, and her handkerchief bound around its head.

At sight of this, one of those present grew pale and fainted to the ground. Upon being revived he confessed that he had murdered the traveler and robbed him of his goods. He was condemned to death for his crime, and the murdered man received burial in the parish churchyard.

The ring, which is peculiarly formed and set with a large grayish chased stone, remains even now in the keeping of the Barkenow family, and is believed to possess miraculous powers in sickness, against evil spirits and other misfortunes. When one of the family dies it is said that a red, bloodlike spot appears upon the stone.

# LJUNGBY HORN AND PIPE

ON THE estates of Ljungby there lies a large stone called Maglestone, under which the Trolls, in olden times, were wont to assemble and, with dancing and games, celebrate their Christmas.

One Christmas night Lady Cissela Ulfstand, sitting in her mansion, listening to the merry-making of the Trolls under the stone, and curious to have a better knowledge of these mysterious mountain people, assembled her menservants and promised the best horse in her stables to him who would ride to Maglestone, at Vesper hour, and bring her a full account of the doings there.

One of her swains, a daring young fellow, accepted the offer, and a little later set out on his way. Arriving at the stone, he discovered it lifted from the ground, supported on pillars of gold, and under it the Trolls in the midst of their revelry.

Upon discovering the horseman a young Troll woman, leaving the others, approached him bearing a drinking horn and pipe. These, upon reaching his side, she placed in the young man's hand, with directions to first drink from the horn to the health of the Mountain King, then blow three times on the pipe, at the same time whispering some words of caution in his ears, whereupon he threw the contents of the horn over his shoulder and set off at the utmost speed, over fields and meadows, toward home. The Trolls followed him closely with great clamor, but he flew before them across the drawbridge, which was at once pulled up, and proceeded to place the horn and pipe in the hands of his mistress.

Outside, across the moat, the Trolls now stood, promising Lady Cissela great happiness and riches if she would return to them their horn and pipe, and declaring that, otherwise, great misfortune and destruction would overtake her and her family, and that it should go especially hard with the young man who had dared to deprive them of the precious articles. True to the predictions, the young man died on the third day thereafter and the horse which he rode fell dead a day later.

During the war of 1645 Field Marshal Gustaf Horn, whose headquarters were at Fjelkinge, having heard this story, and wishing to see the horn and pipe, requested that they be brought to him. The possessor, Axel Gyllerstierna, who then owned Ljungby, forwarded them, accompanied with earnest prayers that they be returned to him as soon as possible. Horn's curiosity was soon satisfied, and he felt no desire to retain them longer in his possession, for while he did he was disturbed every night by unseemly noises about his quarters, which ceased, when, under the escort of a company of cavalry, he sent them back to Ljungby.

Ten years later there took place a still more wonderful circumstance. Henrik Nilsson, the priest at Ljungby, borrowed the strange articles for the purpose of showing them to his brothers-in-law who were then visiting him. During the night the priest's mother-in-law, Lady Anna Conradi, who was one of the family, was awakened by the light of a candle in her room. The bed curtains were drawn back and upon her bed a basket was dropped wherein sat five small children, who in chorus set up a cry:

"O you, who are noted for your kindness, please return to us our horn!"

To her question why they desired it and what value it had to them, they answered:

"For our people's sake."

When she would no longer listen to their pleading they departed, saying they would come again three nights later.

On Thursday night, and the third following their first visit, there was again a light in her room. When Lady Anna drew back the bed curtain she discovered her chamber occupied by a great number of little men, and among them the Troll King himself, approaching her under a canopy of silver cloth upheld on silver poles borne by four servants. His skin was a dark brown and his hair, of which only a tuft was left on his forehead and one by each ear, black and woolly. Softly he neared the bed, holding forth a horn richly adorned with gold chains and massive gold buttons, which he proffered the lady in exchange for the genuine horn. But she was not to be persuaded, and consigned them to God, if they belonged to him, and to the devil, if they were his offspring, whereupon the Trolls quietly and sorrowfully departed.

Soon thereafter it was reported that a peasant's child had been carried off by the Trolls. By means of ringing the church bells it was, however, returned to its mother. The boy related that the Trolls were not pretty, but had large noses and mouths; that the man under Maglestone was called Klausa and his wife Otta. That they sucked the moisture from the food of mankind and so sustained themselves; that they obeyed one king; that they were often at variance with each other, also, that they spoke the language of the country. Lord Chancellor Coyet, who published, "A Narrative of Ljungby Horn and Pipe," dated February 11, 1692, says that he knew this boy, who was then twenty-seven years old, also his mother, but admits that both were disposed to superstition and that their understandings were as feeble as their bodies.

# BLEKINGE

## THE SWAN MAIDEN

A YOUNG peasant, in the parish of Mellby, who often amused himself with hunting, saw one day three swans flying toward him, which settled down upon the strand of a sound near by.

Approaching the place, he was astonished at seeing the three swans divest themselves of their feathery attire, which they threw into the grass, and three maidens of dazzling beauty step forth and spring into the water.

After sporting in the waves awhile they returned to the land, where they resumed their former garb and shape and flew away in the same direction from which they came.

One of them, the youngest and fairest, had, in the meantime, so smitten the young hunter that neither night nor day could he tear his thoughts from the bright image.

His mother, noticing that something was wrong with her son, and that the chase, which had formerly been his favorite pleasure, had lost its attractions, asked him finally the cause of his melancholy, whereupon he related to her what he had seen, and declared that there was no longer any happiness in this life for him if he would not possess the fair swan maiden.

"Nothing is easier," said the mother. "Go at sunset next Thursday evening to the place where you last saw her. When the three swans come

THE SWAN MAIDEN

give attention to where your chosen one lays her feathery garb, take it and hasten away."

The young man listened to his mother's instructions, and, betaking himself, the following Thursday evening, to a convenient hiding place near the sound, he waited, with impatience, the coming of the swans. The sun was just sinking behind the trees when the young man's ears were greeted by a whizzing in the air, and the three swans settled down upon the beach, as on their former visit.

As soon as they had laid off their swan attire they were again transformed into the most beautiful maidens, and, springing out upon the white sand, they were soon enjoying themselves in the water.

From his hiding place the young hunter had taken careful note of where his enchantress had laid her swan feathers. Stealing softly forth, he took them and returned to his place of concealment in the surrounding foliage.

Soon thereafter two of the swans were heard to fly away, but the third, in search of her clothes, discovered the young man, before whom, believing him responsible for their disappearance, she fell upon her knees and prayed that her swan attire might be returned to her. The hunter was, however, unwilling to yield the beautiful prize, and, casting a cloak around her shoulders, carried her home.

Preparations were soon made for a magnificent wedding, which took place in due form, and the young couple dwelt lovingly and contentedly together.

One Thursday evening, seven years later, the hunter related to her how he had sought and won his wife. He brought forth and showed her, also, the white swan feathers of her former days. No sooner were they placed in her hands than she was transformed once more into a swan, and instantly took flight through the open window. In breathless astonishment, the man stared wildly after his rapidly vanishing wife, and before a year and a day had passed, he was laid, with his longings and sorrows, in his allotted place in the village church-yard.

# THE KNIGHT OF ELLENHOLM

MANY, MANY years ago there lived, in Ellenholm Castle, a knight, who, wishing to attend Christmas matins at Morrum's Church, with a long journey before him, and anxious to be present if possible at first matins, set out from the castle, accompanied by his groom, immediately after midnight. Some distance on the way, feeling sleepy, he instructed the groom to ride on while he dismounted and sat down by the roadside, at the foot of a mountain, to take a nap and refresh himself.

He had been sitting only a few minutes when a monster giantess came and bade him follow her into the mountain, which he did, and was conducted to the presence of her giant husband. Here all kinds of tempting viands were set before him, but the Knight, who knew well into what kind of company he had fallen, declined to partake of the food.

Offended at this, the woman drew forth a knife and addressed the Knight:

"Do you recognize this? It is the one with which you chopped me in the thigh when, one time, I was gathering hay for my calves. Father, what do you think we ought to do with him?"

"Let him go," said the Giant. "We can do nothing to him for he invokes the Great Master too much."

"So be it," said the Giantess, "but he shall have something to remember me by." Whereupon she broke the Knight's little finger.

He soon discovered himself in the open air again, and the groom who had returned to search for his master found him in the place where he had left him, but with a little finger broken—a warning to every one not to sleep on the way to church.

# SMÅLAND

# THE TROLLS IN SKURUGATA

IT IS generally understood that Trolls, when their territory is encroached upon by mankind, withdraw to some more secluded place. So when Eksjö was built, those that dwelt in that vicinity moved to Skurugata, a defile between two high mountains whose perpendicular sides rise so near to each other as to leave the bottom in continual semi-darkness and gloom.

Here, it may be supposed, they were left in peace and tranquility. Not so, however, for it is related that upon the occasion of the annual meeting of troops at Ränneslätt, a whole battalion of Småland grenadiers repeatedly marched through, with beating drums and blowing horns, and that sometimes they fired a volley from their guns, which so alarmed the Trolls that it is now a question whether any are still remaining there.

In the neighborhood of the same mountain gulch is a very sacred fountain where those living thereabouts, in former times are said to have offered sacrifices to their patron saint. Whether this custom is now continued is not known. As intelligence increases this and all other peculiar customs will soon belong entirely to the province of tradition. A few decades ago this was not so; then one could, according to the narrations of old men and women, have had the pleasure of both seeing and talking with the Trolls.

There was once a hunter named Pelle Katt, who, one day, went to Skurugata for the purpose of shooting woodcock, but though it was the mating season, when birds are ordinarily plenty and tame, the hunt was unsuccessful. It was as though ordained. The puffy woodcock and his hens kept out of the way of the murderous shot. Pelle was angry, and suspecting that the Trolls had bewitched his gun, he swore and cursed the Trolls generally, and especially those that lived in Skurugata, whose mouth he was just passing, when a woman stepped out, small in stature and peculiar in feature, bearing a little poodle dog in her arms.

"I bring you greeting from my mistress; she says you are to shoot this dog," said she, approaching Pelle.

"Tie it there to that tree and it shall be done before it can get upon its feet," answered Pelle.

This was done, and the little woman disappeared between the mountains. Pelle raised his gun and sent a charge of shot through the dog's head. But what a sight met his gaze when the smoke had disappeared! There lay his own little child wrapped in a dog's hide.

Pelle Katt's habits were not the best. He was fond of drink, quarrelsome and boisterous, and often in his drunken fits declared that he feared neither God nor the devil.

Now, for the first time in his life, he was amazed and crestfallen.

"O God! What have I now done!" he cried.

His knees smote together and the sweat ran copiously from every pore.

"Here you have your reward," said the Troll woman, who now reappeared and threw a dollar piece to Pelle, so that it fell in his open hand, to which it stuck fast, and hastily picking up the dead child bore it away.

In a rage, Pelle threw the dollar piece after the vanishing figure, at the same time calling out:

"I will take no pay from you for such a deed. Here you have your gift again, you detestable Troll."

A hoarse laugh answered from the mountain.

Pelle went home. The child was absent. His wife cried, but Pelle kept still and went to the ale house. He had no money with which to buy brandy in order to drown his sorrows, but after his old custom he stuck his fingers in his vest pocket to feel if there might not be a penny there. Behold! There was the dollar piece which he had recently cast from him. He dropped it upon the ale house counter and received a drink which truly made him forget his dead child, his wife, himself, heaven, hell and all.

When he became sober the coin was again found in his pocket. He again threw it away, and several times thereafter, but always found it in his pocket when searching it for money. So he continued to drink more and more daily, until, finally, he drank himself into that sleep that knows no waking.

So goes the story of Pelle Katt and the Trolls in Skurugata.

# DAME SOÅSAN

IN EARLY times there lived in Soåsan, a range of hills not far from the well-known city of Eksjö, a woman Troll who was called Dame Soåsan.

Trollen i Skurugata.

THE TROLLS OF SKURUGATA

She and her forefathers had, for ages, dwelt there, but when the soldiers came and fired their guns—cracked their nuts, as the mountain folk expressed it—on the camp ground of Ränneslätt, the place became intolerable to her and she departed to her sister's an equally distinguished Troll, who lived in Skurugata, which has been mentioned in a preceding story.

Dame Soåsan was very clever and rich, also the possessor of a very bad temper. It was advisable, therefore, not to anger her in any way, for such as were so unfortunate were instantly punished.

A trooper of that time, belonging to the Hussars of Småland, by name Grevendal, serving under Apelarp in Flisby parish, stood one morning on guard in a distant part of the drill grounds, when he saw, wandering toward him, along the edge of a wood, a very little old woman, whom he rashly assailed with scoffing and vile epithets, whereupon he received a blow on the ear from some unseen hand, which sent him flying to the top of a tall pine tree near by, where he remained unable to descend until assisted down by his comrades.

Toward those who were careful not to offend her the woman exhibited much kindness and extended many favors. A poor old woman of the human family living near Soåsan, in a little hut, was one time in great distress, her table bare and no one near to help her, with famine, already a guest in her hut, menacing her with terrible glare.

Late one evening a knock was heard upon the hut door.

"Come in, in the name of the Lord," answered the old woman, wondering who her visitor might be.

"In that name I can not enter, but here is work for you from the mistress of the mountain. Spin beautiful yarn, but do not wet the threads with spittle, for then it will become christened and that the madam will not tolerate."

"Where shall I leave the yarn?" asked the trembling woman.

"Go straight forward into the woods, where you will find a smooth green lawn. Lay the yarn there and next day you shall have your pay."

The old woman began at once to spin the flax which she found outside the cottage door, but during the work stood a vessel of water beside her with which to wet the thread.

The yarn was soon finished and she betook herself, with profit and pleasure in prospect, to the wood. As the Troll's servant maid had declared she came to a beautiful glade encircled by high trees. She there laid down the yarn and hastened to return home, not daring to look behind her. The next day she went again to the spot and found a new bundle of flax, also several silver pieces.

Now followed a period of prosperity for the poor woman. She accumulated money from her work, became rich, but at the same time avaricious, and forgot the prayers, which she had never before neglected, when she retired to rest.

Finally, she did not even trouble herself to keep faith with the Trolls, but spun the yarn according to general custom, wetting the thread with her spittle.

The skeins of yarn were deposited in the usual place, but when she

Dame Soåsan

went the next day to get her reward she was unable to find the glade again, and in the end went astray in the woods, from which she did not succeed in finding her way home before a whole day later. Upon arriving home, as was her every-day custom, she brought forth and was about to count over her money, when she found that all the silver pieces had been transformed into small stones.

Want pursued her now with greater severity than ever, for none would help one who was known to have had to do with the infamous Soåsan dame, and the old woman died shortly after in great poverty and distress.

———————

A girl who many years ago was a servant in the house of a Senator of Eksjö, named Lind, went one day to find the cattle, which usually grazed in the woods surrounding Soåsan. The animals, for some time back, had not thrived upon the pastures allotted them and were wont to wander far away in search of food, it was supposed, so, at times the girl, notwithstanding the most diligent search, was unable to find them, and when they were found, the cows had already been milked. This day she went plodding sadly along through the dark woods, thinking of the scolding which awaited her at home, when she returned with neither cows nor milk; her mind was also busied with the many stories she had heard about ghosts and Trolls who infested the woods, when she saw two pairs of Pigmies, a boy and girl, sitting under the shadow of a large pine tree.

"It is best to be polite when on the Trolls' own ground," thought the girl. Whereupon she addressed the Troll infants in a very friendly manner and invited each to partake of some bread and butter which she had with her in her little bag. The children ate with exceeding greed, a disgusting sight, as they had extremely large mouths into which the bread and butter vanished rapidly. When the girl was about to depart she heard a voice saying, "As you have taken pity on my children, you shall hereafter escape searching after the cows. Go home! They stand at the gate."

From that day the girl no longer had to search for the cows; they came to the gate every night of their own accord, sweet-laden with a rich tribute of the most excellent milk.

# THE GIANT PUKE

IN THE parish of Lofta in the department of North Tjust there lies, near the sea, a mountain called Puke Mountain. From the land side running into the mountain, there is a long fissure terminating in a cave or hall, where formerly lived a giant called Puke, concerning whom many stories are still quite prevalent among the people.

When the church at Lofta was built the giant was sorely tormented by the church bells. He suffered great discomfort even from the water courses which gurgled out of the mountain, and in a meadow directly north of Lofta Church, was formed a pond, Kofre Spring, in which holy baptism was sometimes performed.

Puke often declared that he must depart from his mountain because of Kofre Spring and Lofta scolding, meaning the church bells in Lofta.

One Sunday the Giant was more than usually disturbed by the long continued bell ringing, and sent his daughter to the top of the mountain, from which, with her apron strings converted into a sling, she threw an enormous stone at the church tower. But the force was too great, and the stone fell upon the other side of the church, where it lies to this day, as large as a good sized cottage.

Some days later the giant maiden, while wandering over the surrounding country, was attracted by three children at play on a hill near by. They had discovered a fallen branch of an oak tree, and to this they had fastened a rope, pretending it was a plow, which one was holding as the other dragged it over the ground. Surprised at this curious implement and the small creatures, she gathered them all into her apron and ran home with them to her giant father. He, however, found no pleasure in the intended playthings but said only:

"Take them out again, our time is past; it is now these who shall rule over us."

In the end Puke became dissatisfied with everything and moved to Götland, where he was some time later found by a ship's master, to whom he gave a box, and bade him offer it upon the altar at Lofta while the people were in church, cautioning him strongly not to open it before.

"If you do as I bid you," said the Giant, "you will find, under the left fore-foot of Lofta's white mare—meaning the church—a key, with which you are to proceed to Puke Mountain. There you will see a door, which you shall open. When you are inside you will meet two black dogs. Do not be afraid of them, but press forward into the room, where you will find a table and upon it many beautiful silver vessels. Of them you may take the largest, but if you take anything more, misfortune will surely overtake you."

The captain kept this all in mind, but when he approached Puke Mountain, on his journey homeward, the conversation of the ship's people was turned to the box. After many deliberations, it was determined to throw it overboard onto a small island which lay near by. This was done, and upon the instant the island was in flames, and even to-day it is brown and desolate as if it had recently been swept by a fire.

# KATRINEHOLM MANOR

In one of the picturesque valleys of romantic Småland and on the Black River is a noted waterfall called Stalpet, which, after placidly winding, by many hundred bends, for a considerable distance, through green meadows, here makes a precipitous descent over a rocky cliff, then quietly pursues its course to a lake a short distance beyond.

Not far from Stalpet lies an old manor, dark, gloomy and unoccupied. A feeling of oppression comes over one in the presence of this large building, barred gates and nailed up windows, and the question is asked, why should this naturally beautiful place be untenanted? Why is there not, at least, a watchman or an attendant? There must be some unusual reason for such a condition of things.

Let us listen to the narration of a good old woman, resident in the neighborhood, who once gave us the story. We use her words, which, may be, enter too much into the detail, but bear with them the natural freshness and coloring that, it is hoped, will not be tedious to the reader. We are given to understand that if we will have the story we must begin at the beginning, and that is, like "Milton's Paradise Lost," with the beginning of all things.

"Know that when Satan was cast out of heaven, on account of his pride, and fell to the earth, there were other spirits, which, like him, were also cast out. These spirits, in their fall, were borne hither and thither on the winds like the golden leaves in the autumn storm, falling to earth finally, some into the sea, some into the forests and some upon the mountains. Where they fell there they remained, so the saying runs, and found there their field of action. After their abiding places they were given different names. Thus we have sea nymphs, mountain fairies, wood fairies, elves and other spirits, all of which are described in the catechism.

Now, it happened, that on that day two spirits fell upon the rock where this old Katrineholm Manor house now stands. In this mountain their offspring lived many hundreds, yes, thousands of years. Though some of them were from time to time killed by lightning and otherwise, they were not exterminated and had not been approached by any human being.

It happened, a long time ago, that a gentleman, who owned this estate, wishing to build himself a residence, and, like a wise architect, to have a solid foundation for it, selected this rock.

The mountain king—for he was a king among his people—was very much displeased with this, but his wife, who was of a milder disposition, pacified her husband and urged him to wait and do their neighbors no harm until it could be known whether harm might be expected from them.

When the house was finished the gentleman married a beautiful young lady whose presence at once filled it with sunshine and joy. But sorrow visits many who little expect it and so it was here.

One day when the young wife was alone in her work-room, a little woman, unexpectedly and unannounced, stood before her. Bowing, she said: "My mistress bids that you visit her, and directs me to say to you that if you consent she will reward you richly." The young wife wondered much at such a request, but having a brave heart and a clear conscience, she promised to follow. The little woman led the way down stairs to the cellar, where she opened a door, until now undiscovered, revealing a passage into the mountain. Entering the passage, which was long and dark, she finally emerged into a large, well-lighted cave, whose walls were sparkling with gold and silver. Here, pacing back and forth, as if in great anguish, was a little man who looked at the new comer searchingly, and with a humble and pleading expression in his eyes, but said nothing. The little woman pushed aside a curtain to an inner cave, at the further end of which the visitor saw, lying upon an elegant bed, another little woman sick and laboring in child-birth. The Christian visitor's presence had the effect to almost immediately still the pains of the suffering woman, whereupon she drew forth a box filled with precious stones, pearls and jewels. "Take this as a memento of your visit to me, but let none know what has happened to you this day, for as surely as you do great misfortune will overtake you and yours," said the Mountain Queen and directed that the young wife be given safe conduct to her room again. As soon as left alone the precious box was carefully secreted.

Time sped on. Everything went well, and in due time the young wife herself became the mother of two beautiful sons. One day, during the mother's absence, the boys discovered the secreted box, and had just begun to play with it when their father entered. He was greatly surprised to find such a treasure in the hands of the children and began at once to question the mother, who had also entered, as to how she became its possessor. At first she refused to betray the secret, and with her refusal the husband became more curious and suspicious, finally angry, when he declared his wife a Troll, and that he himself had seen her come riding through the air on a broomstick. The poor wife was then obliged to reveal her visit to the Troll queen and the circumstances attending it.

"You and I have seen our happiest days, for your curiosity will bring us greater misfortune than you have dreamed of," said she.

A few days later there appeared in the adjacent lake an island, which, strangely enough, seemed to rise from its bosom when anything remarkable was about to take place. It is related that shortly before the death of Charles XII, also before that of Gustav III, the island became visible, and it is even said that a king one time carved his name on a stone on the island, and that stone and name, when, on another occasion the island was visible, were to be seen.

Whether the island was now again visible by some power of the Trolls in unison with the water spirits is not known; it is enough that the island appeared, and that the lord of the manor became possessed with a great desire to go to and inspect it.

He expressed a wish that his wife and boys should accompany him. The mother, who foresaw misfortune, opposed the project with all her energy, and upon her knees begged and prayed her husband to postpone his visit, but without avail.

Finally, the willful man took the boys, leaving his wife at home, and rowed out to the island. Just as the boat touched the enchanted island both boys sprang upon it, and at the same instant both island and boys vanished from the father's sight to be seen no more.

The poor mother mourned herself to death, and the father departed to foreign lands, where he also died, but the building on Katrinesholm has never since been occupied, and there is little probability that any one will in the future prosper in it.

# EBBE SKAMELSON

UPON A small headland which juts from the north into Lake Bolmen, lies an old mansion, Tiraholm, by the peasantry called Tira.

A long time ago there lived here a knight who had a wife and an only child, a beautiful daughter, named Malfred. In the whole country there was not another so fair, and the fame of her beauty traveled far and wide, alluring many suitors to her feet. But Malfred was unmoved by their attentions and turned them away, one after the other.

One day a stately knight, Ebbe Skamelson by name, who had just returned from foreign lands, where he had won his golden spurs, drew up in the court-yard.

With downcast eyes and blushing cheeks the young lady extended her hand when they met, to greet the stranger, who courteously returned her salutation.

The stranger knight became for a time a guest at Tiraholm, and the report soon went out, to the grief of many swains who had indulged in dreams of sooner or later winning the hand of the beautiful maiden, that Ebbe Skamelson and Malfred were betrothed. But, as both were still young, the Knight expressed a desire to join the Crusades to the Holy Land, where he hoped to add to his honors, and stipulated that he be given seven years, at the end of which time he promised to return and celebrate his nuptials.

Some time after Ebbe departed, the old Knight, Malfred's father, died, and it became very lonesome for the daughter and mother in Tiraholm. Year after year passed with no word from Ebbe. The roses of the young maiden's cheeks faded and the dark eyes lost their lustre. The mother advised a remedy and betrothed her to another.

Under the impression that Ebbe had fallen by the sword of the infidels she prepared a wedding feast, and the newly betrothed couple were duly joined according to the rites of the church.

But just as the wedding guests sat themselves at table a gold-laced Knight rode into the court at great speed. The bride became pale under her crown, but the mother, who recognized in the stranger the Knight Ebbe, hastened to meet him in the yard, and reminded him that the seven years had passed, at the same time informing him that his love now sat in the bridal chair with another.

In great anger the Knight sprang to his horse, drew his sword, and after reproaching her for breaking her promise, with one blow he severed her head from her body. His sword still dripping with blood, he sprang from his saddle and into the hall where the festivities were in progress, where the bride sank under his sword, and the bridegroom at another deadly blow fell by her side.

Overtaken by repentance the murderer flung himself upon his horse and rode away into the dark forest, but the pricking of his conscience allowed him no rest. Night and day he saw the apparitions of his victims, and nowhere could he find an escape from them.

Finally he determined to go to Rome, and at the feet of the Holy Father ask absolution from his crimes. A large sum of money procured for him from the Pope the desired indulgence, but absolution from a man did not possess the power to quiet his conscience, still his soul's pain or quell the storm raging in his heart. He then returned to the home of his love, and asked the authorities to impose upon him the severest punishment.

After a long deliberation he was sentenced by the court to be chained hand and foot, in which condition he must visit and pass a day in each one of the three hundred and sixty-five islands in Lake Bolmen. The condemned man went at once about the execution of his sentence. In order that he might get from one island to the other he was given a small boat with which, like a wounded bird, he laboriously propelled himself on his terrible journey.

When, at the end of the year, his sentence was completed he went ashore on the estate of Anglestadt in the district of Sunnebro. Here he went up to a village and rested over night in a barn. Meantime his sorrowful fate had made a deep impression upon the people. A bard had composed a song reciting the woes of Ebbe, and a soothsayer had predicted that upon hearing the song sung Ebbe's chains would fall off and his death follow immediately. While he was lying concealed in the barn, a milkmaid came in the morning to milk the cows. She began to sing "Knight Ebbe's Song," to which he listened with intense interest. At the conclusion of the last verse he cried out with loud voice: "Some is true and some is false."

Thoroughly frightened, the girl sprang into the house and related what had happened. In great haste the people gathered around the barn where Ebbe was lying, commanding him to inform them where he came from and who he was. Still cumbered by his chains he crawled from his shelter and gave his name, at the same time requesting them to conduct him to the churchyard.

Between the village and the church of Anglestadt lies a stone sunken in the ground. When he came to this Ebbe mounted it, raised his eyes to heaven and cried out: "If I am worthy to be buried in consecrated ground, so let it be!"

Instantly the fetters fell from his hands and feet and he sank to the earth a corpse.

Those present took his body and carried it to the church where they buried it in the path outside the churchyard wall, so that all who went into the churchyard should tramp upon his grave. But the next night a long section of the wall, right in front of the grave, was miraculously thrown down. The peasants at once relaid it, but the next night it was again leveled. It was then understood that these happenings were signs that the unfortunate man should be allowed a resting place in consecrated ground, whereupon the churchyard was extended so that the grave was enclosed by its walls, and a low stone even to this day marks the resting place of the outcast. From the fetters, which for a long time hung in Anglestadt church, three iron crosses, resembling the small crosses which were in former times set up in memory of the departed, have been made and placed upon the present church.

# JOHAN AND THE TROLLS*

IN INGELTROP, a parish of North Wedbo, there once lived a farmer who had a servant named Johan.

One day a traveler arrived from Myntorp Inn, and the farmer having been notified that it was his turn to furnish a conveyance for him to the next inn, Johan was sent to the pasture to catch a horse. A halter thrown over his shoulder, he set out, whistling the latest love song. Arriving at the pasture, it was soon clear to him that "Bronte" was in no humor to submit to the halter, and though he now and then allowed himself to be approached, no sooner was the attempt made to lay hold on him than he was off, with head and heels in the air, to a safe distance. Johan persevered, perspiration streaming from his forehead, but in vain. Angered at last, he began to swear in a most ungodly manner, still pursuing the horse until his progress was suddenly checked by a high cliff, to the very base of which he had run before discovering it. Naturally casting his glance upward, as he halted, he saw, sitting upon a crag, a beautiful maiden, apparently combing her hair.

"Are you there, my dear boy?" called the maiden.

Johan, not easily frightened, answered her cheerily:

"Yes, my sweetheart."

"Come here, then," called the maiden.

"I can't," replied Johan.

"Try, Johan." And he did, to his astonishment finding a foothold on the smooth cliff where before no unevenness was discoverable, and soon he was at the maiden's side. She looked at him with great, wondering eyes, then, suddenly, enveloping him in a mist, clouded his understanding so that he was no longer master of his movements, and was, in fact, transformed completely from the Johan he had been to a being like his companion. He forgot horse, home, relatives and friends. Half unconscious, he was conducted into the mountain, and was gone from the sight

*Before the days of railroads and regularly equipped stage lines, it was the duty, established by law, of the farmers and others owning horses to, in their turn, furnish travelers with means of conveyance from the inn of their neighborhood to the next. Upon the arrival of a traveler at an inn a servant was dispatched to the neighbor whose turn it was, and he was expected to promptly furnish horse, wagon and driver.

JOHAN AND THE TROLLS

and power of those who would seek him.

"Bronte" was in harness many good days thereafter, and the farmer became the driver, for, as his sons were growing up, he did not wish to hire another servant in Johan's stead.

One day, many years after Johan's disappearance, it was again the farmer's turn to furnish a horse to a traveler. Grumbling at the fate of Johan, he went to the pasture.

"It was too bad for the boy," said he to himself. "I wonder if he has been caught by the Trolls?" At the same time he chanced to look upward at the cliff where the servant had seen the Troll maiden, and there stood Johan, but with lusterless eyes, staring into vacancy.

"Johan, my dear boy, is that you?" shouted the farmer. "Come down."

"I can not," answered Johan, with husky, unnatural voice.

Hereupon the farmer threw his cap to Johan, which the latter picked up and put on his head.

"Come down," cried the farmer, "before the Trolls come. In the name of the saints, come down."

"I can't," said Johan again.

"Then the farmer threw his clothes up, garment after garment, and when Johan had clothed himself in them he received power enough that he was able to crawl down the cliff. His master took him by the hand, and without looking back they hastened home, the farmer repeating:

"Pshaw! you cunning black Trolls! As a stone, I'll quiet your wicked tongues that they may neither evil think nor speak or do ought against me."

They arrived home, the one dressed the other naked. The traveler was obliged to procure another horse, for in the house of the farmer the joy was so great that none there had a thought of driving him. Johan was never again the same man as before, but remained gloomy and rarely spoke.

His master asked him many times what his occupation was in the mountain, but upon this subject he was silent. It happened that Johan was taken sick and called for a confessor, to whom, when he confessed his sins, he related also his experience in the mountain. His chief employment, he said, had been to steal food for the Trolls. For this purpose the Trolls put a red hat upon him, when he could, in a very short time, fly to Jönkoping through locked doors and into the merchants' stores, where he took corn, salt, fish and whatever he wished. From the Troll cap he received such power that he could take a sack of rye under each arm and a barrel of fish upon his back, and fly as lightly through the air as with no burden whatever.

"It was wrong of me and hard on the merchants," said Johan, "but it was the fault of the Trolls. If there were no Trolls in the world the merchants would become rich, but now they must pay tribute, and so are kept on the verge of bankruptcy." And Johan was done.

# THE LOST TREASURE

MANY HUNDREDS of years ago, at a time when Sweden was invaded by enemies, the people of Stenbrohult gathered their money and jewelry together and concealed them in a large copper kettle, which they sunk to the bottom of Lake Möckeln.

There it lies to-day and will lie for all time, though many have touched it with poles when driving fish into their nets. Meantime, at each touch, it has moved further away until it now lies near the outlet of the lake, where it is so deep that it can not be reached.

When the other residents of the place hid their treasures in the lake there was a rich farmer who buried his silver at Kalfhagsberg in two cans. Shortly after he died so suddenly that no opportunity was given to dig them up. Immediately following his death, two lights were seen every evening over the place where the treasures lay hidden, a sure sign that an evil spirit or dragon had appropriated the treasure.

A poor cottager heard of it, and knowing that man may acquire undisputed possession of the treasures of the earth, if dug up on a Thursday evening and carried away without looking back or uttering a word to any one, he already regarded himself as good as the owner of the wealth. Betaking himself to the place, he succeeded in getting the cans out of the mountain, but on the way home he met one after another of his neighbors who asked where he had been. The old man knew well that the evil spirits had a hand in this, and that what appeared to be his neighbors was nothing less than the spirits transformed, and he was, therefore, stubbornly quiet. But finally he met the priest, who stood by the wayside and greeted him as he was passing with a "good evening, neighbor." Hereupon the old man dared keep quiet no longer, but took his hat off and saluted, "good evening, father," in return, at the same instant he tripped against a root and dropped the cans. When he stopped to pick them up there lay in their stead only a pair of little old birch-bark boxes, and the old man was compelled to go home, his mission fruitless.

# GÖTLAND

## THE TEN FAIRY SERVANTS

MANY YEARS ago there lived in Gullbjers a family of peasants, who had a daughter, Elsa. As she was the only child she was much adored, and her parents sought in every way to anticipate her slightest wish. As soon as she had been confirmed she was sent to the city to learn how to sew, and also city manners and customs. But in the city she acquired little other knowledge than how to adorn herself, and to scorn housework and manual labor.

When she was twenty years old she won the love of an industrious and honorable young farmer, named Gunner, and before many months had gone by they were man and wife.

In the beginning all was pleasure, but she soon began to weary with her many household duties. Early one morning, shortly before Christmas, there was life and activity in Gunner's yard. Elsa had hardly risen from bed when the servant, Olle, sprang in and said:

"Dear mistress, get ready our haversacks, for we are going to the woods, and we must be off if we are to get back before evening."

"Dear mother, the leaven is working," called one of the servant girls, "and if you will come out now we will have more than usually good bread."

The butcher, Zarkis, who had already stuck a large hog and several small pigs, had just stepped in to get the accustomed dram, when old Brita came rushing after material for candle wicks. Lastly came Gunner, out of patience because the servant had not yet started for the woods.

"My departed mother," said he, with kindly earnestness, "always prepared everything the night before when people were expected to go to work early in the morning, and I have requested you to do likewise, Elsa. But do not forget the loom, my dear; there are now only a few yards of cloth remaining to be woven, and it will not do to allow it to lie in the way over the holidays."

Now, wholly out of patience, Elsa rushed in a rage out of the kitchen to the house in which the loom stood, slammed the door furiously behind her and cast herself weeping upon a sofa.

"No!" shrieked she. "I will no longer endure this drudgery. Who could have thought that Gunner would make a common housewife of me, to wear my life out thus? Oh, unhappy me! Is there no one who can help and comfort a poor creature?"

"I can," replied a solemn voice, and before her stood a white-haired man with a broad-brimmed hat upon his head. "Do not be alarmed," continued he, "I came to proffer you the help for which you have just wished. I am called Old Man Hoberg. I know your family to the tenth and eleventh generations. Your first ancestor bade me stand godfather to his first born. I could not be present at the christening, but I gave a suitable godfather's present, for I would by no means be the meanest. The silver I then gave was unfortunately a blessing for no one, for it begot only pride and laziness. Your family long ago lost the riches, but the pride and laziness remain; nevertheless I will help you, for you are at heart good and honest.

"You complain at the life of drudgery you are compelled to lead," continued he, after a short silence; "this comes from your being unaccustomed to work, but I shall give you ten obedient servants, who shall be at your bidding and faithfully serve you in all your undertakings." Whereupon he shook his cloak, and ten comical little creatures hopped out and began to put the room in order.

THE TEN FAIRY SERVANTS

"Reach here your fingers," commanded the old man.

Tremblingly, Elsa extended her hand; whereupon the old man said:

> "Hop O'My Thumb,
> "Lick the Pot,
> "Long Pole,
> "Heart in Hand,
> "Little Peter Funny Man—

"Away, all of you, to your places."

In an instant the little servants had vanished into Elsa's fingers, and even the old man had disappeared.

The young wife sat a long time staring at her hands, but soon she experienced a wonderful desire to work.

"Here I sit and dream," she burst forth with unusual cheerfulness and courage, "and it is already seven o'clock while outside all are waiting for me." And Elsa hastened out to superintend the occupations of her servants.

Not for that day alone, but for all time thereafter Elsa entered into her duties with as much pleasure as she would formerly have found in a dance. No one knew what had happened, but all marveled at the sudden change. None was, however, more pleased and satisfied than the young wife herself, for whom work was now a necessity, and under whose hands everything thereafter flourished, bringing wealth and happiness to the young couple.

# THE SEA NYMPH

ONE NIGHT a number of fishermen quartered themselves in a hut by a fishing village on the northwest shores of an island. After they had gone to bed, and while they were yet awake, they saw a white, dew-besprinkled woman's hand reaching in through the door. They well understood that their visitor was a sea nymph, who sought their destruction, and feigned unconsciousness of her presence.

The following day their number was added to by the coming of a young, courageous and newly married man from Kinnar, in Lummelund. When they related to him their adventure of the night before, he made fun of their being afraid to take a beautiful woman by the hand, and boasted that if he had been present he would not have neglected to grasp the proffered hand.

That evening when they laid themselves down in the same room, the late arrival with them, the door opened again, and a plump, white woman's arm, with a most beautiful hand, reached in over the sleepers.

The young man arose from his bed, approached the door and seized the outstretched hand, impelled, perhaps, more by the fear of his comrades scoffing at his boasted bravery, than by any desire for a closer acquaintance with the strange visitor. Immediately his comrades witnessed him drawn noiselessly out through the door, which closed softly after him. They thought he would return soon, but when morning approached and he did not appear, they set out in search of him. Far and near the search was pursued, but without success. His disappearance was complete.

Three years passed and nothing had been heard of the missing man. His young wife, who had mourned him all this time as dead, was finally persuaded to marry another. On the evening of the wedding day, while the mirth was at its highest, a stranger entered the cottage. Upon closer observation some of the guests thought they recognized the bride's former husband.

The utmost surprise and commotion followed.

In answer to the inquiries of those present as to where he came from and where he had been, he related that it was a sea nymph whose hand he had taken that night when he left the fisherman's hut; and that he was dragged by her down into the sea. In her pearly halls he forgot his wife, parents, and all that was loved by him until the morning of that day, when the sea nymph exclaimed: "There will be a dusting out in Kinnar this evening." Then his senses immediately returned, and, with anxiety, he asked: "Then it is my wife who is to be the bride?" The sea nymph replied in the affirmative. At his urgent request, she allowed him to come up to see his wife as a bride, stipulating that when he arrived at the house he should not enter. When he came and saw her adorned with garland and crown he could, nevertheless, not resist the desire to enter. Then came a tempest and took away half the roof of the house, whereupon the man fell sick and three days later died.

# THE BYSE*

A PEASANT of Svalings, in the parish of Gothem, by the name of Hans, was, one spring day, employed in mending a fence which divided two meadows. It chanced he required a few more willow twigs for bands, whereupon he sprang over the fence to cut them in a neighbor's grove. Entering the thicket, what was his surprise at seeing an old man sitting upon a stump, bowed forward, his face buried in his hands. His astonishment uncontrollable, Hans broke out:

"Who are you?"

---

*In Götland a Byse is the spirit of one who in life was continually on the move around his possessions, or was so covetous of worldly goods that even perjury did not deter him from acquiring property unjustly.

"A wanderer," replied the old man without lifting his head.

"How long have you been a wanderer?" inquired the peasant.

"Three hundred years!" answered the old man.

Still more astonished, the peasant again asked:

"Is it not hard to travel thus?"

"It has never been so hard to me," replied the old man, "for I love the woods."

"Very well, go on then," said Hans.

Hardly were the words uttered than the peasant heard a sound like that from a wild bird startled to wing, and the old man had vanished so suddenly that Hans could not say whether he had sunk into the earth or gone into the air.

# ÖLAND

## THE BRIDGE OVER KALMARSOUND

NORTH OF the village of Wi, in the parish of Källa, lies a large stone called Sekiel's Stone, after a giantess, Sekiel, who is said to have lived in Borgehaga, in the parish of Högo.

The same giantess had a sister, who was married to a giant named Beard, and lived in the parish of Ryssby on the Småland side of the sound.

That they might visit each other oftener it was agreed between the sisters that they should build a stone bridge over Kalmarsound, the one to build from Ryssby shore, the other from Öland.

The giantess of Småland began first upon her work. Every day she came with a great load of stones which she cast into the sea, until, finally, she had completed that point of land now called Skägganäs, reaching a quarter of a mile out into the sea. The giantess on the Öland side also began to build, but when she came with her first load of stones in her apron she was shot through the body with an arrow from a peasant's bow. Overcome by the pain, she sat herself to rest upon the before mentioned Sekiel Stone, which has a shallow depression in the top, marking the resting spot of the giantess.

When she had recovered she again took up her journey, but had proceeded no further than to Persnäs when it began to storm, and she was struck dead by a bolt of lightning. With her fall the stones slipped from her apron, and there they lie to-day, forming the large grave-mound on Persnäs hills.

# HALLAND

## THE YOUNG LADY OF HELLERUP

UPON THE estate of Hellerup, in the parish of Ljungby, there lived, many years ago, a gentleman of rank, who had a daughter renowned for her gentleness as well as for her beauty and intelligence.

One night, while lying awake in her bed, watching the moonbeams dancing upon her chamber floor, her door was opened and a little fairy, clad in a gray jacket and red cap, tripped lightly in and toward her bed.

"Do not be afraid, gracious lady!" said he, and looked her in the eye in a friendly manner. "I have come to ask a favor from you."

"Willingly, if I can," answered the young lady, who began to recover from her fear.

"Oh! it will not be difficult," said the fairy. "I and mine have, for many years, lived under the floor in the kitchen, just where the water tank stands, which has become old and leaky, so that we are continually annoyed by the dripping of water, and the maids spill water upon the floor, which drips through, so that it is never dry in our home."

"That shall be seen to in the morning," promised the lady, and the fairy, making an elegant bow, disappeared as noiselessly as he came.

The next day, at the girl's request, the cask was moved, and the gratitude of the fairies was soon manifested. Never thereafter was a glass or plate broken, and if the servants had work to do that required early rising, they were always awake at the appointed hour.

Some time later the fairy again stood at the young lady's bedside.

"Now I have another request which, in your generosity, you will certainly not refuse to grant."

"What is it, then?" asked the young lady.

"That you will honor me and my house, and tonight stand at the christening of my newly-born daughter."

The young lady arose and clad herself, and followed her unknown conductor through many passages and rooms which she had never before been aware existed, until she finally came to the kitchen. Here she found a host of small folk and priest and father, whereupon the little child was baptized in the usual Christian manner.

When the young lady was about to go the fairy begged permission to put a memento in her apron.

Though what she received looked like a stick and some shavings, she appeared very thankful, and was conducted again through the winding passages back to her room.

Just as the fairy stood ready to leave her, he said: "If we should meet again, and that is probable, bear well in mind not to laugh at me or any of mine. We esteem you for your modesty and goodness, but if you laugh at us, we shall never see each other again." With these words he left the room.

When he had gone the young woman threw her present into the stove and laid herself down to sleep, and the following morning, when the maid went to build the fire, she found in the ashes jewelry of the purest gold and finest workmanship, such as had never before been seen.

Some years later the young woman was about to marry, and preparations were made for a day of pomp and splendor.

For many weeks there was great bustle in the kitchen and bridal chamber. During the day all was quiet under the floor in the kitchen, but through the night one who slept lightly could hear the sounds of work as through the day.

At length the wedding hour arrived.

Decked with laurels and crown, the bride was conducted to the hall where the guests were gathered. During the ceremonies she chanced to cast a glance toward the fireplace in the corner of the hall, where she saw the fairies gathered for a like feast. The bridegroom was a little fairy and the bride her goddaughter, and everything was conducted in the same manner as in the hall.

None of the guests saw what was going on in their vicinity, but it was observed that the bride could not take her eyes from the fireplace. Later in the evening, when she again saw the strange bridal feast, she saw one of the fairies who was acting as waiter stumble and fall over a twig. Unmindful of the caution she had received, she burst out into a hearty laugh. Instantly the scene vanished, and from that time no fairies have been seen at Hellerup.

# ELSTORPS WOODS

DURING THE war between Queen Margarita and Albrecht of Mecklenburg the two armies had an encounter in Southern Halland. The Queen's people had encamped upon the plains of Tjarby, a half mile north of Laholm, while the Prince's adherents were camped in the vicinity of Weinge Church.

One morning the Queen went, as was her custom to morning prayers in Tjarby Church, but took the precaution to set a guard upon the so-called Queen's Mountain to warn her of danger.

While she was buried in her devotions there came a message, informing her that a few unattended knights had been seen in the vicinity.

"There is yet no danger," said the courageous Queen, and continued her prayers at the altar.

In a short time another message was brought, informing her that as many as a hundred knights had made their appearance, but the Queen commanded her people to keep still, that yet there was no occasion for alarm. Finally a message came that all Elstorps Woods seemed to be alive and moving against Tjarby.

"Now, my children, for a hard battle, but God will give us the victory,"

THE YOUNG LADY OF HELLERUP

said the Queen, and springing upon her horse, she marched at the head of her warriors against the enemy.

The enemy had, as is related in the story of Macbeth, made use of stratagem, for each man carried before him a green bush, thinking to come upon the queen's attendants by surprise. But the queen outwitted him and gained a brilliant victory.

In gratitude to God, she rebuilt the old church of Tjarby, and since that day no birches higher than a man's head have grown in Elstorps Woods.

# BOHUSLÄN

## THE GIANT MAIDEN IN BORASEROD MOUNTAIN

In the mountain of Boraserod, which is located in the parish of Svarteborg, there lived, in ancient days, a giant. As with all the giant people, he has disappeared since the coming in of Christianity. Some say that he died, but others believe that he moved to Dovre, in Norway, where giants betook themselves when disturbed by the church bells.

However, there is even to-day a hollow in the mountain which is called "the giant's door," and within the mountain, it is believed there are vaults filled with the giant's gold. No one has, however, dared venture to search for this treasure, and luckily, for with property of giants, blessings do not go.

This giant had a daughter, so beautiful that he who once saw her could never drive thoughts of her from his mind. Among the few whose fortune it was to see her was a young peasant from the estate of Rom, adjacent to the mountain. When he was one day out searching for the horses, which had gone astray, he suddenly came upon the wonderfully beautiful maiden, sitting upon the side of the mountain, in the sunshine, playing on her harp.

The peasant at once understanding who it was, not of the kind to be easily frightened, knowing that her father had an abundance of riches, and thinking it was no worse for him than for many others to marry into the giant family, approached her, under cover of the shrubbery, until he was quite near, when he threw his knife between her and the mountain, and as "steel charms a Troll," or others of the supernatural family, she was obliged, whether or not she would, to follow him to his home.

In the evening, when the giant missed his daughter, he started out in search of her, and in his search came to Rom.

Through the walls he heard the snores of two persons, and, when he had lifted the roof off the cottage, he saw his daughter sleeping in the arms of the young swain.

"Are you there, you whelp!" he hissed. "Has it come to this?" added he. "So be it, then; but I demand that the wedding shall take place before the next new moon. If you can then give me as much food and drink as I want all your offspring shall be made rich and powerful, otherwise I will have nothing to do with you."

Preparations were hastily made by the young man's parents for the wedding, and neighbors and relations came from far and near, laden with provisions. A great number likely to be present, it was determined to have the ceremony performed in the Church of Tosse; but the day before the wedding there came such a great freshet that it seemed impossible for the bridal carriage to cross the swollen creek between Duigle and Barby. The giant was equal to the emergency, and, with his wife, went to Holmasar, in Berffendalen, and fetched a large slab of stone and four boulders to the creek. The giant carried the slab under his arm, and his wife the boulders in her mitten. And thus they built the stone bridge which to this day spans the creek.

When the bridal pair came from the church to the banquet hall, the giant appeared and seated himself at the table with the rest of the guests.

Although the bridal couple did all possible to find him enough to eat, the giant declared when he left the table that he was only half satisfied, and therefore only half of the family should become great people. Wishing to give the bride a becoming bridal present, he cast a sack of gold and silver upon the floor, which the couple was to have if the son-in-law could carry it up to the loft. Stealthily, the bride gave her husband a drink which made him so strong that he threw the sack upon his back, and, to the surprise of all, carried it out of the room. Thus the newly wedded pair became possessors of an abundant treasure with which to begin life.

For some time the young couple lived in plenty and happiness, but soon the husband began to be irritable and abusive. It came, finally, to such a pass that the husband took a whip to his wife. She continued, nevertheless, to be mild and patient as before; but one day he was about to start on a long journey. When the horse was hitched to the wagon he observed that the shoe was gone from one of the hind feet. It would not do to venture on such a journey without first replacing the shoe. Here, however, was a difficulty. He had one shoe only, and that was too large; whereupon he began again to scold and swear.

The wife said nothing, but quietly taking the shoe between her hands, squeezed it together as if it were lead, reducing it to the required size. Her husband looked upon her in astonishment and alarm. Finally he addressed her:

"Why have you, who are so strong, submitted to abuse from me?"

"Because the wife should be submissive to her husband," said the giantess, mildly and pleasantly.

From that hour the man was the most patient and indulgent in the region, and never again was heard a cross word from his mouth.

# THE BRIDAL PRESENT

IN THE parish of Näsinge, two poor sisters once found service with a rich farmer. All through the summer they herded their master's flocks on the mountain sides, whiling away their time in relating legends of kings and abducted princesses.

"If only some prince would carry me away to his gilded palace," said the younger, one day.

"Hush! Do not talk so wickedly," remonstrated the elder. "The Trolls might hear you, when it would go hard with you."

"Oh! there is not much danger of that," replied the first speaker, and continued her story.

Some days later the younger sister disappeared. No one knew where she had gone, and careful search did not reveal. Time went on without the least trace of her whereabouts being discovered. Finally the remaining sister found a sweetheart, but equally poor with herself, wherefore they could not think of marrying yet for many years.

One night in her sleep she dreamed that her absent sister stood at her bedside, and said:

"Make your bed to-morrow night in the barn, past which the Trolls and I shall pass, and I will give you a handsome dower."

The next night when the girl drove her flocks home she made her bed, as her sister had directed, in her master's barn. The barn door she left open, and, laying herself down, she looked out into the night, endeavoring to keep awake until her sister should come. Soon after midnight she heard the sound of hoofs, and saw her sister, accompanied by a Troll, ride up the road at such a speed that the sparks glistened around the horses' feet. When they reached the front of the barn the lost girl threw a purse in at the door, which fell with a ring into the watcher's lap. Hastily the treasure was deposited under her head, and she was soon asleep, wearied with her day's work and night of watching.

The next day, upon examining her strangely acquired gift, what was her astonishment to find it filled with pure gold coins. Before the sun had set she had purchased a splendid farm, and, as may be presumed, the bans were published and a wedding immediately celebrated.


# HALDE HAT*

AT THE extremity of the beautiful valley of Espelund, in the parish of Mo, there rises a wood-covered mountain known as Borgåsa Mountain,

*The belief that giants have two hats, one of which renders the wearer invisible, and another that reveals things otherwise invisible, is widespread in Northern Scandinavia.

from the distance looking like a giant cone; three sides presenting frowning precipices, the fourth (and southern) fortified by a large wall of boulders, which is said to have surrounded, in former times, a king's castle, called Grimslott.

Here, in times gone by, lived a mountain king named Grim. He was, like the rest of his kind, ugly and crafty, and robbed mankind of whatever fell in his way.

For this purpose he had two hats, one of which was called the Dulde hat, and was so endowed that when the king put it on his head both he and his companions became invisible; and the other was called the Halde hat, which possessed a power making all things plainly visible to the wearer that were before invisible.

It happened, during these days, that a farmer of Grimland, preparing a wedding for his daughter, invited guests from near and far to the festivities. Pretending, however, not to know the mountain king, he did not invite him. The latter apparently took no offense at this, but, on the wedding day, putting his Dulde hat upon his head, set out to the wedding feast, followed by all his people, except the queen, who was left at home to watch the castle.

When the wedding guests sat themselves at table everything that was brought in vanished, both food and drink, to the great astonishment of all, as they could not understand where it disappeared; but a young peasant suspected the Trolls were at the bottom of it, and, springing upon a horse, rode straightway to Borgåsa Mountain. On the steps stood the mountain queen, so beautiful and fine, who inquired of the rider how things were going at the wedding feast in Grimland.

"The food is salt and the oil is sour," answered he. "That stingy farmer has hidden the wine and meat in the cellar where no one can find it. Now, your husband sends greeting, and requests that you give me the Halde hat, that he may be able to find its hiding place."

Without mistrust the queen gave him the enchanted hat, whereupon the young peasant hastened back to the festivities. Entering the hall, he donned the hat and saw at once the mountain king and his followers sitting among the guests, seizing upon everything as fast as brought in. The peasant drew his sword, and commanded the others to do likewise.

"Stab as I stab and cut as I cut," cried he, and began to slash around the table. The other guests followed his example and slew the mountain king and all his followers. From that time, so says the story, the castle upon Borgåsa Mountain has been untenanted.

# THE GOLDEN CRADLE

ONE STORMY autumn night, a few years after the death of Charles XII, a ship containing a valuable cargo was wrecked on the island of Tjorn, one of the group of islands on the coast of Bohuslän. Among other things of value in the ship's cargo were many articles of costly jewelry, belonging to King Frederick I, which were being brought to him from Hessia. The most costly, however, was a jewel enclosed in a cradle made of pure gold and richly embellished with pearls and precious stones, sent by a German princess to the king's spouse.

The islanders, as was not unusual in those days, murdered the ship's crew, and, after it had been plundered of its cargo, scuttled and sunk her, so that she was safely out of sight.

Among the priests upon the island was one named Michael Koch, pastor in Klofvedal. He had a hint of the great crime that had been committed, but, fearing the half-barbarous inhabitants, did not dare betray the secret.

Some time after the ship had disappeared a fisherman came one day to the parsonage and presented to the priest a walking stick of great beauty of workmanship and value, which was a part of the cargo of the plundered vessel. Koch accepted the gift, and whether he did not know or did not care where it came from, took it with him, often displaying it upon the streets. When, two years later, he went to Stockholm, as representative to the Diet, King Frederick one day accidentally saw and recognized it as his property. The priest, however, asserted that it was his, and rightfully acquired. But the king could not be deceived, and opening a heretofore concealed hollow in the cane, took therefrom a roll of gold coins. This action attracted attention and aroused suspicion anew that the ship had been plundered. It was not thought that Koch had a hand in it, but, on the assumption that he knew something about it which he ought to have revealed, and that he was trying to conceal the deed, he was escorted from Stockholm.

Meantime further discoveries were made, until they led to finding that the gold cradle was in possession of a peasant in Stordal. At the king's command, soldiers were at once dispatched to Tjorn to arrest the criminals and, possibly, find the jewel. But the command was not kept so secret that the peasant did not get an intimation of what was coming, whereupon he hastened to bury the cradle in Stordal Heath. Under guidance of a police officer the search was prosecuted in all directions, but when the soldiers could not discover the object of their search, they left the island and the offenders escaped.

Some years later the possessor of the cradle became sick. When he found that his case was serious he sent for the priest, and confided to him the whereabouts of his booty, and requested that as soon as he was dead the priest should dig the cradle up and restore it to the king. Hardly had the priest taken his departure when the sick man regretted his simplicity. Gathering his little remaining strength, he rose from his bed, and, with unsteady steps, crept out into the field and concealed his buried treasure in another place. As soon as the man was dead, the priest set out about fulfilling his commission. His digging was in vain, the hidden treasure was not to be found. In his dying hour the peasant had, apparently, endeavored to reveal the new hiding place, but his strength was so near exhausted that his utterances could not be understood.

To this day many of the dwellers on the island are fully persuaded that Queen Elenor's golden cradle may be found somewhere in the Stordal cow pastures, and many have wasted much time and labor in the hope of bringing it to light.

# VESTERGÖTLAND

## THE KNIGHTS OF ÅLLABERG

ONE TIME a peasant, *en route* to Jönköping with a load of rye, came just at dusk to Ållaberg, where he discovered a grand mansion by the way. "Maybe I can sell my rye here," thought he, "and so be spared the journey to Jönköping," and, approaching the door, he knocked for admittance.

The door was at once opened by some unseen power, and the peasant entered.

Upon entering, he found himself in a grand hall. In the middle of the floor stood a large table and upon the table lay twelve golden helmets, grand beyond the power of description, and scattered around the room, deep in slumber, were twelve knights in glittering armor.

The peasant contemplated his beautiful surroundings, but, concluding he could not sell his rye here, went on, coming finally to a large stable, where he found standing twelve most magnificent steeds, bedecked with golden trappings and silver shoes on their hoofs, stamping in their stalls.

Curiosity getting the better of him, he took hold of the bridle of one of the horses in order to learn by what art it was made. Hardly had he touched it when he heard a voice call out, "Is it time now?" and another answer, "No, not yet!"

The peasant had now seen and heard as much as he desired, and, thoroughly frightened, hastened away. When he came out he found that he had been into the mountain instead of into a mansion, and that he had seen the twelve knights who sleep there until the country shall be in some great danger, when they will awake and help Sweden to defend herself against her foreign enemies.

## THE COUNTESS OF HÖJENTORP

SHORTLY AFTER King Charles XI had confiscated most of the property of the nobility to the use of the crown, he came, one day, while upon one of his journeys to Höjentorp, where his aunt on his father's side, Maria Eufrosyna, lived.

On the stairs, as he was about to enter her dwelling, he was met by her and at once saluted with a sound box on the ear. Astounded, the king burst out:

"It is fortunate that it is I whom you have struck! But why are you in such a combative mood, my aunt?"

"Why?" said the countess. "Because you have taken all my possessions from me."

Conducting the king to the dining hall, the countess sat before him to eat a herring's tail and an oat cake.

"Have you no better fare for me than this?" asked the king.

"No," replied the lady; "as you have spread the cloth so must you dine."

"Aunt," said the king, "if you will give me your gold and silver, I will provide for you richly to your death."

"Shame on you!" interrupted the countess. "Will you not allow me to keep so little as my gold and silver, either?" and, advancing upon him, she gave him a second box on the ear, which so alarmed the king that he beat a hasty retreat and commanded that the countess be left in peaceful possession of her property to the end of her days.

# THE GIANT OF SKALUNDA

On Skalunda Hill, near Skalunda Church, there lived, in olden times, a giant, who, much annoyed by the ringing of the church bells, was finally compelled to move away, and took up his residence on an island, far away in the North Sea. One time a ship was wrecked upon this island, and among those of her crew rescued were several men from Skalunda.

"Where are you from?" inquired the giant, who was now old and blind, and was stretched out warming himself before a fire of logs.

"We are from Skalunda, if you wish to know," said one of the men.

"Give me your hand, for I wish to know if still there is warm blood in Sweden," said the giant.

The man, afraid of the grasp of the giant, drew a glowing iron rod from the fire, which he extended to the giant, who, grasping it with great force, squeezed it until the iron ran between his fingers.

"Ah, yes, there is still warm blood in Sweden," exclaimed he, "but does Skalunda Hill still exist?"

"No, the birds have scratched it down," answered the man.

"It could not stand," remarked the giant, "for my wife and daughter built it one Sunday morning. But how is it with Halle and Hunneberg? They remain, surely, for I myself built them."

Upon receiving a reply in the affirmative, he asked if Karin, a giantess, still lived, and when to this he was answered yes, he gave them a belt and

THE GIANT OF SKALUNDA

bade them take it to Karin and say to her that she must wear it in his memory.

The men took the belt, and upon their return home gave it to Karin, but, before she would put it upon herself, she wrapped it around an oak which was growing near by. Hardly was this done when the oak was torn from the ground, and sailed off northward as if in a gale. In the ground where the oak stood, there was left a deep pit, and here to-day is pointed out the best spring in Stommen.

# THE TROLLS IN RESSLARED

IN A mountain called Räfvakullen, Fox Hill, near the Church of Resslared, Trolls, it is said, have lived since long before the building of the church.

When the church was completed and the bell hung in the tower, the priest, as was the custom, proceeded to read prayers over it to protect it from the power of the Trolls. But his prayers lacked the expected efficacy, for he had not yet finished when the Trolls took the bell and sunk it in the "Troll Hole" near the church.

A new bell was cast and hung, and this time the provost, who was more learned, was selected to consecrate it. The provost also failed to hit upon the right prayers, for the following Sunday, when the bell was about to be used for the first time, it flew through the apertures in the tower and was broken on the roof of the church.

Again a bell was cast, and this time, as priest and provost seemed to be powerless against the Trolls, the Bishop of Skara was sent for. His prayers were effectual, and the bell was not again disturbed.

The Trolls thereafter dwelt in harmony with their neighbors, and especially with the parishioners of Resslared. From the latter the Trolls were wont to borrow food and drink, which they always returned two-fold.

In time the first residents died off, and new people took their places. The newcomers were well provided with this world's goods, even to being wealthy, but they were uncharitable.

One day the "mother" of the Trolls went, as was her custom of old, to a cottage, and asked the housewife if she could lend her a measure of meal.

"No, that is out of the question! I have none in the house!" said the woman.

"Very well! it is as you say, of course," replied the Troll, "but maybe you can lend me a can or two of ale. My husband is away, and he will be very thirsty when he returns."

"No, I can't do that. My ale cans are all empty," answered the housewife.

"Very good! Maybe you can lend me a little milk for my little child that is sick in the mountain."

"Milk! Where should I get milk? My cows are all farrow," said the woman.

"Very well," said the Troll woman, and went her way.

The housewife laughed in her sleeve, and thought that she had escaped the Trolls cheaply; but when she inspected her larder it was found that she had really told the truth to the Troll woman. The meal boxes were swept clean, the ale barrels were empty, and the new milch cows, to the last one, farrow. Ever after that the plenty that had heretofore been was wanting, until finally the people were compelled to sell out and move away.

# BISHOP SVEDBERG AND THE DEVIL

BISHOP SVEDBERG, of Skara, was a very pious man and a mighty preacher, therefore, intolerable to the devil.

One night the Bishop set out from Skara to his bishopric in Brunsbo. When he was on the way some distance, the wagon began to run from side to side of the road, and finally one of the hind wheels fell off and rolled away into the ditch.

The driver called the attention of the Bishop to this, and remarked that they could go no farther.

"Don't trouble yourself about that," said the Bishop. "Throw the wheel into the rear of the wagon and we will go along."

The servant thought this was a strange command, but did as directed, and the journey was continued to Brunsbo without further adventure.

Arriving at the inn, the Bishop directed the servant to go to the kitchen and bring a light.

"Look, now," said the Bishop to the servant upon his return, "and you shall see who has been the fourth wheel," at the same time springing from the wagon.

The servant turned the light in the direction indicated, where he saw none other than the devil himself, standing in the place of the wheel, with the axle in his hands.

The devil soon found an opportunity for revenge. One night a great fire spread over Brunsbo, and before morning the whole place was burned to the ground.

The Bishop was at no loss to know who had played him this foul trick, and called the devil to account for the devastation.

"Verily, you shall know," said the devil. "Your maid was down in the pantry, and there snuffed the candle. Passing by, I took the snuffing and with it set fire to the place."

The Bishop was obliged to be content with this answer, but in order that the devil should do him no further harm he sent him, with all his imps, to hell.

# THE TREASURE IN SÄBY CREEK

ON THE estate of Säby, in the parish of Hassle, lived, in former days, a gentleman so rich that he could have purchased half of the territory of Vestergötland, but so miserly that he could not find it in his heart to spend money for necessary food.

When he became aged, and knew that his life was drawing to a close, he began to ponder what he should do with his wealth to prevent its falling into the hands of people not akin to him, and finally he arrived at what he thought a wise determination.

One Sunday, when the people of the house were all in church, he loaded his gold and silver upon a golden wagon and drew it down to Säby Creek, where he sank it in the deepest hole he could find. Reaching home again, he felt more than usually content, and laid himself down upon his bed, where he was found upon the return of the people from church.

When a treasure has been concealed seven years, the Red Spirit is said to take possession of it, and it is then called "Dragon's property." Over the spot where the treasure lies a blue flame is seen to flutter at night time, and it is said the dragons are then polishing their treasure.

When the seven years had passed the dragon light was seen over Säby Creek, now for the first time revealing where the miser had deposited his wealth. Many efforts were made to recover the costly wagon and its load, but neither horses nor oxen were found with strength enough to lift it from the hole.

About this time it happened that a farmer, returning from the market of Skagersholm, where he had been with a load of produce, found quarters for the night with an old man at Tveden. The evening conversation turned upon the hidden treasure, and the many unsuccessful attempts to recover it that had been made, when the old man instructed his guest to procure a pair of bull calves, upon which there should not be a single black hair, and to feed them for three years on skimmed milk, whereby they would acquire the necessary strength to drag the wagon out of the creek.

After great trouble the farmer was fortunate enough to find the desired white calves, and he at once set about rearing them as instructed. But one time the girl who had care of the calves accidentally spilled some of the milk set apart for one of them, and, in order to have the pail full, she replaced the milk with water and gave it to the calf as if nothing had happened. Meantime the calves grew up on their excellent food to large and powerful oxen.

When they were three years old the farmer drove them to the creek and hitched them to the golden wagon. It was heavy, but the calves put their shoulders to it, and had raised it half way from the hole, when one of them fell upon his knees, and the wagon sank back to its old resting-place. The farmer yoked them to it again, but just as the wagon was about to be landed safely, the same bull fell to its knees a second time, so it went time after time, until, finally, the owner saw that one of the bulls was weaker than the other.

When the wagon sank back the last time a bubbling and murmuring came up from the depths and a smothered voice was heard to mutter:

"Your skimmed milk calves can't draw my wagon out." Whereupon the farmer understood that to trouble himself further would be useless, since when no attempts have been made to secure the treasure.

# ÖSTERGÖTLAND

## THE TOMTS

IN DESCRIPTIONS of Tomts we are told that they look like little men well along in years, and in size about that of a child three or four years old, as a rule clad in coarse gray clothes and wearing red caps upon their heads. They usually make the pantry or barn their abiding place, where they busy themselves night and day, and keep watch over the household arrangements. When the servants are to go to threshing, or other work requiring early rising, they are awakened by the Tomts. If there is building going on, it is a good sign if the Tomts are heard chopping and pounding during the hours of rest for the workmen. In the forge where the Tomts have established themselves, the smith may take his rest in confidence that they will awaken him by a blow on the sole of the foot when it is time for him to turn the iron. Formerly no iron was worked on "Tomt night," which they reserved for purposes of their own. On this night, were one to peek through the cracks of the door, the little people would be discovered working silver bars, or turning their own legs under the hammer.

It is believed that in the house or community where there is order and prosperity the Tomts are resident, but in the house where proper respect is lacking, or where there is a want of order and cleanliness, they will not remain, and it will follow that the cup-board and corn-crib will be empty, the cattle will not thrive, and the peasant will be reduced to extreme poverty and want.

It happened thus to a farmer that he had never finished his threshing before spring, although he could not find that he had harvested more grain than others of his neighbors. To discover, if might be, the source of such plenty, he one day hid himself in the barn, whence he saw a multitude of Tomts come, each bearing a stalk of rye, among them one not larger than a man's thumb, bearing a straw upon his shoulders.

"Why do you puff so hard?" said the farmer from his hiding-place, "your burden is not so great."

"His burden is according to his strength, for he is but one night old," answered one of the Tomts, "but hereafter you shall have less."

From 'hat day all luck disappeared from the farmer's house, and finally he was reduced to beggary.

In many districts it has been the custom to set out a bowl of mush for the fairies on Christmas eve.

In the parish of Nyhil there are two estates lying near each other, and both called Tobo. On one was a Tomt, who, on Christmas eve, was usually entertained with wheaten mush and honey. One time the mush was so warm when it was set out that the honey melted. When the Tomt came to the place and failed to find his honey as heretofore, he became so angry that he went to the stable and choked one of the cows to death. After having done this he returned and ate the mush, and, upon emptying the dish, found the honey in the bottom. Repenting his deed of a few minutes before, he carried the dead cow to a neighboring farm and led therefrom a similar cow with which to replace the one he had killed. During his absence the women had been to the barn and returned to the house, where the loss was reported to the men, but when the latter arrived at the cow-shed the missing cow had apparently returned. The next day they heard of the dead cow on the adjoining farm, and understood that the Tomts had been at work.

In one place, in the municipality of Ydre, a housewife remarked that however much she took of meal from the bins there seemed to be no diminution of the store, but rather an augmentation. One day when she went to the larder she espied, through the chinks of the door, a little man sifting meal with all his might.

Noticing that his clothes were very much worn, she thought to reward him for his labor and the good he had brought her, and made him a new suit, which she hung upon the meal bin, hiding herself to see what he would think of his new clothes. When the Tomt came again he noticed the new garments, and at once exchanged his tattered ones for the better, but when he began to sift and found that the meal made his fine clothes dusty he threw the sieve into the corner and said:

"Junker Grand is dusting himself. He shall sift no more."

# THE URKO OF NORTH WIJ

FROM THE point where the river Bulsjö empties into Lake Sommen, extending in a northerly direction for about eight miles, bordering the

THE TOMTS

parishes of North Wij and Asby, nearly up to a point called Hornäs, stretches the principal fjord, one of several branching off from the large lake.

Near Vishult, in the first named of these parishes, descending to the lake from the elevation that follows its west shores, is a wall-like precipice, Urberg, which, from the lake, presents an especially magnificent view, as well in its height and length, and in its wood-crowned top, as in the wild confusion of rocks at its base, where, among the jumble of piled-up slabs of stones, gape large openings, into which only the imagination dares to intrude.

From this point the mountain range extends southward toward Tulleram, and northward, along the shore of Lake Sjöhult, under the name of Tjorgaberg, until it ends in an agglomeration of rocks called Knut's Den.

In this mountain dwells the Urko, a monster cow of traditional massiveness, which, in former times, when she was yet loose, plowed the earth, making what is now Lake Sommen and its many fjords. At last she was captured and fettered by a Troll man from Tulleram, who squeezed a horseshoe around the furious animal's neck and confined her in Urberg. For food she has before her a large cow-hide from which she may eat a hair each Christmas eve, but when all the hairs are consumed, she will be liberated and the destruction of Ydre and all the world is to follow.

But even before this she will be liberated from her prison if Ydre is crossed by a king whom she follows and kills if she can catch him before he has crossed to the confines of the territory.

It happened one time that a king named Frode, or Fluga, passed through Ydre, and, conscious of the danger, hurried to reach the boundaries, but, believing he had already passed them, he halted on the confines at Fruhammer, or, as the place was formerly called, Flude, or Flugehammer, where he was overtaken and gored to death by the monster. In confirmation of this incident, his grave, marked by four stones, is to this day pointed out.

Another narrative, which, however, is known only in the southeastern part of the territory, relates that another king, unconscious of the danger accompanying travel in the neighborhood, passed unharmed over the border, and had reached the estate of Kalleberg, when he heard behind him the dreadful bellowing of the monster in full chase after him. The king hastened away as speedily as possible. The cow monster, unable to check its mad gallop at the border, rushed over some distance to the place where the king first paused, where, in the gravel-mixed field, she pawed up a round hole of several hundred feet in breadth, which became a bog, whose border, especially upon the north side, is surrounded by a broad wall of the upheaved earth.

Still, at times, especially preceding a storm, the Urko is heard rattling its fetters in the mountain, and both upon the mountain and down near the shore of the lake by times.

Extraordinary things are said to happen. One and another of the residents thereabouts assert even that they have seen the Urko in her magnificent rooms and halls, which the neighbors do not for a moment doubt.

# THE TROLL SHOES

NEAR KÖLEFORS, in the jurisdiction of Kinda, lived, a long time ago, an old woman, who, as the saying goes, was accustomed, during Easter week, to go to Blåkulla.

Late one Passion Wednesday evening, as was usual with witches, she lashed her pack in readiness for the night, to follow her comrades in their wanderings. In order that the start should be accompanied by as few hindrances as possible, she had greased her shoes and stood them by the fireplace to dry.

In the dusk of the evening there came to her hut another old woman, tired and wet through from the rain, and asked permission to remain over night. To this the witch would not consent, but agreed to allow the woman to remain until she had dried her soggy shoes before the fire, while she, unwilling to be under the same roof with her guest, remained outside.

After a time the fire died out, and it became so dark in the hut that when the stranger undertook to find her shoes, in order to continue her journey, she got and put on the witch's shoes instead. Hardly had she passed out through the door when the shoes jerked her legs up into the air and stood her head downward, without, however, lifting her into the air and carrying her away as would have been if the witch's broom had been in her hand.

In this condition the old woman and the shoes struggled through the night. Now the shoes stood her on her head and dragged her along the ground, now the woman succeeded in grasping a bush or root, and was able to regain her feet again for a time.

In the end, near morning, a man walking past, noticed her and hastened to her relief. Answering her earnest pleading the man poked off one of the shoes with a stick, whereupon, instantly, shoe and stick flew into the air and vanished in the twinkling of an eye. After the adventures of the night the old Troll woman was so weakened that she fell into a hole, which is pointed out to this day, and is called "The Troll Woman's Pit."

# DAL

## THE WOOD AND SEA NYMPHS*

BOTH WOOD nymphs and sea nymphs belong to the giant family, and thus are related.

They often hold communication with each other, although the wood nymphs always hold themselves a little above their cousins, which frequently occasions differences between them.

A peasant, lying in the woods on the shores of Lake Ömmeln, heard early one morning voices at the lake side engaged in vehement conversation. Conjecturing that it was the wood nymphs and sea nymphs quarreling, he crept through the underbrush to a spot near where they sat, and listened to the following dialogue:

*Sea Nymph*—"You shall not say that you are better than I, for I have five golden halls and fifty silver cans in each hall."

*Wood Nymph*—"I have a mountain which is three miles long and six thousand feet high, and under that mountain is another, ten times higher and formed entirely of bones of the people I have killed."

When the peasant heard this he became so alarmed that he ran a league away, without stopping. Thus he did not learn which was victorious, but it was the wood nymphs without doubt, as they have always been a little superior to the others.

## THE MOUNTAIN KITCHEN

IN THE parish of Bolsta there lived, many years ago, a man named Slottbon. One summer evening he rode his horse to pasture up toward Dalo Mountain. Just as he let the horse go, and was turning to go home, a black man confronted him and asked him if he did not wish to see the mountain kitchen.

Slottbon acquiesced and followed his conductor into the mountain, where it seemed to him certain that he must lose his senses among the glitter of gold and silver utensils of the kitchen, with which he was surrounded.

*The wood nymph dwells in large forests, and is described as a beautiful young woman, when seen face to face, but if her back be turned to one it is hollow, like a dough-trough, or resembles a block stub. Sometimes, instead of a hollow back, she is adorned with a bushy fox tail. The sea nymph dwells, as indicated by the name, at the bottom of seas and lakes, and is clad in a skirt so snow-white that it sparkles in the sunlight. Over the skirt she wears a light blue jacket. Usually her appearance is the forerunner of a storm; she is then seen sitting upon a billow combing her golden hair.

THE TROLL SHOES

The mountain man inquired of his guest if he should order something to eat for him, to which Slottbon assented, and, while his host was absent preparing the repast, improved the opportunity to gather up all the gold and silver his leather apron would hold, and with it hasten away with all possible speed, not slacking his pace until he came to a gravel pit, where it occurred to him to look at his treasure. Seating himself upon a stone, he began to throw the vessels, one after the other, upon the ground, where, as fast as they were thrown down, they were turned into serpents.

Thoroughly frightened at the sight, he dropped his whole burden and took to his heels, followed closely by the wriggling mass of enormous reptiles. Finally, when he had about given himself up for lost, he came to and sprang upon the trunk of a fallen tree and cried out, "God save me, poor sinner!" and in the twinkling of an eye the serpents vanished.

# VERMLAND

## SAXE OF SAXEHOLM

AT THE mouth of the Bay of Olme, upon a little island, which on its west side is connected with the island of Kumel, is situated the castle of Saxeholm.

Here dwelt, in former days, a powerful chief, by name Saxe, the greater part of whose time was spent in bloody warfare, in which occupation he seemed to find great success and pleasure. At home he was gloomy and reserved, and very cruel to his wife.

Finally, becoming wearied by her husband's continued harshness, she determined to elope with another who better understood how to reward her love.

One time when Saxe was at Christmas matins in the church at Varnum, his wife set fire to the castle, shut the gates and threw the key over the wall into the garden outside. Preceding this she had commanded that her horses be shod with shoes reversed, thus hoping to bewilder her pursuers, then, with her lover and a few trusty servants, the castle was deserted, and her way taken over the ice-covered bay.

When Saxe came home, he found his castle wrapped in flames, and the following lines written on the outer gate:

> "Within is burning Saxe's knout,
> And Saxe the cruel must lie without."

What the chief's thoughts were at such a greeting is not related. Meantime his wife, before she left the castle, had deposited, in one of the vaults, a chest filled with valuables, and had declared that no human power should move it therefrom.

Many attempts have since been made to unearth this treasure, and it is said that more than once the searchers have so far succeeded as to get a glimpse of the iron-bound chest, but always at this point they have been frightened away by an awful voice calling out from the depths of the vault, "Don't come here!"

# THE POLITE COAL BURNER

At Vejefors forge, up near the northern frontier, there was, many years ago, a charcoal burner who, however vigilant he might be, always had to rebuild and burn his stacks. Now, the wood was not burned enough, again, poorly burned, and a thousand annoyances pursued him in his work.

One evening, as he sat in his hut mending his tools, a beautiful maiden entered, and, complaining that she was almost frozen, asked permission to warm herself at the fire.

The coal burner, who had been long in the woods, understood at once that his visitor was a wood nymph, beautiful and enchanting when seen face to face, but, when seen behind, is adorned with a bushy fox tail.

When she had warmed herself in front awhile, she turned her back to the fire, and the coal burner was given an opportunity to see the tail, whereupon, with unexpected courtesy, he addressed his guest:

"Miss, look out for your train, please!"

That nice name for her troublesome appendage won the Troll woman's affections, and from that day everything went admirably with the coal burner.

# THE HARVESTERS

In the parish of Ekshärad lies a mountain, Säljeberg, which was formerly the dwelling place of Trolls and giants, now exterminated.

Near the mountain dwelt a farmer, on one of the best farms in the parish. One summer evening he went over his fields admiring the seas of golden grain and exulting at the abundant harvest promised him.

"God be praised for this crop," said he. "If I now could have all these fields harvested by early morning I would give my best cow."

Hereupon he returned to his home and went to bed. Through the whole night the noise of reaping was heard in the fields and the Trolls calling:

"Make bands and bind; let the farmer dry it himself."

As soon as sunrise the farmer was upon his feet and out into the fields, where, to his indescribable amazement, he saw them reaped and the grain lying in bundles upon the ground. Guessing that the Trolls had had a hand in the work, he sprang to the stable, there to find a stall empty and his best cow gone.

# NÄRIKE

## THE ULFGRYT STONES

IN THE peak of Mount Garphytte, one of the many mountain tops that raise themselves over Kilseberger, dwelt, in former days, a giant named Rise.

One morning, as he went from his grotto out into the day, a strange sound, which caused him to pause, greeted his ear. He listened for some time, then returned into the mountain and called his wife.

"Put the smallest of those stones that lie upon the peak into your garter and sling it at that gray cow that goes tinkling along down there by Hjelmaren!" said he, meaning the new church just completed at Orebro, whose bells were that morning ringing for the first time in the service of the Lord.

The giantess, as she was commanded, took a stone as large as a house and threw it at the church, some eight or ten miles distant.

"That was a poor throw," said the giant, when the stone fell down on the plain of Rumbo. "Bring here the band; you shall see a throw that will do its work," whereupon he adjusted a monstrous stone in his wife's garter, and, swinging it a few times through the air, let it go with all his power toward the new church.

"Great in command, but little in power," said the giant woman, when the stone fell upon the one she had thrown, and was broken into a thousand pieces.

At the same time the bell rung out with wonderful clearness. Furious with rage, he tore up two large stones, took one under each arm, and set out for Orebro. Intelligence having reached the residents of Orebro that the giant was coming, consternation was general and good advice dear.

Finally, an old man undertook to save the church. In great haste he gathered up all the worn-out shoes he could find, put them in a sack, and set out to meet the giant. At Ulfgryt, in Toby, he met the giant, who was anything but gentle in appearance.

"How far is it to Orebro?" asked Rise.

THE ULFGRYT STONES

"I can't say exactly," answered the old man, in an innocent manner, "but it is long a way, you will find, for it is seven years since I left there, and I have worn out all these shoes on the way."

"Then let him who will, go there, but I will not," said the giant, and threw the stones from him to the ground with such force that they rang as they struck it.

The stones lie there by the roadside even to-day, but the most remarkable circumstance is that they turn over whenever the church bells in Orebro are rung.

# KATE OF YSÄTTER

THE INHABITANTS of Närike have many stories to relate about an apparition, called Kate of Ysätter, that in olden times dwelt in Öster Närike's forests, but chiefly in the swamps of Ysätter, in the parish of Asker.

According to the belief of the old people, she existed through many generations, although she usually made her appearance as a young girl beautifully clad, and possessing a head of hair of extraordinary length. She was often seen by hunters sitting upon a stump, combing her hair which reached to the ground. Those who went to the swamps to wash their clothes sometimes saw her at a little distance also washing garments which were of an unusual whiteness. To ugly old women she was always a terror, and it seemed to be a pleasure to her to mimic them by keeping time with their motions, but whenever she showed herself it was for a few seconds only, and should one turn his eyes from her, however little, she was gone.

In Öster Närike, the routes she took were shown, and many complaints were heard that she trampled the grain down in her constant journeys back and forth. Often, especially in the night time, her awful laugh was heard from her perch on a tree or top of a rock, when she succeeded in alluring some one from his path, caused him to fall with his load, or break his harness. Her laugh was like a magpie's, and caused the blood of one helpless against her pranks to stand still.

Others who endeavored to stand well with her she assisted in many instances. "She has gone, the lightning has killed her as the others," say the old people, not yet won over to the skepticism of the present time.

Among those who enjoyed her special favor was a hunter, Bottorpa Lasse. He was such a skillful shot that if only he stepped out upon the porch and called a bird, or drew the picture of an animal upon the wall of the barn, the game he wished was brought within range of his gun.

One time Lasse invited his neighbors to accompany him on a hunt, and, expecting to bag an abundance of game, they were not slow to accept the invitation. They betook themselves in the evening to the woods, where they found shelter in a coal burner's hut, and prepared to begin

KATE OF YSÄTTER

the hunt early in the morning.

Along in the night Kate entered the hut, and requested the hunters to show her their guns. She first examined those of the hunter's neighbors, but soon returned them, exclaiming, "Fie!" She then took Lasse's gun, blew down the barrel, examined the priming and handed it back exclaiming, "Good, good, my boy!" What this signified was soon manifested, when Lasse secured a fine lot of game and the others did not so much as get a shot.

It is further related of Kate of Ysätter, that at the burning of the clock tower of Asker, in the year 1750, when even the church was in flames and in great danger of destruction, Kate was seen standing on the roof, opposing their progress.

The last time she made her presence known was at a harvest gathering in the fields of Ysätter. The harvesters had ceased labor to eat their luncheon, and when they had eaten themselves into a good humor, engaging in conversation, which turned upon Kate, a young man declared he would like nothing better than to catch her and give her a good whipping for the vexations she had produced in the world. Instantly a terrific crash was heard in an enclosure near by, and the youth received a blow in the face that caused the blood to gush from mouth and nose over the food of the others, changing their butter to blood. It was after this thought wise to say as little and to have as little as possible to do with Kate of Ysätter.

# THE ELVES' DANCE

UPON THE marshy oak and linden covered island of Sör, when the grass starts forth in the spring, are to be seen, here and there, circles of a deeper green than the surrounding grass, which the people say mark the places where Elves have had their ring dances.

While the provost, Lille Strale, was pastor of the parish church, a servant was sent out late one evening to bring a horse in from a pasture. Plodding along as best he could in the darkness, he had not gone far when it was discovered that he had lost his way, and, turn which way he would, he could not find the sought for meadow.

Exhausted at last by constant walking, he sat down at the foot of an oak to rest himself. Presently strains of lovely music reached his ears, and he saw, quite near, a multitude of little people engaged in a lively ring dance upon the sward. So light were their footsteps that the tops of the grass blades were scarcely moved.

In the middle of the ring stood the Elf Queen herself, taller and more beautiful than the others, with a golden crown upon her head and her clothes sparkling in the moonlight with gold and precious stones.

Beckoning to him, she said: "Come, Anders, and tread a dance with me!" and Anders, thinking it would be impolite not to comply with the request of a woman so beautiful, rose and stepped bowing into the ring.

Poor lad, he did not know what a fate awaited him who ventured to participate in the sports of the Elves. How the dance terminated is not known, but at its conclusion the young man found himself again under the oak, and from that hour he was never again wholly himself. From being the most lively and cheerful young man in the village, he became the dullest and most melancholy, and, before the year had gone, his days were ended.

# THE FIDDLER AND THE SEA NYMPH

MANY YEARS ago a dancing society of Brästa, a village in the parish of Stora Mellösa, planned a great Christmas festival, to which, on the appointed day, old and young flocked from far and near, knowing that Sexton Kant, of Norrbyås, would be there with his fiddle, and assured that fun would run riot. Kant, it is related, was no ordinary fiddler, not a little proud of his skill, and ready at the least word of praise to laud himself to the skies.

When the merry making had gone well into the night and the pleasures were at their height, some one remarked that not many could measure themselves with Father Kant, when he let the bow leap over the strings and played in "four voices," as he himself called it. Nothing further was needed. Kant, always ready to begin where the others left off, declared that the devil, good player as he was reputed to be, could not compete with him in the waltz which they had just heard. This boast came near costing Kant dear. When the dance ended and he set out in the night on his way home, he met, near the hill of Bjurbäcka, a young woman clad in white, who saluted him and addressed him as follows:

"If you will play a polka for me, Father Kant, I will dance for you."

So said, so done. Father Kant sat himself upon a stone and applied the bow to the strings of the instrument. Instantly he lost all control of himself. Such a polka as now came from his fiddle he had never expected to hear, much less play. The tones seemed to come without help from him. The bow bounded over the strings and his arm was forced to follow. One melody followed another; his arm became numb, but the music continued in the same wild measure.

Kant now understood that something was wrong. Finally he burst forth:

"God forgive me, poor sinner. What have I brought upon myself?"

Upon the instant the fiddle strings parted, and an awful-sounding laugh was heard from the brook at the foot of the hill. Heavy of heart, Kant hastened homeward, acknowledging to himself that the devil, after all, was his superior. For a long time he could not be persuaded to again take up his fiddle, but, when he finally complied, he found that one of the beautiful waltzes he had played on the eventful night had fastened itself upon his memory, and he acquired greater renown than before as a fiddler.

# VESTERMANLAND

## THE SNIPE

THE SNIPE, as is well known, is a bird which inhabits low, marshy meadows, and which, in flight, makes a noice with its wings not unlike the neighing of a horse.

A farmer, who himself never looked after his property, had in his employ a lazy and negligent servant. One dry summer the man rode his master's horse, many days in succession, to a pasture where there was no water, without first giving it drink, as he had been instructed. So the poor animal was thus left to suffer through the long dry period.

It happened one day that the farmer would go to the city, and commanded the servant to fetch the horse from the pasture. The man went, but search where he would, no horse could be found. The servant not returning in season, his master set out after him, but neither could he find the animal. It had disappeared from the pasture completely, and was not found again.

Some days later, when the farmer was again out, continuing the search, to his surprise he heard a neighing in the air. Soon after he observed his horse, as he supposed, standing and drinking in an adjoining meadow. "Are you there, Grålle?" cried the farmer, and hastened to catch the horse. His shout was answered with a neigh.

"Grålle, Grålle, my boy!" continued the farmer, in persuasive tones and was about to grasp the halter, when the horse was transformed into a bird, which, with another neigh, flew into the air.

From that day the farmer took care of his own horses, and before all else he saw to it that they did not want for water when they went to pasture.

## TIBBLE CASTLE AND KLINTA SPRING

AT TIBBLE, in the parish of Bedelunda, there stood, in former days, so it is said, a castle, of which the most careful search fails to reveal any remnant now.

THE SNIPE

In the castle dwelt a lady of royal descent, with her young and beautiful daughter. One day there came to it a prince, who was received with great pomp, and it was not long until an ardent love had sprung up between the young people. Knowing that many eyes were upon them, keeping expressions in check, they agreed to meet each other on a certain night at Klinta Spring, situated south of the castle near Klinta Mountain.

Late in the evening, when all its inhabitants were asleep, and it had become quiet in the castle, the young lady crept quietly from her room down to the castle gate, but the porter refused to open it for her. Thinking gold might persuade him, she drew from her hand a ring which she tendered him, but he was not so easily bribed. Then she took a gold chain from her neck, proffering it with the ring; such a temptation the old man could not resist, and quietly allowed her to pass, with the condition that she should return before dawn.

When she arrived at the spring she thought she saw the prince sitting upon a stone near by, and, approaching him, she threw herself into his arms. But, instead of that of her lover, she found herself in the embrace of the Mountain King of Klinta Mountain, who lifted her up and bore her into the mountain. Before reaching the interior of the mountain, however, she succeeded in slipping the crown he wore from the giant's head and hanging it, as she passed, upon the branch of a pine tree so that the prince could see that she had kept her appointment.

When they reached the inside of the mountain, the giant laid the young woman carefully down upon the "star spread" in his chamber, where she fell asleep, after which he went to his mother and told her what a beautiful discovery he had made. Meantime the prince came to the spring. When he failed to find his mistress there he walked around the meadow and came, finally, to the mountain, where his attention was attracted to the crown hanging in the tree. He now understood what had happened, and in anguish drew his sword and pierced his body with it. When the young woman awoke, the giant woman commanded her son to carry her back to the spring. "But," added she, "before you reach there three lives will have been forfeited."

And so it happened. While the giant was carrying the young woman to the spring she breathed her last and was laid by the giant at the side of the prince. Meanwhile the porter, in remorse over his deed, had thrown himself from the tower, and thus ended his days.

The prince and his love were laid upon a golden wagon and conveyed to a beautiful green meadow on an eminence near Gryta and there interred. Even the wagon and sword were buried in the mound, which every spring is surrounded by a hedge of white, blooming bird cherry, but both wagon and sword shall, in time, be dug up, when he who is first to see the latter shall receive his mortal wound therefrom.

# THE COAL BURNER AND THE TROLL

On a point which shoots out into the northwest corner of Lake Råsvalen, in the region of Linde, lived, in days past, a coal burner named Nils. His

THE COAL BURNER AND THE TROLL

little garden patch was left to a servant boy to care for, while he dwelt always in the forest, chopping coal-wood during the summer and burning it in the winter. However he toiled, nothing but bad luck was returned to him, and, leading all other subjects, poor Nils was the talk of the village where his home was.

One day when he was constructing a stack of wood for burning, on the other side of the lake near the dark Harg Mountain, a strange woman came to him and asked him if he needed help in his work.

"Yes, indeed; it would be good to have some assistance," answered Nils, whereupon the woman began to carry logs and wood much faster than Nils could draw with his horse, so that by noon the material was on the ground for a new stack. When evening came she asked Nils what he thought of her day's work, and if she might come again next day.

The coal burner could not well say no, so she returned the following day, and daily thereafter. When the stack was burned she assisted him with the drawing, and never before had Nils had so much nor so good coal as that time.

Thus the woman remained with him in the forest three years, during which time she became the mother of three children, but this did not bother the coal burner, for she took care of them so that he had no trouble from them.

When the fourth year had been entered upon she began to be more presuming, and demanded that he take her home with him and make her his wife. This Nils did not like, but, as she was very useful to him in the coal forest, he was careful not to betray his thoughts, and said he would think over the matter.

One day he went to church, where he had not been for many years, and what he heard there set him to thinking as he had not thought since he was an innocent child. He began to reflect whether he had not made a misstep, and if it might not be a Troll woman who had so willingly lent him her company and help.

Involved in these and similar thoughts, returning to his forest home, he forgot that he had made an agreement with the strange woman when she first entered his service, that always upon his arrival, and before approaching the stack, he would strike three times with an ax against an old pine tree standing a little way from the coal kiln. On he went, when suddenly there burst upon his sight a scene that nearly took his wits from him. As he neared the stack he discovered it in bright flames, and around it stood the mother and her three children drawing the coal. They drew and slacked so that fire, smoke and sparks filled the air high toward the heavens, but instead of pine branches, ordinarily used for slacking, they had bushy tails, with which, after dipping them in the snow, they beat the fire.

When Nils had contemplated this awhile, he crept stealthily back to the pine whose trunk he made echo by three blows from his ax, so that it was heard far away at Harg Mountain. Thereupon he went forward to the stack as if he had seen nothing, and now every thing was as he was accustomed to see it. The stack burned steadily and well, and the woman went about her duties as usual.

When the woman saw Nils again, she renewed her appeals to be allowed to go to his home with him and become his wife.

"Yes, the matter shall be settled now," said Nils, consolingly, and departed for home, ostensibly to fetch his horse, but he went instead to Kallernäs, on the east shores of the lake, where lived a wise old man, whom he asked what course to pursue to free himself from the dilemma. The old man advised him to go home and hitch his horse to the coal cart, but so harness that no loops should be found in the reins or harness. Then he should ride over the ice on the back of the horse; turn at the coal-kiln without pausing; shout to the Troll woman and children to get into the cart; and drive briskly to the ice again.

The coal burner, following the instructions, harnessed his horse and saw to it carefully that there was no loop upon the reins or harness, rode over the ice, up into the woods to the kiln and called to the woman and her children to jump in, at the same time heading for the ice and putting his horse to the best possible speed. When he reached the middle of the lake, he saw, running toward him from the wilderness, a large pack of wolves, whereupon he let slip the harness from the shafts, so that the cart and its contents were left standing on the slippery ice, and rode as fast as the horse could carry him straight to the other shore. When the Troll saw the wolves she began to call and beg. "Come back! come back!" she shrieked. "If you will not do it for my sake, do it for your youngest daughter, Vipa!" But Nils continued his way toward the shore. Then he heard the Trolls calling one to the other, "Brother in Harsberg, sister in Stripa, and cousin in Ringshällen, catch hold of the loops and pull!" "He has no loop," came a reply from the depths of Harsberg.

"Catch him at Härkällarn, then."

"He does not ride in that direction," came from Ringshällen, and Nils did not go that way, but over fields, stones and roads straight to his home, where he had only arrived when the horse fell dead, and a Troll shot came and tore away the corner of the stable.

Nils, himself, fell ill shortly after, and was confined to his bed many weeks. When he recovered his health he sold his cabin in the forest, and cultivated the few acres around his cottage until the end of his days. Thus the Trolls were once caught napping.

# BOLSTRE CASTLE

One evening, a long time ago, a little girl went up through the forest to Bolstre Castle in search of some sheep that had gone astray.

Reaching the inside of the walls, the little girl was met by an old woman, clothed in a red skirt and a gray head covering, who gave into her possession a box, and commanded her to take care of it while she went to invite a number of her friends to become guests at her daughter's wedding.

The girl was so frightened that she did not dare to refuse the charge, and, taking the box, sat down upon a stone to wait the woman's return. When she had thus sat a long time she heard a bird twittering over her head in a tree, and looking up, two leaves fell from the tree in such manner as to form a cross upon the box, whereupon the cover instantly flew open and revealed its contents—a bridal crown of shining gold and many other costly jewels.

The girl waited long and patiently, but the old woman did not return, so, finally she set out on her way home, taking with her the jewel casket. But blessings do not go with Troll property. No bride would wear the crown, it was so fine, and the girl soon after lost her lover. Now that it was clear to every one that a Troll's gold brought only misfortune upon the household, it was carried back to the castle and buried in the ground, where it surely lies to-day.

# SÖDERMANLAND

## THE CHANGELINGS

EVERY INTELLIGENT grandmother knows that the fire must not be allowed to go out in a room, where there is a child not yet christened; that the water in which the new-born child is washed should not be thrown out; also, that a needle, or some other article of steel must be attached to its bandages. If attention is not paid to these precautions it may happen that the child will be exchanged by the Trolls, as once occurred in Bettna many years ago.

A young peasant's wife had given birth to her first child. Her mother, who lived some distance away, was on hand to officiate in the first duties attending its coming, but the evening before the day on which the child should be christened she was obliged to go home for a short time to attend to the wants of her own family, and during her absence the fire was allowed to go out.

No one would have noticed anything unusual, perhaps, if the child had not, during the baptism, cried like a fiend. After some weeks, however, the parents began to observe a change. It became ugly, cried continuously and was so greedy that it devoured everything that came in its way. The people being poor, they were in great danger of being eaten out of house and home. There could no longer be any doubt that the child was a "changeling." Whereupon the husband sought a wise old woman, who, it was said, could instruct the parents what to do to get back their own child.

The mother was directed to build a fire in the bake oven three Thursday evenings in succession, lay the young one upon the bake shovel, then pretend that she was about to throw it into the fire. The advice was followed, and when the woman, the third evening, was in the act of throwing the changeling into the fire, it seemed, a little deformed, evil-eyed woman rushed up with the natural child, threw it in the crib and requested the return of her child. "For," said she, "I have never treated your child so badly and I have never thought to do it such harm as you now propose doing mine," whereupon she took the unnatural child and vanished through the door.

Another changeling story, but with less unfortunate consequences, is told in Södermanland.

A resident of Vingåkir, who made frequent trips to Nyköping with loads of flour, was in the habit of halting for the night at the house of a farmer in Verna. One summer night he arrived later than usual, and, as the people were already in bed and asleep, the weather being pleasant, he did not wish to wake anyone, so unhitched his horse from the wagon, hitched him to a hay stack and laid himself under the wagon to sleep.

He had been some time under the wagon, yet awake, when, from under a stone near by, an ugly, deformed woman, carrying a babe, made her appearance. Looking about her carefully, she laid the child on the stone and went into the house. In a short time she returned, bearing another child; laid it upon the stone, and taking up the first one, returned to the house.

The man observed her actions, and divining their purpose, crept cautiously from his resting place as soon as the woman had disappeared into the house, took the sleeping child and hid it in his coat under the wagon. When the Troll returned and found the child gone she went a third time to the house, from which she returned with the child she had just carried in, whereupon she disappeared under the stone.

The traveler, anxious for the welfare of his little charge, which had in such an extraordinary manner fallen into his hands, could not close his eyes for the rest of the night.

As soon as it dawned he went with his precious burden to the house, where he found the occupants in great consternation over the disappearance of the child, which, as may be presumed, was received with great rejoicing.

# LAKE GOLDRING

ABOUT A mile and a half from Strengnäs lies a narrow valley, between several wood-covered heights and the island upon which in olden times Ingiald Illrada burned herself and all her attendants.

The valley is called Eldsund, and was formerly an open water way connecting two of lake Mälar's bays. Vessels went, then, unhindered through there, and not many years ago a sunken vessel was found, buried in the mud that had one time been at its bottom. Now there is nothing but a small stream winding its way between grass-grown banks, and cows and goats graze where the perch and the pike formerly had their playground.

At one place this little stream spreads its banks until a small lake is formed, which was once of quite respectable size, but is now almost grown over with reeds. Many a poor man has there caught a fish for his pot, that otherwise would have been empty enough.

A good while back there lived a lady on the estate not far from this lake, perhaps as near as Näsbyholm, upon which, near the water-course, lies the notable "cuckoo stone."

This lady was very rich and still more proud, looking with contempt upon all who had less money and lands than she, and were not of as noble blood as she believed herself to be.

One day an old priest visited her. A priest in all respects, not one of those accommodating fellows that could be sent to stir the fire, or one who went with bent back away from home and was painfully straight at home, but a priest who did not hide his thoughts under a chair.

While the priest and his hostess were one day walking along the lake shore, she began, as was her habit, to boast of her riches; to tell how much money she had at interest, and how many tax lists she had complete and incomplete, whereupon the priest asked her how far she thought all that went, or what, after all, it amounted to, for she could not take her riches with her into the grave. At this the lady became angered, and declared that she was so rich that if she should live even many hundreds of years she need not want, and that it was as impossible that she should become poor as it would be to recover her gold ring from the depths of the lake—at the same time drawing a ring from her finger and casting it far out into the water.

The priest maintained that as wonderful things as this had happened in the world, and that it was not more impossible that her ring might be recovered than that she might become poor.

Later in the day an old fisherman came to the house with fish to sell. A number were bought, and the kitchen girl was given the task of cleaning them.

When she cut open the largest pike, she saw something shining, and, upon looking with greater care, she recognized her mistress' most valuable finger ring. In great haste she rushed to the lady, who sat wrangling with the moderate priest because he could think it possible her riches might be taken from her.

"Has my lady lost her ring?" asked the maid.

The lady ceased to talk, and cast a glance at the priest, who sat quietly at the window looking out toward the lake.

"Here it is, any way," said the maid, and laid the ring upon the table.

The lady grew pale, but the priest looked more serious than ever.

How it went with her and her riches thereafter, the story does not relate, but the lake is called Goldring to this day.

# THE TROLL'S GARDEN AT STALLSBACKE

In the forest north of Stora Djulö, in the parish of Stora Malm, lies a hill called Stallsbacke—Stall Hill—because King Charles XI is said to have had his stable there on one of his journeys.

Within the forest near the hill there is an enchanted garden where many a man has gone astray, and has been compelled to wander the whole night through, because he did not know that turning his coat inside out, or throwing fire at the sun, would give him the key to his deliverance.

Many have, during these wanderings, been imprisoned in the enchanted garden, but not all have liberated themselves from the enchantment as old Löfberg, the steward from Stora Djulö, succeeded in doing.

Late one Thursday evening, while traveling the path from the pasture home to the mansion, he found himself suddenly in the presence of a high wall with grated gates, beyond which was visible the most beautiful garden ever seen by man. The moon was high in the heavens, and Löberg could distinguish objects as clearly as in daylight. He saw that the trees hung full of fruit, and that the bushes were bowed with berries, which glistened like precious stones. When he had viewed the magnificent sight a few minutes, and was about to go on, an old man, who proclaimed himself the gardener, presented himself, and invited Löfberg to go in and gather of the fruit what he pleased. But Löfberg was too wise for this. He understood that what he saw was the work of the Trolls, and answered that at home there was a much more beautiful garden, and that he had no occasion to go into strange gardens to get a few rotten, sour apples.

This he should not have said. Suddenly there came up a strong wind, which blew his hat over the wall, and, as Löfberg left it behind him and hastened home, there came a crash in the forest, whereupon the vision suddenly melted away.


# UPLAND

# THE WERWOLF

There was once a king, who ruled over a large kingdom. He was married to a beautiful queen, by whom he had only one child, a daughter. Hence it naturally followed that the little one was to her parents as the apple of their eye, and was dear to them beyond all other things, so that they thought of nothing with such delight as of the pleasure they should have in her when she grew up. But much falls out contrary to expectation; for before the princess was out of her childhood, the queen, her mother, fell sick and died. Now, it is easy to imagine that there was sadness not only in the royal court, but over the whole kingdom, for the queen was greatly beloved by all. The king himself was so deeply afflicted that he resolved never to marry again, but placed all his comfort and joy in the little princess.

In this manner a considerable time passed on; the young princess grew from day to day taller and fairer, and everything she at any time desired was by her father immediately granted her; many attendants being placed about her, for the sole purpose of being at hand to execute all her commands. Among these there was a woman who had been previously married, and had two daughters. She was of an agreeable person, and had a persuasive tongue, so that she well knew how to put her words together; added to all which she was as soft and pliant as silk; but her heart was full of artifices and all kinds of falsehood. No sooner was the queen dead than she began to devise plans how she might become consort to the king, and her daughters be honoured as kings' daughters. With this object she began by winning the affection of the young princess, praised beyond measure all that she said or did, and all her talk ended in declaring how happy they would be if the king would take to himself a new wife. On this subject the conversation oftenest turned both early and late, till at length the princess could not believe otherwise than that all the woman said was true. She therefore asked her what description of wife it were most desirable that the king should select. The woman, in many words, all sweet as honey, answered, "Ill would it become me to give an opinion in such a case, hoping only he may choose for his queen one who will be kind to my little princess. But this I know, that were I so fortunate as to be the object of his choice, I should think only of what might please the princess; and if she wished to wash her hands, one of my daughters should hold the basin, and the other hand her the towel." This and much more she said to the princess, who believed her, as children readily believe all that is told them is true.

Not a day now passed in which the king was free from the solicitations of his daughter, who incessantly besought him to marry the handsome waiting-woman; but he would not. Nevertheless, the princess would not desist from her entreaties, but spoke incessantly precisely as she had been taught by the false waiting-woman. One day, when she was talking in the same strain, the king broke forth: "I see very well that it must at length be as you have resolved, greatly as it is against my wish; but it shall be only on one condition." "What is the condition?" asked the princess, overjoyed. "It is," said the king, "that, as it is for your sake if I marry again, you shall promise me that if at any future time you shall be discontented with your stepmother or your stepsisters, I shall not be troubled with your complaints and grievances." The princess made the promise, and it was settled that the king should marry the waiting-woman, and make her queen over all his realm.

As time passed on the king's daughter grew up to be the fairest maid in all the land; while the queen's daughters were as ugly in person as in disposition, so that no one had a good word for them. There could not, therefore, fail of being a number of young princes and knights, from both east and west, coming to demand the young princess; while not one vouchsafed to woo either of the queen's daughters. At this the step-mother was sorely vexed at heart, however she might conceal her feel-ings, being, to all outward appearance, as smooth and humble as before. Among the suitors there was a king's son from a distant country, who was both young and valorous, and as he passionately loved the princess, she listened to his addresses, and plighted her faith to him in return. The queen observed all this with a jaundiced eye; for she would fain have had the prince marry one of her own daughters, and, therefore, resolved that the young couple should never be united with each other. From that moment her thoughts were solely bent on the destruction of both of them and their love.

An opportunity soon offered itself to her; for just at that time intelli-gence was received that an enemy had invaded the country, so that the king was obliged to take the field. The princess was now soon made to learn what kind of a stepmother she had got; for hardly had the king departed before the queen began to show her true disposition, so that she now was as cruel and malignant as she had previously appeared to be friendly and obliging. Not a day passed on which the princess did not hear maledictions and hard words; nor did the queen's daughters yield to their mother in wickedness. But a lot still more cruel awaited the young prince, the lover of the princess. While engaged in the chase he had lost his way, and got separated from his companions. Availing herself of the opportunity, the queen practised on him her wicked arts, and trans-formed him into a WERWOLF, so that for the remainder of his days he should be a prowler of the forest. When evening drew on, and the prince did not appear, his men returned home; and the sorrow may be easily imagined with which the princess was overwhelmed when she was in-formed how the chase had terminated. She wept and mourned day and night, and would not be comforted. But the queen laughed at her afflic-tion, and rejoiced in her false heart that everything had turned out so agreeably to her wishes.

As the princess was one day sitting alone in her maidenbower, it en-tered her mind that she would visit the forest in which the young prince had disappeared. She went, therefore, to her stepmother, and asked permission to go to the wood, that she might for a little while forget her heavy affliction. To her request the queen would hardly give her consent, as she was always more inclined to say no than yes; but the princess besought her so earnestly that at last her stepmother could no longer withhold her permission, only ordering one of her daughters to accom-pany and keep watch over her. A long dispute now arose between mother and daughters, neither of the stepsisters being willing to go with her, but excusing themselves, and asking what pleasure they could have in follow-ing her who did nothing but weep. The matter ended by the queen insisting that one of her daughters should go with the princess, however much it might be against her will. The maidens then strolled away from the palace and reached the forest, where the princess amused herself with wandering among the trees, and listening to the song of the little birds, and thinking on the friend she loved so dearly, and whom she now had lost; the queen's daughter following all the while, with a heart full of rancorous feeling for the princess and her grief.

After having wandered about for some time they came to a small cottage that stood far in the dark forest. At the same moment the princess was seized with a burning thirst, and entreated her stepsister to accompany her to the cottage, that she might get a draught of water. At this the queen's daughter became only more ill-humoured, and said, "Is it not enough that I follow you up and down in the wild wood? Now, because you are a princess, you require me to go into such a filthy nest. No, my foot shall never enter it. If you will go, go alone." The princess took no long time to consider, but did as her stepsister said, and entered the cabin. In the little apartment she saw an aged woman sitting on a bench, who appeared so stricken with years that her head shook. The princess saluted her, as was her wont, in a friendly tone, with "Good evening, good mother! may I ask you for a little drink of water?" "Yes and right welcome," answered the old woman. "Who are you that come under my humble roof with so kind a greeting?" The princess told her that she was the king's daughter, and had come out to divert herself, with the hope, in some degree, of forgetting her heavy affliction. "What affliction have you, then?" asked the old woman. "Well may I grieve," answered the princess, "and never more feel joyful. I have lost my only friend, and God alone knows whether we shall ever meet again." She then related to the old woman all that had taken place, while the tears flowed from her eyes in such torrents that no one could have refrained from pitying her. When she had concluded, the old woman said, "It is well that you have made your grief known to me; I have experienced much, and can, perhaps, give you some advice. When you go from hence you will see a lily growing in the field. This lily is not like other lilies, but has many wonderful properties. Hasten, therefore, to pluck it. If you can do so, all will be well; for then there will come one who will tell you what you are to do." They then parted; the princess having thanked her, continued her walk, and the old woman remained sitting on her bench and shaking her head. But the queen's daughter had been standing during the whole time outside the door, murmuring and fretting that the princess stayed so long.

When she came out she had to hear much chiding from her stepsister, as was to be expected; but to this she gave very little heed, thinking only how she should find the flower of which the old woman had spoken. She therefore proceeded further into the forest, and in the selfsame moment her eye fell on a spot where there stood a beautiful white lily in full bloom before her. On seeing it she was so glad, so glad, and instantly ran to gather it, but it vanished on a sudden and appeared again at some distance. The princess was now eager beyond measure, and no longer gave heed to the voice of her stepsister, but continued running; though every time she put forth her hand to take the flower it was already away, and immediately afterwards reappeared at a short distance farther off. Thus it continued for a considerable time, and the princess penetrated further and further into the dense forest, the lily all the while appearing and vanishing, and again showing itself, and every time looking taller and more beautiful than before. In this manner the princess at length came to a high mountain, when on casting her eyes up to the summit, there stood the flower on the very edge, as brilliant and fair as the brightest star. She now began to climb up the mountain, caring for neither the stocks nor the stones that lay in the way, so great was her ardour. When she at length had gained the mountain's top, lo! the lily no longer moved, but continued stationary. The princess then stooped and plucked it, and placed it in her bosom, and was so overjoyed that she forgot both stepsister and everything in the world besides.

For a long time the princess could not sufficiently feast her eyes with the sight of the beautiful flower. It then on a sudden entered her mind, what her stepmother would say, when she returned home, for having stayed out so long. She looked about her before returning to the palace, but on casting a glance behind her she saw that the sun had gone down, and that only a strip of day yet tarried on the mountain's summit; while down before her the forest appeared so dark and gloomy, that she did not trust herself to find the way through it. She was now exceedingly weary and exhausted, and saw no alternative but that she must remain for the night where she was. Sitting then down on the rock, she placed her hand under her cheek and wept, and thought on her wicked stepmother and stepsisters, and all the bitter words she must hear when she returned home, and on the king, her father, who was absent, and on the beloved of her heart, whom she should never see again; but abundantly as her tears flowed she noticed them not, so absorbing was her affliction. Night now drew on, all was shrouded in darkness, the stars rose and set, but the princess still continued sitting on the same spot, weeping without intermission. While thus sitting, lost in thought, she heard a voice greeting her with "Good evening, fair maiden! Why do you sit here so lonely and sorrowful?" She started and was greatly surprised, as may be easily imagined; and on looking back there stood a little, little old man, who nodded and looked so truly benevolent. She answered, "I may well be sorrowful, and never more be glad. I have lost my best beloved, and have, moreover, missed my path in the forest, so that I am fearful of being devoured by the wild beasts." "Oh," said the old man, "don't be disheartened for that. If you will obey me in all that I say, I will help you." To this the princess readily assented, seeing herself forsaken by the whole world besides. The old man then drew forth a flint and steel, and said, "Fair maiden! now, in the first place, you shall kindle a fire." The king's daughter did as she was desired, gathered moss, twigs, and dry wood, and kindled a fire on the mountain's brow. When she had done this the old man said to her, "Go now further on the mountain, and you will find a pot full of tar: bring it hither." The princess did so. The old man continued: "Now set the pot on the fire." The princess did so. "When, now, the tar begins to boil," said the old man, "cast your white lily into the pot." This seemed to the princess a very hard command, and she prayed earnestly that she might retain her lily; but the old man said: "Have you not promised to obey me in all that I desire? Do as I tell you; you will not repent." The princess then, with eyes averted, cast the lily into the boiling pot, although it grieved her to the heart; so dear to her was the beautiful flower.

At the same instant a hollow roaring was heard from the forest, like the cry of a wild beast, which came nearer and nearer, and passed into a hideous howl, so that the mountain re-echoed on every side. At the same time was heard a cracking and rustling among the trees, the bushes gave way, and the princess beheld a huge gray wolf come rushing out of the forest just opposite to the spot where they were sitting. In her terror she would gladly have fled from it; but the old man said, "Make haste, run to the brow of the mountain, and the moment the wolf comes before you, empty the tar-pot over him." The princess, although so terrified that she was hardly conscious of what she did, nevertheless followed the old man's direction, and poured the tar over the wolf, just as he came running towards her. But now a wonderful event took place, for scarcely had she done so when the wolf changed his covering, the great gray skin started off from him, and, instead of a ravenous wild beast, there stood a comely youth with eyes directed towards the brow of the mountain; and when the princess had so far recovered from her fright that she could look on him, whom did she behold before her but her own best beloved, who had been transformed into a werwolf!

Now let any one, who can, imagine what the feelings of the princess were at this moment. She stretched out her arms towards him, but could neither speak nor answer, so great were her surprise and joy. But the prince ran up the mountain and embraced her with all the ardour of the truest affection, and thanked her for having restored him. Nor did he forget the little old man, but thanked him in many kind words for his powerful aid. They then sat down on the mountain-top and conversed lovingly with each other. The prince related how he had been changed into a wolf, and all the privations he had suffered while he had to range about the forest; and the princess recounted to him her sorrow and all the tears she had shed during his absence. Thus they sat throughout the night, heedless of the passing hour, until the stars began gradually to retire before the daylight, so that the surrounding objects were visible. When the sun had risen they perceived that a wide road ran from the foot of the hill quite up to the royal palace. Then said the old man, "Fair maiden, turn about. Do you see anything yonder?" "Yes," answered the princess, "I see a horseman on a foaming horse; he rides along the road at full speed." "That," said the old man, "is a messenger from the king, your father. He will follow forthwith with his whole army." Now was the princess glad beyond measure, and wished instantly to descend to meet her father; but the old man held her back, saying "Wait: it is yet too soon. Let us first see how things will turn out."

After some time the sun shone bright, so that its rays fell on the palace down before them. Then said the old man, "Fair maiden, turn about. Do you see anything yonder?" "Yes," answered the princess, "I see many persons coming out of my father's palace, some of whom proceed along the road, while others hasten towards the forest." The old man said, "They are your stepmother's servants. She has sent one party to meet the king and bid him welcome; but the other is going to the forest in search of you." At hearing this the princess was troubled, and was with difficulty induced to remain, but wished to go down to the queen's people: but the old man held her back, saying, "Wait yet a little while; we will first see how things turn out."

For some time the princess continued with her looks directed towards the road by which the king was to come. Then said the old man again, "Fair maiden, turn about. Do you observe anything yonder?" "Yes," answered the princess, "there is a great stir in my father's palace; and see! now they are busy in hanging the whole palace with black." The old man said, "That is your stepmother and her servants. They wish to make your father believe that you are dead." At this the princess was filled with anxiety, and prayed fervently, saying, "Let me go, let me go, that I may spare my father so great an affliction." But the old man detained her, saying, "No, wait. It is still too soon. We will first see how things turn out."

Again another interval passed, the sun rose high in the heaven, and the air breathed warm over field and forest; but the royal children and the little old man continued sitting on the mountain where we left them. They now observed a small cloud slowly rising in the horizon, which grew larger and larger, and came nearer and nearer along the road; and as it moved they saw that it glittered with weapons, and perceived helmets nodding and banners waving, heard the clanking of swords and the neighing of horses, and at length recognised the royal standard. Now it is easy to imagine that the joy of the princess exceeded all bounds, and that she only longed to go and greet her father. But the old man held her back, saying, "Turn about, fair maiden, do you see nothing at the king's palace?" "Yes," answered the princess, "I see my stepmother and my stepsisters coming out clad in deep mourning, and holding white handkerchiefs to their faces, and weeping bitterly." The old man said, "They are now pretending to mourn for your death; but wait a while, we have yet to see how things will turn out."

Some time after, the old man asked again, "Fair maiden, turn about. Do you observe anything yonder?" "Yes," answered the princess, "I see they come bearing a black coffin. Now my father orders it to be opened. And see! the queen and her daughters fall on their knees, and my father threatens them with his sword." The old man said, "The king desired to see your corpse, and so your wicked stepmother has been forced to confess the truth." On hearing this, the princess entreated fervently: "Let me go, let me go, that I may console my father in his great affliction." But the old man still detained her, saying, "Attend to my counsel, and stay here a little while. We have not yet seen how everything will terminate.

Another interval passed, and the princess, and the prince, and the little old man, still continued sitting on the mountain. Then said the old man, "Turn about, fair maiden. Do you observe anything yonder?" "Yes," answered the princess, "I see my father, and my stepmother, and my stepsisters, coming this way with all their attendants." The old man continued, "They have now set out in search of you. Go down now, and bring the wolfskin which is lying below." The king's daughter did so, and

the old man then said, "Place yourself on the brink of the mountain."
The princess did so, and at the same moment perceived the queen and
her daughters coming along the road just beneath the mountain where
they were sitting. "Now," said the old man, "cast the wolfskin straight
down." The princess obeyed, and cast the wolfskin as the old man had
directed. It fell exactly over the wicked queen and her two daughters.
But now a wonderful event took place, for hardly had the skin touched
the three women than they changed their guise, gave a hideous howl,
and were transformed into three fierce werwolves, which at full speed
rushed into the wild forest.

Scarcely had this taken place before the king himself with all his men
came to the foot of the mountain. When he looked up and beheld the
princess, he could not at first believe his eyes, but stood immovable,
thinking it was a spectre. The old man then cried, "Fair maiden, hasten
now down and gladden the heart of your father." The princess did not
wait to be told a second time, but, taking her lover by the hand, was in
an instant at the mountain's foot. When they reached the spot where the
king was standing, the princess fell on her father's breast and wept for
joy; the young prince also wept; even the king himself shed tears, and to
everyone present their meeting was a delightful spectacle. Great joy was
there and many embracings, and the princess related all she had suffered
from her stepmother and stepsisters, and all about her beloved prince,
and the little old man who had so kindly assisted them. But when the
king turned to thank him he had already vanished, and no one could
ever say either who he was or whither he went.

The king and all his suite now returned to the palace, on their way
towards which much was said both about the little old man and what the
princess had undergone. On reaching home the king ordered a sumptuous banquet to be prepared, to which he invited all the most distinguished and exalted persons of his kingdom, and bestowed his daughter
on the young prince; and their nuptials were celebrated with games and
rejoicings for many days. And I, too, was at the feastings; and as I rode
through the forest I was met by a wolf with two young ones; they were
ravenous, and seemed to suffer much. I have since learned that they
were no other than the wicked stepmother and her two daughters.

# THE HERD-BOY

THERE WAS once a poor herd-boy, who had neither kith nor kin except
his stepmother, who was a wicked woman, and hardly allowed him food
or clothing. Thus the poor boy suffered great privation; during all the
livelong day he had to tend cattle, and scarcely ever got more than a
morsel of bread morning and evening.

One day his stepmother had gone out without leaving him any food;

he had, therefore, to drive his cattle to the field fasting, and being very hungry, he wept bitterly. But at the approach of noon he dried his tears, and went up on a green hill, where he was in the habit of resting, while the sun was hot in the summer. On this hill it was always cool and dewy under the shady trees; but now he remarked that there was no dew, that the ground was dry, and the grass trampled down. This seemed to him very singular, and he wondered who could have trodden down the green grass. White thus sitting and thinking, he perceived something that lay glittering in the sunshine. Springing up to see what it might be, he found it was a pair of very, very small shoes of the whitest and clearest glass. The boy now felt quite happy again, forgot his hunger, and amused himself the whole day with the little glass shoes.

In the evening, when the sun had sunk behind the forest, the herd-boy called his cattle and drove them to the village. When he had gone some way, he was met by a very little boy, who in a friendly tone greeted him with "Good evening!" "Good evening again," answered the herd-boy. "Hast thou found my shoes, which I lost this morning in the green grass?" asked the little boy. The herd-boy answered: "Yes, I have found them; but, my good little fellow, let me keep them. I intended to give them to my stepmother, and then, perhaps, I should have got a little meat, when I came home." But the boy prayed so earnestly, "Give me back my shoes; another time I will be as kind to thee," that the herd-boy returned him the shoes. The little one then, greatly delighted, gave him a friendly nod, and went springing away.

The herd-boy now collected his cattle together, and continued his way homewards. When he reached his dwelling it was already dark, and his stepmother chided him for returning so late. "There's still some porridge in the pot," said she; "eat now, and pack thyself off to bed, so that thou canst get up in the morning betimes, like other folks." The poor herd-boy durst not return any answer to these hard words, but ate, and then slunk to bed in the hayloft, where he was accustomed to sleep. The whole night he dreamed of nothing but the little boy and his little glass shoes.

Early in the morning, before the sun shone from the east, the boy was waked by his stepmother's voice: "Up with thee, thou sluggard! It is broad day, and the animals are not to stand hungry for thy sloth." He instantly rose, got a bit of bread, and drove the cattle to the pasture.

When he came to the green hill, which was wont to be so cool and shady, he again wondered to see that the dew was all swept from the grass, and the ground dry, even more so than on the preceding day. While he thus sat thinking, he observed something lying in the grass and glittering in the bright sunshine. Springing towards it, he found it was a very, very little red cap set round with small golden bells. At this he was greatly delighted, forgot his hunger, and amused himself all day with the little elegant cap.

In the evening, when the sun had sunk behind the forest, the herd-boy gathered his cattle together, and drove them towards the village. When on his way, he was met by a very little and, at the same time, very fair damsel. She greeted him in a friendly tone with "Good evening!" "Good evening again," answered the lad. The damsel then said: "Hast

thou found my cap, which I lost this morning in the green grass?" The
boy answered: "Yes, I have found it; but let me keep it, my pretty maid.
I thought of giving it to my wicked stepmother, and then, perhaps, I
shall get a little meat when I go home." But the little damsel entreated so
urgently, "Give me back my cap; another time I will be as good to thee,"
that the lad gave her the little cap, when she appeared highly delighted,
gave him a friendly nod, and sprang off.

On his return home, he was received as usual by his cruel stepmother,
and dreamed the whole night of the little damsel and her little red cap.

In the morning he was turned out fasting, and on coming to the hill,
found it was drier than on either of the preceding days, and that the
grass was trodden down in large rings. It then entered his mind all that
he had heard of the little *elves*, how in the summer nights they were wont
to dance in the dewy grass, and he found that these must be *elfin-rings*,
or *elfin-dances*. While sitting absorbed in thought, he chanced to strike
his foot against a little bell that lay in the grass, and which gave forth so
sweet a sound, that all the cattle came running together, and stood still
to listen. Now the boy was delighted, and could do nothing but play with
the little bell, till he forgot his troubles and the cattle forgot to graze. And
so the day passed much more quickly than can be imagined.

When it drew towards evening, and the sun was level with the tree-
tops, the boy called his cattle and prepared to return home. But let him
entice and call them as he might, they were not to be drawn from the
pasture, for it was a delightful grassy spot. Then thought the boy to
himself, "Perhaps they will pay more heed to the little bell." So drawing
forth the bell, he tingled it as he went along the way. In one moment the
bell-cow came running after him, and was followed by the rest of the
herd. At this the boy was overjoyed, for he was well aware what an
advantage the little bell would be to him. As he was going on, a very little
old man met him, and kindly bade him a good evening. "Good evening
again," said the boy. The old man asked: "Hast thou found my little bell,
which I lost this morning in the green grass?" The herd-boy answered:
"Yes, I have found it." The old man said: "Then give it me back." "No,"
answered the boy, "I am not so doltish as you may think. The day before
yesterday I found two small glass shoes, which a little boy wheedled from
me. Yesterday I found a cap, which I gave to a little damsel; and now you
come to take from me the little bell, which is so good for calling the cattle.
Other finders get a reward for their pains, but I get nothing." The little
man then used many fair words, with the view of recovering his bell, but
all to no purpose. At last he said: "Give me back the little bell, and I will
give thee another, with which thou mayest call thy cattle; thou shalt,
moreover, obtain three wishes." These seemed to the boy no unfavoura-
ble terms, and he at once agreed to them, adding, "As I may wish whatever I will, I will wish to be a king, and I will wish to have a great palace,
and also a very beautiful queen." "Thou hast wished no trifling wishes,"
said the old man, "but bear well in mind what I now tell thee. To-night,
when all are sleeping, thou shalt go hence, till thou comest to a royal
palace, which lies due north. Take this pipe of bone. If thou fallest into
trouble, blow it; if thou afterwards fallest into great trouble, blow it again;
but if, on a third occasion, thou findest thyself in still greater peril,

break the pipe in two, and I will help thee, as I have promised." The boy gave the old man many thanks for his gifts, and the elf-king—for it was he—went his way. But the boy bent his steps homewards, rejoicing as he went along, that he should so soon escape from tending cattle for his wicked stepmother.

When he reached the village it was already dark, and his stepmother had been long awaiting his coming. She was in a great rage, so that the poor lad got blows instead of food. "This will not last long," thought the boy, comforting himself with the reflection, as he went up to his hayloft, where he laid himself down and slumbered for a short time. About midnight, long before the cock crew, he arose, slipped out of the house, and began his journey in a northward direction, as the old man had enjoined. He travelled incessantly, over hill and dale, and twice did the sun rise and twice set, while he was still on his way.

Towards evening on the third day he came to a royal palace, which was so spacious that he thought he should never again see the like. He went to the kitchen and asked for employment. "What dost thou know, and what canst thou do?" inquired the master-cook. "I can tend cattle in the pasture," answered the boy. The master-cook said: "The king is in great want of a herd-boy; but it will, no doubt, be with thee as with the others, that every day thou losest one of the herd." The boy answered: "Hitherto I have never lost any beast that that I drove to the field." He was then taken into the king's service, and tended the king's cattle; but the wolf never got a beast from him: so he was well esteemed by all the king's servants.

One evening, as the herd-boy was driving his cattle home, he observed a beautiful young damsel standing at a window and listening to his song. Though he seemed hardly to notice her, he, nevertheless, felt a glow suffused over him. Some time passed in this manner, the herd-boy being delighted every time he saw the young maiden; though he was still ignorant that she was the king's daughter. It happened one day that the young girl came to him as he was driving the herd to their pasture. She had with her little snow-white lamb, and begged him in a friendly tone to take charge of her lamb, and protect it from the wolves in the forest. At this the herd-boy was so confused that he could neither answer nor speak. But he took the lamb with him, and found his greatest pleasure in guarding it, and the animal attached itself to him, as a dog to its master. From that day the herd-boy frequently enjoyed the sight of the fair princess. In the morning, when he drove his cattle to the pasture, she would stand at the window listening to his song; but in the evening, when he returned from the forest, she would descend to caress her little lamb, and say a few friendly words to the herd-boy.

Time rolled on. The herd-boy had grown up into a comely, vigorous young man; and the princess had sprung up and was become the fairest maiden that could be found far or near. Nevertheless, she came every evening, according to her early custom, to caress her lamb. But one day the princess was missing and could nowhere be found. This event caused a great sorrow and commotion in the royal court, for the princess was beloved by every one; but the king and queen, as was natural, grieved the most intensely of all. The king sent forth a proclamation over the

whole land, that whosoever should recover his daughter should be rewarded with her hand and half the kingdom. This brought a number of
princes, and knights, and warriors from the east and the west. Cased in
steel they rode forth with arms and attendants, to seek the lost princess;
but few were they that returned from their wanderings, and those that
did return brought no tidings of her they went in quest of. The king and
queen were now inconsolable, and thought that they had sustained an
irreparable loss. The herd-boy, as before, drove his cattle to the pasture,
but it was in sadness, for the king's fair daughter engrossed his thoughts
every day and every hour.

One night in a dream the little elfin king seemed to stand before him
and to say: "To the north! to the north! there thou wilt find thy queen."
At this the young man was so overjoyed that he sprang up, and as he
woke, there stood the little man, who nodded to him, and repeated: "To
the north! to the north!" He then vanished, leaving the youth in doubt
whether or not it were an illusion. As soon as it was day he went to the
hall of the palace, and requested an audience of the king. At this all the
royal servants wondered, and the master-cook said: "Thou hast served
for so many years that thou mayest, no doubt, get thy wages increased
without speaking to the king himself." But the young man persisted in
his request, and let it be understood that he had something very different
in his mind. On entering the royal apartment, the king demanded his
errand, when the young man said: "I have served you faithfully for many
years, and now desire permission to go and seek for the princess." Hereupon the king grew angry and said: "How canst thou, a herd-boy, think
of doing that which no warrior nor prince has been able to accomplish?"
But the youth answered boldly, that he would either discover the princess
or, for her sake, lay down his life. The king then let his anger pass, and
called to mind the old proverb: *A heart worthy of scarlet often lies under a
coarse woollen cloak.* He therefore gave orders that the herd-boy should be
equipped with a charger and all things requisite. But the youth said: "I
reck not of riding; give me but your word and permission, together with
means sufficient." The king then wished him success in his enterprise;
but all the boys and other servants in the court laughed at the herd-boy's
rash undertaking.

The young man journeyed towards the north, as he had been instructed by the elf-king, and proceeded on and on until he could not be
far distant from the world's end. When he had thus travelled over mountains and desolate ways, he came at length to a great lake, in the midst of
which there was a fair island, and on the island a royal palace, much
more spacious than the one from whence he came. He went down to the
water's edge, and surveyed the palace on every side. While thus viewing
it, he perceived a damsel with golden locks standing at one of the windows, and making signs with a silken band, such as the princess's lamb
was accustomed to wear. At this sight the young man's heart leaped in
his breast; for it rushed into his mind that the damsel could be no other
than the princess herself. He now began to consider how he should cross
over the water to the great palace; but could hit upon no plan. At last the
thought occurred to him that he would make a trial whether the little

elves would afford him some assistance; and he took forth his pipe, and blew a long-continued strain. He had scarcely ceased, when he heard a voice behind him, saying "Good evening." "Good evening again," answered the youth, turning about; when just before him there stood the little boy whose glass shoes he had found in the grass. "What dost thou wish of me?" asked the elfin boy. The other answered: "I wish thee to convey me across the water to the royal palace." The boy replied: "Place thyself on my back." The youth did so: and at the same instant the boy changed his form and became an immensely huge hawk that darted through the air, and stopped not until it reached the island, as the young man had requested.

He now went up to the hall of the palace and asked for employment. "What dost thou understand and what canst thou do?" inquired the master-cook. "I can take charge of cattle," answered the youth. The master-cook then said: "The giant is just now in great want of a herdsman; but it will, I dare say, be with thee as with the others; for if a beast by chance is lost, thy life is forfeited." The youth answered: "This seems to me a hard condition; but I will, nevertheless, agree to it." The master-cook then accepted his service, and he was to commence on the following day.

The young man now drove the giant's cattle, and sung his song, and rang his little bell, as he had formerly done; and the princess sat at her window, and listened, and made signs to him that he should not appear to notice her. In the evening he drove the herd from the forest, and was met by the giant, who said to him: "Thy life is in the place of any one that may be missing." But not a beast was wanting, let the giant count them as he would. Now the giant was quite friendly, and said: "Thou shalt be my herdsman all thy days." He then went down to the lake, loosed his enchanted ship, and rowed thrice round the island, as he was wont to do.

During the giant's absence the princess stationed herself at the window and sang:—

> "To-night, to-night, thou herdsman bold,
>  Goes the cloud from under my star.
>  And if thou comest hither, then will I be thine,
>  My crown I will gladly give thee."

The young man listened to her song, and understood from it that he was to go in the night and deliver the princess. He therefore went away without appearing to notice anything. But when it was late, and all were sunk in deep sleep, he stealthily approached the tower, placed himself before the window, and sang:—

> "To-night will wait thy herdsman true,
>  Will sad stand under thy window;
>  And if thou comest down, thou mayest one day be mine,
>  While the shadows fall so widely."

The princess whispered: "I am bound with chains of gold, come and break them." The young man now knew no other course than again to blow with his pipe a very long-continued strain; when instantly he heard a voice behind him, saying "Good evening." "Good evening again," answered the youth, looking round; when there stood the little elf-king, from whom he had got the little bell and the pipe. "What wilt thou with me?" inquired the old man. The young man answered: "I beseech you to convey me and the princess hence." The little man said: "Follow me." They then ascended to the maiden's tower: the castle gate opened spontaneously, and when the old man touched the chain, it burst in fragments. All three then went down to the margin of the lake, when the elf-king sang:—

> "Thou little pike in the water must go,
>     Come, come, hastily!
> A princess fair on thy back shall ride,
>     And eke a king so mighty."

At the same moment appeared the little damsel, whose cap the herd-boy had found in the grass. She sprang down to the lake, and was instantly changed into a large pike that sported about in the water. Then said the elf-king: "Sit ye on the back of the pike. But the princess must not be terrified, let what may happen; for then will my power be at an end." Having so said, the old man vanished; but the youth and the fair princess followed his injunctions, and the pike bore them rapidly along through the billows.

While all this was taking place, the giant awoke, looked through the window, and perceived the herd-boy floating on the water together with the young princess. Instantly snatching up his eagle-plumage, he flew after them. When the pike heard the clapping of the giant's wings, it dived far down under the surface of the water, whereat the princess was so terrified that she uttered a scream. Then was the elf-king's power at an end, and the giant seized the two fugitives in his talons. On his return to the island he caused the young herdsman to be cast into a dark dungeon, full fifteen fathoms underground; but the princess was again placed in her tower, and strictly watched, lest she should again attempt to escape.

The youth now lay in the captives' tower, and was in deep affliction at finding himself unable to deliver the princess, and, at the same time, having most probably forfeited his own life. The words of the elfin king now occurred to his memory: "If, on a third occasion, thou findest thyself in great peril, break the pipe in two, and I will help thee." As a last resource, therefore, he drew forth the little pipe and broke it in two. At the same moment he heard behind him the words "Good evening." "Good evening again," answered the youth; and when he looked round there stood the little old man close by him, who asked: "What wilt thou with me?" The young man answered: "I wish to deliver the princess, and to convey her home to her father." The old man then led him through many locked doors and many splendid apartments, till they came to a spacious hall, filled with all kinds of weapons, swords, spears, and axes, of which some shone like polished steel, others like burnished gold. The old man kindled a fire on the hearth, and said: "Undress thyself!" The young man did so, and the little man burnt his old garments. He then went to a large iron chest, out of which he took a costly suit of armour, resplendent with the purest gold. "Dress thyself," said he: the young man did so. When he was thus armed from head to foot, the old man bound a sharp sword by his side, and said: "It is decreed that the giant shall fall by this sword, and this armour no steel can penetrate." The young herdsman felt quite at ease in the golden armour, and moved as gracefully as if he had been a prince of the highest degree. They then returned to the dark dungeon; the youth thanked the elf-king for his timely succour, and they parted from each other.

Till a late hour there was a great bustle and hurrying in the whole palace; for the giant was on that day to celebrate his marriage with the beautiful princess, and had invited many of his kin to the feast. The princess was clad in the most sumptuous manner, and decorated with a crown and rings of gold, and other costly ornaments, which had been worn by the giant's mother. The health of the wedded pair was then drunk amid all kinds of rejoicing, and there was no lack of good cheer, both of meat and drink. But the bride wept without intermission, and her tears were so hot that they felt like fire on her cheeks.

When night approached, and the giant was about to conduct his bride to the nuptial chamber, he sent his pages to fetch the young herdsman, who lay in the dungeon. But when they entered the prison, the captive had disappeared, and in his stead there stood a bold warrior, with sword in hand, and completely armed. At this apparition the young men were frightened and fled; but were followed by the herdsman, who thus ascended to the court of the palace, where the guests were assembled to witness his death. When the giant cast his eyes on the doughty warrior, he was exasperated, and exclaimed: "Out upon thee, thou base Troll!" As he spoke his eyes became so piercing that they saw through the young herdsman's armour; but the youth fearless said: "Here shalt thou strive with me for thy fair bride." The giant was not inclined to stay, and was about to withdraw; but the herdsman drew his sword, which blazed like a flame of fire. When the giant recognised the sword, under which he was doomed to fall, he was terror-struck and sank on the earth; but the young herdsman advanced boldly, swung round his sword, and struck a blow so powerful that the giant's head was separated from his carcass. Such was his end.

On witnessing this exploit, the wedding-guests were overcome with fear, and departed, each to his home; but the princess ran forth and thanked the brave herdsman for having saved her. They then proceeded to the water, loosed the giant's enchanted ship, and rowed away from the island. On their arrival at the king's court, there was great joy that the king had recovered his daughter, for whom he had mourned so long. There was afterwards a sumptuous wedding, and the young herdsman obtained the king's fair daughter. They lived happily for very many years, and had many beautiful children. The bell and the broken pipe are preserved as memorials, aye even to the present day.

# DALARNE

## THE WATER NYMPH

About a mile northwest from Järna Church was located, at one time, a water mill, Snöåqvarn, belonging to the parishioners of Näs.

One Sunday morning, before the church of Järna had a priest of its own, the chaplain of Näs set out for that place, and had just arrived at the mill, when he saw a water man sitting in the rapids below it, playing on a fiddle a psalm from a psalm book.

"What good do you think your playing will do you?" said the priest. "You need expect no mercy!"

Sadly the figure ceased playing, and broke his fiddle in pieces, whereupon the priest regretted his severe condemnation, and again spoke:

"God knows, maybe, after all."

"Is that so?" exclaimed the man in joy, "then I'll pick up my pieces and play better and more charmingly than before."

---

To another mill in the same parish, Lindqvarn, near Lindsnäs, a peasant came one time with his grist. Along in the night he thought he would go and see if it was yet ground. He noticed on his arrival that the mill was not running, and opened the wicket to the wheel-house to learn what the matter might be, when he saw, glaring at him from the water below, two eyes "as large as half moons."

"The devil! what great eyes you have!" cried the peasant, but received no reply.

"Whew! what monstrous eyes you have!" the peasant again cried; again no answer.

Then he sprang into the mill, where he stirred up a large fire brand, with which he returned.

"Are your eyes as large now?" he shouted through the wicket.

"Yes!" came in answer from the stream.

Hereupon the peasant ran the stick through a hole in the floor, where the voice seemed to come from, and at once the wheel began to turn again.

## THE TREASURE SEEKERS

IT IS an established rule that he who seeks buried treasures must carefully maintain the utmost silence, lest his search be in vain and harm befall him, body and soul.

The Water Nymph

They were not ignorant of this—the four men that one time made up a party for the purpose of unearthing treasures said to be buried in Josäterdal.

Making their way, one midsummer night, across Lake Sälen, they saw approaching them a man of strange aspect, behind whose boat dragged a large fir tree, and a little later another, who inquired if they had seen any float-wood on their way.

The treasure seekers, who understood that these rowers were no other than fairies, pretended not to hear the question, and reached Josäterdal finally, without further temptation.

Just as they began to dig in the hill a grand officer approached and addressed them, but no one answered. Soon after a number of soldiers marched up and began to shoot at the diggers, but they did not allow even this to disturb them. Suddenly a red calf hopped up and the soldiers pressed nearer, so that the men soon stood enveloped in powder-smoke so thick that they could not see each other. When this did not frighten them, a tall gallows was raised on the side of the hill. It so happened that one of the diggers wore a red shirt that attracted the attention of the spirits, one of which cried out:

"Shall we begin with him wearing the red shirt?" Whereupon he lost his courage and took to his heels, followed neck over head by the others.

# THE LAPP IN MAGPIE FORM*

A FINN in the forests of Säfsen, having for a long time suffered ill luck with his flock, determined, let the cost be what it would, to find, through a Lapp well versed in the arts of the Trolls, a remedy for the evil he was enduring.

To this end he set out for the home of his to-be-deliverer, and after a long and fatiguing journey through the wilderness, he came at last to a Lapp hut which, with no little quaking, he entered, and there found a man busied with a fire upon the floor.

The Lapp who, through his connection, with the Trolls, already knew the purpose of the visit, and very much flattered thereby, greeted his guest kindly, and said:

"Good morning, Juga, my boy, are you here? I can give you news from home. Everything goes well there. I was there yesterday."

The Finn was terribly frightened at the discovery that he was recognized, but now more when he heard that the Lapp had made the same

---

*The magpie in folk-lore is an ominous bird, and is avoided by the peasantry, because one can not know whether it is the spirit of a Troll, friend or foe. When the magpies build near the house it is regarded as a lucky omen, but if they build on the heath, and meantime come to the house and chatter, it bodes evil.

journey forth and back in one day, that had cost him so many days of wandering.

With assurance of friendship, the Lapp quieted his fears, and continued:

"I had a little matter to attend to yesterday at your home, and sat upon the housetop when your wife went over the garden, but I saw she did not know me, for she threatened me with the house key."

The Finn now made known his errand, and received for answer that his animals were even now doing as well as he could wish. The presents brought by the Finn greatly strengthened their pleasant relations, and the Lapp agreed willingly to initiate him into the mysteries of Trolldom.

When the Finn reached home, the incidents of his journey were circumstantially related to his wife, even to the Lapp's account of his visit, and the threats with the house key.

"Yes, I remember now," said she, "that a magpie sat upon the roof the same day that the animals seemed to revive, but I believed it to be an unlucky bird, therefore tried to frighten it away with the key."

The Finn and his wife now understood that it was their friend, who had transformed himself thus in order to do them a service, and from that time held these creatures in great veneration.

# GESTRIKLAND

## THE VÄTTERS*

VÄTTERS, ACCORDING to the Northern belief, are creatures that live under ground, but often appear above, and then in human form so perfect that they have many times been mistaken for mankind. They live, as do the Trolls and Giants, in mountains, but more often move from one to another, and it is mostly during these journeys that they are seen.

When the parish of Ockilbo was first settled, the Vätters were so plentiful that a peasant who fixed his abode near the Rönn Hills was forced to build his windows high up near the eaves of his cottage to escape seeing the troublesome multitude of these beings that continually swarmed around.

*To the characteristics attributed in this story to the Vätters may be added that they are peaceable and generally inclined to be friendly to mankind, but that they may, nevertheless, be aroused to acts of violence if their wishes are not heeded, or if harm is done them designedly. They are said to have great quantities of gold and silver, but steel is very offensive to them. If, therefore, a knife is stuck into a fissure in a mountain, a piece of gold will, a few days later, be found in its stead. During autumn and in winter they take up their abode in vacated cow barns, where they employ themselves after the manner of mankind.

Despite the disposition of the cottager to have nothing to do with the Vätters, he could not avoid getting into complications with them at times.

One evening, when the wife went to drive the goats into the goat house, she saw among hers two strange goats, having horsehoofs instead of cloven hoofs, as should be. Do her utmost, it was impossible to separate them from the others. They pressed on, and were locked up with the rest.

In the night she was awakened by a heavy pounding upon the walls, and a voice from without called:

"Let us be neighborly, mother, and return my goats to me."

The woman dressed herself and hastened to the goat house, where the strange animals were making a dreadful uproar. Upon her opening the door they sprang out and hurried to the forest, whence she heard the Vätters shouting and calling them.

Thus a friendly feeling was forever established between the cottager and the Vätters, and from that day there were no more disturbances.


# MEDELPAD

## STARKAD AND BALE

THE RENOWNED hero, Starkad, the greatest warrior of the North, had offended a princess, therefore had fallen under the displeasure of the king, to escape whose wrath he wandered northward, where he took up his abode at Rude in Tuna, and it is related in the folk stories that he then took the name of "Ala Dräng," or "Rödu Pilt."

In Balbo, nine miles distant, in the parish of Borgajö, dwelt another warrior, Bale, who was a good friend to Starkad, and a companion in arms.

One morning Starkad climed to the top of Klefberg, in Tuna, and addressed Bale, thus:

"Bale in Balbo, are you awake?"

"Rödu Pilt," answered Bale, nine miles away, "the sun and I always awake at the same time; but how is it with you?"

"Poorly enough! I have only salmon for breakfast, dinner and supper. Bring me a piece of meat."

"All right!" replied Bale, and in a few hours arrived in Tuna with an elk under each arm.

The following morning Bale stood upon a mountain in Balbo and shouted:

"Rödu Pilt, are you awake?"

"The sun and I awake always at the same time," answered Starkad, "but how is it with you?"

THE VÄTTERS

"Oh, I have nothing but meat to eat—elk for breakfast, elk for dinner and elk for supper, come, therefore, and bring me a fish."

"All right," said Starkad, and in a little while he was with his friend, bearing a barrel of salmon under each arm.

In this manner the warriors kept each other supplied with fresh game from forest and sea, meantime spreading desolation and terror through the country, but one evening as they were returning from a plundering expedition to the sea, a black cloud appeared, and it began to thunder and lighten. Both hastened on the way, but reached no further than to Vattjom, when Starkad was struck dead by lightning. His companion buried him in a hill around which he placed five stones, two at his feet, one at each shoulder and one at his head, marking to this day the grave of Starkad forty feet in length.

# HERJEDALEN

## THE VÄTTS STOREHOUSE

IN HERJEDALEN, as in many of the northern regions of our country, where there is yet something remaining of the primitive pastoral life, there are still kept alive reminiscences of a very ancient people, whose occupation was herding cattle, which constituted their wealth and support. It is, however, with a later and more civilized people, though no date is given, that this narrative deals.

In days gone by, so the story goes, it happened that a milkmaid did not produce as much milk and butter from her herd as usual, for which her master took her severely to task. The girl sought vindication by charging it upon the Vätts, who, she claimed, possessed the place and appropriated a share of the product of the herd. This, the master was not willing to believe, but, to satisfy himself, went one autumn evening, after the cattle had been brought home, to the dairy house, where he secreted himself, as he supposed, under an upturned cheese kettle. He had not sat in his hiding place long when a Vätt mother with her family—a large one—came trooping in and began preparation for their meal.

The mother, who was busy at the fireplace, finally inquired if all had spoons.

"Yes," replied one of the Vätts. "All except him under the kettle."

The dairyman's doubts were now dispelled, and he hastened to move his residence to another place.

THE VÄTT'S STOREHOUSE

# VESTERBOTTEN

## THE VOYAGE IN A LAPP SLED

IN THE great forest west of Samsele, a hunter, early one morning, pursued his way in quest of game. About midday he ascended a ridge, where he was overtaken by a Troll-iling—a storm said to be raised by and to conceal a Troll—before which sticks and straws danced in the air. Quickly grasping his knife he threw it at the wind, which at once subsided, and in a few seconds the usual quiet reigned.

Some time later he was again hunting, when he lost his way. After a long and wearisome wandering he reached a Lapp hut, where he found a woman stirring something in a kettle. When she had concluded her cooking, she invited the hunter to dine, and gave him the same knife to eat with that he had thrown at the storm.

The following day he wished to return home, but could not possibly discover the course he should take, whereupon the Troll woman—for his hostess was none other—directed him to get into the Lapp sled, and attach to it a rope, in which he must tie three knots.

"Now, untie one knot at a time," said she, "and you will soon reach home."

The hunter untied one knot, as instructed, and away went the rope, dragging the sled after it into the air. After a time he untied another knot, and his speed was increased. Finally he untied the last knot, increasing the speed to such a rate that when the sled came to a standstill, as it did, suddenly, not long after, he concluded his journey, falling into his own yard with such force as to break his leg.

# LAPPLAND

## THE LAPP GENESIS, OR THE FIRST OF MANKIND

THE LAPPS, like other people, have their legends, and many of them the same, or nearly so, as are found among other nations. Others reflect more particularly the national characteristics of the Lapp folk. Thus, for instance, there is to be found among them a tradition of a general deluge, a universal catastrophe, whereof there still remains a dim reminiscence in the consciences of so many other primitive people.

Before the Lord destroyed mankind, so says the Lapp legend, there were people in Samelads (Lappland), but when the Flood came upon the earth every living creature perished except two, a brother and sister, whom God conducted to a high mountain—Passevare—"The Holy Mountain."

When the waters had subsided and the land was again dry, the brother and sister separated, going in opposite directions in search of others, if any might be left. After three years' fruitless search they met, and, recognizing each other, they once more went into the world, to meet again in three years, but, recognizing one another now, also, they parted a third time. When they met at the end of these three years neither knew the other, whereafter they lived together, and from them came the Lapps and Swedes.

Again, as to the distinct manners and customs of the Lapps and Swedes, they relate that at first both Lapps and Swedes were as one people and of the same parentage, but during a severe storm the one became frightened, and hurried under a board. From this came the Swedes, who live in houses. The other remained in the open air, and he became the progenitor of the Lapps, who, to this day, do not ask for a roof over their heads.

# THE GIANT'S BRIDE

MORE THAN with anything else, the Lapp legends have to do with giants and the adventures of mankind with them. The giant is feared because of his great size and strength and his insatiable appetite for human flesh. His laziness, clumsiness, and that he is inferior to the man in intelligence are, however, often the cause of his overthrow.

It is, therefore, commonly an adventure wherein the giant has been outwitted by a Lapp man or woman that concludes the giant stories.

There was one time a giant who made love to a rich Lapp girl. Neither she nor her father were much inclined toward the match, but they did not dare do otherwise than appear to consent and at the same time thank the Giant for the high honor he would bestow upon them. The father, nevertheless, determined that the union should not take place, and consoled himself with the hope that when the time arrived some means of defeating the Giant's project would be presented. Meantime he was obliged to set the day when the Giant might come and claim his bride. Before the Giant's arrival the Lapp took a block of wood, about the size of his daughter, and clothing it in a gown, a new cap, silver belt, shoes and shoe band, he sat it up in a corner of the tent, with a close veil, such as is worn by Lapp brides, over the head.

When the Giant entered the tent he was much pleased to find the bride, as he supposed, in her best attire awaiting him, and at once asked his prospective father-in-law to go out with him and select the reindeer that should go with the bride as her dower. Meanwhile the daughter was concealed behind an adjacent hill with harnessed reindeer ready for flight. When the reindeer had been counted out the Giant proceeded to kill one of them for supper, while the Lapp slipped off into the woods, and, joining his daughter, they fled with all speed into the mountains.

The Giant, after dressing the reindeer, went into the tent to visit his sweetheart.

"Now, my little darling," said he, "put the kettle over the fire."

But no move in the corner.

"Oh, the little dear is bashful, I'll have to do it myself then," said he.

After the pot had been boiling awhile he again addressed the object in the corner:

"Now my girl, you may cleave the marrow bone," but still no response.

"My little one is bashful, then I must do it myself," thought he.

When the meat was cooked he tried again:

"Come, now, my dear, and prepare the meat." But the bride was as bashful as before, and did not stir.

"Gracious! how bashful she is. I must do it myself," repeated the Giant.

When he had prepared the meal he bade her come and eat, but without effect. The bride remained motionless in her corner.

"The more for me, then," thought he, and sat himself to the repast with a good appetite. When he had eaten, he bade his bride prepare the bed.

"Ah, my love, are you so bashful? I must then do it myself," said the simple Giant.

"Go now and retire." No, she had not yet overcome her bashfulness, whereupon the Giant became angry and grasped the object with great force.

Discovering how the Lapp had deceived him, and that he had only a block of wood instead of a human of flesh and blood, he was beside himself with rage, and started in hot pursuit after the Lapp. The latter, however, had so much the start that the Giant could not overtake him. At the same time it was snowing, which caused the Giant to lose his way in the mountains. Finally he began to suffer from the cold. The moon coming up, he thought it a fire built by the Lapp, and at once set out on a swift run toward it, but he had already run so far that he was completely exhausted. He then climbed to the top of a pine, thinking thereby to get near enough to the fire to warm himself, but he froze to death instead, and thus ends the story.

# THE CUNNING LAPP

A poor Lapp once ran into the hands of a Giant, by whom he knew he would be devoured if he could not conceive some means of outwitting

THE CUNNING LAPP

him. To this end he therefore proposed that they have a contest of strength, the test to be that they should butt against a tree and see which could drive his head farthest into it. He who could make the deepest impression must, of course, be the stronger.

The Giant was first to make the trial. Taking his stand some distance from a tall pine, with a spring forward he drove his head with furious force against the trunk, but the most careful search did not discover a mark caused by the blow. The Lapp then said that he would show his strength the next day. During the night he made a large hollow in the trunks of several trees and re-covered the cavities nicely with the bark. Next morning, when the contest was renewed, the Lapp ran from tree to tree, into each of which he thrust his head to his ears. The Giant looked on, thoroughly crestfallen at the exhibition of strength, but proposed that they have another trial. This time he who could throw an ice ax highest into the air should be declared the victor. The Giant threw first, and to such a height that the ax was almost lost to sight.

"That was a miserable throw," said the Lapp. "When I throw it shall be so high that it will lodge upon a cloud."

"No, my dear!" shouted the Giant. "Rather let me acknowledge myself the weaker, than lose my splendid ax." Thus again the Lapp came off champion.

The next day, as the Lapp and the Giant were out in company, the Lapp gathered a number of willow twigs and began twisting them together.

"What are you about to do with those?" asked the Giant.

"I mean to carry away your treasure house," answered the Lapp.

"Oh, my son," sighed the Giant, "let me retain my house, and I will fill your hat with silver."

"Very well," replied the Lapp.

While the Giant was away after the silver, the Lapp dug a pit, cut a hole in his hat crown and sat the hat over the pit.

"It's a big hat you have," complained the Giant.

"Fill it up!" shouted the Lapp. "Otherwise I'll throw you, as I would have done the ice ax, up into the clouds." And the Giant was compelled to give the Lapp such a sum of money that he was ever after a rich man.

# TALES FROM DENMARK

THE UGLY DUCKLING

# PART ONE

*Tales by Hans Christian Andersen*


# THE UGLY DUCKLING


IT WAS lovely summer weather in the country, and the golden corn, the green oats, and the haystacks piled up in the meadows looked beautiful. The stork walking about on his long red legs chattered in the Egyptian language, which he had learnt from his mother. The corn-fields and meadows were surrounded by large forests, in the midst of which were deep pools. It was, indeed, delightful to walk about in the country. In a sunny spot stood a pleasant old farm-house close by a deep river, and from the house down to the water side grew great burdock leaves, so high, that under the tallest of them a little child could stand upright. The spot was as wild as the centre of a thick wood. In this snug retreat sat a duck on her nest, watching for her young brood to hatch; she was beginning to get tired of her task, for the little ones were a long time coming out of their shells, and she seldom had any visitors. The other ducks liked much better to swim about in the river than to climb the slippery banks, and sit under a burdock leaf, to have a gossip with her. At length one shell cracked, and then another, and from each egg came a living creature that lifted its head and cried, "Peep, peep." "Quack, quack," said the mother, and then they all quacked as well as they could, and looked about them on every side at the large green leaves. Their mother allowed them to look as much as they liked, because green is good for the eyes. "How large the world is," said the young ducks, when they found how much more room they now had than while they were inside the egg-shell. "Do you imagine this is the whole world?" asked the mother; "Wait till you have seen the garden; it stretches far beyond that to the parson's field, but I have never ventured to such a distance. Are you all out?" she continued, rising; "No, I declare, the largest egg lies there still. I wonder how long this is to last, I am quite tired of it;" and she seated herself again on the nest.

"Well, how are you getting on?" asked an old duck, who paid her a visit.

"One egg is not hatched yet," said the duck, "it will not break. But just look at all the others, are they not the prettiest little ducklings you ever saw? They are the image of their father, who is so unkind, he never comes to see me."

"Let me see the egg that will not break," said the duck; "I have no doubt it is a turkey's egg. I was persuaded to hatch some once, and after all my care and trouble with the young ones, they were afraid of the water. I quacked and clucked, but all to no purpose. I could not get them to venture in. Let me look at the egg. Yes, that is a turkey's egg; take my advice, leave it where it is and teach the other children to swim."

"I think I will sit on it a little while longer," said the duck; "as I have sat so long already, a few days will be nothing."

"Please yourself," said the old duck, and she went away.

At last the large egg broke, and a young one crept forth crying, "Peep, peep." It was very large and ugly. The duck stared at it and exclaimed, "It is very large and not at all like the others. I wonder if it really is a turkey. We shall soon find it out, however, when we go to the water. It must go in, if I have to push it myself."

On the next day the weather was delightful, and the sun shone brightly on the green burdock leaves, so the mother duck took her young brood down to the water, and jumped in with a splash. "Quack, quack," cried she, and one after another the little ducklings jumped in. The water closed over their heads, but they came up again in an instant, and swam about quite prettily with their legs paddling under them as easily as possible, and the ugly duckling was also in the water swimming with them.

"Oh," said the mother, "that is not a turkey; how well he uses his legs, and how upright he holds himself! He is my own child, and he is not so very ugly after all if you look at him properly. Quack, quack! come with me now, I will take you into grand society, and introduce you to the farmyard, but you must keep close to me or you may be trodden upon; and, above all, beware of the cat."

When they reached the farmyard, there was a great disturbance, two families were fighting for an eel's head, which, after all, was carried off by the cat. "See, children, that is the way of the world," said the mother duck, whetting her beak, for she would have liked the eel's head herself. "Come, now, use your legs, and let me see how well you can behave. You must bow your heads prettily to that old duck yonder; she is the highest born of them all, and has Spanish blood, therefore, she is well off. Don't you see she has a red flag tied to her leg, which is something very grand, and a great honor for a duck; it shows that every one is anxious not to lose her, as she can be recognized both by man and beast. Come, now, don't turn your toes, a well-bred duckling spreads his feet wide apart, just like his father and mother, in this way; now bend your neck, and say 'quack.'"

The ducklings did as they were bid, but the other duck stared, and said, "Look, here comes another brood, as if there were not enough of us already! and what a queer looking object one of them is; we don't want him here," and then one flew out and bit him in the neck.

"Let him alone," said the mother; "he is not doing any harm."

"Yes, but he is so big and ugly," said the spiteful duck "and therefore he must be turned out."

"The others are very pretty children," said the old duck, with the rag on her leg, "all but that one; I wish his mother could improve him a little."

"That is impossible, your grace," replied the mother; "he is not pretty; but he has a very good disposition, and swims as well or even better than the others. I think he will grow up pretty, and perhaps be smaller; he has remained too long in the egg, and therefore his figure is not properly formed;" and then she stroked his neck and smoothed the feathers, saying, "It is a drake, and therefore not of so much consequence. I think he will grow up strong, and able to take care of himself."

"The other ducklings are graceful enough," said the old duck. "Now make yourself at home, and if you can find an eel's head, you can bring it to me."

And so they made themselves comfortable; but the poor duckling, who had crept out of his shell last of all, and looked so ugly, was bitten and pushed and made fun of, not only by the ducks, but by all the poultry. "He is too big," they all said, and the turkey cock, who had been born into the world with spurs, and fancied himself really an emperor, puffed himself out like a vessel in full sail, and flew at the duckling, and became quite red in the head with passion, so that the poor little thing did not know where to go, and was quite miserable because he was so ugly and laughed at by the whole farmyard. So it went on from day to day till it got worse and worse. The poor duckling was driven about by every one; even his brothers and sisters were unkind to him, and would say, "Ah, you ugly creature, I wish the cat would get you," and his mother said she wished he had never been born. The ducks pecked him, the chickens beat him, and the girl who fed the poultry kicked him with her feet. So at last he ran away, frightening the little birds in the hedge as he flew over the palings.

"They are afraid of me because I am ugly," he said. So he closed his eyes, and flew still farther, until he came out on a large moor, inhabited by wild ducks. Here he remained the whole night, feeling very tired and sorrowful.

In the morning, when the wild ducks rose in the air, they stared at their new comrade. "What sort of a duck are you?" they all said, coming round him.

He bowed to them, and was as polite as he could be, but he did not reply to their question. "You are exceedingly ugly," said the wild ducks, "but that will not matter if you do not want to marry one of our family."

Poor thing! he had no thoughts of marriage; all he wanted was permission to lie among the rushes, and drink some of the water on the moor. After he had been on the moor two days, there came two wild geese, or rather goslings, for they had not been out of the egg long, and were very saucy. "Listen, friend," said one of them to the duckling, "you are so ugly, that we like you very well. Will you go with us, and become a bird of passage? Not far from here is another moor, in which there are some pretty wild geese, all unmarried. It is a chance for you to get a wife; you may be lucky, ugly as you are."

"Pop, pop," sounded in the air, and the two wild geese fell dead among the rushes, and the water was tinged with blood. "Pop, pop," echoed far and wide in the distance, and whole flocks of wild geese rose up from the rushes. The sound continued from every direction, for the sportsmen surrounded the moor, and some were even seated on branches of trees, overlooking the rushes. The blue smoke from the guns rose like clouds over the dark trees, and as it floated away across the water, a number of sporting dogs bounded in among the rushes, which bent beneath them wherever they went. How they terrified the poor duckling! He turned away his head to hide it under his wing, and at the same moment a large terrible dog passed quite near him. His jaws were open, his tongue hung from his mouth, and his eyes glared fearfully. He thrust his nose close to the duckling, showing his sharp teeth, and then, "splash, splash," he went into the water without touching him, "Oh," sighed the duckling, "how thankful I am for being so ugly; even a dog will not bite me." And so he lay quite still, while the shot rattled through the rushes, and gun after gun was fired over him. It was late in the day before all became quiet, but even then the poor young thing did not dare to move. He waited quietly for several hours, and then, after looking carefully around him, hastened away from the moor as fast as he could. He ran over field and meadow till a storm arose, and he could hardly struggle against it. Towards evening, he reached a poor little cottage that seemed ready to fall, and only remained standing because it could not decide on which side to fall first. The storm continued so violent, that the duckling could go no farther; he sat down by the cottage, and then he noticed that the door was not quite closed in consequence of one of the hinges having given way. There was therefore a narrow opening near the bottom large enough for him to slip through, which he did very quietly, and got a shelter for the night. A woman, a tom cat, and a hen lived in this cottage. The tom cat, whom the mistress called, "My little son," was a great favorite; he could raise his back, and purr, and could even throw out sparks from his fur if it were stroked the wrong way. The hen had very short legs, so she was called "Chickie short legs." She laid good eggs, and her mistress loved her as if she had been her own child. In the morning, the strange visitor was discovered, and the tom cat began to purr, and the hen to cluck.

"What is that noise about?" said the old woman, looking round the room, but her sight was not very good; therefore, when she saw the duckling she thought it must be a fat duck, that had strayed from home. "Oh what a prize!" she exclaimed, "I hope it is not a drake, for then I shall have some duck's eggs. I must wait and see." So the duckling was allowed to remain on trial for three weeks, but there were no eggs. Now the tom cat was the master of the house, and the hen was mistress, and they always said, "We and the world," for they believed themselves to be half the world, and the better half too. The duckling thought that others might hold a different opinion on the subject, but the hen would not listen to such doubts. "Can you lay eggs?" she asked. "No." "Then have the goodness to hold your tongue." "Can you raise your back, or purr, or throw out sparks?" said the tom cat. "No." "Then you have no right to express an opinion when sensible people are speaking." So the duckling sat in a corner, feeling very low spirited, till the sunshine and the fresh air came into the room through the open door, and then he began to feel such a great longing for a swim on the water, that he could not help telling the hen.

"What an absurd idea," said the hen. "You have nothing else to do, therefore you have foolish fancies. If you could purr or lay eggs, they would pass away."

"But it is so delightful to swim about on the water," said the duckling, "and so refreshing to feel it close over your head, while you dive down to the bottom."

"Delightful, indeed!" said the hen, "why you must be crazy! Ask the cat, he is the cleverest animal I know, ask him how he would like to swim about on the water, or to dive under it, for I will not speak of my own opinion; ask our mistress, the old woman—there is no one in the world more clever than she is. Do you think she would like to swim, or to let the water close over her head?"

"You don't understand me," said the duckling.

"We don't understand you? Who can understand you, I wonder? Do you consider yourself more clever than the cat, or the old woman? I will say nothing of myself. Don't imagine such nonsense, child, and thank your good fortune that you have been received here. Are you not in a warm room, and in society from which you may learn something. But you are a chatterer, and your company is not very agreeable. Believe me, I speak only for your own good. I may tell you unpleasant truths, but that is a proof of my friendship. I advise you, therefore, to lay eggs, and learn to purr as quickly as possible."

"I believe I must go out into the world again," said the duckling.

"Yes, do," said the hen. So the duckling left the cottage, and soon found water on which it could swim and dive, but was avoided by all other animals, because of its ugly appearance. Autumn came, and the leaves in the forest turned to orange and gold. Then, as winter approached, the wind caught them as they fell and whirled them in the cold air. The clouds, heavy with hail and snow-flakes, hung low in the sky, and the raven stood on the ferns crying, "Croak, croak." It made one shiver with cold to look at him. All this was very sad for the poor little duckling. One evening, just as the sun set amid radiant clouds, there came a large flock of beautiful birds out of the bushes. The duckling had never seen any like them before. They were swans, and they curved their graceful necks, while their soft plumage shown with dazzling whiteness. They uttered a singular cry, as they spread their glorious wings and flew away from those cold regions to warmer countries across the sea. As they mounted higher and higher in the air, the ugly little duckling felt quite a strange sensation as he watched them. He whirled himself in the water like a wheel, stretched out his neck towards them, and uttered a cry so strange that it frightened himself. Could he ever forget those beautiful, happy birds; and when at last they were out of his sight, he dived under the water, and rose again almost beside himself with excitement. He knew not the names of these birds, nor where they had flown, but he felt towards them as he had never felt for any other bird in the world. He was not envious of these beautiful creatures, but wished to be as lovely as they. Poor ugly creature, how gladly he would have lived even with the ducks had they only given him encouragement. The winter grew colder and colder; he was obliged to swim about on the water to keep it from freezing, but every night the space on which he swam became smaller and smaller. At length it froze so hard that the ice in the water crackled as he moved, and the duckling had to paddle with his legs as well as he could, to keep the space from closing up. He became exhausted at last, and lay still and helpless, frozen fast in the ice.

Early in the morning, a peasant, who was passing by, saw what had happened. He broke the ice in pieces with his wooden shoe, and carried the duckling home to his wife. The warmth revived the poor little creature; but when the children wanted to play with him, the duckling thought they would do him some harm; so he started up in terror, fluttered into the milk-pan, and splashed the milk about the room. Then the woman clapped her hands, which frightened him still more. He flew first into the butter-cask, then into the meal-tub, and out again. What a condition he was in! The woman screamed, and struck at him with the tongs; the children laughed and screamed, and tumbled over each other, in their efforts to catch him; but luckily he escaped. The door stood open; the poor creature could just manage to slip out among the bushes, and lie down quite exhausted in the newly fallen snow.

It would be very sad, were I to relate all the misery and privations which the poor little duckling endured during the hard winter; but when it had passed, he found himself lying one morning in a moor, amongst the rushes. He felt the warm sun shining, and heard the lark singing, and saw that all around was beautiful spring. Then the young bird felt that his wings were strong, as he flapped them against his sides, and rose high into the air. They bore him onwards, until he found himself in a large garden, before he well knew how it had happened. The apple-trees were in full blossom, and the fragrant elders bent their long green branches down to the stream which wound round a smooth lawn. Everything looked beautiful, in the freshness of early spring. From a thicket close by came three beautiful white swans, rustling their feathers, and swimming lightly over the smooth water. The duckling remembered the lovely birds, and felt more strangely unhappy than ever.

"I will fly to those royal birds," he exclaimed, "and they will kill me, because I am so ugly, and dare to approach them; but it does not matter: better be killed by them than pecked by the ducks, beaten by the hens, pushed about by the maiden who feeds the poultry, or starved with hunger in the winter."

Then he flew to the water, and swam towards the beautiful swans. The moment they espied the stranger, they rushed to meet him with outstretched wings.

"Kill me," said the poor bird; and he bent his head down to the surface of the water, and awaited death.

But what did he see in the clear stream below? His own image; no longer a dark, gray bird, ugly and disagreeable to look at, but a graceful and beautiful swan. To be born in a duck's nest, in a farmyard, is of no consequence to a bird, if it is hatched from a swan's egg. He now felt glad at having suffered sorrow and trouble, because it enabled him to enjoy so much better all the pleasure and happiness around him; for the great swans swam round the new-comer, and stroked his neck with their beaks, as a welcome.

Into the garden presently came some little children, and threw bread and cake into the water.

"See," cried the youngest, "there is a new one;" and the rest were delighted, and ran to their father and mother, dancing and clapping their hands, and shouting joyously, "There is another swan come; a new one has arrived."

Then they threw more bread and cake into the water, and said. "The new one is the most beautiful of all; he is so young and pretty." And the old swans bowed their heads before him.

Then he felt quite ashamed, and hid his head under his wing; for he did not know what to do, he was so happy, and yet not at all proud. He had been persecuted and despised for his ugliness, and now he heard them say he was the most beautiful of all the birds. Even the elder-tree bent down its bows into the water before him, and the sun shone warm and bright. Then he rustled his feathers, curved his slender neck, and cried joyfully, from the depths of his heart, "I never dreamed of such happiness as this, while I was an ugly duckling."

# THE WILD SWANS

FAR AWAY in the land to which the swallows fly when it is winter dwelt a king who had eleven sons, and one daughter, named Eliza. The eleven brothers were princes, and each went to school with a star on his breast, and a sword by his side. They wrote with diamond pencils on gold slates, and learnt their lessons so quickly and read so easily that every one might know they were princes. Their sister Eliza sat on a little stool of plate-glass, and had a book full of pictures, which had cost as much as half a kingdom. Oh, these children were indeed happy, but it was not to remain so always. Their father, who was king of the country, married a very wicked queen, who did not love the poor children at all. They knew this from the very first day after the wedding. In the palace there were great festivities, and the children played at receiving company; but instead of having, as usual, all the cakes and apples that were left, she gave them some sand in a tea-cup, and told them to pretend it was cake. The week after, she sent little Eliza into the country to a peasant and his wife, and then she told the king so many untrue things about the young princes, that he gave himself no more trouble respecting them.

"Go out into the world and get your own living," said the queen. "Fly like great birds, who have no voice." But she could not make them ugly as she wished, for they were turned into eleven beautiful wild swans. Then, with a strange cry, they flew through the windows of the palace, over the park, to the forest beyond. It was early morning when they passed the peasant's cottage, where their sister Eliza lay asleep in her room. They hovered over the roof, twisted their long necks and flapped their wings, but no one heard them or saw them, so they were at last obliged to fly away, high up in the clouds; and over the wide world they flew till they came to a thick, dark wood, which stretched far away to the seashore. Poor little Eliza was alone in her room playing with a green leaf, for she had no other playthings, and she pierced a hole through the leaf, and looked through it at the sun, and it was as if she saw her brothers' clear eyes, and when the warm sun shone on her cheeks, she thought of all the kisses they had given her. One day passed just like another; sometimes the winds rustled through the leaves of the rose-bush, and would whisper to the roses, "Who can be more beautiful than you!" But the roses would shake their heads, and say, "Eliza is." And when the old woman sat at the cottage door on Sunday, and read her hymn-book, the wind would flutter the leaves, and say to the book, "Who can be more pious than you?" and then the hymn-book would answer "Eliza." And the roses and the hymn-book told the real truth. At fifteen she returned home, but when the queen saw how beautiful she was, she became full of spite and hatred towards her. Willingly would she have turned her into a swan, like her brothers, but she did not dare to do so yet, because the king wished to see his daughter. Early one morning the queen went into the bath-room; it was built of marble, and had soft cushions, trimmed with the most beautiful tapestry. She took three toads with her, and kissed them, and said to one, "When Eliza comes to the bath, seat yourself upon her head, that she may become as stupid as you are." Then she said to another, "Place yourself on her forehead, that she may become as ugly as you are, and that her father may not know her." "Rest on her heart," she whispered to the third, "then she will have evil inclinations, and suffer in consequence." So she put the toads into the clear water, and they turned green immediately. She next called Eliza, and helped her to undress and get into the bath. As Eliza dipped her head under the water, one of the toads sat on her hair, a second on her forehead, and a third on her breast, but she did not seem to notice them, and when she rose out of the water, there were three red poppies floating upon it. Had not the creatures been venomous or been kissed by the witch, they would have been changed into red roses. At all events they became flowers, because they had rested on Eliza's head, and on her heart. She was too good and too innocent for witchcraft to have any power over her. When the wicked queen saw this, she rubbed her face with walnut-juice, so that she was quite brown; then she tangled her beautiful hair and smeared it with disgusting ointment, till it was quite impossible to recognize the beautiful Eliza.

When her father saw her, he was much shocked, and declared she was not his daughter. No one but the watch-dog and the swallows knew her; and they were only poor animals, and could say nothing. Then poor Eliza wept, and thought of her eleven brothers, who were all away. Sorrowfully, she stole away from the palace, and walked, the whole day, over fields and moors, till she came to the great forest. She knew not in what direction to go; but she was so unhappy, and longed so for her brothers, who had been, like herself, driven out into the world, that she was determined to seek them. She had been but a short time in the wood when night came on, and she quite lost the path; so she laid herself down on the soft moss, offered up her evening prayer, and leaned her head against the stump of a tree. All nature was still, and the soft, mild air fanned her forehead. The light of hundreds of glow-worms shone amidst the grass and the moss, like green fire; and if she touched a twig with her hand, ever so lightly, the brilliant insects fell down around her, like shooting-stars.

All night long she dreamt of her brothers. She and they were children again, playing together. She saw them writing with their diamond pencils on golden slates, while she looked at the beautiful picture-book which had cost half a kingdom. They were not writing lines and letters, as they used to do; but descriptions of the noble deeds they had performed, and of all they had discovered and seen. In the picture-book, too, everything was living. The birds sang, and the people came out of the book, and spoke to Eliza and her brothers; but, as the leaves turned over, they darted back again to their places, that all might be in order.

When she awoke, the sun was high in the heavens; yet she could not see him, for the lofty trees spread their branches thickly over her head; but his beams were glancing through the leaves here and there, like a golden mist. There was a sweet fragrance from the fresh green verdure, and the birds almost perched upon her shoulders. She heard water rippling from a number of springs, all flowing in a lake with golden sands. Bushes grew thickly round the lake, and at one spot an opening had been made by a deer, through which Eliza went down to the water. The lake was so clear that, had not the wind rustled the branches of the trees and the bushes, so that they moved, they would have appeared as if painted in the depths of the lake; for every leaf was reflected in the water, whether it stood in the shade or the sunshine. As soon as Eliza saw her own face, she was quite terrified at finding it so brown and ugly; but when she wetted her little hand, and rubbed her eyes and forehead, the white skin gleamed forth once more; and, after she had undressed, and dipped herself in the fresh water, a more beautiful king's daughter could not be found in the wide world. As soon as she had dressed herself again, and braided her long hair, she went to the bubbling spring, and drank some water out of the hollow of her hand. Then she wandered far into the forest, not knowing whither she went. She thought of her brothers, and felt sure that God would not forsake her. It is God who makes the wild apples grow in the wood, to satisfy the hungry, and He now led her to one of these trees, which was so loaded with fruit, that the boughs bent beneath the weight. Here she held her noonday repast, placed props under the boughs, and then went into the gloomiest depths of the forest.

It was so still that she could hear the sound of her own footsteps, as well as the rustling of every withered leaf which she crushed under her feet. Not a bird was to be seen, not a sunbeam could penetrate through the large, dark boughs of the trees. Their lofty trunks stood so close together, that, when she looked before her, it seemed as if she were enclosed within trellis-work. Such solitude she had never known before. The night was very dark. Not a single glow-worm glittered in the moss.

Sorrowfully she laid herself down to sleep; and, after a while, it seemed to her as if the branches of the trees parted over her head, and that the mild eyes of angels looked down upon her from heaven. When she awoke in the morning, she knew not whether she had dreamt this, or if it had really been so. Then she continued her wandering; but she had not gone many steps forward, when she met an old woman with berries in her basket, and she gave her a few to eat. Then Eliza asked her if she had not seen eleven princes riding through the forest.

"No," replied the old woman, "But I saw yesterday eleven swans, with gold crowns on their heads, swimming on the river close by." Then she led Eliza a little distance farther to a sloping bank, and at the foot of it wound a little river. The trees on its banks stretched their long leafy branches across the water towards each other, and where the growth prevented them from meeting naturally, the roots had torn themselves away from the ground, so that the branches might mingle their foliage as they hung over the water. Eliza bade the old woman farewell, and walked by the flowing river, till she reached the shore of the open sea. And there, before the young maiden's eyes, lay the glorious ocean, but not a sail appeared on its surface, not even a boat could be seen. How was she to go farther? She noticed how the countless pebbles on the sea-shore had been smoothed and rounded by the action of the water. Glass, iron, stones, everything that lay there mingled together, had taken its shape from the same power, and felt as smooth, or even smoother than her own delicate hand. "The water rolls on without weariness," she said, "till all that is hard becomes smooth; so will I be unwearied in my task. Thanks for your lessons, bright rolling waves; my heart tells me you will lead me to my dear brothers." On the foam-covered sea-weeds, lay eleven white swan feathers, which she gathered up and placed together. Drops of water lay upon them; whether they were dew-drops or tears no one could say. Lonely as it was on the sea-shore, she did not observe it, for the ever-moving sea showed more changes in a few hours than the most varying lake could produce during a whole year. If a black heavy cloud arose, it was as if the sea said. "I can look dark and angry too;" and then the wind blew, and the waves turned to white foam as they rolled. When the wind slept, and the clouds glowed with the red sunlight, then the sea looked like a rose leaf. But however quietly its white glassy surface rested, there was still a motion on the shore, as its waves rose and fell like the breast of a sleeping child. When the sun was about to set, Eliza saw eleven white swans with golden crowns on their heads, flying towards the land, one behind the other, like a long white ribbon. Then Eliza went down the slope from the shore, and hid herself behind the bushes. The swans alighted quite close to her and flapped their great white wings. As soon as the sun had disappeared under the water, the feathers of the swans fell off, and eleven beautiful princes, Eliza's brothers, stood near her. She uttered a loud cry, for, although they were very much changed, she knew them immediately. She sprang into their arms, and called them each by name. Then, how happy the princes were at meeting their little sister again, for they recognized her, although she had grown so tall and beautiful. They laughed, and they wept, and very soon understood how wickedly their mother had acted to them all. "We brothers," said the eldest, "fly about as wild swans, so long as the sun is in the sky; but as soon as it sinks behind the hills, we recover our human shape. Therefore must we always be near a resting place for our feet before sunset; for if we should be flying towards the clouds at the time we recovered our natural shape as men, we should sink deep into the sea. We do not dwell here, but in a land just as fair, that lies beyond the ocean, which we have to cross for a long distance; there is no island in our passage upon which we could pass the night; nothing but a little rock rising out of the sea, upon which we can scarcely stand with safety, even closely crowded together. If the sea is rough, the foam dashes over us, yet we thank God even for this rock; we have passed whole nights upon it, or we should never have reached our beloved fatherland, for our flight across the sea occupies two of the longest days in the year. We have permission to visit out home once in every year, and to remain eleven days, during which we fly across the forest to look once more at the palace where our father dwells, and where we were born, and at the church, where our mother lies buried. Here it seems as if the very trees and bushes were related to us. The wild horses leap over the plains as we have seen them in our childhood. The charcoal burners sing the old songs, to which we have danced as children. This is our fatherland, to which we are drawn by loving ties; and here we have found you, our dear little sister. Two days longer we can remain here, and then must we fly away to a beautiful land which is not our home; and how can we take you with us? We have neither ship nor boat."

"How can I break this spell?" said their sister. And then she talked about it nearly the whole night, only slumbering for a few hours. Eliza was awakened by the rustling of the swans' wings as they soared above. Her brothers were again changed to swans, and they flew in circles wider and wider, till they were far away; but one of them, the youngest swan, remained behind, and laid his head in his sister's lap, while she stroked his wings; and they remained together the whole day. Towards evening, the rest came back, and as the sun went down they resumed their natural forms. "To-morrow," said one, "we shall fly away, not to return again till a whole year has passed. But we cannot leave you here. Have you courage to go with us? My arm is strong enough to carry you through the wood; and will not all our wings be strong enough to fly with you over the sea?"

"Yes, take me with you," said Eliza. Then they spent the whole night in weaving a net with the pliant willow and rushes. It was very large and strong. Eliza laid herself down on the net, and when the sun rose, and her brothers again became wild swans, they took up the net with their beaks, and flew up to the clouds with their dear sister, who still slept.

The sunbeams fell on her face, therefore one of the swans soared over her head, so that his broad wings might shade her. They were far from the land when Eliza woke. She thought she must still be dreaming, it seemed so strange to her to feel herself being carried so high in the air over the sea. By her side lay a branch full of beautiful ripe berries, and a bundle of sweet roots; the youngest of her brothers had gathered them for her, and placed them by her side. She smiled her thanks to him; she knew it was the same who had hovered over her to shade her with his wings. They were now so high, that a large ship beneath them looked like a white sea-gull skimming the waves. A great cloud floating behind them appeared like a vast mountain, and upon it Eliza saw her own shadow and those of the eleven swans, looking gigantic in size. Altogether it formed a more beautiful picture than she had ever seen; but as the sun rose higher, and the clouds were left behind, the shadowy picture vanished away. Onward the whole day they flew through the air like a winged arrow, yet more slowly than usual, for they had their sister to carry. The weather seemed inclined to be stormy, and Eliza watched the sinking sun with great anxiety, for the little rock in the ocean was not yet in sight. It appeared to her as if the swans were making great efforts with their wings. Alas! she was the cause of their not advancing more quickly. When the sun set, they would change to men, fall into the sea and be drowned. Then she offered a prayer from her inmost heart, but still no appearance of the rock. Dark clouds came nearer, the gusts of wind told of a coming storm, while from a thick, heavy mass of clouds the lightning burst forth flash after flash. The sun had reached the edge of the sea, when the swans darted down so swiftly, that Eliza's head trembled; she believed they were falling, but they again soared onward. Presently she caught sight of the rock just below them, and by this time the sun was half hidden by the waves. The rock did not appear larger than a seal's head thrust out of the water. They sunk so rapidly, that at the moment their feet touched the rock, it shone only like a star, and at last disappeared like the last spark in a piece of burnt paper. Then she saw her brothers standing closely round her with their arms linked together. There was but just room enough for them, and not the smallest space to spare. The sea dashed against the rock, and covered them with spray. The heavens were lighted up with continual flashes, and peal after peal of thunder rolled. But the sister and brothers sat holding each other's hands, and singing hymns, from which they gained hope and courage. In the early dawn the air became calm and still, and at sunrise the swans flew away from the rock with Eliza. The sea was still rough, and from their high position in the air, the white foam on the dark green waves looked like millions of swans swimming on the water. As the sun rose higher, Eliza saw before her, floating on the air, a range of mountains, with shining masses of ice on their summits. In the centre, rose a castle apparently a mile long, with rows of columns, rising one above another, while, around it, palm-trees waved and flowers bloomed as large as mill wheels. She asked if this was the land to which they were hastening. The swans shook their heads, for what she beheld were the beautiful ever-changing cloud palaces of the "Fata Morgana," into which no mortal can

THE WILD SWANS

enter. Eliza was still gazing at the scene, when mountains, forests, and castles melted away, and twenty stately churches rose in their stead, with high towers and pointed gothic windows. Eliza even fancied she could hear the tones of the organ, but it was the music of the murmuring sea which she heard. As they drew nearer to the churches, they also changed into a fleet of ships, which seemed to be sailing beneath her; but as she looked again, she found it was only a sea mist gliding over the ocean. So there continued to pass before her eyes a constant change of scene, till at last she saw the real land to which they were bound, with its blue mountains, its cedar forests, and its cities and palaces. Long before the sun went down, she sat on a rock, in front of a large cave, on the floor of which the over-grown yet delicate green creeping plants looked like an embroidered carpet. "Now we shall expect to hear what you dream of to-night," said the youngest brother, as he showed his sister her bedroom.

"Heaven grant that I may dream how to save you," she replied. And this thought took such hold upon her mind that she prayed earnestly to God for help, and even in her sleep she continued to pray. Then it appeared to her as if she were flying high in the air, towards the cloudy palace of the "Fata Morgana," and a fairy came out to meet her, radiant and beautiful in appearance, and yet very much like the old woman who had given her berries in the wood, and who had told her of the swans with golden crowns on their heads. "Your brothers can be released," said she, "if you have only courage and perseverance. True, water is softer than your own delicate hands, and yet it polishes stones into shapes; it feels no pain as your fingers would feel, it has no soul, and cannot suffer such agony and torment as you will have to endure. Do you see the stinging nettle which I hold in my hand? Quantities of the same sort grow round the cave in which you sleep, but none will be of any use to you unless they grow upon the graves in a churchyard. These you must gather even while they burn blisters on your hands. Break them to pieces with your hands and feet, and they will become flax, from which you must spin and weave eleven coats with long sleeves; if these are then thrown over the eleven swans, the spell will be broken. But remember, that from the moment you commence your task until it is finished, even should it occupy years of your life, you must not speak. The first word you utter will pierce through the hearts of your brothers like a deadly dagger. Their lives hang upon your tongue. Remember all I have told you." And as she finished speaking, she touched her hand lightly with the nettle, and a pain, as of burning fire, awoke Eliza.

It was broad daylight, and close by where she had been sleeping lay a nettle like the one she had seen in her dream. She fell on her knees and offered her thanks to God. Then she went forth from the cave to begin her work with her delicate hands. She groped in amongst the ugly nettles, which burnt great blisters on her hands and arms, but she determined to bear it gladly if she could only release her dear brothers. So she bruised the nettles with her bare feet and spun the flax. At sunset her brothers returned and were very much frightened when they found her dumb. They believed it to be some new sorcery of their wicked step-mother. But when they saw her hands they understood what she was doing on their behalf, and the youngest brother wept, and where his tears fell the pain ceased, and the burning blisters vanished. She kept to her work all night, for she could not rest till she had released her dear brothers. During the whole of the following day, while her brothers were absent, she sat in solitude, but never before had the time flown so quickly. One coat was already finished and she had begun the second, when she heard the huntsman's horn, and was struck with fear. The sound came nearer and nearer, she heard the dogs barking, and fled with terror into the cave. She hastily bound together the nettles she had gathered into a bundle and sat upon them. Immediately a great dog came bounding towards her out of the ravine, and then another and another; they barked loudly, ran back, and then came again. In a very few minutes all the huntsmen stood before the cave, and the handsomest of them was the king of the country. He advanced towards her, for he had never seen a more beautiful maiden.

"How did you come here, my sweet child?" he asked. But Eliza shook her head. She dared not speak, at the cost of her brothers' lives. And she hid her hand under her apron, so that the king might not see how she must be suffering.

"Come with me," he said; "here you cannot remain. If you are as good as you are beautiful, I will dress you in silk and velvet, I will place a golden crown upon your head, and you shall dwell, and rule, and make your home in my richest castle." And then he lifted her on his horse. She wept and wrung her hands, but the king said, "I wish only for your happiness. A time will come when you will thank me for this." And then he galloped away over the mountains, holding her before him on this horse, and the hunters followed behind them. As the sun went down, they approached a fair royal city, with churches, and cupolas. On arriving at the castle the king led her into marble halls, where large fountains played, and where the walls and the ceilings were covered with rich paintings. But she had no eyes for all these glorious sights, she could only mourn and weep. Patiently she allowed the women to array her in royal robes, to weave pearls in her hair, and draw soft gloves over her blistered fingers. As she stood before them in all her rich dress, she looked so dazzingly beautiful that the court bowed low in her presence. Then the king declared his intention of making her his bride, but the archbishop shook his head, and whispered that the fair young maiden was only a witch who had blinded the king's eyes and bewitched his heart. But the king would not listen to this; he ordered the music to sound, the daintiest dishes to be served, and the loveliest maidens to dance. Afterwards he led her through fragrant gardens and lofty halls, but not a smile appeared on her lips or sparkled in her eyes. She looked the very picture of grief. Then the king opened the door of a little chamber in which she was to sleep; it was adorned with rich green tapestry, and resembled the cave in which he had found her. On the floor lay the bundle of flax which she had spun from the nettles, and under the ceiling hung the coat she had made. These things had been brought away from the cave as curiosities by one of the huntsmen.

"Here you can dream yourself back again in the old home in the cave," said the king; "here is the work with which you employed yourself. It will amuse you now in the midst of all this splendor to think of that time."

When Eliza saw all these things which lay so near her heart, a smile played around her mouth, and the crimson blood rushed to her cheeks. She thought of her brothers, and their release made her so joyful that she kissed the king's hand. Then he pressed her to his heart. Very soon the joyous church bells announced the marriage feast, and that the beautiful dumb girl out of the wood was to be made the queen of the country. Then the archbishop whispered wicked words in the king's ear, but they did not sink into his heart. The marriage was still to take place, and the archbishop himself had to place the crown on the bride's head; in his wicked spite, he pressed the narrow circlet so tightly on her forehead that it caused her pain. But a heavier weight encircled her heart—sorrow for her brothers. She felt not bodily pain. Her mouth was closed; a single word would cost the lives of her brothers. But she loved the kind, handsome king, who did everything to make her happy more and more each day; she loved him with all her heart, and her eyes beamed with the love she dared not speak. Oh! if she had only been able to confide in him and tell him of her grief. But dumb she must remain till her task was finished. Therefore at night she crept away into her little chamber, which had been decked out to look like the cave, and quickly wove one coat after another. But when she began the seventh she found she had no more flax. She knew that the nettles she wanted to use grew in the churchyard, and that she must pluck them herself. How should she get out there? "Oh, what is the pain in my fingers to the torment which my heart endures?" said she. "I must venture, I shall not be denied help from heaven." Then with a trembling heart, as if she were about to perform a wicked deed, she crept into the garden in the broad moonlight, and passed through the narrow walks and the deserted streets, till she reached the churchyard. Then she saw on one of the broad tombstones a group of ghouls. These hideous creatures took off their rags, as if they intended to bathe, and then clawing open the fresh graves with their long, skinny fingers, pulled out the dead bodies and ate the flesh! Eliza had to pass close by them, and they fixed their wicked glances upon her, but she prayed silently, gathered the burning nettles, and carried them home with her to the castle. One person only had seen her, and that was the archbishop—he was awake while everybody was asleep. Now he thought his opinion was evidently correct. All was not right with the queen. She was a witch, and had bewitched the king and all the people. Secretly he told the king what he had seen and what he feared, and as the hard words came from his tongue, the carved images of the saints shook their heads as if they would say. "It is not so. Eliza is innocent."

But the archbishop interpreted it in another way; he believed that they witnessed against her, and were shaking their heads at her wickedness. Two large tears rolled down the king's cheeks, and he went home with doubt in his heart, and at night he pretended to sleep, but there came no real sleep to his eyes, for he saw Eliza get up every night and disappear in her own chamber. From day to day his brow became darker, and Eliza saw it and did not understand the reason, but it alarmed her and made her heart tremble for her brothers. Her hot tears glittered like pearls on the regal velvet and diamonds, while all who saw her were wishing they could be queens. In the mean time she had almost finished her task; only one coat of mail was wanting, but she had no flax left, and not a single nettle. Once more only, and for the last time, must she venture to the churchyard and pluck a few handfuls. She thought with terror of the solitary walk, and of the horrible ghouls, but her will was firm, as well as her trust in Providence. Eliza went, and the king and the archbishop followed her. They saw her vanish through the wicket gate into the churchyard, and when they came nearer they saw the ghouls sitting on the tombstone, as Eliza had seen them, and the king turned away his head, for he thought she was with them—she whose head had rested on his breast that very evening. "The people must condemn her," said he, and she was very quickly condemned by every one to suffer death by fire. Away from the gorgeous regal halls was she led to a dark, dreary cell, where the wind whistled through the iron bars. Instead of the velvet and silk dresses, they gave her the coats of mail which she had woven to cover her, and the bundle of nettles for a pillow; but nothing they could give her would have pleased her more. She continued her task with joy, and prayed for help, while the streetboys sang jeering songs about her, and not a soul comforted her with a kind word. Towards evening, she heard at the grating the flutter of a swan's wing, it was her youngest brother—he had found his sister, and she sobbed for joy, although she knew that very likely this would be the last night she would have to live. But still she could hope, for her task was almost finished, and her brothers were come. Then the archbishop arrived, to be with her during her last hours, as he had promised the king. But she shook her head, and begged him, by looks and gestures, not to stay; for in this night she knew she must finish her task, otherwise all her pain and tears and sleepless nights would have been suffered in vain. The archbishop withdrew, uttering bitter words against her; but poor Eliza knew that she was innocent, and diligently continued her work.

The little mice ran about the floor, they dragged the nettles to her feet, to help as well as they could; and the thrush sat outside the grating of the window, and sang to her the whole night long, as sweetly as possible, to keep up her spirits.

It was still twilight, and at least an hour before sunrise, when the eleven brothers stood at the castle gate, and demanded to be brought before the king. They were told it could not be, it was yet almost night, and as the king slept they dared not disturb him. They threatened, they entreated. Then the guard appeared, and even the king himself, inquiring what all the noise meant. At this moment the sun rose. The eleven brothers were seen no more, but eleven wild swans flew away over the castle.

And now all the people came streaming forth from the gates of the city, to see the witch burnt. An old horse drew the cart on which she sat. They had dressed her in a garment of coarse sackcloth. Her lovely hair hung loose on her shoulders, her cheeks were deadly pale, her lips moved silently, while her fingers still worked at the green flax. Even on the way to death, she would not give up her task. The ten coats of mail lay at her feet, she was working hard at the eleventh, while the mob jeered her and said, "See the witch, how she mutters! She has no hymn-book in her hand. She sits there with her ugly sorcery. Let us tear it in a thousand pieces."

And then they pressed towards her, and would have destroyed the coats of mail, but at the same moment eleven wild swans flew over her, and alighted on the cart. Then they flapped their large wings, and the crowd drew on one side in alarm.

"It is a sign from heaven that she is innocent," whispered many of them; but they ventured not to say it aloud.

As the executioner seized her by the hand, to lift her out of the cart, she hastily threw the eleven coats of mail over the swans, and they immediately became eleven handsome princes; but the youngest had a swan's wing, instead of an arm; for she had not been able to finish the last sleeve of the coat.

"Now I may speak," she exclaimed. "I am innocent."

Then the people, who saw what happened, bowed to her, as before a saint; but she sank lifeless in her brothers' arms, overcome with suspense, anguish, and pain.

"Yes, she is innocent," said the eldest brother; and then he related all that had taken place; and while he spoke there rose in the air a fragrance as from millions of roses. Every piece of faggot in the pile had taken root, and threw out branches, and appeared a thick hedge, large and high, covered with roses; while above all bloomed a white and shining flower, that glittered like a star. This flower the king plucked, and placed in Eliza's bosom, when she awoke from her swoon, with peace and happiness in her heart. And all the church bells rang of themselves, and the birds came in great troops. And a marriage procession returned to the castle, such as no king had ever before seen.

# THE OLD HOUSE

A VERY old house stood once in a street with several that were quite new and clean. The date of its erection had been carved on one of the beams, and surrounded by scrolls formed of tulips and hop-tendrils; by this date it could be seen that the old house was nearly three hundred years old. Verses too were written over the windows in old-fashioned letters, and grotesque faces, curiously carved, grinned at you from under the cornices. One story projected a long way over the other, and under the roof ran a leaden gutter, with a dragon's head at the end. The rain was intended to pour out at the dragon's mouth, but it ran out of his body instead, for there was a hole in the gutter. The other houses in the street were new and well built, with large window panes and smooth walls. Any one could see they had nothing to do with the old house. Perhaps they thought, "How long will that heap of rubbish remain here to be a disgrace to the whole street. The parapet projects so far forward that no one can see out of our windows what is going on in that direction. The stairs are as broad as the staircase of a castle, and as steep as if they led to a church-tower. The iron railing looks like the gate of a cemetery, and there are brass knobs upon it. It is really too ridiculous."

Opposite to the old house were more nice new houses, which had just the same opinion as their neighbors.

At the window of one of them sat a little boy with fresh rosy cheeks, and clear sparkling eyes, who was very fond of the old house, in sunshine or in moonlight. He would sit and look at the wall from which the plaster had in some places fallen off, and fancy all sorts of scenes which had been in former times. How the street must have looked when the houses had all gable roofs, open staircases, and gutters with dragons at the spout. He could even see soldiers walking about with halberds. Certainly it was a very good house to look at for amusement.

An old man lived in it, who wore knee-breeches, a coat with large brass buttons, and a wig, which any one could see was a real wig. Every morning an old man came to clean the rooms, and to wait upon him, otherwise the old man in the knee-breeches would have been quite alone in the house. Sometimes he came to one of the windows and looked out; then the little boy nodded to him, and the old man nodded back again, till they became acquainted, and were friends, although they had never spoken to each other; but that was of no consequence.

The little boy one day heard his parents say, "The old man opposite is very well off, but is terribly lonely." The next Sunday morning the little boy wrapped something in a piece of paper and took it to the door of the old house, and said to the attendant who waited upon the old man, "Will you please give this from me to the gentleman who lives here; I have two tin soldiers, and this is one of them, and he shall have it, because I know he is terribly lonely."

And the old attendant nodded and looked very pleased, and then he carried the tin soldier into the house.

Afterwards he was sent over to ask the little boy if he would not like to pay a visit himself. His parents gave him permission, and so it was that he gained admission to the old house.

The brassy knobs on the railings shone more brightly than ever, as if they had been polished on account of his visit; and on the door were carved trumpeters standing in tulips, and it seemed as if they were blowing with all their might, their cheeks were so puffed out. "Tanta-ra-ra, the little boy is coming; Tanta-ra-ra, the little boy is coming."

Then the door opened. All around the hall hung old portraits of knights in armor, and ladies in silk gowns; and the armor rattled, and the silk dresses rustled. Then came a staircase which went up a long way, and then came down a little way and led to a balcony, which was in a very ruinous state. There were large holes and long cracks, out of which grew grass and leaves, indeed the whole balcony, the courtyard, and the walls were so overgrown with green that they looked like a garden. In the balcony stood flower-pots, on which were heads having asses' ears, but the flowers in them grew just as they pleased. In one pot pinks were growing all over the sides, at least the green leaves were shooting forth stalk and stem, and saying as plainly as they could speak. "The air has fanned me, the sun has kissed me, and I am promised a little flower for next Sunday—really for next Sunday."

Then they entered a room in which the walls were covered with leather, and the leather had golden flowers stamped upon it.

> "Gilding will fade in damp weather,
> To endure, there is nothing like leather,"

said the walls. Chairs handsomely carved, with elbows on each side, and with very high backs, stood in the room, and as they creaked they seemed to say, "Sit down. Oh dear, how I am creaking. I shall certainly have the gout like the old cupboard. Gout in my back, ugh."

And then the little boy entered the room where the old man sat.

"Thank you for the tin soldier, my little friend," said the old man, "and thank you also for coming to see me."

"Thanks, thanks," or "Creak, creak," said all the furniture.

There was so much that the pieces of furniture stood in each other's way to get a sight of the little boy.

On the wall near the centre of the room hung the picture of a beautiful lady, young and gay, dressed in the fashion of the olden times, with powdered hair, and a full, stiff skirt. She said neither "thanks" nor "creak," but she looked down upon the little boy with her mild eyes; and then he said to the old man,

"Where did you get that picture?"

"From the shop opposite," he replied. "Many portraits hang there that none seem to trouble themselves about. The persons they represent have been dead and buried long since. But I knew this lady many years ago, and she has been dead nearly half a century."

Under a glass beneath the picture hung a nosegay of withered flowers, which were no doubt half a century old too, at least they appeared so.

And the pendulum of the old clock went to and fro, and the hands turned round; and as time passed on, everything in the room grew older, but no one seemed to notice it.

"They say at home," said the little boy, "that you are very lonely."

"Oh," replied the old man, "I have pleasant thoughts of all that has passed, recalled by memory; and now you are come to visit me, and that is very pleasant."

Then he took from the book-case, a book full of pictures representing long processions of wonderful coaches, such as are never seen at the present time. Soldiers like the knave of clubs, and citizens with waving banners. The tailors had a flag with a pair of scissors supported by two lions, and on the shoemakers' flag there were not boots, but an eagle with two heads, for the shoemakers must have everything arranged so that they can say, "This is a pair." What a picture-book it was; and then the old man went into another room to fetch apples and nuts. It was very pleasant, certainly, to be in that old house.

THE OLD HOUSE

"I cannot endure it," said the tin soldier, who stood on a shelf, "it is so lonely and dull here. I have been accustomed to live in a family, and I cannot get used to this life. I cannot bear it. The whole day is long enough, but the evening is longer. It is not here like it was in your house opposite, when your father and mother talked so cheerfully together, while you and all the dear children made such a delightful noise. No, it is all lonely in the old man's house. Do you think he gets any kisses? Do you think he ever has friendly looks, or a Christmas tree? He will have nothing now but the grave. Oh, I cannot bear it."

"You must not look only on the sorrowful side," said the little boy; "I think everything in this house is beautiful, and all the old pleasant thoughts come back here to pay visits."

"Ah, but I never see any, and I don't know them," said the tin soldier, "and I cannot bear it."

"You must bear it," said the little boy. Then the old man came back with a pleasant face; and brought with him beautiful preserved fruits, as well as apples and nuts; and the little boy thought no more of the tin soldier. How happy and delighted the little boy was; and after he returned home, and while days and weeks passed, a great deal of nodding took place from one house to the other, and then the little boy went to pay another visit. The carved trumpeters blew "Tanta-ra-ra. There is the little boy. Tanta-ra-ra." The swords and armor on the old knight's pictures rattled. The silk dresses rustled, the leather repeated its rhyme, and the old chairs had the gout in their backs, and cried, "Creak;" it was all exactly like the first time; for in that house, one day and one hour were just like another. "I cannot bear it any longer," said the tin soldier; "I have wept tears of tin, it is so melancholy here. Let me go to the wars, and lose an arm or a leg, that would be some change; I cannot bear it. Now I know what it is to have visits from one's old recollections, and all they bring with them. I have had visits from mine, and you may believe me it is not altogether pleasant. I was very nearly jumping from the shelf. I saw you all in your house opposite, as if you were really present. It was Sunday morning, and you children stood round the table, singing the hymn that you sing every morning. You were standing quietly, with your hands folded, and your father and mother were looking just as serious, when the door opened, and your little sister Maria, who is not two years old, was brought into the room. You know she always dances when she hears music and singing of any sort; so she began to dance immediately, although she ought not to have done so, but she could not get into the right time because the tune was so slow; so she stood first on one leg and then on the other, and bent her head very low, but it would not suit the music. You all stood looking very grave, although it was very difficult to do so, but I laughed so to myself that I fell down from the table, and got a bruise, which is there still; I know it was not right to laugh. So all this, and everything else that I have seen, keeps running in my head, and these must be the old recollections that bring so many thoughts with them. Tell me whether you still sing on Sundays, and tell me about your little sister Maria, and how my old comrade is, the other tin soldier. Ah, really he must be very happy; I cannot endure this life."

"You are given away," said the little boy; "you must stay. Don't you see that?" Then the old man came in, with a box containing many curious things to show him. Rouge-pots, scent-boxes, and old cards, so large and so richly gilded, that none are ever seen like them in these days. And there were smaller boxes to look at, and the piano was opened, and inside the lid were painted landscapes. But when the old man played, the piano sounded quite out of tune. Then he looked at the picture he had bought at the broker's, and his eyes sparkled brightly as he nodded at it, and said, "Ah, she could sing that tune."

"I will go to the wars! I will go to the wars!" cried the tin soldier as loud as he could, and threw himself down on the floor. Where could he have fallen? The old man searched, and the little boy searched, but he was gone, and could not be found. "I shall find him again," said the old man, but he did not find him. The boards of the floor were open and full of holes. The tin soldier had fallen through a crack between the boards, and lay there now in an open grave. The day went by, and the little boy returned home; the week passed, and many more weeks. It was winter, and the windows were quite frozen, so the little boy was obliged to breathe on the panes, and rub a hole to peep through at the old house. Snow drifts were lying in all the scrolls and on the inscriptions, and the steps were covered with snow as if no one were at home. And indeed nobody was home, for the old man was dead. In the evening, a hearse stopped at the door, and the old man in his coffin was placed in it. He was to be taken to the country to be buried there in his own grave; so they carried him away; no one followed him, for all his friends were dead; and the little boy kissed his hand to the coffin as the hearse moved away with it. A few days after, there was an auction at the old house, and from his window the little boy saw the people carrying away the pictures of old knights and ladies, the flower-pots with the long ears, the old chairs, and the cup-boards. Some were taken one way, some another. *Her* portrait, which had been bought at the picture dealer's, went back again to his shop, and there it remained, for no one seemed to know her, or to care for the old picture. In the spring, they began to pull the house itself down; people called it complete rubbish. From the street could be seen the room in which the walls were covered with leather, ragged and torn, and the green in the balcony hung straggling over the beams; they pulled it down quickly, for it looked ready to fall, and at last it was cleared away altogether. "What a good riddance," said the neighbors' houses. Very shortly, a fine new house was built farther back from the road; it had lofty windows and smooth walls, but in front, on the spot where the old house really stood, a little garden was planted, and wild vines grew up over the neighboring walls; in front of the garden were large iron railings and a great gate, which looked very stately. People used to stop and peep through the railings. The sparrows assembled in dozens upon the wild vines, and chattered all together as loud as they could, but not about the old house; none of them could remember it, for many years had passed by, so many indeed, that the little boy was now a man, and a really good man too, and his parents were very proud of him. He was just married, and had come, with his young wife, to reside in the new house with the garden in front of it, and now he stood there by her side while she planted a field flower that she thought very pretty. She was planting it herself with her little hands, and pressing down the earth with her fingers. "Oh dear, what was that?" she exclaimed, as something pricked her. Out of the soft earth something was sticking up. It was—only think!—it was really the tin soldier, the very same which had been lost up in the old man's room, and had been hidden among old wood and rubbish for a long time, till it sunk into the earth, where it must have been for many years. And the young wife wiped the soldier, first with a green leaf, and then with her fine pocket-handkerchief, that smelt of such beautiful perfume. And the tin soldier felt as if he was recovering from a fainting fit. "Let me see him," said the young man, and then he smiled and shook his head, and said, "It can scarcely be the same, but it reminds me of something that happened to one of my tin soldiers when I was a little boy." And then he told his wife about the old house and the old man, and of the tin soldier which he had sent across, because he thought the old man was lonely; and he related the story so clearly that tears came into the eyes of the young wife for the old house and the old man. "It is very likely that this is really the same soldier," said she, "and I will take care of him, and always remember what you have told me; but some day you must show me the old man's grave."

"I don't know where it is," he replied; "no one knows. All his friends are dead; no one took care of him, and I was only a little boy."

"Oh, how dreadfully lonely he must have been," said she.

"Yes, terribly lonely," cried the tin soldier; "still it is delightful not to be forgotten."

"Delightful indeed," cried a voice quite near to them; no one but the tin soldier saw that it came from a rag of the leather which hung in tatters; it had lost all its gilding, and look like wet earth, but it had an opinion, and it spoke it thus:—

"Gilding will fade in damp weather,
To endure, there is nothing like leather."

But the tin soldier did not believe any such thing.

# THE ELF OF THE ROSE

IN THE midst of a garden grew a rose-tree, in full blossom, and in the prettiest of all the roses lived an elf. He was such a little wee thing, that no human eye could see him. Behind each leaf of the rose he had a sleeping chamber. He was as well formed and as beautiful as a little child could be, and had wings that reached from his shoulders to his feet. Oh, what sweet fragrance there was in his chambers! and how clean and

THE ELF OF THE ROSE

beautiful were the walls! for they were the blushing leaves of the rose.

During the whole day he enjoyed himself in the warm sunshine, flew from flower to flower, and danced on the wings of the flying butterflies. Then he took it into his head to measure how many steps he would have to go through the roads and cross-roads that are on the leaf of a linden-tree. What we call the veins of a leaf, he took for roads; ay, and very long roads they were for him; for before he had half finished his task, the sun went down: he had commenced his work too late. It became very cold, the dew fell, and the wind blew; so he thought the best thing he could do would be to return home. He hurried himself as much as he could; but he found the roses all closed up, and he could not get in; not a single rose stood open. The poor little elf was very much frightened. He had never before been out at night, but had always slumbered secretly behind the warm rose-leaves. Oh, this would certainly be his death. At the other end of the garden, he knew there was an arbor, overgrown with beautiful honey-suckles. The blossoms looked like large painted horns; and he thought to himself, he would go and sleep in one of these till the morning. He flew thither; but "hush!" two people were in the arbor,—a handsome young man and a beautiful lady. They sat side by side, and wished that they might never be obliged to part. They loved each other much more than the best child can love its father and mother.

"But we must part," said the young man; "your brother does not like our engagement, and therefore he sends me so far away on business, over mountains and seas. Farewell, my sweet bride; for so you are to me."

And then they kissed each other, and the girl wept, and gave him a rose; but before she did so, she pressed a kiss upon it so fervently that the flower opened. Then the little elf flew in, and leaned his head on the delicate, fragrant walls. Here he could plainly hear them say, "Farewell, farewell;" and he felt that the rose had been placed on the young man's breast. Oh, how his heart did beat! The little elf could not go to sleep, it thumped so loudly. The young man took it out as he walked through the dark wood alone, and kissed the flower so often and so violently, that the little elf was almost crushed. He could feel through the leaf how hot the lips of the young man were, and the rose had opened, as if from the heat of the noonday sun.

There came another man, who looked gloomy and wicked. He was the wicked brother of the beautiful maiden. He drew out a sharp knife, and while the other was kissing the rose, the wicked man stabbed him to death; then he cut off his head, and buried it with the body in the soft earth under the linden-tree.

"Now he is gone, and will soon be forgotten," thought the wicked brother; "he will never come back again. He was going on a long journey over mountains and seas; it is easy for a man to lose his life in such a journey. My sister will suppose he is dead; for he cannot come back, and she will not dare to question me about him."

Then he scattered the dry leaves over the light earth with his foot, and went home through the darkness; but he went not alone, as he thought,— the little elf accompanied him. He sat in a dry rolled-up linden-leaf, which had fallen from the tree on to the wicked man's head, as he was digging the grave. The hat was on the head now, which made it very dark, and the little elf shuddered with fright and indignation at the wicked deed.

It was the dawn of morning before the wicked man reached home; he took off his hat, and went into his sister's room. There lay the beautiful, blooming girl, dreaming of him whom she loved so, and who was now, she supposed, travelling far away over mountain and sea. Her wicked brother stopped over her, and laughed hideously, as fiends only can laugh. The dry leaf fell out of his hair upon the counterpane; but he did not notice it, and went to get a little sleep during the early morning hours. But the elf slipped out of the withered leaf, placed himself by the ear of the sleeping girl, and told her, as in a dream, of the horrid murder; described the place where her brother had slain her lover, and buried his body; and told her of the linden-tree, in full blossom, that stood close by.

"That you may not think this is only a dream that I have told you," he said, "you will find on your bed a withered leaf."

Then she awoke, and found it there. Oh, what bitter tears she shed! and she could not open her heart to any one for relief.

The window stood open the whole day, and the little elf could easily have reached the roses, or any of the flowers; but he could not find it in his heart to leave one so afflicted. In the window stood a bush bearing monthly roses. He seated himself in one of the flowers, and gazed on the poor girl. Her brother often came into the room, and would be quite cheerful, in spite of his base conduct; so she dare not say a word to him of her heart's grief.

As soon as night came on, she slipped out of the house, and went into the wood, to the spot where the linden-tree stood; and after removing the leaves from the earth, she turned it up, and there found him who had been murdered. Oh, how she wept and prayed that she also might die! Gladly would she have taken the body home with her; but that was impossible; so she took up the poor head with the closed eyes, kissed the cold lips, and shook the mould out of the beautiful hair.

"I will keep this," said she; and as soon as she had covered the body again with the earth and leaves, she took the head and a little sprig of jasmine that bloomed in the wood, near the spot where he was buried, and carried them home with her. As soon as she was in her room, she took the largest flower-pot she could find, and in this she placed the head of the dead man, covered it up with earth, and planted the twig of jasmine in it.

"Farewell, farewell," whispered the little elf. He could not any longer endure to witness all this agony of grief; he therefore flew away to his own rose in the garden. But the rose was faded; only a few dry leaves still clung to the green hedge behind it.

"Alas! how soon all that is good and beautiful passes away," sighed the elf.

After a while he found another rose, which became his home, for among its delicate fragrant leaves he could dwell in safety. Every morning he flew to the window of the poor girl, and always found her weeping by the flower-pot. The bitter tears fell upon the jasmine twig, and each day, as she became paler and paler, the sprig appeared to grow greener and fresher. One shoot after another sprouted forth, and little white buds blossomed, which the poor girl fondly kissed. But her wicked brother scolded her, and asked her if she was going mad. He could not imagine why she was weeping over that flower-pot, and it annoyed him. He did not know whose closed eyes were there, nor what red lips were fading beneath the earth. And one day she sat and leaned her head against the flower-pot, and the little elf of the rose found her asleep. Then he seated himself by her ear, talked to her of that evening in the arbor, of the sweet perfume of the rose, and the loves of the elves. Sweetly she dreamed, and while she dreamt, her life passed away calmly and gently, and her spirit was with him whom she loved, in heaven. And the jasmine opened its large white bells, and spread forth its sweet fragrance; it had no other way of showing its grief for the dead. But the wicked brother considered the beautiful blooming plant as his own property, left to him by his sister, and he placed it in his sleeping room, close by his bed, for it was very lonely in appearance, and the fragrance sweet and delightful. The little elf of the rose followed it, and flew from flower to flower, telling each little spirit that dwelt in them the story of the murdered young man, whose head now formed part of the earth beneath them, and of the wicked brother and the poor sister. "We know it," said each little spirit in the flowers, "we know it, for have we not sprung from the eyes and lips of the murdered one. We know it, we know it," and the flowers nodded with their heads in a peculiar manner. The elf of the rose could not understand how they could rest so quietly in the matter, so he flew to the bees, who were gathering honey, and told them of the wicked brother. And the bees told it to their queen, who commanded that the next morning they should go and kill the murderer. But during the night, the first after the sister's death, while the brother was sleeping in his bed, close to where he had placed the fragrant jasmine, every flower cup opened, and invisibly the little spirits stole out, armed with poisonous spears. They placed themselves by the ear of the sleeper, told him dreadful dreams and then flew across his lips, and pricked his tongue with their poisoned spears. "Now have we revenged the dead," said they, and flew back into the white bells of the jasmine flowers. When the morning came, and as soon as the window was opened, the rose elf, with the queen bee, and the whole swarm of bees, rushed in to kill him. But he was already dead. People were standing round the bed, and saying that the scent of the jasmine had killed him. Then the elf of the rose understood the revenge of the flowers, and explained it to the queen bee, and she, with the whole swarm, buzzed about the flower-pot. The bees could not be driven away. Then a man took it up to remove it, and one of the bees stung him in the hand, so that he let the flower-pot fall, and it was broken to pieces. Then every one saw the whitened skull, and they knew the dead man in the bed was a murderer. And the queen bee hummed in the air, and sang of the revenge of the flowers, and of the elf of the rose, and said that behind the smallest leaf dwells *One*, who can discover evil deeds, and punish them also.

# SOUP FROM A SAUSAGE SKEWER

"WE HAD such a excellent dinner yesterday," said an old mouse of the female sex to another who had not been present at the feast. "I sat number twenty-one below the mouse-king, which was not a bad place. Shall I tell you what we had? Everything was first rate. Mouldy bread, tallow candle, and sausage. And then, when we had finished that course, the same came on all over again; it was as good as two feasts. We were very sociable, and there was as much joking and fun as if we had been all of one family circle. Nothing was left but the sausage skewers, and this formed a subject of conversation, till at last it turned to the proverb, 'Soup from sausage skins;' or, as the people in the neighboring country call it, 'Soup from a sausage skewer.' Every one had heard the proverb, but no one had ever tasted the soup, much less prepared it. A capital toast was drunk to the inventor of the soup, and some one said he ought to be made a relieving officer to the poor. Was not that witty? Then the old mouse-king rose and promised that the young lady-mouse who should learn how best to prepare this much-admired and savory soup should be his queen, and a year and a day should be allowed for the purpose."

"That was not at all a bad proposal," said the other mouse; "but how is the soup made?"

"Ah, that is more than I can tell you. All the young lady mice were asking the same question. They wished very much to be queen, but they did not want to take the trouble of going out into the world to learn how to make soup, which was absolutely necessary to be done first. But it is not every one who would care to leave her family, or her happy corner by the fire-side at home, even to be made queen. It is not always easy to find bacon and cheese-rind in foreign lands every day, and it is not pleasant to have to endure hunger, and be perhaps, after all, eaten up alive by the cat."

Most probably some such thoughts as these discouraged the majority from going out into the world to collect the required information. Only four mice gave notice that they were ready to set out on the journey. They were young and lively, but poor. Each of them wished to visit one of the four divisions of the world, so that it might be seen which was the most favored by fortune. Every one took a sausage skewer as a traveller's staff, and to remind them of the object of their journey. They left home early in May, and none of them returned till the first of May in the following year, and then only three of them. Nothing was seen or heard of the fourth, although the day of decision was close at hand. "Ah, yes, there is always some trouble mixed up with the greatest pleasure," said the mouse-king; but he gave orders that all the mice within a circle of many miles should be invited at once. They were to assemble in the kitchen, and the three travelled mice were to stand in a row before them, while a sausage skewer, covered with crape, was to be stuck up instead of the missing mouse. No one dared to express an opinion until the king spoke, and desired one of them to go on with her story. And now we shall hear what she said.

## What the First Little Mouse
## Saw and Heard on Her Travels

"When I first went out into the world," said the little mouse, "I fancied, as so many of my age do, that I already knew everything, but it was not so. It takes years to acquire great knowledge. I went at once to sea in a ship bound for the north. I had been told that the ship's cook must know how to prepare every dish at sea, and it is easy enough to do that with plenty of sides of bacon, and large tubs of salt meat and mouldy flour. There I found plenty of delicate food, but no opportunity for learning how to make soup from a sausage skewer. We sailed on for many days and nights; the ship rocked fearfully, and we did not escape without a wetting. As soon as we arrived at the port to which the ship was bound, I left it, and went on shore at a place far towards the north. It is a wonderful thing to leave your own little corner at home, to hide yourself in a ship where there are sure to be some nice snug corners for shelter, then suddenly to find yourself thousands of miles away in a foreign land. I saw large pathless forests of pine and birch trees, which smelt so strong that I sneezed and thought of sausage. There were great lakes also which looked as black as ink at a distance, but were quite clear when I came close to them. Large swans were floating upon them, and I thought at first they were only foam, they lay so still; but when I saw them walk and fly, I knew what they were directly. They belong to the goose species, one can see that by their walk. No one can attempt to disguise family descent. I kept with my own kind, and associated with the forest and field mice, who, however, knew very little, especially about what I wanted to know, and which had actually made me travel abroad. The idea that soup could be made from a sausage skewer was to them such an out-of-the-way, unlikely thought, that it was repeated from one to another through the whole forest. They declared that the problem would never be solved, that the thing was an impossibility. How little I thought that in this place, on the very first night, I should be initiated into the manner of its preparation.

"It was the height of summer, which the mice told me was the reason that the forest smelt so strong, and that the herbs were so fragrant, and the lakes with the white swimming swans so dark, and yet so clear. On the margin of the wood, near to three or four houses, a pole, as large as the mainmast of a ship, had been erected, and from the summit hung wreaths of flowers and fluttering ribbons; it was the Maypole. Lads and lasses danced round the pole, and tried to outdo the violins of the musicians with their singing. They were as merry as ever at sunset and in the moonlight, but I took no part in the merry-making. What has a little mouse to do with a Maypole dance? I sat in the soft moss, and held my sausage skewer tight. The moon threw its beams particularly on one spot where stood a tree covered with exceedingly fine moss. I may almost venture to say that it was as fine and soft as the fur of the mouse-king, but it was green, which is a color very agreeable to the eye. All at once I saw the most charming little people marching towards me. They did not reach higher than my knee; they looked like human beings, but were better proportioned, and they called themselves elves. Their clothes were very delicate and fine, for they were made of the leaves of flowers, trimmed with the wings of flies and gnats, which had not a bad effect. By their manner, it appeared as if they were seeking for something. I knew not what, till at last one of them espied me and came towards me, and the foremost pointed to my sausage skewer, and said, 'There, that is just what we want; see, it is pointed at the top; is it not capital?' and the longer he looked at my pilgrim's staff, the more delighted he became. 'I will lend it to you,' said I, 'but not to keep.'

" 'Oh no, we won't keep it!' they all cried; and then they seized the skewer, which I gave up to them, and danced with it to the spot where the delicate moss grew, and set it up in the middle of the green. They wanted a maypole, and the one they now had seemed cut out on purpose for them. Then they decorated it so beautifully that it was quite dazzling to look at. Little spiders spun golden threads around it, and then it was hung with fluttering veils and flags so delicately white that they glittered like snow in the moonshine. After that they took colors from the butterfly's wing, and sprinkled them over the white drapery which gleamed as if covered with flowers and diamonds, so that I could not recognize my sausage skewer at all. Such a maypole had never been seen in all the world as this. Then came a great company of real elves. Nothing could be finer than their clothes, and they invited me to be present at the feast; but I was to keep at a certain distance, because I was too large for them. Then commenced such music that it sounded like a thousand glass bells, and was so full and strong that I thought it must be the song of the swans. I fancied also that I heard the voices of the cuckoo and the black-bird, and it seemed at last as if the whole forest sent forth glorious melodies— the voices of children, the tinkling of bells, and the songs of the birds; and all this wonderful melody came from the elfin maypole. My sausage peg was a complete peal of bells. I could scarcely believe that so much could have been produced from it, till I remembered into what hands it had fallen. I was so much affected that I wept tears such as a little mouse can weep, but they were tears of joy. The night was far too short for me; there are no long nights there in summer, as we often have in this part of the world. When the morning dawned, and the gentle breeze rippled the glassy mirror of the forest lake, all the delicate veils and flags fluttered away into thin air; the waving garlands of the spider's web, the hanging bridges and galleries, or whatever else they may be called, vanished away as if they had never been. Six elves brought me back my sausage skewer, and at the same time asked me to make any request, which they would grant if in their power; so I begged them, if they could, to tell me how to make soup from a sausage skewer.

" 'How do we make it?' said the chief of the elves with a smile. 'Why you have just seen it; you scarcely knew your sausage skewer again, I am sure.'

"They think themselves very wise, thought I to myself. Then I told them all about it, and why I had travelled so far, and also what promise had been made at home to the one who should discover the method of preparing this soup. 'What use will it be,' I asked, 'to the mouse-king or to our whole mighty kingdom that I have seen all these beautiful things? I cannot shake the sausage peg and say, Look, here is the skewer, and now the soup will come. That would only produce a dish to be served when people were keeping a fast.'

"Then the elf dipped his finger into the cup of a violet, and said to me, 'Look here, I will anoint your pilgrim's staff, so that when you return to your own home and enter the king's castle, you have only to touch the king with your staff, and violets will spring forth and cover the whole of it, even in the coldest winter time; so I think I have given you really something to carry home, and a little more than something.' "

But before the little mouse explained what this something more was, she stretched her staff out to the king, and as it touched him the most beautiful bunch of violets sprang forth and filled the place with perfume. The smell was so powerful that the mouse-king ordered the mice who stood nearest the chimney to thrust their tails into the fire, that there might be a smell of burning, for the perfume of the violets was over-powering, and not the sort of scent that every one liked.

"But what was the something more of which you spoke just now?" asked the mouse-king.

"Why," answered the little mouse, "I think it is what they call 'effect;' " and thereupon she turned the staff round, and behold not a single flower was to be seen upon it! She now only held the naked skewer, and lifted it up as a conductor lifts his baton at a concert. "Violets, the elf told me," continued the mouse, "are for the sight, the smell, and the touch; so we have only now to produce the effect of hearing and tasting;" and then, as the little mouse beat time with her staff, there came sounds of music, not such music as was heard in the forest, at the elfin feast, but such as is often heard in the kitchen—the sounds of boiling and roasting. It came quite suddenly, like wind rushing through the chimneys, and seemed as if every pot and kettle were boiling over. The fire-shovel clattered down on the brass fender; and then, quite as suddenly, all was still,—nothing could be heard but the light, vapory song of the tea-kettle, which was quite wonderful to hear, for no one could rightly distinguish whether the kettle was just beginning to boil or going to stop. And the little pot steamed, and the great pot simmered, but without any regard for each; indeed there seemed no sense in the pots at all. And as the little mouse waved her baton still more wildly, the pots foamed and threw up bubbles, and boiled over; while again the wind roared and whistled through the chimney, and at last there was such a terrible hubbub, that the little mouse let her stick fall.

"That is a strange sort of soup," said the mouse-king; "shall we not now hear about the preparation?"

"That is all," answered the little mouse, with a bow.

"That all!" said the mouse-king; "then we shall be glad to hear what information the next may have to give us."

## WHAT THE SECOND MOUSE HAD TO TELL

"I was born in the library, at a castle," said the second mouse. "Very few members of our family ever had the good fortune to get into the dining-room, much less the store-room. On my journey, and here to-day, are the only times I have ever seen a kitchen. We were often obliged to suffer hunger in the library, but then we gained a great deal of knowledge. The rumor reached us of the royal prize offered to those who should be able to make soup from a sausage skewer. Then my old grandmother sought out a manuscript which, however, she could not read, but had heard it read, and in it was written, 'Those who are poets can make soup of sausage skewers.' She then asked me if I was a poet. I felt myself quite innocent of any such pretensions. Then she said I must go out and make myself a poet. I asked again what I should be required to do, for it seemed to me quite as difficult as to find out how to make soup of a sausage skewer. My grandmother had heard a great deal of reading in her day, and she told me three principal qualifications were necessary—understanding, imagination, and feeling. 'If you can manage to acquire these three, you will be a poet, and the sausage-skewer soup will be quite easy to you.'

"So I went forth into the world, and turned my steps towards the west, that I might become a poet. Understanding is the most important matter in everything. I knew that, for the two other qualifications are not thought much of; so I went first to seek for understanding. Where was I to find it? 'Go to the ant and learn wisdom,' said the great Jewish king. I knew that from living in a library. So I went straight on till I came to the first great ant-hill, and then I set myself to watch, that I might become wise. The ants are a very respectable people, they are wisdom itself. All they do is like the working of a sum in arithmetic, which comes right. 'To work and to lay eggs,' say they, 'and to provide for posterity, is to live out your time properly;' and that they truly do. They are divided into the clean and the dirty ants, their rank is pointed out by a number, and the ant-queen is number ONE; and her opinion is the only correct one on everything; she seems to have the whole wisdom of the world in her, which was just the important matter I wished to acquire. She said a great deal which was no doubt very clever; yet to me it sounded like nonsense. She said the ant-hill was the loftiest thing in the world, and yet close to the mound stood a tall tree, which no one could deny was loftier, much loftier, but no mention was made of the tree. One evening an ant lost herself on this tree; she had crept up the stem, not nearly to the top, but higher than any ant had ever ventured; and when at last she returned home she said that she had found something in her travels much higher than the ant-hill. The rest of the ants considered this an insult to the whole community; so she was condemned to wear a muzzle and to live in perpetual solitude. A short time afterwards another ant got on the tree, and made the same journey and the same discovery, but she spoke of it cautiously and indefinitely, and as she was one of the superior ants and very much respected, they believed her, and when she died they erected an eggshell as a monument to her memory, for they cultivated a great respect for science. I saw," said the little mouse, "that the ants were always running to and fro with her burdens on their backs. Once I saw one of them drop her load; she gave herself a great deal of trouble in trying to raise it again, but she could not succeed. Then two others came up and tried with all their strength to help her, till they nearly dropped their own burdens in doing so; then they were obliged to stop for a moment in their help, for every one must think of himself first. And the ant-queen remarked that their conduct that day showed that they possessed kind hearts and good understanding. 'These two qualities,' she contin-ued, 'place us ants in the highest degree above all other reasonable beings. Understanding must therefore be seen among us in the most prominent manner, and my wisdom is greater than all.' And so saying she raised herself on her two hind legs, that no one else might be mistaken for her. I could not therefore make an error, so I ate her up. We are to go to the ants to learn wisdom, and I had got the queen.

"I now turned and went nearer to the lofty tree already mentioned, which was an oak. It had a tall trunk with a wide-spreading top, and was very old. I knew that a living being dwelt here, a dryad as she is called, who is born with the tree and dies with it. I had heard this in the library, and here was just such a tree, and in it an oak-maiden. She uttered a terrible scream when she caught sight of me so near to her; like many women, she was very much afraid of mice. And she had more real cause for fear than they have, for I might have gnawed through the tree on which her life depended. I spoke to her in a kind and friendly manner, and begged her to take courage. At last she took me up in her delicate hand, and then I told her what had brought me out into the world, and she promised me that perhaps on that very evening she should be able to obtain for me one of the two treasures for which I was seeking. She told me that Phantæsus was her very dear friend, that he was as beautiful as the god of love, that he remained often for many hours with her under the leafy boughs of the tree which then rustled and waved more than ever over them both. He called her his dryad, she said, and the tree his tree; for the grand old oak, with its gnarled trunk, was just to his taste. The root, spreading deep into the earth, the top rising high in the fresh air, knew the value of the drifted snow, the keen wind, and the warm sunshine, as it ought to be known. 'Yes,' continued the dryad, 'the birds sing up above in the branches, and talk to each other about the beautiful fields they have visited in foreign lands; and on one of the withered boughs a stork has built his nest,—it is beautifully arranged, and besides it is pleasant to hear a little about the land of the pyramids. All this pleases Phantæsus, but it is not enough for him; I am obliged to relate to him of my life in the woods; and to go back to my childhood, when I was little, and the tree so small and delicate that a stinging-nettle could over-shadow it, and I have to tell everything that has happened since then till now that the tree is so large and strong. Sit you down now under the green bindwood and pay attention, when Phantæsus comes I will find an opportunity to lay hold of his wing and to pull out one of the little feathers. That feather you shall have; a better was never given to any poet, it will be quite enough for you.'

"And when Phantæsus came the feather was plucked, and," said the little mouse, "I seized and put it in water, and kept it there till it was quite soft. It was very heavy and indigestible, but I managed to nibble it up at last. It is not so easy to nibble one's self into a poet, there are so many things to get through. Now, however, I had two of them, understanding and imagination; and through these I knew that the third was to be found in the library. A great man has said and written that there are novels whose sole and only use appeared to be that they might relieve mankind of overflowing tears—a kind of sponge, in fact, for sucking up feelings and emotions. I remembered a few of these books, they had always appeared tempting to the appetite; they had been much read, and were so greasy, that they must have absorbed no end of emotions in themselves. I retraced my steps to the library, and literally devoured a whole novel, that is, properly speaking, the interior or soft part of it; the crust, or binding, I left. When I had digested not only this, but a second, I felt a stirring within me; then I ate a small piece of a third romance, and felt myself a poet. I said it to myself, and told others the same. I had head-ache and back-ache, and I cannot tell what aches besides. I thought over all the stories that may be said to be connected with sausage pegs, and all that has ever been written about skewers, and sticks, and staves, and splinters came to my thoughts; the ant-queen must have had a wonderfully clear understanding. I remembered the man who placed a white stick in his mouth by which he could make himself and the stick invisible. I thought of sticks as hobby-horses, staves of music or rhyme, of breaking a stick over a man's back, and heaven knows how many more phrases of the same sort relating to sticks, staves, and skewers. All my thoughts ran on skewers, sticks of wood, and staves; and as I am, at last, a poet, and I have worked terribly hard to make myself one, I can of course make poetry on anything. I shall therefore be able to wait upon you every day in the week with a poetical history of a skewer. And that is my soup."

"In that case," said the mouse-king, "we will hear what the third mouse has to say."

"Squeak, squeak," cried a little mouse at the kitchen door; it was the fourth, and not the third, of the four who were contending for the prize, one whom the rest supposed to be dead. She shot in like an arrow, and overturned the sausage peg that had been covered with crape. She had been running day and night. She had watched an opportunity to get into a goods train, and had travelled by the railway; and yet she had arrived almost too late. She pressed forward, looking very much ruffled. She had lost her sausage skewer, but not her voice; for she began to speak at once as if they only waited for her, and would hear her only, and as if nothing else in the world was of the least consequence. She spoke out so clearly and plainly, and she had come in so suddenly, that no one had time to stop her or to say a word while she was speaking. And now let us hear what she said.

## What the Fourth Mouse, Who Spoke Before the Third, Had to Tell

"I started off at once to the largest town," said she, "but the name of it has escaped me. I have a very bad memory for names. I was carried from the railway, with some forfeited goods, to the jail, and on arriving I made my escape, and ran into the house of the turnkey. The turnkey was speaking of his prisoners, especially of one who had uttered thoughtless words. These words had given rise to other words, and at length they were written down and registered: 'The whole affair is like making soup of sausage skewers,' and he, 'but the soup may cost him his neck.'

"Now this raised in me an interest for the prisoner," continued the little mouse, "and I watched my opportunity, and slipped into his apartment, for there is a mouse-hole to be found behind every closed door. The prisoner looked pale; he had a great beard and large, sparkling eyes. There was a lamp burning, but the walls were so black that they only looked the blacker for it. The prisoner scratched pictures and verses with white chalk on the black walls, but I did not read the verses. I think he found his confinement wearisome, so that I was a welcome guest. He enticed me with bread-crumbs, with whistling, and with gentle words, and seemed so friendly towards me, that by degrees I gained confidence in him, and we became friends; he divided his bread and water with me, gave me cheese and sausage, and I really began to love him. Altogether, I must own that it was a very pleasant intimacy. He let me run about on his hand, and on his arm, and into his sleeve; and I even crept into his beard, and he called me his little friend. I forgot what I had come out into the world for; forgot my sausage skewer which I had laid in a crack in the floor—it is lying there still. I wished to stay with him always where I was, for I knew that if I went away the poor prisoner would have no one to be his friend, which is a sad thing. I stayed, but he did not. He spoke to me so mournfully for the last time, gave me double as much bread and cheese as usual, and kissed his hand to me. Then he went away, and never came back. I know nothing more of his history.

"The jailer took possession of me now. He said something about soup from a sausage skewer, but I could not trust him. He took me in his hand certainly, but it was to place me in a cage like a tread-mill. Oh how dreadful it was! I had to run round and round without getting any farther in advance, and only to make everybody laugh. The jailer's granddaughter was a charming little thing. She had curly hair like the brightest gold, merry eyes, and such a smiling mouth.

" 'You poor little mouse,' said she, one day as she peeped into my cage, 'I will set you free.' She then drew forth the iron fastening, and I sprang out on the window-sill, and from thence to the roof. Free! free! that was all I could think of; not of the object of my journey. It grew dark, and as night was coming on I found a lodging in an old tower, where dwelt a watchman and an owl. I had no confidence in either of them, least of all in the owl, which is like a cat, and has a great failing, for she eats mice. One may however be mistaken sometimes; and so was I, for this was a respectable and well-educated old owl, who knew more than the watchman, and even as much as I did myself. The young owls made a great fuss about everything, but the only rough words she would say to them were, 'You had better go and make some soup from sausage skewers.' She was very indulgent and loving to her children. Her conduct gave me such confidence in her, that from the crack where I sat I called out 'squeak.' This confidence of mine pleased her so much that she assured me she would take me under her own protection, and that not a creature

SOUP FROM A SAUSAGE SKEWER

should do me harm. The fact was she wickedly meant to keep me in reserve for her own eating in winter, when food would be scarce. Yet she was a very clever lady-owl; she explained to me that the watchman could only hoot with the horn that hung loose at his side; and then she said he is so terribly proud of it, that he imagines himself an owl in the tower;— wants to do great things, but only succeeds in small; all soup on a sausage skewer. Then I begged the owl to give me the recipe for this soup. 'Soup from a sausage skewer,' said she, 'is only a proverb amongst mankind, and may be understood in many ways. Each believes his own way the best, and after all, the proverb signifies nothing.' 'Nothing!' I exclaimed. I was quite struck. Truth is not always agreeable, but truth is above everything else, as the old owl said. I thought over all this, and saw quite plainly that if truth was really so far above everything else, it must be much more valuable than soup from a sausage skewer. So I hastened to get away, that I might be home in time, and bring what was highest and best, and above everything—namely, the truth. The mice are an enlightened people, and the mouse-king is above them all. He is therefore capable of making me queen for the sake of truth."

"Your truth is a falsehood," said the mouse who had not yet spoken; "I can prepare the soup, and I mean to do so."


## How It Was Prepared

"I did not travel," said the third mouse; "I stayed in this country: that was the right way. One gains nothing by travelling—everything can be acquired here quite as easily; so I stayed at home. I have not obtained what I know from supernatural beings. I have neither swallowed it, nor learnt it from conversing with owls. I have got it all from my reflections and thoughts. Will you now set the kettle on the fire—so? Now pour the water in—quite full—up to the brim; place it on the fire; make up a good blaze; keep it burning, that the water may boil; it must boil over and over. There, now I throw in the skewer. Will the mouse-king be pleased now to dip his tail into the boiling water, and stir it round with the tail. The longer the king stirs it, the stronger the soup will become. Nothing more is necessary, only to stir it."

"Can no one else do this?" asked the king.

"No," said the mouse; "only in the tail of the mouse-king is this power contained."

And the water boiled and bubbled, as the mouse-king stood close beside the kettle. It seemed rather a dangerous performance; but he turned round, and put out his tail, as mice do in a dairy, when they wish to skim the cream from a pan of milk with their tails and afterwards lick it off. But the mouse-king's tail had only just touched the hot steam, when he sprang away from the chimney in a great hurry, exclaiming, "Oh, certainly, by all means, you must be my queen; and we will let the soup question rest till our golden wedding, fifty years hence; so that the poor in my kingdom, who are then to have plenty of food, will have something to look forward to for a long time, with great joy."

And very soon the wedding took place. But many of the mice, as they were returning home, said that the soup could not be properly called "soup from a sausage skewer," but "soup from a mouse's tail." They acknowledged also that some of the stories were very well told; but that the whole could have been managed differently. "I should have told it so—and so—and so." These were the critics who are always so clever *afterwards*.

When this story was circulated all over the world, the opinions upon it were divided; but the story remained the same. And, after all, the best way in everything you undertake, great as well as small, is to expect no thanks for anything you may do, even when it refers to "soup from a sausage skewer."

# THE LITTLE MERMAID

FAR OUT in the ocean, where the water is as blue as the prettiest corn-flower, and as clear as crystal, it is very, very deep; so deep, indeed, that no cable could fathom it: many church steeples, piled one upon another, would not reach from the ground beneath to the surface of the water above. There dwell the Sea King and his subjects. We must not imagine that there is nothing at the bottom of the sea but bare yellow sand. No, indeed; the most singular flowers and plants grow there; the leaves and stems of which are so pliant, that the slightest agitation of the water causes them to stir as if they had life. Fishes, both large and small, glide between the branches, as birds fly among the trees here upon land. In the deepest spot of all, stands the castle of the Sea King. Its walls are built of coral, and the long, gothic windows are of the clearest amber. The roof is formed of shells, that open and close as the water flows over them. Their appearance is very beautiful, for in each lies a glittering pearl, which would be fit for the diadem of a queen.

The Sea King had been a widower for many years, and his aged mother kept house for him. She was a very wise woman, and exceedingly proud of her high birth; on that account she wore twelve oysters on her tail; while others, also of high rank, were only allowed to wear six. She was, however, deserving of very great praise, especially for her care of the little sea-princesses, her grand-daughters. They were six beautiful children; but the youngest was the prettiest of them all; her skin was as clear and delicate as a rose-leaf, and her eyes as blue as the deepest sea; but, like all the others, she had no feet, and her body ended in a fish's tail. All day long they played in the great halls of the castle, or among the living flowers that grew out of the walls. The large amber windows were open, and the fish swam in, just as the swallows fly into our houses when we open the windows, excepting that the fishes swam up to the princesses, ate out of their hands, and allowed themselves to be stroked.

Outside the castle there was a beautiful garden, in which grew bright red and dark blue flowers, and blossoms like flames of fire; the fruit glittered like gold, and the leaves and stems waved to and fro continually. The earth itself was the finest sand, but blue as the flame of burning sulphur. Over everything lay a peculiar blue radiance, as if it were surrounded by the air from above, through which the blue sky shone, instead of the dark depths of the sea. In calm weather the sun could be seen, looking like a purple flower, with the light streaming from the calyx. Each of the young princesses had a little plot of ground in the garden, where she might dig and plant as she pleased. One arranged her flower-bed into the form of a whale; another thought it better to make hers like the figure of a little mermaid; but that of the youngest was round like the sun, and contained flowers as red as his rays at sunset. She was a strange child, quiet and thoughtful; and while her sisters would be delighted with the wonderful things which they obtained from the wrecks of vessels, she cared for nothing but her pretty red flowers, like the sun, excepting a beautiful marble statue. It was the representation of a handsome boy, carved out of pure white stone, which had fallen to the bottom of the sea from a wreck. She planted by the statue a rose-colored weeping willow. It grew splendidly, and very soon hung its fresh branches over the statue, almost down to the blue sands. The shadow had a violet tint, and waved to and fro like the branches; it seemed as if the crown of the tree and the root were at play, and trying to kiss each other. Nothing gave her so much pleasure as to hear about the world above the sea. She made her old grandmother tell her all she knew of the ships and of the towns, the people and the animals. To her it seemed most wonderful and beautiful to hear that the flowers of the land should have fragrance, and not those below the sea; that the trees of the forest should be green; and that the fishes among the trees could sing so sweetly, that it was quite a pleasure to hear them. Her grandmother called the little birds fishes, or she would not have understood her; for she had never seen birds.

"When you have reached your fifteenth year," said the grandmother, "you will have permission to rise up out of the sea, to sit on the rocks in the moonlight, while the great ships are sailing by; and then you will see both forests and towns."

In the following year, one of the sisters would be fifteen; but as each was a year younger than the other, the youngest would have to wait five years before her turn came to rise up from the bottom of the ocean, and see the earth as we do. However, each promised to tell the others what she saw on her first visit, and what she thought the most beautiful; for their grandmother could not tell them enough; there were so many things on which they wanted information. None of them longed so much for her turn to come as the youngest, she who had the longest time to wait, and who was so quiet and thoughtful. Many nights she stood by the open window, looking up through the dark blue water, and watching the fish as they splashed about with the fins and tails. She could see the moon and stars shining faintly; but through the water they looked larger than they do to our eyes. When something like a black cloud passed between her and them, she knew that it was either a whale swimming over her head, or a ship full of human beings, who never imagined that a pretty little mermaid was standing beneath them, holding out her white hands towards the keel of their ship.

As soon as the eldest was fifteen, she was allowed to rise to the surface of the ocean. When she came back, she had hundreds of things to talk about; but the most beautiful, she said, was to lie in the moonlight, on a sandbank, in the quiet sea, near the coast, and to gaze on a large town nearby, where the lights were twinkling like hundreds of stars; to listen to the sounds of the music, the noise of carriages, and the voices of human beings, and then to hear the merry bells peal out from the church steeples; and because she could not go near to all those wonderful things, she longed for them more than ever. Oh, did not the youngest sister listen eagerly to all these descriptions? And afterwards, when she stood at the open window looking up through the dark blue water, she thought of the great city, with all its bustle and noise, and even fancied she could hear the sound of the church bells, down in the depths of the sea.

In another year the second sister received permission to rise to the surface of the water, and to swim about where she pleased. She rose just as the sun was setting, and this, she said, was the most beautiful sight of all. The whole sky looked like gold, while violet and rose-colored clouds, which she could not describe, floated over her; and, still more rapidly than the clouds, flew a large flock of wild swans towards the setting sun, looking like a long white veil across the sea. She also swam towards the sun; but it sunk into the waves, and the rosy tints faded from the clouds and from the sea.

The third sister's turn followed; she was the boldest of them all, and she swam up a broad river that emptied itself into the sea. On the banks she saw green hills covered with beautiful vines; palaces and castles peeped out from amid the proud trees of the forest; she heard the birds singing, and the rays of the sun were so powerful that she was obliged often to dive down under the water to cool her burning face. In a narrow creek she found a whole troop of little human children, quite naked, and sporting about in the water; she wanted to play with them, but they fled in a great fright; and then a little black animal came to the water; it was a dog, but she did not know that, for she had never before seen one. This animal barked at her so terribly that she became frightened, and rushed back to the open sea. But she said she should never forget the beautiful forest, the green hills, and the pretty little children who could swim in the water, although they had not fish's tails.

The fourth sister was more timid; she remained in the midst of the sea, but she said it was quite as beautiful there as nearer the land. She could see for so many miles around her, and the sky above looked like a bell of glass. She had seen the ships, but at such a great distance that they looked like sea-gulls. The dolphins sported in the waves, and the great whales spouted water from their nostrils till it seemed as if a hundred fountains were playing in every direction.

The fifth sister's birthday occurred in the winter; so when her turn came, she saw what the others had not seen the first time they went up. The sea looked quite green, and large icebergs were floating about, each like a pearl, she said, but larger and loftier than the churches built by men. They were of the most singular shapes, and glittered like diamonds. She had seated herself upon one of the largest, and let the wind play with her long hair, and she remarked that all the ships sailed by rapidly, and steered as far away as they could from the iceberg, as if they were afraid of it. Towards evening, as the sun went down, dark clouds covered the sky, the thunder rolled and the lightning flashed, and the red light glowed on the icebergs as they rocked and tossed on the heaving sea. On all the ships the sails were reefed with fear and trembling, while she sat calmly on the floating iceberg, watching the blue lightning, as it darted its forked flashes into the sea.

When first the sisters had permission to rise to the surface, they were each delighted with the new and beautiful sights they saw; but now, as grown-up girls, they could go when they pleased, and they had become indifferent about it. They wished themselves back again in the water, and after a month had passed they said it was much more beautiful down below, and pleasanter to be at home. Yet often, in the evening hours, the five sisters would twine their arms round each other, and rise to the surface, in a row. They had more beautiful voices than any human being could have; and before the approach of a storm, and when they expected a ship would be lost, they swam before the vessel, and sang sweetly of the delights to be found in the depths of the sea, and begging the sailors not to fear if they sank to the bottom. But the sailors could not understand the song, they took it for the howling of the storm. And these things were never to be beautiful for them; for if the ship sank, the men were drowned, and their dead bodies alone reached the palace of the Sea King.

When the sisters rose, arm-in-arm, through the water in this way, their youngest sister would stand quite alone, looking after them, ready to cry, only that the mermaids have no tears, and therefore they suffer more. "Oh, were I but fifteen years old," said she: "I know that I shall love the world up there, and all the people who live in it."

At last she reached her fifteenth year. "Well, now, you are grown up," said the old dowager, her grandmother; "so you must let me adorn you like your other sisters;" and she placed a wreath of white lilies in her hair, and every flower leaf was half a pearl. Then the old lady ordered eight great oysters to attach themselves to the tail of the princess to show her high rank.

"But they hurt me so," said the little mermaid.

"Pride must suffer pain," replied the old lady. Oh, how gladly she would have shaken off all the grandeur, and laid aside the heavy wreath! The red flowers in her own garden would have suited her much better, but she could not help herself: so she said, "Farewell," and rose as lightly as a bubble to the surface of the water. The sun had just set as she raised her head above the waves; but the clouds were tinted with crimson and gold, and through the glimmering twilight beamed the evening star in all its beauty. The sea was calm, and the air mild and fresh. A large ship, with three masts, lay becalmed on the water, with only one sail set; for not a breeze stirred, and the sailors sat idle on deck or amongst the rigging. There was music and song on board; and, as darkness came on, a hundred colored lanterns were lighted, as if the flags of all nations waved in the air. The little mermaid swam close to the cabin windows; and now and then, as the waves lifted her up, she could look in through clear glass window-panes, and see a number of well-dressed people within. Among them was a young prince, the most beautiful of all, with large black eyes; he was sixteen years of age, and his birthday was being kept with much rejoicing. The sailors were dancing on deck, but when the prince came out of the cabin, more than a hundred rockets rose in the air, making it as bright as day. The little mermaid was so startled that she dived under water; and when she again stretched out her head, it appeared as if all the stars of heaven were falling around her, she had never seen such fireworks before. Great suns spurted fire about, splendid fireflies flew into the blue air, and everything was reflected in the clear, calm sea beneath. The ship itself was so brightly illuminated that all the people, and even the smallest rope, could be distinctly and plainly seen. And how handsome the young prince looked, as he pressed the hands of all present and smiled at them, while the music resounded through the clear night air.

It was very late; yet the little mermaid could not take her eyes from the ship, or from the beautiful prince. The colored lanterns had been extinguished, no more rockets rose in the air, and the cannon had ceased firing; but the sea became restless, and a moaning, grumbling sound could be heard beneath the waves; still the little mermaid remained by the cabin window, rocking up and down on the water, which enabled her to look in. After a while, the sails were quickly unfurled, and the noble ship continued her passage; but soon the waves rose higher, heavy clouds darkened the sky, and lightning appeared in the distance. A dreadful storm was approaching; once more the sails were reefed, and the great ship pursued her flying course over the raging sea. The waves rose mountains high, as if they would have overtopped the mast; but the ship dived like a swan between them, and then rose again on their lofty, foaming crests. To the little mermaid this appeared pleasant sport; not so to the sailors. At length the ship groaned and creaked; the thick planks gave way under the lashing of the sea as it broke over the deck; the mainmast snapped asunder like a reed; the ship lay over on her side; and the water rushed in. The little mermaid now perceived that the crew were in danger; even she herself was obliged to be careful to avoid the beams and planks of the wreck which lay scattered on the water. At one moment it was so pitch dark that she could not see a single object, but a flash of lightning revealed the whole scene; she could see every one who had been on board excepting the prince; when the ship parted, she had seen him sink into the deep waves, and she was glad, for she thought he would now be with her; and then she remembered that human beings could not live in the water, so that when he got down to her father's palace he would be quite dead. But he must not die. So she swam about among the beams and planks which strewed the surface of the sea, forgetting that they could crush her to pieces. Then she dived deeply under the dark waters, rising and falling with the waves, till at length she managed to reach the young prince, who was fast losing the power of swimming in that stormy sea. His limbs were failing him, his beautiful eyes were closed, and he would have died had not the little mermaid come to his assistance. She held his head above the water, and let the waves drift them where they would.

In the morning the storm had ceased; but of the ship not a single fragment could be seen. The sun rose up red and glowing from the water, and its beams brought back the hue of health to the prince's cheeks; but his eyes remained closed. The mermaid kissed his high, smooth forehead, and stroked back his wet hair; he seemed to her like the marble statue in her little garden, and she kissed him again, and wished that he might live. Presently they came in sight of land; she saw lofty blue mountains, on which the white snow rested as if a flock of swans were lying upon them. Near the coast were beautiful green forests, and close by stood a large building, whether a church or a convent she could not tell. Orange and citron trees grew in the garden, and before the door stood lofty palms. The sea here formed a little bay, in which the water was quite still, but very deep; so she swam with the handsome prince to the beach, which was covered with fine, white sand, and there she laid him in the warm sunshine, taking care to raise his head higher than his body. Then bells sounded in the large white building, and a number of young girls came into the garden. The little mermaid swam out farther from the shore and placed herself between some high rocks that rose out of the water; then she covered her head and neck with the foam of the sea so that her little face might not be seen, and watched to see what would become of the poor prince. She did not wait long before she saw a young girl approach the spot where he lay. She seemed frightened at first, but only for a moment; then she fetched a number of people, and the mermaid saw that the prince came to life again, and smiled upon those who stood round him. But to her he sent no smile; he knew not that she had saved him. This made her very unhappy, and when he was led away into the great building, she dived down sorrowfully into the water, and returned to her father's castle. She had always been silent and thoughtful, and now she was more so than ever. Her sisters asked her what she had seen during her first visit to the surface of the water; but she would tell them nothing. Many an evening and morning did she rise to the place where she had left the prince. She saw the fruits in the garden ripen till they were gathered, the snow on the tops of the mountains melt away; but she never saw the prince, and therefore she returned home, always more sorrowful than before. It was her only comfort to sit in her own little garden, and fling her arm round the beautiful marble statue which was like the prince; but she gave up tending her flowers, and they grew in wild confusion over the paths, twining their long leaves and stems round the branches of the trees, so that the whole place became dark and gloomy. At length she could bear it no longer, and told one of her sisters all about it. Then the others heard the secret, and very soon it became known to two mermaids whose intimate friend happened to know who the prince was. She had also seen the festival on board ship, and she told them where the prince came from, and where his palace stood.

"Come, little sister," said the other princesses; then they entwined their arms and rose up in a long row to the surface of the water, close by the spot where they knew the prince's palace stood. It was built of bright yellow shining stone, with long flights of marble steps, one of which reached quite down to the sea. Splendid gilded cupolas rose over the roof, and between the pillars that surrounded the whole building stood life-like statues of marble. Through the clear crystal of the lofty windows could be seen noble rooms, with costly silk curtains and hangings of tapestry; while the walls were covered with beautiful paintings which were a pleasure to look at. In the centre of the largest saloon a fountain threw its sparkling jets high up into the glass cupola of the ceiling, through which the sun shone down upon the water and upon the beautiful plants growing round the basin of the fountain. Now that she knew where he lived, she spent many an evening and many a night on the water near the palace. She would swim much nearer the shore than any of the others ventured to do; indeed once she went quite up the narrow channel under the marble balcony, which threw a broad shadow on the water. Here she would sit and watch the young prince, who thought himself quite alone in the bright moonlight. She saw him many times of an evening sailing in a pleasant boat, with music playing and flags waving. She peeped out from among the green rushes, and if the wind caught her long silvery-white veil, those who saw it believed it to be a swan, spreading out its wings. On many a night, too, when the fishermen, with their torches, were out at sea, she heard them relate so many good things about the doings of the young prince, that she was glad she had saved his life when he had been tossed about half-dead on the waves. And she remembered that his head had rested on her bosom, and how heartily she had kissed him; but he knew nothing of all this, and could not even dream of her. She grew more and more fond of human beings, and wished more and more to be able to wander about with those whose world seemed to be so much larger than her own. They could fly over the sea in ships, and mount the high hills which were far above the clouds; and the lands they possessed, their woods and their fields, stretched far away beyond the reach of her sight. There was so much that she wished to know, and her sisters were unable to answer all her questions. Then she applied to her old grandmother, who knew all about the upper world, which she very rightly called the lands above the sea.

"If human beings are not drowned," asked the little mermaid, "can they live forever? do they never die as we do here in the sea?"

"Yes," replied the old lady, "they must also die, and their term of life is even shorter than ours. We sometimes live to three hundred years, but when we cease to exist here we only become the foam on the surface of the water, and we have not even a grave down here of those we love. We have not immortal souls, we shall never live again; but, like the green sea-weed, when once it has been cut off, we can never flourish more. Human beings, on the contrary, have a soul which lives forever, lives after the body has been turned to dust. It rises up through the clear, pure air beyond the glittering stars. As we rise out of the water, and behold all the land of the earth, so do they rise to unknown and glorious regions which we shall never see."

"Why have not we an immortal soul?" asked the little mermaid mournfully; "I would give gladly all the hundreds of years that I have to live, to be a human being only for one day, and to have the hope of knowing the happiness of that glorious world above the stars."

"You must not think of that," said the old woman; "we feel ourselves to be much happier and much better off than human beings."

"So I shall die," said the little mermaid, "and as the foam of the sea I shall be driven about never again to hear the music of the waves, or to see the pretty flowers nor the red sun. Is there anything I can do to win an immortal soul?"

"No," said the old woman, "unless a man were to love you so much that you were more to him than his father or mother; and if all his thoughts and all his love were fixed upon you, and the priest placed his right hand in yours, and he promised to be true to you here and hereafter, then his soul would glide into your body and you would obtain a share in the future happiness of mankind. He would give a soul to you and retain his own as well; but this can never happen. Your fish's tail, which amongst us is considered so beautiful, is thought on earth to be quite ugly; they do not know any better, and they think it necessary to have two stout props, which they call legs, in order to be handsome."

Then the little mermaid sighed, and looked sorrowfully at her fish's tail. "Let us be happy," said the old lady, "and dart and spring about during the three hundred years that we have to live, which is really quite long enough; after that we can rest ourselves all the better. This evening we are going to have a court ball."

It is one of those splendid sights which we can never see on earth. The walls and the ceiling of the large ball-room were of thick, but transparent crystal. Many hundreds of colossal shells, some of a deep red, others of a grass green, stood on each side in rows, with blue fire in them, which lighted up the whole saloon, and shone through the walls, so that the sea was also illuminated. Innumerable fishes, great and small, swam past the crystal walls; on some of them the scales glowed with a purple brilliancy, and on others they shone like silver and gold. Through the halls flowed a broad stream, and in it danced the mermen and the mermaids to the music of their own sweet singing. No one on earth has such a lovely voice as theirs. The little mermaid sang more sweetly than them all. The whole court applauded her with hands and tails; and for a moment her heart felt quite gay, for she knew she had the loveliest voice of any on earth or in the sea. But she soon thought again of the world above her, for she could not forget the charming prince, nor her sorrow that she had not an immortal soul like his; therefore she crept away silently out of her father's palace, and while everything within was gladness and song, she sat in her own little garden sorrowful and alone. Then she heard the bugle sounding through the water, and thought—"He is certainly sailing above, he on whom my wishes depend, and in whose hands I should like to place the happiness of my life. I will venture all for him, and to win an immortal soul, while my sisters are dancing in my father's palace, I will go to the sea witch, of whom I have always been so much afraid, but she can give me counsel and help."

And then the little mermaid went out from her garden, and took the road to the foaming whirlpools, behind which the sorceress lived. She had never been that way before: neither flowers nor grass grew there; nothing but bare, gray, sandy ground stretched out to the whirlpool, where the water, like foaming mill-wheels, whirled round everything that it seized, and cast it into the fathomless deep. Throught the midst of these crushing whirlpools the little mermaid was obliged to pass, to reach the dominions of the sea witch; and also for a long distance the only road lay right across a quantity of warm, bubbling mire, called by the witch her turfmoor. Beyond this stood her house, in the centre of a strange forest, in which all the trees and flowers were polypi, half animals and half plants; they looked like serpents with a hundred heads growing out of the ground. The branches were long slimy arms, with fingers like flexible worms, moving limb after limb from the root to the top. All that could be reached in the sea they seized upon, and held fast, so that it never escaped from their clutches. The little mermaid was so alarmed at what she saw, that she stood still, and her heart beat with fear, and she was very nearly turning back; but she thought of the prince, and of the human soul for which she longed, and her courage returned. She fastened her long flowing hair round her head, so that the polypi might not seize hold of it. She laid her hands together across her bosom, and then she darted forward as a fish shoots through the water, between the supple arms and fingers of the ugly polypi, which were stretched out on each side of her. She saw that each held in its grasp something it had seized with its numerous little arms, as if they were iron bands. The white skeletons of human beings who had perished at sea, and had sunk down into the deep waters, skeletons of land animals, oars, rudders, and chests of ships were lying tightly grasped by their clinging arms; even a little mermaid, whom they had caught and strangled; and this seemed the most shocking of all to the little princess.

She now came to a space of marshy ground in the wood, where large, fat water-snakes were rolling in the mire, and showing their ugly, drab-colored bodies. In the midst of this spot stood a house, built with the bones of ship-wrecked human beings. There sat the sea witch, allowing a toad to eat from her mouth, just as people sometimes feed a canary with a piece of sugar. She called the ugly water-snakes her little chickens, and allowed them to crawl all over her bosom.

"I know what you want," said the sea witch; "it is very stupid of you, but you shall have your way, and it will bring you to sorrow, my pretty princess. You want to get rid of your fish's tail, and to have two supports instead of it, like human beings on earth, so that the young prince may fall in love with you, and that you may have an immortal soul." And then the witch laughed so loud and disgustingly, that the toad and the snakes fell to the ground, and lay there wriggling about. "You are but just in time," said the witch; "for after sunrise to-morrow I should not be able to help you till the end of another year. I will prepare a draught for you, with which you must swim to land to-morrow before sunrise, and sit down on the shore and drink it. Your tail will then disappear, and shrink up into what mankind calls legs, and you will feel great pain, as if a sword were passing through you. But all who see you will say that you are the prettiest little human being they ever saw. You will still have the same floating gracefulness of movement, and no dancer will ever tread so lightly; but at every step you take it will feel as if you were treading upon sharp knives, and that the blood must flow. If you will bear all this, I will help you."

"Yes, I will," said the little princess in a trembling voice, as she thought of the prince and the immortal soul.

"But think again," said the witch; "for when once your shape has become like a human being, you can no more be a mermaid. You will never return through the water to your sisters, or to your father's palace again; and if you do not win the love of the prince, so that he is willing to forget his father and mother for your sake, and to love you with his whole soul, and allow the priest to join your hands that you may be man and wife, then you will never have an immortal soul. The first morning after he marries another your heart will break, and you will become foam on the crest of the waves."

"I will do it," said the little mermaid, and she became pale as death.

"But I must be paid also," said the witch, "and it is not a trifle that I ask. You have the sweetest voice of any who dwell here in the depths of the sea, and you believe that you will be able to charm the prince with it also, but this voice you must give to me; the best thing you possess will I have for the price of my draught. My own blood must be mixed with it, that it may be as sharp as a two-edged sword."

"But if you take away my voice," said the little mermaid, "what is left for me?"

"Your beautiful form, your graceful walk, and your expressive eyes; surely with these you can enchain a man's heart. Well, have your lost your courage? Put out your little tongue that I may cut it off as my payment; then you shall have the powerful draught."

"It shall be," said the little mermaid.

Then the witch placed her cauldron on the fire, to prepare the magic draught.

"Cleanliness is a good thing," said she, scouring the vessel with snakes, which she had tied together in a large knot; then she pricked herself in the breast, and let the black blood drop into it. The steam that rose formed itself into such horrible shapes that no one could look at them without fear. Every moment the witch threw something else into the vessel, and when it began to boil, the sound was like the weeping of a crocodile. When at last the magic draught was ready, it looked like the clearest water. "There it is for you," said the witch. Then she cut off the mermaid's tongue, so that she became dumb, and would never again speak or sing. "If the polypi should seize hold of you as you return through the wood," said the witch, "throw over them a few drops of the potion, and their fingers will be torn into a thousand pieces." But the little mermaid had no occasion to do this, for the polypi sprang back in terror when they caught sight of the glittering draught, which shone in her hand like a twinkling star.

So she passed quickly through the wood and the marsh, and between the rushing whirlpools. She saw that in her father's palace the torches in the ballroom were extinguished, and all within asleep; but she did not venture to go into them, for now she was dumb and going to leave them forever, she felt as if her heart would break. She stole into the garden, took a flower from the flower-beds of each of her sisters, kissed her hand a thousand times towards the palace, and then rose up through the dark blue waters. The sun had not risen when she came in sight of the prince's palace, and approached the beautiful marble steps, but the moon shone clear and bright. Then the little mermaid drank the magic draught, and it seemed as if a two-edged sword went through her delicate body: she fell into a swoon, and lay like one dead. When the sun arose and shone over the sea, she recovered, and felt a sharp pain; but just before her stood the handsome young prince. He fixed his coal-black eyes upon her so earnestly that she cast down her own, and then became aware that her fish's tail was gone, and that she had as pretty a pair of white legs and tiny feet as any little maiden could have; but she had no clothes, so she wrapped herself in her long, thick hair. The prince asked her who she was, and where she came from, and she looked at him mildly and sorrowfully with her deep blue eyes; but she could not speak. Every step she took was as the witch had said it would be, she felt as if treading upon the points of needles or sharp knives; but she bore it willingly, and stepped as lightly by the prince's side as a soap-bubble, so that he and all who saw her wondered at her graceful-swaying movements. She was very soon arrayed in costly robes of silk and muslin, and was the most beautiful creature in the palace; but she was dumb, and could neither speak nor sing.

Beautiful female slaves, dressed in silk and gold, stepped forward and sang before the prince and his royal parents; one sang better than all the others, and the prince clapped his hands and smiled at her. This was great sorrow to the little mermaid; she knew how much more sweetly she herself could sing once, and she thought, "Oh if he could only know that! I have given away my voice forever, to be with him."

The slaves next performed some pretty fairy-like dances, to the sound of beautiful music. Then the little mermaid raised her lovely white arms, stood on the tips of her toes, and glided over the floor, and danced as no one yet had been able to dance. At each moment her beauty became more revealed, and her expressive eyes appealed more directly to the heart than the songs of the slaves. Every one was enchanted, especially the prince, who called her his little foundling; and she danced again quite readily, to please him, though each time her foot touched the floor it seemed as if she trod on sharp knives.

The prince said she should remain with him always, and she received permission to sleep at his door, on a velvet cushion. He had a page's dress made for her, that she might accompany him on horseback. They rode together through the sweet-scented woods, where the green boughs touched their shoulders, and the little birds sang among the fresh leaves. She climbed with the prince to the tops of high mountains; and although her tender feet bled so that even her steps were marked, she only laughed, and followed him till they could see the clouds beneath them looking like a flock of birds travelling to distant lands. While at the prince's palace, and when all the household were asleep, she would go and sit on the broad marble steps; for it eased her burning feet to bathe them in the cold sea-water; and then she thought of all those below in the deep.

Once during the night her sisters came up arm-in-arm, singing sorrowfully, as they floated on the water. She beckoned to them, and then they recognized her, and told her how she had grieved them. After that, they came to the same place every night; and once she saw in the distance her old grandmother, who had not been to the surface of the sea for many years, and the old Sea King, her father, with his crown on his head. They stretched out their hands towards her, but they did not venture so near the land as her sisters did.

As the days passed, she loved the prince more fondly, and he loved her as he would love a little child, but it never came into his head to make her his wife; yet, unless he married her, she could not receive an immortal soul; and, on the morning after his marriage with another, she would dissolve into the foam of the sea.

"Do you not love me the best of them all?" the eyes of the little mermaid seemed to say, when he took her in his arms, and kissed her fair forehead.

"Yes, you are dear to me," said the prince; "for you have the best heart, and you are the most devoted to me; you are like a young maiden whom I once saw, but whom I shall never meet again. I was in a ship that was wrecked, and the waves cast me ashore near a holy temple, where several young maidens performed the service. The youngest of them found me on the shore, and saved my life. I saw her but twice, and she is the only one in the world whom I could love; but you are like her, and you have almost driven her image out of my mind. She belongs to the holy temple, and my good fortune has sent you to me instead of her; and we will never part."

"Ah, he knows not that it was I who saved his life," thought the little mermaid. "I carried him over the sea to the wood where the temple stands: I sat beneath the foam, and watched till the human beings came to help him. I saw the pretty maiden that he loves better than he loves me;" and the mermaid sighed deeply, but she could not shed tears. "He says the maiden belongs to the holy temple, therefore she will never return to the world. They will meet no more: while I am by his side, and see him every day. I will take care of him, and love him, and give up my life for his sake."

Very soon it was said that the prince must marry, and that the beautiful daughter of a neighboring king would be his wife, for a fine ship was being fitted out. Although the prince gave out that he merely intended to pay a visit to the king, it was generally supposed that he really went to see his daughter. A great company were to go with him. The little mer-

THE LITTLE MERMAID

maid smiled, and shook her head. She knew the prince's thoughts better than any of the others.

"I must travel," he had said to her; "I must see this beautiful princess; my parents desire it; but they will not oblige me to bring her home as my bride. I cannot love her; she is not like the beautiful maiden in the temple, whom you resemble. If I were forced to choose a bride, I would rather choose you, my dumb foundling, with those expressive eyes." And then he kissed her rosy mouth, played with her long waving hair, and laid his head on her heart, while she dreamed of human happiness and an immortal soul. "You are not afraid of the sea, my dumb child," said he, as they stood on the deck of the noble ship which was to carry them to the country of the neighboring king. And then he told her of storm and of calm, of strange fishes in the deep beneath them, and of what the divers had seen there; and she smiled at his descriptions, for she knew better than any one what wonders were at the bottom of the sea.

In the moonlight, when all on board were asleep, excepting the man at the helm, who was steering, she sat on the deck, gazing down through the clear water. She thought she could distinguish her father's castle, and upon it her aged grandmother, with the silver crown on her head, looking through the rushing tide at the keel of the vessel. Then her sisters came up on the waves, and gazed at her mournfully, wringing their white hands. She beckoned to them, and smiled, and wanted to tell them how happy and well off she was; but the cabin-boy approached, and when her sisters dived down he thought it was only the foam of the sea which he saw.

The next morning the ship sailed into the harbor of a beautiful town belonging to the king whom the prince was going to visit. The church bells were ringing, and from the high towers sounded a flourish of trumpets; and soldiers, with flying colors and glittering bayonets, lined the rocks through which they passed. Every day was a festival; balls and entertainments followed one another.

But the princess had not yet appeared. People said that she was being brought up and educated in a religious house, where she was learning every royal virtue. At last she came. Then the little mermaid, who was very anxious to see whether she was really beautiful, was obliged to acknowledge that she had never seen a more perfect vision of beauty. Her skin was delicately fair, and beneath her long dark eye-lashes her laughing blue eyes shone with truth and purity.

"It was you," said the prince, "who saved my life when I lay dead on the beach," and he folded his blushing bride in his arms. "Oh, I am too happy," said he to the little mermaid; "my fondest hopes are all fulfilled. You will rejoice at my happiness; for your devotion to me is great and sincere."

The little mermaid kissed his hand, and felt as if her heart were already broken. His wedding morning would bring death to her, and she would change into the foam of the sea. All the church bells rung, and the heralds rode about the town proclaiming the betrothal. Perfumed oil was burning in costly silver lamps on every altar. The priests waved the censers, while the bride and bridegroom joined their hands and received the blessing of the bishop. The little mermaid, dressed in silk and gold, held up the bride's train; but her ears heard nothing of the festive music, and her eyes saw not the holy ceremony; she thought of the night of death which was coming to her, and of all she had lost in the world. On the same evening the bride and her bridegroom went on board ship; cannons were roaring, flags waving, and in the centre of the ship a costly tent of purple and gold had been erected. It contained elegant couches, for the reception of the bridal pair during the night. The ship, with swelling sails and a favorable wind, glided away smoothly and lightly over the calm sea. When it grew dark a number of colored lamps were lit, and the sailors danced merrily on the deck. The little mermaid could not help thinking of her first rising out of the sea, when she had seen similar festivities and joys; and she joined in the dance, poised herself in the air as a swallow when he pursues his prey, and all present cheered her with wonder. She had never danced so elegantly before. Her tender feet felt as if cut with sharp knives, but she cared not for it; a sharper pang had pierced through her heart. She knew this was the last evening she should ever see the prince, for whom she had forsaken her kindred and her home; she had given up her beautiful voice, and suffered unheard-of pain daily for him, while he knew nothing of it. This was the last evening that she would breathe the same air with him, or gaze on the starry sky and the deep sea; an eternal night, without a thought or a dream, awaited her; she had no soul and now she could never win one. All was joy and gayety on board ship till long after midnight; she laughed and danced with the rest, while the thoughts of death were in her heart. The prince kissed his beautiful bride, while she played with his raven hair, till they went arm-in-arm to rest in the splendid tent. Then all became still on board the ship; the helmsman, alone awake, stood at the helm. The little mermaid leaned her white arms on the edge of the vessel, and looked towards the east for the first blush of morning, for that first ray of dawn that would bring her death. She saw her sisters rising out of the flood: they were as pale as herself; but their long beautiful hair waved no more in the wind, and had been cut off.

"We have given our hair to the witch," said they, "to obtain help for you, that you may not die to-night. She has given us a knife: here it is, see it is very sharp. Before the sun rises you must plunge it into the heart of the prince; when the warm blood falls upon your feet they will grow together again, and form into a fish's tail, and you will be once more a mermaid, and return to us to live out your three hundred years before you die and change into the salt sea foam. Haste, then; he or you must die before sunrise. Our old grandmother moans so for you, that her white hair is falling off from sorrow, as our fell under the witch's scissors. Kill the prince and come back; hasten: do you not see the first red streaks in the sky? In a few minutes the sun will rise, and you must die." And then they sighed deeply and mournfully, and sank down beneath the waves.

The little mermaid drew back the crimson curtain of the tent, and beheld the fair bride with her head resting on the prince's breast. She bent down and kissed his fair brow, then looked at the sky on which the rosy dawn grew brighter and brighter; then she glanced at the sharp knife, and again fixed her eyes on the prince, who whispered the name of his bride in his dreams. *She* was in his thoughts, and the knife trembled in the hand of the little mermaid: then she flung it far away from her into the waves; the water turned red where it fell, and the drops that spurted up looked like blood. She cast one more lingering, half-fainting glance at the prince, and then threw herself from the ship into the sea, and thought her body was dissolving into foam. The sun rose above the waves, and his warm rays fell on the cold foam of the little mermaid, who did not feel as if she were dying. She saw the bright sun, and all around her floated hundreds of transparent beautiful beings; she could see through them the white sails of the ship, and the red clouds in the sky; their speech was melodious, but too ethereal to be heard by mortal ears, as they were also unseen by mortal eyes. The little mermaid perceived that she had a body like theirs, and that she continued to rise higher and higher out of the foam. "Where am I?" asked she, and her voice sounded ethereal, as the voice of these who were with her; no earthly music could imitate it.

"Among the daughters of the air," answered one of them. "A mermaid has not an immortal soul, nor can she obtain one unless she wins the love of a human being. On the power of another hangs her eternal destiny. But the daughters of the air, although they do not possess an immortal soul, can, by their good deeds, procure one for themselves. We fly to warm countries, and cool the sultry air that destroys mankind with the pestilence. We carry the perfume of the flowers to spread health and restoration. After we have striven for three hundred years to do all the good in our power, we receive an immortal soul and take part in the happiness of mankind. You, poor little mermaid, have tried with your whole heart to do as we are doing; you have suffered and endured and raised yourself to the spirit-world by your good deeds; and now, by striving for three hundred years in the same way, you may obtain an immortal soul."

The little mermaid lifted her glorified eyes towards the sun, and felt them, for the first time, filling with tears. On the ship, in which she had left the prince, there were life and noise; she saw him and his beautiful bride searching for her; sorrowfully they gazed at the pearly foam, as if they knew she had thrown herself into the waves. Unseen she kissed the forehead of the bride, and fanned the prince, and then mounted with the other children of the air to a rosy cloud that floated through the æther.

"After three hundred years, thus shall we float into the kingdom of heaven," said she. "And we may even get there sooner," whispered one of her companions. "Unseen we can enter the houses of men, where there are children, and for every day on which we find a good child, who is the joy of his parents and deserves their love, our time of probation is shortened. The child does not know, when we fly through the room, that we smile with joy at his good conduct, for we can count one year less of our three hundred years. But when we see a naughty or a wicked child, we shed tears of sorrow, and for every tear a day is added to our time of trial!"

# THE GIRL WHO TROD ON THE LOAF

THERE WAS once a girl who trod on a loaf to avoid soiling her shoes, and the misfortunes that happened to her in consequence are well known. Her name was Ingé; she was a poor child, but proud and presuming, and with a bad and cruel disposition. When quite a little child she would delight in catching flies, and tearing off their wings, so as to make creeping things of them. When older, she would take cockchafers and beetles, and stick pins through them. Then she pushed a green leaf, or a little scrap of paper towards their feet, and when the poor creatures would seize it and hold it fast, and turn over and over in their struggles to get free from the pin, she would say, "The cockchafer is reading; see how he turns over the leaf." She grew worse instead of better with years, and, unfortunately, she was pretty, which caused her to be excused, when she should have been sharply reproved.

"Your headstrong will requires severity to conquer it," her mother often said to her. "As a little child you used to trample on my apron, but one day I fear you will trample on my heart." And, alas! this fear was realized.

Ingé was taken to the house of some rich people, who lived at a distance, and who treated her as their own child, and dressed her so fine that her pride and arrogance increased.

When she had been there about a year, her patroness said to her, "You ought to go, for once, and see your parents, Ingé."

So Ingé started to go and visit her parents; but she only wanted to show herself in her native place, that the people might see how fine she was. She reached the entrance of the village, and saw the young laboring men and maidens standing together chatting, and her own mother amongst them. Ingé's mother was sitting on a stone to rest, with a fagot of sticks lying before her, which she had picked up in the wood. Then Ingé turned back; she who was so finely dressed she felt ashamed of her mother, a poorly clad woman, who picked up wood in the forest. She did not turn back out of pity for her mother's poverty, but from pride.

Another half-year went by, and her mistress said, "You ought to go home again, and visit your parents, Ingé, and I will give you a large wheaten loaf to take to them, they will be glad to see you, I am sure."

So Ingé put on her best clothes, and her new shoes, drew her dress up around her, and set out, stepping very carefully, that she might be clean and neat about the feet, and there was nothing wrong in doing so. But when she came to the place where the footpath led across the moor, she found small pools of water, and a great deal of mud, so she threw the loaf into the mud, and trod upon it, that she might pass without wetting her feet. But as she stood with one foot on the loaf and the other lifted up to step forward, the loaf began to sink under her, lower and lower, till she disappeared altogether, and only a few bubbles on the surface of the muddy pool remained to show where she had sunk. And this is the story.

But where did Ingé go? She sank into the ground, and went down to the Marsh Woman, who is always brewing there.

The Marsh Woman is related to the elf maidens, who are well-known, for songs are sung and pictures painted about them. But of the Marsh Woman nothing is known, excepting that when a mist arises from the meadows, in summer time, it is because she is brewing beneath them. To the Marsh Woman's brewery Ingé sunk down to a place which no one can endure for long. A heap of mud is a palace compared with the Marsh Woman's brewery; and as Ingé fell she shuddered in every limb, and soon became cold and stiff as marble. Her foot was still fastened to the loaf, which bowed her down as a golden ear of corn bends the stem.

An evil spirit soon took possession of Ingé, and carried her to a still worse place, in which she saw crowds of unhappy people, waiting in a state of agony for the gates of mercy to be opened to them, and in every heart was a miserable and eternal feeling of unrest. It would take too much time to describe the various tortures these people suffered, but Ingé's punishment consisted in standing there as a statue, with her foot fastened to the loaf. She could move her eyes about, and see all the misery around her, but she could not turn her head; and when she saw the people looking at her she thought they were admiring her pretty face and fine clothes, for she was still vain and proud. But she had forgotten how soiled her clothes had become while in the Marsh Woman's brewery, and that they were covered with mud; a snake had also fastened itself in her hair, and hung down her back, while from each fold in her dress a great toad peeped out and croaked like an asthmatic poodle. Worse than all was the terrible hunger that tormented her, and she could not stoop to break off a piece of the loaf on which she stood. No; her back was too stiff, and her whole body like a pillar of stone. And then came creeping over her face and eyes flies without wings; she winked and blinked, but they could not fly away, for their wings had been pulled off; this, added to the hunger she felt, was horrible torture.

"If this lasts much longer," she said, "I shall not be able to bear it." But it did last, and she had to bear it, without being able to help herself.

A tear, followed by many scalding tears, fell upon her head, and rolled over her face and neck, down to the loaf on which she stood. Who could be weeping for Ingé? She had a mother in the world still, and the tears of sorrow which a mother sheds for her child will always find their way to the child's heart, but they often increase the torment instead of being a relief. and Ingé could hear all that was said about her in the world she had left, and every one seemed cruel to her. The sin she had committed in treading on the loaf was known on earth, for she had been seen by the

THE GIRL WHO TROD ON THE LOAF

cowherd from the hill, when she was crossing the marsh and had disappeared.

When her mother wept and exclaimed, "Ah, Ingé! what grief thou hast caused thy mother" she would say, "Oh that I had never been born! My mother's tears are useless now."

And when the words of the kind people who had adopted her came to her ears, when they said, "Ingé was a sinful girl, who did not value the gifts of God, but trampled them under her feet."

"Ah," thought Ingé, "they should have punished me, and driven all my naughty tempers out of me."

A song was made about "The girl who trod on a loaf to keep her shoes from being soiled," and this song was sung everywhere. The story of her sin was also told to the little children, and they called her "wicked Ingé," and said she was so naughty that she ought to be punished. Ingé heard all this, and her heart became hardened and full of bitterness.

But one day, while hunger and grief were gnawing in her hollow frame, she heard a little, innocent child, while listening to the tale of the vain, haughty Ingé, burst into tears and exclaim, "But will she never come up again?"

And she heard the reply, "No, she will never come up again."

"But if she were to say she was sorry, and ask pardon, and promise never to do so again?" asked the little one.

"Yes, then she might come; but she will not beg pardon," was the answer.

"Oh, I wish she would!" said the child, who was quite unhappy about it. "I should be so glad. I would give up my doll and all my playthings, if she could only come here again. Poor Ingé! it is so dreadful for her."

These pitying words penetrated to Ingé's inmost heart, and seemed to do her good. It was the first time any one had said, "Poor Ingé!" without saying something about her faults. A little innocent child was weeping, and praying for mercy for her. It made her feel quite strange, and she would gladly have wept herself, and it added to her torment to find she could not do so. And while she thus suffered in a place where nothing changed, years passed away on earth, and she heard her name less frequently mentioned. But one day a sigh reached her ear, and the words, "Ingé! Ingé! what a grief thou hast been to me! I said it would be so." It was the last sigh of her dying mother.

After this, Ingé heard her kind mistress say, "Ah, poor Ingé! shall I ever see thee again? Perhaps I may, for we know not what may happen in the future." But Ingé knew right well that her mistress would never come to that dreadful place.

Time-passed—a long bitter time—then Ingé heard her name pronounced once more, and saw what seemed two bright stars shining above her. They were two gentle eyes closing on earth. Many years had passed since the little girl had lamented and wept about "poor Ingé." That child was now an old woman, whom God was taking to Himself. In the last hour of existence the events of a whole life often appear before us; and this hour the old woman remembered how, when a child, she had shed tears over the story of Ingé, and she prayed for her now. As the eyes of the old woman closed to earth, the eyes of the soul opened upon the hidden things of eternity, and then she, in whose last thoughts Ingé had been so vividly present, saw how deeply the poor girl had sunk. She burst into tears at the sight, and in heaven, as she had done when a little child on earth, she wept and prayed for poor Ingé. Her tears and her prayers echoed through the dark void that surrounded the tormented captive soul, and the unexpected mercy was obtained for it through an angel's tears. As in thought Ingé seemed to act over again every sin she had committed on earth, she trembled, and tears she had never yet been able to weep rushed to her eyes. It seemed impossible that the gates of mercy could ever be opened to her; but while she acknowledged this in deep penitence, a beam of radiant light shot suddenly into the depths upon her. More powerful than the sunbeam that dissolves the man of snow which the children have raised, more quickly than the snowflake melts and becomes a drop of water on the warm lips of a child, was the stony form of Ingé changed, and as a little bird she soared, with the speed of lightning, upward to the world of mortals. A bird that felt timid and shy to all things around it, that seemed to shrink with shame from meeting any living creature, and hurriedly sought to conceal itself in a dark corner of an old ruined wall; there it sat cowering and unable to utter a sound, for it was voiceless. Yet how quickly the little bird discovered the beauty of everything around it. The sweet, fresh air; the soft radiance of the moon, as its light spread over the earth; the fragrance which exhaled from bush and tree, made it feel happy as it sat there clothed in its fresh, bright plumage. All creation seemed to speak of beneficence and love. The bird wanted to give utterance to thoughts that stirred in his breast, as the cuckoo and the nightingale in the spring, but it could not. Yet in heaven can be heard the song of praise, even from a worm; and the notes trembling in the breast of the bird were as audible to Heaven even as the psalms of David before they had fashioned themselves into words and song.

Christmas-time drew near, and a peasant who dwelt close by the old wall stuck up a pole with some ears of corn fastened to the top, that the birds of heaven might have feast, and rejoice in the happy, blessed time. And on Christmas morning the sun arose and shone upon the ears of corn, which were quickly surrounded by a number of twittering birds. Then, from a hole in the wall, gushed forth in song the swelling thoughts of the bird as he issued from his hiding place to perform his first good deed on earth,—and in heaven it was well known who that bird was.

The winter was very hard; the ponds were covered with ice, and there was very little food for either the beasts of the field or the birds of the air. Our little bird flew away into the public roads, and found here and there, in the ruts of the sledges, a grain of corn, and at the halting places some crumbs. Of these he ate only a few, but he called around him the other birds and the hungry sparrows, that they too might have food. He flew into the towns, and looked about, and wherever a kind hand had strewed bread on the windowsill for the birds, he only ate a single crumb himself, and gave all the rest to the rest of the other birds. In the course of the winter the bird had in this way collected many crumbs and given them to other birds, till they equalled the weight of the loaf on which Ingé had trod to keep her shoes clean; and when the last bread-crumb had been found and given, the gray wings of the bird became white, and spread themselves out for flight.

"See, yonder is a sea-gull!" cried the children, when they saw the white bird, as it dived into the sea, and rose again into the clear sunlight, white and glittering. But no one could tell whither it went then, although some declared it flew straight to the sun.

# THE SWINEHERD

Once upon a time lived a poor prince; his kingdom was very small, but it was large enough to enable him to marry, and marry he would. It was rather bold of him that he went and asked the emperor's daughter: "Will you marry me?" but he ventured to do so, for his name was known far and wide, and there were hundreds of princesses who would have gladly accepted him, but would she do so? Now we shall see.

On the grave of the prince's father grew a rose-tree, the most beautiful of its kind. It bloomed only once in five years, and then it had only one single rose upon it, but what a rose! It had such a sweet scent that one instantly forgot all sorrow and grief when one smelt it. He had also a nightingale, which could sing as if every sweet melody was in its throat. This rose and the nightingale he wished to give to the princess; and therefore both were put into big silver cases and sent to her.

The emperor ordered them to be carried into the great hall where the princess was just playing "Visitors are coming" with her ladies-in-waiting; when she saw the large cases with the presents therein, she clapped her hands for joy.

"I wish it were a little pussy cat," she said. But then the rose-tree with the beautiful rose was unpacked.

"Oh, how nicely it is made," exclaimed the ladies.

"It is more than nice," said the emperor, "it is charming."

The princess touched it and nearly began to cry.

"For shame, pa," she said, "it is not artificial, it is natural!"

"For shame, it is natural" repeated all her ladies.

"Let us first see what the other case contains before we are angry," said the emperor; then the nightingale was taken out, and it sang so beautifully that no one could possibly say anything unkind about it.

"*Superbe, charmant,*" said the ladies of the court, for they all prattled French, one worse than the other.

"How much the bird reminds me of the musical box of the late lamented empress," said an old courier, "it has exactly the same tone, the same execution."

"You are right," said the emperor, and began to cry like a little child.

"I hope it is not natural," said the princess.

"Yes, certainly it is natural," replied those who had brought the presents.

"Then let it fly," said the princess, and refused to see the prince.

But the prince was not discouraged. He painted his face, put on common clothes, pulled his cap over his forehead, and came back.

"Good day, emperor," he said, "could you not give me some employment at the court?"

"There are so many," replied the emperor, "who apply for places, that for the present I have no vacancy, but I will remember you. But wait a moment; it just comes into my mind, I require somebody to look after my pigs, for I have a great many."

Thus the prince was appointed imperial swineherd, and as such he lived in a wretchedly small room near the pigsty; there he worked all day long, and when it was night he had made a pretty little pot. There were little bells round the rim, and when the water began to boil in it, the bells began to play the old tune:

> "A jolly old sow once lived in a sty,
> Three little piggies had she," &c.

But what was more wonderful was that, when one put a finger into the steam rising from the pot, one could at once smell what meals they were preparing on every fire in the whole town. That was indeed much more remarkable than the rose. When the princess with her ladies passed by and heard the tune, she stopped and looked quite pleased, for she also could play it—in fact, it was the only tune she could play, and she played it with one finger.

"That is the tune I know," she exclaimed. "He must be a well-educated swineherd. Go and ask him how much the instrument is."

One of the ladies had to go and ask; but she put on pattens.

"What will you take for your pot?" asked the lady.

"I will have ten kisses from the princess," said the swineherd.

"God forbid," said the lady.

"Well, I cannot sell it for less," replied the swineherd.

"What did he say?" said the princess.

"I really cannot tell you," replied the lady.

"You can whisper it into my ear."

"It is very naughty," said the princess, and walked off.

But when she had gone a little distance, the bells rang again so sweetly:

> "A jolly old sow once lived in a sty,
> Three little piggies had she," &c.

"Ask him," said the princess, "if he will be satisfied with ten kisses from one of my ladies."

"No, thank you," said the swineherd: "ten kisses from the princess, or I keep my pot."

"That is tiresome," said the princess. "But you must stand before me, so that nobody can see it."

The ladies placed themselves in front of her and spread out their dresses, and she gave the swineherd ten kisses and received the pot.

That was a pleasure! Day and night the water in the pot was boiling; there was not a single fire in the whole town of which they did not know what was preparing on it, the chamberlain's as well as the shoemaker's. The ladies danced and clapped their hands for joy.

"We know who will eat soup and pancakes; we know who will eat porridge and cutlets; oh, how interesting!"

"Very interesting, indeed," said the mistress of the household. "But you must not betray me, for I am the emperor's daughter."

"Of course not," they all said.

The swineherd—that is to say, the prince—but they did not know otherwise than that he was a real swineherd—did not waste a single day without doing something; he made a rattle, which, when turned quickly round, played all the waltzes, galops, and polkas known since the creation of the world.

"But that is *superbe*," said the princess passing by. "I have never heard a more beautiful composition. Go down and ask him what the instrument costs; but I shall not kiss him again."

"He will have a hundred kisses from the princess," said the lady, who had gone down to ask him.

"I believe he is mad," said the princess, and walked off, but soon she stopped. "One must encourage art," she said. "I am the emperor's daughter! Tell him I will give him ten kisses, as I did the other day; the remainder one of my ladies can give him."

"But we do not like to kiss him" said the ladies.

"That is nonsense," said the princess; "if I can kiss him, you can also do it. Remember that I give you food and employment." And the lady had to go down once more.

"A hundred kisses from the princess," said the swineherd, "or everybody keeps his own."

"Place yourselves before me," said the princess then. They did as they were bidden, and the princess kissed him.

"I wonder what that crowd near the pigsty means!" said the emperor, who had just come out on his balcony. He rubbed his eyes and put his spectacles on.

"The ladies of the court are up to some mischief, I think. I shall have to go down and see." He pulled up his shoes, for they were down at the heels, and he was very quick about it. When he had come down into the courtyard he walked quite softly, and the ladies were so busily engaged in counting the kisses, that all should be fair, that they did not notice the emperor. He raised himself on tiptoe.

"What does this mean?" he said, when he saw that his daughter was kissing the swineherd, and then hit their heads with his shoe just as the swineherd received the sixty-eighth kiss.

"Go out of my sight," said the emperor, for he was very angry; and both the princess and the swineherd were banished from the empire.

THE SWINEHERD

There she stood and cried, the swineherd scolded her, and the rain came down in torrents.

"Alas, unfortunate creature that I am!" said the princess, "I wish I had accepted the prince. Oh, how wretched I am!"

The swineherd went behind a tree, wiped his face, threw off his poor attire and stepped forth in his princely garments; he looked so beautiful that the princess could not help bowing to him.

"I have now learnt to despise you," he said. "You refused an honest prince; you did not appreciate the rose and the nightingale; but you did not mind kissing a swineherd for his toys; you have no one but yourself to blame!"

And then he returned into his kingdom and left her behind. She could now sing at her leisure:

> "A jolly old sow once lived in a sty,
> Three little piggies has she," &c.

# LITTLE CLAUS AND BIG CLAUS

In a village there once lived two men who had the same name. They were both called Claus. One of them had four horses, but the other had only one; so to distinguish them, people called the owner of the four horses, "Great Claus," and he who had only one, "Little Claus." Now we shall hear what happened to them, for this is a true story.

Through the whole week, Little Claus was obliged to plough for Great Claus, and lend him his one horse; and once a week, on a Sunday, Great Claus lent him all his four horses. Then how Little Claus would smack his whip over all five horses; they were as good as his own on that one day. The sun shone brightly, and the church bells were ringing merrily as the people passed by, dressed in their best clothes, with their prayer-books under their arms. They were going to hear the clergyman preach. They looked at Little Claus ploughing with his five horses, and he was so proud that he smacked his whip, and said, "Gee-up, my five horses."

"You must not say that," said Big Claus; "for only one of them belongs to you." But Little Claus soon forgot what he ought to say, and when any one passed he would call out, "Gee-up, my five horses!"

"Now I must beg you not to say that again," said Big Claus; "for if you do, I shall hit your horse on the head, so that he will drop dead on the spot, and there will be an end of him."

"I promise you I will not say it any more," said the other; but as soon as people came by, nodding to him, and wishing him "Good day," he became so pleased, and thought how grand it looked to have five horses ploughing in his field, that he cried out again, "Gee-up, all my horses!"

"I'll gee-up your horses for you," said Big Claus; and seizing a hammer, he struck the one horse of Little Claus on the head, and he fell dead instantly.

"Oh, now I have no horse at all, said Little Claus, weeping. But after a while he took off the dead horse's skin, and hung the hide to dry in the wind. Then he put the dry skin into a bag, and, placing it over his shoulder, went out into the next town to sell the horse's skin. He had a very long way to go, and had to pass through a dark, gloomy forest. Presently a storm arose, and he lost his way, and before he discovered the right path, evening came on, and it was still a long way to the town, and too far to return home before night. Near the road stood a large farmhouse. The shutters outside the windows were closed, but lights shone through the crevices at the top. "I might get permission to stay here for the night," thought Little Claus; so he went up to the door and knocked. The farmer's wife opened the door; but when she heard what he wanted, she told him to go away, as her husband would not allow her to admit strangers. "Then I shall be obliged to lie out here." said Little Claus to himself, as the farmer's wife shut the door in his face. Near to the farmhouse stood a large haystack, and between it and the house was a small shed, with a thatched roof. "I can lie up there," said Little Claus, as he saw the roof; "it will make a famous bed, but I hope the stork will not fly down and bite my legs;" for on it stood a living stork, whose nest was in the roof. So Little Claus climbed to the roof of the shed, and while he turned himself to get comfortable, he discovered that the wooden shutters, which were closed, did not reach to the tops of the windows of the farmhouse, so that he could see into a room, in which a large table was laid out with wine, roast meat, and a splendid fish. The farmer's wife and the sexton were sitting at the table together; and she filled his glass, and helped him plenteously to fish, which appeared to be his favorite dish. "If I could only get some, too," thought Little Claus; and then, as he stretched his neck towards the window he spied a large, beautiful pie,—indeed they had a glorious feast before them.

At this moment he heard some one riding down the road, towards the farmhouse. It was the farmer returning home. He was a good man, but still he had a very strange prejudice,—he could not bear the sight of a sexton. If one appeared before him, he would put himself in a terrible rage. In consequence of this dislike, the sexton had gone to visit the farmer's wife during her husband's absence from home, and the good woman had placed before him the best she had in the house to eat. When she heard the farmer coming she was frightened, and begged the sexton to hide himself in a large empty chest that stood in the room. He did so, for he knew her husband could not endure the sight of a sexton. The woman then quickly put away the wine, and hid all the rest of the nice things in the oven; for if her husband had seen them he would have asked what they were brought out for.

"Oh, dear," sighed Little Claus from the top of the shed, as he saw all the good things disappear.

"Is any one up there?" asked the farmer, looking up and discovering Little Claus. "Why are you lying up there? Come down, and come into the house with me." So Little Claus came down and told the farmer how he had lost his way and begged for a night's lodging.

"All right," said the farmer; "but we must have something to eat first."

The woman received them both very kindly, laid the cloth on a large table, and placed before them a dish of porridge. The farmer was very hungry, and ate his porridge with a good appetite, but Little Claus could not help thinking of the nice roast meat, fish and pies, which he knew were in the oven. Under the table, at his feet, lay the sack containing the horse's skin, which he intended to sell at the next town. Now Little Claus did not relish the porridge at all, so he trod with his foot on the sack under the table, and the dry skin squeaked quite loud. "Hush!" said Little Claus to his sack, at the same time treading upon it again, till it squeaked louder than before.

"Hallo! what have you got in your sack!" asked the farmer.

"Oh, it is a conjuror," said Little Claus; "and he says we need not eat porridge, for he has conjured the oven full of roast meat, fish, and pie."

"Wonderful!" cried the farmer, starting up and opening the oven door; and there lay all the nice things hidden by the farmer's wife, but which he supposed had been conjured there by the wizard under the table. The woman dared not say anything; so she placed the things before them, and they both ate of the fish, the meat, and the pastry.

Then Little Claus trod again upon his sack, and it squeaked as before. "What does he say now?" asked the farmer.

"He says," replied Little Claus, "that there are three bottles of wine for us, standing in the corner, by the oven."

So the woman was obliged to bring out the wine also, which she had hidden, and the farmer drank it till he became quite merry. He would have liked such a conjuror as Little Claus carried in his sack. "Could he conjure up the evil one?" asked the farmer. "I should like to see him now, while I am so merry."

"Oh, yes!" replied Little Claus, "my conjuror can do anything I ask him,—can you not?" he asked, treading at the same time on the sack till it squeaked. "Do you hear? he answers 'Yes,' but he fears that we shall not like to look at him."

"Oh, I am not afraid. What will he be like?"

"Well, he is very much like a sexton."

"Ha!" said the farmer, "then he must be ugly. Do you know I cannot endure the sight of a sexton. However, that doesn't matter, I shall know who it is; so I shall not mind. Now then, I have got up my courage, but don't let him come too near me."

"Stop, I must ask the conjuror," said Little Claus; so he trod on the bag, and stooped his ear down to listen.

"What does he say?"

"He says that you must go and open that large chest which stands in the corner, and you will see the evil one crouching down inside; but you must hold the lid firmly, that he may not slip out."

"Will you come and help me hold it?" said the farmer, going towards the chest in which his wife had hidden the sexton, who now lay inside, very much frightened. The farmer opened the lid a very little way, and peeped in.

LITTLE CLAUS AND BIG CLAUS

"Oh," cried he, springing backwards, "I saw him, and he is exactly like our sexton. How dreadful it is!" So after that he was obliged to drink again, and they sat and drank till far into the night.

"You must sell your conjuror to me," said the farmer; "ask as much as you like, I will pay it; indeed I would give you directly a whole bushel of gold."

"No, indeed, I cannot," said Little Claus; "only think how much profit I could make out of this conjuror."

"But I should like to have him," said the farmer, still continuing his entreaties.

"Well," said Little Claus at length, "you have been so good as to give me a night's lodging, I will not refuse you; you shall have the conjuror for a bushel of money, but I will have quite full measure."

"So you shall," said the farmer; "but you must take away the chest as well. I would not have it in the house another hour; there is no knowing if *he* may not be still there."

So Little Claus gave the farmer the sack containing the dried horse's skin, and received in exchange a bushel of money—full measure. The farmer also gave him a wheelbarrow on which to carry away the chest and the gold.

"Farewell," said Little Claus, as he went off with his money and the great chest, in which the sexton lay still concealed. On one side of the forest was a broad, deep river, the water flowed so rapidly that very few were able to swim against the stream. A new bridge had lately been built across it, and in the middle of this bridge Little Claus stopped, and said, loud enough to be heard by the sexton, "Now what shall I do with this stupid chest; it is as heavy as if it were full of stones: I shall be tired if I roll it any farther, so I may as well throw it in the river; if it swims after me to my house, well and good, and if not, it will not much matter."

So he seized the chest in his hand and lifted it up a little, as if he were going to throw it into the water.

"No, leave it alone," cried the sexton from within the chest; "let me out first."

"Oh," exclaimed Little Claus, pretending to be frightened, "he is in there still, is he? I must throw him into the river, that he may be drowned."

"Oh, no; oh, no," cried the sexton; "I will give you a whole bushel full of money if you will let me go."

"Why, that is another matter," said Little Claus, opening the chest. The sexton crept out, pushed the empty chest into the water, and went to his house, then he measured out a whole bushel full of gold for Little Claus, who had already received one from the farmer, so that now he had a barrow full.

"I have been well paid for my horse," said he to himself when he reached home, entered his own room, and emptied all his money into a heap on the floor. "How vexed Great Claus will be when he finds out how rich I have become all through my one horse; but I shall not tell him exactly how it all happened." Then he sent a boy to Great Claus to borrow a bushel measure.

"What can he want it for?" thought Great Claus; so he smeared the bottom of the measure with tar, that some of whatever was put into it might stick there and remain. And so it happened; for when the measure returned, three new silver florins were sticking to it.

"What does this mean?" said Great Claus; so he ran off directly to Little Claus, and asked, "Where did you get so much money?"

"Oh, for my horse's skin, I sold it yesterday."

"It was certainly well paid for then," said Great Claus; and he ran home to his house, seized a hatchet, and knocked all his four horses on the head, flayed off their skins, and took them to the town to sell. "Skins, skins, who'll buy skins?" he cried, as he went through the streets. All the shoemakers and tanners came running, and asked how much he wanted for them.

"A bushel of money, for each," replied Great Claus.

"Are you mad?" they all cried; "do you think we have money to spend by the bushel?"

"Skins, skins," he cried again, "who'll buy skins?" but to all who inquired the price, his answer was, "a bushel of money."

"He is making fools of us," said they all; then the shoemakers took their straps, and the tanners their leather aprons, and began to beat Great Claus.

"Skins, skins," they cried, mocking him; "yes, we'll mark your skin for you, till it is black and blue."

"Out of the town with him," said they. And Great Claus was obliged to run as fast as he could, he had never before been so thoroughly beaten.

"Ah," said he, as he came to his house; "Little Claus shall pay me for this; I will beat him to death."

Meanwhile the old grandmother of Little Claus died. She had been cross, unkind, and really spiteful to him; but he was very sorry, and took the dead woman and laid her in his warm bed to see if he could bring her to life again. There he determined that she should lie the whole night, while he seated himself in a chair in a corner of the room as he had often done before. During the night, as he sat there, the door opened, and in came Great Claus with a hatchet. He knew well where Little Claus's bed stood; so he went right up to it, and struck the old grandmother on the head, thinking it must be Little Claus.

"There," cried he, "now you cannot make a fool of me again;" and then he went home.

"That is a very wicked man," thought Little Claus; "he meant to kill me. It is a good thing for my old grandmother that she was already dead, or he would have taken her life." Then he dressed his old grandmother in her best clothes, borrowed a horse of his neighbor, and harnessed it to a cart. Then he placed the old woman on the back seat, so that she might not fall out as he drove, and rode away through the wood. By sunrise they reached a large inn, where Little Claus stopped and went to get something to eat. The landlord was a rich man, and a good man too; but as passionate as if he had been made of pepper and snuff.

"Good morning," said he to Little Claus; "you are come betimes to-day."

"Yes," said Little Claus; "I am going to the town with my old grandmother; she is sitting at the back of the wagon, but I cannot bring her into the room. Will you take her a glass of mead? but you must speak very loud, for she cannot hear well."

"Yes, certainly I will," replied the landlord; and, pouring out a glass of mead, he carried it out to the dead grandmother, who sat upright in the cart. "Here is a glass of mead from your grandson," said the landlord. The dead woman did not answer a word, but sat quite still. "Do you not hear?" cried the landlord as loud as he could; "here is a glass of mead from your grandson."

Again and again he bawled it out, but as she did not stir he flew into a passion, and threw the glass of mead in her face; it struck her on the nose, and she fell backwards out of the cart, for she was only seated there, not tied in.

"Hallo!" cried Little Claus, rushing out of the door, and seizing hold of the landlord by the throat; "you have killed my grandmother; see, here is a great hole in her forehead."

"Oh, how unfortunate," said the landlord, wringing his hands. "This all comes of my fiery temper. Dear Little Claus, I will give you a bushel of money; I will bury your grandmother as if she were my own; only keep silent, or else they will cut off my head, and that would be disagreeable."

So it happened that Little Claus received another bushel of money, and the landlord buried his old grandmother as if she had been his own. When Little Claus reached home again, he immediately sent a boy to Great Claus, requesting him to lend him a bushel measure. "How is this? thought Great Claus; "did I not kill him? I must go and see for myself." So he went to Little Claus, and took the bushel measure with him. "How did you get all this money?" asked Great Claus, staring with wide open eyes at his neighbor's treasures.

"You killed my grandmother instead of me," said Little Claus; "so I have sold her for a bushel of money."

"That is a good price at all events," said Great Claus. So he went home, took a hatchet, and killed his old grandmother with one blow. Then he placed her on a cart, and drove into the town to the apothecary, and asked him if he would buy a dead body.

"Whose is it, and where did you get it?" asked the apothecary.

"It is my grandmother," he replied; "I killed her with a blow, that I might get a bushel of money for her."

"Heaven preserve us!" cried the apothecary, "you are out of your mind. Don't say such things, or you will lose your head." And then he talked to him seriously about the wicked deed he had done, and told him that such a wicked man would surely be punished. Great Claus got so frightened that he rushed out of the surgery, jumped into the cart, whipped up his horses, and drove home quickly. The apothecary and all the people thought him mad, and let him drive where he liked.

"You shall pay for this," said Great Claus, as soon as he got into the high-road, "that you shall, Little Claus." So as soon as he reached home he took the largest sack he could find and went over to Little Claus. "You have played me another trick," said he. "First, I killed all my horses, and then my old grandmother, and it is all your fault; but you shall not make a fool of me any more." So he laid hold of Little Claus round the body, and pushed him into the sack, which he took on his shoulders, saying, "Now I'm going to drown you in the river."

He had a long way to go before he reached the river, and Little Claus was not a very light weight to carry. The road led by the church, and as they passed he could hear the organ playing and the people singing beautifully. Great Claus put down the sack close to the church-door, and thought he might as well go in and hear a psalm before he went any farther. Little Claus could not possibly get out of the sack, and all the people were in church; so in he went.

"Oh dear, oh dear," sighed Little Claus in the sack, as he turned and twisted about; but he found he could not loosen the string with which it was tied. Presently an old cattle driver, with snowy hair, passed by, carrying a large staff in his hand, with which he drove a large herd of cows and oxen before him. They stumbled against the sack in which lay Little Claus, and turned it over. "Oh dear," sighed Little Claus, "I am very young, yet I am soon going to heaven."

"And I, poor fellow," said the drover, "I, who am so old already, cannot get there."

"Open the sack," cried Little Claus; "creep into it instead of me, and you will soon be there."

"With all my heart," replied the drover, opening the sack, from which sprung Little Claus as quickly as possible. "Will you take care of my cattle?" said the old man, as he crept into the bag.

"Yes," said Little Claus, and he tied up the sack, and then walked off with all the cows and oxen.

When Great Claus came out of church, he took up the sack, and placed it on his shoulders. It appeared to have become lighter, for the old drover was not half so heavy as Little Claus.

"How light he seems now," said he. "Ah, it is because I have been to a church." So he walked on to the river, which was deep and broad, and threw the sack containing the old drover into the water, believing it to be Little Claus. "There you may lie!" he exclaimed; "you will play me no more tricks now." Then he turned to go home, but when he came to a place where two roads crossed, there was Little Claus driving the cattle. "How is this?" said Great Claus. "Did I not drown you just now?"

"Yes," said Little Claus; "you threw me into the river about half an hour ago."

"But wherever did you get all these fine beasts?" asked Great Claus.

"These beasts are sea-cattle," replied Little Claus. "I'll tell you the whole story, and thank you for drowning me; I am above you now, I am really very rich. I was frightened, to be sure, while I lay tied up in the sack, and the wind whistled in my ears when you threw me into the river from the bridge, and I sank to the bottom immediately; but I did not hurt myself, for I fell upon beautifully soft grass which grows down there; and in a moment, the sack opened, and the sweetest little maiden came towards me. She had snow-white robes, and a wreath of green leaves on her wet hair. She took me by the hand, and said, 'So you are come, Little Claus, and here are some cattle for you to begin with. About a mile farther on the road, there is another herd for you.' Then I saw that the river formed a great highway for the people who live in the sea. They were walking and driving here and there from the sea to the land at the spot where the river terminates. The bed of the river was covered with the loveliest flowers and sweet fresh grass. The fish swam past me as rapidly as the birds do here in the air. How handsome all the people were, and what fine cattle were grazing on the hills and in the valleys!"

"But why did you come up again," said Gread Claus, "if it was all so beautiful down there? I should not have done so."

"Well, said Little Claus, "it was good policy on my part; you heard me say just now that I was told by the sea-maiden to go a mile farther on the road, and I should find a whole herd of cattle. By the road she meant the river, for she could not travel any other way; but I knew the winding of the river, and how it bends, sometimes to the right and sometimes to the left, and it seemed a long way, so I chose a shorter one; and, by coming up to the land, and then driving across the fields back again to the river, I shall save half a mile, and get all my cattle more quickly."

"What a lucky fellow you are!" exclaimed Great Claus. "Do you think I should get any sea-cattle if I went down to the bottom of the river?"

"Yes, I think so," said Little Claus; "but I cannot carry you there in a sack, you are too heavy. However if you will go there first, and then creep into a sack, I will throw you in with the greatest pleasure."

"Thank you," said Great Claus; "but remember, if I do not get any sea-cattle down there I shall come up again and give you a good thrashing."

"No, now, don't be too fierce about it!" said Little Claus, as they walked on towards the river. When they approached it, the cattle, who were very thirsty, saw the stream, and ran down to drink.

"See what a hurry they are in," said Little Claus, "they are longing to get down again."

"Come, help me, make haste," said Great Claus; "or you'll get beaten." So he crept into a large sack, which had been lying across the back of one of the oxen.

"Put in a stone," said Great Claus, "or I may not sink."

"Oh, there's not much fear of that," he replied; still he put a large stone into the bag, and then tied it tightly, and gave it a push.

"Plump!" In went Great Claus, and immediately sank to the bottom of the river.

"I'm afraid he will not find any cattle," said Little Claus, and then he drove his own beasts homewards.

# THE FLYING TRUNK

THERE WAS once a merchant who was so rich that he could have paved the whole street with gold, and would even then have had enough for a small alley. But he did not do so; he knew the value of money better than to use it in this way. So clever was he, that every shilling he put out brought him a crown; and so he continued till he died. His son inherited his wealth, and he lived a merry life with it; he went to a masquerade every night, made kites out of five pound notes, and threw pieces of gold into the sea instead of stones, making ducks and drakes of them. In this manner he soon lost all his money. At last he had nothing left but a pair of slippers, an old dressing-gown, and four shillings. And now all his friends deserted him, they could not walk with him in the streets; but one of them, who was very good-natured, sent him an old trunk with this message, "Pack up!" "Yes," he said, "it is all very well to say 'pack up,'" but he had nothing left to pack up, therefore he seated himself in the trunk. It was a very wonderful trunk; no sooner did any one press on the lock than the trunk could fly. He shut the lid and pressed the lock, when away flew the trunk up the chimney with the merchant's son in it, right up into the clouds. Whenever the bottom of the trunk cracked, he was in a great fright, for if the trunk fell to pieces he would have made a tremendous somerset over the trees. However, he got safely in his trunk to the land of Turkey. He hid the trunk in the wood under some dry leaves, and then went into the town: he could do this very well, for the Turks always go about dressed in dressing-gowns and slippers, as he was himself. He happened to meet a nurse with a little child. "I say, you Turkish nurse," cried he, "what castle is that near the town, with the windows placed so high?"

"The king's daughter lives there," she replied; "it has been prophesied that she will be very unhappy about a lover, and therefore no one is allowed to visit her, unless the king and queen are present."

"Thank you," said the merchant's son. So he went back to the wood, seated himself in his trunk, flew up to the roof of the castle, and crept through the window into the princess's room. She lay on the sofa asleep, and she was so beautiful that the merchant's son could not help kissing her. Then she awoke, and was very much frightened; but he told her he was a Turkish angel, who had come down through the air to see her, which pleased her very much. He sat down by her side and talked to her: he said her eyes were like beautiful dark lakes, in which the thoughts swam about like little mermaids, and he told her that her forehead was a snowy mountain, which contained splendid halls full of pictures. And then he related to her about the stork who brings the beautiful children from the rivers. These were delightful stories; and when he asked the princess if she would marry him, she consented immediately.

"But you must come on Saturday," she said; "for then the king and queen will take tea with me. They will be very proud when they find that I am going to marry a Turkish angel; but you must think of some very pretty stories to tell them, for my parents like to hear stories better than anything. My mother prefers one that is deep and moral; but my father likes something funny, to make him laugh."

"Very well," he replied; "I shall bring you no other marriage portion than a story," and so they parted. But the princess gave him a sword which was studded with gold coins, and these he could use.

Then he flew away to the town and bought a new dressing-gown, and afterwards returned to the wood, where he composed a story, so as to be ready for Saturday, which was no easy matter. It was ready however by Saturday, when he went to see the princess. The king, and queen, and the whole court, were at tea with the princess; and he was received with great politeness.

"Will you tell us a story?" said the queen,—"one that is instructive and full of deep learning."

"Yes, but with something in it to laugh at," said the king.

"Certainly," he replied, and commenced at once, asking them to listen attentively. "There was once a bundle of matches that were exceedingly proud of their high descent. Their genealogical tree, that is, a large pine-tree from which they had been cut, was at one time a large, old tree in the wood. The matches now lay between a tinder-box and an old iron saucepan, and were talking about their youthful days. 'Ah! then we grew on the green boughs, and were as green as they; every morning and evening we were fed with diamond drops of dew. Whenever the sun shone, we felt his warm rays, and the little birds would relate stories to us as they sung. We knew that we were rich, for the other trees only wore their green dress in summer, but our family were able to array themselves in green, summer and winter. But the wood-cutter came, like a great revolution, and our family fell under the axe. The head of the house obtained a situation as mainmast in a very fine ship, and can sail round the world when he will. The other branches of the family were taken to different places, and our office now is to kindle a light for common people. This is how such high-born people as we came to be in a kitchen.'

" 'Mine has been a very different fate,' said the iron pot, which stood by the matches; 'from my first entrance into the world I have been used to cooking and scouring. I am the first in this house, when anything solid or useful is required. My only pleasure is to be made clean and shining after dinner, and to sit in my place and have a little sensible conversation with my neighbors. All of us, excepting the water-bucket, which is sometimes taken into the courtyard, live here together within these four walls. We get our news from the market-basket, but he sometimes tells us very unpleasant things about the people and the government. Yes, and one day an old pot was so alarmed, that he fell down and was broken to pieces. He was a liberal, I can tell you.'

" 'You are talking too much,' said the tinder-box, and the steel struck against the flint till some sparks flew out, crying. 'We want a merry evening, don't we?'

" 'Yes, of course,' said the matches, 'let us talk about those who are the highest born.'

" 'No, I don't like to be always talking of what we are,' remarked the saucepan; 'let us think of some other amusement; I will begin. We will tell something that has happened to ourselves; that will be very easy, and interesting as well. On the Baltic Sea, near the Danish shore'——

" 'What a pretty commencement!' said the plates; 'we shall all like that story, I am sure.'

THE FLYING TRUNK

" 'Yes; well in my youth, I lived in a quiet family, where the furniture was polished, the floors scoured, and clean curtains put up every fortnight.'

" 'What an interesting way you have of relating a story,' said the carpet-broom; 'it is easy to perceive that you have been a great deal in women's society, there is something so pure runs through what you say.'

" 'That is quite true,' said the water-bucket; and he made a spring with joy, and splashed some water on the floor.

"Then the saucepan went on with his story, and the end was as good as the beginning.

"The plates rattled with pleasure, and the carpet-broom brought some green parsley out of the dust-hole and crowned the saucepan, for he knew it would vex the others; and he thought, 'If I crown him to-day he will crown me to-morrow.'

" 'Now, let us have a dance,' said the fire-tongs; and then how they danced and stuck up one leg in the air. The chair-cushion in the corner burst with laughter when she saw it.

" 'Shall I be crowned now?' asked the fire-tongs; so the broom found another wreath for the tongs.

" 'They were only common people after all,' thought the matches. The tea-urn was now asked to sing, but she said she had a cold, and could not sing without boiling heat. They all thought this was affectation, and because she did not wish to sing excepting in the parlor, when on the table with the grand people.

"In the window sat an old quill-pen, with which the maid generally wrote. There was nothing remarkable about the pen, excepting that it had been dipped too deeply in the ink, but it was proud of that.

" 'If the tea-urn won't sing; said the pen, 'she can leave it alone; there is a nightingale in a cage who can sing; she has not been taught much, certainly, but we need not say anything this evening about that.'

" 'I think it highly improper,' said the tea-kettle, who was kitchen singer, and half-brother to the tea-urn, 'that a rich foreign bird should be listened to here. Is it patriotic? Let the market-basket decide what is right.'

" 'I certainly am vexed,' said the basket; 'inwardly vexed, more than any one can imagine. Are we spending the evening properly? Would it not be more sensible to put the house in order? If each were in his own place I would lead a game; this would be quite another thing.'

" 'Let us act a play,' said they all. At the same moment the door opened, and the maid came in. Then not one stirred; they all remained quite still; yet, at the same time, there was not a single pot amongst them who had not a high opinion of himself, and of what he could do if he chose.

" 'Yes, if we had chosen,' they each thought, 'we might have spent a very pleasant evening.'

"The maid took the matches and lighted them; dear me, how they sputtered and blazed up!

" 'Now then,' they thought, 'every one will see that we are the first. How we shine; what a light we give!' Even while they spoke their light went out."

"What a capital story," said the queen, "I feel as if I were really in the kitchen, and could see the matches; yes, you shall marry our daughter."

"Certainly," said the king, "thou shalt have our daughter." The king said *thou* to him because he was going to be one of the family. The wedding-day was fixed, and, on the evening before, the whole city was illuminated. Cakes and sweetmeats were thrown among the people. The street boys stood on tip-toe and shouted "hurrah," and whistled between their fingers; altogether it was a very splendid affair.

"I will give them another treat," said the merchant's son. So he went and bought rockets and crackers, and all sorts of fireworks that could be thought of; packed them in his trunk, and flew up with it into the air. What a whizzing and popping they made as they went off! The Turks, when they saw such a sight in the air, jumped so high that their slippers flew about their ears. It was easy to believe after this that the princess was really going to marry a Turkish angel.

As soon as the merchant's son had come down in his flying trunk to the wood after the fireworks, he thought, "I will go back into the town now, and hear what they think of the entertainment." It was very natural that he should wish to know. And what strange things people did say, to be sure! every one whom he questioned had a different tale to tell, though they all thought it very beautiful.

"I saw the Turkish angel myself," said one; "he had eyes like glittering stars, and a head like foaming water."

"He flew in a mantle of fire," cried another, "and lovely little cherubs peeped out from the folds."

He heard many more fine things about himself, and that the next day he was to be married. After this he went back to the forest to rest himself in his trunk. It had disappeared! A spark from the fireworks which remained had set it on fire; it was burnt to ashes! So the merchant's son could not fly any more, nor go to meet his bride. She stood all day on the roof waiting for him, and most likely she is waiting there still; while he wanders through the world telling fairy tales, but none of them so amusing as the one he related about the matches.

# THE NIGHTINGALE

In China, you know, the emperor is a Chinese, and all those about him are Chinamen also. The story I am going to tell you happened a great many years ago, so it is well to hear it now before it is forgotten. The emperor's palace was the most beautiful in the world. It was built entirely of porcelain, and very costly, but so delicate and brittle that whoever touched it was obliged to be careful. In the garden could be seen the most singular flowers, with pretty silver bells tied to them, which tinkled so that every one who passed could not help noticing the flowers. Indeed, everything in the emperor's garden was remarkable, and it extended so far that the gardener himself did not know where it ended. Those who travelled beyond its limits knew that there was a noble forest, with lofty trees, sloping down to the deep blue sea, and the great ships sailed under the shadow of its branches. In one of these trees lived a nightingale, who sang so beautifully that even the poor fishermen, who had so many other things to do, would stop and listen. Sometimes, when they went at night to spread their nets, they would hear her sing, and say, "Oh, is not that beautiful?" But when they returned to their fishing, they forgot the bird until the next night. Then they would hear it again, and exclaim "Oh, how beautiful is the nightingale's song!"

Travellers from every country in the world came to the city of the emperor, which they admired very much, as well as the palace and gardens; but when they heard the nightingale, they all declared it to be the best of all. And the travellers, on their return home, related what they had seen; and learned men wrote books, containing descriptions of the town, the palace, and the gardens; but they did not forget the nightingale, which was really the greatest wonder. And those who could write poetry composed beautiful verses about the nightingale, who lived in a forest near the deep sea. The books travelled all over the world, and some of them came into the hands of the emperor; and he sat in his golden chair, and, as he read, he nodded his approval every moment, for it pleased him to find such a beautiful description of his city, his palace, and his gardens. But when he came to the words, "the nightingale is the most beautiful of all," he exclaimed, "What is this? I know nothing of any nightingale. Is there such a bird in my empire? and even in my garden? I have never heard of it. Something, it appears, may be learnt from books."

Then he called one of his lords-in-waiting, who was so high-bred, that when any in an inferior rank to himself spoke to him, or asked him a question, he would answer, "Pooh," which means nothing.

"There is a very wonderful bird mentioned here, called a nightingale," said the emperor; "they say it is the best thing in my large kingdom. Why have I not been told of it?"

"I have never heard the name," replied the cavalier; "she has not been presented at court."

"It is my pleasure that she shall appear this evening," said the emperor; "the whole world knows what I possess better than I do myself."

"I have never heard of her," said the cavalier; "yet I will endeavor to find her."

But where was the nightingale to be found? The nobleman went up stairs and down, through halls and passages; yet none of those whom he met had heard of the bird. So he returned to the emperor, and said that it must be a fable, invented by those who had written the book. "Your imperial majesty," said he, "cannot believe everything contained in books; sometimes they are only fiction, or what is called the black art."

"But the book in which I have read this account," said the emperor, "was sent to me by the great and mighty emperor of Japan, and therefore it cannot contain a falsehood. I will hear the nightingale, she must be here this evening; she has my highest favor; and if she does not come, the whole court shall be trampled upon after supper is ended."

"Tsing-pe!" cried the lord-in-waiting, and again he ran up and down stairs, through all the halls and corridors; and half the court ran with him, for they did not like the idea of being trampled upon. There was a great inquiry about this wonderful nightingale, whom all the world knew, but who was unknown to the court.

At last they met with a poor little girl in the kitchen, who said, "Oh, yes, I know the nightingale quite well; indeed, she can sing. Every evening I have permission to take home to my poor sick mother the scraps from the table; she lives down by the sea-shore, and as I come back I feel tired, and I sit down in the wood to rest, and listen to the nightingale's song. Then the tears come into my eyes, and it is just as if my mother kissed me."

"Little maiden," said the lord-in-waiting, "I will obtain for you constant employment in the kitchen, and you shall have permission to see the emperor dine, if you will lead us to the nightingale; for she is invited for this evening to the palace." So she went into the wood where the nightingale sang, and half the court followed her. As they went along, a cow began lowing.

"Oh," said a young courtier, "now we have found her; what wonderful power for such a small creature; I have certainly heard it before."

"No, that is only a cow lowing," said the little girl; "we are a long way from the place yet."

Then some frogs began to croak in the marsh.

"Beautiful," said the young courtier again. "Now I hear it, tinkling like little church bells."

"No, those are frogs," said the little maiden; "but I think we shall soon hear her now:" and presently the nightingale began to sing.

"Hark, hark! there she is," said the girl, "and there she sits," she added, pointing to a little gray bird who was perched on a bough.

"Is it possible?" said the lord-in-waiting, "I never imagined it would be a little, plain, simple thing like that. She has certainly changed color at seeing so many grand people around her."

"Little nightingale," cried the girl, raising her voice, "our most gracious emperor wishes you to sing before him."

"With the greatest pleasure," said the nightingale, and began to sing most delightfully.

"It sounds like tiny glass bells," said the lord-in-waiting, "and see how her little throat works. It is surprising that we have never heard this before; she will be a great success at court."

"Shall I sing once more before the emperor?" asked the nightingale, who thought he was present.

"My excellent little nightingale," said the courtier, "I have the great pleasure of inviting you to a court festival this evening, where you will gain imperial favor by your charming song."

"My song sounds best in the green wood," said the bird; but still she came willingly when she heard the emperor's wish.

The palace was elegantly decorated for the occasion. The walls and floors of porcelain glittered in the light of a thousand lamps. Beautiful flowers, round which little bells were tied, stood in the corridors: what with the running to and fro and the draught, these bells tinkled so loudly that no one could speak to be heard. In the centre of the great hall, a golden perch had been fixed for the nightingale to sit on. The whole court was present, and the little kitchen-maid had received permission to stand by the door. She was not installed as a real court cook. All were in full dress, and every eye was turned to the little gray bird when the emperor nodded to her to begin. The nightingale sang so sweetly that the tears came into the emperor's eyes, and then rolled down his cheeks, as her song became still more touching and went to every one's heart. The emperor was so delighted that he declared the nightingale should have his gold slipper to wear round her neck, but she declined the honor with thanks: she had been sufficiently rewarded already. "I have seen tears in an emperor's eyes," she said, "that is my richest reward. An emperor's tears have wonderful power, and are quite sufficient honor for me;" and then she sang again more enchantingly than ever.

"That singing is a lovely gift;" said the ladies of the court to each other; and then they took water in their mouths to make them utter the gurgling sounds of the nightingale when they spoke to any one, so that they might fancy themselves nightingales. And the footmen and chambermaids also expressed their satisfaction, which is saying a great deal, for they are very difficult to please. In fact the nightingale's visit was most successful. She was now to remain at court, to have her own cage, with liberty to go out twice a day, and once during the night. Twelve servants were appointed to attend her on these occasions, who each held her by a silken string fastened to her leg. There was certainly not much pleasure in this kind of flying.

The whole city spoke of the wonderful bird, and when two people met, one said "nightin," and the other said "gale," and they understood what was meant, for nothing else was talked of. Eleven peddlers' children were named after her, but not of them could sing a note.

One day the emperor received a large packet on which was written "The Nightingale." "Here is no doubt a new book about our celebrated bird," said the emperor. But instead of a book, it was a work of art contained in a casket, an artificial nightingale made to look like a living one, and covered all over with diamonds, rubies, and sapphires. As soon as the artificial bird was wound up, it could sing like the real one, and could move its tail up and down, which sparkled with silver and gold. Round its neck hung a piece of ribbon, on which was written "The Emperor of China's nightingale is poor compared with that of the Emperor of Japan's."

"This is very beautiful," exclaimed all who saw it, and he who had brought the artificial bird received the title of "Imperial nightingale-bringer-in-chief."

"Now they must sing together," said the court, "and what a duet it will be." But they did not get on well, for the real nightingale sang in its own natural way, but the artificial bird sang only waltzes.

"That is not a fault," said the music-master, "it is quite perfect to my taste," so then it had to sing alone, and was as successful as the real bird;

besides, it was so much prettier to look at, for it sparkled like bracelets and breast-pins. Three and thirty times did it sing the same tunes without being tired; the people would gladly have heard it again, but the emperor said the living nightingale ought to sing something. But where was she? No one had noticed her when she flew out at the open window, back to her own green woods.

"What strange conduct," said the emperor, when her flight had been discovered; and all the courtiers blamed her, and said she was a very ungrateful creature.

"But we have the best bird after all," said one, and then they would have the bird sing again, although it was the thirty-fourth time they had listened to the same piece, and even then they had not learnt it, for it was rather difficult. But the music-master praised the bird in the highest degree, and even asserted that it was better than a real nightingale, not only in its dress and the beautiful diamonds, but also in its musical power. "For you must perceive, my chief lord and emperor, that with a real nightingale we can never tell what is going to be sung, but with this bird everything is settled. It can be opened and explained, so that people may understand how the waltzes are formed, and why one note follows upon another."

"This is exactly what we think," they all replied, and then the music-master received permission to exhibit the bird to the people on the following Sunday, and the emperor commanded that they should be present to hear it sing. When they heard it they were like people intoxicated; however it must have been with drinking tea, which is quite a Chinese custom. They all said "Oh!" and held up their forefingers and nodded, but a poor fisherman, who had heard the real nightingale, said, "it sounds prettily enough, and the melodies are all alike; yet there seems something wanting, I cannot exactly tell what."

And after this the real nightingale was banished from the empire, and the artificial bird placed on a silk cushion close to the emperor's bed. The presents of gold and precious stones which had been received with it were round the bird, and it was now advanced to the title of "Little Imperial Toilet Singer," and to the rank of No. 1 on the left hand; for the emperor considered the left side, on which the heart lies, as the most noble, and the heart of an emperor is in the same place as that of other people.

The music-master wrote a work, in twenty-five volumes, about the artificial bird, which was very learned and very long, and full of the most difficult Chinese words; yet all the people said they had read it, and understood it, for fear of being thought stupid and having their bodies trampled upon.

So a year passed, and the emperor, the court, and all the other Chinese knew every little turn in the artificial bird's song; and for that same reason it pleased them better. They could sing with the bird, which they often did. The street-boys sang, "Zi-zi-zi, cluck, cluck, cluck," and the emperor himself could sing it also. It was really most amusing.

One evening, when the artificial bird was singing its best, and the emperor lay in bed listening to it, something inside the bird sounded "whizz." Then a spring cracked. "Whir-r-r-r" went all the wheels, running round, and then the music stopped. The emperor immediately sprang out of bed, and called for his physician; but what could he do? Then they sent for a watchmaker; and, after a great deal of talking and examination, the bird was put into something like order; but he said that it must be used very carefully, as the barrels were worn, and it would be impossible to put in new ones without injuring the music. Now there was great sorrow, as the bird could only be allowed to play once a year; and even that was dangerous for the works inside it. Then the music-master made a little speech, full of hard words, and declared that the bird was as good as ever; and, of course, no one contradicted him.

Five years passed, and then a real grief came upon the land. The Chinese really were fond of their emperor, and he now lay so ill that he was not expected to live. Already a new emperor had been chosen and the people who stood in the street asked the lord-in-waiting how the old emperor was; but he only said, "Pooh!" and shook his head.

Cold and pale lay the emperor in his royal bed; the whole court thought he was dead, and every one ran away to pay homage to his successor. The chamberlains went out to have a talk on the matter, and the ladies'-maids invited company to take coffee. Cloth had been laid down on the halls and passages, so that not a footstep should be heard, and all was silent and still. But the emperor was not yet dead, although he lay white and stiff on his gorgeous bed, with the long velvet curtains and heavy gold tassels. A window stood open, and the moon shone in upon the emperor and the artificial bird. The poor emperor, finding he could scarcely breathe with a strange weight on his chest, opened his eyes, and saw Death sitting there. He had put on the emperor's golden crown, and held in one hand his sword of state, and in the other his beautiful banner. All around the bed, and peeping through the long velvet curtains, were a number of strange heads, some very ugly, and others lonely and gentle-looking. These were the emperor's good and bad deeds, which stared him in the face now Death sat at his heart.

"Do you remember this?" "Do you recollect that?" they asked one after another, thus bringing to his remembrance circumstances that made the perspiration stand on his brow.

"I know nothing about it," said the emperor. "Music! music!" he cried; "the large Chinese drum! that I may not hear what they say." But they still went on, and Death nodded like a Chinaman to all they said. "Music! music!" shouted the emperor. "You little precious golden bird, sing, pray sing! I have given you gold and costly presents; I have even hung my golden slipper round your neck. Sing! sing!" But the bird remained silent. There was no one to wind it up, and therefore it could not sing a note.

Death continued to stare at the emperor with his cold, hollow eyes, and the room was fearfully still. Outside, on the bough of a tree, sat the living nightingale. She had heard of the emperor's illness, and was therefore come to sing to him of hope and trust. And as she sung, the shadows grew paler and paler; the blood in the emperor's veins flowed more rapidly, and gave life to his weak limbs; and even Death himself listened,

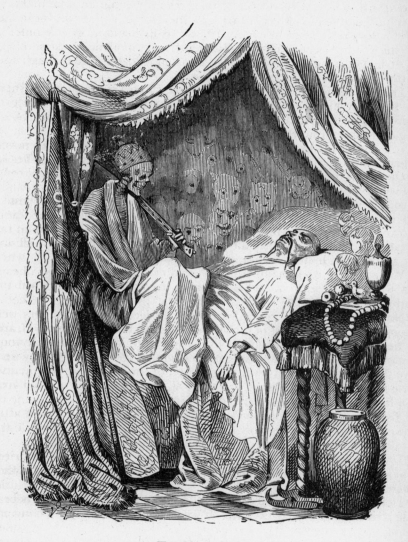

**The Nightingale**

and said, "Go on, little nightingale, go on."

"Then will you give me the beautiful golden sword and that rich banner? and will you give me the emperor's crown?" said the bird.

So Death gave up each of these treasures for a song; and the nightingale continued her singing. She sung of the quiet churchyard, where the white roses grow, where the elder-tree wafts its perfume on the breeze, and the fresh, sweet grass is moistened by the mourners' tears. Then Death longed to go and see his garden, and floated out through the window in the form of a cold, white mist.

"Thanks, thanks, you heavenly little bird. I know you well. I banished you from my kingdom once, and yet you have charmed away the evil faces from my bed, and banished Death from my heart, with your sweet song. How can I reward you?"

"You have already rewarded me," said the nightingale. "I shall never forget that I drew tears from your eyes the first time I sang to you. These are the jewels that rejoice a singer's heart. But now sleep, and grow strong and well again. I will sing to you again."

And as she sung, the emperor fell into a sweet sleep; and how mild and refreshing that slumber was! When he awoke, strengthened and restored, the sun shone brightly through the window; but not one of his servants had returned—they all believed he was dead; only the nightingale still sat beside him, and sang.

"You must always remain with me," said the emperor. "You shall sing only when it pleases you; and I will break the artificial bird into a thousand pieces."

"No; do not do that," replied the nightingale; "the bird did very well as long as it could. Keep it here still. I cannot live in the palace, and build my nest; but let me come when I like. I will sit on a bough outside your window, in the evening, and sing to you, so that you may be happy, and have thoughts full of joy. I will sing to you of those who are happy, and those who suffer; of the good and the evil, who are hidden around you. The little singing bird flies far from you and your court to the home of the fisherman and the peasant's cot. I love your heart better than your crown; and yet something holy lingers round that also. I will come, I will sing to you; but you must promise me one thing."

"Everything," said the emperor, who, having dressed himself in his imperial robes, stood with the hand that held the heavy golden sword pressed to his heart.

"I only ask one thing," she replied; "let no one know that you have a little bird who tells you everything. It will be best to conceal it." So saying, the nightingale flew away.

The servants now came in to look after the dead emperor; when, lo! there he stood, and, to their astonishment, said, "Good morning."

# THE GOBLIN AND THE HUCKSTER

THERE WAS once a regular student, who lived in a garret, and had no possessions. And there was also a regular huckster, to whom the house belonged, and who occupied the ground floor. A goblin lived with the huckster, because at Christmas he always had a large dish full of jam, with a great piece of butter in the middle. The huckster could afford this; and therefore the goblin remained with the huckster, which was very cunning of him.

One evening the student came into the shop through the back door to buy candles and cheese for himself; he had no one to send, and therefore he came himself; he obtained what he wished, and then the huckster and his wife nodded good evening to him, and she was a woman who could do more than merely nod, for she had usually plenty to say for herself. The student nodded in return as he turned to leave, then suddenly stopped, and began reading the piece of paper in which the cheese was wrapped. It was a leaf torn out of an old book, a book that ought not to have been torn up, for it was full of poetry.

"Yonder lies some more of the same sort," said the huckster: "I gave an old woman a few coffee berries for it; you shall have the rest for sixpence, if you will."

"Indeed I will," said the student: "give me the book instead of the cheese; I can eat my bread and butter without cheese. It would be a sin to tear up a book like this. You are a clever man; and a practical man; but you understand no more about poetry than that cask yonder."

This was a very rude speech, especially against the cask; but the huckster and the student both laughed, for it was only said in fun. But the goblin felt very angry that any man should venture to say such things to a huckster who was a householder and sold the best butter. As soon as it was night, and the shop closed, and every one in bed except the student, the goblin stepped softly into the bedroom where the huckster's wife slept, and took away her tongue, which of course, she did not then want. Whatever object in the room he placed his tongue upon immediately received voice and speech, and was able to express its thoughts and feelings as readily as the lady herself could do. It could only be used by one object at a time, which was a good thing, as a number speaking at once would have caused great confusion. The goblin laid the tongue upon the cask, in which lay a quantity of old newspapers.

"Is it really true," he asked, "that you do not know what poetry is?"

"Of course I know," replied the cask: "poetry is something that always stand in the corner of a newspaper, and is sometimes cut out; and I may venture to affirm that I have more of it in me than the student has, and I am only a poor tub of the huckster's."

Then the goblin placed the tongue on the coffee mill; and how it did go to be sure! Then he put it on the butter tub and the cash box, and they all expressed the same opinion as the waste-paper tub; and a majority must always be respected.

"Now I shall go and tell the student," said the goblin; and with these words he went quietly up the back stairs to the garret where the student lived. He had a candle burning still, and the goblin peeped through the keyhole and saw that he was reading in the torn book, which he had brought out of the shop. But how light the room was! From the book shot forth a ray of light which grew broad and full, like the stem of a tree, from which bright rays spread upward and over the student's head. Each leaf was fresh, and each flower was like a beautiful female head; some with dark and sparkling eyes, and others with eyes that were wonderfully blue and clear. The fruit gleamed like stars, and the room was filled with sounds of beautiful music. The little goblin had never imagined, much less seen or heard of, any sight so glorious as this. He stood still on tiptoe, peeping in, till the light went out in the garret. The student no doubt had blown out his candle and gone to bed; but the little goblin remained standing there nevertheless, and listening to the music which still sounded on, soft and beautiful, a sweet cradle-song for the student, who had lain down to rest.

"This is a wonderful place," said the goblin; "I never expected such a thing. I should like to stay here with the student;" and the little man thought it over, for he was a sensible little spirit. At last he sighed, "but the student has no jam!" So he went down stairs again into the huckster's shop, and it was a good thing he got back when he did, for the cask had almost worn out the lady's tongue; he had given a description of all that he contained on one side, and was just about to turn himself over to the other side to describe what was there, when the goblin entered and restored the tongue to the lady. But from that time forward, the whole shop, from the cash box down to the pinewood logs, formed their opinions from that of the cask; and they all had such confidence in him, and treated him with so much respect, that when the huckster read the criticisms on theatricals and art of an evening, they fancied it must all come from the cask.

But after what he had seen, the goblin could no longer sit and listen quietly to the wisdom and understanding down stairs; so, as soon as the evening light glimmered in the garret, he took courage, for it seemed to him as if the rays of light were strong cables, drawing him up, and obliging him to go and peep through the keyhole; and, while there, a feeling of vastness came over him such as we experience by the ever-moving sea, when the storm breaks forth; and it brought tears into his eyes. He did not himself know why he wept, yet a kind of pleasant feeling mingled with his tears. "How wonderfully glorious it would be to sit with the student under such a tree;" but that was out of the question, he must be content to look through the keyhole, and be thankful for even that.

There he stood on the old landing, with the autumn wind blowing down upon him through the trap-door. It was very cold; but the little creature did not really feel it, till the light in the garret went out, and the tones of music died away. Then how he shivered, and crept down stairs again to his warm corner, where it felt home-like and comfortable. And when Christmas came again, and brought the dish of jam and the great lump of butter, he liked the huckster best of all.

Soon after, in the middle of the night, the goblin was awoke by a terrible noise and knocking against the window shutters and the house doors, and by the sound of the watchman's horn; for a great fire had broken out, and the whole street appeared full of flames. Was it in their house, or a neighbor's? No one could tell, for terror had seized upon all. The huckster's wife was so bewildered that she took her gold ear-rings out of her ears and put them in her pocket, that she might save some-

THE GOBLIN AND THE HUCKSTER

thing at least. The huckster ran to get his business papers, and the servant resolved to save her blue silk mantle, which she had managed to buy. Each wished to keep the best things they had. The goblin had the same wish; for, with one spring, he was up stairs and in the student's room, whom he found standing by the open window, and looking quite calmly at the fire, which was raging at the house of a neighbor opposite. The goblin caught up the wonderful book which lay on the table, and popped it into his red cap, which he held tightly with both hands. The greatest treasure in the house was saved; and he ran away with it to the roof, and seated himself on the chimney. The flames of the burning house opposite illuminated him as he sat, both hands pressed tightly over his cap, in which the treasure lay; and then he found out what feelings really reigned in his heart, and knew exactly which way they tended. And yet, when the fire was extinguished, and the goblin again began to reflect, he hesitated, and said at last, "I must divide myself between the two; I cannot quite give up the huckster, because of the jam."

And this is a representation of human nature. We are like the goblin; we all go to visit the huckster "because of the jam."

# THE MARSH KING'S DAUGHTER

THE STORKS relate to their little ones a great many stories, and they are all about moors and reed banks, and suited to their age and capacity. The youngest of them are quite satisfied with "kribble, krabble," or such nonsense, and think it very grand; but the elder ones want something with a deeper meaning, or at least something about their own family.

We are only acquainted with one of the two longest and oldest stories which the storks relate—it is about Moses, who was exposed by his mother on the banks of the Nile, and was found by the king's daughter, who gave him a good education, and he afterwards became a great man; but where he was buried is still unknown.

Every one knows this story, but not the second; very likely because it is quite an inland story. It has been repeated from mouth to mouth, from one stork-mamma to another, for thousands of years; and each has told it better than the last; and now *we* mean to tell it better than all.

The first stork pair who related it lived at the time it happened, and had their summer residence on the rafters of the Viking's* house, which stood near the wild moorlands of Wendsyssell; that is, to speak more correctly, the great moorheath, high up in the north of Jutland, by the Skjagen peak. This wilderness is still an immense wild heath of marshy ground, about which we can read in the "Official Directory." It is said that in olden times the place was a lake, the ground of which had heaved

*Sea Kings, or pirates of the north.

up from beneath, and now the moorland extends for miles in every direction, and is surrounded by damp meadows, trembling, undulating swamps, and marshy ground covered with turf, on which grow bilberry bushes and stunted trees. Mists are almost always hovering over this region, which, seventy years ago, was overrun with wolves. It may well be called the Wild Moor; and one can easily imagine, with such a wild expanse of marsh and lake, how lonely and dreary it must have been a thousand years ago. Many things may be noticed now that existed then. The reeds grow to the same height, and bear the same kind of long, purple-brown leaves, with their feathery tips. There still stands the birch, with its white bark and its delicate, loosely hanging leaves; and with regard to the living beings who frequented this spot, the fly still wears a gauzy dress of the same cut, and the favorite colors of the stork are white, with black and red for stockings. The people, certainly, in those days, wore very different dresses to those they now wear, but if any of them, be he huntsman or squire, master or servant, ventured on the wavering, undulating, marshy ground of the moor, they met with the same fate a thousand years ago as they would now. The wanderer sank, and went down to the Marsh King, as he is named, who rules in the great moorland empire beneath. They also called him "Gunkel King," but we like the name of "Marsh King" better, and we will give him that name as the storks do. Very little is known of the Marsh King's rule, but that, perhaps, is a good thing.

In the neighborhood of the moorlands, and not far from the great arm of the North Sea and the Cattegat which is called the Lumfjorden, lay the castle of the Viking, with its water-tight stone cellars, its tower, and its three projecting storeys. On the ridge of the roof the stork had built his nest, and there the stork-mamma sat on her eggs and felt sure her hatching would come to something.

One evening, stork-papa stayed out rather late, and when he came home he seemed quite busy, bustling, and important. "I have something very dreadful to tell you," said he to the stork-mamma.

"Keep it to yourself then," she replied. "Remember that I am hatching eggs; it may agitate me, and will affect them."

"You must know it at once," said he. "The daughter of our host in Egypt has arrived here. She has ventured to take this journey, and now she is lost."

"She who sprung from the race of the fairies, is it?" cried the mother stork. "Oh, tell me all about it; you know I cannot bear to be kept waiting at a time when I am hatching eggs."

"Well, you see, mother," he replied, "she believed what the doctors said, and what I have heard you state also, that the moor-flowers which grow about here would heal her sick father; and she has flown to the north in swan's plumage, in company with some other swan-princesses, who come to these parts every year to renew their youth. She came, and where is she now!"

"You enter into particulars too much," said the mamma stork, "and the eggs may take cold; I cannot bear such suspense as this."

"Well," said he, "I have kept watch; and this evening I went among the rushes where I thought the marshy ground would bear me, and while I was there three swans came. Something in their manner of flying seemed to say to me, 'Look carefully now; there is one not all swan, only swan's feathers.' You know, mother, you have the same intuitive feeling that I have; you know whether a thing is right or not immediately."

"Yes, of course," said she; "but tell me about the princess; I am tired of hearing about the swan's feathers."

"Well, you know that in the middle of the moor there is something like a lake," said the stork-papa. "You can see the edge of it if you raise yourself a little. Just there, by the reeds and the green banks, lay the trunk of an elder-tree; upon this the three swans stood flapping their wings, and looking about them; one of them threw off her plumage, and I immediately recognized her as one of the princesses of our home in Egypt. There she sat, without any covering but her long, black hair. I heard her tell the two others to take great care of the swan's plumage, while she dipped down into the water to pluck the flowers which she fancied she saw there. The others nodded, and picked up the feather dress, and took possession of it. I wonder what will become of it? thought I, and she most likely asked herself the same question. If so, she received an answer, a very practical one; for the two swans rose up and flew away with her swan's plumage. 'Dive down now!' they cried; 'thou shalt never more fly in the swan's plumage, thou shalt never again see Egypt; here, on the moor, thou wilt remain.' So saying, they tore the swan's plumage into a thousand pieces, the feathers drifted about like a snow-shower, and then the two deceitful princesses flew away."

"Why, that is terrible," said the stork-mamma; "I feel as if I could hardly bear to hear any more, but you must tell me what happened next."

"The princess wept and lamented aloud; her tears moistened the elder stump, which was really not an elder stump but the Marsh King himself, he who in marshy ground lives and rules. I saw myself how the stump of the tree turned round, and was a tree no more, while long, clammy branches like arms, were extended from it. Then the poor child was terribly frightened, and started up to run away. She hastened to cross the green, slimy ground; but it will not bear any weight, much less hers. She quickly sank, and the elder stump dived immediately after her; in fact, it was he who drew her down. Great black bubbles rose up out of the moor-slime, and with these every trace of the two vanished. And now the princess is buried in the wild marsh, she will never now carry flowers to Egypt to cure her father. It would have broken your heart, mother, had you seen it."

"You ought not to have told me," said she, "at such a time as this; the eggs might suffer. But I think the princess will soon find help; some one will rise up to help her. Ah! if it had been you or I, or one of our people, it would have been all over with us."

"I mean to go every day," said he, "to see if anything comes to pass;" and so he did.

A long time went by, but at last he saw a green stalk shooting up out of the deep, marshy ground. As it reached the surface of the marsh, a leaf

THE MARSH KING'S DAUGHTER

spread out, and unfolded itself broader and broader, and close to it came forth a bud.

One morning, when the stork-papa was flying over the stem, he saw that the power of the sun's rays had caused the bud to open, and in the cup of the flower lay a charming child—a little maiden, looking as if she had just come out of a bath. The little one was so like the Egyptian princess, that the stork, at the first moment, thought it must be the princess herself; but after a little reflection he decided that it was much more likely to be the daughter of the princess and the Marsh King; and this explained also her being placed in the cup of a water-lily. "But she cannot be left to lie here," thought the stork, "and in my nest there are already so many. But stay, I have thought of something: the wife of the Viking has no children, and how often she has wished for a little one. People always say the stork brings the little ones; I will do so in earnest this time. I shall fly with the child to the Viking's wife; what rejoicing there will be!"

And then the stork lifted the little girl out of the flower-cup, flew to the castle, picked a hole with his beak in the bladder-covered window, and laid the beautiful child in the bosom of the Viking's wife. Then he flew back quickly to the stork-mamma and told her what he had seen and done; and the little storks listened to it all, for they were then quite old enough to do so. "So you see," he continued, "that the princess is not dead, for she must have sent her little one up here; and now I have found a home for her."

"Ah, I said it would be so from the first," replied the stork-mamma; "but now think a little of your own family. Our travelling time draws near, and I sometimes feel a little irritation already under the wings. The cuckoos and the nightingale are already gone, and I heard the quails say they should go too as soon as the wind was favorable. Our youngsters will go through all the manœuvres at the review very well, or I am much mistaken in them."

The Viking's wife was above measure delighted when she awoke the next morning and found the beautiful little child lying in her bosom. She kissed it and caressed it; but it cried terribly, and struck out with its arms and legs, and did not seem to be pleased at all. At last it cried itself to sleep; and as it lay there so still and quiet, it was a most beautiful sight to see. The Viking's wife was so delighted, that body and soul were full of joy. Her heart felt so light within her, that it seemed as if her husband and his soldiers, who were absent, must come home as suddenly and unexpectedly as the little child had done. She and her whole household therefore busied themselves in preparing everything for the reception of her lord. The long, colored tapestry, on which she and her maidens had worked pictures of their idols, Odin, Thor, and Friga, was hung up. The slaves polished the old shields that served as ornaments; cushions were placed on the seats, and dry wood laid on the fireplaces in the centre of the hall, so that the flames might be fanned up at a moment's notice. The Viking's wife herself assisted in the work, so that at night she felt very tired, and quickly fell into a sound sleep. When she awoke, just before morning, she was terribly alarmed to find that the infant had vanished.

She sprang from her couch, lighted a pine-chip, and searched all round the room, when, at last, in that part of the bed where her feet had been, lay, not the child, but a great, ugly frog. She was quite disgusted at this sight, and seized a heavy stick to kill the frog; but the creature looked at her with such strange, mournful eyes, that she was unable to strike the blow. Once more she searched round the room; then she started at hearing the frog utter a low, painful croak. She sprang from the couch and opened the window hastily; at the same moment the sun rose, and threw its beams through the window, till it rested on the couch where the great frog lay. Suddenly it appeared as if the frog's broad mouth contracted, and became small and red. The limbs moved and stretched out and extended themselves till they took a beautiful shape; and behold there was the pretty child lying before her, and the ugly frog was gone. "How is this?" she cried, "have I had a wicked dream? Is it not my own lovely cherub that lies there." Then she kissed it and fondled it; but the child struggled and fought, and bit as if she had been a little wild cat.

The Viking did not return on that day, nor the next; he was, however, on the way home; but the wind, so favorable to the storks, was against him; for it blew towards the south. A wind in favor of one is often against another.

After two or three days had passed, it became clear to the Viking's wife how matters stood with the child; it was under the influence of a powerful sorcerer. By day it was charming in appearance as an angel of light, but with a temper wicked and wild; while at night, in the form of an ugly frog, it was quiet and mournful, with eyes full of sorrow. Here were two natures, changing inwardly and outwardly with the absence and return of sunlight. And so it happened that by day the child, with the actual form of its mother, possessed the fierce disposition of its father; at night, on the contrary, its outward appearance plainly showed its descent on the father's side, while inwardly it had the heart and mind of its mother. Who would be able to loosen this wicked charm which the sorcerer had worked upon it? The wife of the Viking lived in constant pain and sorrow about it. Her heart clung to the little creature, but she could not explain to her husband the circumstances in which it was placed. He was expected to return shortly; and were she to tell him, he would very likely, as was the custom at that time, expose the poor child in the public highway, and let any one take it away who would. The good wife of the Viking could not let that happen, and she therefore resolved that the Viking should never see the child excepting by daylight.

One morning there sounded a rushing of storks' wings over the roof. More than a hundred pair of storks had rested there during the night, to recover themselves after their excursion; and now they soared aloft, and prepared for the journey southward.

"All the husbands are here, and ready!" they cried; "wives and children also!"

"How light we are!" screamed the young storks in chorus. "Something pleasant seems creeping over us, even down to our toes, as if we were full of live frogs. Ah, how delightful it is to travel into foreign lands!"

"Hold yourselves properly in the line with us," cried papa and mamma.

"Do not use your beaks so much; it tries the lungs." And then the storks flew away.

About the same time sounded the clang of the warriors' trumpets across the heath. The Viking had landed with his men. They were returning home, richly laden with spoil from the Gallic coast, where the people, as did also the inhabitants of Britain, often cried in alarm, "Deliver us from the wild northmen."

Life and noisy pleasure came with them into the castle of the Viking on the moorland. A great cask of mead was drawn into the hall, piles of wood blazed, cattle were slain and served up, that they might feast in reality. The priest who offered the sacrifice sprinkled the devoted parishioners with the warm blood; the fire crackled, and the smoke rolled along beneath the roof; the soot fell upon them from the beams; but they were used to all these things. Guests were invited, and received handsome presents. All wrongs and unfaithfulness were forgotten. They drank deeply, and threw in each other's faces the bones that were left, which was looked upon as a sign of good feeling amongst them. A bard, who was a kind of musician as well as warrior, and who had been with the Viking in his expedition, and knew what to sing about, gave them one of his best songs, in which they heard all their warlike deeds praised, and every wonderful action brought forward with honor. Every verse ended with this refrain,—

> "Gold and possessions will flee away,
> Friends and foes must die one day;
> Every man on earth must die,
> But a famous name will never die."

And with that they beat upon their shields, and hammered upon the table with knives and bones, in a most outrageous manner.

The Viking's wife sat upon a raised cross seat in the open hall. She wore a silk dress, golden bracelets, and large amber beads. She was in costly attire, and the bard named her in his song, and spoke of the rich treasure of gold which she had brought to her husband. Her husband had already seen the wonderfully beautiful child in the daytime, and was delighted with her beauty; even her wild ways pleased him. He said the little maiden would grow up to be a heroine, with the strong will and determination of a man. She would never wink her eyes, even if, in joke, an expert hand should attempt to cut off her eye-brows with a sharp sword.

The full cask of mead soon became empty, and a fresh one was brought in; for these were people who liked plenty to eat and drink. The old proverb, which every one knows, says that "the cattle know when to leave their pasture, but a foolish man knows not the measure of his own appetite." Yes, they all knew this; but men may know what is right, and yet often do wrong. They also knew "that even the welcome guest becomes wearisome when he sits too long in the house." But there they remained; for pork and mead are good things. And so at the Viking's house they stayed, and enjoyed themselves; and at night the bondmen slept in the ashes, and dipped their fingers in the fat, and licked them. Oh, it was a delightful time!

Once more in the same year the Viking went forth, though the storms of autumn had already commenced to roar. He went with his warriors to the coast of Britain; he said that it was but an excursion of pleasure across the water, so his wife remained at home with the little girl. After a while, it is quite certain the foster-mother began to love the poor frog, with its gentle eyes and its deep sighs, even better than the little beauty who bit and fought with all around her.

The heavy, damp mists of autumn, which destroy the leaves of the wood, had already fallen upon forest and heath. Feathers of plucked birds, as they call the snow, flew about in thick showers, and winter was coming. The sparrows took possession of the stork's nest, and conversed about the absent owners in their own fashion; and they, the stork pair and all their young ones, where were they staying now? The storks might have been found in the land of Egypt, where the sun's rays shone forth bright and warm, as it does here at midsummer. Tamarinds and acacias were in full bloom all over the country, the crescent of Mahomet glittered brightly from the cupolas of the mosques, and on the slender pinnacles sat many of the storks, resting after their long journey. Swarms of them took divided possession of the nests—nests which lay close to each other between the venerable columns, and crowded the arches of temples in forgotten cities. The date and the palm lifted themselves as a screen or as a sun-shade over them. The gray pyramids looked like broken shadows in the clear air and the far-off desert, where the ostrich wheels his rapid flight, and the lion, with his subtle eyes, gazes at the marble sphinx which lies half buried in sand. The waters of the Nile had retreated, and the whole bed of the river was covered with frogs, which was a most acceptable prospect for the stork families. The young storks thought their eyes deceived them, everything around appeared so beautiful.

"It is always like this here, and this is how we live in our warm country," said the stork-mamma; and the thought made the young ones almost beside themselves with pleasure.

"Is there anything more to see?" they asked; "are we going farther into the country?"

"There is nothing further for us to see," answered the stork-mamma. "Beyond this delightful region there are immense forests, where the branches of the trees entwine round each other, while prickly, creeping plants cover the paths, and only an elephant could force a passage for himself with his great feet. The snakes are too large, and the lizards too lively for us to catch. Then there is the desert; if you went there, your eyes would soon be full of sand with the lightest breeze, and if it should blow great guns, you would most likely find yourself in a sand-drift. Here is the best place for you, where there are frogs and locusts; here I shall remain, and so must you." And so they stayed.

The parents sat in the nest on the slender minaret, and rested, yet still were busily employed in cleaning and smoothing their feathers, and in sharpening their beaks against their red stockings; then they would stretch out their necks, salute each other, and gravely raise their heads with the high-polished forehead, and soft, smooth feathers, while their brown eyes shone with intelligence. The female young ones strutted about amid the moist rushes, glancing at the other young storks and making acquaintances, and swallowing a frog at every third step, or tossing a little snake about with their beaks, in a way they considered very becoming, and besides it tasted very good. The young male storks soon began to quarrel; they struck at each other with their wings, and pecked with their beaks till the blood came. And in this manner many of the young ladies and gentlemen were betrothed to each other: it was, of course, what they wanted, and indeed what they lived for. Then they returned to a nest, and there the quarrelling began afresh; for in hot countries people are almost all violent and passionate. But for all that it was pleasant, especially for the old people, who watched them with great joy: all that their young ones did suited them. Every day here there was sunshine, plenty to eat, and nothing to think of but pleasure. But in the rich castle of their Egyptian host, as they called him, pleasure was not to be found. The rich and mighty lord of the castle lay on his couch, in the midst of the great hall, with its many colored walls looking like the centre of a great tulip; but he was stiff and powerless in all his limbs, and lay stretched out like a mummy. His family and servants stood round him; he was not dead, although he could scarcely be said to live. The healing moor-flower from the north, which was to have been found and brought to him by her who loved him so well, had not arrived. His young and beautiful daughter who, in swan's plumage, had flown over land and seas to the distant north, had never returned. She is dead, so the two swan-maidens had said when they came home; and they made up quite a story about her, and this is what they told,—

"We three flew away together through the air," said they: "a hunter caught sight of us, and shot at us with an arrow. The arrow struck our young friend and sister, and slowly singing her farewell song she sank down, a dying swan, into the forest lake. On the shores of the lake, under a spreading birch-tree, we laid her in the cold earth. We had our revenge; we bound fire under the wings of a swallow, who had a nest on the thatched roof of the huntsman. The house took fire, and burst into flames; the hunter was burnt with the house, and the light was reflected over the sea as far as the spreading birch, beneath which we laid her sleeping dust. She will never return to the land of Egypt." And then they both wept. And stork-papa, who heard the story, snapped with his beak so that it might be heard a long way off.

"Deceit and lies!" cried he; "I should like to run my beak deep into their chests."

"And perhaps break it off," said the mamma stork, "then what a sight you would be. Think first of yourself, and then of your family; all others are nothing to us."

"Yes, I know," said the stork-papa; "but to-morrow I can easily place myself on the edge of the open cupola, when the learned and wise men assemble to consult on the state of the sick man; perhaps they may come a little nearer to the truth." And the learned and wise men assembled together, and talked a great deal on every point; but the stork could make no sense out of anything they said; neither were there any good results from their consultations, either for the sick man, or for his daughter in the marshy heath. When we listen to what people say in this world, we shall hear a great deal; but it is an advantage to know what has been said and done before, when we listen to a conversation. The stork did, and we know at least as much as he, the stork.

"Love is a life-giver. The highest love produces the highest life. Only through love can the sick man be cured." This had been said by many, and even the learned men acknowledged that it was a wise saying.

"What a beautiful thought!" exclaimed the papa stork immediately.

"I don't quite understand it," said the mamma stork, when her husband repeated it; "however, it is not my fault, but the fault of the thought; whatever it may be, I have something else to think of."

Now the learned men had spoken also of love between this one and that one; of the difference of the love which we have for our neighbor, to the love that exists between parents and children; of the love of the plant for the light, and how the germ springs forth when the sunbeam kisses the ground. All these things were so elaborately and learnedly explained, that it was impossible for stork-papa to follow it, much less to talk about it. His thoughts on the subject quite weighed him down; he stood the whole of the following day on one leg, with half-shut eyes, thinking deeply. So much learning was quite a heavy weight for him to carry. One thing, however, the papa stork could understand. Every one, high and low, had from their inmost hearts expressed their opinion that it was a great misfortune for so many thousands of people—the whole country indeed—to have this man so sick, with no hopes of his recovery. And what joy and blessing it would spread around if he could by any means be cured! But where bloomed the flower that could bring him health? They had searched for it everywhere; in learned writings, in the shining stars, in the weather and wind. Inquiries had been made in every byway that could be thought of, until at last the wise and learned men has asserted, as we have been already told, that "love, the life-giver, could alone give new life to a father;" and in saying this, they had overdone it, and said more than they understood themselves. They repeated it, and wrote it down as a recipe, "Love is a life-giver." But how could such a recipe be prepared—that was a difficulty they could not overcome. At last it was decided that help could only come from the princess herself, whose whole soul was wrapped up in her father, especially as a plan had been adopted by her to enable her to obtain a remedy.

More than a year had passed since the princess had set out at night, when the light of the young moon was soon lost beneath the horizon. She had gone to the marble sphinx in the desert, shaking the sand from her sandals, and then passed through the long passage, which leads to the centre of one of the great pyramids, where the mighty kings of antiquity, surrounded with pomp and splendor, lie veiled in the form of mummies. She had been told by the wise men, that if she laid her head on the breast of one of them, from the head she would learn where to find life and recovery for her father. She had performed all this, and in a dream had learnt that she must bring home to her father the lotus flower, which grows in the deep sea, near the moors and heath in the Danish land. The very place and situation had been pointed out to her, and she was told that the flower would restore her father to health and strength. And, therefore, she had gone forth from the land of Egypt, flying over to the open marsh and the wild moor in the plumage of a swan.

The papa and mamma storks knew all this, and we also know it now. We know, too, that the Marsh King has drawn her down to himself, and that to the loved ones at home she is forever dead. One of the wisest of them said, as the stork-mamma also said, "That in some way she would, after all, manage to succeed;" and so at last they comforted themselves with this hope, and would wait patiently; in fact, they could do nothing better.

"I should like to get away the swan's feathers from those two treacherous princesses," said the papa stork; "then, at least, they would not be able to fly over again to the wild moor, and do more wickedness. I can hide the two suits of feathers over yonder, till we find some use for them."

"But where will you put them?" asked the mamma stork.

"In our nest on the moor. I and the young ones will carry them by turns during our flight across; and as we return, should they prove too heavy for us, we shall be sure to find plenty of places on the way in which we can conceal them till our next journey. Certainly one suit of swan's feathers would be enough for the princess, but two are always better. In those northern countries no one can have too many travelling wrappers."

"No one will thank you for it," said stork-mamma; "but you are master; and, excepting at breeding time, I have nothing to say."

In the Viking's castle on the wild moor, to which the storks directed their flight in the following spring, the little maiden still remained. They had named her Helga, which was rather too soft a name for a child with a temper like hers, although her form was still beautiful. Every month this temper showed itself in sharper outlines; and in the course of years, while the storks still made the same journeys in autumn to the hill, and in spring to the moors, the child grew to be almost a woman, and before any one seemed aware of it, she was a wonderfully beautiful maiden of sixteen. The casket was splendid, but the contents were worthless. She was, indeed, wild and savage even in those hard, uncultivated times. It was a pleasure to her to splash about with her white hands in the warm blood of the horse which had been slain for sacrifice. In one of her wild moods she bit off the head of the black cock, which the priest was about to slay for the sacrifice. To her foster-father she said one day, "If thine enemy were to pull down thine house about thy ears, and thou shouldest be sleeping in unconscious security, I would not wake thee; even if I had the power I would never do it, for my ears still tingle with the blow that thou gavest me years ago. I have never forgotten it." But the Viking treated her words as a joke; he was, like every one else, bewitched with her beauty, and knew nothing of the change in the form and temper of Helga at night. Without a saddle, she would sit on a horse as if she were a part of it, while it rushed along at full speed; nor would she spring from its back, even when it quarrelled with other horses and bit them. She would often leap from the high shore into the sea with all her clothes on, and swim to meet the Viking, when his boat was steering home towards the shore. She once cut off a long lock of her beautiful hair, and twisted it into a string for her bow. "If a thing is to be done well," said she, "I must do it myself."

The Viking's wife was, for the time in which she lived, a woman of strong character and will; but, compared to her daughter, she was a gentle, timid power. It was sometimes as if Helga acted from sheer wickedness; for often when her mother stood on the threshold of the door, or stepped into the yard, she would seat herself on the brink of the well, wave her arms and legs in the air, and suddenly fall right in. Here she was able, from her frog nature, to dip and dive about in the water of the deep well, until at last she would climb forth like a cat, and come back into the hall dripping with water, so that the green leaves that were strewed on the floor were whirled round, and carried away by the streams that flowed from her.

But there was one time of the day which placed a check upon Helga. It was the evening twilight; when this hour arrived she became quiet and thoughtful, and allowed herself to be advised and led; then also a secret feeling seemed to draw her towards her mother. And as usual, when the sun set, and the transformation took place, both in body and mind, inwards and outwards, she would remain quiet and mournful, with her form shrunk together in the shape of a frog. Her body was much larger than those animals ever are, and on this account it was much more hideous in appearance; for she looked like a wretched dwarf, with a frog's head, and webbed fingers. Her eyes had a most piteous expression; she was without a voice, excepting a hollow, croaking sound, like the smothered sobs of a dreaming child.

Then the Viking's wife took her on her lap, and forgot the ugly form, as she looked into the mournful eyes, and often said, "I could wish that thou wouldst always remain my dumb frog child, for thou art too terrible when thou art clothed in a form of beauty." And the Viking woman wrote Runic characters against sorcery and spells of sickness, and threw them over the wretched child; but they did no good.

"One can scarcely believe that she was ever small enough to lie in the cup of the water-lily," said the papa stork; "and now she is grown up, and the image of her Egyptian mother, especially about the eyes. Ah, we shall never see her again; perhaps she has not discovered how to help herself, as you and the wise men said she would. Year after year have I flown across and across the moor, but there was no sign of her being still alive. Yes, and I may as well tell you that each year, when I arrived a few days before you to repair the nest, and put everything in its place, I have spent a whole night flying here and there over the marshy lake, as if I had been an owl or a bat, but all to no purpose. The two suits of swan's plumage, which I and the young ones dragged over here from the land of the Nile, are of no use; trouble enough it was to us to bring them here in three journeys, and now they are lying at the bottom of the nest; and if a fire should happen to break out, and the wooden house be burnt down, they would be destroyed."

"And our good nest would be destroyed, too," said the mamma stork;

"but you think less of that than of your plumage stuff and your moor-princess. Go and stay with her in the marsh if you like. You are a bad father to your own children, as I have told you already, when I hatched my first brood. I only hope neither we nor our children may have an arrow sent through our wings, owing to that wild girl. Helga does not know in the least what she is about. We have lived in this house longer than she has, she should think of that, and we have never forgotten our duty. We have paid every year our toll of a feather, an egg, and a young one, as it is only right we should do. You don't suppose I can wander about the court-yard, or go everywhere as I used to do in old times. I can do it in Egypt, where I can be a companion of the people, without for-getting myself. But here I cannot go and peep into the pots and kettles as I do there. No, I can only sit up here and feel angry with that girl, the little wretch; and I am angry with you, too; you should have left her lying in the water lily, then no one would have known anything about her."

"You are far better than your conversation," said the papa stork; "I know you better than you know yourself." And with that he gave a hop, and flapped his wings twice, proudly; then he stretched his neck and flew, or rather soared away, without moving his outspread wings. He went on for some distance, and then he gave a great flap with his wings and flew on his course at a rapid rate, his head and neck bending proudly before him, while the sun's rays fell on his glossy plumage.

"He is the handsomest of them all," said the mamma stork, as she watched him; "but I won't tell him so."

Early in the autumn, the Viking again returned home laden with spoil, and bringing prisoners with him. Among them was a young Christian priest, one of those who condemned the gods of the north. Often lately there had been, both in hall and chamber, a talk of the new faith which was spreading far and wide in the south, and which, through the means of the holy Ansgarius, had already reached as far as Hedeby on the Schlei. Even Helga had heard of this belief in the teachings of One who was named Christ, and who for the love of mankind, and for their re-demption, had given up His life. But to her all this had, as it were, gone in one ear and out the other. It seemed that she only understood the meaning of the word "love," when in the form of a miserable frog she crouched together in the corner of the sleeping chamber; but the Vi-king's wife had listened to the wonderful story, and had felt herself strangely moved by it.

On their return, after this voyage, the men spoke of the beautiful temples built of polished stone, which had been raised for the public worship of this holy love. Some vessels, curiously formed of massive gold, had been brought home among the booty. There was a peculiar fra-grance about them all, for they were incense vessels, which had been swung before the altars in the temples by the Christian priests. In the deep stony cellars of the castle, the young Christian priest was immured, and his hands and feet tied together with strips of bark. The Viking's wife considered him as beautiful as Baldur, and his distress raised her pity; but Helga said he ought to have ropes fastened to his heels, and be tied to the tails of wild animals.

"I would let the dogs loose after him" she said; "over the moor and across the heath. Hurrah! that would be a spectacle for the gods, and better still to follow in its course."

But the Viking would not allow him to die such a death as that, especially as he was the disowned and despiser of the high gods. In a few days, he had decided to have him offered as a sacrifice on the bloodstone in the grove. For the first time, a man was to be sacrificed here. Helga begged to be allowed to sprinkle the assembled people with the blood of the priest. She sharpened her glittering knife; and when one of the great, savage dogs, who were running about the Viking's castle in great numbers, sprang towards her, she thrust the knife into his side, merely, as she said, to prove its sharpness.

The Viking's wife looked at the wild, badly disposed girl, with great sorrow; and when night came on, and her daughter's beautiful form and disposition were changed, she spoke in eloquent words to Helga of the sorrow and deep grief that was in her heart. The ugly frog, in its monstrous shape, stood before her, and raised its brown mournful eyes to her face, listening to her words, and seeming to understand them with the intelligence of a human being.

"Never once to my lord and husband has a word passed my lips of what I have to suffer through you; my heart is full of grief about you," said the Viking's wife. "The love of a mother is greater and more powerful than I ever imagined. But love never entered thy heart; it is cold and clammy, like the plants on the moor."

Then the miserable form trembled; it was as if these words had touched an invisible bond between body and soul, for great tears stood in the eyes.

"A bitter time will come for thee at last," continued the Viking's wife; "and it will be terrible for me too. It had been better for thee if thou hadst been left on the high-road, with the cold night wind to lull thee to sleep." And the Viking's wife shed bitter tears, and went away in anger and sorrow, passing under the partition of furs, which hung loose over the beam and divided the hall.

The shrivelled frog still sat in the corner alone. Deep silence reigned around. At intervals, a half-stifled sigh was heard from its inmost soul; it was the soul of Helga. It seemed in pain, as if a new life were arising in her heart. Then she took a step forward and listened; then stepped again forward, and seized with her clumsy hands the heavy bar which was laid across the door. Gently, and with much trouble, she pushed back the bar, as silently lifted the latch, and then took up the glimmering lamp which stood in the ante-chamber of the hall. It seemed as if a stronger will than her own gave her strength. She removed the iron bolt from the closed cellar-door, and slipped in to the prisoner. He was slumbering. She touched him with her cold, moist hand, and as he awoke and caught sight of the hideous form, he shuddered as if he beheld a wicked apparition. She drew her knife, cut through the bonds which confined his hands and feet, and beckoned to him to follow her. He uttered some holy names and made the sign of the cross, while the form remained motionless by his side.

"Who art thou?" he asked, "whose outward appearance is that of an animal, while thou willingly performest acts of mercy?"

The frog-figure beckoned to him to follow her, and led him through a long gallery concealed by hanging drapery to the stables, and then pointed to a horse. He mounted upon it, and she sprang up also before him, and held tightly by the animal's mane. The prisoner understood her, and they rode on at a rapid trot, by a road which he would never have found by himself, across the open heath. He forgot her ugly form, and only thought how the mercy and loving-kindness of the Almighty was acting through this hideous apparition. As he offered pious prayers and sang holy songs of praise, she trembled. Was it the effect of prayer and praise that caused this? or, was she shuddering in the cold morning air at the thought of approaching twilight? What were her feelings? She raised herself up, and wanted to stop the horse and spring off, but the Chrisitan priest held her back with all his might, and then sang a pious song, as if this could loosen the wicked charm that had changed her into the semblance of a frog.

And the horse galloped on more wildly than before. The sky painted itself red, the first sunbeam pierced through the clouds, and in the clear flood of sunlight the frog became changed. It was Helga again, young and beautiful, but with a wicked demoniac spirit. He held now a beautiful young woman in his arms, and he was horrified at the sight. He stopped the horse, and sprang from its back. He imagined that some new sorcery was at work. But Helga also leaped from the horse and stood on the ground. The child's short garment reached only to her knee. She snatched the sharp knife from her girdle, and rushed like lightning at the astonished priest. "Let me get at thee!" she cried; "let me get at thee, that I may plunge this knife into thy body. Thou art pale as ashes, thou beardless slave." She pressed in upon him. They struggled with each other in heavy combat, but it was as if an invisible power had been given to the Christian in the struggle. He held her fast, and the old oak under which they stood seemed to help him, for the loosened roots on the ground became entangled in the maiden's feet, and held them fast. Close by rose a bubbling spring, and he sprinkled Helga's face and neck with the water, commanded the unclean spirit to come forth, and pronounced upon her a Christian blessing. But the water of faith has no power unless the wellspring of faith flows within. And yet even here its power was shown; something more than the mere strength of a man opposed itself, through his means, against the evil which struggled within her. His holy action seemed to overpower her. She dropped her arms, glanced at him with pale cheeks and looks of amazement. He appeared to her a mighty magician skilled in secret arts; his language was the darkest magic to her, and the movements of his hands in the air were as the secret signs of a magician's wand. She would not have blinked had he waved over her head a sharp knife or a glittering axe; but she shrunk from him as he signed her with the sign of the cross on her forehead and breast, and sat before him like a tame bird, with her head bowed down. Then he spoke to her, in gentle words, of the deed of love she had performed for him during the night, when she had come to him in the form of an ugly frog, to loosen his bonds, and to lead him forth to life and light; and he told her that she was bound in closer fetters than he had been, and that she could recover also life and light by his means. He would take her to Hedeby* to St. Ansgarius, and there, in that Christian town, the spell of the sorcerer would be removed. But he would not let her sit before him on the horse, though of her own free will she wished to do so. "Thou must sit behind me, not before me," said he. "Thy magic beauty has a magic power which comes from an evil origin, and I fear it; still I am sure to overcome through my faith in Christ." Then he knelt down, and prayed with pious fervor. It was as if the quiet woodland were a holy church consecrated by his worship. The birds sang as if they were also of this new congregation; and the fragrance of the wild flowers was as the ambrosial perfume of incense; while, above all, sounded the words of Scripture, "A light to them that sit in darkness and in the shadow of death, to guide their feet into the way of peace." And he spoke these words with the deep longing of his whole nature.

Meanwhile, the horse that had carried them in wild career stood quietly by, plucking at the tall bramble-bushes, till the ripe young berries fell down upon Helga's hands, as if inviting her to eat. Patiently she allowed herself to be lifted on the horse, and sat there like a somnambulist—as one who walked in his sleep. The Christian bound two branches together with bark, in the form of a cross, and held it on high as they rode through the forest. The way gradually grew thicker of brushwood, as they rode along, till at last it became a trackless wilderness. Bushes of the wild sloe here and there blocked up the path, so that they had to ride over them. The bubbling spring formed not a stream, but a marsh, round which also they were obliged to guide the horse; still there were strength and refreshment in the cool forest breeze, and no trifling power in the gentle words spoken in faith and Christian love by the young priest, whose inmost heart yearned to lead this poor lost one into the way of light and life. It is said that rain-drops can make a hollow in the hardest stone, and the waves of the sea can smooth and round the rough edges of the rocks; so did the dew of mercy fall upon Helga, softening what was hard, and smoothing what was rough in her character. These effects did not yet appear; she was not herself aware of them; neither does the seed in the lap of earth know, when the refreshing dew and the warm sunbeams fall . upon it, that it contains within itself power by which it will flourish and bloom. The song of the mother sinks into the heart of the child, and the little one prattles the words after her, without understanding their meaning; but after a time the thoughts expand, and what has been heard in childhood seems to the mind clear and bright. So now the "Word," which is all-powerful to create, was working in the heart of Helga.

They rode forth from the thick forest, crossed the heath, and again entered a pathless wood. Here, towards evening, they met with robbers.

"Where hast thou stolen that beauteous maiden?" cried the robbers, seizing the horse by the bridle, and dragging the two riders from its back.

The priest had nothing to defend himself with, but the knife he had

*Now the town of Sleswig.

taken from Helga, and with this he struck out right and left. One of the robbers raised his axe against him; but the young priest sprang on one side, and avoided the blow, which fell with great force on the horse's neck, so that the blood gushed forth, and the animal sunk to the ground. Then Helga seemed suddenly to awake from her long, deep reverie; she threw herself hastily upon the dying animal. The priest placed himself before her, to defend and shelter her; but one of the robbers swung his iron axe against the Christian's head with such force that it was dashed to pieces, the blood and brains were scattered about, and he fell dead upon the ground. Then the robbers seized beautiful Helga by her white arms and slender waist; but at that moment the sun went down, and as its last ray disappeared, she was changed into the form of a frog. A greenish white mouth spread half over her face; her arms became thin and slimy; while broad hands, with webbed fingers, spread themselves out like fans. Then the robbers, in terror, let her go, and she stood among them, a hideous monster; and as is the nature of frogs to do, she hopped up as high as her own size, and disappeared in the thicket. Then the robbers knew that this must be the work of an evil spirit or some secret sorcery, and, in a terrible fright, they ran hastily from the spot.

The full moon had already risen, and was shining in all her radiant splendor over the earth, when from the thicket, in the form of a frog, crept poor Helga. She stood still by the corpse of the Christian priest, and the carcase of the dead horse. She looked at them with eyes that seemed to weep, and from the frog's head came forth a croaking sound, as when a child bursts into tears. She threw herself first upon one, and then upon the other; brought water in her hand, which, from being webbed, was large and hollow, and poured it over them; but they were dead, and dead they would remain. She understood that at last. Soon wild animals would come and tear their dead bodies; but no, that must not happen. Then she dug up the earth, as deep as she was able, that she might prepare a grave for them. She had nothing but a branch of a tree and her two hands, between the fingers of which the webbed skin stretched, and they were torn by the work, while the blood ran down her hands. She saw at last that her work would be useless, more than she could accomplish; so she fetched more water, and washed the face of the dead, and then covered it with green leaves; she also brought large boughs and spread over him, and scattered dried leaves between the branches. Then she brought the heaviest stones that she could carry, and laid them over the dead body, filling up the crevices with moss, till she thought she had fenced in his resting-place strongly enough. The difficult task had employed her the whole night; and as the sun broke forth, there stood the beautiful Helga in all her loveliness, with her bleeding hands, and, for the first time, with tears on her maiden cheeks. It was, in this transformation, as if two natures were striving together within her; her whole frame trembled, and she looked around her as if she had just awoke from a painful dream. She leaned for support against the trunk of a slender tree, and at last climbed to the topmost branches, like a cat, and seated herself firmly upon them. She remained there the whole day, sitting alone, like a frightened squirrel, in the silent solitude of the wood, where

THE MARSH KING'S DAUGHTER

the rest and stillness is as the calm of death.

Butterflies fluttered around her, and close by were several ant-hills, each with its hundreds of busy little creatures moving quickly to and fro. In the air, danced myriads of gnats, swarm upon swarm, troops of buzzing flies, lady-birds, dragon-flies with golden wings, and other little winged creatures. The worm crawled forth from the moist ground, and the moles crept out; but, excepting these, all around had the stillness of death: but when people say this, they do not quite understand themselves what they mean. None noticed Helga but a flock of magpies, which flew chattering round the top of the tree on which she sat. These birds hopped close to her on the branches with bold curiosity. A glance from her eyes was a signal to frighten them away, and they were not clever enough to find out who she was; indeed she hardly knew herself.

When the sun was near setting, and the evening's twilight about to commence, the approaching transformation aroused her to fresh exertion. She let herself down gently from the tree, and, as the last sunbeam vanished, she stood again in the wrinkled form of a frog, with the torn, webbed skin on her hands, but her eyes now gleamed with more radiant beauty than they had ever possesed in her most beautiful form of loveliness; they were now pure, mild maidenly eyes that shone forth in the face of a frog. They showed the existence of deep feeling and a human heart, and the beauteous eyes overflowed with tears, weeping precious drops that lightened the heart.

On the raised mound which she had made as a grave for the dead priest, she found the cross made of the branches of a tree, the last work of him who now lay dead and cold beneath it. A sudden thought came to Helga, and she lifted up the cross and planted it upon the grave, between the stones that covered him and the dead horse. The sad recollection brought the tears to her eyes, and in this gentle spirit she traced the same sign in the sand round the grave; and as she formed, with both her hands, the sign of the cross, the web skin fell from them like a torn glove. She washed her hands in the water of the spring, and gazed with astonishment at their delicate whiteness. Again she made the holy sign in the air, between herself and the dead man; her lips trembled, her tongue moved, and the name which she in her ride through the forest had so often heard spoken, rose to her lips, and she uttered the words, "Jesus Christ." Then the frog skin fell from her; she was once more a lovely maiden. Her head bent wearily, her tired limbs required rest, and then she slept.

Her sleep, however, was short. Towards midnight, she awoke; before her stood the dead horse, prancing and full of life, which shone forth from his eyes and from his wounded neck. Close by his side appeared the murdered Christian priest, more beautiful than Baldur, as the Viking's wife had said; but now he came as if in a flame of fire. Such gravity, such stern justice, such a piercing glance shone from his large, gentle eyes, that it seemed to penetrate into every corner of her heart. Beautiful Helga trembled at the look, and her memory returned with a power as if it had been the day of judgment. Every good deed that had been done for her, every loving word that had been said, were vivdly before her mind. She understood now that love had kept her here during the day of her trial; while the creature formed of dust and clay, soul and spirit, had wrestled and struggled with evil. She acknowledged that she had only followed the impulses of an evil disposition, that she had done nothing to cure herself; everything had been given her, and all had happened as it were by the ordination of Providence. She bowed herself humbly, confessed her great imperfections in the sight of Him who can read every fault of the heart, and then the priest spoke. "Daughter of the moorland, thou hast come from the swamp and the marshy earth, but from this thou shalt arise. The sunlight shining into thy inmost soul proves the origin from which thou has really sprung, and has restored the body to its natural form. I am come to thee from the land of the dead, and thou also must pass through the valley to reach the holy mountains where mercy and perfection dwell. I cannot lead thee to Hedeby that thou mayst receive Christian baptism, for first thou must remove the thick veil with which the waters of the moorland are shrouded, and bring forth from its depths the living author of thy being and thy life. Till this is done, thou canst not receive consecration."

Then he lifted her on the horse and gave her a golden censer, similar to those she had already seen at the Viking's house. A sweet perfume arose from it, while the open wound in the forehead of the slain priest, shone with the rays of a diamond. He took the cross from the grave, and held it aloft, and now they rode through the air over the rustling trees, over the hills where warriors lay buried each by his dead war-horse; and the brazen monumental figures rose up and galloped forth, and stationed themselves on the summits of the hills. The golden crescent on their foreheads, fastened with golden knots, glittered in the moonlight, and their mantles floated in the wind. The dragon, that guards buried treasure, lifted his head and gazed after them. The goblins and the satyrs peeped out from beneath the hills, and flitted to and fro in the fields, waving blue, red, and green torches, like the glowing sparks in burning paper. Over woodland and heath, flood and fen, they flew on, till they reached the wild moor, over which they hovered in broad circles. The Christian priest held the cross aloft, and it glittered like gold, while from his lips sounded pious prayers. Beautiful Helga's voice joined with his in the hymns he sung, as a child joins in her mother's song. She swung the censer, and a wonderful fragrance of incense arose from it; so powerful, that the reeds and rushes of the moor burst forth into blossom. Each germ came forth from the deep ground: all that had life raised itself. Blooming water-lilies spread themselves forth like a carpet of wrought flowers, and upon them lay a slumbering woman, young and beautiful. Helga fancied that it was her own image she saw reflected in the still water. But it was her mother she beheld, the wife of the Marsh King, the princess from the land of the Nile.

The dead Christian priest desired that the sleeping woman should be lifted on the horse, but the horse sank beneath the load, as if he had been a funeral pall fluttering in the wind. But the sign of the cross made the airy phantom strong, and then the three rode away from the marsh to firm ground.

At the same moment the cock crew in the Viking's castle, and the dream figures dissolved and floated away in the air, but mother and daughter stood opposite to each other.

"Am I looking at my own image in the deep water?" said the mother.

"Is it myself that I see represented on a white shield?" cried the daughter.

Then they came nearer to each other in a fond embrace. The mother's heart beat quickly, and she understood the quickened pulses. "My child!" she exclaimed, "the flower of my heart—my lotus flower of the deep water!" and she embraced her child again and wept, and the tears were as a baptism of new life and love for Helga. "In swan's plumage I came here," said the mother, "and here I threw off my feather dress. Then I sank down through the wavering ground, deep into the marsh beneath, which closed like a wall around me; I found myself after a while in fresher water; still a power drew me down deeper and deeper. I felt the weight of sleep upon my eyelids. Then I slept, and dreams hovered round me. It seemed to me as if I were again in the pyramids of Egypt, and yet the waving elder trunk that had frightened me on the moor stood ever before me. I observed the clefts and wrinkles in the stem; they shone forth in strange colors, and took the form of hieroglyphics. It was the mummy case on which I gazed. At last it burst, and forth stepped the thousand years' old king, the mummy form, black as pitch, black as the shining wood-snail, or the slimy mud of the swamp. Whether it was really the mummy or the Marsh King I know not. He seized me in his arms, and I felt as if I must die. When I recovered myself, I found in my bosom a little bird, flapping its wings, twittering and fluttering. The bird flew away from my bosom, upwards towards the dark, heavy canopy above me, but a long, green band kept it fastened to me. I heard and understood the tenor of its longings. Freedom! sunlight! to my father! Then I thought of my father, and the sunny land of my birth, my life, and my love. Then I loosened the band, and let the bird fly away to its home—to a father. Since that hour I have ceased to dream; my sleep has been long and heavy, till in this very hour, harmony and fragrance awoke me, and set me free."

The green band which fastened the wings of the bird to the mother's heart, where did it flutter now? whither had it been wafted? The stork only had seen it. The band was the green stalk, the cup of the flower the cradle in which lay the child, that now in blooming beauty had been folded to the mother's heart.

And while the two were resting in each other's arms, the old stork flew round and round them in narrowing circles, till at length he flew away swiftly to his nest, and fetched away the two suits of swan's feathers, which he had preserved there for many years. Then he returned to the mother and daughter, and threw the swan's plumage over them; the feathers immediately closed around them, and they rose up from the earth in the form of two white swans.

"And now we can converse with pleasure," said the stork-papa; "we can understand one another, although the beaks of birds are so different in shape. It is very fortunate that you came to-night. To-morrow we should have been gone. The mother, myself and the little ones, we're about to fly to the south. Look at me now: I am an old friend from the Nile, and a mother's heart contains more than her beak. She always said that the princess would know how to help herself. I and the young ones carried the swan's feathers over here, and I am glad of it now, and how lucky it is that I am here still. When the day dawns we shall start with a great company of other storks. We'll fly first, and you can follow in our track, so that you cannot miss your way. I and the young ones will have an eye upon you."

"And the lotus-flower which I was to take with me," said the Egyptian princess, "is flying here by my side, clothed in swan's feathers. The flower of my heart will travel with me; and so the riddle is solved. Now for home! now for home!"

But Helga said she could not leave the Danish land without once more seeing her foster-mother, the loving wife of the Viking. Each pleasing recollection, each kind word, every tear from the heart which her foster-mother had wept for her, rose in her mind, and at that moment she felt as if she loved this mother the best.

"Yes, we must go to the Viking's castle," said the stork; "mother and the young ones are waiting for me there. How they will open their eyes and flap their wings! My wife, you see, does not say much; she is short and abrupt in her manner; but she means well, for all that. I will flap my wings at once, that they may hear us coming." Then stork-papa flapped his wings in first-rate style, and he and the swans flew away to the Viking's castle.

In the castle, every one was in a deep sleep. It had been late in the evening before the Viking's wife retired to rest. She was anxious about Helga, who, three days before, had vanished with the Christian priest. Helga must have helped him in his flight, for it was her horse that was missed from the stable; but by what power had all this been accomplished? The Viking's wife thought of it with wonder, thought on the miracles which they said could be performed by those who believed in the Christian faith, and followed its teachings. These passing thoughts formed themselves into a vivid dream, and it seemed to her that she was still lying awake on her couch, while without darkness reigned. A storm arose; she heard the lake dashing and rolling from east and west, like the waves of the North Sea or the Cattegat. The monstrous snake which, it is said, surrounds the earth in the depths of the ocean, was trembling in spasmodic convulsions. The night of the fall of the gods was come, "Ragnorock," as the heathens call the judgment-day, when everything shall pass away, even the high gods themselves. The war trumpet sounded; riding upon the rainbow, came the gods, clad in steel, to fight their last battle on the last battle-field. Before them flew the winged vampires, and the dead warriors closed up the train. The whole firmament was ablaze with the northern lights, and yet the darkness triumphed. It was a terrible hour. And, close to the terrified woman, Helga seemed to be seated on the floor, in the hideous form of a frog, yet trembling, and clinging to her foster-mother, who took her on her lap, and lovingly caressed her, hideous and frog-like as she was. The air was filled with the clashing of arms and the hissing of arrows, as if a storm of hail was descending upon the earth. It seemed to her the hour when earth and sky would burst asunder, and all things be swallowed up in Saturn's fiery lake; but she knew that a new heaven and a new earth would arise, and that corn-fields would wave where now the lake rolled over desolate sands, and the ineffable God reign. Then she saw rising from the region of the dead, Baldur the gentle, the loving, and as the Viking's wife gazed upon him, she recognized his countenance. It was the captive Christian priest. "White Christian!" she exclaimed aloud, and with the words, she pressed a kiss on the forehead of the hideous frog-child. Then the frog-skin fell off, and Helga stood before her in all her beauty, more lovely and gentle-looking, and with eyes beaming with love. She kissed the hands of her foster-mother, blessed her for all her fostering love and care during the days of her trial and misery, for the thoughts she had suggested and awoke in her heart, and for naming the Name which she now repeated. Then beautiful Helga rose as a mighty swan, and spread her wings with the rushing sound of troops of birds of passage flying through the air.

Then the Viking's wife awoke, but she still heard the rushing sound without. She knew it was the time for the storks to depart, and that it must be their wings which she heard. She felt she should like to see them once more, and bid them farewell. She rose from her couch, stepped out on the threshold, and beheld, on the ridge of the roof, a party of storks ranged side by side. Troops of the birds were flying in circles over the castle and the highest trees; but just before her, as she stood on the threshold and close to the well where Helga had so often sat and alarmed her with her wildness, now stood two swans, gazing at her with intelligent eyes. Then she remembered her dream, which still appeared to her as a reality. She thought of Helga in the form of a swan. She thought of a Christian priest, and suddenly a wonderful joy arose in her heart. The swans flapped their wings and arched their necks as if to offer her a greeting, and the Viking's wife spread out her arms towards them, as if she accepted it, and smiled through her tears. She was roused from deep thought by a rustling of wings and snapping of beaks; all the storks arose, and started on their journey towards the south.

"We will not wait for the swans," said the mamma stork; "if they want to go with us, let them come now; we can't sit here till the plovers start. It is a fine thing after all to travel in families, not like the finches and the partridges. There the male and the female birds fly in separate flocks, which, to speak candidly, I consider very unbecoming."

"What are those swans flapping their wings for?"

"Well, every one flies in his own fashion," said the papa stork. "The swans fly in an oblique line; the cranes, in the form of a triangle; and the plovers, in a curved line like a snake."

"Don't talk about snakes while we are flying up here," said stork-mamma. "It puts ideas into the children's heads that can not be realized."

"Are those the high mountains I have heard spoken of?" asked Helga, in the swan's plumage.

"They are storm-clouds driving along beneath us," replied her mother.

"What are yonder white clouds that rise so high?" again inquired Helga.

THE MARSH KING'S DAUGHTER

"Those are mountains covered with perpetual snows, that you see yonder," said her mother. And then they flew across the Alps towards the blue Mediterranean.

"Africa's land! Egyptia's strand!" sang the daughter of the Nile, in her swan's plumage, as from the upper air she caught sight of her native land, a narrow, golden, wavy strip on the shores of the Nile; the other birds espied it also and hastened their flight.

"I can smell the Nile mud and the wet frogs," said the stork-mamma, "and I begin to feel quite hungry. Yes, now you shall taste something nice, and you will see the marabout bird, and the ibis, and the crane. They all belong to our family, but they are not nearly so handsome as we are. They give themselves great airs, especially the ibis. The Egyptians have spoilt him. They make a mummy of him, and stuff him with spices. I would rather be stuffed with live frogs, and so would you, and so you shall. Better have something in your inside while you are alive, than to be made a parade of after you are dead. That is my opinion, and I am always right."

"The storks are come," was said in the great house on the banks of the Nile, where the lord lay in the hall on his downy cushions, covered with a leopard skin, scarcely alive, yet not dead, waiting and hoping for the lotus-flower from the deep moorland in the far north. Relatives and servants were standing by his couch, when the two beautiful swans who had come with the storks flew into the hall. They threw off their soft white plumage, and two lovely female forms approached the pale, sick old man, and threw back their long hair, and when Helga bent over her grandfather, redness came back to his cheeks, his eyes brightened, and life returned to his benumbed limbs. The old man rose up with health and energy renewed; daughter and grandchild welcomed him as joyfully as if with a morning greeting after a long and troubled dream.

Joy reigned through the whole house, as well as in the stork's nest; although there the chief cause was really the good food, especially the quantities of frogs, which seemed to spring out of the ground in swarms.

Then the learned men hastened to note down, in flying characters, the story of the two princesses, and spoke of the arrival of the health-giving flower as a mighty event, which had been a blessing to the house and the land. Meanwhile, the stork-papa told the story to his family in his own way; but not till they had eaten and were satisfied; otherwise they would have had something else to do than to listen to stories.

"Well," said the stork-mamma, when she had heard it, "you will be made something of at last; I suppose they can do nothing less."

"What could I be made?" said stork-papa; "what have I done?—just nothing."

"You have done more than all the rest," she replied. "But for you and the youngsters the two young princesses would never have seen Egypt again, and the recovery of the old man would not have been effected. You will become something. They must certainly give you a doctor's hood, and our young ones will inherit it, and their children after them, and so on. You already look like an Egyptian doctor, at least in my eyes."

"I cannot quite remember the words I heard when I listened on the roof," said stork-papa, while relating the story to his family; "all I know is, that what the wise men said was so complicated and so learned, that they received not only rank, but presents; even the head cook at the great house was honored with a mark of distinction, most likely for the soup."

"And what did you receive?" said the stork-mamma. "They certainly ought not to forget the most important person in the affair, as you really are. The learned men have done nothing at all but use their tongues. Surely they will not overlook you."

Late in the night, while the gentle sleep of peace rested on the now happy house, there was still one watcher. It was not stork-papa, who, although he stood on guard on one leg, could sleep soundly. Helga alone was awake. She leaned over the balcony, gazing at the sparkling stars that shone clearer and brighter in the pure air than they had done in the north, and yet they were the same stars. She thought of the Viking's wife in the wild moorland, of the gentle eyes of her foster-mother, and of the tears she had shed over the poor frog-child that now lived in splendor and starry beauty by the waters of the Nile, with air balmy and sweet as spring. She thought of the love that dwelt in the breast of the heathen woman, love that had been shown to a wretched creature, hateful as a human being, and hideous when in the form of an animal. She looked at the glittering stars, and thought of the radiance that had shone forth on the forehead of the dead man, as she had fled with him over the woodland and moor. Tones were awakened in her memory; words which she had heard him speak as they rode onward, when she was carried, wondering and trembling, through the air; words from the great Fountain of love, the highest love that embraces all the human race. What had not been won and achieved by this love?

Day and night beautiful Helga was absorbed in the contemplation of the great amount of her happiness, and lost herself in the contemplation, like a child who turns hurriedly from the giver to examine the beautiful gifts. She was over-powered with her good fortune, which seemed always increasing, and therefore what might it become in the future? Had she not been brought by a wonderful miracle to all this joy and happiness? And in these thoughts she indulged, until at last she thought no more of the Giver. It was the over-abundance of youthful spirits unfolding its wings for a daring flight. Her eyes sparkled with energy, when suddenly arose a loud noise in the court below, and the daring thought vanished. She looked down, and saw two large ostriches running round quickly in narrow circles; she had never seen these creatures before,—great, coarse, clumsy-looking birds with curious wings that looked as if they had been clipped, and the birds themselves had the appearance of having been roughly used. She inquired about them, and for the first time heard the legend which the Egyptians relate respecting the ostrich.

Once, say they, the ostriches were a beautiful and glorious race of birds, with large, strong wings. One evening the other large birds of the forest said to the ostrich, "Brother, shall we fly to the river to-morrow morning to drink, *God willing?*" and the ostrich answered, "I will."

With the break of day, therefore, they commenced their flight; first rising high in the air, towards the sun, which is the eye of God; still higher and higher the ostrich flew, far above the other birds, proudly approaching the light, trusting in its own strength, and thinking not of the Giver, or saying, "*if God will*." When suddenly the avenging angel drew back the veil from the flaming ocean of sunlight, and in a moment the wings of the proud bird were scorched and shrivelled, and they sunk miserably to the earth. Since that time the ostrich and his race have never been able to rise in the air; they can only fly terror-stricken along the ground, or run round and round in narrow circles. It is a warning to mankind, that in all our thoughts and schemes, and in every action we undertake, we should say, "*if God will*."

Then Helga bowed her head thoughtfully and seriously, and looked at the circling ostrich, as with timid fear and simple pleasure it glanced at its own great shadow on the sunlit walls. And the story of the ostrich sunk deeply into the heart and mind of Helga: a life of happiness, both in the present and in the future, seemed secure for her, and what was yet to come might be the best of all, *God willing*.

Early in the spring, when the storks were again about to journey northward, beautiful Helga took off her golden bracelets, scratched her name on them, and beckoned to the stork-father. He came to her, and she placed the golden circlet round his neck, and begged him to deliver it safely to the Viking's wife, so that she might know that her foster-daughter still lived, was happy, and had not forgotten her.

"It is rather heavy to carry," thought stork-papa, when he had it on his neck; "but gold and honor are not to be flung into the street. The stork brings good fortune—they'll be obliged to acknowledge that at last."

"You lay gold, and I lay eggs," said stork-mamma; "with you it is only once in a way, I lay eggs every year But no one appreciates what we do; I call it very mortifying."

"But then we have a consciousness of our own worth, mother," replied stork-papa.

"What good will that do you?" retorted stork-mamma; "it will neither bring you a fair wind, nor a good meal."

"The little nightingale, who is singing yonder in the tamarind grove, will soon be going north, too." Helga said she had often heard her singing on the wild moor, so she determined to send a message by her. While flying in the swan's plumage she had learnt the bird language; she had often conversed with the stork and the swallow, and she knew that the nightingale would understand. So she begged the nightingale to fly to the beechwood, on the peninsula of Jutland, where a mound of stone and twigs had been raised to form the grave, and she begged the nightingale to persuade all the other little birds to build their nests round the place, so that evermore should resound over that grave music and song. And the nightingale flew away, and time flew away also.

In the autumn, an eagle, standing upon a pyramid, saw a stately train of richly laden camels, and men attired in armor on foaming Arabian steeds, whose glossy skins shone like silver, their nostrils were pink, and their thick, flowing manes hung almost to their slender legs. A royal prince of Arabia, handsome as a prince should be, and accompanied by distinguished guests, was on his way to the stately house, on the roof of which the storks' empty nests might be seen. They were away now in the far north, but expected to return very soon. And, indeed, they returned on a day that was rich in joy and gladness.

A marriage was being celebrated, in which the beautiful Helga, glittering in silk and jewels, was the bride, and the bridegroom the young Arab prince. Bride and bridegroom sat at the upper end of the table, between the bride's mother and grandfather. But her gaze was not on the bridegroom, with his manly, sunburnt face, round which curled a black beard, and whose dark fiery eyes were fixed upon her; but away from him, at a twinkling star, that shone down upon her from the sky. Then was heard the sound of rushing wings beating the air. The storks were coming home; and the old stork pair, although tired with the journey and requiring rest, did not fail to fly down at once to the balustrades of the verandah, for they knew already what feast was being celebrated. They had heard of it on the borders of the land, and also that Helga had caused their figures to be represented on the walls, for they belonged to her history.

"I call that very sensible and pretty," said stork-papa.

"Yes, but it is very little," said mamma stork; "they could not possibly have done less."

But, when Helga saw them, she rose and went out into the verandah to stroke the backs of the storks. The old stork pair bowed their heads, and curved their necks, and even the youngest among the young ones felt honored by this reception.

Helga continued to gaze upon the glittering star, which seemed to glow brighter and purer in its light; then between herself and the star floated a form, purer than the air, and visible through it. It floated quite near to her, and she saw that it was the dead Christian priest, who also was coming to her wedding feast—coming from the heavenly kingdom.

"The glory and brightness, yonder, outshines all that is known on earth," said he.

Then Helga the fair prayed more gently, and more earnestly, than she had ever prayed in her life before, that she might be permitted to gaze, if only for a single moment, at the glory and brightness of the heavenly kingdom. Then she felt herself lifted up, as it were, above the earth, through a sea of sound and thought; not only around her, but within her, was there light and song, such as words cannot express.

"Now we must return;" he said; "you will be missed."

"Only one more look," she begged; "but one short moment more."

"We must return to earth; the guests will have all departed. Only one more look!—the last!"

Then Helga stood again in the verandah. But the marriage lamps in the festive hall had been all extinguished, and the torches outside had vanished. The storks were gone; not a guest could be seen; no bridegroom—all in those few short moments seemed to have died. Then a great dread fell upon her. She stepped from the verandah through the empty hall into the next chamber, where slept strange warriors. She opened a side door, which once led into her own apartment, but now, as she passed through, she found herself suddenly in a garden which she had never before seen here, the sky blushed red, it was the dawn of morning. Three minutes only in heaven, and a whole night on earth had passed away! Then she saw the storks, and called to them in their own language.

Then stork-papa turned his head towards her, listened to her words, and drew near. "You speak our language," said he, "what do you wish? Why do you appear,—you—a strange woman?"

"It is I—it is Helga! Dost thou not know me? Three minutes ago we were speaking together yonder in the verandah."

"That is a mistake," said the stork, "you must have dreamed all this."

"No, no," she exclaimed. Then she reminded him of the Viking's castle, of the great lake, and of the journey across the ocean.

Then stork-papa winked his eyes, and said, "Why that's an old story which happened in the time of my grandfather. There certainly was a princess of that kind here in Egypt once, who came from the Danish land, but she vanished on the evening of her wedding day, many hundred years ago, and never came back. You may read about it yourself yonder, on a monument in the garden. There you will find swans and storks sculptured, and on the top is a figure of the princess Helga, in marble."

And so it was; Helga understood it all now, and sank on her knees. The sun burst forth in all its glory, and, as in olden times, the form of the frog vanished in his beams, and the beautiful farm stood forth in all its loveliness; so now, bathed in light, rose a beautiful form, purer, clearer than air—a ray of brightness—from the Source of light Himself. The body crumbled into dust, and a faded lotus-flower lay on the spot on which Helga had stood.

"Now that is a new ending to the story," said stork-papa; "I really never expected it would end in this way, but it seems a very good ending."

"And what will the young ones say to it, I wonder?" said stork-mamma.

"Ah, that is a very important question," replied the stork.

# THE TINDER-BOX

A soldier came marching along the high road: "Left, right—left, right." He had his knapsack on his back, and a sword at his side; he had been to the wars, and was now returning home.

As he walked on, he met a very frightful-looking old witch in the road. Her under-lip hung quite down on her breast, and she stopped and said, "Good evening, soldier; you have a very fine sword, and a large knapsack, and you are a real soldier; so you shall have as much money as ever you like."

"Thank you, old witch," said the soldier.

"Do you see that large tree," said the witch, pointing to a tree which stood beside them. "Well, it is quite hollow inside, and you must climb to the top, when you will see a hole, through which you can let yourself down into the tree to a great depth. I will tie a rope round your body, so that I can pull you up again when you call out to me."

"But what am I to do, down there in the tree?" asked the soldier.

"Get money," she replied; "for you must know that when you reach the ground under the tree, you will find yourself in a large hall, lighted up by three hundred lamps; you will then see three doors, which can be easily opened, for the keys are in all the locks. On entering the first of the chambers, to which these doors lead, you will see a large chest, standing in the middle of the floor, and upon it a dog seated, with a pair of eyes as large as teacups. But you need not be at all afraid of him; I will give you my blue checked apron, which you must spread upon the floor, and then boldly seize hold of the dog, and place him upon it. You can then open the chest, and take from it as many pence as you please, they are only copper pence; but if you would rather have silver money, you must go into the second chamber. Here you will find another dog, with eyes as big as mill-wheels; but do not let that trouble you. Place him upon my apron, and then take what money you please. If, however, you like gold best, enter the third chamber, where there is another chest full of it. The dog who sits on this chest is very dreadful; his eyes are as big as a tower, but do not mind him. If he also is placed upon my apron, he cannot hurt you, and you may take from the chest what gold you will."

"This is not a bad story," said the soldier; "but what am I to give you, you old witch? for, of course, you do not mean to tell me all this for nothing."

"No," said the witch; "but I do not ask for a single penny. Only promise to bring me an old tinder-box, which my grandmother left behind the last time she went down there."

"Very well; I promise. Now tie the rope round my body."

"Here it is," replied the witch; "and here is my blue checked apron."

As soon as the rope was tied, the soldier climbed up the tree, and let himself down through the hollow to the ground beneath; and here he found, as the witch had told him, a large hall, in which many hundred lamps were all burning. Then he opened the first door. "Ah!" there sat the dog, with the eyes as large as teacups, staring at him.

"You're a pretty fellow," said the soldier, seizing him, and placing him on the witch's apron, while he filled his pockets from the chest with as many pieces as they would hold. Then he closed the lid, seated the dog upon it again, and walked into another chamber. And, sure enough, there sat the dog with eyes as big as mill-wheels.

"You had better not look at me in that way," said the soldier; "you will make your eyes water;" and then he seated him also upon the apron, and opened the chest. But when he saw what a quantity of silver money it contained, he very quickly threw away all the coppers he had taken, and filled his pockets and his knapsack with nothing but silver.

Then he went into the third room, and there the dog was really hideous; his eyes were, truly, as big as towers, and they turned round and round in his head like wheels.

"Good morning," said the soldier, touching his cap, for he had never seen such a dog in his life. But after looking at him more closely, he thought he had been civil enough, so he placed him on the floor, and opened the chest. Good gracious, what a quantity of gold there was! enough to buy all the sugar-sticks of the sweet-stuff women; all the tin soldiers, whips, and rockinghorses in the world, or even the whole town itself. There was, indeed, an immense quantity. So the soldier now threw away all the silver money he had taken, and filled his pockets and his knapsack with gold instead; and not only his pockets and his knapsack, but even his cap and boots, so that he could scarcely walk.

He was really rich now; so he replaced the dog on the chest, closed the door, and called up through the tree, "Now pull me out, you old witch."

"Have you got the tinder-box?" asked the witch.

"No; I declare I quite forgot it." So he went back and fetched the tinder-box, and then the witch drew him up out of the tree, and he stood again in the high road, with his pockets, his knapsack, his cap, and his boots full of gold.

"What are you going to do with the tinder-box?" asked the soldier.

"That is nothing to you," replied the witch; "you have the money, now give me the tinder-box."

"I tell you what," said the soldier, "if you don't tell me what you are going to do with it, I will draw my sword and cut off your head."

"No," said the witch.

The soldier immediately cut off her head, and there she lay on the ground. Then he tied up all his money in her apron, and slung it on his back like a bundle, put the tinder-box in his pocket, and walked off to the nearest town. It was a very nice town, and he put up at the best inn, and ordered a dinner of all his favorite dishes, for now he was rich and had plenty of money.

The servant, who cleaned his boots, thought they certainly were a shabby pair to be worn by such a rich gentleman, for he had not yet bought any new ones. The next day, however, he procured some good clothes and proper boots, so that our soldier soon became known as a fine gentleman, and the people visited him, and told him all the wonders that were to be seen in the town, and of the king's beautiful daughter, the princess.

"Where can I see her?" asked the soldier.

"She is not to be seen at all," they said; "she lives in a large copper castle, surrounded by walls and towers. No one but the king himself can pass in or out, for there has been a prophecy that she will marry a common soldier, and the king cannot bear to think of such a marriage."

"I should like very much to see her," thought the soldier; but he could not obtain permission to do so. However, he passed a very pleasant time; went to the theatre, drove in the king's garden, and gave a great deal of money to the poor, which was very good of him; he remembered what it had been in olden times to be without a shilling. Now he was rich, had fine clothes, and many friends, who all declared he was a fine fellow and a real gentleman, and all this gratified him exceedingly. But his money would not last forever; and as he spent and gave away a great deal daily,

THE TINDER-BOX

and received none, he found himself at last with only two shillings left. So he was obliged to leave his elegant rooms, and live in a little garret under the roof, where he had to clean his own boots, and even mend them with a large needle. None of his friends came to see him, there were too many stairs to mount up. One dark evening, he had not even a penny to buy a candle; then all at once he remembered that there was a piece of candle stuck in the tinder-box, which he had brought from the old tree, into which the witch had helped him.

He found the tinder-box, but no sooner had he struck a few sparks from the flint and steel, than the door flew open and the dog with eyes as big as teacups, whom he had seen while down in the tree, stood before him, and said, "What orders, master?"

"Hallo," said the soldier; "well this is a pleasant tinder-box, if it brings me all I wish for.

"Bring me some money," said he to the dog.

He was gone in a moment, and presently returned, carrying a large bag of coppers in his mouth. The soldier very soon discovered after this the value of the tinder-box. If he struck the flint once, the dog who sat on the chest of copper money made his appearance; if twice, the dog came from the chest of silver; and if three times, the dog with eyes like towers, who watched over the gold. The soldier had now plenty of money; he returned to his elegant rooms, and reappeared in his fine clothes, so that his friends knew him again directly, and made as much of him as before.

After a while he began to think it was very strange that no one could get a look at the princess. "Every one says she is very beautiful," thought he to himself; "but what is the use of that if she is to be shut up in a copper castle surrounded by so many towers. Can I by any means get to see her. Stop! where is my tinder-box?" Then he struck a light, and in a moment the dog, with eyes as big as teacups, stood before him.

"It is midnight," said the soldier, "yet I should very much like to see the princess, if only for a moment."

The dog disappeared instantly, and before the soldier could even look round, he returned with the princess. She was lying on the dog's back asleep, and looked so lovely, that every one who saw her would know she was a real princess. The soldier could not help kissing her, true soldier as he was. Then the dog ran back with the princess; but in the morning, while at breakfast with the king and queen, she told them what a singular dream she had had during the night, of a dog and a soldier, that she had ridden on the dog's back, and been kissed by the soldier.

"That is a very pretty story, indeed," said the queen. So the next night one of the old ladies of the court was set to watch by the princess's bed, to discover whether it really was a dream, or what else it might be.

The soldier longed very much to see the princess once more, so he sent for the dog again in the night to fetch her, and to run with her as fast as ever he could. But the old lady put on water boots, and ran after him as quickly as he did, and found that he carried the princess into a large house. She thought it would help her to remember the place if she made a large cross on the door with a piece of chalk. Then she went home to bed, and the dog presently returned with the princess. But when he saw that a cross had been made on the door of the house, where the soldier lived, he took another piece of chalk and made crosses on all the doors in the town, so that the lady-in-waiting might not be able to find out the right door.

Early the next morning the king and queen accompanied the lady and all the officers of the household, to see where the princess had been.

"Here it is," said the king, when they came to the first door with a cross on it.

"No, my dear husband, it must be that one," said the queen, pointing to a second door having a cross also.

"And here is one, and there is another!" they all exclaimed; for there were crosses on all the doors in every direction.

So they felt it would be useless to search any farther. But the queen was a very clever woman; she could do a great deal more than merely ride in a carriage. She took her large gold scissors, cut a piece of silk into squares, and made a neat little bag. This bag she filled with buckwheat flour, and tied it round the princess's neck; and then she cut a small hole in the bag, so that the flour might be scattered on the ground as the princess went along. During the night, the dog came again and carried the princess on his back, and ran with her to the soldier, who loved her very much, and wished that he had been a prince, so that he might have her for a wife. The dog did not observe how the flour ran out of the bag all the way from the castle wall to the soldier's house, and even up to the window, where he had climbed with the princess. Therefore in the morning the king and queen found out where their daughter had been, and the soldier was taken up and put in prison. Oh, how dark and disagreeable it was as he sat there, and the people said to him, "To-morrow you will be hanged." It was not very pleasant news, and besides, he had left the tinder-box at the inn. In the morning he could see through the iron grating of the little window how the people were hastening out of the town to see him hanged; he heard the drums beating, and saw the soldiers marching. Every one ran out to look at them, and a shoemaker's boy, with a leather apron and slippers on, galloped by so fast, that one of his slippers flew off and struck against the wall where the soldier sat looking through the iron grating. "Hallo, you shoemaker's boy, you need not be in such a hurry," cried the soldier to him. "There will be nothing to see till I come; but if you will run to the house where I have been living, and bring me my tinder-box, you shall have four shillings, but you must put your best foot foremost."

The shoemaker's boy liked the idea of getting the four shillings, so he ran very fast and fetched the tinder-box, and gave it to the soldier. And now we shall see what happened. Outside the town a large gibbet had been erected, round which stood the soldiers and several thousands of people. The king and the queen sat on splendid thrones opposite to the judges and the whole council. The soldier already stood on the ladder; but as they were about to place the rope around his neck, he said that an innocent request was often granted to a poor criminal before he suffered death. He wished very much to smoke a pipe, as it would be the last pipe he should ever smoke in the world. The king could not refuse this request, so the soldier took his tinder-box, and struck fire, once, twice, thrice,—and there in a moment stood all the dogs;—the one with eyes as big as teacups, the one with eyes as large as mill-wheels, and the third, whose eyes were like towers. "Help me now, that I may not be hanged," cried the soldier.

And the dogs fell upon the judges and all the councillors; seized one by the legs, and another by the nose, and tossed them many feet high in the air, so that they fell down and were dashed to pieces.

"I will not be touched," said the king. But the largest dog seized him, as well as the queen, and threw them after the others. Then the soldiers and all the people were afraid, and cried, "Good soldier, you shall be our king, and you shall marry the beautiful princess."

So they placed the soldier in the king's carriage, and the three dogs ran on in front and cried "Hurrah!" and the little boys whistled through their fingers, and the soldiers presented arms. The princess came out of the copper castle, and became queen, which was very pleasing to her. The wedding festivities lasted a whole week, and the dogs sat at the table, and stared with all their eyes.

# THE BOTTLE NECK

CLOSE TO the corner of a street, among other abodes of poverty, stood an exceedingly tall, narrow house, which had been so knocked about by time that it seemed out of joint in every direction. This house was inhabited by poor people, but the deepest poverty was apparent in the garret lodging in the gable. In front of the little window, an old bent bird-cage hung in the sunshine, which had not even a proper water-glass, but instead of it the broken neck of a bottle, turned upside down, and a cork stuck in to make it hold the water with which it was filled. An old maid stood at the window; she had hung chickweed over the cage, and the little linnet which it contained hopped from perch to perch and sang and twittered merrily.

"Yes, it's all very well for you to sing," said the bottle neck: that is, he did not really speak the words as we do, for the neck of a bottle cannot speak; but he thought them to himself in his own mind, just as people sometimes talk quietly to themselves.

"Yes, you may sing very well, you have all your limbs uninjured; you should feel what it is like to lose your body, and only have a neck and a mouth left, with a cork stuck in it, as I have: you wouldn't sing then, I know. After all, it is just as well that there are some who can be happy. I have no reason to sing, nor could I sing now if I were ever so happy; but when I was a whole bottle, and they rubbed me with a cork, didn't I sing then? I used to be called a complete lark. I remember when I went out

to a picnic with the furrier's family, on the day his daughter was betrothed,—it seems as if it only happened yesterday. I have gone through
a great deal in my time, when I come to recollect: I have been in the fire
and in the water, I have been deep in the earth, and have mounted
higher in the air than most other people, and now I am swinging here,
outside a bird-cage, in the air and the sunshine. Oh, indeed, it would be
worth while to hear my history; but I do not speak it aloud, for a good
reason—because I cannot."

Then the bottle neck related his history, which was really rather remarkable; he, in fact, related it to himself, or, at least, thought it in his
own mind. The little bird sang his own song merrily; in the street below
there was driving and running to and fro, every one thought of his own
affairs, or perhaps of nothing at all; but the bottle neck thought deeply.
He thought of the blazing furnace in the factory, where he had been
blown into life; he remembered how hot it felt when he was placed in the
heated oven, the home from which he sprang, and that he had a strong
inclination to leap out again directly; but after a while it became cooler,
and he found himself very comfortable. He had been placed in a row,
with a whole regiment of his brothers and sisters all brought out of the
same furnace; some of them had certainly been blown into champagne
bottles, and others into beer bottles, which made a little difference between them. In the world it often happens that a beer bottle may contain
the most precious wine, and a champagne bottle be filled with blacking,
but even in decay it may always be seen whether a man has been well
born. Nobility remains noble, as a champagne bottle remains the same,
even with blacking in its interior. When the bottles were packed our
bottle was packed amongst them; it little expected then to finish its career
as a bottle neck, or to be used as a water-glass to a bird's-cage, which is,
after all, a place of honor, for it is to be of some use in the world. The
bottle did not behold the light of day again, until it was unpacked with
the rest in the wine merchant's cellar, and, for the first time, rinsed with
water, which caused some very curious sensations. There it lay empty,
and without a cork, and it had a peculiar feeling, as if it wanted something it knew not what. At last it was filled with rich and costly wine, a
cork was placed in it, and sealed down. Then it was labelled "first quality,"
as if it had carried off the first prize at an examination; besides, the wine
and the bottle were both good, and while we are young is the time for
poetry. There were sounds of song within the bottle, of things it could
not understand, of green sunny mountains, where the vines grow and
where the merry vine-dressers laugh, sing, and are merry. "Ah, how
beautiful is life." All these tones of joy and song in the bottle were like
the working of a young poet's brain, who often knows not the meaning
of the tones which are sounding within him. One morning the bottle
found a purchaser in the furrier's apprentice, who was told to bring one
of the best bottles of wine. It was placed in the provision basket with ham
and cheese and sausages. The sweetest fresh butter and the finest bread
were put into the basket by the furrier's daughter herself, for she packed
it. She was young and pretty; her brown eyes laughed, and a smile lin-
gered round her mouth as sweet as that in her eyes. She had delicate

hands, beautifully white, and her neck was whiter still. It could easily be seen that she was a very lovely girl, and as yet she was not engaged. The provision basket lay in the lap of the young girl as the family drove out to the forest, and the neck of the bottle peeped out from between the folds of the white napkin. There was the red wax on the cork, and the bottle looked straight at the young girl's face, and also at the face of the young sailor who sat near her. He was a young friend, the son of a portrait painter. He had lately passed his examination with honor, as mate, and the next morning he was to sail in his ship to a distant coast. There had been a great deal of talk on this subject while the basket was being packed, and during this conversation the eyes and the mouth of the furrier's daughter did not wear a very joyful expression. The young people wandered away into the green wood, and talked together. What did they talk about? The bottle could not say, for he was in the provision basket. It remained there a long time; but when at last it was brought forth it appeared as if something pleasant had happened, for every one was laughing; the furrier's daughter laughed too, but she said very little, and her cheeks were like two roses. Then her father took the bottle and the cork-screw into his hands. What a strange sensation it was to have the cork drawn for the first time! The bottle could never after that forget the performance of that moment; indeed there was quite a convulsion within him as the cork flew out, and a gurgling sound as the wine was poured forth into the glasses.

"Long life to the betrothed," cried the papa, and every glass was emptied to the dregs, while the young sailor kissed his beautiful bride.

"Happiness and blessing to you both," said the old people—father and mother, and the young man filled the glasses again.

"Safe return, and a wedding this day next year," he cried; and when the glasses were empty he took the bottle, raised it on high, and said, "Thou hast been present here on the happiest day of my life; thou shalt never be used by others!" So saying, he hurled it high in the air.

The furrier's daughter thought she should never see it again, but she was mistaken. It fell among the rushes on the borders of a little woodland lake. The bottle neck remembered well how long it lay there unseen. "I gave them wine, and they gave me muddy water," he had said to himself, "but I suppose it was all well meant." He could no longer see the betrothed couple, nor the cheerful old people; but for a long time he could hear them rejoicing and singing. At length there came by two peasant boys, who peeped in among the reeds and spied out the bottle. Then they took it up and carried it home with them, so that once more it was provided for. At home in their wooden cottage these boys had an elder brother, a sailor, who was about to start on a long voyage. He had been there the day before to say farewell, and his mother was now very busy packing up various things for him to take with him on his voyage. In the evening his father was going to carry the parcel to the town to see his son once more, and take him a farewell greeting from his mother. A small bottle had already been filled with herb tea, mixed with brandy, and wrapped in a parcel; but when the boys came in they brought with them a larger and stronger bottle, which they had found. This bottle would hold so much more than the little one, and they all said the brandy would be so good for complaints of the stomach, especially as it was mixed with medical herbs. The liquid which they now poured into the bottle was not like the red wine with which it had once been filled; these were bitter drops, but they are of great use sometimes—for the stomach. The new large bottle was to go, not the little one: so the bottle once more started on its travels. It was taken on board (for Peter Jensen was one of the crew) the very same ship in which the young mate was to sail. But the mate did not see the bottle: indeed if he had he would not have known it, or supposed it was the one out of which they had drunk to the felicity of the betrothed and to the prospect of a marriage on his own happy return. Certainly the bottle no longer poured forth wine, but it contained something quite as good; and so it happened that whenever Peter Jensen brought it out, his messmates gave it the name of "the apothecary," for it contained the best medicine to cure the stomach, and he gave it out quite willingly as long as a drop remained. Those were happy days, and the bottle would sing when rubbed with a cork, and it was called a "great lark," "Peter Jensen's lark."

Long days and months rolled by, during which the bottle stood empty in a corner, when a storm arose—whether on the passage out or home it could not tell, for it had never been ashore. It was a terrible storm, great waves arose, darkly heaving and tossing the vessel to and fro. The main mast was split asunder, the ship sprang a leak, and the pumps became useless, while all around was black as night. At the last moment, when the ship was sinking, the young mate wrote on a piece of paper, "We are going down: God's will be done." Then he wrote the name of his betrothed, his own name, and that of the ship. Then he put the leaf in an empty bottle that happened to be at hand, corked it down tightly, and threw it into the foaming sea. He knew not that it was the very same bottle from which the goblet of joy and hope had once been filled for him, and now it was tossing on the waves with his last greeting, and a message from the dead. The ship sank, and the crew sank with her; but the bottle flew on like a bird, for it bore within it a loving letter from a loving heart. And as the sun rose and set, the bottle felt as at the time of its first existence, when in the heated glowing stove it had a longing to fly away. It outlived the storms and the calm, it struck against no rocks, was not devoured by sharks, but drifted on for more than a year, sometimes towards the north, sometimes towards the south, just as the current carried it. It was in all other ways its own master, but even of that one may get tired. The written leaf, the last farewell of the bridegroom to his bride, would only bring sorrow when once it reached her hands; but where were those hands, so soft and delicate, which had once spread the table-cloth on the fresh grass in the green wood, on the day of her betrothal? Ah, yes! where was the furrier's daughter? and where was the land which might lie nearest to her home?

The bottle knew not, it travelled onward and onward, and at last all this wandering about became wearisome; at all events it was not its usual occupation. But it had to travel, till at length it reached land—a foreign country. Not a word spoken in this country could the bottle understand;

it was a language it had never before heard, and it is a great loss not to be able to understand a language. The bottle was fished out of the water, and examined on all sides. The little letter contained within it was discovered, taken out, and turned and twisted in every direction; but the people could not understand what was written upon it. They could be quite sure that the bottle had been thrown overboard from a vessel, and that something about it was written on this paper: but what was written? that was the question,—so the paper was put back into the bottle, and then both were put away in a large cupboard of one of the great houses of the town. Whenever any strangers arrived, the paper was taken out and turned over and over, so that the address, which was only written in pencil, became almost illegible, and at last no one could distinguish any letters on it at all. For a whole year the bottle remained standing in the cupboard, and then it was taken up to the loft, where it soon became covered with dust and cobwebs. Ah! how often then it thought of those better days—of the times when in the fresh, green wood, it had poured forth rich wine; or, while rocked by the swelling waves, it had carried in its bosom a secret, a letter, a last parting sigh. For full twenty years it stood in the loft, and it might have stayed there longer but that the house was going to be rebuilt. The bottle was discovered when the roof was taken off; they talked about it, but the bottle did not understand what they said—a language is not to be learnt by living in a loft, even for twenty years. "If I had been down stairs in the room," thought the bottle, "I might have learnt it." It was now washed and rinsed, which process was really quite necessary, and afterwards it looked clean and transparent, and felt young again in its old age; but the paper which it had carried so faithfully was destroyed in the washing. They filled the bottle with seeds, though it scarcely knew what had been placed in it. Then they corked it down tightly, and carefully wrapped it up. There not even the light of a torch or lantern could reach it, much less the brightness of the sun or moon. "And yet," thought the bottle, "men go on a journey that they may see as much as possible, and I can see nothing." However, it did something quite as important; it travelled to the place of its destination, and was unpacked.

"What trouble they have taken with that bottle over yonder!" said one, "and very likely it is broken after all." But the bottle was not broken, and, better still, it understood every word that was said: this language it had heard at the furnaces and at the wine merchant's; in the forest and on the ship,—it was the only good old language it could understand. It had returned home, and the language was as a welcome greeting. For very joy, it felt ready to jump out of people's hands, and scarcely noticed that its cork had been drawn, and its contents emptied out, till it found itself carried to a cellar, to be left there and forgotten. "There's no place like home, even if it's a cellar." It never occurred to him to think that he might lie there for years, he felt so comfortable. For many long years he remained in the cellar, till at last some people came to carry away the bottles, and ours amongst the number.

Out in the garden there was a great festival. Brilliant lamps hung in festoons from tree to tree; and paper lanterns, through which the light

THE BOTTLE-NECK

shone till they looked like transparent tulips. It was a beautiful evening, and the weather mild and clear. The stars twinkled; and the new moon, in the form of a crescent, was surrounded by the shadowy disc of the whole moon, and looked like a gray globe with a golden rim: it was a beautiful sight for those who had good eyes. The illumination extended even to the most retired of the garden walks, at least not so retired that any one need lose himself there. In the borders were placed bottles, each containing a light, and among them the bottle with which we are acquainted, and whose fate it was, one day, to be only a bottle neck, and to serve as a water-glass to a bird's-cage. Everything here appeared lovely to our bottle, for it was again in the green wood, amid joy and feasting; again it heard music and song, and the noise and murmur of a crowd, especially in that part of the garden where the lamps blazed, and the paper lanterns displayed their brilliant colors. It stood in a distant walk certainly, but a place pleasant for contemplation; and it carried a light; and was at once useful and ornamental. In such an hour it is easy to forget that one has spent twenty years in a loft, and a good thing it is to be able to do so. Close before the bottle passed a single pair, like the bridal pair—the mate and the furrier's daughter—who had so long ago wandered in the wood. It seemed to the bottle as if he were living that time over again. Not only the guests but other people were walking in the garden, who were allowed to witness the splendor and the festivities. Among the latter came an old maid, who seemed to be quite alone in the world. She was thinking, like the bottle, of the green wood, and of a young betrothed pair, who were closely connected with herself; she was thinking of that hour, the happiest of her life, in which she had taken part, when she had herself been one of that betrothed pair; such hours are never to be forgotten, let a maiden be as old as she may. But she did not recognize the bottle, neither did the bottle notice the old maid. And so we often pass each other in the world when we meet, as did these two, even while together in the same town.

The bottle was taken from the garden, and again sent to a wine merchant, where it was once more filled with wine, and sold to an aeronaut, who was to make an ascent in his balloon on the following Sunday. A great crowd assembled to witness the sight; military music had been engaged, and many other preparations made. The bottle saw it all from the basket in which he lay close to a live rabbit. The rabbit was quite excited because he knew that he was to be taken up, and let down again in a parachute. The bottle, however, knew nothing of the "up," or the "down;" he saw only that the balloon was swelling larger and larger till it could swell no more, and began to rise and be restless. Then the ropes which held it were cut through, and the aerial ship rose in the air with the aeronaut and the basket containing the bottle and the rabbit, while the music sounded and all the people shouted "Hurrah."

"This is a wonderful journey up into the air," thought the bottle; "it is a new way of sailing, and here, at least, there is no fear of striking against anything."

Thousands of people gazed at the balloon, and the old maid who was in the garden saw it also; for she stood at the open window of the garret, by which hung the cage containing the linnet, who then had no water-glass, but was obliged to be contented with an old cup. In the window-sill stood a myrtle in a pot, and this had been pushed a little on one side, that it might not fall out; for the old maid was leaning out of the window, that she might see. And she did see distinctly the aeronaut in the balloon, and how he let down the rabbit in the parachute, and then drank to the health of all the spectators in the wine from the bottle. After doing this, he hurled it high into the air. How little she thought that this was the very same bottle which her friend had thrown aloft in her honor, on that happy day of rejoicing, in the green wood, in her youthful days. The bottle had no time to think, when raised so suddenly; and before it was aware, it reached the highest point it had ever attained in its life. Steeples and roofs lay far, far beneath it, and the people looked as tiny as possible. Then it began to descend much more rapidly than the rabbit had done, made somersaults in the air, and felt itself quite young and unfettered, although it was half full of wine. But this did not last long. What a journey it was! All the people could see the bottle; for the sun shone upon it. The balloon was already far away, and very soon the bottle was far away also; for it fell upon a roof, and broke in pieces. But the pieces had got such an impetus in them, that they could not stop themselves. They went jumping and rolling about, till at last they fell into the court-yard, and were broken into still smaller pieces; only the neck of the bottle managed to keep whole, and it was broken off as clean as if it had been cut with a diamond.

"That would make a capital bird's glass," said one of the cellar-men; but none of them had either a bird or a cage, and it was not to be expected they would provide one just because they had found a bottle neck that could be used as a glass. But the old maid who lived in the garret had a bird, and it really might be useful to her; so the bottle neck was provided with a cork, and taken up to her; and, as it often happens in life, the part that had been uppermost was now turned downwards, and it was filled with fresh water. Then they hung it in the cage of the little bird, who sang and twittered more merrily than ever.

"Ah, you have good reason to sing," said the bottle neck, which was looked upon as something very remarkable, because it had been in a balloon; nothing further was known of its history. As it hung there in the bird's-cage, it could hear the noise and murmur of the people in the street below, as well as the conversation of the old maid in the room within. An old friend had just come to visit her, and they talked, not about the bottle neck, but of the myrtle in the window.

"No, you must not spend a dollar for your daughter's bridal bouquet," said the old maid; "you shall have a beautiful little bunch for a nosegay, full of blossoms. Do you see how splendidly the tree has grown? It has been raised from only a little sprig of myrtle that you gave me on the day after my betrothal, and from which I was to make my own bridal bouquet when a year had passed: but that day never came; the eyes were closed which were to have been my light and joy through life. In the depths of the sea my beloved sleeps sweetly; the myrtle has become an old tree, and I am a still older woman. Before the sprig you gave me faded, I took a spray, and planted it in the earth; and now, as you see, it has become a large tree, and a bunch of the blossoms shall at last appear at a wedding festival, in the bouquet of your daughter."

There were tears in the eyes of the old maid, as she spoke of the beloved of her youth, and of their betrothal in the wood. Many thoughts came into her mind; but the thought never came, that quite close to her, in that very window, was a remembrance of those olden times,—the neck of the bottle which had, as it were, shouted for joy when the cork flew out with a bang on the betrothal day. But the bottle neck did not recognize the old maid; he had not been listening to what she had related, perhaps because he was thinking so much about her.

# LITTLE TUK

YES, THEY called him Little Tuk, but it was not his real name; he had called himself so before he could speak plainly, and he meant it for Charles. It was all very well for those who knew him, but not for strangers.

Little Tuk was left at home to take care of his little sister, Gustava, who was much younger than himself, and he had to learn his lessons at the same time, and the two things could not very well be performed together. The poor boy sat there with his sister on his lap, and sung to her all the songs he knew, and now and then he looked into his geography lesson that lay open before him. By the next morning he had to learn by heart all the towns in Zealand, and all that could be described of them.

His mother came home at last, and took little Gustava in her arms. Then Tuk ran to the window, and read so eagerly that he nearly read his eyes out; for it had become darker and darker every minute, and his mother had no money to buy a light.

"There goes the old washerwoman up the lane," said the mother, as she looked out of the window; "the poor woman can hardly drag herself along, and now she had to drag a pail of water from the well. Be a good boy, Tuk, and run across and help the old woman, won't you?"

So Tuk ran across quickly, and helped her, but when he came back into the room it was quite dark, and there was not a word said about a light, so he was obliged to go to bed on his little truckle bedstead, and there he lay and thought of his geography lesson, and of Zealand, and of all the master had told him. He ought really to have read it over again, but he could not for want of light. So he put the geography book under his pillow, for he had heard that this was a great help towards learning a lesson, but not always to be depended upon. He still lay thinking and thinking, when all at once it seemed as if some one kissed him on his eyes and mouth. He slept and yet he did not sleep; and it appeared as if the old washerwoman looked at him with kind eyes and said, "It would be a great pity if you did not know your lesson to-morrow morning; you

LITTLE TUK

helped me, and now I will help you, and Providence will always keep those who help themselves;" and at the same time the book under Tuk's pillow began to move about. "Cluck, cluck, cluck," cried a hen as she crept towards him. "I am a hen from Kjöge,"* and then she told him how many inhabitants the town contained, and about a battle that had been fought there, which really was not worth speaking of.

"Crack, crack," down fell something. It was a wooden bird, the parrot which is used as a target as Prästöe.† He said there were as many inhabitants in that town as he had nails in his body. He was very proud, and said, "Thorwalsden lived close to me,‡ and here I am now, quite comfortable."

But now little Tuk was no longer in bed; all in a moment he found himself on horseback. Gallop, gallop, away he went, seated in front of a richly-attired knight, with a waving plume, who held him on the saddle, and so they rode through the wood by the old town of Wordingburg, which was very large and busy. The king's castle was surrounded by lofty towers, and radiant light streamed from all the windows. Within there were songs and dancing; King Waldemar and the young gayly-dressed ladies of the court were dancing together. Morning dawned, and as the sun rose, the whole city and the king's castle sank suddenly down together. One tower after another fell, till at last only one remained standing on the hill where the castle had formerly been.§

The town now appeared small and poor, and the school-boys read in their books, which they carried under their arms, that it contained two thousand inhabitants; but this was a mere boast, for it did not contain so many.

And again little Tuk lay in his bed, scarcely knowing whether he was dreaming or not, for some one stood by him.

"Tuk! little Tuk!" said a voice. It was a very little person who spoke. He was dressed as a sailor, and looked small enough to be a middy, but he was not one. "I bring you many greetings from Corsör.§§ It is a rising town, full of life. It has steamships and mail-coaches. In times past they used to call it ugly, but that is no longer true. I lie on the sea-shore," said Corsör; "I have high-roads and pleasure-gardens; I have given birth to a poet who was witty and entertaining, which they are not all. I once wanted to fit out a ship to sail round the world, but I did not accomplish it, though most likely I might have done so. But I am fragrant with

*Kjöge, a little town on Kjöge Bay. Lifting up children by placing the hands on each side of their heads, is called "showing them Kjöge hens."

†Prästöe, a still smaller town.

‡About a hundred paces from Prästöe lies the estate of Nysöe, where Thorwalsden usually resided while in Denmark, and where he executed many memorable works.

§Wordingburg under King Waldemar was a place of great importance; now it is a very insignificant town: only a lonely tower and the remains of a well show where the castle once stood.

§§Corsör, on the Great Belt, used to be called the most tiresome town in Denmark before the establishment of steamers. Travellers had to wait for a favorable wind. The title of "tiresome" was ingeniously added to the Danish escutcheon by a witticism of Vaudeville Heibergs. The poet Baggesen was born here.

perfume, for close to my gates most lovely roses bloom."

Then before the eyes of little Tuk appeared a confusion of colors, red and green; but it cleared off, and he could distinguish a cliff close to the bay, the slopes of which were quite overgrown with verdure, and on its summit stood a fine old church with pointed towers. Springs of water flowed out of the cliff in thick waterspouts, so that there was a continual splashing. Close by sat an old king with a golden crown on his white head. This was King Hroar of the Springs* and near the springs stood the town of Roeskilde, as it is called. Then all the kings and queens of Denmark went up the ascent to the old church, hand in hand, with golden crowns on their heads, while the organ played and the fountains sent forth jets of water.

Little Tuk saw and heard it all. "Don't forget the names of these towns," said King Hroar.

All at once everthing vanished; but where! It seemed to him like turning over the leaves of a book. And now there stood before him an old peasant woman, who had come from Soröe,† where the grass grows in the marketplace. She had a green linen apron thrown over her head and shoulders, and it was quite wet, as if it had been raining heavily. "Yes, that it has," said she, and then, just as she was going to tell him a great many pretty stories from Holberg's comedies, and about Waldemar and Absalom, she suddenly shrunk up together, and wagged her head as if she were a frog about to spring. "Croak," she cried; "it is always wet, and as quiet as death in Soröe." Then little Tuk saw she was changed into a frog. "Croak," and again she was an old woman. "One must dress according to the weather," said she. "It is wet, and my town is just like a bottle. By the cork we must go in, and by the cork we must come out again. In olden times I had beautiful fish, and now I have fresh, rosy-cheeked boys in the bottom of the bottle, and they learn wisdom, Hebrew and Greek."

"Croak." How it sounded like the cry of the frogs on the moor, or like the creaking of great boots when some one is marching,—always the same tone, so monotonous and wearing, that little Tuk at length fell fast asleep, and then the sound could not annoy him. But even in this sleep came a dream or something like it. His little sister Gustava, with her blue eyes, and fair curly hair, had grown up a beautiful maiden all at once, and without having wings she could fly. And they flew together over Zealand, over green forests and blue lakes.

"Hark, so you hear the cock crow, little Tuk. 'Cock-a-doodle-doo.' The fowls are flying out of Kjöge. You shall have a large farm-yard. You shall never suffer hunger or want. The bird of good omen shall be yours, and you shall become a rich and happy man; your house shall rise up like

*Roeskilde (from Roesquelle, rose-spring, falsely called Rothschild), once the capital of Denmark. The town took its name from King Hroar, and from the numerous springs in the neighborhood. In its beautiful cathedral most of the kings and queens of Denmark are buried. In Roeskilde the Danish States used to assemble.

†Soröe, a very quiet little town in a beautiful situation, surrounded by forests and lakes. Holberg, the Molière of Denmark, founded a noble academy here. The poets Hanck and Jugeman were professors here. Letztern lives there still.

King Waldemar's towers, and shall be richly adorned with marble statues, like those at Prästöe. Understand me well; your name shall travel with fame round the world like the ship that was to sail from Corsör, and at Roeskilde,—Don't forget the names of the towns, as King Hroar said,— you shall speak well and clearly little Tuk, and when at last you lie in your grave you shall sleep peacefully, as—"

"As if I lay in Soröe," said little Tuk awaking. It was bright daylight, and he could not remember his dream, but that was not necessary, for we are not to know what will happen to us in the future. Then he sprang out of bed quickly, and read over his lesson in the book, and knew it all at once quite correctly. The old washerwoman put her head in at the door, and said, "Many thanks, you good child, for your help yesterday. I hope all your beautiful dreams will come true."

Little Tuk did not at all know what he had dreamt, but One above did.


# SHE WAS GOOD FOR NOTHING


THE MAYOR stood at the open window. He looked smart, for his shirt-frill, in which he had stuck a breast-pin, and his ruffles, were very fine. He had shaved his chin uncommonly smooth, although he had cut himself slightly, and had stuck a piece of newspaper over the place. "Hark 'ee, youngster!" cried he.

The boy to whom he spoke was no other than the son of a poor washer-woman, who was just going past the house. He stopped, and respectfully took off his cap. The peak of this cap was broken in the middle, so that he could easily roll it up and put it in his pocket. He stood before the mayor in his poor but clean and well-mended clothes, with heavy wooden shoes on his feet, looking as humble as if it had been the king himself.

"You are a good and civil boy," said the mayor. "I suppose your mother is busy washing the clothes down by the river, and you are going to carry that thing to her that you have in your pocket. It is very bad for your mother. How much have you got in it?"

"Only half a quartern," stammered the boy in a frightened voice.

"And she has had just as much this morning already?"

"No, it was yesterday," replied the boy.

"Two halves make a whole," said the mayor. "She's good for nothing. What a sad thing it is with these people. Tell your mother she ought to be ashamed of herself. Don't you become a drunkard, but I expect you will though. Poor child! there, go now."

The boy went on his way with his cap in his hand, while the wind fluttered his golden hair till the locks stood up straight. He turned round the corner of the street into the little lane that led to the river, where his mother stood in the water by her washing bench, beating the linen with a heavy wooden bar. The floodgates at the mill had been drawn up, and

SHE WAS GOOD FOR NOTHING

as the water rolled rapidly on, the sheets were dragged along by the stream, and nearly overturned the bench, so that the washerwoman was obliged to lean against it to keep it steady. "I have been very nearly carried away," she said; "it is a good thing that you are come, for I want something to strengthen me. It is cold in the water, and I have stood here six hours. Have you brought anything for me?"

The boy drew the bottle from his pocket, and the mother put it to her lips, and drank a little.

"Ah, how much good that does, and how it warms me," she said; "it is as good as a hot meal, and not so dear. Drink a little, my boy; you look quite pale; you are shivering in your thin clothes, and autumn has really come. Oh, how cold the water is! I hope I shall not be ill. But no, I must not be afraid of that. Give me a little more, and you have a sip too, but only a sip; you must not get used to it, my poor, dear child." She stepped up to the bridge on which the boy stood as she spoke, and came on shore. The water dripped from the straw mat which she had bound round her body, and from her gown. "I work hard and suffer pain with my poor hands," said she, "but I do it willingly, that I may be able to bring you up honestly and truthfully, my dear boy."

At the same moment, a woman, rather older than herself, came towards them. She was a miserable-looking object, lame of one leg, and with a large false curl hanging down over one of her eyes, which was blind. This curl was intended to conceal the blind eye, but it made the defect only more visible. She was a friend of the laundress, and was called, among the neighbors, "Lame Martha, with the curl." "Oh, you poor thing; how you do work, standing there in the water!" she exclaimed. "You really do need something to give you a little warmth, and yet spiteful people cry out about the few drops you take." And then Martha repeated to the laundress, in a very few minutes, all that the mayor had said to her boy, which she had overheard; and she felt very angry that any man could speak, as he had done, of a mother to her own child, about the few drops she had taken; and she was still more angry because, on that very day, the mayor was going to have a dinner-party, at which there would be wine, strong, rich wine, drunk by the bottle. "Many will take more than they ought, but they don't call that drinking! *They* are all right, you are good for nothing indeed!" cried Martha indignantly.

"And so he spoke to you in that way, did he, my child?" said the washerwoman, and her lips trembled as she spoke. "He says you have a mother who is good for nothing. Well, perhaps he is right, but he should not have said it to my child. How much has happened to me from that house!"

"Yes," said Martha; "I remember you were in service there, and lived in the house when the mayor's parents were alive; how many years ago that is. Bushels of salt have been eaten since then, and people may well be thirsty," and Martha smiled. "The mayor's great dinner-party to-day ought to have been put off, but the news came too late. The footman told me the dinner was already cooked, when a letter came to say that the mayor's younger brother in Copenhagen is dead."

"Dead!" cried the laundress, turning pale as death.

"Yes, certainly," replied Martha; "but why do you take it so much to heart? I suppose you knew him years ago, when you were in service there?"

"Is he dead?" she exclaimed. "Oh, he was such a kind, good-hearted man, there are not many like him," and the tears rolled down her cheeks as she spoke. Then she cried, "Oh, dear me; I feel quite ill: everything is going round me, I cannot bear it. Is the bottle empty?" and she leaned against the plank.

"Dear me, you are ill indeed," said the other woman. "Come, cheer up; perhaps it will pass off. No, indeed, I see you are really ill; the best thing for me to do is to lead you home."

"But my washing yonder?"

"I will take care of that. Come, give me your arm. The boy can stay here and take care of the linen, and I'll come back and finish the washing; it is but a trifle."

The limbs of the laundress shook under her, and she said, "I have stood too long in the cold water, and I have had nothing to eat the whole day since the morning. O kind Heaven, help me to get home; I am in a burning fever. Oh, my poor child," and she burst into tears. And he, poor boy, wept also, as he sat alone by the river, near to and watching the damp linen.

The two women walked very slowly. The laundress slipped and tottered through the lane, and round the corner, into the street where the mayor lived; and just as she reached the front of his house, she sank down upon the pavement. Many persons came round her, and Lame Martha ran into the house for help. The mayor and his guests came to the window.

"Oh, it is the laundress," said he; "she has had a little drop too much. She is good for nothing. It is a sad thing for her pretty little son. I like the boy very well; but the mother is good for nothing."

After a while the laundress recovered herself, and they led her to her poor dwelling, and put her to bed. Kind Martha warmed a mug of beer for her, with butter and sugar—she considered this the best medicine—and then hastened to the river, washed and rinsed, badly enough, to be sure, but she did her best. Then she drew the linen ashore, wet as it was, and laid it in a basket. Before evening, she was sitting in the poor little room with the laundress. The mayor's cook had given her some roasted potatoes and a beautiful piece of fat for the sick woman. Martha and the boy enjoyed these good things very much; but the sick woman could only say that the smell was very nourishing, she thought. By-and-by the boy was put to bed, in the same bed as the one in which his mother lay; but he slept at her feet, covered with an old quilt made of blue and white patchwork. The laundress felt a little better by this time. The warm beer had strengthened her, and the smell of the good food had been pleasant to her.

"Many thanks, you good soul," she said to Martha. "Now the boy is asleep, I will tell you all. He is soon asleep. How gentle and sweet he looks as he lies there with his eyes closed! He does not know how his mother has suffered; and Heaven grant he never may know it. I was in service at the counsellor's, the father of the mayor, and it happened that the youngest of his sons, the student, came home. I was a young wild girl then, but honest; that I can declare in the sight of Heaven. The student was merry and gay, brave and affectionate; every drop of blood in him was good and honorable; a better man never lived on earth. He was the son of the house, and I was only a maid; but he loved me truly and honorably, and he told his mother of it. She was to him as an angel upon earth; she was so wise and loving. He went to travel, and before he started he placed a gold ring on my finger; and as soon as he was out of the house, my mistress sent for me. Gently and earnestly she drew me to her, and spake as if an angel were speaking. She showed me clearly, in spirit and in truth, the difference there was between him and me. 'He is pleased now,' she said, 'with your pretty face; but good looks do not last long. You have not been educated like he has. You are not equals in mind and rank, and therein lies the misfortune. I esteem the poor,' she added. 'In the sight of God, they may occupy a higher place than many of the rich; but here upon earth we must beware of entering upon a false track, lest we are overturned in our plans, like a carriage that travels by a dangerous road. I know a worthy man, an artisan, who wishes to marry you. I mean Eric, the glovemaker. He is a widower, without children, and in a good position. Will you think it over?' Every word she said pierced my heart like a knife; but I knew she was right, and the thought pressed heavily upon me. I kissed her hand, and wept bitter tears, and I wept still more when I went to my room, and threw myself on the bed. I passed through a dreadful night; God knows what I suffered, and how I struggled. The following Sunday I went to the house of God to pray for light to direct my path. It seemed like a providence that as I stepped out of church Eric came towards me; and then there remained not a doubt in my mind. We were suited to each other in rank and circumstances. He was, even then, a man of good means. I went up to him, and took his hand, and said, 'Do you still feel the same for me?' 'Yes; ever and always,' said he. 'Will you, then, marry a maiden who honors and esteems you, although she cannot offer you her love? but that may come.' 'Yes, it will come,' said he; and we joined our hands together, and I went home to my mistress. The gold ring which her son had given me I wore next to my heart. I could not place it on my finger during the daytime, but only in the evening, when I went to bed. I kissed the ring till my lips almost bled, and then I gave it to my mistress, and told her that the banns were to be put up for me and the glovemaker the following week. Then my mistress threw her arms round me, and kissed me. She did not say that I was 'good for nothing;' very likely I was better then than I am now; but the misfortunes of this world were unknown to me then. At Michael-mas we were married, and for the first year everything went well with us. We had a journeyman and an apprentice, and you were our servant, Martha."

"Ah, yes, and you were a dear, good mistress," said Martha, "I shall never forget how kind you and your husband were to me."

"Yes, those were happy years when you were with us, although we had no children at first. The student I never met again. Yet I saw him once, although he did not see me. He came to his mother's funeral. I saw him, looking pale as death, and deeply troubled, standing at her grave; for she was his mother. Sometime after, when his father died, he was in foreign lands, and did not come home. I know that he never married, I believe he became a lawyer. He had forgotten me, and even had we met he would not have known me, for I have lost all my good looks, and perhaps that is all for the best." And then she spoke of the dark days of trial, when misfortune had fallen upon them.

"We had five hundred dollars," she said, "and there was a house in the street to be sold for two hundred, so we thought it would be worth our while to pull it down and build a new one in its place; so it was bought. The builder and carpenter made an estimate that the new house would cost ten hundred and twenty dollars to build. Eric had credit, so he borrowed the money in the chief town. But the captain, who was bringing it to him, was shipwrecked, and the money lost. Just about this time, my dear sweet boy, who lies sleeping there, was born, and my husband was attacked with a severe lingering illness. For three quarters of a year I was obliged to dress and undress him. We were backward in our payments, we borrowed more money, and all that we had was lost and sold, and then my husband died. Since then I have worked, toiled, and striven for the sake of the child. I have scrubbed and washed both coarse and fine linen, but I have not been able to make myself better off; and it was God's will. In His own time He will take me to Himself, but I know He will never forsake my boy." Then she fell asleep. In the morning she felt much refreshed, and strong enough, as she thought, to go on with her work. But as soon as she stepped into the cold water, a sudden faintness seized her; she clutched at the air convulsively with her hand, took one step forward, and fell. Her head rested on dry land, but her feet were in the water; her wooden shoes, which were only tied on by a wisp of straw, were carried away by the stream,and thus she was found by Martha when she came to bring her some coffee.

In the meantime a messenger had been sent to her house by the mayor, to say that she must come to him immediately, as he had something to tell her. It was too late; a surgeon had been sent for to open a vein in her arm, but the poor woman was dead.

"She has drunk herself to death," said the cruel mayor. In the letter, containing the news of his brother's death, it was stated that he had left in his will a legacy of six hundred dollars to the glovemaker's widow, who had been his mother's maid, to be paid with discretion, in large or small sums to the widow or her child.

"There was something between my brother and her, I remember," said the mayor; "it is a good thing that she is out of the way, for now the boy will have the whole. I will place him with honest people to bring him up, that he may become a respectable working man." And the blessing of God rested upon these words. The mayor sent for the boy to come to him, and promised to take care of him, but most cruelly added that it was a good thing that his mother was dead, for "she was good for nothing." They carried her to the churchyard, the churchyard in which the poor were buried. Martha strewed sand on the grave and planted a rose-tree upon it, and the boy stood by her side.

"Oh, my poor mother!" he cried, while the tears rolled down his cheeks. "Is it true what they say, that she was good for nothing?"

"No, indeed, it is not true," replied the old servant, raising her eyes to heaven; "she was worth a great deal; I knew it years ago, and since the last night of her life I am more certain of it than ever. I say she was a good and worthy woman, and God, who is in heaven, knows I am speaking the truth, though the world may say, even now she was good for nothing."

# PART TWO
## *Traditional Tales*

### TOLLER'S NEIGHBORS

ONCE UPON a time a young man and a young girl were in service together at a mansion down near Klode Mill, in the district of Lysgaard. They became attached to each other, and as they both were honest and faithful servants, their master and mistress had a great regard for them, and gave them a wedding dinner the day they were married. Their master gave them also a little cottage with a little field, and there they went to live.

This cottage lay in the middle of a wild heath, and the surrounding country was in bad repute; for in the neighbourhood were a number of old grave-mounds, which it was said were inhabited by the Mount-folk; though Toller, so the peasant was called, cared little for that. "When one only trusts in God," thought Toller, "and does what is just and right to all men, one need not be afraid of anything." They had now taken possession of their cottage and moved in all their little property. When the man and his wife, late one evening, were sitting talking together as to how they could best manage to get on in the world, they heard a knock at the door, and on Toller opening it, in walked a little little man, and wished them "Good evening." He had a red cap on his head, a long beard and long hair, a large hump on his back, and a leathern apron before him, in which was stuck a hammer. They immediately knew him to be a Troll; notwithstanding he looked so good-natured and friendly, that they were not at all afraid of him.

"Now hear, Toller," said the little stranger, "I see well enough that you know who I am, and matters stand thus: I am a poor little hill-man, to whom people have left no other habitation on earth than the graves of fallen warriors, or mounds, where the rays of the sun never can shine down upon us. We have heard that you are come to live here, and our king is fearful that you will do us harm, and even destroy us. He has, therefore, sent me up to you this evening, that I should beg of you, as amicably as I could, to allow us to hold our dwellings in peace. You shall never be annoyed by us, or disturbed by us in your pursuits."

"Be quite at your ease, good man," said Toller, "I have never injured any of God's creatures willingly, and the world is large enough for us all, I believe; and I think we can manage to agree, without the one having

479

any need to do mischief to the other."

"Well, thank God!" exclaimed the little man, beginning in his joy to dance about the room, "that is excellent, and we will in return do you all the good in our power, and that you will soon discover; but now I must depart."

"Will you not first take a spoonful of supper with us?" asked the wife, setting a dish of porridge down on the stool near the window; for the Man of the Mount was so little that he could not reach up to the table. "No, I thank you," said the mannikin, "our king is impatient for my return, and it would be a pity to let him wait for the good news I have to tell him." Hereupon the little man bade them fare well and went his way.

From that day forwards, Toller lived in peace and concord with the little people of the Mount. They could see them go in and out of their mounds in daylight, and no one ever did anything to vex them. At length they became so familiar, that they went in and out of Toller's house, just as if it had been their own. Sometimes it happened that they would borrow a pot or a copper-kettle from the kitchen, but always brought it back again, and set it carefully on the same spot from which they had taken it. They also did all the service they could in return. When the spring came, they would come out of their mounds in the night, gather all the stones off the arable land, and lay them in a heap along the furrows. At harvest time they would pick up all the ears of corn, that nothing might be lost to Toller. All this was observed by the farmer, who, when in bed, or when he read his evening prayer, often thanked the Almighty for having given him the Mount-folk for neighbors. At Easter and Whitsuntide, or in the Christmas holidays, he always set a dish of nice milk-porridge for them, as good as it could be made, out on the mound.

Once, after having given birth to a daughter, his wife was so ill that Toller thought she was near her end. He consulted all the cunning people in the district, but no one knew what to prescribe for her recovery. He sat up every night and watched over the sufferer, that he might be at hand to administer to her wants. Once he fell asleep, and on opening his eyes again towards morning, he saw the room full of the Mount-folk: one sat and rocked the baby, another was busy in cleaning the room, a third stood by the pillow of the sick woman and made a drink of some herbs, which he gave his wife. As soon as they observed that Toller was awake they all ran out of the room; but from that night the poor woman began to mend, and before a fortnight was past she was able to leave her bed and go about her household work, well and cheerful as before.

Another time, Toller was in trouble for want of money to get his horses shod before he went to the town. He talked the matter over with his wife, and they knew not well what course to adopt. But when they were in bed his wife said: "Art thou asleep, Toller?" "No," he answered, "what is it?" "I think," said she, "there is something the matter with the horses in the stable, they are making such a disturbance." Toller rose, lighted his lantern, and went to the stable, and, on opening the door, found it full of the little Mount-folk. They had made the horses lie down, because the mannikins could not reach up to them. Some were employed in taking off the old shoes, some were filing the heads of the nails, while others were tacking on the new shoes; and the next morning, when Toller took his horses to water, he found them shod so beautifully that the best of smiths could not have shod them better. In this manner the Mount-folk and Toller rendered all the good services they could to each other, and many years passed pleasantly. Toller began to grow an old man, his daughter was grown up, and his circumstances were better every year. Instead of the little cottage in which he began the world, he now owned a large and handsome house, and the naked wild heath was converted into fruitful arable land.

One evening just before bed-time, some one knocked at the door, and the Man of the Mount walked in. Toller and his wife looked at him with surprise; for the mannikin was not in his usual dress. He wore on his head a shaggy cap, a woollen kerchief round his throat, and a great sheep-skin cloak covered his body. In his hand he had a stick, and his countenance was very sorrowful. He brought a greeting to Toller from the king, who requested that he, his wife, and little Inger would come over to them in the Mount that evening, for the king had a matter of importance, about which he wished to talk with him. The tears ran down the little man's cheeks while he said this, and when Toller tried to comfort him, and inquired into the source of his trouble, the Man of the Mount only wept the more, but would not impart the cause of his grief.

Toller, his wife and daughter, then went over to the Mount. On descending into the cave, they found it decorated with bunches of sweet willow, crowfoots, and other flowers, that were to be found on the heath. A large table was spread from one end of the cave to the other. When the peasant and his family entered, they were placed at the head of the table by the side of the king. The little folk also took their places, and began to eat, but they were far from being as cheerful as usual; they sat and sighed and hung down their heads; and it was easy to see that something had gone amiss with them. When the repast was finished, the king said to Toller: "I invited you to come over to us because we all wished to thank you for having been so kind and friendly to us, during the whole time we have been neighbors. But now there are so many churches built in the land, and all of them have such great bells, which ring so loud morning and evening, that we can bear it no longer; we are, therefore, going to leave Jutland and pass over to Norway, as the greater number of our people have done long ago. We now wish you farewell, Toller, as we must part."

When the king had said this, all the Mount-folk came and took Toller by the hand, and bade him farewell, and the same to his wife. When they came to Inger, they said: "To you, dear Inger, we will give a remembrance of us, that you may think of the little Mount-people when they are far away." And as they said this, each took up a stone from the ground and threw it into Inger's apron. They left the Mount one by one, with the king leading the way.

Toller and his family remained standing on the Mount as long as they could discern them. They saw the little Trolls wandering over the heath, each with a wallet on his back and a stick in his hand. When they had gone a good part of the way, to where the road leads down to the sea, they all turned round once more, and waved their hands, to say farewell. Then they disappeared, and Toller saw them no more. Sorrowfully he returned to his home.

The next morning Inger saw that all the small stones the Mount-folk had thrown into her apron shone and sparkled, and were real precious stones. Some were blue, others brown, white, and black, and it was the Trolls who had imparted the colour of their eyes to the stones, that Inger might remember them when they were gone; and all the precious stones which we now see, shine and sparkle only because the Mount-folk have given them the color of their eyes, and it was some of these beautiful precious stones which they once gave to Inger.

# THE TROLL'S HAMMER

THERE WAS once a great famine in the country; the poor could not procure the necessaries of life, and even the rich suffered great privation. At that time a poor peasant dwelt out on the heath. One day he said to his son, that he could no longer support him, and that he must go out in the world, and provide for himself. Niels, therefore, left home and wandered forth.

Towards evening he found himself in a large forest, and climbed up into a tree, lest the wild beasts might do him harm during the night. When he had slept about an hour or perhaps more, a little man came running towards the tree. He was hunch-backed, had crooked legs, a long beard, and a red cap on his head. He was pursued by a werwolf, which attacked him just under the tree in which Niels was sitting. The little man began to scream; he bit and scratched, and defended himself as well as he could, but all to no purpose, the werwolf was his master, and would have torn him in pieces, if Niels had not sprung down from the tree, and come to his assistance. As soon as the werwolf saw that he had two to contend with, he was afraid, and fled back into the forest.

The Troll then said to Niels: "Thou hast preserved my life, and done me good service; in return I will also give thee something that will be beneficial to thee. See! here is a hammer, with which all the smith's work thou doest, no one shall be able to equal. Continue thy way, and things will go better than thou thinkest." When the Troll had spoken these words, he sank into the ground before Niels.

The next day the boy wandered on, until he came in the neighbourhood of the royal palace, and here he engaged himself to a smith.

Now it just happened, that a few days previously a thief had broken into the king's treasury and stolen a large bag of money. All the smiths in the city were, therefore, sent for to the palace, and the king promised that he who could make the best and securest lock, should be appointed court locksmith, and have a considerable reward into the bargain. But the lock must be finished in eight days, and so constructed that it could not be picked by any one.

When the smith, with whom Niels lived, returned home and related this, the boy thought he should like to try whether his hammer really possessed those qualities which the Troll had said. He therefore begged his master to allow him to make a lock, and promised that it should be finished by the appointed time. Although the smith had no great opinion of the boy's ability, he, nevertheless, allowed him to make the trial. Niels then requested to have a separate workshop, locked himself in, and then began hammering the iron. One day went, and then another, and the master began to be inquisitive; but Niels let no one come in, and the smith was obliged to remain outside, and peep through the keyhole. The work, however, succeeded far better than the boy himself had expected; and, without his really knowing how it came to pass, the lock was finished on the evening of the third day.

The following morning he went down to his master and asked him for some money. "Yesterday I worked hard," said he, "and to-day I will make myself merry." Here-upon he went out of the city, and did not return to the workshop till late in the evening. The next day he did the same, and idled away the rest of the week. His master was, consequently, very angry, and threatened to turn him away, unless he finished his work at the appointed time. But Niels told him to be quite easy, and engaged that his lock should be the best. When the day arrived. Niels brought his work forth, and carried it up to the palace, and it appeared that his lock was so ingenious and delicately made, that it far excelled all the others. The consequence was, that Niels' master was acknowledged as the most skil-ful, and received the promised office and reward.

The smith was delighted, but he took good care not to confess to any one who it was that had made the curious lock. He now received one work after another from the king, and let Niels do them all, and he soon became a wealthy man.

In the meantime, the report spread from place to place of the inge-nious lock the king had got for his treasury. Travellers came from a great distance to see it, and it happened that a foreign king came also to the palace. When he had examined the work for a long time, he said, that the man who could make such a lock deserved to be honoured and respected. "But however good a smith he may be," added the king, "I have got his master at home." He continued boasting in this manner, till at length the king offered to wager with him which could execute the most skilful piece of workmanship. The smiths were sent for, and the two kings determined, that each smith should make a knife. He who won was to have a considerable reward. The smith related to Niels what had passed, and desired him to try whether he could not make as good a knife as he had a lock. Niels promised that he would, although his last work had not benefited him much. The smith was in truth an avaricious man, and treated him so poorly that at times he had not enough to eat and drink.

It happened one day, as Niels was gone out to buy steel to make the knife, that he met a man from his own village, and, in the course of conversation, learnt from him that his father went begging from door to door, and was in great want and misery. When Niels heard this he asked his master for some money to help his father; but his master answered, that he should not have a shilling, before he had made the knife. Hereupon Niels shut himself up in the workshop, worked a whole day, and, as on the former occasion, the knife was made without his knowing how it happened.

When the day arrived on which the work was to be exhibited, Niels dressed himself in his best clothes, and went with his master up to the palace, where the two kings were expecting them. The strange smith first showed his knife. It was so beautiful, and so curiously wrought, that it was a pleasure to look at it; it was, moreover, so sharp and well tempered, that it could cut through a millstone to the very centre, as if it had been only a cheese, and that without the edge being in the least blunted. Niels' knife, on the contrary, looked very poor and common. The king already began to think he had lost his wager, and spoke harshly to the master-smith, when his boy begged leave to examine the stranger's knife a little more closely. After having looked at it for some time, he said: "This is a beautiful piece of workmanship which you have made, and shame on those who would say otherwise; but my master is, nevertheless, your superior, as you shall soon experience." Saying this, he took the stranger's knife and split it lengthwise from the point to the handle with his own knife, as easily as one splits a twig of willow. The kings could scarcely believe their eyes; and the consequence was, that the Danish smith was declared the victor, and got a large bag of money to carry home with him.

When Niels asked for payment, his master refused to give him anything, although he well knew that the poor boy only wanted the money to help his father. Upon this Niels grew angry, went up to the king, and related the whole story to him, how it was he who had made both the lock and the knife. The master was now called, but he denied everything, and accused Niels of being an idle boy, whom he had taken into his service out of charity and compassion.

"The truth of this story we shall soon find out," said the king, who sided with the master. "Since thou sayest it is thou who has made this wonderful knife, and thy master says it is he who has done it, I will adjudge each of you to make a sword for me within eight days. He who can make the most perfect one shall be my master-smith; but he who loses, shall forfeit his life."

Neils was well satisfied with this agreement. He went home, packed up all his things, and bade his master farewell. The smith was now in great straits, and would gladly have made all good again; but Niels appeared not to understand him, and went his way, and engaged with another master, where he cheerfully began to work on the sword.

When the appointed day arrived, they both met at the palace, and the master produced a sword of the most elaborate workmanship that any one could wish to see, besides being inlaid with gold, and set with precious stones. The king was greatly delighted with it.

"Now, little Niels," said he, "what dost thou say to this sword?"

"Certainly," answered the boy, "it is not so badly made as one might expect from such a bungler."

"Canst thou show anything like it?" asked the king.

"I believe I can," answered Niels.

"Well, produce thy sword; where is it?" said the king.

"I have it in my waistcoat pocket," replied Niels.

Hereupon there was a general laugh, which was increased when they saw the boy take a little packet out of his waistcoat pocket. Niels opened the paper, in which the blade was rolled up like a watch-spring. "Here is my work," said he, "will you just cut the thread, master?"

The smith did it willingly, and in a moment the blade straightened itself and struck him in the face.

Niels took out of his other pocket a hilt of gold, and screwed it fast to the blade; then presented the sword to the king; and all present were obliged to confess that they never before had seen such matchless workmanship.

Niels was unanimously declared the victor, and the master was obliged to acknowledge that the boy had made both the lock and the knife.

The king in his indignation would have had the master executed, if the boy had not begged for mercy on the culprit. Niels received a handsome reward from the king, and from that day all the work from the palace was intrusted to him. He took his old father to reside with him, and lived in competence and happiness till his death.

# THE MAGICIAN'S PUPIL

THERE WAS once a peasant who had a son, whom, when of a proper age, his father apprenticed to a trade; but the boy, who had no inclination for work, always ran home again to his parents; at this the father was much troubled, not knowing what course to pursue. One day he entered a church, where, after repeating the Lord's Prayer, he said: "To what trade shall I apprentice my son? He runs away from every place."

The clerk, who happened at that moment to be standing behind the altar, hearing the peasant utter these words, called out in answer: "Teach him witchcraft; teach him witchcraft!"

The peasant, who did not see the clerk, thought it was our Lord who gave him this advice, and determined upon following it.

The next day he said to his son, that he should go with him, and he would find him a new situation. After walking a good way into the country, they met with a shepherd tending his flock.

"Where are you going to, good man?" inquired the shepherd.

"I am in search of a master, who can teach my son the black art," answered the peasant. "You may soon find him," said the shepherd:

"keep straight on and you will come to the greatest wizard that is to be found in all the land." The peasant thanked him for this information, and went on. Soon after, he came to a large forest, in the middle of which stood the wizard's house. He knocked at the door, and asked the Troll-man whether he had any inclination to take a boy as a pupil. "Yes," answered the other; "but not for a less term than four years; and we will make this agreement, that at the end of that time, you shall come, and if you can find your son, he shall belong to you, but should you not be able to discover him, he must remain in my house, and serve me for the rest of his life."

The peasant agreed to these conditions, and returned home alone. At the end of a week he began to look for his son's return; thinking that in this, as in all former cases, he would run away from his master. But he did not come back, and his mother began to cry, and say her husband had not acted rightly in giving their child into the power of the evil one, and that they should never see him more.

After four years had elapsed the peasant set out on a journey to the magician's, according to their agreement. A little before he reached the forest, he met the same shepherd, who instructed him how to act so as to get his son back. "When you get there," said he, "you must at night keep your eyes constantly turned towards the fireplace, and take care not to fall asleep, for then the Troll-man will convey you back to your own house, and afterwards say you did not come at the appointed time. To-morrow you will see three dogs in the yard, eating milk-porridge out of a dish. The middle one is your son, and he is the one you must choose."

The peasant thanked the shepherd for his information, and bade him farewell.

When he entered the house of the magician, everything took place as the shepherd had said. He was conducted into the yard, where he saw three dogs. Two of them were handsome with smooth skins, but the third was lean and looked ill. When the peasant patted the dogs, the two handsome ones growled at him, but the lean one, on the contrary, wagged his tail. "Canst thou now tell me which of these three dogs is thy son?" said the Troll-man; "if so thou canst take him with thee; if not, he belongs to me."

"Well then I will choose the one that appears the most friendly," answered the peasant; "although he looks less handsome than the others." "That is a sensible choice," said the Troll-man; "he knew what he was about who gave thee that advice."

The peasant was then allowed to take his son home with him. So, putting a cord round his neck, he went his way, bewailing that his son was changed into a dog. "Oh! why are you bewailing so?" asked the shepherd as he came out of the forest, "it appears to me you have not been so very unlucky."

When he had gone a little way, the dog said to him: "Now you shall see that my learning has been of some use to me. I will soon change myself into a little tiny dog, and then you must sell me to those who are coming past." The dog did as he said, and became a beautiful little creature. Soon after a carriage came rolling along with some great folks in it. When they saw the beautiful little dog that ran playing along the road, and heard that it was for sale, they bought it of the peasant for a considerable sum, and at the same moment the son changed his father into a hare, which he caused to run across the road, while he was taken up by those who had bought him. When they saw the hare they set the dog after it, and scarcely had they done so, than both hare and dog ran into the wood and disappeared. Now the boy changed himself again, and this time both he and his father assumed human forms. The old man began cutting twigs and his son helped him. When the people in the carriage missed the little dog, they got out to seek after it, and asked the old man and his son if they had seen anything of a little dog that had run away. The boy directed them further into the wood, and he and his father returned home, and lived well on the money they had received by selling the dog.

When all the money was spent, both father and son resolved upon going out again in search of adventures. "Now I will turn myself into a boar," said the youth, "and you must put a cord round my leg and take me to Horsens market for sale; but remember to throw the cord over my right ear at the moment you sell me, and then I shall be home again as soon as you."

The peasant did as his son directed him, and went to market; but he set so high a price on the boar, that no one would buy it, so he continued standing in the market till the afternoon was far advanced. At length there came an old man who bought the boar of him. This was no other than the magician, who, angry that the father had got back his son, had never ceased seeking after them from the time they had left his house. When the peasant had sold his boar he threw the cord over its right ear as the lad had told him, and in the same moment the animal vanished; and when he reached his own door he again saw his son sitting at the table.

They now lived a pleasant merry life until all the money was spent, and then again set out on fresh adventures. This time the son changed himself into a bull, first reminding his father to throw the rope over his right ear as soon as he was sold. At the market he met with the same old man, and soon came to an agreement with him about the price of the bull. While they were drinking a glass together in the alehouse, the father threw the rope over the bull's right horn, and when the magician went to fetch his purchase it had vanished, and the peasant upon reaching home again found his son sitting by his mother at the table. The third time the lad turned himself into a horse, and the magician was again in the market and bought him. "Thou hast already tricked me twice," said he to the peasant; "but it shall not happen again." Before he paid down the money he hired a stable and fastened the horse in, so that it was impossible for the peasant to throw the rein over the animal's right ear. The old man, nevertheless, returned home, in the hope that this time also he should find his son; but he was disappointed, for no lad was there. The magician in the meantime mounted the horse and rode off. He well knew whom he had bought, and determined that the boy should pay with his life the deception he had practised upon him. He led the horse through swamps and pools, and galloped at a pace that, had he long continued it, he must have ridden the animal to death; but the horse was a hard trotter, and the magician being old he at last found he had got his master, and was therefore obliged to ride home.

When he arrived at his house he put a magic bridle on the horse and shut him in a dark stable without giving him anything either to eat or drink. When some time had elapsed, he said to the servant-maid: "Go out and see how the horse is." When the girl came into the stable the metamorphosed boy (who had been the girl's sweetheart while he was in the Troll's house) began to moan piteously, and begged her to give him a pail of water. She did so, and on her return told her master that the horse was well. Some time after he again desired her to go out and see if the horse were not yet dead. When she entered the stable the poor animal begged her to loose the rein and the girths, which were strapped so tight that he could hardly draw breath. The girl did as she was requested, and no sooner was it done than the boy changed himself into a hare and ran out of the stable. The magician, who was sitting in the window, was immediately aware of what had happened on seeing the hare go springing across the yard, and, instantly changing himself into a dog, went in pursuit of it. When they had run many miles over corn-fields and meadows, the boy's strength began to fail and the magician gained more and more upon him. The hare then changed itself into a dove, but the magician as quickly turned himself into a hawk and pursued him afresh.

In this manner they flew towards a palace where a princess was sitting at a window. When she saw a hawk in chase of a dove she opened the window, and immediately the dove flew into the room, and then changed itself into a gold ring. The magician now became a prince, and went into the apartment for the purpose of catching the dove. When he could not find it, he asked permission to see her gold rings. The princess showed them to him, but let one fall into the fire. The Troll-man instantly drew it out, in doing which he burnt his fingers, and was obliged to let it fall on the floor. The boy now knew of no better course than to change himself into a grain of corn.

At the same moment the magician became a hen, in order to eat the corn, but scarcely had he done so than the boy became a hawk and killed him.

He then went to the forest, fetched all the magician's gold and silver, and from that day lived in wealth and happiness with his parents.

# TEMPTATIONS

In Vinding, near Veile, lived once a poor cottager, who went out as day labourer; his son was employed by the priest at Skjærup to run on errands, for which he received his board and lodging. One day the boy was sent with a letter for the priest at Veile. It was in the middle of summer, and the weather was very hot; when he had walked some distance he became tired and drowsy, and lay down to sleep. On awaking he saw a willow, from the roots of which the water had washed away all the earth, whereby the tree was on the point of perishing. "I am but little, it is true," said John, for such was the boy's name, "and can do but little, still I can help thee." He then began to throw mould on the bare roots, and ceased not till they were quite covered and protected. When he had finished, he heard a soft voice proceeding from the tree, which said to him: "Thou shalt not have rendered me this good service for nothing; cut a pipe from my branches, and everything for which thou blowest shall befall thee."

Although the boy did not give much credit to this, he, nevertheless, cut off a twig for a pipe. "As such a fine promise has been made me," thought he to himself, "I will wish that I could blow myself into a good situation by Michaelmas, that I might be of some use to my poor old father." He blew, but saw nothing, and then, putting his pipe in his pocket, hurried on to make up for the time he had loitered away at the willow-tree. Not long after he found a pocket-book full of money lying in the road. Now John by keeping it, could at once have relieved both his own and his father's necessities, but such a thought never entered his mind; on the contrary, he ran back to the town, inquired of all that he met, whether they had not lost a pocket-book. At length there came a horseman galloping along the road, and when John also asked him, the stranger replied that he had that morning dropped his pocket-book on his way from home, at the same time giving a description of it.

John delivered the pocket-book to him, and the horseman, who was a proprietor from Ostedgaard, near Fredericia, was so gratified, that he immediately gave the boy a handsome reward, and asked him if he would like to enter his service. "Yes, I should indeed," answered John, quite pleased at the thought. He then parted from the gentleman with many thanks for his kindness, after having agreed between them that John should come down to Osted at Michaelmas. He then executed his errand for the priest, and felt convinced, that it was alone owing to the pipe that he had met with such a lucky adventure; he therefore concealed it carefully, and let no one know anything of the matter.

Now this gentleman was an adept in the black art, and had only offered to take the lad into his service that he might see how far his honesty would be proof against the temptations into which he purposed to lead him.

At the appointed time John went to Ostedgaard, and was summoned by the master, who inquired of him what he could do. "I am not fit for much," said John, "as I am so little; but I will do my best at all times to perform whatever my good master requires of me." "That is well, with that I am contented," answered the master; "I have twelve hares, these thou must take to the wood every morning, and if thou bringest back the full number every evening I will give thee house and home in remuneration; but if thou allowest them to run away, thou wilt have a reckoning to settle with me." "I will do my best," answered John.

The next morning his master came down to the inclosure, and counted the hares. As soon as he opened the door and gave the animals their liberty, away they all ran, one to the east, another to the west, and John remained standing alone; he was not, however, so disheartened as might be imagined; for he had his willow pipe in his pocket. As soon, therefore, as he came into a lonely part of the wood, he took out his pipe and began to blow, and no sooner had he put it to his mouth, than all the twelve hares came running and assembled round him. As John now felt he could rely on the virtues of his pipe, he let them all go again, and passed his time in amusing himself. In the evening he took out his pipe again, and as he walked up to the manor continued blowing it. All the hares then came forth and followed him one by one. The master was standing at the gate, to see what would take place. He could not recover from his astonishment, when he saw the little herd-boy blowing his pipe as he approached the house, and all the hares following him as gently and quietly as if it were a flock of sheep he was driving home. "Thou art more clever than thou appearest," said the master; "the number is right, go in and get some food; for to-day thou hast done a good piece of work: we shall now see whether thou art as fortunate to-morrow."

The next day everything passed in exactly the same manner. As soon as the inclosure was opened, all the hares ran out in different directions, and the boy let them enjoy their liberty, as he now felt certain that he could bring them back whenever he wished. But this time his master had prepared a harder trial for him.

At noon he desired his daughter to disguise herself in a peasant's dress, and to go and ask the boy to give her a hare. The young maiden was so beautiful that he did not think John could refuse her request.

When the daughter had thus disguised herself, she went into the field and began talking to John, asking him what he was doing there. "I am taking care of hares," answered the boy.

"What has become of thy hares?" said the maiden, "I see nothing of them." "Oh, they are only gone a little way into the wood," said he; "but as soon as I call them they will all come back again." When the young girl pretended to doubt this, he blew on his pipe, and instantly all the twelve came running towards him. She now begged and prayed him to give her one of them. The boy at first refused, but as she was very importunate, he at length told her that she should have a hare for a kiss. In short, the maiden got the hare, and carried it up to the manor; but when John thought she must be near home, he blew on his pipe, and immediately the hare came bounding back to him, and so he brought all the twelve home that evening.

On the third day, the lord of Osted was determined to try whether he could not trick the boy. He therefore dressed himself like a peasant and went in search of John. When they had conversed some time, he requested him to call his hares together, and when they came, he wished to purchase one of them, but the boy answered, that he did not dare to sell what did not belong to him. As the lord continued to entreat him most urgently, John promised him a hare, if he would give him the ring that was on his finger. The lord, it must be observed, had forgotten to take off his ring when he put on the peasant's dress, and now found that he was known. He, nevertheless, gave the boy the ring and got one of the hares. When he had nearly reached Osted, John blew on his pipe, and, although the master held the hare as firmly as he could, it got away and ran back, just as on the preceding day. When the master found he could not get the better of the boy by fair means, he had recourse to the black art, and ascertained that the willow pipe was the cause of the hares always obeying John.

When the boy returned on the fourth evening, his master gave him plenty of food and strong drink, and being unaccustomed to such things, he soon fell asleep, so that it was no difficult matter to steal his pipe from him. The next day the hares were turned out as usual; but this time John could not bring them back; he, consequently, durst not show himself at Osted, but continued wandering about the wood, crying and sobbing. His master had now gained his point. When it began to grow dark, he went to seek for John, and asked him why he remained away so long that evening. John scarcely ventured to confess his misfortune; but as his master continued urging him to tell him, he at length acknowledged that the hares had run away, and that it was not in his power to get them back again.

The lord took pity on him and told him to return home, for the loss was not very great. "A house and home I see thou wilt not get at present," said he as they walked back, "unless thou canst fulfil a condition, which I will propose to-morrow." John was glad to hear these words; for his sorrow was less at losing what his master had promised him than at forfeiting his benefactor's favour, and being turned out of the house. The next day there were guests at Ostedgaard, and when they were all assembled, the lord of the manor, calling John, told him he should have what had been promised him, if he could relate a bagful of untruths. "No," replied John, "to untruths I have never been addicted; but, if my good master pleases, I can, perhaps, tell him a bagful of truths."

"Well then," said his master, "here is a bag, and now begin thy story."

John began to recite about his lot as a little boy, how he had passed all his life in indigence and misery. Then he recited about his adventure with the willow-tree, how he had obtained his pipe, and had afterwards found the pocket-book, which was the cause of his master taking him into his service. Lastly, he recited how a maiden had come to him and given him a kiss for a hare. As he was continuing his master called out (as he did not wish his own fruitless attempt should be known): "Stop, John, thou hast kept thy word—the bag is full." He then let the boy go out of the room, and told his guests how faithfully and honourably John had always conducted himself, adding, that it was not possible to seduce him to deceive or to tell an untruth."

"Still I think it is to be done," said the proprietor of Nebbegaard. "I will answer for it that he will not be able to withstand, if he is seriously tempted."

His host felt offended by this doubting, and immediately offered to lay as large a wager as his neighbour pleased, that he could not get John either to deceive him or to tell an untruth. The challenge was accepted, and their estates were pledged for and against the boy.

The proprietor of Nebbegaard wrote a letter to his daughter, in which he explained to her what had taken place, and how important it was for him to win the wager. He desired her, therefore, to entertain John in the best manner possible, and to appear as affable and friendly towards him as she could, with the view of prevailing on him to give her the horse on which he rode.

The lad was then sent to Nebbegaard with this letter. His master lent him a horse, that he might the more expeditiously perform his errand; but warned him not to ride too fast, or by any means to lose the horse, which was the finest and most valuable animal he had in his stable. John promised to follow his instructions, and rode away. When he had ridden a short way from home, he dismounted, and led the horse, in order to comply, as much as possible, with his master's wish. In this manner he proceeded but slowly, and it was evening before he reached Nebbegaard.

When the young lady had read her father's letter, she sent for John, and behaved in the kindest and most friendly manner towards him. The maiden was very handsome, and treated the young lad as her equal in condition and rank. She entertained him sumptuously, and said not a word about the horse till he had drunk much more than he could bear. Without knowing what he did, John promised (after she had long entreated him in vain) that he would give her the horse, and the young girl behaved yet more friendly towards him; so the next morning John finding he had no longer a horse, took the saddle and bridle and wandered back to Ostedgaard. As he walked along it struck him how wrongly he had acted, and he began to repent bitterly of what he had done. "What shall I now say when I reach home, and my master finds that the horse is gone?" said he to himself, as he hung the saddle and bridle on the hedge. " 'Well, John,' master will say, 'hast thou executed my errand?' Then I shall answer, 'Yes,' 'But what then is become of my horse, with which I entrusted thee?' Then I will say, 'that I met a band of robbers on the way, and they took the horse from me.' No, that will never do," continued he, "never have I told a lie yet, and I will not do it now." Not long after another thought rose to his mind: "I can say that the horse fell, and that I buried it in a ditch. That won't do either—Lord knows what I, poor fellow, had best do." When he had gone on a little further, he resolved within himself that he would say that the horse had run away, and had shaken off his saddle and bridle.

Long before he reached Ostedgaard, the guests saw him approaching with the saddle on his head and the bridle on his arm.

"Here comes our truthful boy," exclaimed the proprietor of Nebbegaard, "look only how slowly he approaches; who do you now think has won the wager?"

The lord of Osted had already recognised John, and was highly incensed at seeing him return without the horse. As soon as the boy entered the house, he was called up where all the guests were assembled, and his master said: "Well, John, hast thou executed my errand?" "Yes, I have, gracious master," answered the boy, trembling with fear. "What then is become of my good horse, which I ordered thee to take such care of?"

John did not dare to meet the look of his master, but cast his eyes on the ground and said, in a whimpering voice:—

> "Dainty the fare, sweet was the mead,
> The lady's arm was soft and round,
> The sparkling cup my senses drown'd,
> And thus I lost my master's steed."

When he had recited this, his master embraced him in his joy, and exclaimed: "See now! I knew well enough that he would speak the truth. Which of us two has won the wager?"

John did not comprehend the meaning of these words, and continued sorrowful, till his master said to him: "Be of good heart, my boy! as thou hast always kept to truth and right, I will give thee both house and land, and when thou art old enough, I will give thee my daughter to wife."

The following day John was allowed to fetch his old father to live with him, and some years after he was married to his master's daughter.

# THE GIRL CLAD IN MOUSESKIN

THERE WAS once a nobleman who had an only daughter, whom he placed in a mount,* there to remain as long as there was war in the country. The father had secretly caused a room to be built for her in the mount, and had laid in a stock of provisions, and wood enough to last for seven years; and she was not to come out until he fetched her; but if at the end of seven years he did not come for her, she might conclude that he was dead, and might then leave the mount. Her little dog was the only companion she was to have. The father kissed her when they parted, and comforted her by saying, that he had lodged her in a secure place, while the dissolute soldiery were spread over the land. He then collected all his retainers, and went forth to fight for his country.

The young damsel occupied herself in the mount with spinning, weaving, and sewing; and thus one year passed after another. She made a great number of fine clothes, some of which were embroidered with gold, and others with silver; but when she had no longer anything to spin or employ her, the time began to be tedious. Her stock of food was also nearly exhausted, and she was fearful that her father would not return. As the time that she was to remain in the mount had nearly expired, and he had not come to fetch her, she concluded that he was dead. She now

*A mound, or little hill of earth.

began to dig her way out of the mount, but this was a very slow work, and no easy task for her.

In the meantime all her provisions were consumed, but the mount was full of mice, and her little dog destroyed a great many every day; these she skinned, roasted, and ate the meat, and gave the bones to her little dog; but she stitched all the skins together, and made herself a cloak or garment, which was so large, that she could quite wrap herself up in it. Every day she laboured at the aperture, and at length succeeded so far as to be able once more to see the light of day. When she had made an opening large enough, she went out, accompanied by her little faithful dog. On finding herself on the outside, she knelt down, and returned thanks for her deliverance. She then closed up the opening, and the mouseskins that remained over she hung round the mount upon little sticks, which she stuck in the earth.

She now left the hill with her little dog, and went through the wood, and there was much she found changed in the seven years she had lived underground. She had her silver and her gold dresses on, and over them she wore the mouseskin cloak, which quite covered her, so that she had more the appearance of a poor man's child than a young lady of rank. At the first house she came to, she inquired who lived at the manor. She was told it was the young lord, who had inherited it after the death of the former proprietor. "How then did he die?" asked she, hardly able to conceal her feelings. She received for answer, that he was a brave soldier, and drove the enemy out of the country, but in the last battle that was fought he was killed. That his only child was a daughter who had been carried off before that time, and no one had since ever heard anything of her.

The young maiden then asked, if they could tell her where she could be employed, as she wanted work. "Our young master is soon to be married," said the people; "his bride, with her father and mother, are arrived at the mansion to make preparations for the wedding; if you only go up there, you may be sure they will find something for you to do."

The young girl in the mouseskin dress then went up to her late father's abode, and her little dog was so happy; for it knew the place again; but its mistress wept with grief, as she humbly knocked at the door. When the people heard that she wished to be employed, they gladly engaged her, and set her to sweep the yard, and the steps, and do other menial kinds of work. But she did everything willingly and well, so that everybody was satisfied with her. Many as they passed her were amused at the sight of her mouseskin dress, but no one could get a glimpse of her face; for she wore a long hood which hung down and completely concealed it, and this she never would throw aside.

The day before the wedding the bride sent for her, and told her that she had a great favour to ask: "Thou art of the same height as I am," said she; "thou must to-morrow put on my bridal dress and veil, and drive to the church, and be wedded to the bridegroom, instead of me." The young girl could not imagine why the other objected to be wedded to the handsome young lord. The bride then told her, that there was another lover, to whom she had previously betrothed herself; but that her parents wanted to force her to marry this rich young lord; that she was afraid of disobeying them, but that she had agreed with her first beloved, that on the wedding day she would elope with him. This she could not do, if she were wedded at the altar to another; but if she sent some one in her place, everything might end well. The young maiden promised to do all that the bride requested of her.

The next day the bride was attired in the most costly dress, and all the people in the house came into her chamber to look at her; at length she said: "Now call that poor young girl that sweeps the yard, and let her also see me." The girl in the mouseskin dress came up accordingly, and when they were alone together, the bride locked the door, dressed her in the beautiful clothes, with the bridal veil over her head, and then wrapped herself in the young girl's large mouseskin cloak.

The late lord's daughter was then conducted to a chariot, in which was the bridegroom, and they drove to church together, accompanied by all the bridal guests. On the road they passed the mount, where she had lived so long concealed. She sighed beneath her veil, and said:—

> "Yonder stands yet every pin,
> With every little mouse's skin,
> Where seven long years I pined in sadness
> In the dark mount, and knew no gladness."

"What sayest thou, dearest of my heart?" asked the bridegroom. "Oh! I am only talking a little to myself," answered the bride.

When she entered the church, she saw the portraits of her parents suspended on each side of the altar; but it appeared to her as if they turned from her, as she wept beneath her veil while gazing on them; she then said:—

> "Turn, turn again, ye pictures dear; dear father and
> mother, turn again;"

and then the pictures turned again. "What sayest thou, my dear bride?" asked the bridegroom. "Oh! I am only talking a little to myself," answered she again. They were then wedded in the church, the young lord put a ring upon her finger, and they drove home. As soon as the bride alighted from the carriage she hurried up into the lady's chamber, as they had agreed, where they changed dresses once more, but the wedding-ring which she had on her finger she kept. When standing in her mouseskin dress again among all the servants, little did any one think that she had just before stood at the altar as a bride.

In the evening there was dancing, and the young lord danced with her who he thought was his bride; but when he took her hand, he said: "Where is the ring I put on your finger in the church?" The bride was at first embarrassed, but said quickly: "I took it off and left it in my chamber, but now I will run and fetch it." She then ran out of the room, called the real bride, and demanded the ring. "No," answered the maiden, "the ring I will not part with, it belongs to the hand that was given away at the altar. But I will go with you to the door, then you can call him, and we will both stand in the passage; when he comes we will extinguish the light that is there, and I will stretch forth my hand in at the door, so that he can see the ring." Thus it was arranged.

The bridegroom was standing near the door, when the bride called him into the passage, and said: "See! here is the ring." At the same moment as the one damsel extinguished the light, the other stretched forth her hand with the ring.

But the bridegroom was not satisfied with merely seeing the ring, he seized the hand, and drew the young girl into the room, and then, to his astonishment, saw it was the damsel in the mouseskin dress. All the guests flocked round them, and were eager to know how it had all happened.

She then threw off her mouseskin dress, and stood clad in her beautiful gold embroidery, and was more lovely to look at than the other bride. Every one was impatient to hear her story; and she was obliged to relate to them, how long she had remained concealed in the mount, and that her father had been their former lord. The little dog was fetched from her miserable room, and many of the neighbours knew it again.

Hereupon there was great joy and wonder. Everybody revered her father, who had fought so bravely for his country, and all were unanimous that the estate belonged to her. Her sorrow was now turned into joy, and as she wished every one to be as happy as herself, she bestowed land and money on the other bride, that she might marry the man of her choice, to whom she had secretly given her heart. The parents were contented with this arrangement, and now the marriage-feast was gay, when the young lord danced with his true bride, to whom he had been wedded in the church, and given the ring.

# THE OUTLAW

At PALSGAARD, in the district of Bjerge, lived once a knight, whose name was Eisten Brink. He was addicted to the belief in supernatural agency, and kept an astrologer in his house, that he might foretell him his fate. As Eisten had been many years a widower, he resolved to marry again, and with that object courted the daughter of Jens Grib of Barritskov. Although the young maiden was not very favourably inclined towards her old suitor, her father forced her to give the consenting "Yes" to his proposals.

Two nights before the wedding was to take place, Eisten went up to the Astrologer's tower, and requested him to foretell what his fate would be in the married state.

The Astrologer took out his instruments, and after having for some time consulted the heavens, he told the knight, "that there always ap-

peared a little black spot upon his star, which signified some secret, and
with this he must become acquainted before he could possibly foretell
his future."

At first Eisten would divulge nothing; but as the Astrologer refused to
proceed before he made a full confession, the knight was at last obliged
to acknowledge, that Palsgaard had unjustly come into his possession in
the following manner. His brother-in-law, a knight named Palle, had,
many years ago, made him the superintendent of the castle, and, at the
same time, committed to his care his little son, while he went to join in
the war. A few years after this, Eisten received intelligence of Palle's
death, and a year later his son also disappeared one day, when he had
been seen playing near the lake. The people in the neighbourhood believed that the boy had fallen into the water and been drowned; but the
truth was, that Eisten Brink had got an old woman to kidnap the child,
and conceal him, so that he might be no impediment in the way of his
becoming master of Palsgaard.

When Eisten had related this tale, the Astrologer asked him, if he had
never since heard what had become of Palle's son. "Yes," replied the
knight, "old Trude (so the woman was called) sent him first to Sleswig, to
live with a sister of hers, but at her death he returned to Trude, and she
got him placed as huntsman to my future father-in-law."

"And is he there now?" asked the Astrologer.

"No, that he is not; for a day or two ago, as Grib observed that Abel
was paying too much attention to Inger, who is to be my wife to-morrow,
he turned him out of doors, and forbade him ever to appear again at
Barritskov."

When the Astrologer had heard all he wished to know, he predicted
much happiness to Eisten in the married state. The next day the knight,
richly attired, and attended by a numerous retinue, rode over to Jens
Grib's at Barritskov. Jens immediately told his son-in-law in confidence,
that Abel, although forbidden the house and grounds, was still lingering
about, and that Inger did not appear to be unfavourably disposed towards him. He therefore advised Eisten to have all his eyes about him
when they were married, and to be cautious whom he admitted to Palsgaard. Eisten smiled at this warning, and thought that he could very well
manage matters.

In the afternoon of that day, he rode down to Rosenvold, or Staxesvold, as it was then called. This place belonged at that time to a noted
freebooter who roamed about in Middlefart Sound, and plundered all
the vessels he could master. Eisten, through good works and good pay,
got a promise that two of the freebooters would waylay and murder Abel,
whom they knew by sight, having often met him, as Jens Grib's wood
reached down to theirs. They agreed to do their work the following
night, so that the knight should never more be troubled with the huntsman. With regard to Abel, Jens Grib's suspicions were well founded.
Inger and he had been attached to each other for some time, long, in
fact, before Eisten thought of becoming her suitor. The young lover was,
therefore, much grieved at finding himself suddenly dismissed from Barritskov, and knew not how to find an opportunity of speaking to Inger.

In his distress he went in the evening down to the wood, where old Trude, his foster-mother, lived. He confided to her his secret, and asked her what course she thought he had best pursue. After they had had some conversation together, the old woman advised him to accompany her into the wood, to a mount in which lived a Troll, and if he could be brought to interest himself in the matter, Abel need have no fear, either for the father or lover of Inger. The young huntsman felt no great inclination to follow this advice; yet what else could he do? He at length consented, and they set out together, taking the road that led to the Troll's Mount.

The real cause why Trude was desirous of inducing Abel to go with her to the Troll was, that she had sold herself to him, body and soul, after a certain period, unless she could find another willing to enter into the same conditions. This period expired on the very evening of Abel's visit, and the wicked woman resolved in her evil heart to save herself by the sacrifice of her foster-son. When they came to the spot the old woman began to summon forth the Troll. She made a circle of human bones about the hill, within which she placed herself and Abel. A great noise was then heard around them; the mount rose on four pillars of fire, and the Troll appeared.

The woman made known her errand, and presented Abel to him. The Troll was just laying hold of the young man, when a loud cry was heard in the wood, and the Astrologer from Palsgaard rushed towards Abel, but could not enter the circle which the crone had made. He cried again with all his might: "This boy is mine, take him not from me, he is my only son."

To this appeal the Troll gave little heed, and it would have fared ill with the huntsman, had not the Astrologer again cried with a powerful voice: "In the name of our Lord, I conjure you to spare my son!" No sooner had he uttered these words, than the Troll gave a horrible scream, and, seizing old Trude round the waist, disappeared with her in the mount, which immediately closed upon them and sank down again; but Abel remained behind and was saved.

The Astrologer was no other than the old knight Palle, the brother-in-law of Eisten Brink. He had been outlawed for having joined the king's enemies, hence the reason of his living in concealment at Palsgaard. No sooner had Eisten informed him how he had acted towards his son than he went down to Trude's cottage. Not finding her at home, he wandered into the wood, where he fortunately came to the Troll's Mount, just as Abel was in the greatest danger. When he had made himself known to his son, and they had embraced each other, and thanked God for their happy deliverance, they consulted together as to the course they should pursue, then lay down in the wood to sleep.

That same night the two freebooters left Staxesvold in quest of Abel, as had been agreed between them and Eisten Brink. They first took the road to old Trude's house, then proceeded further along the same path which the Astrologer had taken just before. On the same day, it happened that the king had been out hunting from a neighbouring manor. He had found a white hind, and pursued it throughout the day, over hill and through dale, until it reached the wood of Palsgaard. He thus became separated from his followers, and as the evening was drawing on, he could neither find his way out of the wood, nor any path through it. He rode about for some time at a venture, when the voices of Abel and his father talking together attracted his attention. He went in the direction of the sound, and came to the spot where they had lain down to rest.

Here he was met by the freebooters, who, believing they had found the man they were in search of, entered into discourse with the king, who did not dream of any mischief. Abel looked up on hearing voices, and saw one of the miscreants draw forth a knife and steal softly behind the king. He immediately saw that murder was intended, and sprang up, exclaiming: "Defend yourself, sir! for your life is threatened."

Old Palle rushed to the assistance of his son, and it cost them but little trouble to overpower the two freebooters. One was killed in the fray, the other threw away his weapon and begged for mercy. The king ordered him immediately to confess what inducement he had for making this murderous attack; when the assassin, without reserve, acknowledged how Eisten had instigated them to murder Abel.

The king now turned to the Astrologer, and asked him who he was. The old man laid his sword at the king's feet, and said: "Kneel down with me, my son, for you stand before Denmark's king." Hereupon he related his history; and also the manner in which Eisten Brink had acted towards him and his son Abel.

The king pardoned him; and when he heard that Eisten's wedding was to be celebrated at Barritskov on the following day, he determined on being present at the festival, taking with him the captured robber. Palle and his son also accompanied him to the castle.

At Barritskov all was mirth and glee; the bridemaids were adorning Inger and twining the bridal wreath in her hair. Jens Grib was busied in receiving the congratulations of his neighbours. But Eisten had not yet made his appearance; he was sitting alone in his chamber, impatiently waiting to hear tidings from the two assassins, who had undertaken to murder Abel.

At once he thought he heard a great and unusual noise in the castle-yard. He approached the door to ascertain the cause, when his future father-in-law burst into the room with the intelligence, that the king had arrived at the castle, in company with Abel, the Astrologer, and a prisoner.

Eisten Brink could scarcely believe his own ears, but still more astounded was he upon finding that the king had suspended all the festivities, and commanded every one to meet him in the knights' hall.

Here the king related to the astonished company how Eisten had acted towards his brother-in-law, the old Palle, and requested the assembled guests to pass judgment upon such a criminal.

Eisten was deprived of his honours. Palle was restored to his power and dignity; but the best of all was, that Abel was wedded to Inger, and lived with her many years in splendour and felicity.

# THE LITTLE CHICKEN KLUK AND HIS COMPANIONS

THERE WAS once a little chicken called Kluk. A nut fell on his back, and gave him such a blow that he fell down and rolled on the ground. So he ran to the hen, and said: "Henny Penny, run, I think all the world is falling!" "Who has told thee that, little chicken Kluk?" "Oh, a nut fell on my back, and struck me so that I rolled on the ground." "Then let us run," said the hen.

So they ran to the cock, and said: "Cocky Locky, run, I think all the world is falling." "Who has told thee that, Henny Penny?" "Little chicken Kluk." "Who told thee that, little chicken Kluk?" "Oh, a nut fell on my back, and struck me so that I rolled on the ground." "Then let us run," said the cock.

So they ran to the duck, and said: "Ducky Lucky, run, I think all the world is falling." "Who told thee that, Cocky Locky?" "Henny Penny." "Who has told thee that, Henny Penny?" "Little chicken Kluk." "Who has told thee that, little chicken Kluk?" "Oh, a nut fell on my back, and struck me so that I rolled on the ground." "Then let us run," said the duck.

So they ran to the goose. "Goosy Poosy, run, I think all the world is falling." "Who has told thee that, Ducky Lucky?" "Cocky Locky." "Who has told thee that, Cocky Locky?" "Henny Penny." "Who has told thee that, Henny Penny?" "Little chicken Kluk." "Who has told thee that, little chicken Kluk?" "Oh, a nut fell on my back, and struck me so, that I rolled on the ground." "Then let us run," said the goose.

Then they ran to the fox, and said; "Foxy Coxy, run, I think all the world is falling." "Who has told thee that, Goosy Poosy?" "Ducky Lucky." "Who has told thee that, Ducky Lucky?" "Cocky Locky." "Who has told thee that, Cocky Locky?" "Henny Penny." "Who has told thee that, Henny Penny?" "Little chicken Kluk." "Who has told thee that, little chicken Kluk?" "Oh, a nut fell on my back, and struck me so, that I rolled on the ground." "Then let us run," said the fox.

So they all ran into the wood. Then the fox said: "I must now count and see if I have got you all here. I, Foxy Coxy, one; Goosy Poosy, two; Ducky Lucky, three; Cocky Locky, four; Henny Penny, five; and little chicken Kluk, six; Hei! that one I'll snap up." He then said: "Let us run."

So they ran further into the wood. Then said he: "Now I must count and see if I have got you all here. I, Foxy Coxy, one; Goosy Poosy, two; Ducky Lucky, three; Cocky Locky, four; Henny Penny, five; Hei! that one I'll snap up." And so he went on till he had eaten them all up.

# TALES FROM FINLAND

JACK OF SJÖHÖLM AND THE GAN-FINN

# PART ONE

*Weird Tales from Northern Seas*
*(told by Norwegians about Finns)*

## JACK OF SJÖHOLM AND THE GAN[1]-FINN

IN THE days of our forefathers, when there was nothing but wretched boats up in the North, and folks must needs buy fair winds by the sackful from the Gan-Finn, it was not safe to tack about in the open sea in wintry weather. In those days a fisherman never grew old. It was mostly women-folk and children, and the lame and halt, who were buried ashore.

Now there was once a boat's crew from Thjöttö in Helgeland, Norway, which had put to sea, and worked its way right up to the East Lofotens.

But that winter the fish would not bite.

They lay to and waited week after week, till the month was out, and there was nothing for it but to turn home again with their fishing gear and empty boats.

But Jack of Sjöholm, who was with them, only laughed aloud, and said that, if there were no fish there, fish would certainly be found higher northwards. Surely they hadn't rowed out all this distance only to eat up all their victuals, said he.

He was quite a young chap, who had never been out fishing before. But there was some sense in what he said for all that, thought the head-fisherman.

And so they set their sails northwards.

On the next fishing-ground they fared no better than before, but they toiled away so long as their food held out.

And now they all insisted on giving it up and turning back.

"If there's none here, there's sure to be some still higher up towards the north," opined Jack; "and if they had gone so far, they might surely go a little further still," quoth he.

So they tempted fortune from fishing-ground to fishing-ground, till they had ventured right up to Finmark.[2] But there a storm met them, and, try as they might to find shelter under the headlands, they were obliged at last to put out into the open sea again.

[1]This untranslatable word is a derivative of the Icelandic *Gandr,* and means magic of the black or malefic sort.

[2]The northernmost province of Norway, right within the Arctic circle.

There they fared worse than ever. They had a hard time of it. Again and again the prow of the boat went under the heavy rollers, instead of over them, and later on in the day the boat foundered.

There they all sat helplessly on the keel in the midst of the raging sea, and they all complained bitterly against that fellow Jack, who had tempted them on, and led them into destruction. What would now become of their wives and children? They would starve now that they had none to care for them.

When it grew dark, their hands began to stiffen, and they were carried off by the sea one by one.

And Jack heard and saw everything, down to the last shriek and the last clutch; and to the very end they never ceased reproaching him for bringing them into such misery, and bewailing their sad lot.

"I must hold on tight now," said Jack to himself, for he was better even where he was than in the sea.

And so he tightened his knees on the keel, and held on fast till he had no feeling left in either hand or foot.

In the coal-black gusty night he fancied he heard yells from one or other of the remaining boats' crews.

"They, too, have wives and children," thought he. "I wonder whether they have also a Jack to lay the blame upon!"

Now while he thus lay there and drifted and drifted, it seemed to him to be drawing towards dawn, he suddenly felt that the boat was in the grip of a strong shoreward current; and, sure enough, Jack got at last ashore. But whichever way he looked, he saw nothing but black sea and white snow.

Now as he stood there, speering and spying about him, he saw, far away, the smoke of a Norwegian Finn's hut, which stood beneath a cliff, and he managed to scramble right up to it.

The Finn was so old that he could scarcely move. He was sitting in the midst of the warm ashes, and mumbling into a big sack, and neither spoke nor answered. Large yellow humble-bees were humming about all over the snow, as if it were Midsummer; and there was only a young lass there to keep the fire alight, and give the old man his food. His grandsons and grand-daughters were with the reindeer, far far away on the *Fjeld*.

Here Jack got his clothes well dried, and the rest he so much wanted. The Finn girl, Seimke, couldn't make too much of him; she fed him with reindeer milk and marrow-bones, and he lay down to sleep on silver fox-skins.

Cosy and comfortable it was in the smoke there. But as he thus lay there, 'twixt sleep and wake, it seemed to him as if many odd things were going on round about him.

There stood the Finn in the doorway talking to his reindeer, although they were far away in the mountains. He barred the wolf's way, and threatened the bear with spells; and then he opened his skin sack, so that the storm howled and piped, and there was a swirl of ashes into the hut. And when all grew quiet again, the air was thick with yellow humble-bees, which settled inside his furs, whilst he gabbled and mumbled and wagged his skull-like head.

But Jack had something else to think about besides marvelling at the old Finn. No sooner did the heaviness of slumber quit his eyes than he strolled down to his boat.

There it lay stuck fast on the beach and tilted right over like a trough, while the sea rubbed and rippled against its keel. He drew it far enough ashore to be beyond the reach of the sea-wash.

But the longer he walked around and examined it, the more it seemed to him as if folks built boats rather for the sake of letting the sea in than for the sake of keeping the sea out. The prow was little better than a hog's snout for burrowing under the water, and the planking by the keel-piece was as flat as the bottom of a chest. Everything, he thought, must be arranged very differently if boats were to be really seaworthy. The prow must be raised one or two planks higher at the very least, and made both sharp and supple, so as to bend before and cut through the waves at the same time, and then a fellow would have a chance of steering a boat smartly.

He thought of this day and night. The only relaxation he had was a chat with the Finn girl of an evening.

He couldn't help remarking that this Seimke had fallen in love with him. She strolled after him wherever he went, and her eyes always became so mournful when he went down towards the sea; she understood well enough that all his thoughts were bent upon going away.

And the Finn sat and mumbled among the ashes till his fur jacket regularly steamed and smoked.

But Seimke coaxed and wheedled Jack with her brown eyes, and gave him honeyed words as fast as her tongue could wag, till she drew him right into the smoke where the old Finn couldn't hear them.

The Gan-Finn turned his head right round.

"My eyes are stupid, and the smoke makes 'em run," said he; "what has Jack got hold of there?"

"Say it is the white ptarmigan you caught in the snare," whispered she.

And Jack felt that she was huddling up against him and trembling all over.

Then she told him so softly that he thought it was his own thoughts speaking to him, that the Finn was angry and muttering mischief, and chanting against the boat which Jack wanted to build. If Jack were to complete it, said she, the Gan-Finn would no longer have any sale for his fair-winds in all Nordland. And then she warned him to look to himself and never get between the Finn and the Gan-flies.

Then Jack felt that his boat might be the undoing of him. But the worse things looked, the more he tried to make the best of them.

In the grey dawn, before the Finn was up, he made his way towards the sea-shore.

But there was something very odd about the snow-hills. They were so many and so long that there was really no end to them, and he kept on trampling in deep and deeper snow and never got to the sea-shore at all. Never before had he seen the northern lights last so long into the day. They blazed and sparkled, and long tongues of fire licked and hissed after him. He was unable to find either the beach or the boat, nor had he the least idea in the world where he really was.

At last he discovered that he had gone quite astray inland instead of down to the sea. But now, when he turned round, the sea-fog came close up against him, so dense and grey that he could see neither hand nor foot before him.

By the evening he was well-nigh worn out with weariness, and was at his wits' end what to do.

Night fell, and the snowdrifts increased.

As now he sat him down on a stone and fell a brooding and pondering how he should escape with his life, a pair of snow-shoes came gliding so smoothly towards him out of the sea-fog and stood still just in front of his feet.

"As you have found me, you may as well find the way back also," said he.

So he put them on, and let the snow-shoes go their own way over hillside and steep cliff. He let not his own eyes guide him or his own feet carry him, and the swifter he went the denser the snowflakes and the driving sea-spray came up against him, and the blast very nearly blew him off the snow-shoes.

Up hill and down dale he went over all the places where he had fared during the daytime, and it sometimes seemed as if he had nothing solid beneath him at all, but was flying in the air.

Suddenly the snow-shoes stood stock still, and he was standing just outside the entrance of the Gan-Finn's hut.

There stood Seimke. She was looking for him.

"I sent my snow-shoes after thee," said she, "for I marked that the Finn had bewitched the land so that thou should'st not find the boat. Thy *life* is safe, for he has given thee shelter in his house, but it were not well for thee to see him this evening."

Then she smuggled him in, so that the Finn did not perceive it in the thick smoke, and she gave him meat and a place to rest upon.

But when he awoke in the night, he heard an odd sound, and there was a buzzing and a singing far away in the air:

> "The Finn the boat can never bind,
>   The Fly the boatman cannot find,
>   But round in aimless whirls doth wind."

The Finn was sitting among the ashes and chanting, and muttering till the ground quite shook, while Seimke lay with her forehead to the floor and her hands clasped tightly round the back of her neck, praying against him to the Finn God. Then Jack understood that the Gan-Finn was still seeking after him amidst the snowflakes and sea-fog, and that his life was in danger from magic spells.

So he dressed himself before it was light, went out, and came tramping in again all covered with snow, and said he had been after bears in their winter retreats. But never had he been in such a sea-fog before; he had groped about far and wide before he found his way back into the hut again, though he stood just outside it.

The Finn sat there with his skin-wrappings as full of yellow flies as a beehive. He had sent them out searching in every direction, but back they had all come, and were humming and buzzing about him.

When he saw Jack in the doorway, and perceived that the flies had pointed truly, he grew somewhat milder, and laughed till he regularly shook within his skin-wrappings, and mumbled, "The bear we'll bind fast beneath the scullery-sink, and his eyes I've turned all awry, so that he can't see his boat, and I'll stick a sleeping-peg in front of him till spring time."

But the same day the Finn stood in the doorway, and was busy making magic signs and strange strokes in the air.

Then he sent forth two hideous Gan-flies, which flitted off on their errands, and scorched black patches beneath them in the snow wherever they went. They were to bring pain and sickness to a cottage down in the swamps, and spread abroad the Finn disease, which was to strike down a young bride at Bodö with consumption.

But Jack thought of nothing else night and day but how he could get the better of the Gan-Finn.

The lass Seimke wheedled him and wept and begged him, as he valued his life, not to try to get down to his boat again. At last, however, she saw it was no use—he had made up his mind to be off.

Then she kissed his hands and wept bitterly. At least he must promise to wait till the Gan-Finn had gone right away to Jokmok in Sweden.

On the day of his departure, the Finn went all round his hut with a torch and took stock.

Far away as they were, there stood the mountain pastures, with the reindeer and the dogs, and the Finn's people all drew near. The Finn took the tale of the beasts, and bade his grandsons not let the reindeer stray too far while he was away, and could not guard them from wolves and bears. Then he took a sleeping potion and began to dance and turn round and round till his breath quite failed him, and he sank moaning to the ground. His furs were all that remained behind of him. His spirit had gone—gone all the way over to Jokmok.

There the magicians were all sitting together in the dark sea-fog beneath the shelter of the high mountain, and whispering about all manner of secret and hidden things, and blowing spirits into the novices of the black art.

But the Gan-flies, humming and buzzing, went round and round the empty furs of the Gan-Finn like a yellow ring and kept watch.

In the night Jack was awakened by something pulling and tugging at him as if from far away. There was as it were a current of air, and something threatened and called to him from the midst of the snow-flakes outside—

> "Until thou canst swim like the duck or the drake,
> The egg[1] thou'dst be hatching no progress shall make;

[1] *I.e.*, the boat he would be building.

The Finn shall ne'er let thee go southwards with sail,
For he'll screw off the wind and imprison the gale."

At the end of it the Gan-Finn was standing there, and bending right over him. The skin of his face hung down long and loose, and full of wrinkles, like an old reindeer skin, and there was a dizzying smoke in his eyes. Then Jack began to shiver and stiffen in all his limbs, and he knew that the Finn was bent upon bewitching him.

Then he set his face rigidly against it, so that the magic spells should not get at him; and thus they struggled with one another till the Gan-Finn grew green in the face, and was very near choking.

After that the sorcerers of Jokmok sent magic shots after Jack, and clouded his wits. He felt so odd; and whenever he was busy with his boat, and had put something to rights in it, something else would immediately go wrong, till at last he felt as if his head were full of pins and needles.

Then deep sorrow fell upon him. Try as he would, he couldn't put his boat together as he would have it; and it looked very much as if he would never be able to cross the sea again.

But in the summer time Jack and Seimke sat together on the headland in the warm evenings, and the gnats buzzed and the fishes spouted close ashore in the stillness, and the eider-duck swam about.

"If only some one would build me a boat as swift and nimble as a fish, and able to ride upon the billows like a sea-mew!" sighed and lamented Jack, "then I could be off."

"Would you like me to guide you to Thjöttö?" said a voice up from the sea-shore.

There stood a fellow in a flat turned-down skin cap, whose face they couldn't see.

And right outside the boulders there, just where they had seen the eider-duck, lay a long and narrow boat, with high prow and stern; and the tar-boards were mirrored plainly in the clear water below; there was not so much as a single knot in the wood.

"I would be thankful for any such guidance," said Jack.

When Seimke heard this, she began to cry and take on terribly. She fell upon his neck, and wouldn't let go, and raved and shrieked. She promised him her snow-shoes, which would carry him through everything, and said she would steal for him the bone-stick from the Gan-Finn, so that he might find all the old lucky dollars that ever were buried, and would teach him how to make salmon-catching knots in the fishing lines, and how to entice the reindeer from afar. He should become as rich as the Gan-Finn, if only he wouldn't forsake her.

But Jack had only eyes for the boat down there. Then she sprang up, and tore down her black locks, and bound them round his feet, so that he had to wrench them off before he could get quit of her.

"If I stay here and play with you and the young reindeer, many a poor fellow will have to cling with broken nails to the keel of a boat,"[1] said he.

---

[1]Meaning that he would never have a chance of building the new sort of boat that his mind was bent on.

"If you like to make it up, give me a kiss and a parting hug, or shall I go without them?"

Then she threw herself into his arms like a young wild cat, and looked straight into his eyes through her tears, and shivered and laughed, and was quite beside herself.

But when she saw she could do nothing with him, she rushed away, and waved her hands above her head in the direction of the Finn's hut.

Then Jack understood that she was going to take counsel of the Gan-Finn, and that he had better take refuge in his boat before the way was closed to him. And, in fact, the boat had come so close up to the boulders, that he had only to step down upon the thwarts. The rudder glided into his hand, and aslant behind the mast sat some one at the prow, and hoisted and stretched the sail; but his face Jack could not see.

Away they went.

And such a boat for running before the wind Jack had never seen before. The sea stood up round about them like a deep snow-drift, although it was almost calm. But they hadn't gone very far before a nasty piping began in the air. The birds shrieked and made for land, and the sea rose like a black wall behind them.

It was the Gan-Finn who had opened his windsack, and sent a storm after them.

"One needs a full sail in the Finn-cauldron here," said something from behind the mast.

The fellow who had the boat in hand took such little heed of the weather that he did not so much as take in a single clew.

Then the Gan-Finn sent a tempest after them.

They sped along in a wild dance right over the firth, and the sea whirled up in white columns of foam, reaching to the very clouds.

Unless the boat could fly as quick and quicker than a bird, it was lost.

Then a hideous laugh was heard to larboard—

"Anfinn Ganfinn gives mouth,
And blows us right south;
There's a crack in the sack,
With three clews we must tack."

And heeling right over, with three clews in the sail, and the heavy foremost fellow astride on the sheer-strake, with his huge sea-boots dangling in the sea-foam, away they scudded through the blinding spray right into the open sea, amidst the howling and roaring of the wind.

The billowy walls were so vast and heavy that Jack couldn't even see the light of day across the yards, nor could he exactly make out whether they were going under or over the sea-trough.

The boat shook the sea aside as lightly and easily as if its prow were the slippery fin of a fish, and its planking was as smooth and fine as the shell of a tern's egg; but, look as he would, Jack couldn't see where these planks ended; it was just as if there was only half a boat and no more; and at last it seemed to him as if the whole of the front part came off in the sea-foam, and they were scudding along under sail in half a boat.

When night fell, they went through the sea-fire, which glowed like hot embers, and there was a prolonged and hideous howling up in the air to windward.

And cries of distress and howls of mortal agony answered the wind from all the upturned boat keels they sped by, and many hideously pale-looking folks clutched hold of their thwarts. The gleam of the sea-fire cast a blue glare on their faces, and they sat, and gaped, and glared, and yelled at the blast.

Suddenly he awoke, and something cried, "Now thou art at home at Thjöttö, Jack!"

And when he had come to himself a bit, he recognised where he was. He was lying over against the boulders near his boathouse at home. The tide had come so far inland that a border of foam gleamed right up in the potato-field, and he could scarcely keep his feet for the blast. He sat him down in the boathouse, and began scratching and marking out the shape of the Draugboat in the black darkness till sleep overtook him.

When it was light in the morning, his sister came down to him with a meat-basket. She didn't greet him as if he were a stranger, but behaved as if it were the usual thing for her to come thus every morning. But when he began telling her all about his voyage to Finmark, and the Gan-Finn, and the Draugboat he had come home in at night, he perceived that she only grinned and let him chatter. And all that day he talked about it to his sister and his brothers and his mother, until he arrived at the conclusion that they thought him a little out of his wits. When he mentioned the Draugboat they smiled amongst themselves, and evidently went out of their way to humour him. But they might believe what they liked, if only he could carry out what he wanted to do, and be left to himself in the out-of-the-way old boathouse.

"One should go with the stream," thought Jack; and if they thought him crazy and out of his wits, he ought to behave so that they might beware of interfering with him, and disturbing him in his work.

So he took a bed of skins with him down to the boathouse, and slept there at night; but in the day-time he perched himself on a pole on the roof, and bellowed out that now he was sailing. Sometimes he rode astraddle on the roof ridge, and dug his sheath-knife deep into the rafters, so that people might think he fancied himself at sea, holding fast on to the keel of a boat.

Whenever folks passed by, he stood in the doorway, and turned up the whites of his eyes so hideously, that every one who saw him was quite scared. As for the people at home, it was as much as they dared to stick his meat-basket into the boathouse for him. So they sent it to him by his youngest sister, merry little Malfri, who would sit and talk with him, and thought it such fun when he made toys and playthings for her, and talked about the boat which should go like a bird, and sail as no other boat had ever sailed.

If any one chanced to come upon him unexpectedly, and tried to peep and see what he was about in the boathouse there, he would creep up into the timberloft and bang and pitch the boards and planks about, so that they didn't know exactly where to find him, and were glad enough to be off. But one and all made haste to climb over the hill again when they heard him fling himself down at full length and send peal after peal of laughter after them.

So that was how Jack got folks to leave him at peace.

He worked best at night when the storm tore and tugged at the stones and birchbark of the turf roof, and the sea-wrack came right up to the boathouse door.

When it piped and whined through the fissured walls, and the fine snowflakes flitted through the cracks, the model of the Draugboat stood plainest before him. The winter days were short, and the wick of the train-oil lamp, which hung over him as he worked, cast deep shadows, so that the darkness came soon and lasted a long way into the morning, when he sought sleep in his bed of skins with a heap of shavings for his pillow.

He spared no pains or trouble. If there was a board which would not run into the right groove with the others, though never so little, he would take out a whole row of them and plane them all round again and again.

Now, one night, just before Christmas, he had finished all but the uppermost planking and the gabs. He was working so hard to finish up that he took no count of time.

The plane was sending the shavings flying their briskest when he came to a dead stop at something black which was moving along the plank.

It was a large and hideous fly which was crawling about and feeling and poking all the planks in the boat. When it reached the lowest keel-board it whirred with its wings and buzzed. Then it rose and swept above it in the air till, all at once, it swerved away into the darkness.

Jack's heart sank within him. Such doubt and anguish came upon him. He knew well enough that no good errand had brought the Gan-fly buzzing over the boat like that.

So he took the train-oil lamp and a wooden club, and began to test the prow and light up the boarding, and thump it well, and go over the planks one by one. And in this way he went over every bit of the boat from stem to stern, both above and below. There was not a nail or a rivet that he really believed in now.

But now neither the shape nor the proportions of the boat pleased him any more. The prow was too big, and the whole cut of the boat all the way down the gunwale had something of a twist and a bend and a swerve about it, so that it looked like the halves of two different boats put together, and the half in front didn't fit in with the half behind. As he was about to look into the matter still further (and he felt the cold sweat bursting out of the roots of his hair), the train-oil lamp went out and left him in blank darkness.

Then he could contain himself no longer. He lifted his club and burst open the boathouse door, and, snatching up a big cow-bell, he began to swing it about him and ring and ring with it through the black night.

"Art chiming for me, Jack?" something asked. There was a sound behind him like the surf sucking at the shore, and a cold blast blew into the boathouse.

There on the keel-stick sat some one in a sloppy grey sea-jacket, and with a print cap drawn down over its ears, so that its skull looked like a low tassel.

Jack gave a great start. This was the very being he had been thinking of in his wild rage. Then he took the large baling can and flung it at the Draug (demon.)

But right through the Draug it went, and rattled against the wall behind, and back again it came whizzing about Jack's ears, and if it had struck him he would never have got up again.

The old fellow, however, only blinked his eyes a little savagely.

"Fie!" cried Jack, and spat at the uncanny thing—and back into his face again he got as good as he gave.

"There you have your wet clout back again!" cried a laughing voice.

But the same instant Jack's eyes were opened and he saw a whole boat-building establishment on the sea-shore.

And, there, ready and rigged out on the bright water, lay an *Ottring*,[1] so long and shapely and shining that his eyes could not feast on it enough.

The old 'un blinked with satisfaction. His eyes became more and more glowing.

"If I could guide you back to Helgeland," said he, "I could put you in the way of gaining your bread too. But you must pay me a little tax for it. In every seventh boat you build 'tis *I* who must put in the keel-board."

Jack felt as if he were choking. He felt that the boat was dragging him into the very jaws of an abomination.

"Or do you fancy you'll worm the trick out of me for nothing?" said the gaping grinning Draug.

Then there was a whirring sound, as if something heavy was hovering about the boathouse, and there was a laugh: "If you want the *seaman's* boat you must take the *dead man's* boat along with it. If you knock three times to-night on the keel-piece with the club, you shall have such help in building boats that the like of them will not be found in all Nordland."

Twice did Jack raise his club that night, and twice he laid it aside again.

But the Ottring lay and frisked and sported in the sea before his eyes, just as he had seen it, all bright and new with fresh tar, and with the ropes and fishing gear just put in. He kicked and shook the fine slim boat with his foot just to see how light and high she could rise on the waves above the water-line.

And once, twice, thrice, the club smote against the keel-piece.

So that was how the first boat was built at Sjöholm.

Thick as birds together stood a countless number of people on the headland in the autumn, watching Jack and his brothers putting out in the new Ottring.

It glided through the strong current so that the foam was all round it.

Now it was gone, and now it ducked up again like a sea-mew, and past skerries and capes it whizzed like a dart.

Out in the fishing grounds the folks rested upon their oars and gaped. Such a boat they had never seen before.

But if in the first year it was an Ottring, next year it was a broad heavy

---

[1]An eight-oared boat.

*Femböring* for winter fishing which made the folks open their eyes.

And every boat that Jack turned out was lighter to row and swifter to sail than the one before it.

But the largest and finest of all was the last that stood on the stocks on the shore.

This was the *seventh*.

Jack walked to and fro, and thought about it a good deal; but when he came down to see it in the morning, it seemed to him, oddly enough, to have grown in the night and, what is more, was such a wondrous beauty that he was struck dumb with astonishment. There it lay ready at last, and folks were never tired of talking about it.

Now, the Bailiff who ruled over all Helgeland in those days was an unjust man who laid heavy taxes upon the people, taking double weight and tale both of fish and of eider-down, nor was he less grasping with the tithes and grain dues. Wherever his fellows came they fleeced and flayed. No sooner, then, did the rumour of the new boats reach him than he sent his people out to see what truth was in it, for he himself used to go fishing in the fishing grounds with large crews. When thus his fellows came back and told him what they had seen, the Bailiff was so taken with it that he drove straightway over to Sjöholm, and one fine day down he came swooping on Jack like a hawk. "Neither tithe nor tax has thou paid for thy livelihood, so now thou shalt be fined as many half-marks of silver as thou hast made boats," said he.

Ever louder and fiercer grew his rage. Jack should be put in chains and irons and be transported northwards to the fortress of Skraar, and be kept so close that he should never see sun or moon more.

But when the Bailiff had rowed round the *Femböring,* and feasted his eyes upon it, and seen how smart and shapely it was, he agreed at last to let Mercy go before Justice, and was content to take the *Femböring* in lieu of a fine.

Then Jack took off his cap and said that if there was one man more than another to whom he would like to give the boat, it was his honour the Bailiff.

So off the magistrate sailed with it.

Jack's mother and sister and brothers cried bitterly at the loss of the beautiful *Femböring;* but Jack stood on the roof of the boat-house and laughed fit to split.

And towards autumn the news spread that the Bailiff with his eight men had gone down with the *Femböring* in the West-fjord.

But in those days there was quite a changing about of boats all over Nordland, and Jack was unable to build a tenth part of the boats required of him. Folks from near and far hung about the walls of his boat-house, and it was quite a favour on his part to take orders, and agree to carry them out. A whole score of boats soon stood beneath the pent-house on the strand.

He no longer troubled his head about every *seventh* boat, or cared to know which it was or what befell it. If a boat foundered now and then, so many the more got off and did well, so that, on the whole, he made a very good thing indeed out of it. Besides, surely folks could pick and choose their own boats, and take which they liked best.

But Jack got so great and mighty that it was not advisable for any one to thwart him, or interfere where he ruled and reigned.

Whole rows of silver dollars stood in the barrels in the loft, and his boat-building establishment stretched over all the islands of Sjöholm.

One Sunday his brothers and merry little Malfri had gone to church in the *Femböring*. When evening came, and they hadn't come home, the boatman came in and said that some one had better sail out and look after them, as a gale was blowing up.

Jack was sitting with a plumb-line in his hand, taking the measurements of a new boat, which was to be bigger and statelier than any of the others, so that it was not well to disturb him.

"Do you fancy they're gone out in a rotten old tub, then?" bellowed he. And the boatman was driven out as quickly as he had come.

But at night Jack lay awake and listened. The wind whined outside and shook the walls, and there were cries from the sea far away. And just then there came a knocking at the door, and some one called him by name.

"Go back whence you came," cried he, and nestled more snugly in his bed.

Shortly afterwards there came the fumbling and the scratching of tiny fingers at the door.

"Can't you leave me at peace o'nights?" he bawled, "or must I build me another bedroom?"

But the knocking and the fumbling for the latch outside continued, and there was a sweeping sound at the door, as of some one who could not open it. And there was a stretching of hands towards the latch ever higher and higher.

But Jack only lay there and laughed. "The *Fembörings* that are built at Sjöholm don't go down before the first blast that blows," mocked he.

Then the latch chopped and hopped till the door flew wide open, and in the doorway stood pretty Malfri and her mother and brothers. The sea-fire shone about them, and they were dripping with water.

Their faces were pale and blue, and pinched about the corners of the mouth, as if they had just gone through their death agony. Malfri had one stiff arm round her mother's neck; it was all torn and bleeding, just as when she had gripped her for the last time. She railed and lamented, and begged back her young life from him.

So now he knew what had befallen them.

Out into the dark night and the darker weather he went straightway to search for them, with as many boats and folk as he could get together. They sailed and searched in every direction, and it was in vain.

But towards day the *Femböring* came drifting homewards bottom upwards, and with a large hole in the keel-board.

Then he knew who had done the deed.

But since the night when the whole of Jack's family went down, things were very different at Sjöholm.

In the daytime, so long as the hammering and the banging and the planing and the clinching rang about his ears, things went along

JACK OF SJÖHÖLM AND THE GAN-FINN

swimmingly, and the frames of boat after boat rose thick as sea fowl on an *Æggevær*.[1]

But no sooner was it quiet of an evening than he had company. His mother bustled and banged about the house, and opened and shut drawers and cupboards, and the stairs creaked with the heavy tread of his brothers going up to their bedrooms.

At night no sleep visited his eyes, and sure enough pretty Malfri came to his door and sighed and groaned.

Then he would lie awake there and think, and reckon up how many boats with false keel-boards he might have sent to sea. And the longer he reckoned the more draug-boats he made of it.

Then he would plump out of bed and creep through the dark night down to the boathouse. There he held a light beneath the boats, and banged and tested all the keel-boards with a club to see if he couldn't hit upon the *seventh*. But he neither heard nor felt a single board give way. One was just like another. They were all hard and supple, and the wood, when he scraped off the tar, was white and fresh.

One night he was so tormented by an uneasiness about the new *Sek-string*,[2] which lay down by the bridge ready to set off next morning, that he had no peace till he went down and tested its keel-board with his club.

But while he sat in the boat, and was bending over the thwart with a light, there was a gulping sound out at sea, and then came such a vile stench of rottenness. The same instant he heard a wading sound, as of many people coming ashore, and then up over the headland he saw a boat's crew coming along.

They were all crooked-looking creatures, and they all leaned right forward and stretched out their arms before them. Whatever came in their way, they went right through it, and there was neither sound nor shriek.

Behind them came another boat's crew, big and little, grown men and little children, rattling and creaking.

And crew after crew came ashore and took the path leading to the headland.

When the moon peeped forth Jack could see right into their skeletons. Their faces glared, and their mouths gaped open with glistening teeth, as if they had been swallowing water. They came in heaps and shoals, one after the other: the place quite swarmed with them.

Then Jack perceived that here were all they whom he had tried to count and reckon up as he lay in bed, and a fit of fury came upon him.

He rose in the boat and spanked his leather breeches behind and cried: "You would have been even more than you are already if Jack hadn't built his boats!"

But now like an icy whizzing blast they all came down upon him, staring at him with their hollow eyes.

They gnashed their teeth, and each one of them sighed and groaned for his lost life.

---

[1] A place where sea-birds' eggs abound.
[2] A contraction of *Sexæring, i.e.*, a boat with six oars.

Then Jack, in his horror, put out from Sjöholm.

But the sail slackened, and he glided into dead water. There, in the midst of the still water, was a floating mass of rotten swollen planks. All of them had once been shaped and fashioned together, but were now burst and sprung, and slime and green mould and filth and nastiness hung about them.

Dead hands grabbed at the corners of them with their white knuckles and couldn't grip fast. They stretched themselves across the water and sank again.

Then Jack let out all his clews and sailed and sailed and tacked according as the wind blew.

He glared back at the rubbish behind him to see if those *things* were after him. Down in the sea all the dead hands were writhing, and tried to strike him with gaffs astern.

Then there came a gust of wind whining and howling, and the boat drove along betwixt white seething rollers.

The weather darkened, thick snowflakes filled the air, and the rubbish around him grew greener.

In the daytime he took the cormorants far away in the grey mist for his landmarks, and at night they screeched about his ears.

And the birds flitted and flitted continually, but Jack sat still and looked out upon the hideous cormorants.

At last the sea-fog lifted a little, and the air began to be alive with bright, black, buzzing flies. The sun burned, and far away inland the snowy plains blazed in its light.

He recognized very well the headland and shore where he was now able to lay to. The smoke came from the Gamme up on the snow-hill there. In the doorway sat the Gan-Finn. He was lifting his pointed cap up and down, up and down, by means of a thread of sinew, which went right through him, so that his skin creaked.

And up there also sure enough was Seimke.

She looked old and angular as she bent over the reindeer-skin that she was spreading out in the sunny weather. But she peeped beneath her arm as quick and nimble as a cat with kittens, and the sun shone upon her, and lit up her face and pitch-black hair.

She leaped up so briskly, and shaded her eyes with her hand, and looked down at him. Her dog barked, but she quieted it so that the Gan-Finn should mark nothing.

Then a strange longing came over him, and he put ashore.

He stood beside her, and she threw her arms over her head, and laughed and shook and nestled close up to him, and cried and pleaded, and didn't know what to do with herself, and ducked down upon his bosom, and threw herself on his neck, and kissed and fondled him, and wouldn't let him go.

But the Gan-Finn had noticed that there was something amiss, and sat all the time in his furs, and mumbled and muttered to the Gan-flies, so that Jack dare not get between him and the doorway.

The Finn was angry.

Since there had been such a changing about of boats over all Nordland,

and there was no more sale for his fair winds, he was quite ruined, he complained. He was now so poor that he would very soon have to go about and beg his bread. And of all his reindeer he had only a single doe left, who went about there by the house.

Then Seimke crept behind Jack, and whispered to him to bid for this doe. Then she put the reindeer-skin around her, and stood inside the Gamme door in the smoke, so that the Gan-Finn only saw the grey skin, and fancied it was the reindeer they were bringing in.

Then Jack laid his hand upon Seimke's neck, and began to bid.

The pointed cap ducked and nodded, and the Finn spat in the warm air; but sell his reindeer he would not.

Jack raised his price.

But the Finn heaved up the ashes all about him, and threatened and shrieked. The flies came as thick as snow-flakes; the Finn's furry wrappings were alive with them.

Jack bid and bid till it reached a whole bushel load of silver, and the Finn was ready to jump out of his skins.

Then he stuck his head under his furs again, and mumbled and chanted till the amount rose to seven bushels of silver.

Then the Gan-Finn laughed till he nearly split. He thought the reindeer would cost the purchaser a pretty penny.

But Jack lifted Seimke up, and sprang down with her to his boat, and held the reindeer-skin behind him, against the Gan-Finn.

And they put off from land, and went to sea.

Seimke was so happy, and smote her hands together, and took her turn at the oars.

The northern light shot out like a comb, all greeny-red and fiery, and licked and played upon her face. She talked to it, and fought it with her hands, and her eyes sparkled. She used both tongue and mouth and rapid gestures as she exchanged words with it.

Then it grew dark, and she lay on his bosom, so that he could feel her warm breath. Her black hair lay right over him, and she was as soft and warm to the touch as a ptarmigan when it is frightened and its blood throbs.

Jack put the reindeer-skin over Seimke, and the boat rocked them to and fro on the heavy sea as if it were a cradle.

They sailed on and on till night-fall; they sailed on and on till they saw neither headland nor island nor sea-bird in the outer skerries more.

# FINN BLOOD

In Svartfjord, north of Senje, in Norway, dwelt a lad called Eilert. His neighbours were seafaring Finns, and among their children was a pale little girl, remarkable for her long black hair and her large eyes. They dwelt behind the crag on the other side of the promontory, and fished for a livelihood, as also did Eilert's parents; wherefore there was no particular goodwill between the families, for the nearest fishing ground was but a small one, and each would have liked to have rowed there alone.

Nevertheless, though his parents didn't like it at all, and even forbade it, Eilert used to sneak regularly down to the Finns. There they had always strange tales to tell, and he heard wondrous things about the recesses of the mountains, where the original home of the Finns was, and where, in the olden time, dwelt the Finn Kings, who were masters among the magicians. There, too, he heard tell of all that was beneath the sea, where the Mermen and the Draugs hold sway. The latter are gloomy evil powers, and many a time his blood stood still in his veins as he sat and listened. They told him that the Draug usually showed himself on the strand in the moonlight on those spots which were covered with sea-wrack; that he had a bunch of seaweed instead of a head, but shaped so peculiarly that whoever came across him absolutely couldn't help gazing into his pale and horrible face. They themselves had seen him many a time, and once they had driven him, thwart by thwart, out of the boat where he had sat one morning, and turned the oars upside down. When Eilert hastened homewards in the darkness round the headland, along the strand, over heaps of seaweed, he dare scarcely look around him, and many a time the sweat absolutely streamed from his forehead.

In proportion as hostility increased among the old people, they had a good deal of fault to find with one another, and Eilert heard no end of evil things spoken about the Finns at home. Now it was this, and now it was that. They didn't even row like honest folk, for, after the Finnish fashion, they took high and swift strokes, as if they were womenkind, and they all talked together, and made a noise while they rowed, instead of being "silent in the boat." But what impressed Eilert most of all was the fact that, in the Finnwoman's family, they practised sorcery and idolatry, or so folks said. He also heard tell of something beyond all question, and that was the shame of having Finn blood in one's veins, which also was the reason why the Finns were not as good as other honest folk, so that the magistrates gave them their own distinct burial-ground in the churchyard, and their own separate "Finn-pens" in church. Eilert had seen this with his own eyes in the church at Berg.

All this made him very angry, for he could not help liking the Finn folks down yonder, and especially little Zilla. They two were always together: she knew such a lot about the Merman. Henceforth his conscience always plagued him when he played with her; and whenever she stared at him with her large black eyes while she told him tales, he used to begin to feel a little bit afraid, for at such times he reflected that she and her people belonged to the Damned, and that was why they knew so much about such things. But, on the other hand, the thought of it made him so bitterly angry, especially on her account. She, too, was frequently taken aback by his odd behaviour towards her, which she couldn't understand at all; and then, as was her wont, she would begin laughing at and teasing him by making him run after her, while she went and hid herself.

One day he found her sitting on a boulder by the sea-shore. She had in her lap an eider duck which had been shot, and could only have died quite recently, for it was still warm, and she wept bitterly over it. It was, she sobbed, the same bird which made its nest every year beneath the shelter of their outhouse—she knew it quite well, and she showed him a red-coloured feather in its white breast. It had been struck dead by a single shot, and only a single red drop had come out of it; it had tried to reach its nest, but had died on its way on the strand. She wept as if her heart would break, and dried her face with her hair in impetuous Finnish fashion. Eilert laughed at her as boys will, but he overdid it, and was very pale the whole time. He dared not tell her that that very day he had taken a random shot with his father's gun from behind the headland at a bird a long way off which was swimming ashore.

One autumn Eilert's father was downright desperate. Day after day on the fishing grounds his lines caught next to nothing, while he was forced to look on and see the Finn pull up one rich catch after another. He was sure, too, that he had noticed malicious gestures over in the Finn's boat. After that his whole house nourished a double bitterness against them; and when they talked it over in the evening, it was agreed, as a thing beyond all question, that Finnish sorcery had something to do with it. Against this there was only one remedy, and that was to rub corpse-mould on the lines; but one must beware of doing so, lest one should thereby offend the dead, and expose oneself to their vengeance, while the sea-folk would gain power over one at the same time.

Eilert bothered his head a good deal over all this; it almost seemed to him as if he had had a share in the deed, because he was on such a good footing with the Finn folks.

On the following Sunday both he and the Finn folks were at Berg church, and he secretly abstracted a handful of mould from one of the Finn graves, and put it in his pocket. The same evening, when they came home, he strewed the mould over his father's lines unobserved. And, oddly enough, the very next time his father cast his lines, as many fish were caught as in the good old times. But after this Eilert's anxiety became indescribable. He was especially cautious while they were working of an evening round the fireside, and it was dark in the distant corners of the room. He sat there with a piece of steel in his pocket. To beg "forgiveness" of the dead is the only helpful means against the conse-quences of such deeds as his, otherwise one will be dragged off at night, by an invisible hand, to the churchyard, though one were lashed fast to the bed by a ship's hawser.

When Eilert, on the following "Preaching Sunday," went to church, he took very good care to go to the grave, and beg forgiveness of the dead.

As Eilert grew older, he got to understand that the Finn folks must, after all, be pretty much the same sort of people as his own folks at home; but, on the other hand, another thought was now uppermost in his mind, the thought, namely, that the Finns must be of an inferior stock, with a taint of disgrace about them. Nevertheless, he could not very well do without Zilla's society, and they were very much together as before, especially at the time of their confirmation.

But when Eilert became a man, and mixed more with the people of the parish, he began to fancy that this old companionship lowered him somewhat in the eyes of his neighbours. There was nobody who did not believe as a matter of course that there was something shameful about Finn blood, and he, therefore, always tried to avoid her in company.

The girl understood it all well enough, for latterly she took care to keep out of his way. Nevertheless, one day she came, as had been her wont from childhood, down to their house, and begged for leave to go in their boat when they rowed to church next day. There were lots of strangers present from the village, and so Eilert, lest folks should think that he and she were engaged, answered mockingly, so that every one could hear him, "that church-cleansing was perhaps a very good thing for Finnish sorcery," but she must find some one else to ferry her across.

After that she never spoke to him at all, but Eilert was anything but happy in consequence.

Now it happened one winter that Eilert was out all alone fishing for Greenland shark. A shark suddenly bit. The boat was small, and the fish was very big; but Eilert would not give in, and the end of the business was that his boat capsized.

All night long he lay on the top of it in the mist and a cruel sea. As now he sat there almost fainting for drowsiness, and dimly conscious that the end was not far off, and the sooner it came the better, he suddenly saw a man in seaman's clothes sitting astride the other end of the boat's bottom, and glaring savagely at him with a pair of dull reddish eyes. He was so heavy that the boat's bottom began to slowly sink down at end where he sat. Then he suddenly vanished, but it seemed to Eilert as if the sea-fog lifted a bit; the sea had all at once grown quite calm (at least, there was now only a gentle swell); and right in front of him lay a little low grey island, towards which the boat was slowly drifting.

The skerry was wet, as if the sea had only recently been flowing over it, and on it he saw a pale girl with such lovely eyes. She wore a green kirtle, and round her body a broad silver girdle with figures upon it, such as the Finns use. Her bodice was of tar-brown skin, and beneath her stay-laces, which seemed to be of green sea-grass, was a foam-white chemise, like the feathery breast of a sea-bird.

When the boat came drifting on to the island, she came down to him and said, as if she knew him quite well, "So you're come at last, Eilert; I've been waiting for you so long!"

It seemed to Eilert as if an icy cold shudder ran through his body when he took the hand which helped him ashore; but it was only for the moment, and he forgot it instantly.

In the midst of the island there was an opening with a brazen flight of steps leading down to a splendid cabin. Whilst he stood there thinking things over a bit, he saw two heavy dog-fish swimming close by—they were, at least, twelve to fourteen ells long.

As they descended, the dog-fish sank down too, each on one side of the brazen steps. Oddly enough, it looked as if the island was transparent. When the girl perceived that he was frightened, she told him that they were only two of her father's bodyguard, and shortly afterwards they disappeared. She then said that she wanted to take him to her father, who was waiting for them. She added that, if he didn't find the old gentleman precisely as handsome as he might expect, he had, nevertheless, no need to be frightened, nor was he to be astonished too much at what he saw.

He now perceived that he was under water, but, for all that, there was no sign of moisture. He was on a white sandy bottom, covered with chalk-white, red, blue, and silvery-bright shells. He saw meadows of sea-grass, mountains thick with woods of bushy seaweed and sea-wrack, and the fishes darted about on every side just as the birds swarm about the rocks that sea-fowl haunt.

As they two were thus walking along together she explained many things to him. High up he saw something which looked like a black cloud with a white lining, and beneath it moved backwards and forwards a shape resembling one of the dog-fish.

"What you see there is a vessel," said she; "there's nasty weather up there now, and beneath the boat goes he who was sitting along with you on the bottom of the boat just now. If it is wrecked, it will belong to us, and then you will not be able to speak to father to-day." As she said this there was a wild rapacious gleam in her eyes, but it was gone again immediately.

And, in point of fact, it was no easy matter to make out the meaning of her eyes. As a rule, they were unfathomably dark with the lustre of a night-billow through which the sea-fire sparkles; but, occasionally, when she laughed, they took a bright sea-green glitter, as when the sun shines deep down into the sea.

Now and again they passed by a boat or a vessel half buried in the sand, out and in of the cabin doors and windows of which fishes swam to and fro. Close by the wrecks wandered human shapes which seemed to consist of nothing but blue smoke. His conductress explained to him that these were the spirits of drowned men who had not had Christian burial— one must beware of them, for dead ones of this sort are malignant. They always know when one of their own race is about to be wrecked, and at such times they howl the death-warning of the Draug through the wintry nights.

Then they went further on their way right across a deep dark valley. In the rocky walls above him he saw a row of four-cornered white doors, from which a sort of glimmer, as from the northern lights, shot downwards through the darkness. This valley stretched in a north-eastwardly direction right under Finmark, she said, and inside the white doors dwelt the old Finn Kings who had perished on the sea. Then she went and opened the nearest of these doors—here, down in the salt ocean, was the last of the kings, who had capsized in the very breeze that he himself had conjured forth, but could not afterwards quell. There, on a block of stone, sat a wrinkled yellow Finn with running eyes and a polished dark-red crown. His large head rocked backwards and forwards on his withered neck, as if it were in the swirl of an ocean current. Beside him, on the same block, sat a still more shrivelled and yellow little woman, who also had a crown on, and her garments were covered with all sorts of

FINN BLOOD

coloured stones; she was stirring up a brew with a stick. If she only had fire beneath it, the girl told Eilert, she and her husband would very soon have dominion again over the salt sea, for the thing she was stirring about was magic stuff.

In the middle of a plain, which opened right before them at a turn of the road, stood a few houses together like a little town, and, a little further on, Eilert saw a church turned upside down, looking, with its long pointed tower, as if it were mirrored in the water. The girl explained to him that her father dwelt in these houses, and the church was one of the seven that stood in his realm, which extended all over Helgeland and Finmark. No service was held in them yet, but it would be held when the drowned bishop, who sat outside in a brown study, could only hit upon the name of the Lord that was to be served, and then all the Draugs would go to church. The bishop, she said, had been sitting and pondering the matter over these eight hundred years, so he would no doubt very soon get to the bottom of it. A hundred years ago the bishop had advised them to send up one of the Draugs to Rödö church to find out all about it; but every time the word he wanted was mentioned he couldn't catch the sound of it. In the mountain "Kunnan" King Olaf had hung a church-bell of pure gold, and it is guarded by the first priest who ever came to Nordland, who stands there in a white chasuble. On the day the priest rings the bell, Kunnan will become a big stone church, to which all Nordland, both above and below the sea, will resort. But time flies, and therefore all who come down here below are asked by the bishop if they can tell him that name.

At this Eilert felt very queer indeed, and he felt queerer still when he began reflecting and found, to his horror, that he also had forgotten that name.

While he stood there in thought, the girl looked at him so anxiously. It was almost as if she wanted to help him to find it and couldn't, and with that she all at once grew deadly pale.

The Draug's house, to which they now came, was built of boat's keels and large pieces of wreckage, in the interstices of which grew all sorts of sea-grass and slimy green stuff. Three monstrously heavy green posts, covered with shell-fish, formed the entrance, and the door consisted of planks which had sunk to the bottom and were full of clincher-nails. In the middle of it, like a knocker, was a heavy rusty iron mooring-ring, with the worn-away stump of a ship's hawser hanging to it. When they came up to it, a large black arm stretched out and opened the door.

They were now in a vaulted chamber, with fine shell-sand on the floor. In the corners lay all sorts of ropes, yarn, and boating-gear, and among them casks and barrels and various ship's inventories. On a heap of yarn, covered by an old red-patched sail, Eilert saw the Draug, a broad-shouldered, strongly built fellow, with a glazed hat shoved back on to the top of his head, with dark-red tangled hair and beard, small tearful dog-fish eyes, and a broad mouth, round which there lay for the moment a good-natured seaman's grin. The shape of his head reminded one somewhat of the big sort of seal which is called Klakkekal—his skin about the neck looked dark and shaggy, and the tops of his fingers grew together. He sat there with turned-down sea-boots on, and his thick grey woollen stockings reached right up to his thigh. He wore besides, plain freize clothes with bright glass buttons on his waistcoat. His spacious skin jacket was open, and round his neck he had a cheap red woollen scarf.

When Eilert came up, he made as if he would rise, and said good naturedly, "Good day, Eilert—you've certainly had a hard time of it to-day! Now you can sit down, if you like, and take a little grub. You want it, I'm sure;" and with that he squirted out a jet of tobacco juice like the spouting of a whale. With one foot, which for that special purpose all at once grew extraordinarily long, he fished out of a corner, in true Nord-land style, the skull of a whale to serve as a chair for Eilert, and shoved forward with his hand a long ship's drawer full of first-rate fare. There was boiled groats with sirup, cured fish, oatcakes with butter, a large stack of flatcakes, and a multitude of the best hôtel dishes besides.

The Merman bade him fall to and eat his fill, and ordered his daughter to bring out the last keg of Thronhjem *aqua vitœ*. "Of that sort the last is always the best," said he. When she came with it, Eilert thought he knew it again: it was his father's, and he himself, only a couple of days before, had bought the brandy from the wholesale dealer at Kvæford; but he didn't say anything about that now. The quid of tobacco, too, which the Draug turned somewhat impatiently in his mouth before he drank, also seemed to him wonderfully like the lead on his own line. At first it seemed to him as if he didn't quite know how to manage with the keg— his mouth was so sore; but afterwards things went along smoothly enough.

So they sat for some time pretty silently, and drank glass after glass, till Eilert began to think that they had had quite enough. So, when it came to his turn again, he said no, he would rather not; whereupon the Merman put the keg to his own mouth and drained it to the very dregs. Then he stretched his long arm up to the shelf, and took down another. He was now in a better humour, and began to talk of all sorts of things. But every time he laughed, Eilert felt queer, for the Draug's mouth gaped ominously wide, and showed a greenish pointed row of teeth, with a long interval between each tooth, so that they resembled a row of boat stakes.

The Merman drained keg after keg, and with every keg he grew more communicative. With an air as if he were thinking in his own mind of something very funny, he looked at Eilert for a while and blinked his eyes. Eilert didn't like his expression at all, for it seemed to him to say: "Now, my lad, whom I have fished up so nicely, look out for a change!" But instead of that he said, "You had a rough time of it last night, Eilert, my boy, but it wouldn't have gone so hard with you if you hadn't streaked the lines with corpse-mould, and refused to take my daughter to church"— here he suddenly broke off, as if he had said too much, and to prevent himself from completing the sentence, he put the brandy-keg to his mouth once more. But the same instant Eilert caught his glance, and it was so full of deadly hatred that it sent a shiver right down his back.

When, after a long, long draught, he again took the keg from his mouth, the Merman was again in a good humour, and told tale after tale. He stretched himself more and more heavily out on the sail, and laughed and grinned complacently at his own narrations, the humour of which was always a wreck or a drowning. From time to time Eilert felt the breath of his laughter, and it was like a cold blast. If folks would only give up their boats, he said, he had no very great desire for the crews. It was driftwood and ship-timber that he was after, and he really couldn't get on without them. When his stock ran out, boat or ship he *must* have, and surely nobody could blame him for it either.

With that he put the keg down empty, and became somewhat more gloomy again. He began to talk about what bad times they were for him and her. It was not as it used to be, he said. He stared blankly before him for a time, as if buried in deep thought. Then he stretched himself out backwards at full length, with feet extending right across the floor, and gasped so dreadfully that his upper and lower jaws resembled two boats' keels facing eath other. Then he dozed right off with his neck turned towards the sail.

Then the girl again stood by Eilert's side, and bade him follow her.

They now went the same way back, and again ascended up to the skerry. Then she confided to him that the reason why her father had been so bitter against him was because he had mocked her with the taunt about church-cleansing when she had wanted to go to church—the name the folks down below wanted to know might, the Merman thought, be treasured up in Eilert's memory; but during their conversation on their way down to her father, she had perceived that he also had forgotten it. And now he must look to his life.

It would be a good deal later on in the day before the old fellow would begin inquiring about him. Till then he, Eilert, must sleep so as to have sufficient strength for his flight—she would watch over him.

The girl flung her long dark hair about him like a curtain, and it seemed to him that he knew those eyes so well. He felt as if his cheek were resting against the breast of a white sea-bird, it was so warm and sleep-giving—a single reddish feather in the middle of it recalled a dark memory. Gradually he sank off into a doze, and heard her singing a lullaby, which reminded him of the swell of the billows when it ripples up and down along the beach on a fine sunny day. It was all about how they had once been playmates together, and how later on he would have nothing to say to her. Of all she sang, however, he could only recollect the last words, which were these—

> "Oh, thousands of times have we played on the shore,
> And caught little fishes—dost mind it no more?
> We raced with the surf as it rolled at our feet,
> And the lurking old Merman we always did cheat.

> "Yes, much shalt thou think of at my lullaby,
> Whilst the billows do rock and the breezes do sigh.
> Who sits now and weeps o'er thy cheeks? It is she
> Who gave thee her soul, and whose soul lived in thee.

> "But once as an eider-duck homeward I came
> Thou didst lie 'neath a rock, with thy rifle didst aim;

In my breast thou didst strike me; the blood thou dost see
Is the mark that I bear, oh! beloved one, of thee."

Then it seemed to Eilert as if she sat and wept over him, and that, from time to time, a drop like a splash of sea-water fell upon his cheek. He felt now that he loved her so dearly.

The next moment he again became uneasy. He fancied that right up to the skerry came a whale, which said that he, Eilert, must now make haste; and when he stood on its back he stuck the shaft of an oar down its nostril, to prevent it from shooting beneath the sea again. He perceived that in this way the whale could be steered accordingly as he turned the oar to the right or left; and now they coasted the whole land of Finmark at such a rate that the huge mountain islands shot by them like little rocks. Behind him he saw the Draug in his half-boat, and he was going so swiftly that the foam stood mid-mast high. Shortly afterwards he was again lying on the skerry, and the lass smiled so blithely; she bent over him and said, "It is I, Eilert."

With that he awoke, and saw that the sunbeams were running over the wet skerry, and the Mermaid was still sitting by his side. But presently the whole thing changed before his eyes. It was the sun shining through the window-panes, on a bed in the Finn's hut, and by his side sat the Finn girl supporting his back, for they thought he was about to die. He had lain there delirious for six weeks, ever since the Finn had rescued him after capsizing, and this was his first moment of consciousness.

After that it seemed to him that he had never heard anything so absurd and presumptuous as the twaddle that would fix a stigma of shame or contempt on Finn blood, and the same spring he and the Finn girl Zilla were betrothed, and in the autumn they were married.

There were Finns in the bridal procession, and perhaps many said a little more about that than they need have done; but every one at the wedding agreed that the fiddler, who was also a Finn, was the best fiddler in the whole parish, and the bride the prettiest girl.

# PART TWO
## *Traditional Finnish Tales*

## TALES OF MAGIC

## VAINO AND THE SWAN PRINCESS

ONCE UPON a time there was a young man named Vaino. He lived all alone in the deep forest, in a *tupa* (cottage) beside a small lake. One morning as he sat resting under a tree, all at once he heard a beating of wings, and nine snow-white swans swooped down from the sky and settled upon the water near the shore. But when they caught sight of Vaino, away they all flew again.

Vaino was so excited that the next morning he hid behind a stump to see if they would return. Sure enough they did, and this time a strange thing happened. The nine swans laid down their feathery robes on the shore, and Vaino saw that they were nine beautiful maidens who had come to bathe in the lake.

They were all beautiful, but one was more beautiful than the rest, with long golden hair and blue eyes. Vaino knew that she must be under the evil spell of some witch, and as he had fallen in love with her at first sight he wanted very much to free her.

As soon as the nine maidens left the water, they put on their feathery robes again and at once they became nine white swans that flapped their wings and flew off into the sky. Vaino hurried to the hut of an old Lapland woman who lived on the edge of the forest.

"How can I break the spell and free this beautiful maiden?" he asked her.

The old woman sat on her bench, her chin in her hand, rocking her body slowly back and forth. After mumbling to herself for a long time she said:

"Tomorrow, while the maiden is in the water, steal her feathery robe and burn it. Then the spell will be broken."

"But how can I win her love?" Vaino wanted to know.

"When the maiden calls to you the first time, you must answer with this charm:

> Pala tuli, pala mieli,
> Kaunis neitosen.

528

> Burn, O fire, burn, O heart
> Of maiden beautiful!

and at once her heart will burn with love for you."

Vaino thanked the old woman, and next morning he again hid himself behind the stump and waited. Before long he once more heard the beating of wings, and saw the glitter of white pinions against the sun. Once more the nine swan maidens swooped down, cast off their robes and began swimming in the water. Vaino, watching his chance, snatched up the robe belonging to the maiden he loved, and burned it. When the maidens smelled the burning and saw the smoke that filled the air, they were seized with terror; they rushed to their robes and eight of them flew off into the sky as swans.

But the ninth maiden ran about on the sands weeping.

"Who has stolen my robe!" she wailed. And in her despair she began to repeat a charm:

"If you are older than I, you shall be my father. If you are younger, you shall be my brother. If you are as old, and no older, you shall be my husband."

Vaino heard her voice, soft and pitiful, and answered her:

> Pala tuli, pala mieli
> Kaunis neitosen.

> Burn, O fire, burn, O heart
> Of maiden beautiful.

As he finished singing, he stepped from his hiding place, and when the maiden saw how strong and handsome he was she gladly gave him her hand.

"How glad I am," she cried, "that that witch's evil spell is broken!"

"But how came you to be changed into a swan?" Vaino asked.

The maiden told him that the witch had hated her father, who was a king, and had wreaked her spite on his nine daughters.

"Come with me now to my father's castle," she said to Vaino, "for you shall be my husband from now on."

The King was delighted to see his daughter back again in her true form, but when it came to Vaino he was not so well pleased, for Vaino was of lowly birth. He thought a while, and said:

"First you must go into the heavens and fetch me the golden chains that hang from the clouds. Then we will talk about marrying my daughter."

Vaino set out on his journey with a heavy heart. He had never even heard of the golden chains that hang from the clouds, and had not the least idea how to set about finding them. But after he had walked a long way, thinking and thinking about it, he remembered the old Lapland woman who lived on the edge of the forest, and he hurried to her hut.

"How can I find the golden chains that hang from the clouds?" he asked her.

Again the old Lapland woman sat with her chin in her hands and rocked slowly back and forth for a long time, saying at last:

"Take the horse I shall give you. Close your eyes, and ride over mountain and valley, through river and forest. Ride without stopping until you feel your horse slipping from beneath you. Keep your eyes tight shut but stretch your two hands upward. Clutch at the air as the horse slips away, and you will feel the golden chains in your hands."

Vaino did as the old woman bade him. He rode over mountain and plain, over land and sea. All the time he kept his eyes tightly closed, though he was very curious to know where his horse was carrying him. At last he felt the horse slip from beneath him; he reached his arms upward and clutched at the air. And suddenly the heavy golden chains were in his hands.

In the same breath he felt himself falling—down, down and ever down— through the empty air. He held his breath and clutched the gold chains tightly. When he opened his eyes again, he was in a strange country. Everywhere about him stretched a barren plain, with only a few dead stunted trees and here and there a withered flower. For this was the land of death.

In confusion Vaino walked this way and that, staring hopelessly about him. Presently he heard a clatter, and saw two skeletons fighting with drawn swords. Shivering with fear, Vaino drew near and asked them:

"Brothers, why are you fighting?"

"*Ka!*" shrieked one of the skeletons. "Here is a man at last who can settle our quarrel! It is like this. My neighbor here wants me to pay a debt which I have already paid to him, but he will not believe me."

"That's a queer thing," said Vaino. "But since you are both dead, there can be no question of debt between you. For surely the dead have nothing left to divide!"

"*Ka*, are we both dead?" cried the second skeleton.

"You speak truth," shrieked the first skeleton. "We will fight no more. Let us agree."

"And to you, O wise one," they said to Vaino, "here is a reward."

Then one of the skeletons thrust a cold gray stone into Vaino's hand, saying:

"Carry this stone with you, for you will find use for it before you again set foot in the land of the living."

And twining their bony arms about each other's necks, the two skeletons disappeared.

Vaino went his way, but soon he came upon two more skeletons, fighting just like the first. This time the quarrel was because one claimed the land belonging to the other. When they saw Vaino they asked him:

"Can you settle our quarrel for us?"

"How stupid you are to fight," said Vaino. "For since you are both of you dead, you can't have any land to fight about!"

This surprised them both, but they agreed that Vaino was right. So they made up their quarrel, giving Vaino another cold gray stone.

Presently Vaino came upon yet another pair of dead men, fighting because they could not agree whose wife was the cleverer and more beautiful. Again Vaino settled their quarrel, and for reward they, too, gave him a cold gray stone.

"I have enough of these cold gray stones," said Vaino to himself. "I must escape from this dreadful place, full of dead men fighting. But how?"

It happened that, as he spoke, he rattled the heavy golden chains he was still holding. And at the sound, at once there appeared before him every kind of sea creature, from a barnacle to a whale.

"What brings you here?" Vaino asked.

"You called us," said the sea creatures. "Do you not need us?"

"*Ka,* I need you indeed," Vaino said. "Carry me back from this pit of death to the land of the living."

"We are sorry," said the sea creatures, "but we cannot help you."

"Then go your ways!" cried Vaino, and he rattled the chains again.

This time there came running every kind of animal that dwells in the forest. From the rabbit and the squirrel to the wolf and the moose, they all gathered before him.

"Why do you gather?" Vaino asked them.

"You called us."

"What can you do?"

"Whatever you ask."

"Then carry me back to the land of the living," said Vaino.

"That we cannot do."

"Then you may go your ways," Vaino said, and they all disappeared.

A third time he rattled the heavy golden chains, and this time all the birds of the air fluttered down beside him.

"Why did you call us?" they asked.

"Carry me back to the land of the living," Vaino begged.

The birds looked at one another. Not one of them had the courage for such a flight. But at last a bald eagle flapped his great wings, and stepped forward.

"Have you the gold chains tight in your hands?" he asked.

"You can see for yourself," said Vaino.

"And have you the three cold gray stones?"

"I have them, too."

"Then climb on my back," said the bald eagle. "Put the golden chains in my beak for reins. Clutch the three stones tight in your hand and we will be off."

Vaino did as he was bid, and the eagle flapped his great wings and soared into the sky, cutting the winds and scraping the clouds. For a long time they flew, until the eagle grew tired. They were over the wide ocean now. The eagle said to Vaino:

"Drop your first cold gray stone into the water."

Vaino dropped the stone, and where it struck the water, there grew a huge mountain. The eagle settled down upon the mountain top and there they rested for the night.

In the morning the eagle took Vaino on his back again and they set forth, flying high above the clouds toward the land of the living. They were still above the wide ocean when the eagle again grew weary.

"Drop your second cold gray stone into the water," he said.

Vaino dropped his second stone. Again a tall mountain rose where the stone fell, and again they rested the night.

On the third day the eagle once more grew weary, and Vaino dropped his last cold gray stone into the sea. And once more they rested on the tall mountain that grew from the waters.

On the fourth day the eagle brought Vaino to the garden by the King's castle, setting him safely down among the flowers. Then he flapped his wings and flew off.

And there was Vaino's princess waiting for him, her golden hair shining in the sun and her eyes bluer than the blue sky.

"Whatever the King my father says, never will I let you go again!" she cried as she caught Vaino by the hand.

"Don't be afraid," said Vaino. "I have had my fill of long lonely journeys."

Together the lovers laid the golden chains at the King's feet, and the King was overjoyed.

"At last!" he cried. "With this golden chain I can break the spell that binds my eight other daughters!"

Then he gave Vaino and the Princess his blessing, and they all lived happily ever after.

# LIPPO AND TAPIO

There was once a famous hunter named Lippo. All winter long he used to travel in search of game, and he was as much at home on his skiis as a bird is in the air.

One day Lippo and two of his friends set out to the Northland to hunt moose. All day long they followed tracks in the snow, but without meeting any game. At dusk they came to a small hut where they slept the night. Next morning they started out bright and early, again on their skiis. Lippo, who was setting the pace, kicked one ski against the other and said in fun:

"Today we must get a moose for each ski, and one for the ski-staff!"

New snow had fallen during the night, and presently sure enough they saw before them the fresh tracks of three large moose. They hastened their pace and soon caught up with two of the moose, who were fighting so hard that they paid no attention to the hunters. But the third moose saw them coming, and galloped off through the forest.

"Here's a piece of luck," whispered Lippo to his friends. "You shoot these two, and I will track down the third."

His friends killed the two moose and dragged them homeward, while Lippo swept forward on his skiis, light-hearted and alone. He flew swiftly over the snow, but however swiftly he travelled the tracks still stretched ahead of him, farther than his eyes could reach. At last, as night was falling, they led him through a fence and into a garden.

There, in the doorway of his house, stood Tapio, God of the Forests. His long beard was the color of moss and he wore a cap of leaves on his head. The moose, grunting with fright, stood beside him.

When Tapio saw Lippo he shouted angrily:

"How dare you hunt my moose, and drive him into a foaming sweat!"

"How could I tell he was your moose?" said Lippo. "He had strayed far into the forest."

When Tapio saw that Lippo was a plain, honest man his anger left him. He said:

"It is late and you are far from home. Come into my *tupa* and stay the night."

Lippo shook the snow from his skiis and set them up against the wall. When he followed the old man into the house, he was surprised to see the room crowded with wild animals. Elk, bear, moose, wolf and fox, rabbit and weasel, there they all sat round the fire, talking each in his own tongue.

Tapio called in a loud voice like the sound of wind in the fir trees:

"Daughter! We have a guest!"

And there entered a lovely girl dressed in a robe of green leaves. She set a supper of honey, milk and bread on the birch-log table, and Lippo ate hungrily.

When he had eaten he turned to the girl, who was sitting now beside the fire, holding a fox in her arms, and asked her: "Who are you, and what is the name of this far north country?"

She answered: "I am Tellervo, daughter of Tapio, God of the Forests. My father takes care of every living creature in the woods. And this country is Pohjola, far to the north of your native Finland."

As darkness drew on and the first star came into the skies, the wild creatures began to file out into the forest, each to his own home. When the last had disappeared through the doorway, Tapio gave Lippo a bed of fir boughs beside the fire.

In the morning Lippo was up early, all ready to start out again in search of game, but nowhere could he find his skiis. They were gone as if by magic. When he asked Tapio what had happened to them the old man said:

"You will find them when you wish to go back to your own people. I have but one daughter, Tellervo. How would you like to stay here as my son-in-law?"

"I would gladly stay," said Lippo, "but I am only a poor man."

"*Ho* (Ho), don't let that worry you," Tapio said. "Lack of money is no crime. Here we need no gold."

So Lippo, the forest-wanderer, married Tellervo, and together they lived in the hut in the woods, with the old man, her father. Soon Lippo learned to speak the language of every creature living in the forest.

After three years a son was born to Lippo and Tellervo. Lippo was so proud that he wanted at once to go back to his family for a visit and tell them all the good news. He begged Tapio to go with him but Tapio said:

"First you must make me a pair of skiis. If the skiis are to my liking, then I will come with you."

Lippo went into the forest and began to hew out wood for the skiis. A little titmouse sat on a branch over his head, singing!

> Tii, tii, tiiainen,
> Vati, kuti, varpunen.

> Tit, tit, titmouse,
> Spicker, spacker, sparrow,
> Set the branch upon the shoulder,
> Form a head upon the foot-rest.

The titmouse made Lippo so fidgetty with its chirping that he did not even listen to what it said. He flung a stick at it and shouted: "Stop your noise, you chatterbox!"

Then he forgot all about the bird so intent was he on fashioning his skiis. He made them as beautifully as he knew how. And when at last they were finished, he brought them to his father-in-law. Tapio fastened the skiis to his feet and took a turn round the garden on them, saying: "These skiis are not for me. They don't fit me. You will have to make me a better pair."

Again Lippo went into the forest. And again the titmouse flew to a branch over his head and sang:

> Tii, tii, tiiainen,
> Vati, kuti, varpunen.

> Tit, tit, titmouse,
> Spicker, spacker, sparrow,
> Set the branch upon the shoulder,
> Form a head upon the foot-rest.

Again Lippo was very annoyed by this chattering. "Why must you be always chirping and chattering, you scamp!" he shouted, and this time he threw a chip of wood to frighten the bird away.

When the second pair of skiis were finished, Tapio tried them out and said: "These skiis are not for me, either. You'll have to keep on trying till you can do better."

Lippo went a third time into the forest, determined to please his father-in-law. And a third time the titmouse sang:

> Tii, tii, tiiainen,
> Vati, kuti, varpunen.

This time Lippo stood listening.

"What are you trying to tell me, you little fidget? I'll try your advice. You can't be singing the same thing over and over for no reason at all."

He worked fast, and did as the bird said. In the center of the ski he fashioned a shoulder for Tapio to stand upon. He bent the front end of the ski slightly upward into a head, so that it would glide more easily over the snow.

When Tapio tried this new pair of skiis he was delighted.

"*Ka,* these are the skiis for me! They fit me perfectly. You must have learned at last to listen to the words of your little forest friends, my Lippo, or you would never have known how to please me. Now you may go home!"

So they started, Tapio first, Lippo with his child strapped to his back, and Tellervo his wife close behind him.

When they had gone far into the deep wild forest Tapio stopped and said: "From now on I shall travel ahead of you. Follow my tracks in the snow. Each time you see the hole of my pointed ski-staff, there make your camp for the night. Weave the roof of your lodge carefully of fir boughs, and be sure that no light from the stars can shine through to work you harm."

And he set off ahead like a flash of light on his skiis, and was gone.

All day long Lippo followed the ski tracks, with Tellervo and his child. Night was falling when they saw the first hole made by Tapio's staff. Here they found a moose broiled and steaming for their supper.

Lippo built a lodge as Tapio had told him. He wove the fir branches carefully so that no starlight could shine through. He took the birch bark pack from his shoulders and set his child in the lodge before the fire. Here they all three slept the night.

In the morning they ate again, took enough moose meat for a meal during the day, and set out to follow Tapio's ski tracks.

Again at nightfall they saw the second hole made by Tapio's staff. Beside it was a deer roasted and steaming. They ate, built a lodge of fir boughs as before, and slept the night.

The third day they pushed forward on their skiis, and at nightfall found only a wood grouse fried and steaming. They were so hungry that no morsel remained for next day's meal.

Lippo was greatly disheartened. He said:

"Tellervo, we cannot travel without food. My bow and arrows I left in the hut. Tapio and his magic have failed us, and my home is still far away."

That night he took no heed how he built their lodge. He wove the fir boughs carelessly, and through the bare chinks the starlight shone through on them.

In the morning when Lippo rose to stir the camp fire, he found that his wife, Tellervo, was gone. Far and near Lippo searched, but he could not find her. He asked the birds in the trees where she had gone but, when they answered him, he found he could no longer understand their language.

He went into the hut and took his child upon his knee. Sad and hopeless he sat there before the fire. He saw moose and deer outside in the forest but he had no weapons to hunt them.

The next morning and the next and the next, every morning when he awoke, Lippo found a wood grouse cooked and steaming before the door. Many years passed, and still Lippo lived in his lodge of fir boughs before the open fire in the forest. He dreamed of home, but he no longer had courage to set out on the search for it.

Lippo's son grew into a tall boy, and from boyhood he grew to manhood. He asked Lippo to teach him about the stars, so that he could travel alone and learn more about the world.

One day when he came back from exploring the forest he said: "Father, we are not far from your home. To the south lie your home fields."

Then he took his father, who was now an old man, and together they set out on the journey. After a day's travel they found themselves at Lippo's old home. Tears came to Lippo's eyes at the sight of his old country after all these years, but the boy was not content to stay there. He left his father behind and travelled north once more to make a home for himself.

And to this very day the Laplanders proudly trace their descent from this wise and restless son of Lippo, the mighty hunter.

# THE WOOING OF SEPPO ILMARINEN

Seppo Ilmarinen stood at his anvil in the smithy, beating out a piece of red hot iron. Clang, clang, went his hammer. He looked up, and there before him stood a queer little woman, as tiny as a dwarf. Just like a jointed wooden doll she looked, and her movements were quick and jerky. And she piped up in a voice like the chirping of a cricket:

"If you knew what I know, Seppo Ilmarinen, you wouldn't stand there hammering iron!"

"And what is it you know?" said Seppo. "If it's good news I'll give you my blessing, but if it's bad news all you get is a curse!"

"What I say is the truth," returned the little woman. "At this very moment there are two suitors rowing in boats to Hiitola. They are after the hand of Katrina, the King's daughter, and no less!"

When he heard this Seppo dropped his hammer on the floor, shut up his blacksmith shop and rushed home as fast as his legs would carry him.

"Aiti, Aiti," he shouted to his mother, "build a fire in the *sauna*, quick. Make the water sizzle on the bathhouse stones! Give me a clean shirt and new bark shoes!"

When he had taken his bath he shouted to his servant:

"Catch the three-year-old colt, and put the iron harness on him with the new reins. Hitch him up to the painted sledge."

The servant harnessed the colt, but the colt was so wild that it took the two of them to get him between the shafts. He kicked and he plunged as Seppo gathered up the reins.

"Give me your blessing, Mother," Seppo cried. "I'm going a-wooing!"

"I bless you indeed," called his mother. "May no charm come near you to work you harm!"

THE WOOING OF SEPPO ILMARINEN

Seppo went swishing along over the open sea in his painted sledge, with the wild colt pulling it. He flew so fast that no wave touched him, and the sledge runners left no track in the water. After a long time he caught up with the two suitors in their boats. So the queer little woman had told him the truth! They were on their way to woo the beautiful Katrina. Seppo shouted a greeting to them, and together they hurried on.

The beautiful Katrina was sitting before the castle, on the third terrace of the King's garden, looking out across the sea. When she saw the three specks on the water she called to her old nurse.

"See, nurse, my three suitors are coming! Two are rowing in boats, but the third one comes in a sledge."

When the three suitors reached the castle door, the King greeted them kindly. He gave them meat and drink. When they had eaten the three young men knelt before the King and said:

"Noble King, we have come to pay court to your beautiful daughter, Katrina."

The King replied: "Answer me this question. Which of you can plow my field of snakes, with unshod feet and unbound ankles?"

When the two suitors who had come by boat heard these words, they were very much upset. They stammered their excuses and went their ways. But Seppo stood bravely before the King and said:

"I will plow your field of snakes barefoot, if that is your wish."

"Good," said the King. "My servants will show you the field."

Seppo hitched his wild colt to the King's plow, took off his shoes and set to work. When the snakes saw him coming they reared high on their tails and hissed, striking with their poisonous fangs. But Seppo whispered to his colt, and they ran so fast that the snakes flew beneath the plowshare and over his head, but not one touched him.

"O King," said Seppo, "your field is plowed."

"You've made a good beginning," said the King," But now I want you to make a sparkling pool in my garden, where big fish may swim and small fish flicker and glitter in the sun. And this you must do not with tools, but by the power of song alone."

"It shall be as you wish," said Seppo.

He walked straightway into the garden, and there he sang a brave song.

Luonotar, oi Ilman Neiti,


Luonotar, Lady of Creation,
Grant me the power of winged song.
Sparkle water in the pool,
Flicker minnows in the sun.


And by magic there lay a sparkling pool where a moment ago had been smooth green grass. He could plainly see the large fish swimming and the silver flicker of the darting minnows. Again Seppo stood before the King.

"O King, my task is done. There lies your pool and there swim your fishes."

The King looked kindly at Seppo, and said: "You have indeed made a good beginning. But there is one thing more you must do. My daughter has need of the *Huomenlahja Lipas*, the hope chest which has long lain hidden under the sea. Bring her this, and you shall have her hand in marriage."

"It shall be as you wish," Seppo answered.

With a strong heart he strode forth from the King's palace, and soon reached the sea shore. Here he saw three strange women, robed in green seaweed. They were sitting on the shore, sifting the sand through their long fingers. Seppo called to them:

"O maidens, where is the *huomenlahja lipas* for the beautiful Katrina? Tell me where it lies hidden under the waves."

"To find that," answered the maidens, "you must go to Ukko Untamoinen, the sleepy old man of the sea who keeps all dreams hidden from mortal eyes. You can just see his *tupa* across the waves. Go and ask him, but be sure to keep your wits about you. For many have gone to Ukko, but few have returned."

Seppo hurried on to the hut of the old man of the sea, there he looked in through the window. There lay Ukko Untamoinen, the great drowsy giant, stretched out along the floor sound asleep. He was so big that his feet and head stuck out through the doorway and his body filled the whole *tupa*. Seppo jumped over the old man's feet and into the hut. He shouted:

"Ukko Untamoinen, give me the hidden hope chest for my beautiful Katrina."

Ukko Untamoinen rubbed his eyes with his huge green fists drowsily, and said:

"First you must climb up and dance on my tongue, so that it tickles. Then I will give you the hope chest."

The giant stuck out his great tongue as he spoke, and Seppo climbed up on it and began to dance. But no sooner had he begun to dance than Ukko opened his huge mouth wide and tilted his head, and Seppo went tumbling headlong down into his belly. The drowsy giant smiled, and closed his eyes again. He had finished with Seppo.

But Seppo had not finished with him. Instead of being frightened, Seppo kept his wits about him. He drew from his shirt a forge, and from his sleeve a bellows; from his right boot a pair of tongs and from his left boot a great hammer. He rolled up his sleeves and he started to work. From his bosom he drew forth a piece of copper. This he heated in his forge and hammered out a bird with hard claws and a sharp pointed beak. Then Seppo sang one of his brave songs, and blew into the copper bird the breath of life. The bird tore with its claws and beak, and flapped with its wings, and soon the drowsy old man of the sea was doubled up with pain. He clutched at his belly and cried to Seppo:

"If you'll only come out of my belly I'll give you the hope chest!"

Seppo climbed out on the giant's tongue once more, and jumped to the ground.

"Go back to the sea shore," Ukko Untamoinen grumbled. "You will see there three maidens sifting sand between their fingers. Repeat this charm, and they will tell you where the chest is hidden:

Ukko Untamoisen onnella.
By the luck of Ukko Untamoinen.

Seppo found the three maidens again. They were sifting sand through their fingers.

"O good maidens," he called to them, "give me the hope chest which you guard for my beautiful Katrina. Ukko Untamoinen promised it to me . . . Ukko Untamoisen onnella."

"Here it is, hidden under the sand," the maidens answered, "and very glad we are that you've come to fetch it. We are tired of guarding it."

Seppo dug through the sand and uncovered the hope chest. Then he hoisted it to his shoulder, hurrying back to the King's palace.

"Here, King," he said, "is the *huomenlahja lipas* which you sent me to seek for Katrina."

When the King saw that Seppo had brought the chest he was satisfied at last. Sending for the fair rosy-cheeked Katrina, he gave her to Seppo for his wife, with his blessing upon them both.

Seppa once more harnessed his wild colt with the iron harness and the stout reins and started out with Katrina in the painted sledge, swishing across the open sea. The wild colt flew so fast that no wave touched them, and the sledge runners left no track on the water.

Hard they drove, till night overtook them in the midst of the sea. Then Seppo sang a brave song, and by the magic of his song there rose a beautiful island before them. Here they stopped for the night.

With the coming of dawn Seppo awoke. He looked about him, but nowhere could he see Katrina. She had disappeared. He looked here, he looked there, and saw only the wild ducks circling in the air. He counted them and found there was one duck too many. So he sang:

"Do not try to hide, Katrina, I have found you."

At once one of the wild ducks turned into a fair rosy-cheeked girl, and Katrina stood before him, smiling. Seppo took Katrina into his painted sledge and once more they drove across the open sea. When night overtook them Seppo sang another brave song, and again an island rose before them.

Again, when Seppo awoke in the morning, there was no Katrina. He searched the island, and counted all the trees. There was one tree too many. He sang:

"Do not try to hide, Katrina, I have found you."

And when the trees heard his song, one of them stepped forth, and there stood Katrina.

The third day Seppo took Katrina once more into his painted sledge, and once more they drove across the sea. When night overtook them, he sang a third time, and a third time an island rose before them. When day dawned Seppo awoke and saw that his Katrina was once more missing.

This time he grew hot with anger.

"No more shall Katrina deceive me!" he shouted.

He counted the rocks along the shore, and found that there was one rock too many.

"Do not hide, Katrina, I have found you," he called.

But when Katrina stood before him, he said with a bitter heart:

"Long have I paid court to you, Katrina. For the King, your father, I have done many tasks, and is this my pay, that you should deceive and mock me? For this you shall live forever upon the sea. I will make you into a tern, and every day shall you fly against the wind."

Then he sang a brave song, and as he sang Katrina turned into a gray bird and flew away.

But as he saw her flying away upon the wind Seppo grew sad. His heart was empty. He felt that he could not live alone. So he set up his forge, drew a piece of copper from his breast, and began to hammer out a woman to suit his fancy. And when he had finished he sang a brave song, and there came into the copper the breath of life.

At first Seppo was pleased with this woman of his own handiwork. She obeyed him in everything. But soon he grew tired of being obeyed. He grew tired of his cold copper woman and cast her away.

After long days of wandering and loneliness, Seppo heard a soft knocking within his heart. A voice said:

"I am wisdom. Listen to me, and know the truth. A man should not try to make a woman after his own dreams. He should learn to be happy with the wife Hiisi has given him."

Then Seppo sang his brave song for the last time. And as he sang a gray sea-bird swooped down beside him, and there stood his wife, Katrina.

Seppo wasted no time. He took Katrina into his painted sledge, whipped up his wild colt, and with laughter in his heart swept homeward.


# THE MOUSE BRIDE


ONCE THERE was a laborer named Pekka, who was always worried about the future. He was so anxious to know what might be going to happen that one day he went to an old Lapland woman, and asked her to tell him his fortune.

The old Laplander woman said:

"You will have three sons. As each is born, you must plant a tree for him, and you must call that tree by the same name that you give your son. When the boys are grown to manhood and want to marry, tell each one to cut down his own name tree, and in whichever direction the tree falls, that way must he travel to find his wife. Mark my words well, and you will have good fortune."

Pekka did as the old Laplander woman told him. When his first son was born he planted a birch tree, and called it Onni, after the baby's own name. When his second child was born a year later he planted an oak tree, and he named both the boy and the tree Arne. When the third child was born, Pekka planted a fir tree, and named both the child and the tree Jukka.

As the boys grew, the trees grew, and by the time the three sons were grown men there stood their name trees, tall and fair with spreading branches.

One day Pekka's three sons came to him and said:

"Father, surely it is time now for each of us to seek a wife."

"It is time," said Pekka. "But before you set out, each one of you must fell his own name tree. And whichever way the tree points as it falls, that way must you set out to seek your wife."

It so happened that Onni's, the eldest son's tree, fell in the direction of a rich man's house. Arne's oak tree fell in the direction of a farmer's *tupa*. But when it came to Jukka, the youngest son's name tree, that fell in the direction of no house at all, but only by the deep forest.

Each son accepted his fate, and set forth in the direction his tree had pointed.

As Jukka walked on and on into the forest, he wondered what sort of bride he would find there. After walking for three days and seeing no one at all he came at last to a little clearing hidden among the trees, and there he saw a tiny *tupa* built of grey logs. He knocked at the door, but no one answered. Then he lifted the latch to look inside. The room was quite empty.

Jukka was tired after his long journey, and when he found no one at home he was very disappointed. But there on the table in the middle of the room sat a little gray mouse with blue eyes and a queer white-tipped nose, looking at him.

"Welcome, stranger," said the little mouse. "Why are you so sad?"

"You would be sad, too," said Jukka, "if you had travelled three days and three nights, only to find that your bride was not at home."

"Then marry me," piped the little gray mouse.

"*Ka* (See)!" laughed Jukka bitterly. "Marry you, indeed! Why, you aren't even human."

"Marry me," said the little gray mouse again. "Marry me, and you will never be sorry for your bargain."

"*Ka,* I couldn't be worse off than I am now," said Jukka, "even if I did marry you."

"It's a bargain, then," said the mouse, and she began to dance about the table on her little gray feet. "When you come back, I'll be here waiting for you."

Jukka shut the door behind him and trudged sadly home again. When he reached the house his father and his two brothers asked him:

"What kind of wife did you find in the forest?"

THE MOUSE BRIDE

"A very fine wife indeed," Jukka told them.

"Tell us all about her."

"There's nothing to tell, except that her eyes are very blue and her nose is very white."

"Blue eyes and a white nose! That's funny!" And they all began to laugh.

Then Onni and Arne began to tell their luck, bragging all evening about the wonderful brides they had found. But poor Jukka could only sit silent, and presently he went sadly to bed.

Next morning Pekka called his three sons to him, and said:

"Today you must each go and bring me back some piece of your bride's handiwork, so that I may judge which is the best. What do you say to a loaf of bread?"

"That's a good idea," agreed Onni and Arne, and they set out in haste. Poor Jukka trudged back to his mouse.

When he opened the door of the tiny gray *tupa*, there was his mouse bride sitting on the table.

"Do you seek something from me, *Kultani* (my dear one)," she asked, "or have you come to marry me?"

"My father has sent me to fetch a sample of your handiwork," Jukka answered. "Will you make me a loaf of bread?"

"All right," said the mouse bride. And she took a tiny reindeer bell in her paws and began ringing it. At the very first sound of the bell, in came a thousand mice all dancing on their toes. The mouse bride said to them:

"Each of you mice must bring me the finest grain of wheat you can find. Hurry up!"

Away scampered the thousand mice, and in no time at all there they were back again, each bringing a single grain of wheat. Then Jukka's bride took the grains of wheat, ground them up, and made a loaf of bread.

Jukka thought it very strange that a mouse could do all this, but he asked no questions. He merely thanked the mouse bride, took the loaf of bread under his arm and went home.

Onni had proudly brought a loaf of rye bread from his bride. Arne's loaf was of barley. But when their father saw that Jukka's loaf was baked from the finest wheat flour, he opened his eyes very wide. He examined each loaf in turn, then said:

"Now you must fetch me a piece of cloth woven by each of your brides. I wish to see which is the most skilful with her hands."

When Jukka opened the door of the tiny gray *tupa*, his mouse bride asked:

"Do you seek something from me, *Kultani*, or have you come to marry me?"

"My father has sent me," answered Jukka, "to fetch a piece of cloth that you have woven with your own hands."

"*Vai niin* (Is that so)!" cried the mouse bride. "That won't take long!"

Again she rang the tiny reindeer bell. Again the thousand mice came dancing in on their toes.

"Each of you mice must fetch me the finest shred of flax you can find," said the mouse bride. "And remember there's no time to waste!"

Away scampered the thousand mice, and in a moment back they all came again, each with his shred of the finest flax.

"Now you must all help me to weave it," said the mouse bride.

The mice all set to work busily. Some carded, others spun, the mouse bride herself wove, and in no time at all the piece of cloth was finished. Jukka was very surprised when his mouse bride folded up the cloth neatly, tucked it inside a nutshell and put the nutshell in his hand. He thanked her, thrust the nutshell in his pocket and hurried home.

His father and his two brothers were there waiting for him. Onni proudly showed his square of cloth, but it was hard and stiff. The cloth that Arne's bride had made was uneven and loosely woven. The father examined the two pieces, but said nothing. Then he turned to Jukka and asked:

"*Ka,* and where is your cloth?"

"There is so little of it, it is hardly worth the showing," Jukka said, taking the nutshell from his pocket.

When they saw the nutshell, Onni and Arne burst out laughing. But when their father opened it and drew out the cloth, so finely was the linen woven that there were fifty yards of it folded there! Pekka's eyes opened wide in wonder, for never had he seen anything to compare with this handiwork, but still he said nothing.

A few days after he again called his sons together.

"It is now the summer month," he told them, "and time for each of you to go and fetch his bride. I wish to see which of you has made the wisest choice. It is fitting that my sons be wed on Midsummer's Day!"

Onni and Arne fairly jumped for joy, and ran each to fetch his bride. But poor Jukka scarcely knew what to do. He set off slowly like a man who walks in a bad dream.

When he reached the tiny gray *tupa* he said to his mouse bride:

"Come now with me. My father wants to meet you."

"*Ka,* since it is his wish, let us go together," piped the mouse bride in her tiny treble voice.

She rang her reindeer bell, and this time there danced into the room five sleek gray mice harnessed to a carriage made of a chestnut burr with a toadstool for a canopy.

The mouse bride seated herself in the tiny carriage as stately as any queen, all ready to start.

"But how can I bring you to my father like this?" Jukka asked. "When my brothers see how small you are they will make fun of me, and my father will be angry."

"Don't be afraid," said the mouse bride. "If only you do as I tell you, dear Jukka, you'll be a happy man yet!"

The five sleek mice started off at a gallop, and Jukka walked slowly along beside the chestnut burr carriage. He did not know whether to laugh or cry.

On the second day of their journey they came to a bridge that crossed a river. The five gray mice started at a quick trot, with Jukka walking beside them. In the middle of the bridge they met a big peasant boy with a hard ugly face and broad shoulders. The boy growled:

"What do you think you're doing, walking beside this crazy mouse-carriage?"

And before Jukka could stop him, the peasant boy had given a kick with his clumsy foot. Pell-mell, the five gray mice and the tiny chestnut burr carriage and the little mouse bride all flew out into the running water. There was a splash, and they were gone.

Jukka was ready to fight, but when he looked round the boy had disappeared. So he turned to peer again into the running water. And then he saw five sleek gray horses drawing a glittering carriage out of the stream and up the bank. In the carriage, holding the reins, sat a lovely maiden. She drove the carriage up to the bridge and stopped beside Jukka, who stood tongue-tied with surprise.

"Aren't you coming with me the rest of the way?" she asked. But Jukka could only look stupid and rub his eyes.

"Don't you know me?" the maiden went on. "I am the mouse bride whom you agreed to marry. Get up here and ride beside me, and on the way I'll tell you how it all happened."

Jukka climbed into the carriage beside her. He took the reins into his own hands and as they drove along his bride told her story.

"I was once a king's daughter," she said. "But a Lapland witch-woman became envious of my beauty, and when I was fifteen she changed me and all of my servants into mice. The spell could not be broken until one young man should ask to marry me, and another should try to kill me by casting me into water. You, Jukka, became betrothed to me, and the peasant lad we just met on the bridge kicked me into the water to drown. So now the spell has been broken and here I am, my own self once more!"

When he heard this, Jukka was the happiest man in the whole world.

"And what shall I say," he asked, "when my father wants to know your name?"

"Call me Olga," said his bride.

"And now, Olga my sweetheart," Jukka said, "we must waste no time in getting home to keep our wedding feast. The village folk will all be there and we'll dance all day and all night."

As usual, Onni and Arne had returned first, and were there waiting with their father, but this time they had their brides with them. When they saw Jukka driving up in that grand carriage with his five fine horses, they couldn't believe their eyes. But the sight of Olga surprised them still more, for she was the most beautiful woman they had ever seen. As for their father, he couldn't keep his eyes off her, which made both Onni and Arne very jealous.

So the three sons were married in their father's house, which was all decked with green boughs and flowers. The village musician came and played on his *kantele* (A Finnish harp) and sang while all the young folk of the village danced by moonlight. And old Pekka nodded his head in happiness to see his sons and daughters so gay.

When the last tune had been played and the last dance was over and the last toast drunk, Jukka and Olga climbed into their carriage and the five grey horses bore them swiftly back to the valley hidden away between the trees.

And there was a new surprise for Jukka, for the tiny grey *tupa* had turned into a King's castle.

"This is just as it all was when I was a child," smiled Olga, "before the Laplander woman worked her witchcraft on me."

And there it was, far from the busy world, that Jukka and his mouse bride lived happily ever after.

# ANTTI AND THE WIZARD'S PROPHECY

MANY YEARS ago it happened that two wizards were journeying through Finland. One evening they came to the *tupa* of a small farmer and asked if they might spend the night. As luck would have it the farmer's wife had that very evening given birth to a baby. So as the household was all upset and there was no room for strangers, the farmer asked the two wizards if they would mind sleeping in the *sauna* (bathhouse). They were both very tired so they readily agreed.

The farmer was so excited about the new baby he quite forgot to tell the wizards that he had already given the upper berth in the *sauna* to a travelling merchant who had also asked for a night's lodging earlier in the evening. The wizards saw the merchant lying there, but thought he was asleep, so they made up their own bed on the lower berth just beneath him, talking in whispers while they undressed.

"The farmer's wife has a new-born son," said the first wizard. "Let us repeat a charm so that she may rest easy during the night."

And together they repeated:

> "Mene kipu kauas täältä
> Lenna mustilla siivilla."
> Go forth, O pain!
> Fly on black wings
> Over Tuonela's dark river
> To Mountain of Misery, Kipuvuori.

"What kind of man do you think the child will be when he grows up?" asked the second wizard.

The first wizard repeated another charm which helped him to look into the future, and said:

"It is written that the boy will become the heir of Ahnas, the wealthy merchant who is now sleeping on the upper berth just over our heads."

But it happened that the merchant was not asleep, and he heard everything the wizards said. Their prophecy worried him so much that he lay awake all night planning how to rid himself of the child. When morning

came, he again pretended to be asleep until he was quite sure that the
two wizards had started on their way. Then he got up and went to speak
to the farmer.

"You are poor," he said, "and have already many children to feed and
clothe. I am rich. If you will give me your new-born son, I will pay you a
hundred roubles. I will make him my heir, and he will be a comfort to
me in my old age."

The poor farmer was quite dazzled by this offer, for a hundred roubles
seemed to him a great deal of money. He thought, too, that it would
be a very good thing for his son, so he sold the child to Ahnas then
and there.

The farmer's wife sewed the baby into a warm leather bag so that only
its tiny pink face showed, and with tears in her eyes put it into the
merchant's arms. Ahnas laid the child on a bed of pine boughs in the
bottom of his sleigh and set off for home.

But as soon as he was well out of sight of the house, he turned his
horse and drove into the deep wild forest. There he left the child in the
crotch of a gnarled pine tree and as he whipped his horse and drove
hastily away he said to himself:

"Now I'm rid of you for good! You won't threaten my fortune any
more."

But he was scarcely out of sight before a hunter happened to pass that
way, and heard the baby crying. He took it down tenderly, carrying it
in his arms to his *tupa* in the village. There he told the neighbors what
had happened and they named the child Antti Puuhaara, which means
"tree crotch."

Antti proved a strong healthy child, and as the years passed he grew
into a strong and handsome young man.

It so happened that Ahnas, the merchant, stopped one day at the
hunter's *tupa* to buy furs, and the hunter invited him to spend the night.
During the evening the family gathered round the open hearth. They
played the *kantele* and sang old-time songs and ballads. Ahnas became
interested in the handsome youth whose voice was so clear and whose
smile was so honest.

"What is your son's name?" he asked.

"Antti Puuhaara," the hunter told him. "It is a strange story. Many
years ago, when he was a tiny baby, I found him sewed into a leather bag
and hanging from the fork of a tree in the deep wild forest. I brought
him home and he has become the joy and life of our household."

The merchant turned pale and his hands began to tremble, for again
the fear of the wizard's prophecy was upon him. He disguised his feelings, but all that night he lay awake planning how he might make an end
of Antti. In the morning he said to the hunter:

"I have to send an important message home. I am too busy buying
furs to go myself, but if you will let Antti carry it for me I will pay you
well for the trouble."

"*Ka*, indeed," said the hunter. "Antti will be only too glad to help you."

So Ahnas give Antti a sealed letter to carry, and the youth started off gayly on his errand, never dreaming what the letter contained. Ahnas had written:

> DEAR WIFE,
>
> Command my servants to hang by the neck the messenger Antti who brings you this letter. Fasten the rope to the limb of the birch tree that grows behind the garden wall.

Antti went whistling on his way. It was a long journey, and by the time he reached the foot of the mountains he was tired, so he lay down to rest. While he was sleeping two rogues happened along. They saw the letter, and thinking that it might contain money they opened it.

These two rogues knew Ahnas very well, for he had often cheated them in buying their furs. Here was a chance to pay him back. They guessed that he was playing a trick on the innocent Antti, so they changed the letter to read:

> DEAR WIFE,
>
> Give the messenger Antti, who brings this letter, our daughter Alli for his wife without delay. Tell my servants to hang Musti, my dog, by the neck to the birch tree that grows behind the garden wall.

Then they made off, leaving Antti still sleeping. Presently Antti woke, not knowing that anything had happened, and continued his journey to the merchant's house. When he arrived the merchant's wife read the letter. She obediently gave her daughter to Antti in marriage and poor Musti, the dog, was duly hanged.

Many weeks later, when Ahnas returned home, he saw from a distance something black dangling from the birch tree.

"Ka," he said to himself. "Now I'm through with you. *You* will never be my heir!"

But when he drew nearer he had a great shock, for it was not Antti hanging from the tree branch, but Musti, his favorite hound. Worse still, when he entered the house there was Antti, his son-in-law, already taking his place in command of the household. Every one was very pleased and happy about it too.

Ahnas was a clever man, so he pretended that everything was just as he had expected. When he was alone with his wife he asked to see the letter, and all that night he lay awake planning how he might rid himself of Antti.

The next morning he greeted Antti very pleasantly, and said:

"Now that you're my son-in-law and heir to my estate, you must prove to me that you are really worthy of the honor. All my life long I have wondered what trade brings a man the greatest happiness. I'm tired of travelling here and there about the country buying furs, and I would like to change to some pleasanter business, if I only knew what. The only person in the world who can answer my question is Louhi, Mistress of the Northland. I myself am too old to make the long journey to her kingdom, so you must go for me."

Antti was quite willing to go. He was sorry to leave Alli, his happy bride, but he felt it a duty to do any service he could for this kind father-in-law. So he took a spear in his hand and set off with a brave heart.

After many days he came to Hiisi, the mountain where the gnomes dwell. At the very top of this mountain stood a tall giant, who carried clouds on his head and in his cap held imprisoned the eight winds of heaven. The giant saw Antti coming, and called to him:

"Where are you going, my lad?"

"I am bound for the far Northland, to ask Louhi what trade will bring a man most happiness."

"I have a question I'd like to have answered, too," the giant shouted. "My orchard used to bear fine fruit, but now the fruit molds before it is ripe. If you will ask Louhi what I can do about it, I will lend you my stallion to ride so you can travel faster."

"Surely I'll ask Louhi your question," said Antti, and he leapt on the stallion's back and galloped on.

As he rode, he heard ahead of him a great rumbling like thunder, and felt the earth tremble. Antti wondered what it could be. Presently he came to a stone castle. Outside the door stood a giant with an enormous key; he was trying to open the door, but the key would not turn in the lock. After trying a little while, he would lose patience and begin pounding on the door with his huge fists, so that the ground shook for miles around.

Antti was so frightened that it was all he could do to keep on his horse's back, but he managed to say:

"Good day and good luck to you!"

The giant turned round, scratched his ear angrily and returned:

"Where are you going, my lad?"

"I'm on my way to ask a question of Louhi, Mistress of the far Northland."

"*Ka,* then you can ask Louhi a question for me, too. I have lost the keys to my castle. If she can tell you where I can find them again, I'll make you a present of my own best handiwork."

"Surely I'll ask her that," said Antti, and he rode on with the speed of the wind.

Soon he came to another castle, on a high mountain in the land of Hiitola. Here stood a huge birch tree that reached to the skies, and on a branch of the tree sat a giant roasting an elk, which he held on the point of his lance over the fire. As soon as the giant saw Antti he called:

"Hurry, hurry, my lad, and I'll give you a dinner of roasted meat."

Antii was hungry, and gladly ate his fill. When he had finished the giant said: "Where are you going at such a pace?"

"I'm going to Louhi, to ask her a question."

"Ask her one for me, too. Ask her why I must needs sit in this tree all my life. Sometimes I am lucky enough to spear an elk but more often I nearly starve to death, for I'm held here a prisoner and cannot move."

"Surely I will ask her that," said Antti, and he leapt astride the black stallion again and hurried on his way.

At last he came to a wide river. By the shore was a little boat and in the boat an old woman, bent and toothless.

"If you will leave your horse here with me," said the old woman, "I will row you over to the other side. It is only a step from there to the castle of Louhi, and I'll be glad to show you the way."

"But shall I find my horse waiting for me when I come back?" Antti asked.

"If you bring me back an answer to my question from Louhi herself, I'll promise that your horse will be here waiting for you."

"Surely I will ask her your question," said Antti, and he stepped into the boat.

"Find out from Louhi," said the old woman as she bent over the creaking oars, "why I must be forever ferrying people across this river. For hundreds of years I've had to do this, and I am getting very tired."

Antii took the path which the old woman pointed out to him, and after a little while he came to tilled fields, and then a castle. He knocked at the door and the Daughter of the Rainbow, a lovely maiden with rosy cheeks, asked him in. Antti said:

"May I ask a few questions of Louhi, your mother?"

"My mother is not home today," the maiden answered, "but I expect her back at nightfall."

"I have come a long way," said Antti, "and I have many questions to ask. May I please wait here till your mother returns?"

The Daughter of the Rainbow looked at Antti's honest face and his kindly smile, and was curious to know what questions he had to ask. So Antti repeated them, one by one, and when he had finished she clapped her hands in laughter.

"O-ho, you want to know a great deal! But I'm afraid my mother will never answer all those questions for you."

Antti looked so sad at this that she added quickly: "Never mind, perhaps I can help you. When we hear Louhi coming, you must hide behind the cupboard. I will ask my mother the questions for you. Listen carefully, and then in the night you can slip out and hurry home again, without her being any the wiser."

By-and-by Louhi came home. When they heard her step, Antti crept behind the cupboard to listen.

"Did anyone come while I was gone?" asked Louhi as soon as she had opened the door.

"A man came early this morning with questions," answered her daughter, "but you were not at home, so I sent him on his way to ask elsewhere."

"O-ho! I could have told him anything he wanted to know," said Louhi. "What sort of questions did he ask?"

"He first asked in what trade a man would be happiest."

"He must have been a wise man to ask about happiness. I could have told him the old saying: Man is happiest when he plows the fields, clears the soil, piles the rocks in heaps, and plants seeds that will grow into food for himself and his cattle."

"He also asked why the fruit belonging to a certain giant is always covered with mold."

"Only a fool would ask such a question! He should know that there lives a worm in the giant's garden that breathes upon the fruit. If the giant only has sense to crush this worm between two stones, his fruit will no longer be blighted."

"Another giant has lost the keys to his castle, and wants to know where to find them."

"How simple!" Louhi laughed contemptuously. "The giant will find his key fast enough if he looks between the stones leading to his own door."

"The man had still another question. A third giant has spent his life sitting fast in a birch tree, and wants to know how he can break his bonds."

"All he need do is to strike the foot of the tree with his lance. That will break the charm, and the limbs of the tree will fall to the ground and turn to pure gold."

"Last of all he wanted to know how the old woman who ferries people to and fro across the river may escape from her bondage."

"It's a pity the old woman is so stupid! All she has to do is to jump ashore when she next rows someone across, push the boat off with her left heel and repeat this charm:

Minä lähden tästä, sinä jäät siihen.

I leave here, you stay there.

Whoever happens to be in the boat at the time will then become the ferryman and the old woman will be free to do as she likes."

"Well, those were all the questions," said the Daughter of the Rainbow, with a ripple of laughter.

"The man must be a fool," Louhi said, "or he would have known the answers for himself. But if he ever comes back again, mind you don't tell them to him, for simple questions like these are considered the greatest secrets in the world of men."

When Louhi had finished, Antti felt so full of wisdom that he feared his head would burst with it all before he could get away. Time dragged, and it seemed a year before Louhi at last went to sleep. As soon as Antti heard her deep breathing, he crept from his hiding place, thanked the Daughter of the Rainbow, and ran back to the river.

"What did Louhi answer to my question?" the old woman wanted to know.

"I'll tell you as soon as you set me ashore on the opposite bank," Antti said.

When he had set foot on the sand he jumped astride his stallion and shouted:

Minä lähden tästa, sinä jäät siihen.

I leave here, you stay there.

This is Louhi's answer. You can work the charm on the next traveller who asks you to row him across!"

The old woman thanked Antti, and he rode away.

Soon he reached the giant who sat fidgeting in the birch tree, and told him Louhi's answer. The giant struck the foot of the tree with his lance, and to his surprise the branches fell to the ground and he with them. The fallen branches turned to pure gold and the giant was so happy that he gave Antti half of his riches to take with him.

Antti, riding happily on, met the next giant and told him where to find the keys of his castle. This giant was so glad that he gave Antti more gold.

As for the third giant, who carried the clouds upon his head, he was so happy to know how he could make his trees bear good fruit again that he gave Antti the stallion for his very own.

And now Antti rode like the wind back to the house of Ahnas, for he could scarcely wait to tell his wife, Alli, all his adventures and the good fortune that had befallen him.

When Ahnas saw that Antti had returned, he was furious. He said:

"Have you really been to Louhi, and has she truly told you in which trade a man is happiest?"

"These are Louhi's words," Antti replied. " 'Man is happiest when he plows the fields, clears the soil, piles the rocks in heaps, and plants seed that will grow into food for himself and his cattle.' "

This answer did not please Ahnas at all, for he hated to work or to stay in one place and besides, he was very greedy. He wanted to know at once where Antti had found all the gold that he brought home. And when Antti told him about his adventures, Ahnas made up his mind to set out himself on a journey through the land of Hiitola, and to ask Louhi how he might find more gold.

Antti offered to share his wealth. But the greedy merchant would not listen to him.

So Ahnas set off to visit Louhi. After a long journey, he at last came to the river where the old woman sat waiting in her boat. She rowed him across, then jumped ashore, gave the boat a shove with her left heel and said:

"I leave here, you stay there."

Then the charm fell upon Ahnas, and like it or not, he had to stay there in her stead.

Soon every man in Finland heard of Antti's great adventure and of Louhi's answer to the age-old question of mankind, how to find the greatest happiness, and from that time forth they became content to till the soil. For this reason Ahnas has had no passengers to row across the river to the land of Louhi, the ancient sorceress. From that day to this, he has remained in the boat.

And so the prophecy of the two wizards was fulfilled, for Antti fell heir to the merchant's estate and for many years lived happily with his gentle wife Alli.

# JURMA AND THE SEA GOD

THERE WAS once a farmer named Jurma, who lived by the sea. One hot day while he was plowing in the fields he grew tired, so he sat down on the rocks and dangled his feet in the cool waves to rest them.

While he was sitting there a Sea God caught him by the ankles and said:

"Unless you give me your eldest daughter, Impi, I will drag you under the water and drown you."

The farmer tried to kick the Sea God's long scaly fingers from his ankles but the more he struggled the tighter the Sea God held on.

"I have never harmed you," begged the farmer. "Let me go. I love Impi too much to give her to you."

"All right," laughed the Sea God as he gave Jurma's ankles another tug. "Come yourself, then."

Jurma was very frightened as he clutched at the rocks.

"Let me go, let me go," he cried, "and I will give you my daughter!"

As Jurma spoke, the Sea God let go of his ankles, and for one moment stood up in the water. The green scales of his body glittered in the sun as he said:

"You must not forget your promise."

Then he dived under the waters and was gone.

When Jurma reached his *tupa* he dared not tell his wife what had happened. He simply said:

"Impi, I forgot to bring the horse's reins from the rocks where I was resting. Run and fetch them for me, for I'm very tired."

Impi did as he told her, and ran gaily down to the shore. The Sea God, who was waiting under the water, saw her standing there on the rocks. He caught her in his long green arms and carried her off to his palace under the waves. When he came to his sea kingdom, he set Impi on her feet again and knelt before her. And he said a charm:

> Kultani kallihin,
> Minum Sydämeni sinulle,
> Sinun sydämesi minulle.

> Golden one, priceless one,
> My heart to you, yours to me.

And at once Impi fell in love with the Sea God.

At first Impi was so dazed by the world under the sea that she thought she was dreaming. All about her was a blue haze. In the Sea King's palace the chairs and tables were made of finest green coral, and the walls of flowing green tapestry. The door yard of the palace was planted with great fronds of waving sea weeds, and paved with all kinds of shells. Strangest of all was the fence of shining eels that enclosed the castle.

Here we shall be at home," said the Sea God. "You are now my wife and shall rule my palace as you choose."

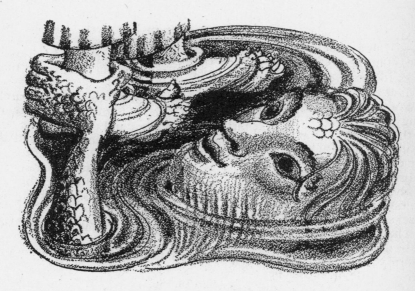

JURMA AND THE SEA GOD

Impi smiled, for she loved the Sea God, but she longed for the light of the sun and the stars, for the sweet clean air of the upper world. The green shadows amused her, but she still felt strange and lonely.

Years passed, and Impi grew used to this strange world under the waters. But the Sea God became restless and wanted to go away for a time. One day he said to Impi:

"I must make a long journey, and shall be gone for many days. Here are the keys to all the chambers of the palace. Amuse yourself until my return. You can do anything you like, and go anywhere you wish, only do not enter the last chamber at the back of the palace. This is my private room, and no one ever crosses its threshold but myself."

After the Sea God had gone, Impi wandered through the palace from room to room. She opened and closed every door a dozen times, and at length became curious to enter the Sea God's private chamber.

"My husband will never know, if I enter his chamber," she said to herself, "but what would it matter, even if he did!"

She put the great key into the lock and drew it out again two or three times to see if anything would happen. Then she put her ear to the keyhole each time, but all was silent.

When Impi entered the room, she was surprised to see only bare, dingy walls. There was a wide shelf and two large bottles. In the center of the floor stood a huge keg filled with black tar, and on top of the tar floated a beautiful golden ring. Impi tried the ring on her finger, and as she did so, a large drop of tar touched her hand and burned like fire.

Impi was frightened, and threw the ring back into the tar. She ran out of the room, and locked the door behind her. She tried to rub the tar stain from her finger and to ease the burn. But the more she rubbed, the blacker the stain became, and the more it pained her.

That evening the Sea God returned, tired with his journey and glad to be at home.

"Impi," he said, "take my head in your lap, and lay your hands on my brow to ease my headache."

When Impi's stained finger touched the Sea God's forehead, he leapt to his feet and cried:

"What is that, a coal of fire on my brow?"

"I have no fire in my hands," said Impi, holding out her palms to him.

Then the Sea God saw the stain on Impi's finger, and said angrily:

"You have tricked me. I gave you the keys to every room in the palace, and you have gone into my secret chamber."

Impi begged for mercy, but the Sea God was furious. He carried her into the secret chamber, and threw her into the great keg of tar.

While all these things were happening under the sea, Impi's father continued to dwell with his wife and his two remaining daughters on the sea-shore. One day while Impi's father was fishing in his boat in the bay, the boat caught on the sand. He tried in every way to free it, but the boat would not move. While he was pushing with his oar, the Sea God lifted his shining green head above the water, and said, smiling:

"My good man, this is not the first time I have met you. Give me your second daughter, Hella, and I will set you free."

"Cruel Sea God!" shouted Jurma. "Have you no pity? Haven't you already harmed me enough?"

But as he spoke, his boat began to sink.

"I have a beautiful palace, and Hella will be very happy," said the Sea God. "Make haste and decide, for your boat is already shipping water."

The father began to weep. "Save me, and I'll give you my daughter!"

"Very well, I will be waiting at the shore," said the Sea God and he dived under the waves.

When Hella's father reached his *tupa*, he could not bear to tell what had happened. He simply said:

"Hella, I have forgot my fishing spear in the boat. Fetch it to me."

Hella ran down to the boat, whereupon the Sea God seized her, and carried her quickly under the water to his palace.

Years passed, and the Sea God decided to go on another journey. He gave his keys to Hella and said:

"While I am gone, you may do as you like. You may have the freedom of the entire palace, but do not enter my private chamber."

When he had left, Hella too became curious, and entered the chamber. She tried on the ring as her sister had done, and stained her finger. When the Sea God returned, he threw Hella, too, into the keg of tar.

In the Upper World, time had passed slowly for Hella's father and mother, and for the younger sister, Vieno. The father had learned his lesson, and stayed away from the sea. When his wife and daughter asked him to bring them fish, he always found some excuse. But one day, after his wife had begged him to set his nets on the shallow sand at low tide, he went down to the shore.

As he approached his boat, he saw a pair of the most finely woven birch bark shoes he had ever seen. He decided to try them on his feet.

No sooner were the shoes on his feet, than they began to slide with him toward the water. He realized too late that the shoes were bewitched, for when he tried to kick them off, they carried him quickly into the waves. He was in the water up to his waist, then up to his neck.

As he struggled, there stood the Sea God beside him, smiling.

"Is there nothing I can do for you, my good man?"

"Free me from these cursed birch bark shoes," cried Jurma. "They are carrying me to a watery grave."

"This should teach you not to take what does not belong to you," laughed the Sea God. "Now you are in my power, and unless you give me your third daughter, Vieno, I will not help you."

The father was now broken-hearted, and begged for mercy.

"Your Vieno will be happier with me," said the Sea God, "than she is with you. I shall give her every treasure that her heart wishes."

When the father went back to his *tupa* he said wearily:

"Vieno, I have forgotten my birch bark shoes on the shore beside the boat. Fetch them to me."

Vieno feared nothing, and ran happily down to the water. The Sea God caught her in his arms, and carried her joyfully away to his green shadowed palace. He gave her of his wealth and jewels, and at last she became accustomed to the strange, dreamy land under the sea.

One day the Sea God said to Vieno:

"My dear wife, I am going on a long journey. Here are the keys to my palace. You are welcome to enter every room but one . . . "

When he had gone, Vieno entered the forbidden chamber, as her sisters had done, and looked cautiously about her, for she suspected some sort of trickery.

She examined the two large bottles on the shelf. One was labelled THE WATER OF LIFE, and the other THE WATER OF DEATH.

Then she noticed the keg and the golden ring floating on the top of the thick black tar. She looked closely at the tar, and suddenly discovered the eyes of her two sisters staring coldly at her.

Vieno was weak with fright. She wondered what she could do. She remembered, then, the Water of Life, and lifted the great bottle down from the shelf.

She sprinkled the Water of Life upon the tar, and when she had shaken the last drop from the bottle, there stood her two sisters before her, rubbing their eyes as if awakened from a bad dream.

Vieno then poured all the Water of Death into the bottle labelled the Water of Life, and placed the two bottles again on the shelf. When she told her sisters all that had happened, she led them from the terrible secret chamber, and locked the door.

For a time the three sisters stood, trembling with fear lest the Sea God should return and find them. They thought hard, and finally decided upon a plan of escape. Vieno placed Impi and Hella in two large sea chests, and fastened them securely.

When the Sea God returned, Vieno said sweetly:

"My lord, you look tired, and your hair and beard are tangled. Lay your head upon my knees, and I will bring my golden comb."

This pleased the Sea God, and as she smoothed his temples, and ran the comb through his hair, he grew gentle and said:

"My dear wife, is there not something I can do to make you happy?"

"I have been wondering," said Vieno, "if you would mind doing a little errand for me. My parents are poor, while we have plenty and to spare. Will you not carry this sea chest, and place it on the shore by their *tupa* where they will find it? I had rather you would not open it, for I am ashamed to have you see the women's trifles that I am sending to my mother."

The Sea God laughed, but took the sea chest upon his shoulder, and set it down before Jurma's *tupa*.

When the Sea God returned, Vieno again took his head upon her knees until he became gentle.

"I know it has made you happy to carry the sea chest to my parents. Will you not make two more journeys for me? The chests are so small, and my parents are so sorely in need, that three chests will be little to pay for all that I owe them. Do these errands for me, and I shall never ask you another favor."

The Sea God gladly took the second chest, in which was hidden Hella, and set it down on the sand before Jurma's *tupa*.

While he was gone, Vieno gathered many treasures together into the third chest. Then she made a dummy of pillows, and dressed it in her own clothes. This she set upon the balcony where the Sea God would see it upon his return.

Vieno then climbed into the third chest, and clamped down the lid. When she heard the Sea God coming, she said in a loud voice:

"Carry this third chest at once to my parents without opening it, and they will be very grateful for the good turn you have done them."

The Sea God peered upward through the green shadows, and saw the figure upon the balcony. He thought it was his Vieno, and so he took the third chest upon his shoulders and started off. After he had gone a little way he set the chest down.

"This chest is so heavy," he said to himself, "that I must see what it contains before I go any farther."

"Do not look inside," called a strange voice. "Did you not promise me that?"

"She can still see me," said the Sea God. "That is why she climbed up to the balcony, so that she could watch what I am doing."

Again he struggled a long time under his burden, and again set the sea chest down to open it. But a strange voice, half in a whisper, said:

"Do not deceive me. Remember your promise. Do not look inside, but keep on your way."

"Never again will I go on an errand for my wife," swore the Sea God as he again set out. "She is too clever."

As soon as he had set the third chest upon the sand, he returned in high spirits. He entered his castle shouting:

"Hurry the dinner, for I have a ravenous appetite."

He looked up at the silent dummy upon the balcony. He started up the steps at a bound, saying:

"Something must have happened to Vieno, that she does not move or answer."

When he saw how he had been tricked, he struck at the dummy in his anger, but lost his balance, and tumbled headlong down the stairs. The Sea God was so badly bruised that he went to his secret chamber, and taking down the bottle labelled THE WATER OF LIFE, drank deeply. But, alas, this was the Water of Death, and so the Sea God never knew what happened.

In the farmer's *tupa* there was great rejoicing when Jurma and his wife found their three daughters in the chests upon the shore. They sold the treasures and jewels that Vieno had brought with her, and forever after had plenty, and to spare.

And now that the Sea God had come to his well-deserved end, there was no one left to spoil their happiness.

# SEVERI AND VAPPU

THERE WAS a young man named Severi who set out one spring morning to find his fortune.

The sun shone, the birds sang, and Severi felt so lighthearted that he too sang for joy, and so eager that his feet fairly ran away with him. Over hills and meadows, through deep woods he wandered, until at last he came to the wide ocean, where he saw a little rowboat dancing on the tide.

"Now I will sail to some far country," cried Severi. "Who knows what adventures I may meet!"

So he jumped into the little boat and set forth. For many days and nights Severi battled against waves and tide, but he was young and strong and he feared nothing. Then one day a great wind began to blow and a black storm beat down upon him. The rain fell in sheets, the thunder and lightning flashed and rumbled. All at once a huge wave swept over Severi's head and hurled him into the water.

But still Severi did not lose heart. He swam day and night, until at last the tide washed him upon a shining white beach at the foot of a tall black cliff. Severi saw a rope hanging over the edge of the cliff. He caught hold of the rope and climbed hand over hand until he reached the top. There before him lay a new strange country, with distant icy mountains glittering in the sun.

After he had rested for a while, Severi noticed a little path which ran along the edge of the cliff and between the hills. In and out it wound, and Severi followed it, until presently it led him to a stairway that went deep into the very heart of the black cliff.

Severi walked down and down the stone steps until he thought he must have reached the very center of the earth. There at the bottom was a golden door. He lifted his hand to knock, but as he did so the door swung open all by itself and Severi stepped through. There he stood in a wonderful world of green meadows with beautiful flowers and shining trees all laden with golden fruit.

In the distance rose the turrets of a copper castle, shining like red gold in the sun. Straight to the castle Severi walked, and stood before it wondering. As he gazed and wondered, suddenly he saw an old man standing beside him, with glittering white hair. He was a strange old man, but Severi saw that his cheeks were young.

"Where are you travelling, my boy?" the old man asked him.

"That is not easy to say," Severi answered. "First I wandered for days across mountain and valley and woodland. Then I rowed on the broad blue back of the ocean. A storm overturned my boat and I swam for many days. At last the tide washed me up on the sands at the foot of your cliff, and here I am."

"*Ka!*" laughed the old man. "Since you have come so far, why not stay here? If you like, you can be my servant."

"It is a bargain," cried Severi. "I ask nothing better."

So the old man took Severi into his shining copper castle. There he gave him food fit for the gods—all that he could eat and more. When at length Severi rose from the table, the old man said:

"Here are the keys to my castle. There are twenty-four rooms and twenty-four keys. You may use every key and open every room except one. The twenty-fourth room you enter at your own risk. If ever you unlock that door I will not be to blame for anything that may happen to you."

"Good," said Severi, already beginning to feel very curious.

Next day the old man set out on a long journey, and Severi was left all alone in the great copper castle. He said to himself:

"I have twenty-three rooms to explore. I know that each will be filled with a different wonder."

He took the first key and, turning it in the first lock, threw open the first gleaming door. At once his eyes were so dazzled he thought the whole room was on fire. Then he saw that the room and everything in it was of new, shining copper. The sun, pouring through the window and striking on the walls and floor and tables and chairs, nearly blinded him.

All this was fine, but it was not adventure, and it was adventure that Severi sought. So he turned the second key in the lock. The second room was all of heavy silver. This, too, so dazzled his eyes that he rushed to see what the third room was like. Here the walls were all of purest leaf gold, but their glitter so nearly blinded him that he hurried on to the other rooms, each in turn.

One of the rooms was of black ebony, one of warm Italian marble. One seemed to be cut from the heart of a cold green emerald, another from topaz and still another from red garnet. There was a room of blue sapphire and one of lapis lazuli.

After gazing on so many wonders Severi began to grow tired and hungry and thirsty. He wished he were back in his native *tupa* (cottage) with his bed of straw and his supper of black bread.

The next door opened into a room of mother-of-pearl. Severi felt as though he were standing in the middle of a great gleaming sea-shell. On the floor stood a carved couch covered with the softest silk. Severi stepped eagerly toward it but the silk covers were so smooth and beautiful that he dared not lay hands upon them.

A little sadly Severi walked to the door of the next room. When he had flung it open, he saw a table of gold laden with strange fruits. Some gave forth a golden fragrance and some were transparent as emerald. There were red berries with the fresh dew still upon them. But they were so perfect Severi was afraid to touch them.

There was a beaker of sparkling wine, too, and some of this Severi poured into a crystal goblet. But when he lifted the glass the sun from the window filled it with such a strange and lovely light that he feared to drink.

And now Severi grew sad, for he knew that he had entered every one of the three and twenty rooms.

"What is there left for me?" he thought. "All my adventures are over and done."

Turning back now, like one in a dream he laid a hand on the fruit and ate it, and he drank the wine at a single gulp. And suddenly he felt very weary. He thought of the silken couch, and throwing himself down upon it he fell into a heavy sleep.

When he awoke, he found that the key to the twenty-fourth room was clasped in his hand. Severi began looking at it curiously, turning over in his mind what might happen if he opened the twenty-fourth door.

"What can there be in this last room?" he wondered. "I think I shall open it and find out. I don't believe anything very terrible will happen. . . . The old man didn't really forbid me to open the door. He only said I would enter at my own risk."

Bravely he set the twenty-fourth key into the lock, and threw open the heavy door.

There in the middle of the room, on a high throne, sat the loveliest maid in all the world. Her eyes were as blue as the deepest sea, her hair shone golden like the sun, and her smile was like the warm red south.

For a time Severi could only stare and stare. Then at last he said in a soft whisper. "What is your name?"

"Vappu," answered the maiden, her voice like the rippling music of a *kantele* (harp).

"And why do you sit here?"

"For a very good reason. So far no one has ever come to take me away."

"Would you leave your throne if you could?" Severi asked, gaining courage as he spoke.

"It has been told in an old prophecy," said Vappu, "that whoever should open the door of this room, with him should I go and to him alone should I belong."

Proudly Severi stepped forward and held out his hand. Vappu placed her soft fingers within his as he helped her down, then she whispered:

"I have been waiting for you a very long time, *kultani* (my dear one)."

Days and nights passed as in a dream, while Vappu and Severi dwelt together in the copper castle. The new moon rose and waned, and not once did they think of the old man, who was still away on his journey.

One day after they had eaten their noon-day meal Vappu led Severi into a deep orchard where cool winds swept through the swaying boughs. Red and golden birds sang among the trees. A brook rippled in the sunlight and beside its clear waters blossomed the Tree of Life.

Severi and Vappu sat beneath the Tree of Life. They ate of its golden fruit and drank from the sparkling brook beside it.

After a while Severi fell into a deep sleep. When at last he awoke and opened his eyes, Vappu was gone.

Severi was frightened. In and out between the trees he ran, calling: "Vappu, Vappu, Vappu!" But the only sound he could hear was the song of the red and golden birds that flittered among the branches.

For a long while Severi searched and called. He ran in and out of the twenty-four doors of the castle crying over and over again: "Vappu, Vappu, Vappu!"

But only the echo of his own voice mocked him, and the sound of his own footsteps.

Again and again Severi searched the garden but nowhere could he find Vappu. At last he flung himself down on a rock to weep.

As he lay there sobbing, all at once the old man with his shining white hair stood beside him and asked:

"Why are you weeping, my boy?"

"I weep because I have lost what is dearer to me than the whole wide world. It is like this: I unlocked the twenty-fourth room and there I found the most beautiful of all beautiful maidens. She came with me and we lived together in this castle and all my life was pure joy. Only an hour ago, it seems, we were in this orchard together. I fell asleep, and when I woke up she was gone. Come help me to find her, for I cannot live without her."

"Ha-ha-ho-ho-he-he!" laughed the old man. "Ho-ho-ho-ho! That's the way it always happens when you do what you should have left undone."

"You forget I am a man grown," answered Severi. "Besides, you did not forbid me to enter the twenty-fourth room."

"I told you that you went at your own risk."

"Have it as you will," said Severi. "Only help me to find my Vappu. That is all I ask."

"That's as may be," said the old man. "But tell me, are you wiser now?"

"My sorrow has made me older," Severi answered. "It has made me wiser, too."

Then the old man muttered words of magic under his breath and there stood Vappu before him, radiant as a sunbeam.

"Were you lonesome for me, Severi?" she asked.

"All my happiness went with you," said Severi. "You must promise never to leave me again."

"I promise, but on one condition. I will never leave you again if you can but once hide from me so that I cannot find you. Then, and then only, will I be always with you."

Severi was puzzled. He did not understand what Vappu meant. But the old man whispered in his ear.

"Here is a charm for you. Whenever you wish to hide beyond all seeing, repeat these words, and in the twinkling of an eye you will become invisible. First try hiding in the heart of a fleeing rabbit."

Now the last thing in the world that Severi wanted to do was to hide from Vappu, but he knew that if he were to win her he must do as she bade him.

So he ran as fast as his legs could carry him. He ran through fields and meadows, over hills and valleys, and at last he found a rabbit that fled before him through the forest.

"Little Rabbit, Grey Rabbit," Severi called. And the rabbit stood still to listen to his words.

Thrice I knock at the door of your heart,
Let me in, Grey Rabbit, let me in.

And the Grey Rabbit opened the door of his heart to Severi, and Severi became invisible and leaped inside.

In the morning when Vappu awoke, she had only to look into her crystal pool. In its clear depths she saw the path that Severi had taken across the meadows and the hills. She saw how he had leapt into the heart of a little grey rabbit. She ran like the wind over the path he had taken, and soon she found him.

"You are not very good at playing hide-and-seek," she laughed, "but you must try again. Perhaps next time you will do better."

This time Severi thought he would enter the heart of a growling bear. He ran until he came to a wild mountain, and there in a deep cave he found a bear. He said:

> Thrice I knock at the door of your heart,
> Let me in, Honeypaw, let me in.

Then he jumped into the warm heart of the bear, and waited.

Next morning Vappu looked again into her crystal pool, and saw the path Severi had taken. Once more she ran like the wind until she came to the cave and stood before the growling bear. But when the bear saw Vappu in her beauty he knelt before her, and she cried out laughing:

"Severi, Severi, you cannot hide from me. I have found you, I have found you!"

So Severi came out from his hiding place and walked sadly back with her to the castle.

Again the old man with glistening white hair stood beside Severi.

"Why don't you hide this time within Vappu's own heart?" he asked.

"Thank you for helping me," Severi whispered back, and the next moment he repeated softly:

> Thrice I knock at your door, dear heart,
> Let me in, heart's jewel, let me in!

Then Vappu stared about her in amazement and cried: "Why, Severi was here beside me, and now he is gone!"

She ran to look in her crystal pool but this time it was of no use; she could not see where Severi was hidden.

"*Kultani,* my golden one," cried Severi, "can you not find me?"

"But where are you?" Vappu asked.

"Here in your heart."

"Who led you here?"

"You, Vappu, you led me here."

"And what will you have for your reward?"

"You, Vappu, only you!" cried Severi as he leapt from his hiding place and stood before her.

And from that day forward Severi and Vappu lived in peace in their copper castle, beneath the golden blossoms of the trees and beside the crystal brook.

# LEPPÄ PÖLKKY AND THE BLUE CROSS

THERE WAS once a man, named Jukka. He and his wife were sorely troubled because no child had come to bless their home. But even in their old age they did not give up hope. They went into the deep forest, found an alder stump, and placed it in the waiting cradle. For three years they rocked the cradle gently, but nothing happened. Then one day while the father was plowing in the field and the mother was milking the cows, a wizard, passing by, changed the alder stump into a boy.

That evening when Jukka and his wife came home for supper, there was the boy walking across the floor. He called:

"Mother, give me bread."

"At last our wish has come true," cried Jukka.

Years passed, and the boy grew by leaps and bounds into manhood. He was taller by a head than other men, and his muscles were of iron. The people of the village called him Leppä Pölkky, which means "alder stump."

One day it happened that darkness suddenly covered the whole earth. The King in Leppä's country sent forth his soldiers to find a wise man who could tell how to bring back the dawn, the moonlight, and sunshine to the world. At last a Laplander wizard was found, who came to the King's castle and told the King that an evil witch, Loviatar, with her three serpent sons, had pulled the moon, the sun, and the dawn out of the sky, and imprisoned them in the sea. Thus it was that the world was always in darkness.

The wizard also told the King that he must find three men strong enough to journey to the farthest north, to bring the dawn, the moon, and the sun back again. He told the King to test the men by seeing how much strong wine they could drink.

Once more the King sent his heralds throughout the land, and at last two men were found stronger than all the others. One of these men could drink three bottles of wine, the other, six.

"We yet need a man who can drink nine bottles of wine," said the King.

The King's messengers searched everywhere, but they found no man who could drink more than six bottles. So the King called the Laplander wizard to him again, and asked his advice.

"There is no man but Leppä Pölkky in all your kingdom," replied the wizard, "who can drink nine bottles of your powerful wine."

The King then ordered Leppä Pölkky to be brought before him. And Leppä Pölkky gulped down nine bottles of the wine as if it were water, and asked for more.

The King was satisfied, and gave each of the three strong men a horse, a dog, and money for the journey. He asked each to carry as many bottles of the wine as he could drink.

"You will need these bottles in your time of trial," said the King. "So don't waste them along the way."

After the King had blessed the three men, the three horses, and the three wolfhounds, Leppä Pölkky and his companions set off through the darkness to rescue the moon and the sun from their grave in the sea. At the end of many days, *Päivänkoitto*, the dawn, began to glimmer faintly. They took hope and rode faster until they saw a feeble reflection of *Kuu*, the moon. But they did not stop until they met *Aurinko*, the sun, above the edge of the sea.

Presently they came to the home of the wise widow, Leski-Akka. She was seated in a hut made of the skins of polar bears.

"*Ka,* how is it that you have sunlight here, while the rest of the world is dark?" the men asked the widow.

"O-ho, my lads," she answered, "the day is not always golden here, either. The Paha-Sydamiset, the evil-hearted sons of the old witch Loviatar, have put a curse on the day. They are all thieves, and cannot steal in the light. When they go into the sea they take the sun, the moon, and the dawn with them. Then it becomes night, and we do not see the sun again until they return to shore."

"Who is this old witch Loviatar?" Leppä asked.

"You from Finland should know her," said the widow. "It is she who brought the nine sicknesses to Finland. These wicked sons of hers who steal the dawn, the moon and the sun are three serpents even more evil-hearted than their ugly mother."

The three men walked on. Presently they saw a castle, one half of which wept while the other half laughed. This amazed them, and they went back to Leski-Akka to ask what the strange sight could mean.

"It is like this," said Leski-Akka. "The King of our country has just taken his eldest daughter as a sacrifice to the three-headed serpent, Loviatar's eldest son. This he must do, for otherwise the serpent will destroy one half of the castle, one half of the people, and one half of the shining jewels. If any man could slay the monster, then once more would dawn rise over the world."

"I will try my strength to make an end of this three-headed serpent," answered the man who could drink the three bottles.

When they were again alone, the three-bottle drinker said to his companions:

"If, in fighting, I let fly my boot toward you, loose the three dogs we brought with us to help me."

He drank three bottles of wine to strengthen his courage, and rode off alone to slay the monster.

On the shore of the sea he found the serpent, and fought with it. When he was hard pressed, he let fly his boot, and his companions loosed the three dogs. The fight grew more and more furious, but in the end the three-headed serpent, the first son of Loviatar, the witch, lay dead; and dawn had begun to spread over the whole earth.

When it was dark again, the three men walked once more toward the King's castle. Again one half of the castle wept and the other half laughed. They hurried back to Leski-Akka, and the man who could drink six bottles asked:

"Why does one side of the castle again weep, and the other side laugh? Did we not kill the three-headed serpent?"

"*Oi* (oh) my boy!" answered Leski-Akka. "The six-headed serpent, the second son of the witch, now threatens to destroy one half of the castle, one half of the people, and one half of the shining jewels. To prevent this, the King has just taken his second daughter as a sacrifice. If a man were found strong enough to slay the monster, not only would the king's daughter be saved, but moonlight and dreams would return to the earth."

"I will make an end to this six-headed monster," answered the man who could drink six bottles.

When they were alone in the garden, he said:

"If you see my boot fly, loose the dogs to aid me."

He then drank the six bottles, and rode off with courage to slay the monster.

The next day the silver moon shone around the whole world, and the six-bottle man rode back to the castle with the second daughter of the King.

A third time the men walked in the garden, and once again they saw the strange sight. One side of the castle wept, the other laughed. For the third time the men returned to Leski-Akka. This time it was Leppä Pölkky who asked:

"Why does one part of the castle still weep and the other laugh?"

"This is the truth of the matter," said Leski-Akka. "The King has just taken his youngest daughter as a sacrifice to the third son of the witch, the nine-headed monster. He has threatened to devour half the castle with its people and wealth. If a man could be found strong enough to kill this most terrible of the three sons of the ogress, the sun would shine upon the earth, and again day would be golden."

"I shall see what I can do," answered Leppä.

When the three men were alone, Leppä told his two companions, if they saw his boot fly through the air, to loose the three dogs to aid him. He then gulped down the nine bottles of wine, and rode off without fear on his fiery steed to slay the monster.

There was dawn and moonlight over all the world, but the sun still lay hidden in the sea. For a long while the people waited, until they almost gave up hope.

Then, suddenly, to the joy of all, golden day flowed over the earth, and Leppä came riding from the seashore with the King's youngest daughter unharmed.

The King was so grateful to these brave men who had slain the three terrible serpent sons of Loviatar, that he gave a great feast, and in the midst of the rejoicing, he said to Leppä Pölkky and his two companions:

"My distinguished guests, I desire to give each of you the daughter of mine whom he has saved. The half of my castle and gold and jewels will I also divide with you if you will make your home with me."

The three brave men bowed low to the King, and Leppä answered for all of them:

"We thank you, O King, for your gracious hospitality! We are sorry that we cannot accept your gifts, but we have come as messengers from another King who dwells far away from this country. To him we are pledged to return. If you will give us meat and drink for our journey homeward, we shall ask no more."

The King gave Leppä and his two companions food for their journey, and they set out for home. Through moonlight, dawn and day they rode, for the journey was long.

Presently they saw a hut of willow boughs by the road side. Within they could hear harsh voices quarrelling. It was Loviatar and her witch cronies. Leppä crept to the window to listen.

"The men who killed my three sons are coming down the road," Loviatar raged. "They think they'll get home safely, but destroy them I will!"

Leppä turned cold with fright, for the witches were the ugliest hags he had ever seen. They had long yellow teeth and finger nails of iron, and Loviatar's face was a deep purple.

A second witch cried in a shrill voice: "You cannot do this, old Loviatar! They are too strong for you."

"I will put the spell of hunger on them," Loviatar screamed. "When they are starving I will set tables of rich food before them, and when they stop to eat I'll catch them."

"But suppose they think to strike a cross on the table with their sword?" jeered another witch. "Then your spell would be broken."

"Then I'll charm them with thirst. I'll set a sparkling pool before them, and destroy them when they stoop to drink."

"But if they cut the pool with two sword strokes in the form of a cross, then they'd escape you!"

"I'll burden them with sleep, and set beds for them," Loviatar screeched. "That way I'll catch them surely!"

"Unless they break the charm by striking the beds with their sword!"

"They will never know how to break my charms unless one of you witches tells them," shouted Loviatar furiously, "and whoever reveals these words of mine shall be changed into a blue cross!"

When he heard all this, Leppä hurried back to his companions.

"What were they quarrelling about?" his companions asked.

Leppä did not dare to tell, for fear he should be changed into a blue cross forthwith. He answered:

"They were quarrelling over nothing at all, as all old women do."

The three men mounted their horses, but before they had gone very far they were taken with a great hunger. It seemed that they could not go another step for weakness. At that very moment they saw before them a table all set with food and drink.

Leppä jumped to the ground and struck the table three strokes with his sword, in the form of a cross, and instantly the table vanished.

His two comrades were very angry. They began to abuse Leppä, but he dared not tell them the truth for fear of the witch's spell. He said:

"What do we want with food—our hunger has left us. Food will taste far better when we reach our journey's end."

Again they rode, and now a great thirst came upon them. They saw a pool of sparkling water with three birch bark dippers set beside it.

The two men jumped from their horses, but Leppä was quicker still. He struck the water with his sword and the pool vanished, and with it their thirst. But the two men were nearly beside themselves with rage. Leppä said:

"We have no need for water. In our own country we can find the best and the clearest water in the world."

They rode on, farther and still farther. And now a great drowsiness overcame them, till they were ready to drop from the saddle for sheer weariness. And there by the wayside they saw three comfortable beds.

LEPPÄ POLKKY AND THE BLUE CROSS

Leppä sprang from his horse, and slashed one bed with three strokes of his sword. It disappeared, but before he could touch the other two beds his companions had flung themselves down. And then Loviatar destroyed them before Leppä's very eyes. She stole Leppä's horse and drove it back to the stable beside her hut, and tied it there with an iron chain. Poor Leppä was forced to flee for his life on foot.

Leppä was now alone in the woods, and far from home. He wept for the fate of his two companions as he walked forward, footsore and weary. At last he sat down beside a tree to rest. Here he discovered an eye watching him through a hole in the bark. And as he sat wondering at it, he heard the heart-broken wail of a maiden.

This maiden had come under the power of the old witch, Loviatar, who had blinded her so that she could not find her way. Leppä called the maiden to him, recovered her eye from the tree, and told her who he was. The maiden was so grateful that she led Leppä back to the witch's stable.

"If you strike the chain three blows with your sword in the form of a cross," she whispered, "your horse will be free."

Leppä struck the heavy chain three blows, and it fell to the ground. The witch heard the noise and rushed to the stable. When she saw Leppä with his sword drawn, she shrieked:

"I have a mind to kill you. But I will spare your life on the one condition, that you will go and bring me Katrina of Kiijoki, the most beautiful princess in the world."

"*Ka,*" said Leppä, "get her I will!"

Loviatar then hollowed out a birch log, and gave it to Leppä for a boat. And so there was nothing left for him to do but to set out on the sea in search of the beautiful Katrina.

When he had rowed a short way he heard a man calling from the shore:

"Hoo-hoo! Wherever are you going, Leppä? Take me with you, by God's will!"

Leppä rowed to the shore and asked:

"Who are you among men?"

"Hurttinen-hosuja, the Dog-chaser," the man answered.

"Very well, come along," Leppä replied.

They had rowed but a short distance farther when they heard another man calling:

"Hoo-hoo! Take me with you, Leppä, wherever you are going, by God's will!"

Leppä again rowed to the shore, and asked:

"Who are you?"

"I am Unen-makaaja, the Dream-sleeper."

"Come along," said Leppä.

The three men rowed a little way farther when they heard a call from another part of the shore:

"Take me with you, Leppä, by God's will!"

"And who are you?"

"I am Kylyn-kylpijä, the Bath-bather."

"Come, you are welcome," laughed Leppä.

And now they made a fresh start, but they heard two other men calling:

"Hoo-hoo! Take us with you, Leppä, by God's will!"

One of these was Ruokien-syöjä, the Food-eater, and the other Veden-kantaja, the Water-carrier. These also Leppä took with him.

And now Leppä and his five companions rowed forward as fast as their oars would carry them, and after many hours, they reached Kiijoki.

As their boat scraped the sand, the people saw them coming and set their savage dogs upon them. The dogs snarled and barked with such a din that the men were afraid of being torn to pieces.

Then Leppä said to the first man who had come into the boat:

"Go you, since you are Hurttinen-hosuja, the Dog-chaser, and call off these hounds."

Hurttinen-hosuja leapt from the boat. He waved his hat three times in the air, and the dogs ran in every direction, disappearing as by magic.

Then Leppä and his companions pulled their boat high on the sand and walked bravely into the King's castle. The guards looked at them in wonder, and said:

"You are the first guests who have ever entered this castle. Every time that visitors have come to our shores, our dogs have destroyed them."

"We did not come here to be food for dogs," said Hurttinen-hosuja.

The guards permitted them to enter the castle, and at last they stood before the King. Leppä said:

"I have come from a far country to Kiijoki, to win your beautiful daughter, Katrina."

"If you think she is so easily won, you make a great mistake," answered the King. "First you must sleep away our dreams."

At this, Unen-makaaja, the Dream-sleeper, stepped forward and answered:

"Gladly we will sleep away your dreams."

The King then asked Leppä and his men to spend the night in his barn. As they stretched upon the floor to sleep, Unen-makaaja covered the men with his body. In the middle of the night, the King sent guards to set fire to the barn. Unen-makaaja slept on top and the burning brands fell upon him, and did the men no harm.

The barn burned to ashes, but the men were not even awakened. When morning came, they all went into the King's castle, and Leppä again spoke to the King:

"You were foolish to try to harm us. See, you have only burned your own barn!'

The King was silent a long time, then he said:

"We will not give Katrina to you unless you first bathe in our bath-house."

"It is as you wish," answered Leppä. "Make the fires hot upon the hearth."

The King commanded his guards to make the *kylpy* (bath) red hot. This was done, but it made little difference. First entered Kylyn-kylpijä, the Bath-bather. He blew his cold breath into the center of the room, and there came by magic a mound of snow, and before the hearth, a pool of water. The bathhouse walls were covered with frost.

After Leppä and his men had bathed, they went together to the King's castle and said:

"You don't treat your guests very well. The stones in the hearth were so cold that there was no steam on the stones for our bath."

Now the King began to be frightened. After a long while he said:

"We will not give you Katrina in spite of your magic, until you have eaten all the food that we set before you."

"Be it as you wish," said Leppä.

The King called his guards, and commanded them to kill cows and lambs, and to set a huge feast. When the piles were high, Ruokien-syöjä, Food-eater, stepped forward, and alone gulped down all that was set before him. When he had finished, he asked:

"*Ka,* and is this all your food? I am still hungry, and my comrades have had nothing at all."

By this time the King and his people were trembling with fear.

"This is all," they answered. "We have no more grain, and all of our cattle are killed."

Ruokien-syöjä felt sorry for them. He lifted his pack from his shoulders and gave the King and his people a feast.

But the King was still stubborn. When he and all his people had eaten their fill, he grumbled:

"We will not give you our daughter Katrina until first you carry water in a sieve."

It was now the turn of Veden-kantaja, Water-carrier, to step forward:

"Give me a sieve, O King, and I will carry as much water as you wish."

The sieve was brought, and Veden-kantaja took it down to the shore of the sea, filled it with water, and brought it, brimming full, to the King.

When this work was finished, the King and his people talked a long time among themselves.

"*Ka,*" they said. "It is useless to try and conquer such a man as Leppä. He laughs at our hardest labors. We shall give to him our beautiful Katrina."

At last Katrina was brought. Her eyes were the color of the sea at midday. Her cheeks were like the rosy dawn, and her hair hung about her in ringlets of gold. When Leppä saw her, he knew she was so beautiful that her equal could not be found on land or sea.

Leppä thanked the King, took Katrina into the boat, and together with his companions set out from Kiijoki. Continuing their voyage, each companion left at the place on the shore where he had first met Leppä, until finally Leppä and Katrina were alone in the boat. As Leppä rowed, he noticed that the waves splashed Katrina's beautiful blue gown, and he lifted the folds with his forefinger from the water.

Leppä and Katrina found Loviatar waiting for them. She held out her skinny hand to Katrina, and bit off Leppä's forefinger.

"Since you touched the maiden with that finger," she screamed, "I have bitten it off."

This made Leppä hot with anger. He drew his sword as quick as lightning, struck the witch three strokes in the form of the cross, and so destroyed her.

When Katrina saw that Leppä had rescued her from the charm of the witch, she said:

"You are a brave man, and since you have saved me, I will gladly be your bride."

At these words Leppä was filled with joy. He ran to Loviatar's empty hut and took her gold and jewels. He mounted his horse, lifted Katrina before him on the saddle, and together they rode happily back to Leppä's own country.

But, alas, their joy was short! The King of Leppä's country and the Courtiers began to ask Leppä what had happened to his comrades, the three-bottle drinker and the six-bottle drinker, who had ridden out with him on his far journey. Leppä could not tell them, for if he did, he would be changed into a blue cross. And so he made up a strange story out of his brain, and expected the people to believe it.

But the people did not believe his story. Instead, they began to gossip and to imagine the worst. They all came to believe that Leppä had killed his faithful companions. When the King heard this, he gave a command to have Leppä put to death.

And so at last Leppä was forced to tell the truth. But as he came to tell how he had broken the spells of Loviatar by striking with his sword, he was changed instantly into a blue cross.

Katrina became the King's bride, for she was still the most beautiful woman in the world. And to this day travellers to that far northern land are still shown the blue cross that stands there upon a lonely hillside, a witness to the truth of Leppä's strange story.

# LIISA AND THE PRINCE

THERE WAS once an old man, Māki, who lived in a *tupa* on the edge of the deep wild forest, with his wife and his small daughter, Liisa. He had a cow and a flock of sheep, and spent most of his time in the pastures.

One day when he was not watching, it chanced that his black lamb, Musti, strayed into the woods and was lost. Māki called his wife, and together they started to hunt for it, each going a different way through the trees.

The wife had gone but a short way when she met a spiteful Ogress in disguise.

"What is it you search for, my good woman?" asked the Ogress.

And when the wife looked up, the Ogress spat in her face and mumbled quickly:

"My body to you, yours to me."

The charm worked, and the wife became ugly and brown and wrinkled, while the Ogress looked exactly like Māki's wife, with yellow hair, and smooth skin, and rosy cheeks.

It was the Ogress who had hidden the black lamb, and now she ran and brought it to Māki, shouting:

"Māki, hoi! Hoi, ukko (Ho, Māki! Ho, old man)! See, I have found our lost lamb!"

Māki took the Ogress for his own wife, and together they carried Musti home to the fold.

The real wife was left behind in the forest. She wandered about, weeping, for the Ogress had left her so dazed that she could not find her way home. Presently she came to a flock of sparrows chirping in a tree. She spoke to them, begging them to help her, but the birds only looked at her and flew away in terror.

At last she came to a brook. She stooped down beside it to quench her thirst, and there saw for the first time, how ugly her face had become. Then she knew she could never rejoin her family, for Māki would never believe that she was his wife.

She sat by the river bank under a birch tree for three days and nights, and wept. And at last her spirit left her and became the spirit of the tree.

Meantime the Ogress lived in the *tupa* with Māki and his pretty daughter, Liisa. After a year she had a daughter of her own whom she named Kirjo. This daughter at first was brown and wrinkled and ugly, but the Ogress by magic gave her a family resemblance to Liisa, so that it would seem she was her sister.

As soon as Kirjo was born, the Ogress hated Liisa and plagued her in every way to make her unhappy. She dressed her in ragged threadbare homespun, and made her sleep alone in the *sauna*. During the day, poor Liisa did all the heavy work about the house, and at night she could do nothing but weep, for she knew that the Ogress was not her real mother.

As for Kirjo, the Ogress dressed her up in the finest linen, and set her beside Māki at the table. At night she gave her the softest, warmest bed in the *tupa*.

Some years later the King gave a great feast at the castle. The young prince had just come of age, and his father wanted him to choose a bride. So he sent his soldiers out to gather all the people together. Into every village, along every highway the soldiers went singing:

> Come all ye people far and wide,
> Come high, come low, from every side,
> Come rich, come poor, none are denied.

When the Ogress heard the invitation, she said to Māki:

"Take Kirjo, and start on ahead. I'll give Liisa some work here at home, so she won't be lonesome while we are away, and then I will join you along the road."

The Ogress took Liisa into the bath house. She turned over the hearthstones, and scattered barley seeds everywhere on the floor and among the ashes.

"If you don't gather up every one of these seeds into this basket before

I return from the castle," she said, "I will beat you every day as long as you live!"

Poor Liisa dried her tears when the Ogress had gone, and began to pick the barley seeds, one by one, from the ashes and from among the black hearth stones. After she had worked for hours, she saw that the task was hopeless. It was as if she had been set to pick the sand grains from the seashore. Tears blinded her eyes, and she decided to run away.

As Liisa was running through the forest, a great birch tree called after her:

"Liisa, Liisa, where do you run?"

Liisa stopped to see who was speaking.

"Do not be afraid," the tree continued. "I am the spirit of your mother. Dry your eyes and take one of my branches, and make a brush. With this sweep the hearthstones, and the barley seeds will all fly into the basket as if by magic. When you have finished, bring the brush to me, and I will show you a great wonder."

Soon the barley seeds were all in the basket, and Liisa hurried back to the forest. Then her mother's spirit said:

"Bathe now in the river, and return to me and I will give you clothes such as you have never seen."

As Liisa came out of the water, she was transformed into the most beautiful woman in the kingdom. And then she returned to the birch tree. There she found a dress of the finest linen, and shoes of the softest white leather. Brilliant jewels glittered in her yellow hair, and rarest pearls were about her smooth white throat, and upon her slender fingers sparkled great diamonds. A prancing horse trapped in gold and silver stood waiting beside her. Liisa leapt to the saddle, and before she knew what was happening, the horse carried her to the garden beside the King's castle.

When the Prince Uvanto saw how beautiful Liisa was, he came running across the garden to meet her. He lifted her down from the saddle, tied her horse by the reins, and led her into the castle. Here he presented her to the King and the Court.

All the people of the countryside were assembled there, according to the King's order. When they saw Liisa they began whispering. Everyone wondered who this beautiful stranger was and where she had come from, for not even Māki, her own father, knew her.

This made the Ogress very angry, for she was trying hard to catch the Prince's attention herself, so he would ask Kirjo to sit beside him. But after a while he was so annoyed by their smirks and gestures that he ordered his guards to put the Ogress out of the room and to send Kirjo to sit in the stable with the servants, where she had only the left-over scraps to eat.

When the feast was over, and all the people were starting for their homes, Liisa asked the Prince if he would not help her to her horse.

"First you must give me some keepsake to remember you by," smiled the Prince, "for I hope to see you again very soon."

"Take this ring from my finger," said Liisa.

The Prince kissed her hand as he took the ring, and said to himself:

"It is a good thing you don't know how beautiful you really are."

The Prince led Liisa through the garden between the flowers and told her how he loved her. Then he lifted her to her saddle, and she rode off.

When Liisa reached the birch tree by the river, she left her fine horse and her clothes and her jewels, and told her mother's spirit all that had happened.

"One of the rings is lacking," she said, "because the Prince begged it as a remembrance."

"All is well," answered the mother's spirit. "Go back to the bath house, and don't worry."

Liisa did as her mother's spirit bade her, and when Māki and the Ogress and Kirjo arrived at the *tupa*, she pretended that she was just dropping the last barley seed into the basket. The Ogress was surprised to find the work finished, and she pretended to be sorry for Liisa.

"My poor Liisa," she said, "you have missed the feast at the King's castle, but such things are not for the like of you. My Kirjo, now, was quite at home. She had a wonderful time. Prince Uvanto asked her to sit beside him at the feast, and he kissed her hand, and invited her to come again."

Liisa knew this was not true, for she had seen all that had happened. Yet she said nothing, but did the hard work in silence, for the Ogress was now even more cruel.

As soon as Liisa had ridden away from the castle, the Prince looked at the sparkling diamond ring, and sighed for her return. If he had only known where she dwelt, he would have sent for her. And after a few weeks he felt so lonely that he begged the King to send his soldiers to search for Liisa.

"But the soldiers don't know who she is!" said the King.

"I have her ring," answered the Prince. "Take it and make a ring the same size for each of the soldiers to carry, and let them try the finger of every girl in the kingdom. In this way they can surely find the girl I love."

The rings were made, and the soldiers went out with them. One of the soldiers came to Māki's *tupa* and said:

"It is the King's wish that each girl shall hold her finger out to see if the ring fits."

The Ogress by magic changed the size of Kirjo's finger so that the ring seemed to belong to it, but she hid Liisa behind her skirts so that the soldier did not notice her.

When the soldier saw how perfectly the ring fitted, he said to Kirjo:

"It is the King's wish that you come with me to the castle, for the Prince wishes to speak with you."

Kirjo gladly went with the soldier, and after they had gone, the Ogress turned sharply to Liisa.

"Dry your tears, you lazy girl! Stop dreaming, and get to work and finish scrubbing the floor. You were not meant for a Prince. The worst man alive would never marry you if he knew how lazy you were."

The next day Kirjo returned in tears:

"The Prince would have nothing to do with me," she complained. "There were forty other girls from every part of the realm. Our fingers all fitted the ring, but our faces did not please the Prince."

Now Liisa knew that the Prince was surely searching for her. He heart leapt, but she held her tongue.

Five days later the King's soldiers were again sent out to call the people together. They went everywhere chanting:

> Come all ye people, far and wide,
> Come high, come low, from every side,
> Come rich, come poor, none be denied.

Again before she started with Māki and Kirjo to the King's castle, the Ogress took Liisa into the bath house. She kicked over the hearthstones, and scattered ashes about the floor, and then flung about a basket of the finest flax seed. As the seed flew everywhere, the Ogress said to Liisa:

"If every one of these flax seeds is not in the basket, and if the ashes are not in the hearth, and if the hearthstones are not in their places when I return from the castle, I will beat you with willow boughs morning and night as long as you live. Dry your tears, you lazy girl, and set to work."

As the Ogress left the bath house she slapped Liisa sharply across the cheek. Liisa tried to gather the flax seeds, but it was hopeless, for they were finer than needle points. Her eyes again filled with tears. And then she remembered her mother's spirit, and ran to the forest.

"Take another of my branches and make a broom," her mother's spirit whispered sweetly, "and sweep the flax seeds into the basket, the ashes into the hearth, and the heart stones into place. When you have finished, return, and I will show you another wonder."

Soon Liisa was running back to the birch tree with a happy face, her work all done.

"Bathe again in the river," said her mother's spirit.

When Liisa came from the river this time, she was more beautiful than ever. The most gorgeous clothes awaited her, and when she was dressed, the same prancing steed in its gold and silver trappings stood before her. Liisa leapt into the saddle, and was soon at the King's castle.

The Prince was watching at the window, and when he caught the first glimpse of Liisa, he dashed across the garden to greet her.

"This time I will keep you, if I may," he said as he lifted her from her saddle.

Then he led Liisa into the castle and set her down beside him at the table.

Again all the people marvelled at her beauty. All tried to guess who she was, and where she came from. When the feast was finished and all the people were starting for their homes, the Prince tried to keep Liisa with him.

"Stay with me," he said, "and I will make you my princess."

"But you don't understand," replied Liisa. "I cannot stay today. Let me go, I pray you, for I must not be home late!"

"Then leave me something to remember you by," he pleaded.

"Here, then," said Liisa, "Take this earring."

After a few days the Prince was so sorry he had let Liisa go this second time that he begged the King to send out his soldiers to see if he could not find her.

"Father, tell your goldsmiths to make an earring for each of your soldiers like this one I have for a keepsake. When a woman is found who has the fellow to the earring, she will surely be the woman that I love."

This time when the soldiers came to Māki's *tupa*, the Ogress by magic made a fellow to the earring, and placed it in Kirjo's ear. The soldier was sure he had found the right woman, and carried Kirjo off to talk with the Prince.

Next day Kirjo returned again in tears.

"I was the only woman who had an earring to match," she said, "but the minute the Prince looked at me, he was angry, and sent me away."

Again Liisa's heart leapt within her, but she said nothing. The Ogress was so angry that she made Liisa work twice as hard.

When the soldiers failed to find the right woman, the earrings were thrown away, and the Prince begged the King to call all the people to another feast.

Again the King's soldiers went chanting throughout the land:

> Come all ye people, far and wide,
> Come high, come low, from every side,
> Come rich, come poor, none be denied.

This time before leaving for the castle with Māki and Kirjo, the Ogress spilled a bowl of milk among the ashes and over the hearth stones, and said to Liisa:

"If you do not gather the milk into the bowl before I return you'll be sorry, for I will plague you day and night without mercy."

Her mother's spirit again helped Liisa, and when the milk was safely in the bowl to the last drop, she bathed, dressed, leapt upon the prancing steed, and was the third time carried to the King's castle.

The Prince Uvanto was waiting in the King's rose garden, and when Liisa arrived, he cried: "This time I shall keep you for my very own!"

And when the others were leaving, the Prince tried his best to keep Liisa by him.

"I cannot stay today," said Liisa. "A cruel Ogress is to blame for your not finding me."

"Then we must break the spiteful witch's charm," the Prince answered. "Leave me a keepsake so that I may search you out."

"Here is my slipper," answered Liisa.

The Prince looked at the dainty jewelled slipper, and sighed. He called together the wisest fortune tellers and magicians in the realm, and asked their advice. At last an old gypsy man tottered to the Prince's side and whispered:

"Come, Prince Uvanto, with me, and I will take you to the woman of your heart. You must bring twelve of your most trusted servants. Four shall carry tar and tinder, four shall carry fire, and four a blue carpet."

After a long winding journey, the old gypsy wise man, the Prince, and his twelve servants, came in sight of Māki's *tupa*.

"O Prince," said the gypsy, "command your servants to dig a pit before the door of the bath house. Fill it with tinder and tar, lay a platform of rotten wood over it, and spread on the platform the blue carpet. You and I will approach the *tupa*, and see what is happening."

The gypsy whispered a charm, and disguised himself and the Prince as two woodcutters. Through the window of the *tupa* they saw Liisa scrubbing the floor on her knees, while the Ogress scolded and Kirjo sat by on a silken cushion and sipped milk.

When the Ogress came to the door, the gypsy said:

"We found this strange jewelled slipper as we came near your *tupa*. Is there a girl here whose foot it fits?"

The Ogress examined the slipper, and by magic changed Kirjo's foot so that the slipper seemed exactly made for it. The Prince saw that this was the girl he had twice sent away from his castle, and Liisa felt her heart thump as she listened.

But the gypsy said:

"Good! The Prince would like you to go with your daughter to the castle, for he has something to say to her. But first you must take her to the bath house. There dress her in the finest linen, and make ready for the journey."

The Ogress did as she was bid, but when she and Kirjo stepped on the blue rug which the twelve servants had spread, the boards gave way, and they both fell into the burning tar, and were destroyed.

When Liisa saw all that was happening, she ran to the forest, bathed in the river, put on the gorgeous gown and the one jewelled slipper, and leapt upon the prancing steed. She heard the spirit of her mother saying:

"Now I shall rest in peace, for I know you are happy at last!"

The Prince Uvanto saw Liisa coming. He saw too that one of her tiny feet was bare. He placed the jewelled slipper which he had brought where it belonged, and off they rode to the castle. And now that the Ogress was dead, there they lived happily ever after.


# DROLL STORIES


## THE PIG-HEADED WIFE


WHEN MATTI married Liisa, he thought she was the pleasantest woman in the world. But it wasn't long before Liisa began to show her real character. Headstrong as a goat she was, and as fair set on having her own way.

Matti had been brought up to know that a husband should be the head of his family, so he tried to make his wife obey. But this didn't work with Liisa. It just made her all the more stubborn and pigheaded. Every time that Matti asked her to do one thing, she was bound to do the opposite, and work as he would she generally got her own way in the end.

Matti was a patient sort of man, and he put up with her ways as best he could, though his friends were ready enough to make fun of him for being henpecked. And so they managed to jog along fairly well.

But one year as harvest time came round, Matti thought to himself:

"Here am I, a jolly good-hearted fellow, that likes a bit of company. If only I had a pleasant sort of wife, now, it would be a fine thing to invite all our friends to the house, and have a nice dinner and drink and a good time. But it's no good thinking of it, for as sure as I propose a feast, Liisa will declare a fast."

And then a happy thought struck him.

"I'll see if I can't get the better of Liisa, all the same. I'll let on I want to be quiet, and then she'll be all for having the house full of guests." So a few days later he said:

"The harvest holidays will be here soon, but don't you go making any sweet cakes this year. We're too poor for that sort of thing."

"Poor! What are you talking about?" Liisa snapped. "We've never had more than we have this year. I'm certainly going to bake a cake, and a good big one, too."

"It works," thought Matti. "It works!" But all he said was:

"Well, if you make a cake, we won't need a pudding too. We mustn't be wasteful."

"Wasteful, indeed!" Liisa grumbled. "We shall have a pudding, and a big pudding!"

Matti pretended to sigh, and rolled his eyes.

"Pudding's bad enough, but if you take it in your head to serve stuffed pig again, we'll be ruined!"

"You'll kill our best pig," quoth Liisa, "and let's hear no more about it."

"But wine, Liisa," Matti went on. "Promise me you won't open a single bottle. We've barely enough to last us through the winter as it is."

Liisa stamped her foot.

"Are you crazy, man? Who ever heard of stuffed pig without wine! We'll not only have wine, but I'll buy coffee too. I'll teach you to call me extravagant by the time I'm through with you!"

"Oh dear, oh dear," Matti sighed. "If you're going to invite a lot of guests, on top of everything else, that'll be the end of it. We can't possibly have guests."

"And have all the food spoil with no one to eat it, I suppose?" jeered Liisa. "Guests we'll have, and what's more, you'll sit at the head of the table, whether you like it or not."

"Well, at any rate I'll drink no wine myself," said Matti, growing bolder. "If I don't drink the others won't, and I tell you we'll need that wine to pull us through the winter."

Liisa turned on him, furious.

"You'll drink with your guests as a host should, till every bottle is empty. There! Now will you be quiet?"

When the day arrived, the guests came, and great was the feasting. They shouted and sang round the table, and Matti himself made more noise than any of his friends. So much so, that long before the feast was over Liisa began to suspect he had played a trick on her. It made her furious to see him so jolly and carefree.

As time went on she grew more and more contrary, until there was no living with her. Now, it happened one day in the spring when all the streams were high, that Matti and Liisa were crossing the wooden bridge over the little river which separated two of their meadows. Matti crossed first, and noticing that the boards were badly rotted, he called out without thinking:

"Look where you step, Liisa! The plank is rotten there. Go lightly or you'll break through."

"Step lightly!" shouted Liisa. "I'll do as . . ."

But for once Liisa didn't finish what she had to say. She jumped with all her weight on the rotted timbers, and fell plop into the swollen stream.

Matti scratched his head for a moment: then he started running up-stream as fast as he could go.

Two fishermen along the bank saw him, and called: "What's the matter, my man? Why are you running upstream so fast?"

"My wife fell in the river," Matti panted, "and I'm afraid she's drowned."

"You're crazy," said the fishermen. "Anyone in his right mind would search downstream, not up!"

"Ah," said Matti, "but you don't know my Liisa! All her life she's been so pig-headed that even when she's dead she'd be bound to go against the current!"

# STUPID PEIKKO

## I

PEIKKO WAS a gnome who lived in the old days. He was very ugly, with a short, crooked body and bandy legs, like all gnomes, and he had a great idea of his own cleverness. He liked to spend his time with human beings and prided himself on being a great deal smarter than they were. But as a matter of fact he was really very stupid.

Among the young men in the village Peikko had one particular friend named Matti, whom he was always trying to outwit. One day he said to him:

"Listen, my friend, since you are so clever, make me a bridge across this brook here. But you must use neither wood nor stone nor iron."

Matti scratched his head and considered. The brook was very narrow. All at once he leaned over, braced his feet on one bank and his hands on the other.

"There's your bridge, Peikko," he laughed. "It is neither wood nor stone nor iron. Walk across and try it!"

Peikko was outdone that time, but the next time he thought he would surely get the better of Matti. There was to be a wedding in the village. Matti was always a great favorite with the girls at dancing, and Peikko who was a bit jealous of him thought it would be a grand trick to keep Matti from going to the wedding at all. So he said to him:

"Matti, I want you to do something for me this evening, and it's a job I wouldn't trust to everyone, either. I have a storehouse where I keep my sacks of gold. I don't dare leave it unwatched, but I have an important engagement tonight, so I want you to stand guard over my storehouse door while I'm away."

"I'll be glad to watch it for you," said Matti, "if you show me where it is."

"Come with me," said Peikko, and he led him to the building. "Now you stand guard, and be sure you don't leave the door once, while I go to the wedding."

"Wedding?" cried Matti. "Why didn't you tell me where you were going? I want to go to the wedding, too."

"I can't help that. You promised to guard my storehouse door, and mind you don't leave it one instant!"

"But I didn't know about the wedding."

All the same Matti had to sit down beside the door while Peikko pranced off to the wedding with a merry heart, thinking he'd got the better of Matti for once.

Matti thought and thought, and the more he thought the more he wanted to go to the wedding. After a while he had a bright idea. He pulled the door from its leather hinges, lifted it on his back and hurried off.

When he arrived he found the guests feasting gaily. Peikko was there with the others, eating, drinking and shouting with laughter. When he looked up and saw Matti he was very surprised.

"Why Matti, what are you doing here?" he cried. "You've broken your promise. You swore you wouldn't leave that door for a single instant."

"Well, neither I have," said Matti. "I've brought it here on my back!"

Peikko stared at him. Then he lifted his glass.

"I drink your health, Matti," he said. "You're certainly smarter than I am."


## II


It chanced another time that Matti had spent all his money. He knew that Peikko was very rich, like all gnomes, so he thought he would try to get some of that wealth for himself.

So he walked through the forest till he came to Peikko's hut, which was on the shore of a very pretty lake. There he sat himself down on the shore in front of the house and began to whistle softly. When he saw that Peikko had heard him and was coming, he leaned forward and began to drink the lake water in great gulps.

"You must be very thirsty," said Peikko, watching him. "Come into my *tupa* and I'll give you something better than water to drink."

"I'm not drinking the water because I'm thirsty," said Matti, "but because I want to drink the lake dry. It's like this, Peikko. Whenever I want to go anywhere, this lake is always in my way. I have no boat to cross it, so I have to walk around, and that's a nuisance. Besides, I'm always afraid someone will drown. So I've decided to drink the lake dry, and get rid of it once and for all."

As he spoke, Matti leaned down and began lapping the water again.

"Don't do that," cried Peikko. "I love this lake. I couldn't live without it. If you promise not to drink it dry I'll give you a bag of silver."

"Will you, indeed?" said Matti. "It'll need be a large bag to pay me for all the trouble I've been put to on account of this wretched lake of yours!"

"At least stop drinking till I go to my garden and fetch it!"

"I can't promise unless you hurry."

Foolish Peikko hobbled off to his garden as fast as his bandy legs would carry him, terrified lest Matti would drink the lake dry before he got back. But when he returned, the lake was still there, laughing in the sun.

And Matti laughed, too, as he hurried off with the bag of silver.

## III

Some days after it happened that Peikko needed a man to help him roof his *tupa*. So he went to Matti, promising to fill his hat with silver as soon as the job was finished.

Matti agreed, and when the work was over he held his hat out and said:

"Your money is heavy, Peikko, and my hat is old and likely to tear. I'd better rest it on a stump while you fill it."

"Just as you like, Matti. While I fetch the silver, you find the stump."

Matti soon found a stump to his liking. It was old and rotten, and hollow to the root. Matti's hat too was old, and there was a hole in the crown which Peikko had not seen.

Matti held the hat over the hole in the stump, and Peikko began to pour the money in.

"Your hat holds a lot," Peikko said as he began to empty the second bag.

The third bag just filled the hat to the brim. Peikko nodded as he looked at it.

"You are a wise man, Matti. It must be because your head is so large. Three sacks of silver it would hold. But I promise you I'll never bargain to fill your shirt."

"That's right," said Matti, trying to keep a straight face. "One of us has a hole in the side of his head and the other hasn't."

But this was too deep for stupid Peikko to understand. He could only shake his head as he walked away.

## IV

Among other things Peikko was always bragging to Matti about his strength. By-and-by Matti grew tired of this, so to cure Peikko of boasting he proposed they have some contests.

First they went into the forest near Peikko's house to see which could fell the largest tree. Peikko wound his arms around the trunk of a tall white birch, and tugged and pushed until he was black in the face. But for all his tugging the tree stood firm and solid, and at last poor Peikko had to give it up.

It was Matti's turn. He too seized the birch in his arms. Then he shouted:

"It's giving, Peikko, it's giving! Stand out of the way!"

Peikko took to his heels and ran so that the tree would not fall on him. When he was out of sight Matti took his axe from the hollow stump where he had hidden it, and chopped the tree down in a couple of strokes. He called:

"Where are you, Peikko? It's quite safe now, the tree's down!"

Sure enough, when Peikko came back there lay the tree on the ground.

"Now we'll try our strength at lifting it," Matti said.

He seized one end of the tree and dragged it a few paces. Then Peikko lifted the end of the tree, too, but Matti, hidden by the leaves, set his foot on one of the trailing branches. Peikko puffed and tugged till he was tired, but the tree would not budge.

"You've won again," he grumbled.

"What shall we try next?" Matti teased him.

"We'll try breaking a rock with our fingers. You won't beat me at that, for my fingers are stronger than yours."

"All right," said Matti, for he remembered that he had slipped a boiled potato into his pocket that morning for lunch.

Peikko found a white cobblestone, and Matti pretended to find one, too, and put it in his pocket. "You crush your stone first," he said.

Peikko took the cobble in his strong right hand and squeezed with all his might. Tears came to his eyes from the effort, but the stone didn't break.

"You needn't grin," he said peevishly to Matti. "You won't do any better yourself!"

"Watch me," Matti returned.

He drew out the boiled potato, set his teeth and pretended to squeeze very hard, while Peikko watched. Presently a few drops of water trickled from between his fingers. He took a long breath, then opened his fist and showed Peikko the crumbled pieces.

"That's strange," said Peikko. "It begins to look as if you were a wizard!"

"I'm no wizard," Matti laughed. "It's just that I'm stronger than you, though our stones were both the same size."

"How about throwing a stone?" said Peikko then. "I can throw farther than anyone I know."

As he spoke, he picked up a stone and hurled it very high into the air. It fell a long distance off, and Peikko smiled. "Try and beat that," he said.

Matti picked a stone up, balanced it a moment in his hand, then pretended to hurl it at the very instant that a bird darted past them up into the air.

STUPID PEIKO

"There, see that?" he shouted.

Peikko blinked in astonishment, for he had caught only a glimpse of something that flew through the air and out of sight into the clouds.

"You may be a wizard," he said, "but I don't believe you can throw my iron hammer further than I can."

Matti seized the hammer and swung it a few times as though to gauge its weight.

"Watch, Peikko. I'll throw it right into the sky. I'll make it lodge on top of that cloud over there."

"Then I won't be able to get it back again," Peikko cried.

"Of course you won't. Not unless the hammer should break the cloud and come down with the hailstones," said Matti very seriously. "But I don't think that's very likely to happen. At least, it never has happened with me yet."

"Stop! Don't throw it, Matti," Peikko begged, and he snatched the hammer from Matti's hand. "I'll believe you. I'm sure you are a wizard!"

"Wrong again, Peikko," Matti laughed. "I'm just stronger than you are, that's all. You have to give in!"

## V

When the miller's daughter was married, the miller gave a grand wedding feast, and Peikko was invited. Peikko loved good food, and when they all sat down round the table he began to eat like a wolf. Meat, cakes and honey all began to disappear at a great rate, and all the other guests stared, for they had never seen a man so greedy. As the meal went on, the host began to worry for fear the food would not last out to the end. Yet Peikko ate and ate and ate.

At last the miller whispered to his wife: "We must get rid of Peikko, or there won't be a crumb for anyone else."

By this time the guests had begun to tell stories, seeing that Peikko gave them no chance at the food, and someone had spoken of snakes.

"The only thing in the world I'm afraid of is a snake. I can't bear to hear one hiss, even. Just the very thought of a snake makes me shiver!"

This gave the miller an idea. He ran for some green willow twigs, and threw them on the hot embers in the open fireplace. They burned slowly at first but soon burst into a blaze, and as they caught one by one the fresh sap in them began to hiss. "Ssss-sss-ss," they went as the flames swept them.

Peikko was emptying a great jug of mead down his throat when the sound caught his ear. He set the jug down in a great hurry.

"What's that noise?" he whispered.

"It's nothing," said Matti, who was sitting beside him. "Someone must have brought a snake into the house."

"I—I think I'd better go home," Peikko said as he pushed his chair back. "I don't feel very well."

Just then the hissing of the willow twigs grew louder.

"Yes, I must go—I must go at once," Peikko said, his teeth fairly chattering.

And without saying good-bye he jumped through the window and made off as fast as he could pelt, leaving the wedding feast to continue merrily without him.

## VI

One day Peikko happened to meet a man with a handsome red beard. He turned to Matti, who was standing beside him, and said:

"How did that man get such a fine red beard?"

"Oh, that's easy," laughed Matti. "He just gilded it."

"I wish I had a red beard," said Peikko. "If I had, all the girls would fall in love with me."

"Come with me," said Matti, "and I'll see what can be done."

He prepared a great pot of tar, and when it was hot he told Peikko to dip his beard in it, and hold it there. Peikko did, and when the tar had cooled he tried to lift his head to see how fine his beard had become. But instead of turning color, his beard stuck fast in the tar, and he had to call for help.

Matti came and cut the beard off with a sharp knife, but it was months before Peikko dared to show his face again, for the story got around and all the girls in the village were laughing at him. After that he was quite content with his own black beard.

## VII

As Peikko grew older, he grew more and more grasping. Often he took what did not belong to him. The miller, who was his nearest neighbor, began to miss things, and knew that Peikko must have stolen them. Tools, leather straps, everything, even his stock of grain began to dwindle.

One day Peikko came creeping to the miller's oat bin, and filled his cap and his pockets with oats. This time the miller saw him, but he said nothing. Instead, he made a pair of birch-bark shoes huge enough for a giant, and left them leaning against the wall of his *tupa*, in full view.

The next night when Peikko came to carry off more of the miller's grain, he saw the huge pair of shoes leaning there.

"*Ka,*" said Peikko to himself. "Whoever wears those shoes must be a giant. It'll be a pretty bad job for me if he catches me. I'd better be going!"

And without more ado he took to his heels and ran home as fast as he could.

## VIII

In his old age Peikko began to grow childish. He became curious about little things, and often asked foolish questions. He was greedier than ever, too; he could let nothing alone.

One day he was walking with Matti when he saw a haystack in the field near by, and pointed at it with a foolish smile.

"What's that?"

"That's a reed from my mother's loom," Matti told him.

"Can I have it?"

"Certainly," Matti laughed.

With great effort Peikko managed to balance the haycock on his back, and they walked on. Presently Peikko saw an old boat rocking at anchor.

"What's that?"

"Oh, that's my mother's old shoe," said Matti.

"Can I have it?"

"Surely!"

With still more effort, Peikko balanced the boat on his shoulder beside the hay.

A little later they passed a disused millstone, and Peikko asked again with his foolish grin:

"What's that?"

"That's my mother's old spinning wheel," said Matti, laughing till his sides shook.

"Can I have it?"

"Surely."

"But how can I carry it?" Peikko asked him.

"Tie it to a rope round your neck."

Peikko tied the millstone about his neck and hobbled on as best he could.

At last they came to the edge of a lake.

"And what's that?" Peikko asked.

Matti was beginning to get tired of his foolish questions. He said: "*Ka,* it's a lake. What did you think it was?"

"How can I get across?" Peikko asked.

"Use the boat you've got on your shoulder, stupid," cried Matti impatiently.

"A boat!" cried Peikko delightedly, for he had forgotten all about it. "A boat! So I have. I'll cross in the boat. Won't you come with me, Matti?"

"I'll walk around," said Matti. "Your boat isn't strong enough to hold two. And take care yourself, if you're going to put all that load in it!"

But Peikko paid no heed to his warnings. The addled old gnome jumped into the boat before Matti could stop him.

"*Hyvasti* (Good-bye)!" he piped.

When he reached the middle of the lake, the boat filled with water and sank. Some say that Peikko stood on the haycock and shouted for help and that his friends rescued him, and that he still lived to a ripe old age. Others say that he still dwells in the palace of the Water God at the bottom of the lake, and that there he has been restored to everlasting youth.

# FABLES

## THE END OF THE WORLD

THE LITTLE brown hen was out walking in the wood. Presently an acorn fell on her head.

"Goodness, what a crash!" cried the hen. "The sky is falling to pieces. Yes, that is what hit me! The world is coming to an end!"

And off she rushed, squawking. Presently she met the pig.

"Hurry, hurry," she screamed. "The world is coming to an end. A big piece of sky fell down and hit me. Let's run, quick."

"Oh dear," squealed the pig, and he began to run, too. "We must warn all our friends."

When the cow, the dog and the rooster heard what was happening, they all began to scream and run. "The world is coming to an end! What shall we do?"

They made such a noise that the fox, the wolf and the bear heard them shouting, and came running to see.

"Where are you rushing to?" the bear asked. "What is happening?"

"Haven't you heard?" chattered the hen. "The world is coming to an end. We are going to hide in the forest. Hurry, if you want to save your lives!"

"Heavens!" cried the wolf, the fox and the bear, and they all began running.

At last they came to a hollow in the forest, hidden by tall trees.

"Here is a good place to hide," said the hen.

And here they all hid. They waited and they waited, but nothing happened, and by-and-by they all began to feel very hungry.

"What shall we eat?" they asked one another.

The fox looked around, and saw the hen.

"*Ka*," he said, licking his chops. "It was the hen that started all this foolishness. We'll eat the hen first."

And before the hen could say a single word they all fell on her and gobbled her up.

But they were still hungry.

"We'll eat the pig next," cried the fox, "because he's so stupid he believed every word the hen told him."

So they ate the pig, too. By this time all the other barnyard animals were too frightened to move, and one by one the fox, the wolf and the bear ate them all up in turn, first the rooster, then the dog and then the cow.

"This has been a very pleasant excursion," said the fox.

"I feel as full as a tick," the bear grinned.

"I've eaten so much I must lie down and sleep," said the wolf.

They all curled up and slept, but when they woke up they were as hungry as ever.

"What shall we eat now?" asked the bear and the wolf, and they both looked at the fox, because he was the smallest.

"I," said the fox, "am going to eat myself."

And he turned his head and pretended to gnaw at his own tail.

The bear and the wolf thought that was a good idea, so they began to do the same. But while they were busy gnawing away the fox jumped out of the hollow and shouted:

"You are fools to eat yourselves up, but I'd be crazier still if I stayed with you!"

And off he galloped through the forest.

# FARMERS THREE

ONCE A fox, a wolf and a bear decided to become farmers.

"We will till the fields just as the men do," said the fox.

So they planned to cut down trees, burn brush, plow the ground, sow seed and reap the grain.

But when it came to felling the trees, the wolf and the bear found that they had chosen a very hard task. The fox slipped away, and only peeped out once in a while to see how they were getting on. He was no help at all. The bear could only wrestle with the stumps and drag boulders from the ground. So it fell to the wolf to hold the axe between his paws, as best he could.

When the trees were finally cut, the fox came back to say he was very sorry he had been too busy to help. He'd do better next time, he assured them.

But when it came time to burn the brush, the fox said: "I'm sorry, but I shall have to leave you again. The smoke makes me so dizzy I can't see anything."

The bear and the wolf went on working. The bear fell in the hot ashes and singed his fur and blistered his paws, and the wolf's eyes smarted so from the smoke that tears ran down his cheeks.

After the brush was burned, there was all the plowing to do. The bear was the horse, and pulled the plow till his shoulders ached, while the wolf's paws were sore from holding the plow handle. By the time the field was all harrowed and the seed sown, the wolf and the bear were completely worn out.

When harvest time came, back came the fox.

"Now I'll make up for lost time," he told the others. "I'll do my share of the work, and more. I'll gather all the grain while you thrash it."

So again the wolf blistered his paws wielding the flail, while the bear was nearly blinded by the dust and the flying chaff. All that the fox had to do was to bite the stalks with his sharp teeth.

"Now our harvest is gathered," said the fox when the threshing was all over, "I suggest that we divide the crop according to our sizes. The bear is the largest, so he must have the largest share. You, wolf, come next, so you shall have the next largest. I am the smallest, so I'll be content with the least."

"Agreed, agreed!" cried the two others, for they thought the fox was being very generous. And they let him make the division.

The straw was by far the largest part of the harvest, so he gave that to the bear. The wolf got the chaff, for that was the next largest heap. And the smallest pile of all, the ripe yellow kernels of grain, the clever fox kept for himself.


# THE VAIN BEAR


THE BEAR was not always vain. There was a time when he paid very little attention to his looks. One day, however, he happened to notice what a beautiful red coat the fox had, and he grew very envious. He asked the fox:

"Cousin, where did you get such a beautiful red coat?"

"My coat?" said the fox. "Why, I climbed on a hay stack one day, and my friends set fire to the hay underneath me. I let my coat burn a little, and ever since it has been this beautiful color that you see."

"Really?" said the bear. "I wish you'd do the same for me. I'd like to have a red coat, too."

"Gladly," said the fox, laughing to himself. "There is a hay stack over in that field. Climb up on it and I'll light the fire."

The bear clambered up to the top of the stack, shouting: "Hurry, cousin, hurry!"

So the fox set fire to the hay, and soon the bear was nearly smothered in smoke.

"It's burning," he cried. "It's burning! Shall I jump down?"

"It's not ready yet, wait a little longer!" the fox called back.

Just then a wind sprang up and the hay burst into flame. The bear's long fur caught fire and he jumped from the hay stack and dived into the stream.

"Wait till I catch you!" he called to the fox. But the fox had already run away.

And ever since that day the bear's fur has been dark and coarse, and singed at the tips.

# THE WISDOM OF THE RABBIT

ONE DAY the rabbit was feeling particularly pleased with himself. He thought he was the finest fellow alive and could match his wits with anyone. He was prancing along, flapping his ears and twitching his whiskers, when he met a fox.

"Good morning, Mr. Fox," said the rabbit. "How would you like to have a bet with me?"

"I'd be delighted," said the fox, "especially to make a bet with you."

"*Ka,*" said the rabbit. "You flatter me. However, let's mark a straight line on the ground. Whoever jumps over the line first shall win half the other's possessions."

"Fine," said the fox. "Are you ready to begin?"

"Not yet," answered the rabbit. "I want to think a moment first."

"Think as long as you like, my friend," said the fox gaily, "if you hope that thinking will mend your wits."

"I am thinking," answered the rabbit.

Just then a crow flew past and the fox turned his head to see where he was going. While the fox was looking the other way the rabbit shouted suddenly: "I'm ready!"

And before the fox could turn around, he had jumped over the line.

# TALES FROM ICELAND

TÚNGUSTAPI

# STORIES OF ELVES

## TÚNGUSTAPI

In the olden times, many years ago, a rich farmer lived at Sœlíngsdal-stúnga. Of his children, two were sons, by name Arnór and Sveinn. These brothers were both full of promise, though as different in character from one another as day and night. Arnór was a brave, stirring, and active youth; Sveinn, a quiet, gentle, and timid one.

Arnór, who was full of life and spirits, spent all his time in out-door sports and games, in company with the other young men who lived in that valley, and who used to meet together at a rocky hill standing near the farm Túnga, which was called Túngustapi. Their favorite amusement in the winter was to slide in sleighs down the snowy sides of the hill, and in the evenings, the rocks used to echo again with their shouts and merriment, Arnór being always ringleader.

Sveinn scarcely ever took part in their sports, but was wont generally to pass his time in the church, and to wander alone about the foot of the hill, when the rest were not playing there. People used to point to him, and to say that he had to do with the elves who dwelt in the mountain.

Certain it was that, without fail, every new year's night, he used to disappear, and nobody knew where he went to. He often warned his brother not to make such riot on the hill, but Arnór always laughed at him for his pains, and said that "no doubt the elves were none the worse for it. As for stopping their sports on the hill, he saw no fun in that, and go on he would." And go on he did, just the same as ever, though Sveinn assured him, over and over again, that harm would come of his folly.

One new year's night Sveinn had disappeared as usual, but stayed much longer away from home than was his custom. Arnór offered to go and look for him, saying in joke, "He is certainly enjoying the company of his friends the elves." So starting out, he took his way to the mountain.

The night was dark and stormy. When he had arrived at that side of the hill which faced the farm, the rock opened suddenly before him of its own accord, and he saw, within, endless rows of the brightest lamps. At the same time he heard the sound of music, and bethought himself that this must surely be the time for the elves' public worship. And drawing nearer he came to an open door, through which he looked, and saw

595

vast crowds of people assembled within. One, who seemed to be a priest, stood, dressed in splendid robes, by an altar, round which were placed numberless burning candles. Arnór then went further in still, and saw his brother Sveinn kneeling before the altar, while the priest, laying his hands on his head, was speaking some words over him. Round about him stood many others, all in sacred robes, so that Arnór guessed at once that they were making his brother an elfin-priest.

Then he cried aloud, "Sveinn! Come! Come with me! You are running the risk of death!"

Whereupon Sveinn started up, and, turning towards the door near which his brother stood, made as if he would hurry to him. But the priest, who stood before the altar, said:

"Shut instantly the door! and let us wreak vengeance upon the man who has dared to place his feet within our holy place. But thou, Sveinn, must go from among us for thy brother's fault; and, inasmuch as thou wert willing to go to him, and loved more his shameless call than these our sacred rites, thou shalt fall down dead whenever thine eyes again see me standing in my robes before this altar."

Arnór now saw those who had been standing round the altar, lift his brother in their arms and vanish with him through a distant arch of rock. At the same moment the sound of a bell rang out above him, and all the assembled crowd rushed with one accord to the doorway. He himself ran through it first, back into the outer night, and sped towards his home. But soon he heard behind him the sound of following feet, and the weird tramp of fleet elfin horses. And one of the foremost riders cried with a loud voice—

> "Ride! Ride! Ride on!
> For the slopes are dark and the path is dim;
> He flees before, ride after him!
> Let us, with fell enchantment, spread
> Confusion o'er his feet and head,
>   In order that he
>   May never see
> To-morrow's sun! Ride! Ride! Ride on!"

Then the whole troop rode between Arnór and the farm and drove him back. On they went over hill and rock and morass, Arnór, whose dread clogged his feet, knowing not whither he fled. At last he came to some slopes far east of his home, and there, his strength forsaking him, he fell down fainting, and the whole elfin-troop rode over him, bruising him with the hoofs of their goblin-horses, till he was more dead than alive.

As to Sveinn, he came home just when the household, tired of waiting, were going to bed. He did not utter a word about himself or his own long absence, but bade them at once make search for his brother Arnór. All the servants, therefore, went out and spent the rest of the night in vainly trying to find him. But he was found at last by a farmer who lived to the eastward, and who, as he rode to early worship, at Túnga, next morning, stumbled across him lying at the foot of the slopes. Arnór was sensible, but dying, and so weak that he only found strength and words to tell the farmer what had happened, and to beg him not to take him home again, but leave him, before he fell back dead.

Ever since that those mounds have been called "the slopes of death!"

Sveinn was never himself again, but became more sullen, silent, and strange than he had been before. And it was noticed from that time forth he neither went near nor looked towards the rocky mountain, Túngustapi. He seemed to care no more for worldly things, and at last gave them up with their interests for ever, by becoming a monk, and shutting himself up in the monastery of Helgafell. He was so learned that none of the brethren were by any means a match for him, and he sang the mass so sweetly that the like of it—they said—had never been heard before. So they looked at him with awe, and as on one who is not of this world, and he was, as it were, head over them all.

Now, after a while, his father, at Túnga, being far on in years, fell sick for the last time, and yearning to see his son before he died, sent for Sveinn to come to him. Sveinn at once obeyed the bidding, but, as he departed, said sadly to the monks who had assembled to wish him God-speed:

"May it fare well with you all for ever, for perchance I may never come back with life again."

He arrived at Túnga the Saturday before Easter, and found his father so void of strength as to be scarcely able to speak. But the old man made it understood that he wished his son to sing the mass on Easter day in the church, whither he himself would be carried to die. Sveinn, strangely loth, consented, but only on condition that the church door should be kept firmly shut during the whole service, for upon the fulfilment of this something told him that his life depended.

Easter morning has arrived, and the dying man is borne by his servants into the church. Then Sveinn, attired in his priestly robes, stands upon the steps of the altar and sweetly sings the mass. So sweetly, that all there present think that never before have they heard a voice like this, and they kneel with the very breath hushed upon their lips to listen to him the better.

But when, at the close of the service, the priest turns from the altar, and with outstretched hands pronounces solemnly the blessing, suddenly a strong wind from the west strikes the church, and the door, bursting from its fastenings, falls heavily inwards. All turn to look, and they see through the empty frame that the rocky hill near at hand yawns open, and that within it gleam countless rows of burning lamps. And when they turn again towards the altar, Sveinn has fallen down and lies dead where he has just pronounced the blessing. And his father has fallen also from his couch, his face likewise white with death.

Then the people knew whence the west wind came, and how Sveinn has been slain by the revengeful elves.

For the farmer, who had found Arnór at the foot of the slopes, has long ago told them the story; and they whisper to one another that Sveinn has seen the elfin-priest standing robed at his altar.

So the father and son were buried on the same day.

But the church at Túnga now stands elsewhere, that it may be out of sight of the elfin temple, whose altar is to the west and whose door to the east.

# THE GENESIS OF THE HID-FOLK

ONCE UPON a time, God Almighty came to visit Adam and Eve. They received him with joy, and showed him everything they had in the house. They also brought their children to him, to show him, and these He found promising and full of hope. Then He asked Eve whether she had no other children than these whom she now showed him. She said "None."

But it so happened that she had not finished washing them all, and, being ashamed to let God see them dirty, had hidden the unwashed ones. This God knew well, and said therefore to her, "What man hides from God, God will hide from man." These unwashed children became forthwith invisible, and took up their abode in mounds, and hills, and rocks. From these are the elves descended, but we men from those of Eve's children whom she had openly and frankly shown to God. And it is only by the will and desire of the elves themselves that men can ever see them.

A traveller once lost his way, and knew not whither to turn or what to do. At last, after wandering about for some time, he came to a hut, which he had never seen before; and on his knocking at the door, an old woman opened it, and invited him to come in, which he gladly did. Inside, the house seemed to be a clean and good one. The old woman led him to the warmest room, where were sitting two young and beautiful girls. Besides these there were none else in the house. He was well received and kindly treated, and having eaten a good supper was shown to bed.

He asked whether one of the girls might stay with him, as his companion for the night, and his request was granted.

And now wishing to kiss her, the traveller turned towards her, and placed his hand upon her; but his hand sank through her, as if she had been of mist, and though he could well see her lying beside him, he could grasp nothing but the air. So he asked what this all meant, and she said, "Be not astonished, for I am a spirit. When the devil, in times gone by, made war in heaven, he, with all his armies, was driven into outer darkness. Those who turned their eyes to look after him as he fell, were also driven out of heaven; but those who were neither for nor against him, were sent to the earth and commanded to dwell there in the rocks and mountains. These are called Elves and Hid-folk. They can live in company with none but their own race. They do either good or evil, which they will, but what they do they do thoroughly. They have no bodies as you other mortals, but can take a human form and be seen of men when they wish. I am one of these fallen spirits, and so you can never hope to embrace me."

To this fate the traveller yielded himself, and has handed down to us this story.

# THE FISHERMAN OF GÖTUR

IT IS told, that long ago, a peasant living at Götur in Mýrdalur, went out fishing round the island of Dyrhólar. In returning from the sea, he had to cross a morass. It happened once, that, on his way home, after nightfall, he came to a place where a man had lost his horse in the bog, and was unable to recover it without help. The fisherman, to whom this man was a stranger, aided him in freeing his horse from the peat.

When the animal stood again safe and sound upon the dry earth, the stranger said to the fisherman, "I am your neighbour, for I live in Hvammsgil, and am, as you, returning from the sea. But I am so poor, that I cannot pay you for this service, as you ought to be paid. I will promise you, however, this much—that you shall never go to sea without catching fish, nor ever, if you will take my advice, return with empty hands. But you must never put to sea without having first seen me pass your house as if going towards the shore. Obey me in this matter and I promise you that you shall launch, at no time, your boat in vain."

The fisherman thanked him for this advice, and sure enough it was, that, for three years afterwards, never putting to sea till he had first seen his neighbour pass his door, he always launched his boat safely, and always came home full-handed.

But at the end of the three years, it fell out that one day, in the early morning, the fisherman looking out from his house, saw the wind and weather favourable and all other fishers hurrying down to the sea, to make the best of so good a time. But though he waited hour after hour, in the hope of seeing his neighbour pass, the man of Hvammsgil never came. At last losing his patience, he started out without having seen him go by. When he came down to the shore, he found that all the boats were launched and far away.

Before night the wind rose and became a storm, and every boat that had that day put to sea was wrecked, and every fisher drowned, the peasant of Götur alone escaping, for he had been unable to go out fishing. The next night he had a strange dream, in which his neighbour from Hvammsgil came to him and said, "Although you did not yesterday follow my advice, I yet so far felt kindly towards you, that I hindered you from going out to sea, and saved you thus from drowning; but look no more forth to see me pass, for we have met for the last time." And never again did the peasant see his neighbour pass his door.

# THE GRATEFUL ELFWOMAN

A PEASANT'S wife once dreamed that a woman came to her bedside, whom she knew to be a Huldukona (elfwoman) and who begged her to give her milk for her child, two quarts a day, for the space of a month, placing it always in a part of the house which she pointed out. The goodwife promised to do so, and remembered her promise when she awoke. So she put a milkbowl every morning in the place which the other had chosen, and left it there, always on her return finding it empty. This went on for a month; and at the end of the month she dreamed that the same woman came to her, thanked her for her kindness, and begged her to accept the belt which she should find in the bed when she awoke, and then vanished. In the morning the goodwife found beneath her pillow, a silver belt, beautifully and rarely wrought, the promised gift of the grateful elfwoman.

# THÓRDUR OF THRASTASTADIR

A CERTAIN man named Thórdur lived at Thrastastadir, in Skagafiördur.

One day, in the winter, he started from home, intending to go to the trading-town of Hofsós, but the snow had drifted so deeply that the way was thought unsafe. Not caring for this, he carried his merchandise in a bag and walked off across a bog, which he knew to be his shortest path to Hofsós. When he had gone a little way, he quite lost the track, but still walked straight on till nightfall, when he saw before him some warehouses, so lofty and so beautiful that they filled him with surprise. Going up to them he discovered a light in one of the windows, and at the same time heard some delightful music. So he looked in at the window and saw a number of people dancing. He then went to the door and knocked, and immediately it was opened by a well-dressed man, who asked him what he would? Thórdur told him how he had lost his way, and begged, if it were possible, for a night's shelter.

"Come in and be welcome," said the man, "you shall have shelter here. Bring in your bag too, and to-morrow I will trade with you, and I promise you that you shall not find the bargains of Hofsós better than mine."

Thórdur could scarcely believe his ears, but thought he must be dreaming. So the man let him into the chief room, spite of Thórdur's plain and muddy dress. There were many assembled there; the lady of the house, her children, and her servants, all gaily and brightly drest, making merry.

The man who had opened the door to Thórdur, and who was no other than the master of the house, said to the lady, "Wife, here is a man who has lost his way and who needs both rest and food: treat him well."

"I grieve to hear of his distress," replied she, and rising, brought in a good and plentiful supper, which she set before Thórdur, while the master of the house fetched wine and glasses, and begged Thórdur to drink with him. Thórdur did so, and thought he had never tasted such wine in all his life, nor ever met such goodly company, though he could not, for all that, help wondering at the strangeness of the adventure. Glass after glass of wine he drank, and by-and-by, becoming tipsy, went to bed and fell into a deep sleep.

Next morning, at breakfast, he was offered wine even better than that of the night before, and having drunk it, was conducted by the master to the trading-room, which was well filled with every kind of merchandise. Then and there Thórdur showed the man his wares, and received from him in exchange more than half again what he would have got for them at Hofsós. With the money he bought corn and linen, and many other small things, at a much lower price than he was wont to pay elsewhere for the like, and filled with them his sack.

When the trading was finished the master offered him as a gift, a cloak for his wife and cakes for his children, saying to him, "These and many other good turns shall you have at my hands, as tokens of my gratitude to you for having saved my son from death." Thórdur wondered what the man could mean, but the other said, "Once, you were standing under the rock called Thórdarhöfdi, in company with other young men, waiting for a good wind to take your boat to Drángey. Your companions amused themselves by throwing stones against the rock, under which, as the sun was very hot, my son had laid himself down to sleep; for he was tired, having been up all the night. You bade them cease their sport, for it was a foolish one, you said, and a useless. They laughed at you for this notion of yours, and called you strange and fanciful for your pains. But had you not prevented them from throwing stones, they would have killed my son."

After this Thórdur took leave of all in the house, for the sky was now clear and the path good, and started on his homeward way, the master walking some steps with him, to wish him "God-speed." Thórdur marched on steadily for a while; but chancing to look back for the house wherein he had passed the night, he saw nothing of it, but, in its place, the rocks of the Thórdarhöfdi. Then he understood that the kind merchant was an elf, and hastening home, told his wife all that had befallen him, and gave her the cloak. As for the wares he had got instead of his own, he showed them to all his neighbours, and never were the like of them, for goodness, seen in all that country, nor in any other country under the sun.

# GRÍMSBORG

IN THE north country, near a farm called Keta, stands a high and steep rock, named Grímsborg. It is said that, in this wild castle, elves have dwelt for many ages, and that their chief has always been called Grímur. Certain old folk, not long dead, used to declare that in their time, four elves dwelt in the Grímsborg, two men and two women, and that of these each pair went in turn to church at Keta, when there was worship, leaving the others at home.

It happened that a bad season, for a long time prevailing, cut off from the inhabitants of that district their supply of food, and drove them into the very jaws of death. Once, during the famine, the farmer of Keta, chancing to pass the Elf-castle, bethought him of what hope might lie in an appeal to the good-will of the chief elf, and going close to the foot of the borg, said in a loud voice:—

> "Rich Grímur of the castle, hear our sorrow!
> And, of they pity, ere shall dawn to-morrow,
> Cast up beneath the rocks, upon the shore,
> A mighty whale, that we may starve no more."

Then he waited to hear if there should be any answer to these words. In a few minutes a voice came from the Elf-castle, saying:—

> "Whale, come to land!
> Lie stretched upon the sand
> In death, that those who fear to die
> From famine, find salvation nigh."

As soon as he heard these words, the farmer returned home joyfully, knowing that the days of the famine were ended, since the elves vouchsafed their help. And next morning, going with a large band of men down to the beach, what should he see lying dead upon the rocks, but a fine whale, which had been driven up by the surf in the night!

So ended the famine of Keta, for before the people had finished the flesh of the whale, the season changed and good days came back again.

# THE FATHER OF EIGHTEEN ELVES

At a certain farm, long ago, it happened that all the household were out one day, making hay, except the goodwoman and her only child, a boy of four years old. He was a strong, handsome, lusty little fellow, who could already speak almost as well as his elders, and was looked upon by his parents with great pride and hope. But as his mother had plenty of other work to do besides watching him, she was obliged to leave him alone for a short time, while she went down to the brook to wash the milk-pails. So she left him playing in the door of the cottage, and came back again as soon as she had placed the milk-pails to dry.

Directly she spoke to the child, it began to cry in a strange and unnatural way, which amazed her not a little, as it had always been so quiet and sweet-tempered. When she tried to make the child speak to her, as it was wont to do, it only yelled the more, and so it went on for a long time, always crying and never would be soothed, till the mother was in despair at so wonderful a change in her boy, who now seemed to have lost his senses.

Filled with grief, she went to ask the advice of a learned and skilful woman in the neighbourhood, and confided to her all her trouble.

Her neighbour asked her all sorts of questions—How long ago this change in the child's manner had happened? What his mother thought to be the cause of it? and so forth. To all of which the wretched woman gave the best answers she could. At last the wise woman said:

"Do you not think, my friend, that the child you now have is a changeling? Without doubt it was put at your cottage door in the place of your son, while you were washing the milk-pails."

"I know not," replied the other, "but advise me how to find it out."

So the wise woman said, "I will tell you. Place the child where he may see something he has never seen before, and let him fancy himself alone. As soon as he believes no one to be near him, he will speak. But you must listen attentively, and if the child says something that declares him to be a changeling, then beat him without mercy."

That was the wise woman's advice, and her neighbour, with many thanks for it, went home.

When she got to her house, she set a cauldron in the middle of the hearth, and taking a number of rods, bound them end to end, and at the bottom of them fastened a porridge-spoon. This she stuck into the cauldron in such a way that the new handle she had made for it reached right up the chimney: as soon as she had prepared everything, she fetched the child, and placing him on the floor of the kitchen left him and went out, taking care, however, to leave the door ajar, so that she could hear and see all that went on.

When she had left the room, the child began to walk round and round the cauldron, and eye it carefully, and after a while he said:

"Well! I am old enough, as anybody may guess from my beard, and the father of eighteen elves, but never, in all my life, have I seen so long a spoon to so small a pot."

On hearing this the goodwoman waited not a moment, but rushed into the room and snatching up a bundle of fire-wood flogged the changeling with it, till he kicked and screamed again. In the midst of all this, the door opened, and a strange woman, bearing in her arms a beautiful boy, entered and said, "See how we differ! I cherish and love your son, while you beat and illuse my husband;" with these words, she gave back to the farmer's wife her own son, and taking the changeling by the hand, disappeared with him.

But the little boy grew up to manhood, and fulfilled all the hope and promise of his youth.

# THE BISHOP AND THE ELVES

A BISHOP, travelling to visit the various parts of his diocese, took with him, among other servants, as was the custom in those times (for this was long ago), a maid-servant to cook his meals for him. One evening he rested and caused the tents to be pitched, and the camp for the night to be made upon a certain mountain.

Next morning the maid was missing. Search was made, high and low, far and wide, for her, but all in vain, and the bishop shrewdly suspected that she had been stolen by the elves.

Now he had in his retinue of servants a certain man, who, from his great stature and strength, went by the name of "John the Giant." Accordingly he called John the Giant to him, and said to him:

"Sit you here, upon my bed, while I go out, and do not stir for an instant from the tent. If it should happen that the maid come in, seize her and hold her fast; and, above all things, do not let her go till I return, however much she may struggle, and however much she may beg. Take care, too, how you believe what she says, for to deceive you into leaving her free, she will not stick at a lie."

With these words, the bishop took his staff, and going out drew with it three circles, one within the other, on the ground outside the tent, and went away without anybody seeing in what direction.

Meanwhile John the Giant sat upon the bed and waited, listening and looking intently, but moving neither hand nor foot. After a little while the maid, who had been lost, appeared near the tent, without any shoes upon her feet, and running into it, went up to the pillow of the bishop's bed as if to get something from underneath it. But John the Giant was too quick for her, and starting up flung his arms round her and held her tight. At first she begged him to let her go, saying that the bishop had sent her, and that she must make haste back to him again. Then, as soon as she saw that John the Giant turned a deaf ear to all her entreaties, and did not believe or care for a word she said, she began to struggle, and fought so sturdily, that it was almost more than he could do to hold her.

Just at this time the other servants outside saw twelve mounted men, dressed in blue, ride towards the tent, stopping, however, suddenly, as if they had been shot, when they came to the circles which were drawn round it, and immediately vanishing away.

For these were magic circles which the bishop had made with his holy staff, and nothing evil or ungodly could pass beyond them.

Soon afterwards the bishop himself returned and told his serving men to bind the maid until such time as her temper should be less perverse. Then he again went away, and before long the girl came to her own good senses again. When the others saw this they asked her to tell them what had befallen her, and how she had left the camp without awakening anybody. She declared that in the night a man had come to her bedside, taken her hand and led her out, she not knowing why or whither they were going till they came to a certain mound, into which they entered. That here she found a great many people assembled in a large hall, at the end of which was a raised daïs, with many women collected together upon it. That these women had made her go to bed, and placed beside her couch a spinning-wheel and bundle of hemp, bidding her spin it when she awoke. "But," she said, "in the morning the bishop, with his staff in his hand, came to my bedside and bade me run back here and fetch his keys from under his pillow. I rose and ran in such haste that I had not even time to put on my shoes."

And this was the end of the matter. The bishop came back soon afterwards, not ill-pleased with his morning's work; for being pretty well skilled in magic and the like, and being, moreover, a very holy man, and a right-determined one to boot, he had played the elves a pretty trick that day, in getting his maid-servant out of their hands almost as soon as they had got her into theirs. And, as far as that went, he could have done it a hundred times just as easily as once; and in a different way each time.

# WHO BUILT REYNIR CHURCH?

A CERTAIN farmer once lived at Reynir, in the district of Mýrdal. He was ordered by the bishop to build a good church hard by his farm-house, but had so much difficulty in getting enough timber before the hay-making season, and then so much trouble in finding proper builders, that he feared he should be unable to finish the work before the winter.

One day as he was walking in his field, thinking sadly over the matter, and how he should excuse himself to the bishop for failing to obey his bidding, a strange man, whom he had never seen before, met him, and stopping him, offered him his services in building the church, declaring that he should require the services of no other workman. Then the farmer asked him what payment he would think the due meed of such labour, and the man made the following condition—that the farmer should either find out his name before he had finished the church, or else give him his son, who was then a little boy six years old. The farmer thought these easy terms enough, forsooth, and laughing in his sleeve, gladly consented to them.

So the strange builder set to work, and worked with a will, by day and by night, speaking but little to anybody, until the church rose beneath his hands as quickly as if by magic, and the farmer plainly foresaw that it would be finished even before the hay-making was over.

But by this time he had rather changed his mind about the payment he had before thought so easy, and was very far from feeling glad that the end of the church-building was so near; for do what he would, ask whom he would, and search the country round as he would, and had done, he could not, for the life of him, find out the name of his quick-handed mason. Still the church went on not a whit slower for his anxiety, and autumn came, and a very little more labour would finish the building.

One day, the last day of the work, he happened to be wandering outside his field, brooding, in deep grief, over what now seemed to be the heavy price he would have to pay to his master-builder, and threw himself down upon a grass-mound which he came to; he had scarcely lain there a minute, when he heard some one singing, and listening, he found that the voice was that of a mother lulling her child, and came from inside the mound upon which he had flung himself down. This is what it said:

> "Soon will thy father Finnur come from Reynir,
> Bringing a little playmate for thee, here."

And these words were repeated over and over again; but the farmer, who pretty soon guessed what they meant, did not wait to hear how many times the mother thought fit to sing them, or what the child seemed to think of them, but started up and ran with all speed, his heart filled with joy, to the church, in which he found the builder just nailing the last plank over the altar.

"Well done, friend Finnur!" said he, "how soon you have finished your work!"

No sooner had these words passed his lips than friend Finnur, letting the plank fall from his hand, vanished, and was never seen again.

# KATLA'S DREAM

A CERTAIN chief, named Már, lived, long ago, at Reykhólar. His wife, who was of noble family, was called Katla. Once, as was his custom, Már had ridden to the legislature, leaving his wife at home.

One morning, during his absence, Katla, feeling tired and heavy, went to bed, not very long after she had risen from it, and fell into a deep sleep. At noon her attendants went to her to call her, but, try as they would, could not wake her; so, fearing that she was dead, they called her foster-father, who lived in the house, and told him of her state. He went to the side of her bed, and himself endeavoured to rouse her, but quite in vain. Then, looking attentively at her, he said, "She is not dead: the flame of life is still flickering in her bosom, but I am no more able to wake her than you were." And, with these words, he sat down beside her couch, and kept close watch over her for four whole days and nights.

On the fifth day Katla awoke, and seemed to be overcome with sorrow; but no one dared to ask her what was the cause of it.

Soon after this her husband came back home from the legislature; but his wife was no longer the same that he had left behind him. She was changed. She neither went to meet him, as she was wont to do, nor when he came did she say "Welcome" to him, nor salute him with her usual love, nor show joy to see him safe.

Wondering and grieved at her strange manner, he asked her attendants apart what had befallen her, and why she behaved thus; but they could only tell him that she had slept unceasingly for four days and four nights, and on awaking had shown this sorrow, without ever telling anybody the reason of it, or what ailed her. On hearing this, Már took Katla herself apart, and urged her to tell him what ailed her,—whether aught had befallen her in her long sleep, assuring her that she would lighten her load of sorrow in thus giving him the half of it. At last, yielding to her husband's prayers, she spoke as follows:—

"As you know, my husband, I fell into a deep sleep early one morning while you were away. I had not slept long, when there came to my bedside a beautiful lady, richly dressed, who spoke sweetly to me, and telling me that she lived at the farm Thverá, not far hence, begged me to go back with her some part of the way thither. As soon as I rose to comply with her wish, she placed her gloves in my bed, saying, 'These shall take your place while you are away.' Then we went out, and came soon to a large lake, as clear and as smooth as glass, upon which, near the shore, a gaily-painted boat was moored. Here I would part from the lady, and wished her God-speed; but she, thanking me for having come so far with her, held out her hand, as if to bid me farewell, crying, 'Will you not say farewell to Alvör?'

"No sooner had I stretched forth mine in return, than she grasped it tightly, and leaping from the shore into the skiff with me, rowed it swiftly to a small island which stood in the midst of the lake. Now, indeed, I felt only too well that she had all power over me, and that I was unable to resist her. She saw that I was filled with dread, and tried to calm my fears, showing me every kindness and courtesy, and assuring me that it was Fate alone which had compelled her to treat me thus. 'I will,' she said, 'soon take you safely home again.'

"When we had come to the island, I saw that there stood upon it a castle, more beautiful than anything I had ever seen or heard of before. 'This is mine,' said Alvör; and leading me into it by the hand, she took me to her own room, where many ladies were sitting. There she made me enter a bath of sweet water, and when I had bathed, she took me to a beautiful bed which stood in the room, covered with curtains of the richest stuff, and filled with soft down. In this I fell asleep after I had drunk a cup of some rare wine which was handed me. When I awoke, I found on a couch near me a mantle worked richly in gold, which the lady who sat by my side bade me put on, together with an embroidered dress which she gave me. When I was dressed, she threw also over me her own mantle, which was daintily wrought in gold and lined with fur. Besides all this, she gave me five rings of red gold, a golden band for my hair, and a costly belt, begging me to keep them all as gifts. After I had thus attired myself, she bade me follow her to the dining-hall, and we went there with her, eight ladies in all.

"All the walls of the room were hung with cloth of woven gold, and the tables were crowded with silver vessels and flagons, and with gold inlaid horns; and round the table sat many handsome men, splendidly attired. At the high table stood a throne, and near this I saw a man, dressed in rich silk, lying asleep on a couch. Alvör went up to him and woke him, and I heard that she called him Kári.

"He started up from his slumber, and said to her, 'Why have you broken my rest? Have you aught of good tidings to tell me? or, perchance, have you brought Katla hither?'

"As soon as he saw that I was in the hall, he came to me, and taking me by the hand, led me to the throne, where he made me sit, and sat beside me. Then the Lady Alvör pointed to us, and cried out to the guests, 'See! the bride and bridegroom!' Whereupon they shouted, as with one voice, and drank and made merry till nightfall. And through all this din of revel, Alvör told me that for that night I was to share the couch of Kári; but I, full wroth, withdrawing myself from her side, said:

" 'Never will I do this thing! Far too dearly do I love my husband to share the love of any other.'

"The lady answered, 'If you say nay, bale and bann will cling to you for ever: be wise, therefore, and consent.'

"Wretched that I was, I knew not what to do, or whither to turn myself, for neither comfort nor aid was near, and I was as a lamb in the midst of a herd of wolves. They led me to the couch in which I had slept before, and then Kári came to me, and offered me all he had, if I would only love him. I told him that his love was hopeless, but he would not hear me. Then he brought me a horn of wine; and after he had tasted it himself first, made me drink of it, saying:

" 'Rather would I struggle with Helja than see sorrow in your eyes. Be comforted; you shall soon return to your home.'

"With these words he lay beside me; and whether it were the force of his entreaties, or the beauty of his presence, or the weight of the wine upon my soul, I cannot tell, but I no longer opposed his love, though the while my heart was filled with grief.

"And so in sorrow passed two days and nights; nor could all the kindness of the attendants, and of all around me, comfort me. At last Kári said to me, 'Call the son whom you shall bear to me by my name, and give him from his father, whom he shall never see, this belt of wrought gold, and this knife with the haft of cunning workmanship, and let them be heirlooms in his family.' And he bade me place the belt and knife, together with the embroidered garments and costly ornaments which I had worn while with him, in a sack, and take them home with me.

" 'Show them,' he said, 'to your husband Már, and tell him the whole truth, though it be a grief and woe to your heart to do so; for it is but just, and your duty. Let him aid you in building a farm at Thverá, where you shall see two small hillocks, which shall be your money-mounds. In that place you shall found a great and noble family. Now I must leave you, and you will never see me again, for,' said he sadly, 'the hours of my life are numbered.'

"When he had finished speaking, Alvör the lady took my hand and led me out; and as I left the hall I heard a loud and echoing sound, and turning my head to see whence it came, behold Kári lay dead, for his heartstrings had broken with exceeding love and sorrow. So the lady rowed me again in the boat across the lake and brought me home, and took the gloves out of my bed.

"As she left me she said, 'May it fare well with you, though you have caused but sorrow to me in breaking my son's heart for love and anguish. Enjoy all the wealth you have, and be happy.' So saying, she was no more with me.

"This is the end of my dream. Therefore, my husband, as you are a just and true man, weigh my fault against its causes, and forgive me. Truly my love for you has not one whit departed."

So she showed Már all the beautiful and costly things that she had brought with her from Alvör's castle.

In the summer she gave birth to a son, a lovely child, and exceeding all other children in mind and form, whom she called, as she had promised his father—Kári. But she never loved the boy with a true mother's love; though on the other hand Már doted upon him as if he had been his own son. Soon after, they built a new farm at Thverá, where they found the two money-mounds, as Kári had promised, and, unestranged by Katla's dream, dwelt there happy and prosperous to a ripe old age.

# THE MAN-WHALE

In ancient times, in the south part of the country, it was the custom to go in a boat, at a certain season of the year, from the mainland to the cliffs, Geirfuglasker, to procure sea-birds and the eggs which they were in the habit of laying there. The passage to these rocks was always looked upon as an unsafe one, as they stood some way out at sea, and a constant and heavy surf beat upon them.

It happened once that some men went thither in a boat at the proper season for the purpose, as the weather seemed to promise a long calm. When they arrived at the rocks, some of them landed, the rest being left to take care of the boat. Suddenly a heavy wind came on, and the latter were forced to leave the island in haste, as the sea became dangerous and the surf beat furiously upon the cliffs. All those who had landed were enabled to reach the boat in time, at the signal from their companions, except one, a young and active man, who, having gone in his zeal higher and farther than the others, was longer in getting down to the beach again. By the time he did get down, the waves were so high, that though those in the boat wrought their best to save him, they could not get near enough to him, and so were compelled for their own lives' sake to row to shore. They determined, however, when the storm should abate its fury, to return to the rocks and rescue him, knowing that unless they did so and the wind were soon spent, the youth could not but perish from cold and hunger. Often they tried to row to the Geirfuglasker, but, the whole season through, they were unable to approach them, as the wind and surf always drove them back. At last, deeming the young man dead, they gave up the attempt and ceased to risk their lives in seas so wrathful.

So time passed away, until the next season for seeking sea-birds came round, and the weather being now calm, the peasants embarked in their boat for the Geirfuglasker. When they landed upon the cliffs, great was their astonishment at seeing come towards them a man, for they thought that no one could live in so wild and waste a spot. When the man drew near them, and they recognized him as the youth who had been left there the year before, and whom they had long ago given up as lost, their wonder knew no bounds, and they guessed that he had the elves to thank for his safety. They asked him all sorts of questions. What had he lived upon? Where had he slept at night? What had he done for fire in the winter? and so forth, but he would give them none but vague replies, which left them just as wise as they were before. He said, however, he had never once left the cliff, and that he had been very comfortable there, wanting for nothing. They than rowed him to land, where all his friends and kin received him with unbounded amazement and joy, but, question him as they would, could get but mighty little out of him concerning his life on the cliffs the whole year through. With time, the strangeness of this event and the wonder it had awakened passed away from men's minds, and it was little if at all more spoken of.

One Sunday in the summer, certain things that took place in the church at Hvalsnes filled people with astonishment. There were large numbers there, and among them the young man who had passed a year on the cliffs of the Geirfuglasker. When the service was over and the folk began to leave the church, what should they find standing in the porch but a beautiful cradle with a baby in it. The coverlet was richly embroidered, and wrought of a stuff that nobody had ever seen before. But the strangest part of the business was, that though everybody looked at the cradle and child, nobody claimed either one or the other, or seemed to know anything whatever about them. Last of all came the priest out of church, who, after he had admired and wondered at the cradle and child as much as the others, asked whether there was no one present to whom they belonged. No one answered. Then he asked whether there was no one present who had enough interest in the child to desire him to baptize it. No one either answered or came forward.

At this moment the priest happened to cast his eyes on the young peasant, concerning whose sojourn on the Geirfuglasker rocks he had always felt particularly suspicious, and calling him aside, asked him whether he had any idea who its father was, and whether he would like the child baptized. But the youth turning angrily from him declared that he knew nothing whatever about the child or its father.

"What care I," he said, "whether you baptize the child or no? Christen it or drown it, just which you think fit; neither it, nor its father, nor its mother, are aught to me."

As these words left his lips, there suddenly appeared in the porch a woman, handsomely apparelled, of great beauty and noble stature, whom no one had ever seen before. She snatched the coverlet from the cradle, and flinging it in through the door of the church, said:

"Be witnesses all, that I wish not the church to lose its dues for this child's baptism."

Then turning to the young peasant, and stretching out her hands towards him, she cried, "But thou, O faithless coward, disowner of thy child, shalt become a whale, the fiercest and most dreaded in the whole wide sea!"

With these words, she seized the cradle and disappeared.

The priest, however, took the coverlet which she had flung into the church, and made of it an altar-cloth, the handsomest that had ever been seen. As for the young peasant, he went mad on the spot; and, rushing down to the Holmur Cliffs, which rise sheer from the deep water, made as if he would throw himself from them. But while he hesitated for a moment on the brink, lo! a fearful change came over him, and he began to swell to a vast size, till, at last, he became so large, that the rock could no longer bear him, but crumbling beneath him hurled him into the sea. There he was changed into a great whale, and the red cap which he had been wearing, became a red head.

After this, his mother confessed that her son had spent the year with the elves upon the Geirfuglasker. On his being left on the rocks by his companions (so he had declared to her), he had at first wandered about in despair, filled only with the thought of throwing himself into the waves to die a speedy death rather than suffer all the pangs of hunger and cold; but a lovely girl had come to him, and telling him she was an elf, had asked him to spend the winter with her. She had borne him a child before the end of the year, and only allowed him to go to shore when his companions came again to the cliffs, on condition that he would have this child baptized when he should find it in the church-porch, threatening him, if he failed in the fulfilment of this, with the severest punishment and most hapless fate.

Now Redhead, the whale, took up his abode in the Faxafjörd, and wrought mischief there without end, destroying boats innumerable, and drowning all their crews, so that at last it became unsafe to cross any part of the bay, and nothing could either prevent his ravages or drive him away. After matters had gone on like this for some time, the whale began to haunt a narrow gulf between Akranes and Kjarlarnes, which is now called after him, Hvalfjördur.

At that time there lived at Saurbœr, in Hvalfjardarströnd, an aged priest, who, though hale and hearty, was blind. He had two sons and a daughter, who were all in the flower of their youth, and who were their father's hope and stay, and, as it were, the very apple of his eye. His sons were in the habit of fishing in Hvalfjördur, and one day when they were out they encountered the whale, Redhead, who overthrew their boat and drowned them both. When their father heard of their death, and how it had been brought about, he was filled with grief, but uttered not a word at the time.

Now it must be known that this old priest was well skilled in all magical arts.

Not long after this, one fine morning in the summer, he bade his daughter take his hand and guide him down to the sea-shore. When he arrived there, he planted the end of the staff which he had brought with him, in the waves, and leaning on the handle fell into deep thought.

After a few minutes he asked his daughter, "How looks the sea?"

She answered, "My father, it is as bright and smooth as a mirror."

Again, a few minutes, and he repeated, "How looks the sea?"

She replied, "I see on the horizon a black line, which draws nearer and nearer, as it were a shoal of whales, swimming quickly into the bay."

When the old man heard that the black line was approaching them, he bade the girl lead him along the shore towards the inland end of the bay. She did so, and the black surging sea followed them constantly. But as the water became shallower, the girl saw that the foam arose, not from a shoal of whales, as she had thought at first, but from the swimming of a single huge whale with a red head, who came rapidly towards them along the middle of the bay, as if drawn to them by some unseen power. A river ran into the extreme end of the gulf, and the old priest begged his daughter to lead him still on along its banks. As they went slowly up the stream, the old man feeling every footstep before him, the whale followed them, though with a heavy struggle, as the river contained but little water for so vast a monster to swim in. Yet forward they went, and the whale still after them, till the river became so narrow between its high walls of rock, that the ground beneath their feet quaked as the whale followed them. After a while they came to a waterfall, up which the monster leaped with a spring that made the land tremble far and wide, and the very rocks totter. But they came at last to a lake, from which the river rose, whose course they had followed from the sea; the lake Hvalvatn. Here the heart of the monster broke from very toil and anguish, and he disappeared from their eyes.

When the old priest returned home, after having charmed the whale thus to his death, all the people from far and near thanked him for having rid their coasts of so dread a plague.

And in case anybody should doubt the truth of this story of Redhead, the man-whale, we may as well say that on the shores of the lake Hvalvatn, mighty whale-bones were found lying long after the date of this tale.

# VALBJÖRG THE UNELFED

IN THE east country, not far from the Lakes of Wool, as they are called, lived a certain farmer, who had a son named Sigurdur.

It happened one year, that this peasant had lost all his sheep upon the mountains, and, as his flocks were nearly all that he had to depend upon for his livelihood, had taken the loss very much to heart, and sent four

The Man-Whale

or five men in succession to search far and near, through hill and valley, for the missing sheep, which could not, in the short time that had passed since they were lost sight of, have strayed very far.

But to the farmer's great distress neither sheep nor shepherds ever came to light again.

One fine day Sigurdur, who was a sturdy fellow and brave to boot, said to his father, "My father, I will go and try my luck in searching for your lost servants and flocks; give me God speed."

His parents were mightily against this, "for," said they, "we would rather lose a thousand servants and a thousand flocks than our son."

But Sigurdur laughed at their fears, and said go he would, and go he must. Accordingly, go he did, having asked the blessing of his parents. Over hill and through valley he went, just as he had heard his father bid the shepherds go; but though he looked far and near, and though he toiled himself well weary, nothing did he see of either men or sheep. At last he came to some large lakes, round the shores of which lay vast masses of wool spread out for drying. On the other side of these, lay some pasture lands of the richest grass, upon which he saw flocks grazing and shepherds watching them. Thinking, at once, that they must be the sheep that had been lost and of which he was in search, he made his way, with all speed, towards them. But he had scarcely gone near enough to count them, when a woman of handsome presence walked up to him and saluted him kindly. When he had returned her greeting, he asked her what she was called.

"I am called," she said, "Vandrád or Valbjörg, which you please, and am glad to see you here and welcome you, friend Sigurdur."

"Surely I have never seen you before," replied he; "how then do you know my name?"

The woman answered, "I know well both you and your father Andres, and what is more, I know that you are now in search of his missing flocks and herdsmen. To tell you the truth, it was I that both lost your father his sheep and killed his shepherds. And you, since you have been foolhardy enough to wander about on the same errand, shall lose your life in the same way as the others have done, if you will not agree, better than they, to what I ask you."

"What is your will?" said Sigurdur. "Tell me what you wish me to do."

Then she said, "My will is that you stay here and live with me and never try to escape."

"But," replied Sigurdur again, "I must know first to what manner of woman I pledge myself; and if you refuse to tell me I will rather die, for I know not fear, than say you yea."

Upon this she answered, "I am one of the race of elves, and I dwell in yonder hillock."

Then Sigurdur consented to live with her, on condition that she would, firstly, let him build a house for himself after his own manner; secondly, that she would let his father know that he still lived and did well; and lastly, that she would restore safe and sound his father's flocks. All these things she promised to do, and bade Sigurdur follow her. Pretty well content with the bargain he had made, and not altogether cold to Valbjörg's charms, he followed her till they came to the hillock, into which they entered through a door of carved wood. As Sigurdur was looking round him and admiring the beauty of the rooms and the traces of wealth which they contained, Valbjörg said to him:

"Two years have I lived here quite alone, since I lost my parents, and weary and lonely have I been. And I have been unwilling to dwell with one of my own race, as my father prophesied that I should have children by a human being. Therefore, when the herdsmen came here to look after the lost flocks, I asked them to stay with me and comfort me, and when each refused, I slew him by magic art. But I am well pleased, Sigurdur, that your heart has inclined towards me, as now my father's words will be accomplished."

So Sigurdur built himself a hut close to the hillock, and lived with Valbjörg; and though, at first, he found his new life irksome to him, and his soul yearned for home, yet after a short time he became accustomed to everything about him, and his love for Valbjörg increased.

One morning, when Andres, Sigurdur's father, rose from sleep and looked forth from the farm, he saw the flock of sheep which he had lost grazing in the home-field, and on going to count them, he found that not one was missing. Much rejoiced at this, he thought that Sigurdur, and perhaps the missing shepherds, had come back during the night, and were now in the family room. But no! nothing had either been seen or heard of them, and Andres was constrained to send out twenty of his neighbours to search for them. All in vain, however; for search as they would, far and near, high and low, over hill and through valley, not a trace was to be found of the lost men. When they all came back to the farm with this bad news, the farmer took it so much to heart, that he fell ill and kept to his bed.

It happened one night, some little time after this, that Andres had a dream, in which he saw a woman of handsome presence come to him, who said—

"Fear not, my friend, for your son's life. He is well, and lives happily with me, who am an elfwoman. It was I who stole your sheep, but your son made me restore them."

Upon this she left him, and he woke, full of joy that his son was still alive; and in the morning he rose again, restored to health by these happy tidings, and went about among his servants, attending to the management of the farm, as he had done before the illness smote him.

Three years went by, and still nothing was heard of Sigurdur. In the autumn of the third year, however, the farmer Andres had a dream, in which his son came to him, and after he had saluted him, said:

"Come, my father, I entreat you, on Christmas-eve, to the Lakes of Wool, and bring with you the priest Eiríkur. By the shores of the lakes you will see my house standing, and will find the door thrown open. Come into the house yourself, but bid Eiríkur stand in the entrance and grasp tightly the woman who shall run out from the family-room as if to leave the house. On no account must he let her go, do or say what she will, as on his holding her fast depend my safety and happiness. If she escape him that Christmas-eve, you will never see me more."

With these words he vanished, and Andres woke. After pondering a while over this dream, which he felt to be no idle fancy, but well fraught with meaning, he determined to do as Sigurdur had bidden him, and rising went forthwith to Eiríkur's house to take counsel with him. When the priest had heard the dream, he said to the farmer:

"My friend, this but confirms what I have always thought, namely, that the elves withhold your son from you, and right willingly will I aid you in this matter, whatever turn it may take."

According in due time Andres and Eiríkur addressed themselves to their journey, and on Christmas-eve arrived at the shores of the Lakes of Wool. They at once saw Sigurdur's house, and going up to it found the door thrown open. Then Andres went in, leaving the priest in the doorway, as his son had told him in the dream to do. When he entered the family-room he saw, by the light of a candle that was burning there, his son Sigurdur carding wool upon a wooden chest. Near him was a bed, on which sat a woman with a child in her arms, and another child lying in a cradle before her feet.

So the farmer saluted them, saying, "God be here."

No sooner were the words out of his mouth than the woman, flinging down the child she held in her arms, and leaping over the cradle which lay at her feet, ran hastily from the family-room, and made as if she would leave the house. But Eiríkur, the priest, who stood in the doorway, was too quick for her, and seizing her in his arms, held her fast. And that was no easy matter, for she struggled so that the priest, who had the strength of two men, and who was moreover skilled in wrestling and manly arts, had much ado to resist her. When they heard the noise, Sigurdur and his father went out from the family-room, taking the light with them, and helped the priest to bring her back into the house and lay her down on the bed. After Eiríkur had laid his hand gently upon her she became quieter, and he watched over her all that night. From time to time she fainted, and when she came again to her senses, wept till it made the blood of all who heard her run cold. And she entreated the priest to let her go free, by all he loved best; but he was not to be moved from his firm though gentle watch and ward. At last, after day had broken, Sigurdur and his father collected all the house-wealth together, packed it on horses, and set forth, taking the priest and Valbjörg and the children with them, and driving the flocks before them. When they had left the hut and the mound a little way behind them, Sigurdur turned round and cast a spell over the place, which is the reason why nobody can find it.

Now the weather being fine and the nights bright and calm, the whole company travelled without resting till they came to Andres' farm, where the priest Eiríkur dwelt with them a week, trying, through much watching and prayer, to tame the savage temper of Valbjörg.

But at the end of that time Sigurdur and his father thought best that he should take the woman to his own house for the remainder of the winter, which he did; and before the spring time, he had quite subdued her elfin nature.

In the meantime Sigurdur took care of his two children at the farm, and his flocks wandered about the hills, taking care of themselves and trusting to kind neighbours.

In the spring Eiríkur joined Sigurdur and Valbjörg in marriage, and a very loving and happy couple they were, now that all Valbjörg's elfin nature had left her. So they dwelt to a good age in the parish of which the worthy Eiríkur was priest, and Valbjörg was much loved and looked up to, as a Christian woman and a good housewife. Four children they had, whose decendants may no doubt be found in the East of Iceland, by anybody who cares to look for them.

# UNA THE ELFWOMAN

A CERTAIN man named Geir lived at a farm called Raudafell, and was rich, young, and active, and a widower at the time to which this story refers. Once, in the haymaking season, a large quantity of hay being left for the women to rake up—almost more than they could do, for he kept but few maid-servants—Geir saw a young and fair woman enter the field, and begin raking up the hay with the others. She uttered not a word to anybody, but worked quietly, and so quickly, that, very soon after she arrived, the hay was all got in, till the farmer fancied there must be some magic power in the rake she used. Every evening, when the work was over, she went away, but came on the morrow, and every day through the season, always doing more work than all the rest, and always departing at nightfall without exchanging a syllable with anybody. On the last night of the hay-cutting, however, the farmer went up to her, and thanked her for having worked so diligently all the summer. She received his thanks kindly, and they talked a long time together, the farmer concluding by asking her to come to his house and act thenceforth as his housekeeper. She consented, and went away.

Next morning she came to Raudafell, bringing with her a large chest, and at once entered upon her duties in the house. The chest was put into one of the outhouses, as she was unwilling, for some reasons of her own, to keep it in the farm itself. She stayed there through the winter, and Geir had every cause to be pleased with her management of the house, for she was clean and thrifty, and an active manager. She never would tell the farmer whence she came, but went so far as to allow that her name was Una: nor would she ever enter the church, though urged to do so over and over again by the farmer; and this was the only cause of offence which he could find in her.

It was the custom on Christmas-eve for every inmate of the farm to go to church except one, who was left behind to take care of the house. On this occasion Una always refused to go with the rest, which much displeased the farmer; she remained at home, and when the family returned from church, had finished all the household work.

Three years passed, during which time Una remained with the farmer, who became so fond of her, that were it not for her one fault—her dislike of going to church—he would have married her.

On Christmas-eve in the third winter Una was, as usual, while the others went to service, left alone in the house. When the family had gone some little distance from home on their way to church, one of the men-servants declared himself unwell, and, sitting on a stone, said that he would remain there till the illness passed over, and that he did not wish anyone to remain behind with him. The farmer, therefore, and the rest of the family left him there, and went on to the church.

When they were out of sight, the man got up and went back to the farm—for his illness was only feigned in order to enable him to play the spy upon Una. On arriving there he saw that Una was sweeping and washing the whole house, and seemed in great haste to finish her work. He hid himself so that Una should not know of his return, and, when she had finished her work, saw her leave the house. He followed her, and saw her go to the outhouse and unlock her chest, from which she took out handsome and cunningly-embroidered clothes, and, having dressed herself in them, she looked so lovely, that the man-servant thought he had never seen anybody so beautiful before. Then she took out of the chest a red cloth, which she put under her arm, and, locking the box, left the outhouse, and closed the door behind her. She ran across the meadow near the farm till she came to a soft swamp, upon the surface of which she spread the scarlet cloth, and stepped into the centre of it, just leaving room by chance at one of the corners for the man-servant, who (having by magical arts, in which he was well skilled, made himself quite invisible) stepped on to the cloth after her.

No sooner was he there than the cloth sank with them through the earth, which seemed like smoke round them, until they came to some wide and fair green fields, where Una stepped off the cloth and put it again under her arm. Some little way off stood a vast and stately palace, into which Una went, and the man after her. Here he found a great number of people assembled, who rose at her entrance, and received her with every show of love and respect. The whole hall in which they stood was adorned as if for a feast. When they had greeted Una they all sat down again, Una amongst them, and the most costly dainties, and rarest wines in gold and silver vessels, were set before them.

But as for our invisible friend, the man-servant, all he could get hold of was a rib-bone of smoked mutton, wonderfully fat and good, which he, without tasting, thrust into his pocket.

When the supper was over, the guests amused themselves with drink-ing and various games, and kept up the revel all night with a great show of joy. About day-break Una rose and declared that she must now depart, as the farmer, her master, and his family would by this time be leaving church. Then bidding a courteous farewell to all, she went out again into the fair green fields, where she spread the cloth out once more, and stepped upon it, and the man-servant on to the corner, as before. The cloth rose with them through the earth, till they arrived at the swamp, whence they had started. And now, gathering up the cloth under her arm, Una ran into the outhouse, where she locked it, together with her handsome clothes in the chest, and again donning her every-day apparel, went back to the farmer's house. Pretty well content with having seen all this, the man-servant took his visible form, and hastened back to the stone, where he had feigned illness the evening before. On their way homewards from church, the farmer and his family found him; and inquiring how he was, received for answer that he had passed a wretched night, but was much better, and was now able to return home with them, which he did.

When they were all assembled at breakfast, and were eating, the farmer (suspecting nothing) took up a rib-bone of mutton from his plate, and holding it up, said:

"Did any of you ever see so fat a rib-bone as this?"

"Possibly, my master," replied the man-servant; and taking from his pocket the rib-bone of mutton he had stolen from the elfin-feast, held it up.

Directly she saw it, Una changed colour, and without a word vanished from their sight: nor was she ever seen afterwards. So the man told the farmer all that he had seen in the night, and Geir no longer wondered why Una should avoid going to church.

# HILDUR, THE QUEEN OF THE ELVES

Once, in a mountainous district, there lived a certain farmer, whose name and that of his farm have not been handed down to us; so we cannot tell them. He was unmarried, and had a housekeeper named Hildur, concerning whose family and descent he knew nothing whatever. She had all the indoor affairs of the farm under her charge, and managed them wondrous well. All the inmates of the house, the farmer himself to boot, were fond of her, as she was clean and thrifty in her habits, and kind and gentle in speech.

Everything about the place flourished exceedingly, but the farmer always found the greatest difficulty in hiring a herdsman; a very important matter, as the well-being of the farm depended not a little on the care taken of the sheep. This difficulty did not arise from any fault of the farmer's own, or from neglect on the part of the housekeeper to the comforts of the servants, but from the fact, that no herdsman who entered his service lived more than a year, each one being without fail found dead in his bed, on the morning of Christmas-day. No wonder, therefore, the farmer found herdsmen scarce.

In those times it was the custom of the country to spend the night of Christmas-eve at church, and this occasion for service was looked upon as a very solemn one. But so far was this farm from the church, that the herdsmen, who did not return from their flocks till late in the evening, were unable to go to it on that night until long after the usual time; and as for Hildur, she always remained behind to take care of the house, and always had so much to do in the way of cleaning the rooms and dealing out the rations for the servants, that the family used to come home from church and go to bed long before she had finished her work, and was able to go to bed herself.

The more the reports of the death of herdsman after herdsman, on the night of Christmas-eve, were spread abroad, the greater became the difficulty the farmer found in hiring one, although it was never supposed for an instant that violence was used towards the men, as no mark had ever been found on their bodies; and as, moreover, there was no one to suspect. At length the farmer declared that his conscience would no longer let him thus hire men only in order that they might die, so he determined in future to let luck take care of his sheep, or the sheep take care of themselves.

Not long after he had made this determination, a bold and hardy-looking man came to him and made him a proffer of his services. The farmer said:

"My good friend, I am not in so great need of your services as to hire you."

Then the man asked him, "Have you, then, taken a herdsman for this winter?"

The farmer said, "No; for I suppose you know what a terrible fate has hitherto befallen every one I have hired."

"I have heard of it," said the other, "but the fear of it shall neither trouble me nor prevent my keeping your sheep this winter for you, if you will but make up your mind to take me."

But the farmer would not hear of it at first; "For," said he, "it is a pity, indeed, that so fine a fellow as you should lose your chance of life. Begone, if you are wise, and get work elsewhere."

Yet still the man declared, again and again, that he cared not a whit for the terrors of Christmas-eve, and still urged the farmer to hire him.

At length the farmer consented, in answer to the man's urgent prayer, to take him as herdsman; and very well they got along together. For everyone, both high and low, liked the man, as he was honest and open, zealous in everything he laid his hands to, and willing to do anyone a good turn, if need were.

On Christmas-eve, towards nightfall, the farmer and all his family went (as has been before declared to be the custom) to church, except Hildur, who remained behind to look after household matters, and the herdsman, who could not leave his sheep in time. Late in the evening, the latter as usual returned home, and after having eaten his supper, went to bed. As soon as he was well between the sheets, the remembrance struck him of what had befallen all the former herdsmen in his position on the same evening, and he thought it would be the best plan for him to lie awake and thus to be ready for any accident, though he was mighty little troubled with fear. Quite late at night, he heard the farmer and his family return from church, enter the house, and having taken supper, go to bed. Still, nothing happened, except that whenever he closed his eyes for a moment, a strange and deadly faintness stole over him, which only acted as one reason the more for his doing his best to keep awake.

Shortly after he had become aware of these feelings, he heard some one creep stealthily up to the side of his bed, and looking through the gloom at the figure, fancied he recognized Hildur the housekeeper. So he feigned to be fast asleep, and felt her place something in his mouth, which he knew instantly to be the bit of a magic bridle, but yet allowed her to fix it on him, without moving. When she had fastened the bridle, she dragged him from his bed with it, and out of the farmhouse, without his being either able or willing to make the least resistance. Then mounting on his back, she made him rise from the ground as if on wings, and rode him through the air, till they arrived at a huge and awful precipice, which yawned, like a great well, down into the earth.

She dismounted at a large stone, and fastening the reins to it, leaped into the precipice. But the herdsman, objecting strongly to being tied to this stone all night, and thinking to himself that it would be no bad thing to know what became of the woman, tried to escape, bridle and all, from the stone. This he found, however, to be impossible, for as long as the bit was in his mouth, he was quite powerless to get away. So he managed, after a short struggle, to get the bridle off his head, and having so done, leapt into the precipice, down which he had seen Hildur disappear. After sinking for a long, long time, he caught a glimpse of Hildur beneath him, and at last they came to some beautiful green meadows.

From all this, the man guessed that Hildur was by no means a common mortal, as she had before made believe to be, and feared if he were to follow her along these green fields, and she turn round and catch sight of him, he might, not unlikely, pay for his curiosity with his life. So he took a magic stone which he always carried about him, the nature of which was to make him invisible when he held it in his palm, and placing it in the hollow of his hand, ran after her with all his strength.

When they had gone some way along the meadows, a splendid palace rose before them, with the way to which Hildur seemed perfectly well acquainted. At her approach a great crowd of people came forth from the doors, and saluted Hildur with respect and joy. Foremost of these walked a man of kingly and noble aspect, whose salutation seemed to be that of a lover or a husband: all the rest bowed to her as if she were their queen. This man was accompanied by two children, who ran up to Hildur, calling her mother, and embraced her. After the people had welcomed their queen, they all returned to the palace, where they dressed her in royal robes, and loaded her hands with costly rings and bracelets.

The herdsman followed the crowd, and posted himself where he would be least in the way of the company, but where he could catch sight easily of all that passed, and lose nothing. So gorgeous and dazzling were the hangings of the hall, and the silver and golden vessels on the table, that he thought he had never, in all his life before, seen the like; not to mention the wonderful dishes and wines which seemed plentiful there, and which, only by the look of them, filled his mouth with water, while he would much rather have filled it with something else.

After he had waited a little time, Hildur appeared in the hall, and all the assembled guests were begged to take their seats, while Hildur sat on her throne beside the king; after which all the people of the court ranged themselves on each side of the royal couple, and the feast commenced.

When it was concluded, the various guests amused themselves, some by dancing, some by singing, others by drinking and revel; but the king and queen talked together, and seemed to the herdsman to be very sad.

While they were thus conversing, three children, younger than those the man had seen before, ran in, and clung round the neck of their mother. Hildur received them with all a mother's love, and, as the youngest was restless, put it on the ground and gave it one of her rings to play with.

After the little one had played a while with the ring he lost it, and it rolled along the floor towards the herdsman, who, being invisible, picked it up without being perceived, and put it carefully into his pocket. Of course all search for it by the guests was in vain.

When the night was far advanced, Hildur made preparations for departure, at which all the people assembled showed great sorrow, and begged her to remain longer.

The herdsman had observed, that in one corner of the hall sat an old and ugly woman, who had neither received the queen with joy nor pressed her to stay longer.

As soon as the king perceived that Hildur addressed herself to her journey, and that neither his entreaties nor those of the assembly could induce her to stay, he went up to the old woman, and said to her:

"Mother, rid us now of thy curse; cause no longer my queen to live apart and afar from me. Surely her short and rare visits are more pain to me than joy."

The old woman answered him with a wrathful face.

"Never will I depart from what I have said. My words shall hold true in all their force, and on no condition will I abolish my curse."

On this the king turned from her, and going up to his wife, entreated her in the fondest and most loving terms not to depart from him.

The queen answered, "The infernal power of thy mother's curse forces me to go, and perchance this may be the last time that I shall see thee. For lying, as I do, under this horrible ban, it is not possible that my constant murders can remain much longer secret, and then I must suffer the full penalty of crimes which I have committed against my will."

While she was thus speaking the herdsman sped from the palace and across the fields to the precipice, up which he mounted as rapidly as he had come down, thanks to the magic stone.

When he arrived at the rock he put the stone into his pocket, and the bridle over his head again, and awaited the coming of the elf-queen. He had not long to wait, for very soon afterwards Hildur came up through the abyss, and mounted on his back, and off they flew again to the farmhouse, where Hildur, taking the bridle from his head, placed him again in his bed, and retired to her own. The herdsman, who by this time was well tired out, now considered it safe to go to sleep, which he did, so soundly as not to wake till quite late on Christmas-morning.

Early that same day the farmer rose, agitated and filled with the fear that, instead of passing Christmas in joy, he should assuredly, as he so often had before, find his herdsman dead, and pass it in sorrow and mourning. So he and all the rest of the family went to the bedside of the herdsman.

When the farmer had looked at him and found him breathing, he praised God aloud for his mercy in preserving the man from death.

Not long afterwards the man himself awoke and got up.

Wondering at his strange preservation the farmer asked him how he had passed the night, and whether he had seen or heard anything.

The man replied, "No; but I have had a very curious dream."

"What was it?" asked the farmer.

Upon which the man related everything that has passed in the night, circumstance for circumstance, and word for word, as well as he could remember. When he had finished his story every one was silent for wonder, except Hildur, who went up to him and said:

"I declare you to be a liar in all that you have said, unless you can prove it by sure evidence."

Not in the least abashed, the herdsman took from his pocket the ring which he had picked up on the floor of the hall in Elf-land, and showing it to her said:

"Though my dream needs no proof, yet here is one you will not doubtless deem other than a sure one; for is not this your gold ring, Queen Hildur?"

Hildur answered, "It is, no doubt, my ring. Happy man! may you prosper in all you undertake, for you have released me from the awful yoke which my mother-in-law laid, in her wrath, upon me, and from the curse of a yearly murder."

And then Hildur told them the story of her life as follows:—

"I was born of an obscure family among the elves. Our king fell in love with me and married me, in spite of the strong disapproval of his mother. She swore eternal hatred to me in her anger against her son, and said to him, 'Short shall be your joy with this fair wife of yours, for you shall see her but once a year, and that only at the expense of a murder. This is my curse upon her, and it shall be carried out to the letter. She shall go and serve in the upper world, this queen, and every Christmas-eve shall ride a man, one of her fellow-servants, with this magic bridle, to the confines of Elf-land, where she shall pass a few hours with you, and then ride him back again till his very heart breaks with toil, and his very life leaves him. Let her thus enjoy her queenship.'

"And this horrible fate was to cling to me until I should either have these murders brought home to me, and be condemned to death, or should meet with a gallant man, like this herdsman, who should have nerve and courage to follow me down into Elf-land, and be able to prove afterwards that he had been there with me, and seen the customs of my people. And now I must confess that all the former herdsmen were slain by me, but no penalty shall touch me for their murders, as I committed them against my will. And as for you, O courageous man, who have dared, the first of human beings, to explore the realms of Elf-land, and have freed me from the yoke of this awful curse, I will reward you in times to come, but not now.

"A deep longing for my home and my loved ones impels me hence. Farewell!"

With these words Hildur vanished from the sight of the astonished people, and was never seen again.

But our friend the herdsman, leaving the service of the farmer, built a farm for himself, and prospered, and became one of the chief men in the country, and always ascribed, with grateful thanks, his prosperity to Hildur, Queen of the Elves.

# THE MAN-SERVANT AND THE WATER-ELVES

IN A large house, where all the chief rooms were panelled, there lived, once upon a time, a farmer, whose ill fate it was that every servant of his that was left alone to guard the house on the night of Christmas-eve, while the rest of the family went to church, was found dead when the family returned home. As soon as the report of this was spread abroad, the farmer had the greatest difficulty in procuring servants who would consent to watch alone in the house on that night; until at last one day a man, a strong fellow, offered him his services to sit up alone and guard the house. The farmer told him what fate awaited him for his rashness, but the man despised such a fear, and persisted in his determination.

On Christmas-eve, when the farmer and all his family, except the new man-servant, were preparing for church, the farmer said to him:

"Come with us to church; I cannot leave you here to die."

But the other replied, "I intend to stay here, for it would be unwise in you to leave your house unprotected; and, besides, the cattle and sheep must have their food at the proper time."

"Never mind the beasts," answered the farmer. "Do not be so rash as to remain in the house this night, for whenever we have returned from church on this night, we have always found every living thing in this house dead, with all its bones broken."

But the man was not to be persuaded, as he considered all these fears beneath his notice; so the farmer and the rest of the servants went away and left him behind, alone in the house.

As soon as he was by himself, he began to consider how to guard against anything that might occur, for a dread had stolen over him, in spite of his courage, that something strange was about to take place. At last he thought that the best thing to do was, first of all to light up the family room, and then to find some place in which to hide himself. As soon as he had lighted all the candles, he moved two planks out of the wainscot at the end of the room, and, creeping into the space between it and the wall, restored the planks to their places, so that he could see plainly into the room, and yet avoid being himself discovered.

He had scarcely finished concealing himself, when two fierce and strange-looking men entered the room and began looking about.

One of them said, "I smell a human being."

"No," replied the other, "there is no human being here."

Then they took a candle and continued their search, until they found the man's dog asleep under one of the beds. They took it up, and, having dashed it on the ground till every bone in its body was broken, hurled it from them. When the man-servant saw this, he congratulated himself on not having fallen into their hands.

Suddenly the room was filled with people, who were laden with tables and all kinds of table furniture, silver, cloths, and all, which they spread out, and having done so, sat down to a rich supper, which they had also brought with them. They feasted noisily, and spent the remainder of the night in drinking and dancing. Two of them were appointed to keep guard, in order to give the company due warning of the approach either of anybody, or of the day. Three times they went out, always returning with the news that they saw neither the approach of any human being, nor yet of the break of day.

But when the man-servant suspected the night to be pretty far spent, he jumped from his place of concealment into the room, and clashing the two planks together with as much noise as he could make, shouted like a madman:

"The day! the day! the day!"

On these words the whole company rose scared from their seats, and rushed headlong out, leaving behind them not only their tables and all the silver dishes, but even the very clothes they had taken off for ease in dancing. In the hurry of flight many were wounded and trodden under foot, while the rest ran into the darkness, the man-servant after them, clapping the planks together, and shrieking, "The day! the day! the day!" until they came to a large lake, into which the whole party plunged headlong and disappeared.

From this, the man knew them to be water-elves.

Then he returned home, cleaned up the house and took possession of all the treasures the elves had left behind them.

On the farmer's return, his servant told him all that had occurred, and showed him the spoils. The farmer praised him for a brave fellow, and congratulated him on having escaped with his life. The man gave him half the treasures of the elves, and ever afterwards prospered exceedingly.

This was the last visit the water-elves ever paid to *that* house.


# THE CROSSWAYS


IT IS supposed that among the hills there are certain cross-roads from the centre of which you can see four churches, one at the end of each road.

If you sit at the crossing of these roads, on Christmas-eve (or as others say, on New Year's-eve), elves come from every direction and cluster round you, and ask you, with all sorts of blandishments and fair promises, to go with them; but you must continue silent. Then they bring to you rarities and delicacies of every description, gold, silver, and precious stones, meats and wines, of which they beg you to accept; but you must neither move a limb nor accept a single thing they offer you. If you get so far as this without speaking, elfwomen come to you in the likeness of your mother, your sister, or any other relation, and beg you to come with them, using every art and entreaty; but beware you neither move nor speak. And if you can continue to keep silent and motionless all the night, until you see the first streak of dawn, then start up, and cry aloud:

"Praise be to God! His daylight filleth the heavens!"

As soon as you have said this, the elves will leave you, and with you, all the wealth they have used to entice you, which will now be yours.

But should you either answer, or accept of their offers, you will from that moment become mad.

On the night of one Christmas-eve, a man named Fusi was out on the cross-roads, and managed to resist all the entreaties and proffers of the elves, until one of them offered him a large lump of mutton-suet, and begged him to take a bite of it. Fusi, who had up to this time gallantly resisted all such offers as gold and silver and diamonds, and such filthy lucre, could hold out no longer, and crying, "Seldom have I refused a bite of mutton-suet," he went mad.

# STORIES OF WATER-MONSTERS

## THE MERMAN

LONG AGO a farmer lived at Vogar, who was a mighty fisherman, and, of all the farms round about, not one was so well situated with regard to the fisheries as his.

One day, according to custom, he had gone out fishing, and having cast down his line from the boat, and waited awhile, found it very hard to pull up again, as if there were something very heavy at the end of it. Imagine his astonishment when he found that what he had caught was a great fish, with a man's head and body! When he saw that this creature was alive, he addressed it and said, "Who and whence are you?"

"A merman from the bottom of the sea," was the reply.

The farmer then asked him what he had been doing when the hook caught his flesh.

The other replied, "I was turning the cowl of my mother's chimney-pot, to suit it to the wind. So let me go again, will you?"

"Not for the present," said the fisherman. "You shall serve me awhile first."

So without more words he dragged him into the boat and rowed to shore with him.

When they got to the boat-house, the fisherman's dog came to him and greeted him joyfully, barking and fawning on him, and wagging his tail. But his master's temper being none of the best, he struck the poor animal; whereupon the merman laughed for the first time.

Having fastened the boat, he went towards his house, dragging his prize with him, over the fields, and stumbling over a hillock, which lay in his way, cursed it heartily; whereupon the merman laughed for the second time.

When the fisherman arrived at the farm, his wife came out to receive him, and embraced him affectionately, and he received her salutations with pleasure; whereupon the merman laughed for the third time.

Then said the farmer to the merman, "You have laughed three times, and I am curious to know *why* you have laughed. Tell me, therefore."

"Never will I tell you," replied the merman, "unless you promise to take me to the same place in the sea wherefrom you caught me, and there to let me go free again." So the farmer made him the promise.

"Well," said the merman, "I laughed the first time because you struck your dog, whose joy at meeting you was real and sincere. The second time, because you cursed the mound over which you stumbled, which is full of golden ducats. And the third time, because you received with pleasure your wife's empty and flattering embrace, who is faithless to you, and a hypocrite. And now be an honest man and take me out to the sea whence you have brought me.'

The farmer replied: "Two things that you have told me I have no means of proving, namely, the faithfulness of my dog and the faithlessness of my wife. But the third I will try the truth of, and if the hillock contain gold, then I will believe the rest."

Accordingly he went to the hillock, and having dug it up, found therein a great treasure of golden ducats, as the merman had told him. After this the farmer took the merman down to the boat, and to that place in the sea whence he had caught him. Before he put him in, the latter said to him:

"Farmer, you have been an honest man, and I will reward you for restoring me to my mother, if only you have skill enough to take possession of property that I shall throw in your way. Be happy and prosper."

Then the farmer put the merman into the sea, and he sank out of sight.

It happened that not long after, seven sea-grey cows were seen on the beach, close to the farmer's land. These cows appeared to be very unruly, and ran away directly the farmer approached them. So he took a stick and ran after them, possessed with the fancy that if he could burst the bladder which he saw on the nose of each of them, they would belong to him. He contrived to hit out the bladder on the nose of one cow, which then became so tame that he could easily catch it, while the others leaped into the sea and disappeared. The farmer was convinced that this was the gift of the merman. And a very useful gift it was, for better cow was never seen nor milked in all the land, and she was the mother of the race of grey cows so much esteemed now.

And the farmer prospered exceedingly, but never caught any more merman. As for his wife, nothing further is told about her, so we can repeat nothing.

# NENNIR, OR THE ONE WHO
# FEELS INCLINED

THERE WAS once a girl who had been charged by her master to look after some ewes which were lost. She had gone a long way after them, until she was quite tired, when suddenly she saw before her a grey horse. Much delighted at this, she went up to it and bound her garter into its mouth for a bridle, but just as she was going to mount she said, "I feel afraid, I am half-inclined not to mount this horse." As soon as the animal heard these words it leaped into some water that stood near, and disappeared.

Then the girl saw that this was a river-horse.

Now the nature of this animal is that it cannot bear to hear its own name "Nennir, or the one who feels inclined," which is the reason why it jumped into the water when the girl said, "I feel afraid, I am half-inclined not to mount this horse."

The same is the effect on the river-horse if it hears the name of the devil.

Listen to another story.

Three children were playing together on the shingly bank of a river, when they saw a grey horse standing near them and went up to it to look at it. One of the children mounted on its back and after him another, to have a ride for pleasure, and only the eldest one was left. They asked him to follow, "for," they said, "the horse's back is surely long enough for all three of us."

But the child refused, and said, "I do not feel inclined." No sooner were the words out of his mouth, than the horse leaped into the river with the two other children, who were both drowned, while only the eldest survived to tell us this story of Nennir the grey river-horse.


# THE LAKE-MONSTER

IN THE last century a man lived in the north country, called Kolbeinn, who was very poor. But everybody liked him for his good heart, and treated him with kindness.

Once, on the day before Christmas-eve, late at night, he went over the lake of Vesturhóp, which was frozen, to beg some food for the next day, from one of the farmers on the other side. The farmer gave him a smoked carcase of mutton, with which Kilbeinn returned joyfully homewards.

When he was about the middle of the lake, he heard a noise behind him, and turning round saw the ice crack and a monster rise from it, having eight feet, and looking like two horses joined by their tails, with their heads facing opposite ways. This monster ran after Kilbeinn, who saw no chance of escape, so he dropped the carcase of mutton and took to his heels with all the speed he could muster.

Next morning he went out again on to the ice to see how much might be left of his mutton, but only found a few chewed bones. He took some of his neighbours to look at these bones, and they pitied him so much that they soon made up his loss to him.

# NADDI

IN ANCIENT times there was a main road from Njardvik, to Borgar-fjördur, which passed over a very steep mountain, sloping down to the sea. But this road became unfrequented because a monster, half-man, half-beast, took up his abode upon it, and after nightfall used to destroy so many travellers that the way was at length considered impassable. This creature hid itself in a rocky gulf on the sea-side of the mountains, which has since been called the gulf of Naddi. This name arose from the fact that as people passed, a strange rattling was heard among the stones at the bottom.

It happened once, in autumn, that a certain man stopped at a farm in the neighbourhood, who intended late in the evening to cross this part of the mountain, and was not to be dissuaded from his determination by the entreaties of the farmer and his family. So he started off with the words "as long as I fear nothing, nothing can harm me."

When he came to the gulf he met with the monster, and at once attacked it, and they had a long and fearful struggle together. In their fight they came together to the verge of a precipice which has been since called Krossjadar. Over this the man hurled the monster. Afterwards upon this very spot was raised a cross, with this inscription:—

"Effigiem Christi, qui prodis, pronus honora."

The man came to Njardvík, black and blue with his struggle, and, after having kept his bed for a month, recovered.

Never was this fearful sea-monster seen after it had been vanquished by a human being. The man soon forgot his bruises in the glory of having rid his country of such a plague.

# STORIES OF TROLLS

## TROLL'S STONE

IN THE neighbourhood of Kirkjubœr, in Hróarstúnga, stand some curious rocks under which is a cave. In this cave, ages ago, dwelt a troll named Thórir, with his wife. Every year, these trolls contrived to entice into their clutches, by magic arts, either the priest or the herdsmen, from Kirkjubœr, and thus matters went on until a priest arrived at the place, named Eiríkur, a spiritual man, who was able by his prayers to protect both himself and his herdsmen from the magic spells of this worthy couple.

One Christmas-eve, the female troll had tried her incantations quite in vain, and went to her husband, saying, "I have tried my utmost to entice the priest or the herdsman, but to no purpose, for, as soon as ever I begin my spells, a hot wind blows upon me which forces me by the scorching heat to desist, as if it would consume all my joints. So you must go and procure something for our Christmas dinner, as we have nothing left to eat in the cave."

The giant expressed great unwillingness to trouble himself, being rather lazy, but was at length compelled to go, by the entreaties of his wife, and accordingly marched off to a lake in the neighbourhood which since was called by his name. There he broke a hole through the ice, and lying down on his face, cast in a line and caught trout. When he thought he had caught enough for the Christmas dinner, he wanted to get up again, in order to take them home; but the frost had been so hard while he was intent upon his fishing that it had frozen him tight to the ice, so that he could not rise from it. He struggled desperately to escape, but in vain, and the frost seized upon his heart and killed him where he lay.

The female troll finding her husband rather long in returning, and becoming very hungry, sallied out in search of him, and discovered him lying dead upon the ice. She ran to him and tried to tear his body up from the ice, but failing in this, seized the string of trout, and placing it over her shoulder started off.

Before she went, she said, "A curse on thee, thou wicked lake! Never shall a living fish be caught in thee again."

Which words have indeed proved fatal to the fishery, for the lake since then has never yielded a single fish.

Then she went back homewards with great strides. As she came, however, to the edge of the neighbouring hill, she saw the day-break in the east, and heard from the south the sound of the Kirkjubœr church-bells (two things, which, as everyone knows, are fatal to trolls), upon which she was instantly changed into the rock which now bears the name of Troll's Stone.

# GELLIVÖR

NEAR THE end of the Roman Catholic times, a certain married couple lived at a farm named Hvoll, situated on a firth (river estuary) in the east part of the country. The farmer was well to do, and wealthy in sheep and cattle. It was commonly reported that a female troll lived on the south side of the firth, who was supposed to be mild and not given to mischief.

One Christmas-eve, after dark, the farmer went out and never returned again, and all search for him was in vain. After the man's disappearance one of the servants took the management of the farm, but was lost in the same manner, after dark on the Christmas-eve following. After this the widow of the farmer determined to remove all her goods from the house and live elsewhere for the winter, leaving only the sheep and herds under the charge of shepherds, and returning to pass the summer there. As soon as the winter approached she made preparations for leaving Hvoll, until the next spring, and set the herdsmen to take care of the sheep and cattle, and feed them during the cold season.

For home-use she always kept four cows, one of which had just had a calf.

Two days before her intended departure, a woman came to her in her dreams, who was dressed in an old-fashioned dress of poor appearance. The stranger addressed her with these words: "Your cow has just calved, and I have no hope of getting nourishment for my children, unless you will every day, when you deal out the rations, put a share for me in a jug in the dairy. I know that your intention is to move to another farm in two days, as you dare not live here over Christmas, for you know not what has become of your husband and of the servant, on the last two Christmas-eves. But I must tell you that a female troll lives in the opposite mountains, herself of mild temper, but who, two years ago, had a child of such curious appetite and disposition, that she was forced to provide fresh human flesh for it each Christmas. If, however, you will do willingly for me what I have asked you to do, I will give you good advice as to how you may get rid of the troll from this neighbourhood."

With these words the woman vanished. When the widow awoke she remembered her dream, and getting up, went to the dairy, where she filled a wooden jug with new milk and placed it on the appointed spot. No sooner had she done so than it disappeared. The next evening the jug stood again in the same place, and so matters went on till Christmas.

On Christmas-eve she dreamt again that the woman came to her with a friendly salutation, and said, "Surely you are not inquisitive, for you have not yet asked to whom you give milk every day. I will tell you. I am an elfwoman, and live in the little hill near your house. You have treated me well all through the winter, but henceforth I will ask you no more for milk, as my cow had yesterday a calf. And now you must accept the little gift which you will find on the shelf where you have been accustomed to place the jug for me; and I intend, also, to deliver you from the danger which awaits you to-morrow night. At midnight you will awake and feel yourself irresistibly urged to go out, as if something attracted you; do not struggle against it, but get up and leave the house. Outside the door you will find a giantess standing, who will seize you and carry you in her arms across your grass-field, stride over the river, and make off with you in the direction of the mountains in which she lives. When she has carried you a little way from the river, you must cry, 'What did I hear then?' and she will immediately ask you, 'What did you hear?' You must answer, 'I heard some one cry, "Mamma Gellivör, Mamma Gellivör!" ' which she will think very extraordinary, for she knows that no mortal ever yet heard her name. She will say, 'Oh, I suppose it is that naughty child of mine,' and will put you down and run to the mountains. But in the meantime, while she is engaged with you, I will be in the mountain and will thump and pinch her child without mercy. Directly she has left you, turn your back upon the mountain and run as fast as you possibly can towards the nearest farm along the river banks. When the troll comes back and overtakes you, she will say, 'Why did you not stand still, you wretch?' and will take you again in her arms and stride away with you. As soon as you have gone a little way you must cry again, 'What did I hear then?' She will ask as at first, 'What did you hear?' Then you shall reply again, 'I thought I heard some one calling "Mamma Gellivör, Mamma Gellivör!" ' on which she will fling you down as before, and run towards the mountain. And now you must make all speed to reach the nearest church before she can catch you again, for if she succeeds in doing so she will treat you horribly in her fury at finding that I have pinched and thumped her child to death. If, however, you fail in getting to the church in time, I will help you."

When, after this dream, the widow awoke, the day had dawned, so she got up and went to the shelf upon which the jug was wont to stand. Here she found a large bundle, which contained a handsome dress and girdle, and cap, all beautifully embroidered.

About midnight on Christmas-day, when all the rest of the farm people at Hvoll were asleep, the widow felt an irresistible desire to go out, as the elfwoman had warned her, and she did so. Directly she had passed the threshold, she felt herself seized and lifted high in the air by the arms of the gigantic troll, who stalked off with her over the river and towards the mountain. Everything turned out exactly as the elf had foretold, until the giantess flung down her burden for the second time, and the widow made speed to reach the church. On the way, it seemed to her as if some one took hold of her arms and helped her along. Suddenly she heard the sound of a tremendous land-slip on the troll's mountain, and turning round saw in the clear moonlight the giantess striding furiously towards her over the morasses. At this sight she would have fainted with fear, had not she felt herself lifted from the ground and hurried through the air into the church, the door of which closed immediately behind her. It happened that the priests were about to celebrate early mass, and all the people were assembled. Directly after she came into the church the bells began to ring, and the congregation heard the sound of some heavy fall outside. Looking from one of the windows they saw the troll hurry away from the noise of the bells, and, in her flight, stumble over the wall of the churchyard, part of which fell. Then the troll said to it. "Never stand again," and hurrying away took up her abode in another mountain beyond the confines of the parish of Hvoll.

# THE SHEPHERDESS

ONCE UPON a time, in Dalasyslu, a little shepherdess went to church and took the sacrament. When she left the church, instead of going home to dinner, she went to look after her ewes. As she was passing some rocks, she heard a voice from one of them say:

"Ragnhildur in the Red rock!"

Then a voice from the opposite side answered:

"What is the matter, O giant, in the triple rocks?"

"There is a tender little steer running along the road; let us take her; let us eat her."

"Faugh," replied the other, "leave her alone; she looks as if she had been chewing coals."

So the little girl ran away as fast as she could, and heard no more about it.

# JÓRA THE TROLL

A FARMER'S daughter, young and hopeful, but gifted with a fearful temper, acted as housekeeper to her father. Her name was Jóra.

One day it happened that a horse-fight was held near the farm at which she lived, and one of the combatants was a horse of her father's, of which she was very fond. She was present at the fight, together with many other women; but at the commencement she saw that her favourite horse was getting the worst of it. So she jumped furiously down from her seat, and running up to the victor, seized one of its hind-legs and tore it off. Then she ran off with the leg so quickly, that nobody could catch her. When she came to the river Ólfusá, where it forms in a deep gulf a waterfall called Laxfoss, she seized a large rock from the wall of the abyss, and hurling it into the middle of the fall, used it as a stepping-stone, and leaped over, with these words—

> "Here is a jump for a maiden like me,
> Though soon comes the time when a wife I shall be."

Ever after this, that passage of the river has been called "Troll's-leap."

From this place she ran on for a long way, till she came to a mountain called Heingill, where she took up her abode in a cave (since called "Jóra's Cave"), and became the most malignant troll possible: killing man and beast without mercy. She used to sit on a high peak, which has since been called "Jóra's-seat," and from this eminence looked out for passers-by in all directions; and if she saw one, killed him and ate him up. At last, nearly the whole neighbourhood had fallen victims to her, and the roads became void, except when, from time to time, large troops of people came, with the vain idea of destroying her.

In this state of affairs, when no means could be found of destroying this wicked troll, a young man, who had been a sailor, went to the King of Norway, and told him of this monster who lived in the Mountain Heingill, at the same time asking his advice how to overcome her.

The king answered, "You must attack Jóra at sunrise on Whit-Sunday; for there is no monster, however fearful, and no troll, however strong, that is not fast asleep at that time. You will find her sleeping with her face to the ground. Here is an axe of silver, which I will give you. With this you must make a chop between her shoulder-bones. Then Jóra, feeling the pain, will turn and say to you, 'May your hands grow to the handle.' But you must instantly answer—'Blade, leave the handle.' Then she will roll down into a lake near the foot of the peak, and be drowned."

With these words he dismissed the young man, who returned to the Heingill, and did as the King of Norway had told him, and killed Jóra.

So that was the end of Jóra the Troll.

# KATLA

ONCE IT happened that the Abbot of the Monastery of Thykkvabœ had a housekeeper whose name was Katla, and who was an evil-minded and hot-tempered woman. She possessed a pair of shoes whose peculiarity was, that whoever put them on was never tired of running. Every body was afraid of Katla's bad disposition and fierce temper, even the Abbot himself. The herdsman of the monastery farm, whose name was Bardi, was often dreadfully ill-treated by her, particularly if he had chanced to lose any of the ewes.

One day in the autumn the Abbot and his housekeeper went to a wedding, leaving orders with Bardi to drive in the sheep and milk them before they came home. But unhappily, when the time came, the herdsman could not find all the ewes; so he went into the house, put on Katla's magic shoes, and sallied out in search of the stray sheep. He had a long way to run before he discovered them, but felt no fatigue, so drove all the flock in quite briskly.

When Katla returned, she immediately perceived that the herdsman had been using her shoes, so she took him and drowned him in a large tubful of curds. Nobody knew what had become of the man, and as the winter went on, and the curds in the tub sank lower and lower, Katla was heard to say these words to herself: "Soon will the waves of milk break upon the foot-soles of Bardi!"

Shortly after this, dreading that the murder should be found out, and that she would be condemned to death, she took her magic shoes, and ran from the monastery to a great ice-mountain, into a rift of which she leaped, and was never seen again.

As soon as she had disappeared, a fearful eruption took place from the mountain, and the lava rolled down and destroyed the monastery at which she had lived. People declared that her witchcraft had been the cause of this, and called the crater of the mountain "The Rift of Katla."

# OLAFUR AND THE TROLLS

SOME PEOPLE who lived in the south part of the country, at Biskupstúngur, once went into the forest to cut wood for charcoal, and took with them a young lad to hold their horses. While he was left to look after the animals he disappeared, and, though they searched in every direction for him, they failed in finding him.

After three years had passed, the same people were cutting wood in exactly the same place, when the lost boy Olafur came running to them. They asked him where he had been all this time, and how he had gone away.

He said, "While I was looking after the horses, and had strolled a short distance from them, I suddenly met a gigantic troll-woman, who came rushing towards me and seized me in her arms, and ran off with me until she came into the heart of the wilderness to some great rocks. In these rocks was her cave, into which she carried me. When I was there I saw another giantess coming towards me, of younger appearance than the former, but both were immensely tall. They were dressed in tunics of horse-leather, falling to their feet in front, but very short behind. Here they kept me, and fed me with trout, which one was always out catching, while the other watched me. During the night they forced me to sleep between them on their bed of horse-skins. Sometimes they used to lull me to sleep by singing magical songs in my ears, so that I was enchanted by wonderful dreams. They both were very kind to me, and watched me carefully lest I should wish to escape from them. One day when I had been left alone, I was standing outside the cave, and saw, on the other side of the wilderness, the smoke of the charcoal-burners; so, as I knew that neither of the trolls was at home, I ran off in the direction of the smoke. But I had gone very few paces when one of the trolls saw me, and, running after me, struck me on the cheek, so that I have never lost the bruise, and seizing me in her arms, took me back again to the cave. After this, they looked after me diligently enough.

"Once the younger troll said to the elder, 'How is it that whenever I touch the bare cheek of Olafur, it seems to burn me like fire?'

"The other replied, 'Do not wonder at that; it is on account of the prayer which Oddur the wry-faced* has taught him.'

*So called by the troll, as he was a bishop and good Christian, two equally abominable qualities in the eyes of a troll.

"In this way I passed three years; and when I knew that the season for charcoal-burning was come, and that there would be people on the other side of the wilderness assembled for the purpose, I pretended that I was sick, and could not eat any food. They tried every means in their power to cure me, but all in vain, I only became worse.

"Once they asked me whether I could not mention any delicacy for which I had a fancy.

"I said, 'No, except it were shark-flesh, which had been dried in the wind for nine years.'

"The elder one said, 'This will be very difficult to get you, for it is not to be found anywhere in the whole country, but at one farmer's house in the west, Ögur. At any rate, I will try to get it.'

"Then she strode off in search of it. Directly I saw that she was gone, and that the younger troll was busily engaged in catching trout, I took to my heels, and never ceased running towards the smoke of the charcoal-fires until I arrived here safely."

When they had heard his story, the burners mounted their horses and took Olafur as speedily as possible to Skálholt. On the way, when they had just crossed the Brúará, whom should they meet but the ugly old troll herself, who came tearing down the rocks towards them, and crying, "Aha! there you are, you wretch!"

Olafur, at the sound of her voice, went mad, and tried to break away from the men, so that it was all they could do to hold him back.

Then the troll seized hold of a horse which stood near her on the rocks, and tearing it asunder, threw the pieces over her shoulder in her fury, and ran back to her cave.

When the news arrived at Skálholt, they took Olafur to the bishop, who kept him by him for a few days, and then sent him into the east part of the country, out of the reach of the trolls, having cured him of his madness.


# THE TROLL IN THE SKRÚDUR


Long ago, the priest's daughter at Hólmar, near the Reidarfjördur, was lost from her father's house, and though search was made for her in all directions, both by sea and land, was not found again.

At the mouth of the Reidarfjördur there is a high rocky island called Skrúdur, upon which the priest used to graze his sheep, from the end of the autumn till the spring. But after he had lost his daughter, it happened that every winter, for several years, his best wethers always disappeared.

Once, in the winter, some fishermen were caught in a storm at sea, and were compelled to take shelter under this rocky island. When they had fastened their boats, they sat down near the beach, drenched as they

THE TROLL IN THE SKRÚDUR

were, and to while away the time, sang songs about the Virgin Mary,—when suddenly the rock opened, and a gigantic hand came out, with a ring on each finger, and the arm clad in a scarlet velvet sleeve, which thrust down towards them a large bowl full of porridge, with as many spoons in it as there were fishermen.

At the same time they heard a voice saying, "My wife is pleased now, but not I."

When the men had eaten the porridge, the bowl disappeared into the rock in the same way as it had appeared. The next day the storm had abated, and they rowed safely to the main land.

At the same season in the year following, the fishermen were again driven to seek shelter on this island by violent winds; and while they sat near the beach, they amused themselves by singing songs about Andri the Hero; when the same hand appeared from the rock, holding out to them a great dish full of fat smoked mutton, and they heard these words, "Now am I pleased, but not my wife."

So the fishermen ate the meat, and the dish was taken back into the rock. Soon afterwards the wind fell, and they were enabled to row safely to shore.

Some years passed away, until Bishop Gudmundur visited that part of his diocese, in order to bind the malignant monsters in rocks and waters and mountains, by his prayers. When he came to Hólmar, he was asked by the priest to consecrate the island Skrúdur; but the same night, the bishop had a dream, in which a tall and splendidly dressed man came to him and said, "Do not obey the priest's injunction, nor consecrate Skrúdur, for it will be very difficult for me to move away with all my chattels before your arrival. Besides this, I may as well tell you, that if you come out to visit that island, it will be your last journey in this life." So the bishop refused, on the morrow, to consecrate the island at all, and the troll was left in peace.

# THE SHEPHERD OF SILFRÚNARSTADIR

A MAN named Gudmundur lived once upon a time at a farm called Silfrünarstadir, in the bay of Skagafjördur. He was very rich in flocks, and looked upon by his neighbours as a man of high esteem and respectability. He was married, but had no children.

It happened one Christmas-eve, at Silfrünarstadir, that the herdsman did not return home at night, and, as he was not found at the sheep-pens, the farmer caused a diligent search to be made for him all over the country, but quite in vain.

Next spring Gudmundur hired another shepherd, named Grímur, who was tall and strong, and boasted of being able to resist anybody. But the farmer, in spite of the man's boldness and strength, warned him to be careful how he ran risks, and on Christmas-eve bade him drive the sheep early into the pens, and come home to the farm while it was still daylight. But in the evening Grímur did not come, and though search was made far and near for him, was never found. People made all sorts of guesses about the cause of his disappearance, but the farmer was full of grief, and after this could not get any one to act as shepherd for him.

At this time there lived a very poor widow at Sjávarborg, who had several children, of whom the eldest, aged fourteen years, was named Sigurdur.

To this woman the farmer at last applied, and offered her a large sum of money if she would allow her son to act as shepherd for him. Sigurdur was very anxious that his mother should have all this money, and declared himself most willing to undertake the office; so he went with the farmer, and during the summer was most successful in his new situation, and never lost a sheep.

At the end of a certain time the farmer gave Sigurdur a wether, a ewe, and a lamb as a present, with which the youth was much pleased.

Gudmundur became attached to him, and on Christmas-eve begged him to come home from his sheep before sunset.

All day long the boy watched the sheep, and when evening approached, he heard the sound of heavy footsteps on the mountains. Turning round he saw coming towards him a gigantic and terrible troll.

She addressed him, saying, "Good evening, my Sigurdur. I am come to put you into my bag."

Sigurdur answered, "Are you cracked? Do you not see how thin I am? Surely I am not worth your notice. But I have a sheep and a fat lamb here which I will give you for your pot this evening."

So he gave her the sheep and the lamb, which she threw on to her shoulder, and carried off up the mountain again. Then Sigurdur went home, and right glad was the farmer to see him safe, and asked him whether he had seen anything.

"Nothing whatever, out of the common," replied the boy.

After New Year's day the farmer visited the flock, and, on looking over them, missed the sheep and lamb which he had given the youth, and asked him what had become of them. The boy answered that a fox had killed the lamb, and that the wether had fallen into a bog; adding, "I fancy I shall not be very lucky with *my* sheep."

When he heard this, the farmer gave him one ewe and two wethers, and asked him to remain another year in his service. Sigurdur consented to do so.

Next Christmas-eve, Gudmundur begged Sigurdur to be cautious, and not run any risks, for he loved him as his own son.

But the boy answered, "You need not fear, there are no risks to run."

When he had got the sheep into the pens about nightfall, the same troll came to him, and said:

"As sure as ever I am a troll, you shall not, this evening, escape being boiled in my pot."

"I am quite at your service," answered Sigurdur, intrepidly; "but you see that I am still very thin; nothing to be compared even to one wether.

I will give you, however, for your Christmas dinner, two old and two young sheep. Will you condescend to be satisfied with this offer of mine?"

"Let me see," said the troll; so the lad showed her the sheep, and she, hooking them together by their horns, threw them on to her shoulder, and ran off with them up the mountain. Then Sigurdur returned to the farm, and, when questioned, declared, as before, that he had seen nothing whatever unusual upon the mountain.

"But," he said, "I have been dreadfully unlucky with *my* sheep, as I said I should be." Next summer the farmer gave him four more wethers.

When Christmas-eve had come again, just as Sigurdur was putting the sheep into their pens, the troll came to him, and threatened to take him away with her. Then he offered her the four wethers, which she took, and hooking them together by their horns, threw them over her shoulder. Not content with this, however, she seized the lad too, tucked him under her arm, and ran off with her burthen to her cave in the mountains.

Here she flung the sheep down, and Sigurdur after them, and ordered him to kill them and shave their skins. When he had done so, he asked her what task she had now for him to perform.

She said, "Sharpen this axe well, for I intend to cut off your head with it."

When he had sharpened it well, he restored it to the troll, who bade him take off his neckerchief; which he did, without changing a feature of his face.

Then the troll, instead of cutting off his head, flung the axe down on the ground, and said, "Brave lad! I never intended to kill you, and you shall live to a good old age. It was I that caused you to be made herdsman to Gudmundur, for I wished to meet with you. And now I will show you in what way you shall arrive at good-fortune. Next spring you must move from Silfrúnarstadir, and go to the house of a silversmith, to learn his trade. When you have learned it thoroughly, you shall take some specimens of silver-work to the farm where the church dean's three daughters live; and I can tell you that the youngest of them is the most promising maiden in the whole country. Her elder sisters love dress and ornaments, and will admire what you bring them, but Margaret will not care about such things. When you leave the house, you shall ask her to accompany you as far as the door, and then as far as the end of the grass-field, which she will consent to do. Then you shall give her these three precious things—this handkerchief, this belt, and this ring; and after that she will love you. But when you have seen me in a dream you must come here, and you will find me dead. Bury me, and take for yourself everything of value that you find in my cave."

Then Sigurdur bade her farewell and left her, and returned to the farm, where Gudmundur welcomed him with joy, having grieved at his long absence, and asked him whether he had seen nothing.

"No," replied the boy; and declared that he could answer for the safety of all future herdsmen. But no more questions would he answer, though the family asked him many. The following spring he went to a silversmith's house, and in two years made himself master of the trade. He often visited Gudmundur, his old master, and was always welcome. Once he went to the trading town of Hofsós, and buying a variety of glittering silver ornaments, took them to Miklïbœr, and offered them for sale to the dean's daughters, as the troll had told him. When the elder sisters heard that he had ornaments for sale, they begged him to let them see them first, in order that they might choose the best of them. Accordingly he showed them his wares, and they bought many trinkets, but Margaret would not even so much as look at the silver ornaments.

When he took leave, he asked the youngest sister to accompany him as far as the door, and when they got there, to come with him as far as the end of the field. She was much astonished at this request, and asked him what he wanted with her, as she had never seen him before. But Sigurdur entreated her the more the more she held back, and at last she consented to go with him. At the end of the field Sigurdur gave her the belt and handkerchief, and put the ring on to her finger.

This done, Margaret said, "I wish I had never taken these gifts, but I cannot now give them you back."

Sigurdur then took leave and went home. But Margaret, as soon as she had received the presents, fell in love with their giver; and finding after a while that she could not live without him, told her father all about it. Her father bade her desist from such a mad idea, and declared that she should never marry the youth as long as he lived to prevent it. On this Margaret pined away, and became so thin from grief, that the father found he would be obliged to consent to her request; and going to the farm at which Sigurdur lived, engaged him as his silversmith.

Not long after, Sigurdur and Margaret were betrothed.

One day the youth dreamed that he saw the old troll, and felt sure from this that she was dead; so he asked the dean to accompany him as far as Silfrúnarstadir, and sleep there one night. When they arrived there, they told Gudmundur that Sigurdur was betrothed to Margaret. When the farmer heard this, he said that it had long been his intention to leave Sigurdur all his property, and offered him the management of the farm the ensuing spring. The youth thanked him heartily, and the dean was glad to see his daughter so soon, and so well, provided for.

Next day Sigurdur asked the farmer and the dean to go with him as far as the middle of the mountain, where they found a cave into which he bade them enter without fear. Inside they saw the troll lying dead on the floor with her face awfully distorted. Then Sigurdur told them all about his interviews with the troll, and asked them to help him to bury her. When they had done so, they returned to the cave and found there as many precious things as ten horses could carry, which Sigurdur took back to the farm.

Not long after, he married the dean's daughter, and prospered to the end of his life, which, as the old troll had prophesied, was a long one.

# THE NIGHT-TROLLS

Two TROLLS, who, quite contrary to the custom of trolls in general, had taken a great fancy to a church in their neighbourhood, determined to do it a service by taking an island out of the sea and adding it on to the church property. So they waded out one night till they reached one of a group of islands which suited their notions, and having rooted it up they proceeded to take it to shore, the man pulling before, and the wife pushing behind.

But before they could accomplish their task, dawn broke in the east, and they were both suddenly turned into stones.

And there they stand in Breidifjördur, to this day, the husband troll a tall and thin rock, the wife troll a short and broad one, and are called still "old man," and "old woman."

# THE STORY OF BERGTHÓR OF BLÁFELL

IN HEATHEN times a troll named Bergthór married a wife, and lived in a cave called Hundahellir, on Bláfell. He was well skilled in the black art, but a very mild-tempered and harmless troll, except when provoked. Near the mountains stood a farm called Haukadalur, where an old man then lived.

One day the troll came to him and said, "I wish, when I die, to be buried where I can hear the sound of bells and running water; promise, therefore, to place me in the churchyard at Haukadalur. As a sign of my death, my large staff shall stand at your cottage-door; and, as a reward for burying me, you may take what you find in the kettle by the side of my body."

The farmer made him the promise, and Bergthór took leave of him.

Some time afterwards when the servants went out of the farmhouse at Haukadalur early in the morning, they found standing by the door a great wooden staff, and told the farmer of it. As soon as he saw it he recognised it as that of Bergthór, and having caused a coffin to be made, rode in company with some of his men to Bláfell. When they entered the cave, they found Bergthór dead, and placed him in the coffin, wondering among themselves to find so large a corpse so light as his seemed to be. By the side of the bed the farmer discovered a large kettle, and opened it, expecting it to be full of gold. But when he saw that it contained nothing but dead leaves, he fancied that the troll had played him false, and was much wroth. One of the men, however, filled both his gloves with these leaves, and then they carried the coffin with Bergthór in it down to the level ground.

At the foot of the hill they stopped to rest, and the man who had taken the leaves opened his gloves and found that they were full of money.

The farmer seeing this, was struck with astonishment, and turned back with some of his servants to get the rest of it; but, search as they would, they could find no traces of either cave or kettle, and were obliged to leave the mountain disappointed, as everybody else, who made the same search, was too.

They buried the body of the troll, and the mound which marked where they placed him is called "Bergthór's barrow" to this day.

# GRYLA

WE CANNOT conclude our stories of trolls without giving a description of Grýla, a bugbear used to frighten children quiet, which is almost horrible enough to frighten them to death.

Grýla had three hundred heads, six eyes in each head, besides two livid and ghostly blue eyes at the back of each neck. She had goat's horns, and her ears were so long as to hang down to her shoulders at one end, and at the other to join the ends of her three hundred noses. On each forehead was a tuft of hair, and on each chin a tangled and filthy beard. Her teeth were like burnt lava. To each thigh she had bound a sack, in which she used to carry naughty children, and she had, moreover, hoofs like a horse. Besides all this, she had fifteen tails, and on each tail a hundred bags of skin, every one of which bags would hold twenty children.

Grýla had a husband named Leppalúdi, a scarecrow, and they had twenty children. In addition to these, they had thirteen more (whom Grýla is reported to have borne before she was married to Leppalúdi the scarecrow) called Christmas-men, as they were supposed to come to human abodes about Christmas time, and take away the naughty children.

More is told about all these trolls which is not worth repeating.

# STORIES OF GHOSTS AND GOBLINS

## MURDER WILL OUT

ONCE UPON a time, in a certain churchyard, some people who were digging a grave, found a skull with a knitting-pin stuck through it from temple to temple. The priest took the skull and preserved it until the next Sunday, when he had to perform service.

When the day came, the priest waited until all the people were inside the church, and then fastened up the skull to the top of the porch. After the service the priest and his servant left the church first, and stood outside the door, watching carefully everybody that came out. When all the congregation had passed out without anything strange occurring, they looked in to see if there was any one still remaining inside. The only person they saw was a very old woman sitting behind the door, who was so unwilling to leave the church, that they were compelled to force her out. As she passed under the porch, three drops of blood fell from the skull on to her white head-dress, and she exclaimed, "Alas, murder will out at last!" Then she confessed, that having been compelled to marry her first husband against her will, she had killed him with a knitting-pin and married another.

She was tried for the murder, though it had happened so many years back, and condemned to death.

# KETILL, THE PRIEST OF HÚSAVÍK

THERE ONCE lived a priest at Húsavík, whose name was Ketill. Finding the churchyard rather crowded, he dug up a good many of the coffins, saying, "that they were no use where they were, but only took up room," and used them for firewood.

Some time after, in a kitchen, three old women were sitting round the fire where some of the coffin-planks were burning. A spark flew out and set fire to the dress of one of them, and, as they were sitting close together, the flame quickly caught the dresses of the other two, and burnt so fiercely, that all three were dead before any one could come to their assistance.

Next night the priest saw a man come to his bedside who said, "Do not endeavour to make room in the churchyard by taking out our coffins and burning them; you see that I have already killed three old women, and if you go on in this way I will kill many more, and fill up your graves for you quicker than you will like."

The priest took the warning, burnt no more coffins, and saw no more ghosts, nor were any more old women killed.

# WHITE CAP

A CERTAIN boy and girl, whose names this tale telleth not, once lived near a church. The boy being mischievously inclined, was in the habit of trying to frighten the girl in a variety of ways, till she became at last so accustomed to his tricks, that she ceased to care for anything whatever, putting down everything strange that she saw and heard to the boy's mischief.

One washing-day, the girl was sent by her mother to fetch home the linen, which had been spread to dry in the churchyard. When she had nearly filled her basket, she happened to look up, and saw sitting on a tomb near her a figure dressed in white from head to foot, but was not the least alarmed, believing it to be the boy playing her, as usual, a trick. So she ran up to it, and pulling its cap off said, "You shall not frighten me, *this* time." Then when she had finished collecting the linen she went home; but, to her astonishment—for he could not have reached home before her without her seeing him—the boy was the first person who greeted her on her arrival at the cottage.

Among the linen, too, when it was sorted, was found a mouldy white cap, which appeared to be nobody's property, and which was half full of earth.

The next morning the ghost (for it was a ghost that the girl had seen) was found sitting with no cap upon its head, upon the same tombstone as the evening before; and as nobody had the courage to address it, or knew in the least how to get rid of it, they sent into the neighbouring village for advice.

An old man declared that the only way to avoid some general calamity, was for the little girl to replace on the ghost's head the cap she had seized from it, in the presence of many people, all of whom were to be perfectly silent. So a crowd collected in the churchyard, and the little girl, going forward, half afraid, with the cap, placed it upon the ghost's head, saying, "Are you satisfied now?"

But the ghost, raising its hand, gave her a fearful blow, and said, "Yes; but are *you* now satisfied?"

The little girl fell down dead, and at the same instant the ghost sank into the grave upon which it had been sitting, and was no more seen.

# A GHOST'S VENGEANCE

SOME YEARS ago, two friends were conversing together on various subjects, and, among others, on corpses.

"If ever I happen to find a dead man," said the one, "I shall do my best for it, and bury it."

"For my part," replied the other, "I shall take no such trouble, but pass it by like any other carrion."

Some time passed away, and one day Ketill (that was the name of the latter), while out walking, found the corpse of an old woman lying in the road, but passed by without paying the slightest attention to it.

Next night, after he was in bed, this old woman appeared to him and said, "No thanks to you for your neglect of me; for you did me neither good nor evil."

And she looked so horrible, that he jumped out of bed, grasped a large knife that lay near him, and chased the spectre from the house, cursing and swearing, and crying, "Shall I stab you, you old witch?"

After this he went to bed again, and fell asleep; then he saw the old woman a second time, holding her lungs, all clotted with blood, in her hand, and making as if she was going to strike him with them. So he jumped out of bed with the knife, but before he could reach her, she had disappeared.

When he had got into bed again, and was asleep, she came a third time, and made as if she would strangle him. So a third time he jumped out of bed with the knife, but failed in reaching her before she vanished.

And this hag's ghost followed the unhappy Ketill all his life, and drove him with her wrath and spite into an untimely grave. Whether Ketill's friend ever found a corpse and had a chance of carrying out his charitable intentions with regard to it, this story narrates not, neither does it so much as hint at what reward he would have got for his pains.

# THE BOY WHO DID NOT KNOW WHAT FEAR WAS

THERE WAS once a boy so courageous and spirited that his relations despaired of ever frightening him into obedience to their will, and took him to the parish priest to be brought up. But the priest could not subdue him in the least, though the boy never showed either obstinacy or ill-temper towards him.

Once in the winter three dead bodies were brought to be buried, but as it was late in the afternoon they were put into the church till next day, when the priest would be able to bury them. In those days it was the custom to bury people without coffins, and only wrapped up in grave-clothes. The priest ordered these three bodies to be laid a little distance apart, across the middle of the church.

After nightfall the priest said to the boy, "Run into the church and fetch me the book which I left on the altar."

With his usual willingness he ran into the church, which was quite dark, and half way to the altar stumbled against something which lay on the floor, and fell down on his face. Not in the least alarmed, he got up again, and, after groping about, found that he had stumbled over one of the corpses, which he took in his arms and pushed into the side-benches out of his way. He tumbled over the other two, and disposed of them in like manner. Then, taking the book from the altar, he left the church, shut the door behind him, and gave the volume to the priest, who asked him if he had encountered anything extraordinary in the church.

The Boy Who Did Not Know What Fear Was

"Not that I can remember," said the boy.

The priest asked again, "Did you not find three corpses lying across your passage?"

"Oh yes," replied he, "but what about them?"

"Did they not lie in your way?"

"Yes, but they did not hinder me."

The priest asked, "How did you get to the altar?"

The boy replied, "I stuck the good folk into the side benches, where they lie quietly enough."

The priest shook his head, but said nothing more that night.

Next morning he said to the boy, "You must leave me; I cannot keep near me any longer one who is shameless enough to break the repose of the dead."

The boy, nothing loth, bade farewell to the priest and his family, and wandered about some little time without a home.

Once he came to a cottage, where he slept the night, and there the people told him that the Bishop of Skálholt was just dead. So next day he went off to Skálholt, and arriving there in the evening, begged a night's lodging.

The people said to him, "You may have it and welcome, but you must take care of yourself."

"Why take care of myself so much?" asked the lad.

They told him that after the death of the bishop, no one could stay in the house after nightfall, as some ghost or goblin walked about there, and that on this account every one had to leave the place after twilight.

The boy answered, "Well and good; that will just suit me."

At twilight the people all left the place, taking leave of the boy, whom they did not expect to see again alive.

When they had all gone, the boy lighted a candle and examined every room in the house till he came to the kitchen, where he found large quantities of smoked mutton hung up to the rafters. So, as he had not tasted meat for some time, and had a capital appetite, he cut some of the dried mutton off with his knife, and placing a pot on the fire, which was still burning, cooked it.

When he had finished cutting up the meat, and had put the lid on the pot, he heard a voice from the top of the chimney, which said, "May I come down?"

The lad answered, "Yes, why not?"

Then there fell down on to the floor of the kitchen half a giant,—head, arms, hands, and body, as far as the waist, and lay there motionless.

After this he heard another voice from the chimney, saying, "May I come down?"

"If you like," said the boy; "why not?"

Accordingly down came another part of the giant, from the waist to the thighs, and lay on the floor motionless.

Then he heard a third voice from the same direction, which said, "May I come down?"

"Of course," he replied; "you must have something to stand upon."

So a huge pair of legs and feet came down and lay by the rest of the body, motionless.

After a bit the boy, finding this want of movement rather tedious, said, "Since you have contrived to get yourself all in, you had better get up and go away."

Upon this the pieces crept together, and the giant rose on his feet from the floor, and, without uttering a word, stalked out of the kitchen. The lad followed him, till they came to a large hall, in which stood a wooden chest. This chest the goblin opened, and the lad saw that it was full of money. Then the goblin took the money out in handfuls, and poured it like water over his head, till the floor was covered with heaps of it; and, having spent half the night thus, spent the other half in restoring the gold to the chest in the like manner. The boy stood by and watched him filling the chest again, and gathering all the stray coins together by sweeping his great arms violently over the floor, as if he dreaded to be interrupted before he could get them all in, which the lad fancied must be because the day was approaching.

When the goblin had shut up the coffer, he rushed past the lad as if to get out of the hall; but the latter said to him, "Do not be in too great a hurry."

"I must make haste," replied the other, "for the day is dawning."

But the boy took him by the sleeve and begged him to remain yet a little longer for friendship's sake.

At this the goblin waxed angry, and, clutching hold of the youth, said, "Now you shall delay me no longer."

But the latter clung tight to him, and slipped out of the way of every blow he dealt, and some time passed away in this kind of struggle. It happened, however, at last, that the giant turned his back to the open door, and the boy, seeing his chance, tripped him up and butted at him with his head, so that the other fell heavily backwards, half in and half out of the hall, and broke his spine upon the threshold. At the same moment the first ray of dawn struck his eyes through the open house door, and he instantly sank into the ground in two pieces, one each side of the door of the hall. Then the courageous boy, though half dead from fatigue, made two crosses of wood and drove them into the ground where the two parts of the goblin had disappeared. This done, he fell asleep till, when the sun was well up, the people came back to Skálholt. They were amazed and rejoiced to find him still alive, asking him whether he had seen anything in the night.

"Nothing out of the common," he said.

So he stayed there all that day, both because he was tired, and because the people were loth to let him go.

In the evening, when the people began as usual to leave the place, he begged them to stay, assuring them that they would be troubled by neither ghost nor goblin. But in spite of his assurances they insisted upon going, though they left him this time without any fear for his safety. When they were gone, he went to bed and slept soundly till morning.

On the return of the people he told them all about his struggle with the goblin, showed them the crosses he had set up, and the chestful of money in the hall, and assured them that they would never again be troubled at night, so need not leave the place. They thanked him most heartily for his spirit and courage, and asked him to name any reward he would like to receive, whether money or other precious things, inviting him, in addition, to remain with them as long as ever he chose. He was grateful for their offers, but said, "I do not care for money, nor can I make up my mind to stay longer with you."

Next day he addressed himself to his journey, and no persuasion could induce him to remain at Skálholt. For he said, "I have no more business here, as you can now, without fear, live in the bishop's house." And taking leave of them all, he directed his steps northwards, into the wilderness.

For a long time nothing new befell him, until one day he came to a large cave, into which he entered. In a smaller cave within the other he found twelve beds, all in disorder and unmade. As it was yet early, he thought he could do no better than employ himself in making them, and having made them, threw himself on to the one nearest the entrance, covered himself up, and went to sleep.

After a little while he awoke and heard the voices of men talking in the cave, and wondering who had made the beds for them, saying that, whoever he was, they were much obliged to him for his pains. He saw, on looking out, that they were twelve armed men of noble aspect. When they had had supper, they came into the inner cave and eleven of them went to bed. But the twelfth man whose bed was next to the entrance, found the boy in it, and calling to the others they rose and thanked the lad for having made their beds for them, and begged him to remain with them as their servant, for they said that they never found time to do any work for themselves, as they were compelled to go out every day at sunrise to fight their enemies, and never returned till night. The lad asked them why they were forced to fight day after day? They answered that they had over and over again fought, and overcome their enemies, but that though they killed them over-night they always came to life again before morning, and would come to the cave and slay them all in their beds if they were not up and ready on the field at sunrise.

In the morning the cave-men went out fully armed, leaving the lad behind to look after the household work.

About noon he went in the same direction as the men had taken, in order to find out where the battle-field was, and as soon as he had espied it in the distance, ran back to the cave.

In the evening the warriors returned weary and dispirited, but were glad to find that the boy had arranged everything for them, so that they had nothing more to do than eat their supper and go to bed.

When they were all asleep, the boy wondered to himself how it could possibly come to pass that their enemies rose every night from the dead. So moved with curiosity was he, that as soon as he was sure that his companions were fast asleep he took what of their weapons and armour he found to fit him best, and stealing out of the cave, made off in the direction of the battle-field. There was nothing at first to be seen there but corpses and trunkless heads, so he waited a little time to see what would happen. About dawn he perceived a mound near him open of itself, and an old woman in a blue cloak come out with a glass phial in her hand. He noticed her go up to a dead warrior, and having picked up his head, smear his neck with some ointment out of the phial and place the head and trunk together. Instantly the warrior stood erect, a living man. The hag repeated this to two or three, until the boy seeing now the secret of the thing, rushed up to her and stabbed her to death as well as the men she had raised, who were yet stupid and heavy as if after sleep. Then taking the phial, he tried whether he could revive the corpses with the ointment, and found on experiment that he could do so successfully. So he amused himself for a while in reviving the men and killing them again, till, at sunrise, his companions arrived on the field.

They were mightily astonished to see him there, and told him that they had missed him as well as some of their weapons and armour; but they were rejoiced to find their enemies lying dead on the field instead of being alive and awaiting them in battle array, and asked the lad how he had got the idea of thus going at night to the battle-field, and what he had done.

He told them all that had passed, showed them the phial of ointment, and, in order to prove its power, smeared the neck of one of the corpses, who at once rose to his feet, but was instantly killed again by the cave-men. They thanked the boy heartily for the service he had rendered them, and begged him to remain among them, offering him at the same time money for his work. He declared that he was quite willing, paid or unpaid, to stay with them, as long as they liked to keep him. The cave-men were well pleased with his answer, and having embraced the lad, set to work to strip their enemies of their weapons: made a heap of them with the old woman on the top and burned them; and then, going into the mound, appropriated to themselves all the treasures they found there. After this they proposed the game of killing each other, to try how it was to die, as they could restore one another to life again. So they killed each other, but by smearing themselves with the ointment, they at once returned to life.

Now this was great sport for a while.

But once, when they had cut off the head of the lad, they put it on again wrongside before. And as the lad saw himself behind, he became as if mad with fright, and begged the men to release him by all means from such a painful sight.

But when the cave-folk had run to him and, cutting off his head, placed it on all right again, he came back to his full senses, and was as fearless as ever before.

The boy lived with them ever afterwards, and no more stories are told about him.


# THE TWO SIGURDURS


A FARMER once had a son named Sigurdur, who was so ill-tempered that no one could live in peace with him.

One day it happened that a man whose name was also Sigurdur, came to the farmer's house and asked shelter of him for the winter, which the farmer consented to give him. The stranger did nothing but play the flute, and the farmer's son became so fond of him that he cared for nobody else.

In the spring the stranger went away, and Sigurdur became so sick of home-life that he also left the farm and went in search of his beloved namesake. From house to house, from parish to parish, and from district to district, he went, continually asking for Sigurdur. At last at a certain priest's house where he made the same inquiry, they told him that a man of that name had just died there, and lay in the church. On being admitted into the church the boy sat down by the open coffin, intending to watch over it all night.

At midnight the corpse of Sigurdur (for it really was his friend) rose from the coffin and left the church, but his namesake sat still and awaited his return. At dawn the corpse came back, but Sigurdur would not let him, in spite of his entreaties, return to his coffin before telling him how he had spent the night outside the church.

So the dead man said, "I have been looking over my money. Now I must get into the coffin."

"No," replied the other; "you must first tell me where your money is."

"In one of the corners of the family-room," said the other.

"How much is there of it?"

"One barrelful."

"Did you do nothing," again inquired the youth, "besides counting your money?"

The corpse denied it, but when the living Sigurdur pressed him to tell him how he had been employed, on pain of refusing to admit him into his coffin again, the other answered, "Well, then! I have killed the priest's lady, who had just had a child."

"Why did you commit so mean a crime?" asked Sigurdur.

"Because," replied the corpse, "during her lifetime I tried to seduce her, but she always resisted my persuasions."

"How did you kill her?"

The dead Sigurdur answered, "I drove all the life in her body into her little finger."

"Can she not be revived?" asked the youth.

"Yes! If you can untie the thread that is round her finger without shedding any blood, she will come to life. And now I really must get into my coffin."

The other only allowed him to do so on his promising that he would not ever try to move again.

In the morning, as soon as the sun was fully risen, Sigurdur left the church and entered the family-room where he found everybody plunged in grief, and, on his asking them what was the matter, they told him that the priest's wife had died in the night, and nobody could tell her complaint. So he asked permission to see her, which was granted him, and having gone up to the dead woman and undone the cord which he found round her little finger, he urged back the life from it into her body, and she sat up alive and well. Then he told the priest about his interview with the corpse of Sigurdur, and, to prove his words still further, showed him the money hidden in the corner of the family-room. The priest thanked him cordially for the good service he had done him, and after this Sigurdur became as much beloved as he had before been hated.

# THE DEACON OF MYRKÁ

A LONG time ago, a deacon lived at Myrká, in Egafjördur. He was in love with a girl named Gudrún, who dwelt in a farm on the opposite side of the valley, separated from his house by a river.

The deacon had a horse with a grey mane, which he was always in the habit of riding, and which he called Faxi.

A short time before Christmas, the deacon rode to the farm at which his betrothed lived, and invited her to join in the Christmas festivities at Myrká, promising to fetch her on Christmas-eve. Some time before he had started out on this ride, there had been heavy snow and frost; but this very day there came so rapid a thaw, that the river over which the deacon had safely ridden, trusting to the firmness of the ice, became impassable during the short time he spent with his betrothed; the floods rose, and huge masses of drift-ice were whirled down the stream.

When the deacon had left the farm, he rode on to the river, and being deep in thought did not perceive at first the change that had taken place. As soon, however, as he saw in what state the stream was, he rode up the banks until he came to a bridge of ice, on to which he spurred his horse. But when he arrived at the middle of the bridge, it broke beneath him, and he was drowned in the flood.

Next morning, a neighbouring farmer saw the deacon's horse grazing in a field, but could discover nothing of its owner, whom he had seen the day before cross the river, but not return. He at once suspected what had occurred, and going down to the river, found the corpse of the deacon, which had drifted to the bank, with all the flesh torn off the back of his head, and the bare white skull visible. So he brought the body back to Myrká, where it was buried a week before Christmas.

Up to Christmas-eve the river continued so swollen, that no communication could take place between the dwellers on the opposite banks, but that morning it subsided, and Gudrún, utterly ignorant of the deacon's death, looked forward with joy to the festivities to which she had been invited by him.

In the afternoon Gudrún began to dress in her best clothes, but before she had quite finished, she heard a knock at the door of the farm. One of the maid-servants opened the door, but seeing nobody there, thought it was because the night was not sufficiently light, for the moon was hidden for the time by clouds. So saying, "Wait there till I bring a light," went back into the house; but she had no sooner shut the outer door behind her, than the knock was repeated, and Gudrún cried out from her room, "It is some one waiting for me."

As she had by this time finished dressing, she slipped only one sleeve of her winter cloak on, and threw the rest over her shoulders hurriedly. When she opened the door, she saw the well-known Faxi standing outside, and by him a man whom she knew to be the deacon. Without a word he placed Gudrún on the horse, and mounted in front of her himself, and off they rode.

When they came to the river it was frozen over, all except the current in the middle, which the frost had not yet hardened. The horse walked on to the ice, and leaped over the black and rapid stream which flowed in the middle. At the same moment the head of the deacon nodded forward, so that his hat fell over his eyes, and Gudrún saw the large patch of bare skull gleam white in the midst of his hair. Directly afterwards, a cloud moved from before the moon, and the deacon said—

> "The moon glides,
>     Death rides,
>     Seest thou not the white place
>     In the back of my head,
>     Garún, Garún?"

Not a word more was spoken till they came to Myrká, where they dismounted.

Then the man said:

> "Wait here for me, Garún, Garún,
>     While I am taking Faxi, Faxi,
>     Outside the hedges, the hedges!"

When he had gone, Gudrún saw near her in the churchyard, where she was standing, an open grave, and half sick with horror, ran to the church porch, and seizing the rope, tolled the bells with all her strength. But as she began to ring them, she felt some one grasp her and pull so fiercely at her cloak that it was torn off her, leaving only the one sleeve into which she had thrust her arm before starting from home. Then turning round, she saw the deacon jump headlong into the yawning grave, with the tattered cloak in his hand, and the heaps of earth on both sides fall in over him, and close the grave up to the brink.

Gudrún knew now that it was the deacon's ghost with whom she had had to do, and continued ringing the bells till she roused all the farm-servants at Myrká.

That same night, after Gudrún had got shelter at Myrká and was in bed, the deacon came again from his grave and endeavoured to drag her away, so that no one could sleep for the noise of their struggle.

This was repeated every night for a fortnight, and Gudrún could never be left alone for a single instant, lest the goblin deacon should get the better of her. From time to time, also, a neighbouring priest came and sat on the edge of the bed, reading the Psalms of David to protect her against this ghostly persecution.

But nothing availed, till they sent for a man from the north country, skilled in witchcraft, who dug up a large stone from the field, and placed it in the middle of the guest-room at Myrká. When the deacon rose that night from his grave and came into the house to torment Gudrún, this man seized him, and by uttering potent spells over him, forced him beneath the stone, and exorcised the passionate demon that possessed him, so that there he lies in peace to this day.

# THE SON OF THE GOBLIN

THE FARM Bakki (now called Prestbakki, in Hrútafjördur) once stood further north than it does now, and the reasons of its being moved from its ancient to its present position are as follows.

It happened that a certain farmer's son courted the daughter of the priest who lived at Bakki, but met with a refusal of his offers, which grieved him so sorely, that he fell sick and died, and was buried at the church near the priest's house. This had happened in summer. The winter following, people noticed a certain strangeness in the demeanour of the priest's daughter, for which they could not account.

One evening, it happened that her foster-mother, an old woman and a wise one withal, went out to the churchyard with her knitting, as it was warm enough, and the moon had but few clouds to wade through.

Some time before this, her foster-child had told her that since his death her old lover had often been to see her, and that she found herself now with child, whose father had assured her that the infant would prove an ill-fated one; and the unfortunate girl had asked the old woman to try to prevent, from that time forth, her ghostly lover's visits; and it was for this purpose that the good dame had gone out into the churchyard. She went to the grave of the young man, which was yawning wide open, and threw her ball of thread down into it, and having done so, sat down on its edge to knit. There she sat until the ghost came, who at once begged her to take up the ball of thread from the grave, so that he might enter his coffin and take his rest.

But the old woman said, "I have no mind to do so, unless you tell me what you do out of your grave thus at night."

He answered, "I visit the priest's daughter, for he has no means of preventing my doing so. Ere long she will be delivered of a boy."

Then the old woman said, "Tell me this boy's fate."

"His fate," replied the other, "is, that he will be a priest at Bakki, and the church with all its congregation will sink down to hell the first time he pronounces the blessing from the altar, and then my vengeance will be complete, for the injury the priest did me in not allowing me to marry his daughter during my lifetime."

"Your prophecy is, indeed, a great one, if it meets with a fulfilment," answered the old woman; "but are there no means by which so horrible a curse can be prevented?"

The ghost replied, "The only means are for some one to stab the priest the moment he begins to pronounce the blessing; but I do not fancy that anybody will undertake that task."

When she had gathered this information, the old woman said to him, "Go now into your grave, and be sure never again to come out of it."

After this the old woman drew up her ball of thread, and the corpse leaped into the grave, over which the earth closed itself. Then she recited over the grave some magic spells, which bound the corpse in its last rest for ever; and returning home, told nobody what had passed between her and the goblin-lover.

Some time afterwards, the girl was delivered of a fine and healthy boy, who was brought up at Bakki by his mother and his grandfather (though the latter did not know who its father was). In his early youth people saw that he excelled all his companions both in mind and body; and when his education was complete, and he had arrived at the proper age, he became his grandfather's curate.

Now, the old woman saw that something must be done to prevent the approaching ill-fate, so she went to her son, who was a man of great courage, and one who did not shrink from trifles, and told him the whole story of her interview with the goblin, and begged him to stab the young priest directly he began to pronounce his blessing from the altar, promising herself to take all the consequences of the deed. He was at first very unwilling to do this, but when she pressed him with earnest entreaties, he at last made the promise she required, and confirmed it with an oath.

At length the day came on which the young curate was to perform service for the first time, and the large congregation assembled in the church were struck with his eloquence and sweet voice. But when the youth stood at the altar and raised his hands for the benediction, the old woman signed to her son, who rushed forward and stabbed him, so that he fell dead on the spot. Horror-struck at this fearful act, many rushed forward and seized the murderer, but those who went to the altar to raise the priest found nothing of him but the top bone of his neck, which lay where he had been standing. Every one now saw that what had happened was no every-day murder, but that some goblin had had to do with it; and the old woman, standing in the midst of them, told them the whole story. When they had heard it they recovered from their panic, and thanked her for her foresight, and her son for his quickness and courage. They then perceived that the east end of the church had sunk down a little into the ground, because the priest had had time to pronounce the first few syllables of the blessing.

After this, the farm of Bakki was so haunted by goblins that it was removed from its old to its present situation.

# MISCELLANEOUS TALES

## THE STORY OF JÓN ASMUNDSSON

IN THE district of Boyarfjördur, once lived a poor married couple. The man's name was Asmundur. They had many children, whose names have not been handed down to us, except that of the eldest, and he was called Jón. At this time, so severe a season was prevailing, that Asmundur was obliged to leave his home and his children, who were scattered about the country and brought up, one here and one there, at the houses of various farmers.

Now there lived at Reykjavík a priest, named Christján, and he it was that took Jón into his house, and brought him up as his own son. Jón grew into a fine and handsome lad, and was stronger than any of his fellows. But he was always very quiet, and seldom opened his mouth, unless first spoken to. He was, moreover, hardworking and willing, and became before long a great favourite, not only with the priest himself, but with every member of the household.

One summer, according to yearly custom, a trading vessel arrived at Reykjavík. Its owner was a foreign merchant, who carried on a large business at this season; but of his name no mention is made. Among other people with whom he had dealings was Christján, the priest. One day while Christján was on board the ship, it fell out that they came to talk about strong men. The merchant, being himself well-built and powerful, went up to where four barrels of rye lay bound together, and, seizing them by the rope which was round them, lifted them all together as high as his knee. When he had put them down again, he said, "There! let anyone prove himself my match in lifting, and I will give him three half-pounds of gold by weight."

When the priest returned home, he told his foster-son what he had seen, and how the merchant had promised three half-pounds of gold by weight to any man that should match him in lifting, and encouraged the boy to make the trial. To this Jón agreed without wasting many words. So they went together to the ship, and Christján told the captain that the lad would like to try his strength. The merchant pointed out the rye barrels to Jón, who, going up to them, lifted them on to his shoulder as if they were but a handful of feathers, and when he had walked with them to and fro upon the deck, put them down again in their place.

When he saw this, the merchant changed colour, but weighed out the three half-pounds of gold, and paid them over to Jón, begging him, as he took leave, to come and pay him one more visit on board the ship before he sailed away. This Jón promised to do.

One day, shortly before the time the merchant had fixed for sailing, the priest came to Jón, and reminded him of his promise to visit the ship. Accordingly Jón went, and Christján with him, and the merchant received them with all due honour, begging Jón to come with him into the cabin for a few words he wished to say in his ear.

657

But when he saw that the priest was going to make one of their party, he turned round to him, and said, "Friend, you can stay up here a while; we have no need of you."

Christján, however, was not to be put off, but assuring the merchant that he would not disturb them, or be in their way, followed them down into the cabin.

Then the merchant said to Jón, "You have not yet done with me; for next year I shall bring with me a boy for you to wrestle with, and if you get the better of him in that game, I will weigh you out five pounds of gold."

Jón agreed to this, and when he and Christján had taken leave, the merchant sailed away.

For some time everything went on quietly, and the winter set in. One day the priest asked Jón whether he remembered the agreement he had made with the foreign merchant before his departure.

Jón answered, that it was so slight a matter that he had never yet given it a thought.

But the priest said, "Indeed it is no such child's play as you think; for the boy that this merchant will bring for you to wrestle with, is none other than a monstrous black man, and get the better of you he surely will, unless you employ craft against him. I will find out speedily some means for gaining you the victory, for ere three weeks of the summer be over the merchant-ship will come into harbour."

Jón nodded, but said nothing, and seemed in no way troubled by the news; nor did he give himself the least pains about it till the time came.

Before three weeks of the summer were over, as Christján had foretold, a vessel was seen making for the harbour of Reykjavík from the open ocean. It was no sooner in sight than the priest went to Jón, and, warning him of what he now might expect, dressed him in a peasant's frock of black wool, and clasped a belt round his waist; when he had thus equipped him, he gave him a little, bright, sharp-edged dagger, which he bade him keep ready to his hand, hidden in the sleeve of the woollen frock. He further told Jón, not to attempt to resist the black man's attacks, as the latter would fling him easily over his shoulder.

"I," said he, "will take good care that you fall on your feet. But, after a while, challenge the black man to take off his shaggy mantle, and do you make ready in your hand the dagger, that when he rushes upon you a second time you may thrust it into his chest."

The anchor was scarcely dropped before a boat sped from the vessel, and set on shore a black man of giant's build, dressed in a shaggy mantle, who, direcctly he saw the priest and the lad standing close to the sea, rushed at Jón, and, seizing him in his arms, flung him like a pebble over his head, high into the air. But the boy fell on his feet, and forthwith challenged the black to fight without his woolly mantle, that they might the more easily try their skill in wrestling. To this the man consented; but while he was doffing his cloak, Jón made ready in his right hand the sharp-edged dagger which the priest had given him, and when the other ran blindly upon him, thrust it into his breast once and again. But yet they wrestled together for a while, and assuredly even now Jón would have got the worst of it, were it not that his black woollen frock served him as armour against the heavy blows.

At last the fight came to an end, and Jón slew his enemy.

Then he and Christján went on board the vessel, where they found the merchant, and saluted him.

"Well," said the latter, "and how went the fight?"

The priest answered, "If you will look towards the shore, you will see the black lying dead close to the waves. That is how the fight went."

Then the merchant was exceeding wroth, and said, "Aha! you have not acted like brave and true-hearted men. This lad has but fought by craft and with steel."

"But," replied the priest, "however that may be, he has deserved fairly the prize; for, whereas you promised to bring a lad to wrestle with him, you have brought a giant-built black."

To this the merchant had no answer ready, so, as needs must be, paid into Jón's hand the five pounds of weighed-out gold, which he had promised to the winner in the wrestling. Then, smoothing his angry brows, he begged Jón to come and see him once more before the ship sailed, which would be in the latter end of the summer.

Everything went on as usual till a short time before the merchant had determined to sail from Reykjavík, and then the priest reminded Jón of his promise to visit the merchant before his departure, offering at the same time to accompany him, and be present during the interview. They went, therefore, to the vessel and greeted the merchant, who received them with great politeness, but, as before, begged Jón to go a little aside with him, as he had something particular to tell him. Christján, however, followed close upon their heels, and the merchant, seeing him, said, "You need not trouble yourself to come so close; what we speak about has nought to do with you."

But the priest was not to be put off so, and saying, "I will neither leave the side of my foster-son, nor will I interrupt your converse," kept still close to them.

Then the merchant said to Jón, "Next summer I will bring with me a little whelp against which you shall try your strength, and if you get the best of the fight, I will weigh out into your hand seven-and-a-half pounds of good gold."

Upon this they parted; Jón and Christján returning on shore, and the merchant sailing away.

Now the summer passed away, and a great part of the winter passed away without Jón making any preparations for, or saying a word about, the next visit of the merchant.

One day the priest asked him whether or no he remembered the merchant's words and promise.

"Not I," replied Jón.

"But," said the priest, "this visit of his will bring almost as much difficulty as his last one. The whelp he promised to match against you, ere half a month of the summer be past, is nothing less than a large and cruel deer-hound, and to get the best of the fight we must devise some wile, for your strength will be as nothing."

But Jón only answered, "Devise, then, for me," and there he let the matter rest, occupying himself no further about it.

Ere half a month of the summer was over, a vessel appeared in sight, sailing from the open sea towards Reykjavík.

Then the priest went to Jón and said, "The merchant will now soon be in harbour, and you must be ready for him." And he made him put on again the black woollen frock which he had now woven through and through with links of iron. He gave him, at the same time, a spear, with moveable barbs, which would spread out and tear the flesh into which they had been thrust, and, placing on the point of this a piece of meat, bade Jón watch his chance and thrust it with all his strength down the dog's throat.

When he had thus equipped him he led him down to the shore.

Scarcely was the anchor dropped, when a boat sped from the vessel, and placed upon the beach a large and evil-eyed deer-hound, who, directly he saw Jón advancing towards him, rushed at him with mad fury, and would have torn him to pieces on the spot had not the frock, with its links of mail, saved Jón from his teeth. Over and over again the brute rushed upon him, each time with greater rage and strength. But Jón, who escaped unscathed from each attack, watched his chance, and keeping the piece of meat always before the dog till the beast opened its mouth to snap at it, thrust it with all his force down its throat, till, in a short while, it lay dead at his feet.

Then they went out to the ship and saluted the merchant, who received and returned their greeting surlily enough. But feign and conceal as he would, he could not hide from them the wrathful red blood that filled his cheek and brow and swelled his lip.

"We have come to claim the gold," said the priest; "my foster-son has fairly earned it."

"Fairly, forsooth!" replied the merchant. "He has fought like a brave man in truth, by wile and craft and steel. He has no claim to the gold, he has not kept to our agreement."

"Neither have you," the priest returned, "for you promised to bring a whelp, and have brought a wild beast to match it against this lad." So the merchant, who could not deny this, put the smoothest face he could upon the matter and weighed into Jón's hand the gold. Just before Jón and the priest left the ship, the merchant begged the former to come once more to see him before he weighed anchor and sailed away at the summer's end. Jón promised to come.

Now the time came round at which the merchant had fixed to sail, and Christján reminded Jón of his promise to go once more and visit him, saying, at the same time, that he himself would take good care to be present at their meeting. Accordingly they went on board the ship, whose anchor was even now being weighed. Just as before, the merchant begged Jón to come down with him into the cabin, as he had something particular to say to him, and when he saw Christján following them, turned round to him with a fierce look and cried, "Stand back, and meddle not where nothing concerns you."

"I do not wish to meddle," said the priest, "but I will not leave my foster-son." And as he seemed firm about this the merchant said no more; so they went all three down to the cabin.

Then the merchant took down from one of the shelves a book, out of which he pulled a leaf and waved it quickly before Jón's eyes, as if to prevent the priest from seeing its contents. But Christján caught a glance of some of the words written upon it, without the merchant's knowledge. Then he returned the leaf to the book and the book to its place, saying to Jón, "If you do not bring me next summer, when I come back here, the book from which this leaf was taken, I will brand you as a fool and a faint heart; but if you bring the book I will weigh you out fifteen full pounds of good gold."

With these words they parted, Jón and Christján going home, and the merchant putting at once to sea.

When one week of the summer was still left, the priest asked Jón whether he had yet given a thought to the task with which the merchant had charged him for the next year.

Jón answered that it had never entered his head.

Then the other asked him whether he had known the leaf that the merchant had shown him, but Jón said, "No."

"No wonder," answered Christján, "for it was none other than a leaf from the devil's manual, which the merchant has bidden you bring him, and this is surely no slight or easy matter. But I have a brother who is a priest in the worlds below, and who is the only man that can help you to procure this book. Make yourself ready, therefore, at once for the journey, for you must spend with him in the lower regions the whole winter, from the first day to the last."

So Jón addressed himself to his journey, and when he was all ready for starting, the priest gave him a letter to his brother down below, and a ball of thread which would run before him and guide him. When he wished him Godspeed, he warned him most strictly never once to look back on the way, and never to utter a single word the whole winter through. The youth promised, saying, he thought this surely easy enough.

Bidding his friend and foster-father, Christján, farewell, he flung down on the ground the ball of thread, keeping one end in his hand, and it ran quickly along before him, he following and never looking back. After a while they came to a mountain which lay north of Reykjavík, and in which appeared a passage leading deep into the earth. Into this the ball ran. Soon it became so dark, and the passage so rough and difficult, that more than once Jón stopped, doubting whether to go any further or to turn back. But every time he paused the ball pulled so hard that he was encouraged to go on, and still followed it in spite of difficulties. Thus, for a long way, they went on, till all at once the place became light, and Jón saw lying before him a vast and charming green plain over which the ball still rolled till it came to a farm as big as a town, and stopped at the door of one of the houses, where Jón picked it up from the ground. At this door Jón knocked , and a girl came out, neatly and plainly dressed, and of modest mien, and, as Jón thought, the most winsome he had ever seen. Jón nodded to her, and gave her the letter, which she took without speaking, as well as the ball of thread, and went with them into the house, leaving Jón standing at the door. In a few minutes she came back, and with her another girl younger than herself, who looked hard at Jón, and turned back into the house. But the other took him by the hand and led him through some passages into a room, where stood one small table, one chair, a bench, and a bed.

In this room Jón lived for a long time, till he thought the winter must be far advanced. He saw no one but the young girl, who came every day into the room, brought him his meals, and made his bed, but never spoke to him, nor did he, the whole time, hear the sound of a human voice.

One day, however, there entered the room a tall and handsome man, dressed in a long black cassock. This was the brother of Christján, the priest in the infernal world. He bade Jón good-day in a sweet and courteous voice, but Jón merely nodded in reply.

Then the other asked him if he knew how long he had, by this time, remained in the worlds below.

But Jón was still silent, and only shook his head.

The priest then said to him, "You have done well to keep so long and so firmly silent. But you may speak now, as the winter is over, and this is the first day of summer. Your task is accomplished, for here is the book you came to seek. Take care of it, and give it safely into my brother's hands. You must start hence to-day, as the merchant will arrive before a week of the summer be fully past. The owner of this book will miss it just about the same time, and claim it first from the merchant's hands. Therefore bid my brother buy every scrap of the merchandise on board the ship, and beware to land it before he delivers the volume into the captain's hands. Be bearer, too, of my love to my brother. My daughter shall go with you to point out the way." And with those words he took leave of him.

Then the girl who had served Jón all the winter, came to him and led him from the house, and they walked on sadly, holding one another by the hand. What they talked about now that Jón's tongue was loosed, nobody knows. However, at last the girl stopped and said she could go no further, as it was now easy enough for him to find his own way home. And these were her last words, "Now we must part, though it go nigh to break our hearts for sorrow. We cannot live together, for neither can you dwell here below, nor I in the world above. But, in the course of some months, I shall bear you a child. If it be a boy, I will send it you when it is six years old; but if a girl, when it is twelve. I pray you, receive it well." She then gave him the ball of thread. And when she had embraced him, with many tears, left him.

He, sad at heart, flung down the ball, which rolled before him, leading him this time, not through dark and difficult caverns, but along such a smooth and smiling country, that Jón knew not when he had left the one world and entered the other. Towards the close of the first week in summer he arrived at Reykjavík and was received joyfully by Christján, to whom he gave the book, and his brother's love and message.

The very next day the merchant arrived in harbour, and he had no sooner dropped anchor than the priest hurried on board and saluted him, but their greetings were just about as warm and cordial as the north-

THE STORY OF JÓN ASMUNDSSON

east wind. These over, the priest told him that, as a harsh and severe season had just prevailed and provisions were scant all through the near country, he wished to buy the whole stock that lay on board, and land it at once. They soon came to an agreement, and in a few days all the merchandise was landed.

No sooner was the last bale on shore than Christján and Jón went on board the vessel. When they had saluted, the merchant immediately asked Jón how he had succeeded in fulfilling the task wherewith he had been charged.

"Pretty well," said Jón.

Then Christján gave the book to the merchant, in the name of Jón, and mightily astonished the man was when he saw that it was the right one, but paid out the gold at the priest's request without saying any more about it. This Jón took, and after they had bidden adieu to the merchant, he and Christján jumped into their own boat and rowed quickly to shore.

But they had no sooner stepped out on to the beach, than the sea became, all at once, rough and stormy, and when they looked towards the merchant's vessel, lo! it was no more to be seen. The devil had claimed his manual.

After this they returned to the priest's house, where no small wealth was now stored up, and Jón stayed there for another half-year. Always quiet and reserved, he was ten-fold more so since his return from the lower worlds. At the end of that time the priest, who had noted the youth's melancholy, taxed him with having fallen in love with one of the daughters of his brother, the priest in the subterranean world. But to this Jón made no reply. Then Christján went on to offer him one of his own daughters (he had three, whose names we know not), whichever he loved the best, as a wife, thinking that this would perhaps free him from the thrall of his sadness. Jón chose the youngest of the three, and the priest married them, and giving his daughter no mean marriage present, settled them in a neighbouring farm, which could boast of the best land for many a long mile round.

Here they lived for many years in unbroken love and great prosperity, and had not a few children, but never the whole time did Jón lose one jot of his sadness.

At the end of twelve years, it happened one day that, as all the household were assembled in the family-room, a knock was heard at the door. Jón sent one of his sons, a lad about six years old, to the door to see who was there. The child returned, saying that there stood outside a little girl of wonderful beauty, who had asked him sweetly to say in the house that she wished to speak to her father.

At these words, it was as if a ray of sunshine had passed across Jón's face. He rose from his seat and ran eagerly to the outer door. The little girl, directly she saw him, ran up to him, and throwing her arms round his neck, kissed him fondly, calling him her own dear father. Jón returned her embrace with the greatest joy and love. She told him that her mother, the daughter of the priest in the worlds below, had sent her to him, bearing her sweetest love. Jón took the child by the hand and led her in to his wife, to whom he told the whole story of her parentage, begging her at the same time, as she loved him, so to treat the little girl as one of her own. The woman, being of true heart, welcomed the child with open arms and became a fond mother to her, from that day forth. They called her Sigrídur, and she grew up among them, a sister to the other children, and was lovelier by far and by far more accomplished than any girl of her own age, round about for many a stretch of long miles.

At the end of three years, Sigrídur, whose beauty was in everybody's mouth, asked her father's leave to pay her mother a visit in the worlds below. Jón granted it willingly, telling her that, if she would, she might stay a whole year with her mother, and making her the bearer of his sweetest love.

The year over, Sigrídur came back and was welcomed with delight by her father and all the family. She told Jón that she brought him her mother's dying farewell, together with the message that he himself had but one month more to live. Far from being grieved by this news, Jón seemed glad, and for the whole month no one noticed any change in his conduct, except that his heart was lighter than heretofore.

At last Jón made a settlement of all he possessed, giving by far the greater part of his property to Sigrídur, and his personal wealth to his wife and other children, who were well off with it. And every one thus saw that he was most fond of his daughter from the lower regions; and what, all things considered, was the wonder? When Jón died, many felt deeply his loss and wept bitterly for him; for he had been a good man and a warm friend.

Some years afterwards Sigrídur married a young and hopeful peasant, and their farm throve till none in the district could compare with it. They lived happily and everybody looked up to them with respect and fondness. Of their many children the descendants are scattered widely through the south country.

# THE SKELETON IN HÓLAR CHURCH

ONCE, ON a winter evening, it happened that Jón Arason, Bishop of Hólar, wanted a book which he had left lying on the altar in the church, so called his household folk together, and asked which of them would do him the favour of fetching the book for him. They all shuddered at the idea, and all drew back except one maid-servant, who declared herself quite willing to go, and not in the least afraid.

Now the bishop having enemies—as who has not?—had made a tunnel from his own house, which was called the Palace, underground to the church, with a view to being able, if need should ever be, to take sanctuary at a moment's notice, and unobserved.

Through this tunnel the maid went, having procured the keys of the church; but when she had taken the book from the altar, she determined not to go back through the tunnel, which she had found dismal and ghostly, but rather round the other way. So she walked down the church with the keys to the outer door; and looking towards the benches where the women were wont to sit, she saw there a human skeleton with long yellow hair! Amazed at this, but in no way frightened, she went up to the figure and said, "Who are you?"

Upon which the skeleton said, "I am a woman, and have long been dead. But my mother cursed me so that I can never corrupt, and return to the dust whence I sprung. Now, therefore, my good girl, I entreat you to release me from this ban, if it lies in your power."

"But," answered the girl, "it does *not* lie in my power, as far as I now know. Tell me how I can help you."

Then the skeleton replied, "You must ask my mother to forgive me my faults, and to annul her curse; for she may very likely do for the living what she refuses to do for the dead. It is a rare thing indeed for the living to ask favours of the dead."

"Where is your mother, then?" asked the maiden.

"Oh," said the other, "she is here, there, and everywhere. Now, for example, she is yonder in the choir."

Then the maiden went through the door into the choir, and saw sitting there on one of the benches a wondrous ugly old woman in a red hat, to whom she addressed herself, asking her to be good enough to forgive her daughter, and remove from her the curse. After pausing a while, plainly unwilling, the old hag answered—"Well! it is not often that you living people ask favours of me, so for once I will say to you yea!"

Having thanked her for her goodness, the maiden went back towards the outer door, but when she came to the place where she had seen the skeleton, found there only a heap of dust. So she went on towards the door, and as she opened it she heard a voice from the inner part of the church, which cried after her, "Look at my red eyes, how red they are!" And without looking round, she answered, "Look at my black back, how black it is!"

As soon as she had shut the door behind her, she found that the churchyard seemed to swarm with people who were shouting and screaming direfully, and who made as if they would stop her. But she, summoning up courage, rushed through the middle of them, without looking either to the right or to the left, and reached the home-building in safety.

As she delivered the book to the bishop, she said:

> "So loud were the voices of the Goblin band
> That five echoes for each were found
> In the mountain-rocks, though far they stand
> From Hólar burying-ground."